Lars Pearson

mad norwegian press | des moines, iowa
www.madnorwegian.com

Also available from Mad Norwegian Press...

Redeemed: The Unauthorized Guide to Angel
by Lars Pearson and Christa Dickson

Dusted: The Unauthorized Guide to Buffy the Vampire Slayer
by Lawrence Miles, Lars Pearson and Christa Dickson

I, Who: The Unauthorized Guide to the Doctor Who Novels and Audios
by Lars Pearson (vols. 1-3)

Running Through Corridors: Rob and Toby's Marathon Watch of Doctor Who
by Robert Shearman and Toby Hadoke (Vol. 1: The 60s) and (Vol. 2: The 70s)

Space Helmet for a Cow: The Mad, True Story of Doctor Who
by Paul Kirkley (Vol. 1: 1963-1990) and (Vol. 2: 1990-2013)

Wanting to Believe: A Critical Guide to The X-Files, Millennium and the Lone Gunmen
by Robert Shearman

The AHistory Series by Lance Parkin and Lars Pearson
AHistory: An Unauthorized History of the Doctor Who Universe [4th Edition]
Unhistory: Stories Too Strange for Even Ahistory: An Unauthorized History of the Doctor Who Universe
(ebook only)

The About Time Series by Tat Wood and Lawrence Miles
About Time 1: The Unauthorized Guide to Doctor Who (Seasons 1 to 3)
About Time 2: The Unauthorized Guide to Doctor Who (Seasons 4 to 6)
About Time 3: The Unauthorized Guide to Doctor Who (Seasons 7 to 11) [2nd Ed]
About Time 4: The Unauthorized Guide to Doctor Who (Seasons 12 to 17)
About Time 5: The Unauthorized Guide to Doctor Who (Seasons 18 to 21)
About Time 6: The Unauthorized Guide to Doctor Who (Seasons 22 to 26)
About Time 7: The Unauthorized Guide to Doctor Who (Series 1 to 2)
About Time 8: The Unauthorized Guide to Doctor Who (Series 3)
About Time 9: The Unauthorized Guide to Doctor Who (Series 4, The 2009 Specials)

Essay Collections
Chicks Dig Comics: A Celebration of Comic Books by the Women Who Love Them

Chicks Dig Gaming: A Celebration of All Things Gaming by the Women Who Love It

Chicks Dig Time Lords: A Celebration of Doctor Who by the Women Who Love It
2011 Hugo Award Winner, Best Related Work

Chicks Unravel Time: Women Journey Through Every Season of Doctor Who

Companion Piece: Women Celebrate the Humans, Aliens and Tin Dogs of Doctor Who

Queers Dig Time Lords: A Celebration of Doctor Who by the LGBTQ Fans Who Love It

Published by Mad Norwegian Press (www.madnorwegian.com).

ISBN: 9781570329029
First Edition: September 2002. First print-on-demand version: August 2021.

Table of Contents

Table of Contents

Action Force (1987-1988)

European Missions (1988-1989)

Sidebars

TV SERIES

COMIC SERIES

How to Use This Book

My father was fortunate. He served in World War II as an Air Force captain and returned home in complete health. Yet despite spending the next quarter century doing nothing more dangerous than selling insurance, he'd don his military uniform every Memorial Day – without fail – and march in the local parade.

That's more relevant to *G.I. Joe* than you think, because it serves – certainly for me – as a constant reminder of the overwhelming sense of camaraderie that exists between military men. I don't pretend to fully understand this bond, but it's more than simple fraternity, because it's hard to feel only *friendship* toward the person who guards your back with an AK-47 during a combat situation.

If we're taking a moment – just a *moment* – to be serious before we begin, it's likely that sense of teamwork that makes *G.I. Joe* stand out from other 1980s properties. The comics, cartoons and action figures respectively hammer home this ethic in their own fashion, fusing the Joes into a team, even a *family* at points. That said, I've discovered – as an adult – that there comes a point when you've got to put the action figures aside and focus on the heroic ethic inherent in the stories themselves.

And that's a tough job to do, given *A Real American Hero*'s 20-year history. So, since you've been busy, we've watched – and read – this for you.

WHAT 'NOW YOU KNOW' DOES FOR YOU

In a dazzling display of journalism worthy of "Nightline," *Now You Know* catalogues the fact and fancy that makes up the *G.I. Joe* cartoon and comic book series. The result is a thorough guide to the plot twists and turns that compose the *G.I. Joe* universe (or *universes*, if you treat the TV and comic series as separate... which we do).

As you've probably guessed, we're most interested in the *stories* of *G.I. Joe,* not the hundreds of figures that made up the 1980s toy line. Although we've included a price guide in the appendix, if the toys are your fixation, this isn't the book for you. We can only recommend the *G.I. Joe Hall of Fame* by James DeSimone, a handy-dandy toy identification guide.

SPOILER WARNING

Spoilers, which freely spill the beans about plot twists and the like, tend to make some fans' nostrils flare worse than naked pictures of Jar-Jar Binks. But let's be honest: Reference guides that fail to deliver all the story's goods are about as useful as refrigerator manuals. Ergo, if spoilers give you epileptic fits, this isn't the book for you.

By the way, Darth Vader is Luke's father.

MISCELLANEOUS STUFF!

G.I. JOE'S TV HISTORY

• **G.I. Joe: A Real American Hero (Sunbow)** – Animation studio Sunbow initially debuted the *G.I. Joe* cartoon in 1983 as a five-part mini-series. Dubbed "The M.A.S.S. Device," it garnered enough attention (and, presumably, enough toy sales) to warrant a second mini-series ("The Revenge of Cobra") the following year.

Two full seasons followed in 1985, kicked off by – you guessed it – yet another mini-series ("The Pyramid of Darkness"). Finally, *G.I. Joe: The Movie*, starring such well-known actors as Don Johnson and Burgess Meredith, hit the silver screen in 1987. All told, these 95 Sunbow-made episodes (plus the movie), compose what vast droves of fandom deem the halcyon days of *A Real American Hero.* Unlike, for example...

• **G.I. Joe: A Real American Hero (DIC)** – In 1989, cartoon studio DIC hooked the "G.I. Joe" license and set about producing a string of cartoons for USA Network. An initial mini-series ("Operation Dragonfire") bridged the gap between *G.I. Joe: The Movie* and the DIC stories, with two full DIC seasons quickly hitting the airwaves in 1990 and 1991.

Although it sounds obvious, the DIC series was decidedly made *for children*, revolving around plots such as kindergartners defeating Cobra ("Kindergarten Commandos") and games of football ("Pigskin Commandos") or something equally as banal. If we're stereotyping, *G.I. Joe* fans seem largely to abhor the DIC series with a passion usually reserved for relatives at Thanksgiving. Certainly, the Internet contains no end of *Joe* advocates who spit on the DIC stories – if they mention them at all – with all the verve of camels.

Since we happen to share this opinion, we've truncated the DIC coverage considerably. Some fans would argue that *any* coverage is too good for the DIC stuff, but it's better – as Dr. Evil once said – to throw a frickin' bone to the possible DIC fans out there (we hear they *do* exist).

• **G.I. Joe Extreme (Sunbow)** – *G.I. Joe* in name only, *G.I. Joe Extreme* spawned from a failed pilot for a *Sgt. Savage and His Screaming Eagles* cartoon (1994) and produced two seasons in 1995 and 1996. The series pitted Lt. Stone and his "G.I. Joe" team against the dictatorial Iron Klaw, but to reiterate, this has *nothing* to do with the *A Real American Hero* mythos. As such, we've opted to ignore both the *G.I. Joe Extreme* cartoons and their short-lived tie-in comic series from Dark Horse.

Now You Know

THE CATEGORIES

Hopefully, most of the categories are self-explanatory. But a few probably warrant further description:

BATTLE ROSTER A list of each story's *main* characters – i.e. the characters who actually *do* something other than suck air – in each story. We *don't* list every single background character, since even our geekdom has limits.

OR THE ONE WHERE... It has come to our attention that a certain flavor of *G.I. Joe* viewers remember a story's *plot* far quicker than its title. Accordingly, *Or the One Where...* serves as your *Cliffs Notes* to the TV show, providing a one-sentence summation of each episode.

THE CRUCIAL BITS Whereas the cartoons mostly feature stand-alone stories, the *G.I. Joe* comic series sports a 20-year-long continuity. As such, *The Crucial Bits* concisely lists the comics' keystone events – the most important first appearances, deaths, promotions, etc.

MEMORABLE MOMENTS The juiciest, sexiest and most poignant tidbits – i.e. the scenes that make you leap out of your seat and cheer as if Green Bay's just scored while the clock expires.

LOVE AND WAR This category notes the characters' romantic relationships, as well as brief flirtations among the Joe and Cobra agents. Oh, and since we're reviewing this material as *adults*, there's a fair amount of double-entendres thrown in for good measure.

ASS-WHUPPINGS A rundown of the series' shootings, stabbings, maimings, throat-slittings, horsewhippings, keel-haulings and more (i.e. the stuff you *really* care about).

NOW YOU KNOW... To give *G.I. Joe* a sense of realism, comic book writer Larry Hama often marbled his stories with tidbits of practical knowledge, such as how to dynamite a ravenous bear. Think of this as the advice column written by your neighborhood Marine.

PREPOSTEROUS PHYSICS Keeping in mind that we're here to praise *G.I. Joe*, not bury it, there's times when it butchers all the laws of physics and makes Einstein squirm in his grave. Accordingly, this category mentions all the physical impossibilities that crop up in the series.

GOOFS ... whereas *this* category relates to animation glitches, implausible motives, blatant plot holes and other such screw-ups.

SAVE THEM! A TV-only section, cataloging the extraordinary and exhausting lengths that the kid-friendly *G.I. Joe* cartoon resorts to in guaranteeing, on pain of death, that nobody dies. (*Please note:* Given that G.I. Joe and Cobra airplane pilots safely parachute to freedom every five minutes, we've ignored the more mundane saves.)

G.I. JOE: THE MUSICAL With *G.I. Joe* hailing from the era of Madonna, Michael Jackson and MTV, we're lucky that *every* cartoon episode didn't include a musical rendition. Nonetheless, this category chronicles the Joes' musical mishaps in all their glory.

CHARACTER PROFILE Scads of information pertaining to various Joe, Cobra and independently-affiliated characters, mostly relating to personality quirks and the like. We've ignored rather commonplace facts such as "Roadblock wears yellow pants" or "Duke carries a rifle."

THE COMMAND DECISION The review section, discussing in an over-the-coffee fashion which stories make our blood thunder, which are watchable and which should be forever boxed up and sealed in a Pentagon vault, never again to see the light of day. Some kids' advocates will undoubtedly cry foul at the thought of Generation X'ers who're nearly 30 (and let's stress the *nearly*) reviewing a property originally intended for children. But let's admit a certain truth: Most *G.I. Joe* fans today are in our age group, and certainly the often-visceral comic book series was never exactly targeted at five-year-olds. For better or worse, we *are* the market.

How to Use This Book

THE COMIC SERIES

How the 'G.I. Joe' comics and TV series fuse together

... in short, they don't.

G.I. Joe fans will probably be debating until their dying day whether the comics are superior to the TV series or vice versa. Either way, both camps readily agree that the *G.I. Joe* TV and comic series exist in separate universes. Indeed, the cartoons' lightheartedness and the comics' visceral tone often rub each other raw, meaning there's times you'd swear the two were entirely unrelated save for having the same title and characters.

DO THE BRITISH COMICS COUNT?

Produced purely for a UK audience, the weekly *Action Force* (50 issues, March 1987 to Feb. 1988) reprinted the American *G.I. Joe* series in a haphazard order, along with a scant five pages of original material – starring Flint, Lady Jaye and the like against Cobra legions in Britain – with each issue.

After *Action Force*'s demise, *Action Force Monthly* – titled *G.I. Joe European Missions* for its American release (15 issues, June 1988 to August 1989) – made an already snarled continuity even worse by adding even *more* reprints and original material. (Trust us, it's *really* complicated.) All told, the British series hopelessly rearranges crucial events in its American counterpart, then creates even more paradoxes in trying to patch the resultant problems. As such, any attempt to merge the European and American comic continuities ends in disaster. That leaves us in the regrettable position of dubbing *Action Force* and *G.I. Joe European Missions* – however interesting their content – as apocrypha.

SHUFFLING THE COMIC SERIES

To the best of our ability, we've interwoven the main *G.I. Joe* issues with the spin-off *G.I. Joe Special Missions*. That said, the self-contained tales that compose the vast bulk of *Special Missions* make a proper continuity order virtually impossible. Sometimes, we lucked out when issues such as *Special Missions* #6, #7 and #26 directly impacted the main title. But we freely admit that everything else is arbitrary.

DID THE MOVIE HAPPEN?

Certainly not so far as the comics are concerned, given Larry Hama's self-professed loathing for the Cobra-La characters. Only *G.I. Joe European Missions* #6 carries anything by way of a solid movie tie-in – and even that's apocrypha (*see above*).

MISCELLANEOUS STUFF!

THE COMIC BOOK HOEDOWN

Again, purely to help any *G.I. Joe* newbies in the audience, here's a run-down of the comic series covered by *Now You Know*:

- **G.I. Joe (Marvel)** – The lodestone of *G.I. Joe* in comic-book form. It lasted a mind-bending 155 issues, from 1982 to 1994.
- **G.I. Joe Special Missions (Marvel)** – During *G.I. Joe*'s heyday, Marvel launched a spin-off title named *G.I. Joe Special Missions*, featuring the Joes in (mostly) stand-alone stories. It petered out after 28 issues.
- **Action Force (Marvel)** – The British counterpart to *G.I. Joe*, extremely interesting at points, but ultimately the stuff of apocrypha (*see the main text*).

LARRY HAMA

Practically no discussion of the comic would be adequate without mentioning Larry Hama, *G.I. Joe*'s godfather, in whispered and respectful tones. Hama served a tour of duty in Vietnam, and the military apparently empowered his life to such an extent that – certainly the last time I visited his office – he still wears dog tags and keeps a mounted rifle above his desk.

As one might expect, Hama's experiences helped him endow *G.I. Joe* with a clear-cut sense of military realism. While working for Hasbro, Hama created most of the *G.I. Joe* characters, writing the filecards that appeared with each action figure. More notably, he authored the whole of Marvel's *G.I. Joe* and *G.I. Joe Special Missions* series – more than 180 issues over a 12-year span – with scarcely a fill-in issue.

Critically speaking, Larry Hama wrote the most highly inspired and creative *G.I. Joe* comics you're ever likely to experience. But if we're being honest, he also wrote some truly horrendous issues – especially during the end of Marvel's *G.I. Joe* run. That said, if there's any goodness in *G.I. Joe*, it's due to Hama's vision and military savvy.

P.S. Unless otherwise noted, Hama is the sole writer of *the entirety* of *G.I. Joe*, *Special Missions* and the *G.I. Joe Yearbooks*. Amen.

The Episodes

Mini-Series No. 1: "The M.A.S.S. Device"

Episodes: *Five*
Titles: *"The Cobra Strikes" (Pt. 1), "Slave of the Cobra Master" (Pt. 2), "The Worms of Death" (Pt. 3), "Duel in the Devil's Cauldron" (Pt. 4), "A Stake in the Serpent's Heart" (Pt. 5)*
US Transmission Dates: *Sept. 12-16, 1983*
Writer: *Ron Friedman*

BATTLE ROSTER/FIRST APPEARANCES ***Joes:*** Duke (first sergeant), Scarlett (counter intelligence), Snake-Eyes (commando), Stalker (ranger), Breaker (communications officer), Short-Fuze (mortar soldier), Gung Ho (marine), Rock 'n Roll (machine gunner), Wild Bill (helicopter pilot), Flash (laser rifle trooper), Clutch (VAMP driver), Snow Job (arctic trooper), Trip-Wire (mine detector), Cover Girl (Wolverine driver), Torpedo (SEAL), Doc (medic), Steeler (tank commander), Zap (bazooka soldier), Timber (wolf), General Flagg; ***Cobra:*** Cobra Commander (Cobra commander), Destro (weapons supplier), the Baroness (intelligence officer), Major Bludd (mercenary).

MISSION BRIEF ***Part 1:*** Endowed with a thirst for conquest, a rogue terrorist organization named Cobra starts accruing troops and weaponry, hoping to amass enough military might to conquer the world. In response, the American government assembles G.I. Joe, a special mission force composed of code-named military specialists, to thwart Cobra's goals. Steeled with the American military's best operatives, G.I. Joe handily whips Cobra forces on multiple fronts.

Unable to triumph solely through military might, the top Cobra leader – creatively named "Cobra Commander" – turns to more devious methods. Accordingly, Cobra's arms supplier, a genius engineer named Destro, creates a powerful matter teleporter named "The M.A.S.S. Device," raiding the four corners of the globe for the three rare catalytic elements needed to fuel such a contraption.

Meanwhile, the Joes oversee security for the launch of a new American satellite (code-named "The Relay Star") designed to transmit energy instantly around the world. Hoping to augment the M.A.S.S. Device's capabilities, Destro plots with an undercover Cobra spy named the Baroness to teleport the Relay Star back to Cobra Headquarters, but the untested M.A.S.S. Device overheats before the transfer occurs. Quickly improvising, Destro instead teleports Cobra troops – led by a mercenary named Major Bludd – into the Relay Star's launch bay.

Caught off guard, the Joes stagger under a combined assault from Bludd and the Baroness. As Bludd's soldiers secure the Relay Star, Destro feverishly recalibrates the M.A.S.S. Device to beam Major Bludd, the Baroness, their subordinates and the Relay Star back to Cobra Headquarters. Unfortunately, the M.A.S.S. beam also snags Joe top sergeant Duke – allowing Cobra troops to pistol-whip and capture the Joe leader.

Working with blinding speed, Cobra engineers adapt the orbital Relay Star to re-route the M.A.S.S. Device's energy output, greatly enhancing the range and efficiency of Destro's teleport beam. Meanwhile, the Joes analyze the M.A.S.S. Device's energy signature – tagging it as a molecular deconstruction process – and ally themselves with Nobel Prize winner Dr. Lazlo Vandermeer, the world's leading authority on the topic.

Using the M.A.S.S. Device and Relay Star in conjunction, Cobra demonstrates its newfound power by stealing the Eiffel Tower, demanding that the world's governments surrender within 24 hours or risk further hostilities. Dr. Vandermeer offers to build a M.A.S.S. Device identical to Cobra's weapon, but stresses that the Joes must search the world for the three catalytic elements needed to effect molecular transport.

Back at Cobra H.Q., Cobra Commander and Destro fit Duke with a headband that slaves his movements to a remote joystick, then toss him into a battle arena for sport. With Destro directing Duke's actions, Cobra Commander unveils his champion – a giant slave who reaches out his beefy hands toward Duke's throat.

Part 2: While Duke struggles against his mammoth slave opponent, Destro and Cobra Commander trade wagers on who will win the fight. Destro backs Duke, then craftily puts his controller aside to let Duke fight for himself, knowing that the hapless Joe will easily triumph on his own. Duke downs the giant, but Destro immediately re-dominates Duke's mobility.

At Joe Headquarters, Dr. Vandermeer briefs the Joes on the first of three elements needed to fuel their duplicate M.A.S.S. Device: a radioactive crystal buried near an arctic expanse known as "The Sea of Ice." Alerted to the Joes' maneuvers, Destro and Cobra Commander prep battalions to hinder the Joes and, more crucially, replenish Cobra's diminishing supply of catalytic elements.

Led by a female intelligence officer named Scarlett and a commando called Snake-Eyes, a Joe team reaches the radioactive crystal mine, then tangles with Major Bludd-led Cobra troops. While the Joes provide covering fire, Snake-Eyes uses radiation-proof mine equipment to harvest a canisterful of the crystals. Unfortunately, Major Bludd triggers an explosion, sending a cloud of radioactive dust hurling up the mine toward the Joes.

With his teammates pinned, Snake-Eyes spots the approaching cloud and drops an emergency shield – saving the Joes but trapping himself with the lethal dust. Left with little choice, Scarlett's team sadly declares Snake-Eyes and his cache of crystals lost, escaping up an emergency ladder and returning to Joe Headquarters.

Meanwhile, Cobra Commander delivers further ultimatums, ordering world leaders to gather at Tanu Island and surrender to Cobra rule. Various governments send representatives for the purpose of unanimously rejecting Cobra's demands, but Cobra Commander uses the M.A.S.S. Device to kidnap the delegates, thereby gaining valuable hostages.

Back at Cobra Headquarters, a young woman named Selena – part of a resistance movement brewing among Cobra's slaves – helps Duke escape. Duke pauses long enough to give Selena his ring, promising to return, then endures a harrowing chase with Cobra trackers dogging his every step. Duke eventually makes his way to Joe Headquarters, but the stress of his escape induces short-term memory loss. With Cobra whipping the Joes left and right, Duke's teammates lament their leaders' inability to remember the location of Cobra Headquarters.

Part 3: At the radioactive cavern near "The Sea of Ice," Major Bludd's forces dispatch a mining robot to harvest some crystals for Cobra, reopening the mine shaft enough for Snake-Eyes – dying from radiation poisoning – to exit with his canister of crystals. Major Bludd deems Snake-Eyes doomed, allows the ailing Joe to depart, then withdraws his own forces back to Cobra Headquarters.

Lost in the snow, Snake-Eyes frees a wolf clamped in a trap, thereby gaining the beast's gratitude. Exhausted, Snake-Eyes collapses, but a reclusive blind Scottish man happens across the comatose Joe and drains away his radiation sickness with a cocoon of leaves and herbs. Fully recovered, Snake-Eyes takes his crystal cache and newfound wolf ally – whom the Scottish man names "Timber" – and departs for civilization.

Meanwhile, G.I. Joe and Cobra mobilize to retrieve the second catalytic element: a pool of heavy water, located at the deepest part of the ocean floor. The Joes battle the Baroness' underwater Cobra troops for the prize, but giant tubeworms native to the ocean depths besiege both parties. Agreeing to combat their common enemy, Joe and Cobra soldiers blast away the tube-like structures anchoring the worms to the ocean floor – shunting the worms up to a lesser depth and rupturing them from the sudden pressure shift. Mission accomplished, the two factions split the heavy water and go their separate ways.

Now possessing a re-supply of two catalytic elements – but running dangerously low on the third – an undaunted Cobra Commander threatens to obliterate New York City with a concentrated M.A.S.S. energy bolt unless G.I. Joe surrenders. Luckily, Snake-Eyes returns to Joe Headquarters with his canister of radioactive crystals, momentarily giving his teammates renewed hope. But seconds later, the crystal-holding canister – previously booby-trapped by Cobra – releases paralyzing fumes that nearly asphyxiates the whole of Joe command. Worse, an explosive device within the canister primes itself – threatening to annihilate the unconscious Joes.

Part 4: Joe member Cover Girl fights against the incapacitating fumes, safely disposing the bomb outside the perimeter of Joe Headquarters. Recovering from their close call, the Joes depart to retrieve the third and last catalytic element: a unique meteorite that crashed 100,000 years ago in a volcanic South American region known as "the Ring of Fire." Destro hurriedly assembles a Cobra retrieval squad, sparking a fierce clash near the fallen meteorite's volcanic home.

In Destro's absence, Cobra Commander over-zealously decides to prove his supremacy by M.A.S.S.-eradicating New York City. Although it completely drains Destro's original supply of the third catalytic element, the M.A.S.S. Device fires off a cataclysmic energy bolt toward Manhattan. Thankfully, Duke's ally, the slave girl Selena, shorts out the M.A.S.S. Device controls with a well-placed jug of water, thereby dissipating the fatal bolt. Lacking the third catalytic element to try again, Cobra Commander slates Selena for a vague but terrible punishment.

In South America, Destro's fighters haul the rare meteorite aboard a flying Cobra aircraft carrier, but Joe commandoes wearing rocket packs overrun the Cobra dreadnought. With seconds to spare, Destro grabs some meteorite fragments and escapes in a small jet vessel. Working at breakneck speed, the Joes fly the Cobra aircraft carrier back to headquarters, delivering the meteorite to Dr. Vandermeer.

Equally in possession of the required catalytic elements, G.I. Joe and Cobra race like mad to prep their M.A.S.S. devices for activation. However, Destro finds himself aghast at Cobra Commander's failure to destroy New York, dethroning the commander and seizing command of Cobra. With his M.A.S.S. Device fully charged, Destro attempts to succeed where Cobra Commander failed – launching a destructive M.A.S.S. bolt that zips toward Manhattan and its millions of inhabitants.

Part 5: With seconds to spare, the Joes bring their M.A.S.S. Device online and fire off a counter-strike, neutralizing Cobra's death ray at the last minute. Incensed, Destro threatens to execute the kidnapped world leaders one by one – starting with G.I. Joe liaison General Flagg – unless the Joes surrender.

Left with few options, the Joes employ hypnosis as a last-ditch effort to make Duke remember the location of Cobra Headquarters. Suitably mesmerized, Duke remembers giving the slave girl Selena his ring – enabling the Joes to lock onto the ring's electronic chips and pinpoint the main Cobra Temple. In rapid succession, the Joes use their M.A.S.S. Device to teleport multiple squadrons right onto Cobra's doorstep, liberating the slaves and overrunning Cobra H.Q..

Intractable to the end, Destro programs Cobra's M.A.S.S. Device to tunnel into the Earth's core, attempting to rupture the entire planet in a final act of defiance. G.I. Joe marine Gung Ho elegantly solves the problem by blowing up M.A.S.S. Device's controls, even as Destro escapes and the Joes capture Cobra Commander.

Triumphant, the Joes combine the last of their catalytic elements with Cobra's supplies to teleport the Eiffel Tower back to Paris. Unfortunately, Joe communications expert Breaker botches the coordinates – materializing the structure in London. Having run dry of catalytic elements – but safe at last from Cobra's threat – the Joes happily set about rectifying the mistake and move the tower back home with heavy equipment.

MEMORABLE MOMENTS Scarlett weeps when Snake-Eyes seals himself behind a drop-down shield – thereby sparing his teammates fatal radiation poisoning at the cost of his own life (thankfully, nobody quotes *Star Trek II:* "He'll die!" "He's dead already!"). Celebrating a victory over Cobra, an over-excited Gung Ho nearly punches Scarlett's lights out by accident, then resorts to a calmer high-five and awkwardly tells her: "Way to go, Scarlett!" Destro lectures Cobra Commander on the need to make good on his threats, sharpening the Cobra leaders' resolve to succeed. Reflecting the Cold War era that spawned *G.I. Joe*, a Russian leader calls Destro a "monstrous imperialist!"

LOVE AND WAR Scarlett flirts with Duke, admitting that she missed him while he was away. For his part, Duke pushes Scarlett aside during a firefight rather than simply shouting, "Look out!" (Any excuse to cop a feel...) Duke gives Selena his ring in Part 2, but it's likely more a keepsake than a token of love. Still, when a gleeful Selena locks lips with Duke in Part 5, a jealous Scarlett comments: "Later, sister. We've got a war to win." In turn, Duke tells Scarlett that he thought about bringing flowers, but opted for her crossbow instead (how romantic). Ever the lucky bastard, Duke ends the story with a girl – Selena and Scarlett – on each arm.

Oh, and it's nothing more then a double-entendre, but Scarlett tells Stalker during a battle: "Shall we do our thing?"

Finally, Duke floats in a special sensory deprivation tank in only his undies (shades of Luke Skywalker's dip in the Bacta tank in *The Empire Strikes Back*).

SAVE THEM! Cobra hang-gliders fall into a yawning chasm but miraculously land on a cushiony row of trees. Cobra Commander's slave champion Ramar, freed from his shackles, tosses a Cobra ATV and its drivers through a barred window – but the thugs harmlessly land in a moat.

ASS-WHUPPINGS Cobra opens this story by evoking Pearl Harbor and blowing up a grounded G.I. Joe Skystriker squadron. There's a few rare (and we do mean rare) instances in this story of the Joes blowing a few Cobra jets and tanks to smithereens without their pilots bailing out.

A Cobra-controlled Ramar hauls Duke about in the arena like a sack of wheat. Snake-Eyes endures radiation poisoning and a spontaneous polar bear attack (the blind Scottish man chases the offending bear off, possibly following Shakespeare's infamous stage direction from *The Winter's Tale* of "Exeunt a bear."). Joe and Cobra divers work in unison to massacre a mess of giant tubeworms.

In Part 4, Scarlett jabs Destro's boot with her heel and smacks his face with her crossbow, but the fiend captures her anyway. Cobra troopers who haven't met their torture quota randomly toss Scarlett down a stone stairwell.

GOOFS On his original mission to find the three catalytic elements, why didn't Destro procure a larger supply? (The obvious answer: Because then we wouldn't have a story.)

Cobra M.A.S.S.-beams two HISS tanks to capture the Relay Star, but the Joes blow up at least three of 'em in the resultant mêlée.

Selena gives Duke a contraband gold strip – that Cobra guards entirely miss when they frisk the Joe leader. Cobra Commander's impossibly strong tournament champion Ramar, able to knock down stone pillars with his bare hands, evidently eats Wheaties by the case.

The Joes oddly decide that going after the catalytic elements one at a time is preferable to simultaneous missions ("The Revenge of Cobra" mini-series pretty much rectifies this pacing problem.)

During a cliffhanger in Part 2, automated guns point at the Joes, compelling Trip-Wire to shout, "Stay back!", but everything's normal after the commercial break. Joes in the arctic tundra ditch their winter parkas and strut about in flimsy costumes for no readily apparent reason. Flash, a Joe laser rifle trooper, fights Cobra robots... with a blowtorch. Trip-Wire and Flash whirl a giant Cobra robot, presumably weighing multiple tons, like a top.

Duke clambers down a wall with his bare hands (perhaps a radioactive spider bit him). It's never explained how Cobra slaves such as Selena deduce that gold strips can override their Cobra control headbands, or indeed, how the slaves found gold strips just lying about the place.

World leaders unanimously refuse Cobra's demands for power, then gather at a Cobra-dictated meeting place and stupidly make a nice, big target for Cobra. If Duke's ring contained the equivalent of a homing beacon, why the hell didn't the Joes locate him with it in the first place? Snake-Eyes literally glows red from radiation poisoning but somehow survives thanks to a witch-doctor concoction of leaves and herbs. Oh, and polar bears live at the South Pole, not the Arctic.

In Part 3, Cobra uses the last of their catalytic elements to beam space troopers up the relay satellite – then fail to ever bring them back down (presumably, they're still up there). Having previously retrieved heavy water from the ocean's bottom, Cobra doesn't bother telling the Baroness' follow-up team: "By the way, watch out for the giant tube worms."

An animation goof makes Cobra's depleted levels of elements magically replenish themselves at one point. Rather than contacting the U.S. military for a state-of-the-art weapon to eliminate the Cobra-controlled Relay Star, the Joes favor a Steeler, Short-Fuze and Clutch-made rocket that's presumably stapled together.

At the opening of Part 4, Snake-Eyes' pet wolf Timber – who's lived his entire life in the wild – miraculously gains enough knowledge of chemistry to find Cover Girl a liquid that filters Cobra's lethal fumes. We see Cobra Commander at dinner eating a chicken leg – with his helmet on. Selena shorts out the controls of Cobra's M.A.S.S. Device, which somehow dissipates an already fired M.A.S.S. energy bolt.

Scarlett's "thermal arrow" oddly coats things in green ooze. Cobra lets its mind-controlled slaves walk about with guns – a brilliant policy, considering their brainwashing can't be failure-proof. In Part 5, Cobra lets the Joes M.A.S.S.-teleport into Cobra Temple without using their own M.A.S.S. Device to blow the in-transit Joes into tofu.

Taking a hint from Megatron of *Transformers* fame, Cobra Commander insanely thinks that constructing the M.A.S.S. Device is "...the first step toward Cobra domination of the Universe!" (Errrr, there's no alien life in *G.I. Joe*...)

Last point – and this question has kept Joe fans awake for years – how does Destro's metal face plate move when he talks?

PREPOSTEROUS PHYSICS Joe and Cobra laser rifles blow up tanks and crash windmills. HISS tanks run through water and pop wheelies as adeptly as hovercraft.

In Part 3, the Joes and Cobras hear the giant tube worms scream underwater. In the same scene, Joe and Cobra scuba divers happily talk over the radio while wearing mouthpieces. If we're to believe Destro, tunneling into a volcano's base and releasing some of its molten lava will, in fact, trigger an eruption.

A few Joes – perhaps numbering 10 at most – overrun Destro's heavily fortified Cobra aircraft carrier with the inhuman strength and verve of Arnold Schwarzenegger.

TV TIE-INS Cover Girl waltzes about with long blonde hair, but in "The Revenge of Cobra," she wears short, red hair to match her Hasbro toy. Eye markings on the blind man who rescues Snake-Eyes in Part 3 resemble those of Zartan (who debuts in "The Revenge of Cobra"), but it's coincidental. Cobra Commander punctuates his words with a hiss, much moreso than in subsequent episodes. Here captured, Cobra Commander walks about free – without a word of explanation – in "The Revenge of Cobra."

CHARACTER PROFILE: JOES

• *Duke:* G.I. Joe's leader directly reports to General Flagg. Duke's 6'2" with blue eyes, and often crabs about Scarlett's piloting skills.

• *General Flagg:* Serves as a liaison between G.I. Joe and the Pentagon, also acting as the President's appointee during various crises.

• *Scarlett:* Uses a crossbow as her weapon of choice, sometimes firing arrows with explosive charges or towing lines. Scarlett's trained with exceptional karate skills.

• *Snake-Eyes:* Joe commando who wears a black face mask, presumably disguising a terrible injury or hideous facial scarring. Although mute, Snake-Eyes possesses an intuitive sixth sense.

• *Stalker:* He last acted onstage as a pumpkin in the school Thanksgiving show.

• *Trip-Wire:* His mine-detecting device also picks up life signs, although radioactivity messes up its readings.

• *Torpedo:* G.I. Joe's top SEAL (Sea, Air and Land) trooper, who pilots a personal submarine.

• *Wild Bill:* Top-rated helicopter pilot who also flies jets.

CHARACTER PROFILE: COBRA

• *Cobra Commander:* Decently nutty and pompous leader of Cobra, often more interested in games, banquets and diversions than focusing on victory. He's armed with a "video game controller" that directs giant robots with lasers and claws.

• *Cobra Commander and Destro:* Destro doesn't think much of Cobra Commander, but needs Cobra's resources to achieve further power (Destro's an arms supplier and technical expert, but presumably lacks Cobra Commander's troops and monetary resources).

• *Destro:* He wears gloves strong enough to punch holes in concrete.

• *The Baroness:* Powerful espionage agent, able to disguise her identity with latex face masks (á là *Mission: Impossible*).

• *Major Bludd:* Also wears latex face masks for masquerade purposes.

ORGANIZATIONS *Cobra:* Possesses a communications system capable of overriding every TV and radio station in the world. Cobra keeps a slave labor force with unknown origins.

• *Cobra and G.I. Joe:* Despite their respective specialties, pretty much every Joe and Cobra member possesses certain military skills such as how to fly helicopters and airplanes, plus weapons training and marksmanship. Although certain characters get tagged as pilots (Wild Bill, etc.) or "drivers" (Clutch, etc.), take it as given that the Joes and Cobras are by-and-large interchangeable during battle. "The M.A.S.S. Device" claims that few Joes are trained for deep sea diving (Torpedo being an obvious exception), although truth to tell, pretty much every Joe and Cobra member can scuba-dive.

• *G.I. Joe:* "Condition White" signals a unilateral Joe surrender. Some Joes fly using personal rocket packs. Nutty-looking robotic "rock walkers" (that look like giant cookie sheets with legs) carry Joe tanks up rock walls.

• *The Soviet Union:* Currently ruled by Premier Ivan Vlancov.

STUFF YOU NEED *Cobra RATTLER Jets:* Can rotate their engines to hover in place.

• *G.I. Joe Dragonfly Helicopters:* Equipped with auto-pilots.

• *G.I. Joe Magnet Grenades:* Sneaky devices that latch onto enemy metal and obliterate it.

• *The M.A.S.S. Device:* Looks like a large cannon with a jeweled tip.

• *The Relay Star:* Is shaped like a giant onion.

THE COMMAND DECISION Obviously the prototype *G.I. Joe* story, but also – and we say this regret – one of the most outrageously lumbering and clunky Joe tales, "The M.A.S.S. Device" stands a good chance of making even the most zealous 1980s fans find religion. The characters are little more than caricatures at this early stage, plus there's a disturbing failure to outlay any sort of mythology (á là *Transformers*' debut story, "More than Meets the Eye"), dampening *G.I. Joe*'s momentum in the long run. In short, however much you're pining to re-watch *G.I. Joe*, make peace with your childhood – and sedate yourself – before viewing "The M.A.S.S. Device."

Mini-Series No. 2: "The Revenge of Cobra"

a.k.a. "The Weather Dominator"
Episodes: *Five*
Titles: *"In the Cobra's Pit" (Pt. 1), "The Vines of Evil" (Pt. 2), "The Palace of Doom" (Pt. 3), "Battle on the Roof of the World" (Pt. 4), "Amusement Park of Terror" (Pt. 5)*
US Transmission Dates: *Sept. 10-14, 1984*
Writer: *Ron Friedman*

BATTLE ROSTER ***Joes:*** Duke, Snake-Eyes, Gung Ho, Snow Job, Scarlett, Doc; ***Cobras***: Cobra Commander, Destro, the Baroness, Major Bludd.

FIRST APPEARANCES ***Joes:*** Flint (warrant officer), Lady Jaye (covert operations), Spirit (tracker), Shipwreck (sailor), Mutt (dog handler) and Junkyard (dog), Roadblock (heavy machine gunner), Recondo (jungle trooper), Ripcord (HALO jumper), Sparks (communications), Cutter (hovercraft pilot), Thunder (self-propelled gun artilleryman), Colonel Sharpe; ***Cobra:*** Zartan (master of disguise), Buzzer, Ripper and Torch (Dreadnoks), Storm Shadow (ninja), Scrap Iron (anti-armor specialist), Firefly (saboteur).

MISSION BRIEF ***Part 1:*** When G.I. Joe oversees transport of a super-energy generator named "the laser core" – slated to become part of a new defense cannon – Cobra forces overwhelm the Joes and steal the device, capturing Duke and Snake-Eyes as a bonus. In turn, Joe member Lady Jaye nabs Cobra Commander, prompting warrant officer Flint – who assumes Joe leadership in Duke's absence – to authorize Cobra Commander's incarceration in Louisiana's Blackwater Prison.

Unfortunately, a bayou-based master of disguise named Zartan, assisted by a trio of rowdy British and Australian rogues named the Dreadnoks, infiltrates the prison. Following a previously established contract with Cobra, Zartan nets himself a hefty payment by freeing Cobra Commander.

Meanwhile, Destro affixes the stolen laser core to his newest invention, the so-called "Weather Dominator" – a device capable of spontaneously generating any type of weather across the globe. To test the Weather Dominator's capabilities, Destro unleashes a formidable tornado against a squadron of G.I. Joe Skystriker jets. The maelstrom hurls Flint, Roadblock and Mutt's planes into a huge cavern named "The Pit of Chaos," even as Scarlett orders the remaining Joes back to headquarters.

Drunk with success, Destro informs Cobra Commander that he previously seeded the arid "Pit of Chaos" with bio-engineered creeper vines that, when given a single drop of water, sprout iron-strong, strangling fronds. As Flint emerges from his downed Skystriker, rain activates the pre-planted creepers. Flint tries to hack through the constricting vegetation, initially denying the creepers a chokehold, but quickly loses ground and falls into a mass of seething plants.

Part 2: Roadblock aids Flint, gaining a brief respite, but the plants surge on until Mutt re-ignites his downed Skystriker's engines – keeping the creepers at bay with a wall of fire. Working quickly, the three stranded Joes construct a makeshift helicopter from bits of Mutt's Skystriker. But as the jury-rigged helicopter takes off, the creepers renew their attack and snag Roadblock's ankle. With the helicopter unable to pull free, Roadblock leaps back into the canyon, sacrificing himself to let Flint and Mutt soar to freedom.

Meanwhile, in Cobra Headquarters, Cobra Commander and Destro discuss plans to deploy the Weather Dominator against Washington D.C. as a show of strength. Seeking cheap amusement, Cobra Commander and Destro pit the captive Duke and Snake-Eyes against each other in a battle arena – inadvertently enabling the two Joes to overhear Cobra Commander's plans. Duke and Snake-Eyes stage a mad dash for freedom, gaining a few seconds to radio their fellow Joes a warning on Snake-Eyes' hidden communicator.

As Cobra troopers re-subdue Duke and Snake-Eyes, Joe medic Doc scrambles for some type of defense against Cobra's

Weather Dominator, cobbling together a network of "energy mirrors" – polished surfaces designed to absorb, reflect and redirect energy. Thanks to Duke and Snake-Eyes' alert, Scarlett rallies the Joes to evacuate Washington D.C., then deploys teams with dozens of energy mirrors.

Destro drives home the inevitable weather-based assault, hammering the Joes in Washington with freak tornadoes and killer-size hailstones. At Cobra Commander's urging, Destro taps the stolen laser core to make lightning, intending to fry the Joes with an electrical assault. But braced for impact, the Joes absorb the lightning attack into their surviving energy mirrors, then redirect and concentrate the soaked-up energy into a central mirror.

With the flip of a lever, Doc releases the stored energy in a single jolt – sending it on a reverse trajectory. Instantly, the Joe energy pulse races around the planet and strikes the Weather Dominator head-on, instigating a chain reaction. Completely overloaded, the Weather Dominator rockets into orbit – triggering freakish weather patterns around the globe. Above Earth, the Weather Dominator explodes into its three main components – the ion correlator, the Hydromaster and the laser core – with the various fragments landing in remote locations. Separately tracking the fragments' trajectories, G.I. Joe and Cobra both ready retrieval teams to travel around the world and hopefully retrieve the Weather Dominator components.

Back in the creeper-laden pit, a sudden outbreak of sunny weather kills off the creeper vines, enabling Roadblock to climb to safety. Meanwhile, Flint and Mutt's improvised helicopter conks out, marooning them in the middle of the desert. The two Joes soon arrive at a wretched hive of scum and villainy known as "The Cobra Café," where a ne'er-do-well mercenary sailor named Shipwreck offers to take them out of Cobra territory for a sizeable fee. Flint and Mutt agree, setting off with Shipwreck in his wind-powered sand skimmer. But just as the Joes and Shipwreck get underway, a nightmarish sandstorm appears and pummels their vessel, knocking Mutt overboard.

Part 3: Anchoring himself with a towline and shoveling like mad, Flint rescues Mutt and pulls him back to Shipwreck's downed "sailing" ship. The three of them take cover under their ship's fallen sail, waiting until the sandstorm burns itself out before repairing Shipwreck's skimmer and returning to Joe Headquarters.

Meanwhile, Cobra Commander agonizes over the Weather Dominator's loss, ordering the Baroness to search for the first Weather Dominator component – the ion correlator – at a tropical location called "The Island of No Return." The Baroness obliges, but G.I. Joe forces led by Cutter and Wild Bill quickly move to intercept. Pinned down, Cutter authorizes G.I. Joe tracker Spirit to sneak past the battle lines and recover the ion correlator. Spirit easily locates the fallen fragment, but finds himself confronting a skilled Cobra ninja named Storm Shadow. Brawling for the Weather Dominator component, Spirit and Storm Shadow plunge down a raging waterfall with their prize, vanishing from sight.

Elsewhere, Cobra's Major Bludd begins a campaign to retrieve the second Weather Dominator fragment – the Hydromaster – from an Aztec-reminiscent edifice dubbed "the Palace of Doom." As Flint's troops provide covering fire, Lady Jaye, Shipwreck and Gung Ho sneak inside the palace and locate the Hydromaster in a central chamber. Unfortunately, Gung Ho treads on a pressure-sensitive stone, activating a trap that awakens a giant stone guardian from its slumber.

Designed to defend the palace against intruders, the stone giant moves to trample the Joes, but an enormous serpent-headed Cobra robot engages the rocky guardian. As the Weather Dominator-spurred freakish weather intensifies and creates a vicious earthquake, opening a chasm, Gung Ho drops the Hydromaster. Pouncing, Major Bludd snatches the component and immediately retreats. The Joes attempt to withdraw, but the chasm widens, isolating Gung Ho's trio. Flint's party stops to pull Lady Jaye to safety, but another tremor rumbles – hurling Shipwreck and Gung Ho into the abyss.

Part 4: With lightning speed, Lady Jaye hurls a net-projecting javelin into the gorge, saving Gung Ho and Shipwreck from a fatal drop. Pulling their teammates clear, Flint's forces – having lost the day to Cobra – regroup at Joe Headquarters.

Meanwhile, on the "Island of No Return," a half-drowned Spirit and Storm Shadow emerge in an underwater alcove with the ion correlator. Nervously realizing that the rising tide will submerge the entire cavern, Spirit and Storm Shadow wisely join forces.

Spirit reasons that the rising water must displace the cavern's air through a blowhole on the surface, diving under water and hauling the Weather Dominator fragment through said blowhole with Storm Shadow's help. Acknowledging that Spirit saved his life, Storm Shadow relinquishes the ion correlator and departs. Soon after, Spirit escapes the island with his teammates – scoring a win for the Joes.

Completely oblivious to the Weather Dominator quest, the still-missing Roadblock stows himself aboard a convoy of Cobra trucks and arrives at the main Cobra Temple. Bursting into the command center, Roadblock whips Cobra Commander about like a bale of hay, but waves of Cobra troopers quickly down the wayward Joe. Soon after, Roadblock, Duke and Snake-Eyes find themselves back in the Cobra battle arena, tensed for combat as the arena generates giant, video game-esque, electrically charged battle snakes. (*Author's Note:* So help me, I'm not making this up.)

Each possessing one piece of the Weather Dominator, G.I. Joe and Cobra send teams to retrieve the final Weather Dominator component – the laser core – from its landing point in a snowy location called "the Roof of the World." But unknown to both factions, the mercenary Zartan leads his Dreadnoks on a private expedition, hoping to snag the laser core for himself.

As Flint and Destro's parties indulge in a pitched firefight for the laser core, Storm Shadow saves Spirit from a falling boulder, evening the score between them. Suddenly, Zartan and his Dreadnoks race into the mayhem, hauling the laser core to a secure outcropping. While the Joes and Cobras turn slack-jawed, Zartan announces his intention to auction the vital laser core to the highest bidder. Seconds later, Zartan lasers a nearby glacier, triggering an avalanche. Destro's troops quickly summon circling Cobra jets and escape, but Flint's ground-based soldiers look up in terror as an all-consuming tidal wave of snow rushes toward them.

Part 5: In desperation, Flint's group discharges their lasers upward, melting part of the oncoming avalanche and burrowing a hidey-hole to survive the onslaught. Freed when Lady Jaye uses a diamond-tipped javelin to carve a path through the ice, the Joes yet again return to base.

Meanwhile, Zartan and the Dreadnoks withdraw with the laser core to their back-up headquarters, a rebuilt "Bayou World Theme Park" in Louisiana. Contacting both G.I. Joe and Cobra, Zartan makes a further demand that the two sides duel – with their wallets – to acquire the laser core. Unluckily for Zartan, the G.I Joe team and Cobra both track his transmission and mobilize against his location.

Led by Destro, a Cobra battalion unwisely blusters into the theme park – coming under heavy fire from laser-mounted kiddie rides – but the Joes more sensibly blow up Zartan's power generator. As the Joes secure the theme park's control room, Zartan and his Dreadnoks head for their swamp vehicles with the laser core. The Dreadnoks rev their swamp skimmers and charge to freedom, but Destro cuts off Zartan at the last instant, bagging the laser core for Cobra.

Having paid his debt to Spirit, Storm Shadow infiltrates Joe Headquarters and steals back the Hydromaster – granting Cobra possession of all three Weather Dominator components. Meanwhile, in the Cobra Temple, the captive Duke, Snake-Eyes and Roadblock cross the battle arena's electrical poles, shorting out the computer-generated snakes. Duke's trio quickly escapes into the temple's sewer systems, planting a homing device for their teammates.

Returning to headquarters, Destro advocates extreme punishment for the treacherous Zartan – then despairs when Cobra Commander, gleeful for the Weather Dominator's return, pardons the rogue. Locking onto Duke's signal, a massive G.I. Joe air and ground assault mobilizes toward Cobra H.Q., but Destro reactivates the Weather Dominator, blistering the Joes with a fury of snow, ice, wind and lightning.

Just when all seems lost, Duke, Snake-Eyes and Roadblock locate a stash of Destro's bio-engineered creeper vine sprigs. By seeding creeper springs beneath the Weather Dominator and finding a convenient fire hose, Duke's party spurs massive creeper vine growth. With a ruthless efficiency, the steel-strong creeper vines unseat Destro and snag the Weather Dominator controls – luckily calming the erratic weather.

Finally granted an opening, the Joes capture Cobra Commander and Cobra Temple, leaving Destro and Zartan to escape in the confusion. Using the reassembled Weather Dominator, the Joes hail the end of Cobra's mad weather schemes.

MEMORABLE MOMENTS The scruffy Dreadnoks scrap like dogs over a freshly killed squirrel when Cobra Commander tosses them a bag of gold coins. Flint bravely struggles against the killer creeper vines, hacking away with his knife before being overwhelmed in a glorious cliffhanger to Part 1.

Resuming their battle in the underwater cavern, Spirit and Storm Shadow slug each other with an equal number of hits and kicks. Upon realizing they're accomplishing nothing, Spirit suggests, "We must dwell upon this," prompting them to assume the position of Rodin's "Thinker" statue.

An outraged, over-the-top Cobra Commander smashes a control screen with a chair, then declares the battered equipment "defective" and orders his communications chief punished (he pulls the same trick in Part 5, mostly out of boredom).

Snuggly in possession of the laser core, a boastful Zartan proclaims to his rivals: "The crucial, final fragment of the weather dominator – the laser core itself! – is now entirely in my possession… a prize which I offer to the highest bidder. G.I. Joe? Cobra? The world belongs to one of you – the one with the greatest bank account!"

LOVE AND WAR Lady Jaye tells Flint how much she missed his company, making him awkwardly sputter: "Well, that means a lot… knowing your buddies miss you, I mean." A heartbeat later, Flint introduces Shipwreck and adds how the renegade sailor "saved his neck," making Shipwreck unabashedly add to Lady Jaye: "I'd rather save yours …"

On "the Roof of the World," Shipwreck laments not being paired with Lady Jaye for a toboggan ride, causing Gung Ho to gruffly remark: "Get a date some other time. This ain't the Tunnel of Love."

Oh, and it's a double-entendre, but Cobra armament expert Scrap Iron orders his troops: "Take [Roadblock] from behind!"

ASS-WHUPPINGS Because it just wouldn't be a *G.I. Joe* mini-series without Duke getting beat to paste, Cobra troopers pistol-whip him and Snake-Eyes – twice. Flint and Mutt cleans up "The Cobra Café" with a furious bar brawl (the piano player, seemingly oblivious to the fury, does little more than turn his pages).

Automated Joe Packrat robots take a heavy toll on armored

Cobra robots, then bob and beep to each other like R2-D2. The mêlée at "The Palace of Doom" ends with the stone guardian and the giant Cobra robot falling to their (we have to say it once) *doom!*

Duke and Snake-Eyes mash a couple of Cobra troopers beneath a bookcase.

"The Revenge of Cobra" makes the viewer endure the presence of truck owner (and Southern-talking) Honda Lou West, who fires off comments such as "Cobra trucks, my hush puppies!" (Trust us – on behalf of anyone watching, this is an ass-whupping of epic proportions.)

SAVE THEM! During a jailbreak, Duke and Snake-Eyes shoot guns out of Cobra troopers' hands at point-blank range. At "the Island of No Return" battle, shot-down pilots nicely parachute into the water.

GOOFS The Joes previously captured Cobra Commander in "The M.A.S.S. Device," but he inexplicably frees himself in the interim.

An animation overlay glitch makes a Joe missile impact under a Cobra HISS tank – complete with devastating explosion – with zero damage. Attempting to stop Cobra goons from making off with the laser core, Duke ditches his one-man Sky Hawk fighter in favor of hand-to-hand combat. G.I. Joe dog Junkyard miraculously gains enough engineering knowledge to gather spare parts.

While dueling in the Cobra battle arena, Duke and Snake-Eyes somehow acquire the hearing of a bat and overhear every word of Cobra Commander's private chat with Destro. Cobra soldiers stupidly fail to divest the captive Snake-Eyes of his G.I. Joe communicator (used in Part 2). Then, having realized that Snake-Eyes got one over on them, the soldiers *even more stupidly* fail to search Duke and find his homing beacon (used in Part 5). For that matter, if Duke had such a homing beacon, why didn't he use it before the final episode?

Cutter's Joes deploy a smoke screen to cover their movements, compelling the Baroness to order her troops to do the same (why the hell didn't Cobra just move under cover of the Joe smoke screen?).

Storm Shadow and Spirit escape drowning in an alcove by breathing "air trapped beneath the Weather Dominator fragment." (Trapped where? It's a rectangular box.) Oh, and don't even get us started about the giant stone idol in "The Palace of Doom" that inexplicably comes to life.

The Dreadnoks undertake a perilous climb to "The Roof of the World," somehow carrying enough equipment in their backpacks to assemble three-wheel ATVs at the top. Flint and his allies survive an avalanche by lasering the oncoming snow into water and burrowing themselves a hidey-hole within the re-freezing ice (an optimistic solution, to say the least).

Duke, Snake-Eyes and Roadblock gain super-strength in the Cobra battle arena, ripping up the floor tiling for use as a weapon (thank you, steroids). For an encore, they hurl Southern belle Honda Lou through the air like she was a football en route to a field goal. By the way, nobody monitors the Joes or even watches their death match, failing to guard against the chance (however slim) that they might survive and simply walk free.

A small hand-operated lever on the outside of Cobra Temple (without even a "Do not pull except in case of genuine G.I. Joe attack" sign) makes the entire workings lower into the ground.

PREPOSTEROUS PHYSICS Possessing biceps of steel, Lady Jaye hand-throws javelins hard enough to hit flying gliders. Doc, the G.I. Joe team *medic*, almost off-handedly devises the ultra-powerful energy refracting mirror system – a landmark of physics that could revolutionize science and make Einstein squirm in his grave. Snake-Eyes smacks a guard in the face with a trident – but doesn't cause so much as a nosebleed.

TV TIE-INS Cover Girl's hair, formerly long and blonde in "The M.A.S.S. Device," here turns short and red to match her toy incarnation. Duke previously commented at the end of "The M.A.S.S. Device" that the Joes "weren't perfect but do okay," – words of wisdom that Flint re-utters during the finale of this story.

Crafted solely for the *G.I. Joe* TV series, Colonel Sharpe returns in "Cobra Stops the World."

Spirit and Storm Shadow renew their feud in "Countdown for Zartan." Disliking each others' goals and *modus operandi*, Zartan and Destro here begin their long-running rivalry ("Countdown to Zartan," "The Synthoid Conspiracy," etc.).

Sparks, a Joe communications officer who never got the action figure treatment, returns in "Cobra Stops the World."

CHARACTER PROFILE: JOES

• *Gung Ho:* He's prone to disobeying orders in order to log more battle time.

• *Lady Jaye*: Carries javelins as her main weapon, some of which explode or extend into high-jump poles at a moment's notice.

• *Mutt:* G.I. Joe dog trainer who growls like a dog himself. He's normally accompanied by a dog named Junkyard.

• *Roadblock:* Beefy, bald black machine gunner who annoyingly speaks with rhyme. He's a gourmet chef in his spare time.

• *Spirit:* American Indian tracker who's disgusted by pointless violence. Spirit's usually accompanied by his eagle Freedom, who's fast enough to beak-catch Storm Shadow's throwing stars. Spirit's evenly matched with Storm Shadow in a one-on-one fight.

• *Trip-Wire:* His mine detector device also gauges seismic activity.

CHARACTER PROFILE: COBRA

• *Destro:* He's still looking to dethrone Cobra Commander, but currently bows to his leadership.

• *Destro and Zartan:* Destro deems Zartan a repugnant mercenary, (rightly) questioning his loyalty and despising how much Zartan sucks up to Cobra Commander.

• *Major Bludd:* Favors Cobra Commander over Destro.

• *Storm Shadow:* Slippery Cobra ninja whose throwing stars unleash a gas attack.

• *Zartan:* Freelance mercenary who leads the rowdy Dreadnoks and holds standing contracts with Cobra Commander (presumably guarding against the likelihood that none of Cobra Commander's lieutenants will jump to his rescue as needed). Zartan possesses a chameleon-like talent that allows him to blend in with his surroundings, although direct sunlight greatly weakens him. Zartan's chest plate glows red when he's angered.

Aside from his color-shifting talent, Zartan disguises himself with latex masks. Zartan also equips himself with electronic voice replicators.

ORGANIZATIONS *Cobra:* Publishes a paper named the Cobra News. Cobra sensors can't detect wind power, explaining why Shipwreck operates his sand skimmer near Cobra bases in secrecy.

• *Dreadnoks:* Zartan's lackeys, composed of the flame-throwing Torch, the buzzsaw-wielding Buzzer and the bayonet-equipped Ripper. The Dreadnoks aren't exactly Rhodes Scholar material and often foil themselves by acting like childish prats. They're paid in gold, operate out of the Louisiana bayou and answer only to Zartan.

STUFF YOU NEED *Destro's Creeper Vines:* Innocently look like tiny sprigs – until you add a drop of water, making the sprigs suddenly shoot out tensile-strength fronds that choke the life out of you. Deprived of a continued water source, the creepers quickly wither and die.

THE COMMAND DECISION A drastic improvement over "The M.A.S.S. Device," crucially expanding G.I. Joe's cast (Flint, Lady Jaye, Zartan, etc.) while sticking to a ripping pace. Unfortunately, some profitless digressions (the painfully jokey, Southern-talking Honda Lou West) and abhorrent science (the stone giant, etc.) trip this mini-series long before the finish line, leaving the stylish "Revenge of Cobra" a reasonable effort – for a first draft.

1.1 to 1.5: "The Pyramid of Darkness"

Episodes: *Five*
Titles: *"The Further Adventures of G.I. Joe" (Pt. 1), "Rendezvous in the City of the Dead" (Pt. 2), "Three Cubes to Darkness" (Pt. 3), "Chaos in the Sea of Lost Souls" (Pt. 4), "Knotting Cobra's Coils" (Pt. 5)*
US Transmission Dates: *Sept. 16-20, 1985*
Order: *Season 1 #1-#5*
Writer: *Ron Friedman*

BATTLE ROSTER *Joes:* Flint, Lady Jaye, Snake-Eyes, Shipwreck, Mutt, Roadblock, Duke, Scarlett; *Cobra:* Cobra Commander, Destro, Zartan and the Dreadnoks, the Baroness, Major Bludd.

FIRST APPEARANCES *Joes:* Ace (fighter pilot), Alpine (mountain trooper), Bazooka (missile specialist), Dusty (desert trooper), Quick Kick (silent weapons specialist), Footloose (infantry trooper), Airtight (hostile environment specialist), Tollbooth (Bridge Layer driver), Admiral Ledger (*USS Flagg* commander); *Cobra:* Tomax and Xamot (Crimson Guard commanders).

MISSION BRIEF *Part 1:* Having established Space Station Delta, a new command center in geo-stationary orbit above Earth, G.I. Joe prepares to send up a shuttle containing additional Delta personnel and equipment. But suddenly, Cobra launches a massive air and ground assault on the shuttle's launch pad – a diversion to smuggle two secret cargo containers aboard the shuttle. Unaware of the deception, the Joes "easily" repel the enemy and celebrate as the shuttle – along with its contraband – launches to safety.

Mission complete, Cobra Commander flees underwater with his Crimson Guard commanders – twin brothers named Tomax and Xamot. Unwilling to let the Cobra brass escape, Snake-Eyes and Shipwreck pursue the villains, but lose time fighting a giant Cobra robot. Unable to capture the Cobra officers, Shipwreck and Snake-Eyes opt instead to explore a newly constructed tunnel, hopefully scouting out Cobra operations.

Meanwhile, the G.I. Joe shuttle crew discovers one of Cobra's illicit cargo pods, rallying Duke and his Joes aboard Space Station Delta to the defense. Braced for combat, the Joes tear open Cobra's container – only to uncover adorable, knee-high fuzzy animals resembling bears. The Joes breathe a sigh of relief, but Cobra espionage agent Zartan, having infiltrated the Delta shuttle crew, stealthily releases his Dreadnoks from the second pod and readies them for battle.

Now You Know

The cooing bears charm the Joes, but Zartan suddenly blows a high frequency whistle. Instantly, the Cobra-engineered fuzzy bears – dubbed "Fatal Fluffies" – writhe in agony as the whistle activates a pre-set mnemonic, expanding them into eight-feet-tall demonic-looking monstrosities. Completely surrounded, Duke's Joes yield control of Space Station Delta to Zartan.

Mostly for sport, Zartan unloads the full clip of Delta's laser cannons at Joe Headquarters – largely scrapping the Joe command center. Determined to take the battle to Cobra, Flint leaves a skeleton crew to repair Joe Headquarters and works at setting up a temporary base elsewhere.

Meanwhile, Cobra Commander and his officers rejoice, deeming the acquisition of Space Station Delta as the first step toward a more ambitious plan. Using Delta as a relay point, Cobra Commander schemes to plant four large control cubes across the Earth. When linked in an electric circuit with Delta, the four control cubes will create a formation named the "Pyramid of Darkness" – a region capable of neutralizing all electrical and combustion power within its boundaries. Cobra Commander anticipates that the world's nations, once divested of energy, will quickly surrender.

Respectively accompanied by their animal buddies – the wolf Timber and a parrot named Polly – Snake-Eyes and Shipwreck ditch their SHARC vessels and explore a Cobra-made subway line beneath Enterprise City. Overpowering two Cobras and taking their uniforms, Snake-Eyes and Shipwreck find themselves at a Cobra factory. Unfortunately, the automatic security system fails to recognize Shipwreck's voice, causing a lockdown that targets the hapless Joes for extermination.

Part 2: Shipwreck and Snake-Eyes indulge in sweaty panic as the security zone's walls start squeezing down on them, but the security system responds to Shipwreck's parrot Polly's shrieks and lets them through. Relived to be alive (and not flat), Shipwreck and Snake-Eyes explore the Cobra factory, finding it busily producing the four control cubes for the Pyramid of Darkness. Breaking into the factory's main office, Shipwreck, Snake-Eyes and their pets swipe a laser disc containing schematics for the control cubes. Discovered, Shipwreck's group barely evades capture and emerges – as hunted men and animals – into the slums of Enterprise City.

Aboard Space Station Delta, Zartan and the Dreadnoks use the Joes as slave labor, modifying the station to work as a focal point for the Pyramid of Darkness. Unable to re-gain control, Joes Dusty and Mutt settle for hot-wiring the station's communications array with a circuit breaker, allowing their Earth-bound teammates to eavesdrop on Cobra transmissions. In this fashion, the Joes learn about deployments of Cobra teams with control cubes to various locations on Earth.

Taking command, Flint relocates his Joes to the *USS Flagg* aircraft carrier, then readies an intercept team to tackle Destro-led forces intent on planting the first control cube in a molten area known as "The Devil's Playground." The Joes draw Destro's fire, allowing Flint and Lady Jaye to position themselves on a ridge behind Destro's troops. Unfortunately, Destro spots the duo and blasts the ground beneath their feet – plunging Flint and Lady Jaye beneath a pool of heated mud.

Part 3: Out of options – not to mention oxygen – Lady Jaye deploys a custom-made javelin, extending a life-sustaining bubble around herself and Flint. Rising through the ooze, the two Joes renew their attack, but the control cube suddenly sprouts a series of laser defenses, holding the Joes at bay while Destro's forces retreat.

Meanwhile, Shipwreck, Snake-Eyes and their animals find themselves at a Cobra-run nightclub named "The Snake Café." Cobra henchmen soon arrive, still following the Joes after their escape from the control cube factory, but the Café's lead singer – a sultry blonde named Satin – surprisingly hides the Joes in her dressing room.

Elsewhere, Crimson Guard commanders Tomax and Xamot arrive with the second control cube in a long-past Asian settlement known as "The City of the Dead." Extremely careful not to awaken the city's guardians – a massive contingent of inert, stone-cast warriors – the twins detect a platoon of G.I. Joe pursuers and quickly conceal themselves. As the twins anticipated, a Joe force led by Roadblock blunders in and carelessly sets off a Trip-Wire, rousing the guardians from their centuries-old slumber. With waves of stone samurais hellishly pounding at Roadblock's troops, the twins set about programming their control cube.

To the twins' dismay, a second vanguard of city defenders rallies to assault their position. Moments later, Roadblock's party bursts onto the scene and proceeds to laser everybody – annihilating the guardians and grabbing Tomax in the confusion – but Xamot succeeds in activating the control cube.

Instantly, the Cube fires a titanic electrical beam up through Earth's atmosphere, connecting with Space Station Delta. Moments later, Zartan activates Delta's augmented equipment and completes the circuit – locking the control cube in an unbreakable chain of energy and rendering it invulnerable to attack. A gloating Xamot retreats with his forces, vowing to return for his captured brother Tomax.

In "The Devil's Playground," Destro's control cube responds to a preset program and ceases attacking the Joes, establishing a secondary connection with Space Station Delta and constructing half of the "Pyramid of Darkness."

Across the world at a snowy peak dubbed "The Mountain of Glass," a team of Joes led by mountain climber Alpine and his bazooka-toting bud Bazooka engage Major Bludd's forces, intent on planting the third control cube. Separated from their allies, Alpine and Bazooka try to reach base camp, but Cobra ninja Storm Shadow spots them. Unable to hit the two Joes directly, Storm Shadow settles for shooting away the ice beneath their feet and setting the two Joes adrift on a tiny ice floe. Half-frozen and stranded, Alpine and Bazooka ponder their dwindling options – just as a pack of hungry killer leopard seals suddenly appears to assault the hapless heroes. (*Author's Note:* Please. I couldn't concoct this stuff if I tried.)

Part 4: As Alpine and Bazooka prepare to kick the oxygen habit, a martial arts expert named Quick Kick shows up, throws a line and hauls the Joes to freedom. Besting Storm Shadow in one-on-one combat, Quick Kick introduces himself as a movie stuntman, left by a crooked producer in the snow while filming a commercial for "Frozen Fudgie" bars.

Seconds later, Major Bludd finishes his task, activating the third control cube and establishing yet another unbreakable energy chain with Space Station Delta. Still isolated from the main Joe force, Alpine, Quick Kick and Bazooka pigeonhole themselves aboard the under-carriage of a HISS tank, taking a ride with Major Bludd back to Cobra Headquarters.

As Cobra comes perilously close to victory, the haggard Joes relocate the *Flagg to* "The Sea of Lost Souls" – the intended location for the fourth and final control cube. Cobra Commander grants Xamot's request to delay the Pyramid's activation until he liberates his brother Tomax from the *Flagg*'s brig, then gives Destro and the Baroness secret orders to activate the Pyramid ASAP – hopefully stranding the Crimson Twins and taking their spoils.

Xamot's Crimson Guardsmen successfully rescue Tomax, but Destro and the Baroness fend off the Joes' counter-assault and trigger the fourth control cube. Finally complete, the Pyramid of Darkness – in full conjunction with Space Station Delta – cancels out all electrical power within its boundaries. Marooned in the darkness, the Joes quickly rig the *Flagg* with sails, traveling back to the mainland via wind power.

Having anticipated Cobra Commander's treachery, Tomax and Xamot travel outside the Pyramid's boundaries in rafts, then shoot off an enormous flare – signaling their covert agents aboard Space Station Delta. Secretly in Tomax and Xamot's employ from the very start, the Dreadnoks turn on Zartan and usurp control of the space station.

Meanwhile, Satin tells Shipwreck and Snake-Eyes that she helped them because Cobra once framed her father for crimes he didn't commit. Satin helps smuggle the lost Joes and their pets out of Enterprise City, quickly departing despite Shipwreck's entreaties.

Pompously planning to deliver his victory speech, Cobra Commander turns stunned when Tomax and Xamot return to Cobra Headquarters and announce their acquisition of the Pyramid of Darkness – seizing Cobra leadership as a result. Cobra Commander sputters for a response, but the twins, delivering demands for surrender to the world's governments, allow the ex-Cobra leader to stay onboard as a toady.

Nearby, Major Bludd's division nears Cobra Headquarters, located in a remote tropical area outside the Pyramid's boundaries. Sensing they've reached the end of the line, the stowaway Alpine, Bazooka and Quick Kick bail out and steal a Cobra airplane. The Joes manage a smooth takeoff, but Cobra troopers hidden aboard the airplane jump them – starting a fight that causes the plane to spin perilously out of control.

Part 5: Alpine, Bazooka and Quick Kick briefly overpower their attackers and level out the plane, then abandon ship in one-man Cobra jet pods. Seizing control of a nearby Cobra helicopter, the Joes mop their brows and race for headquarters.

Aboard Space Station Delta, the Joes completely turn the tables when Mutt snatches the Fatal Fluffy control whistle from around Dreadnok Torch's neck. Hurriedly blowing into the whistle, Mutt triggers the mnemonic that defaults the Fluffies to their harmless, mewing, fuzzy bear incarnations. Easily overpowering the troop-less Dreadnoks, the Joes wrest back control of Space Station Delta and shut down the Pyramid of Darkness circuit – returning the four control cubes on Earth to a dormant standby mode.

Decrying the Pyramids' loss as "Calamity most foul!", Cobra Commander seizes back control of Cobra from the Crimson Twins, then flails about for a new strategy. Hoping to gain breathing space, Cobra Commander orders Destro to fly an augmented helicopter to a lofty mountain peak and link up with the control cubes – establishing a half-power, low altitude Pyramid of Darkness.

Having restored Joe Headquarters to minimal operation, the Joes rejoice as Shipwreck and Snake-Eyes finally arrive home with the control cube schematics. Studying the control cube designs, the Joes learn that the top-secret Cobra Headquarters contains a self-destruct switch for the Pyramid of Darkness. Clueless as to Cobra Headquarters' location, the Joes further celebrate when Alpine, Bazooka and Quick Kick waltz through the door with the required information.

With the low-altitude Pyramid of Darkness fading in and out, the Joes mobilize at half speed, eventually overwhelming Cobra Headquarters' defenses and activating the Pyramid's self-destruct. Across the world, the four control cubes obliterate themselves into a pile of smoking metal – again ending Cobra's mad schemes.

Zartan escapes from detention aboard Space Station Delta, briefly pausing to free his Dreadnoks and forgive their treachery. As a small token of punishment, Zartan ejects the Dreadnoks back to Earth in a garbage container, then comfortably returns to Earth himself aboard a one-man shuttle pod. Greatly diminished in resources and credibility, the rest of the Cobra leadership – including Cobra Commander, Destro, the Baroness and the Crimson Twins – withdraw into Enterprise City's underworld and trade blame for the Pyramid of Darkness debacle.

Now You Know

MEMORABLE MOMENTS *Part 1:* Shipwreck spouts philosophical nonsense and acts nutty (actually, it's not much of a act) so that Cobra subway workers won't question him and Snake-Eyes. The two Joes later trip a Cobra security system that simultaneously tries to mash them between two spike-covered walls (shades of the trash compactor in Star Wars) and dice them with floor-mounted buzz saws (Cobra, it seems, can't do anything simple).

• *Part 2:* Shipwreck tells a Cobra goon that parrot Polly and wolf Timber belong to Destro, further elaborating: "Hitler had a canary, Attila the Hun liked goldfish..." There's an surprisingly hilarious bit where a lava bubble pops and covers Destro's metal face plate with slime. In response, Destro calmly demands a sander from his aide, takes the device and polishes his face back to perfection.

Alpine waxes poetic about going to the Mountain of Glass: "... dangling in space, thousands of feet in the air... ain't that exciting?" (Bazooka quickly retorts: "No, sickening.")

• *Part 3:* The narrator recaps the action, uttering Sentence No. 584 we thought we'd never hear: "Using Fatal Fluffies, Cobra captures Space Station Delta!" Stone-cast guardians in "The City of the Dead" sneak up behind Roadblock's party and quietly nab several nameless Joes – their legs mutely kicking in protest – from behind. Satin intimidates Cobra Colonel Slash with, "Get out, Slush!", before pitching a lamp at him. Best of all, upon the first control cube's activation, Zartan ominously announces to his captive: "Savor this moment, Duke. It marks the beginning of your end."

• *Part 5:* Having traveled the final miles to Joe Headquarters on the back of a cow (thanks to the Pyramid of Darkness neutralizing all vehicle power), Shipwreck asks Wild Bill to "milk my pony and bring me a glass." The turncoat Dreadnoks beg for Zartan's forgiveness – by groveling at his feet. Cobra Commander bemoans the loss of the Pyramid of Darkness with his usual restraint: "I've lost my beautiful cubes! Now I'll never rule the world! I hate this job!"

LOVE AND WAR Flint and Lady Jaye plunge beneath lava-like ooze, then huddle close within a life-saving air bubble – a situation that Lady Jaye deems "cozy." Referring to the pink goo surrounding them, Flint tells her, "Pink is your color," then nervously blathers: "So, where do we go from here... not us personally ... I mean the mission." (Lady Jaye cattily answers, "Why, to the top," and lifts them out of the lava pool.)

For the first time on TV, Destro and the Baroness openly acknowledge a relationship, notably playing tonsil-hockey in Part 4 (Cobra Commander, catching them in the act, spouts: "I see you both clearly and I am stunned!"). Still, fallout from the "Pyramid of Darkness" debacle leaves Destro and the Baroness bitching at each other by story's end.

Shipwreck seems taken with hottie singer Satin (granted, her "Cobra that Got Away" song is one of the more tolerable *G.I. Joe* musical moments), but only gets a smooch for his effort.

Quick Kick sizes up Alpine and Bazooka as being less handsome than Robert Redford, making us wonder if Q-Kick's the type of man who walks across eggshells without cracking a single one.

"The Pyramid of Darkness" sports a decent amount of double-entendres, including Destro's barked order: "Commence implantation!" A Cobra trooper, hot on Snake-Eyes and Shipwreck's tail, shouts: "Increase thrust!" Tomax tells his Joe captors: "Thank you for making my pursuit so... physical," then belts out a hearty laugh. Perhaps worst of all, Bazooka asks for a Frozen Fudgie snack bar and frequently babbles: "Fudgies!!"

ASS-WHUPPINGS For the third mini-series in a row, Duke gets pistol-whipped (this time by a Fatal Fluffy). Scarlett tosses a monstrous Fatal Fluffy aside, squishing Zartan. Rebellious Joes variously activate/deactivate Space Station Delta's artificial gravity, leading to a Dreadnok three-wheeler pile-up.

During a chase over the train tracks, Snake-Eyes smacks his pursuers in the head with a signal sign. Mingling with Satin's can-can crew, Shipwreck and Snake-Eyes nail their pursuers with a high-flying kick worthy of *Moulin Rouge*.

Roadblock shoots loose a large decorative stone ball that bowls over a number of "City of the Dead" guardians (shades of *Raiders of the Lost Ark*). Roadblock also gives Tomax a furious shaking, making his twin brother Xamot (*see Character Profile*) twist about like an epileptic. Shipwreck punches one twin in Part 5, allowing Snake-Eyes to follow up with a belly kick.

Bazooka twists his ankle on "The Mountain of Glass," hobbling his way through a couple episodes. Joe wannabe Quick Kick and Cobra ninja Storm Shadow rush at each other and trade kicks – both of them look perfectly fine for a moment afterward, then Storm Shadow falls flat on his face.

Satin drops off Shipwreck and Snake-Eyes in Part 4, but briefly returns in Part 5 to mash Cobra Commander's face plate into a console. Space Station Delta eradicates the Crimson Twins' giant rocket (which isn't terribly relevant to the plot – *see Places to Go*).

SAVE THEM! Alpine, Bazooka and Quick Kick use one-man Cobra jet pods to storm a Cobra helicopter, overpowering the crew in five seconds flat. The Cobra troops in question evidently wear parachutes at all times, because the Joes toss 'em out and the Cobras easily chute to safety.

PREPOSTEROUS PHYSICS Tomax and Xamot plant hand-held rockets that pack enough wallop to alter the Joe

Friedman Repeats Himself...

Keeping in mind that writer Ron Friedman penned all three of the initial G.I. Joe mini-series ("The M.A.S.S. Device," "The Revenge of Cobra" and "The Pyramid of Darkness") – and that the stories in question were produced with year-long intervals between them, it's not hard to speculate why the stories contain so many familiar elements. For anyone who's watched the three mini-series in a row – and felt like a temporal loop's taken hold of your VCR – here's a rundown of the mini-series' most striking similarities:

The M.A.S.S. Device	The Revenge of Cobra	The Pyramid of Darkness
Cobra embarks on an over-complicated scheme to rule the world with the "M.A.S.S. Device," a doo-hickey that teleport matter.	Cobra embarks on an over-complicated scheme to rule the world with the "Weather Dominator," a doo-hickey that controls weather patterns.	Cobra embarks on an over-complicated scheme to rule the world with the "Pyramid of Darkness," a doo-hickey that cancels out electricity.
The Joes madly race around the world, contesting with Cobra for possession of three ultra-rare elements needed to fuel the M.A.S.S. Device.	The Joes madly race around the world, contesting with Cobra for possession of three Weather Dominator components.	The Joes madly race around the world, contesting with Cobra over placement of four "Pyramid of Darkness" control cubes.
The Joes and Cobra clash in geographic locations with fanciful names such as "The Sea of Ice."	The Joes and Cobra clash in geographic locations with fanciful names such as "The Palace of Doom."	The Joes and Cobra clash in geographic locations with fanciful names such as "The City of the Dead."
Duke gets captured, thrown into a fiendish Cobra battle arena.	Duke gets captured, thrown into a fiendish Cobra battle arena.	Duke gets captured, tossed into a cell aboard Space Station Delta and near-forgotten.
The Joes keep overly intelligent animals such as the wolf Timber, who's got a knowledge of chemistry (Part 4).	The Joes keep overly intelligent animals such as the dog Junkyard, who knows which spare Skystriker parts to gather (Part 2).	The Joes keep overly intelligent animals such as the parrot Polly, who somehow fools a Cobra security system (Part 2).
Destro briefly gets one over on Cobra Commander, usurps Cobra leadership.	Zartan briefly gets one over on Cobra Commander, steals a vital laser core.	Tomax and Xamot briefly get one over on Cobra Commander, usurp Cobra leadership.
G.I. Joe discovers Cobra Headquarters mostly by luck (Duke's madcap escape), thereby insuring Cobra's defeat.	G.I. Joe discovers Cobra Headquarters mostly by luck (Duke's homing device), thereby insuring Cobra's defeat.	G.I. Joe discovers Cobra Headquarters mostly by luck (Alpine, Bazooka and Quick Kick hitch a ride from Major Bludd), thereby insuring Cobra's defeat.
Cobra Commander gets captured, walks about in "The Revenge of Cobra" without an explanation of his escape.	Cobra Commander gets captured, walks about in "The Pyramid of Darkness" without an explanation of his escape.	Cobra Commander breaks with tradition, surprisingly ends the story disguised as a bag lady.

space shuttle's course. Various characters aboard the gravityless Space Station Delta "airwalk" from location to location (Sorry, zero-gee doesn't work like that). Flint carves a Cobra HISS tank in half with his Skystriker's jet wing, which was evidently manufactured by Ginsu.

Lady Jaye deploys a life support bubble around herself and Flint, failing to take into account that they're already immersed in ooze. (In other words, the bubble's deployment should have also encased a bunch of gunk, suffocating the pair of them. Excellent.) Moreover, Flint and Lady Jaye emerge from the ooze without a drop on them.

Airtight steps on a pressure-sensitive stone in "The City of the Dead" – which seems odd, considering Cobra successfully drove a control cube-laden support truck over it in the previous scene.

On the "Mountain of Glass," Alpine's yodeling brings down a snowcap that repeated noise from discharging laser rifles failed to shift. It's wildly optimistic that the Joes could move their massive aircraft carrier, adrift in the "Pyramid of Darkness," by simply adding sails.

Space Station Delta variously hovers above one of Earth's poles and the equator. Destro's low-level "Pyramid of Darkness," established in Part 4, has about a spittle's chance of working – no matter which mountain he chooses to sit atop.

Perhaps oddest of all, Tomax and Xamot escape in Part 4 in rafts pulled by *killer sharks.*

GOOFS "The Pyramids of Darkness" debuts a very strange G.I. Joe tradition: Every single episode in the first two seasons opens with Flint screaming "Yo, Joe!" – in Duke's voice.

Cobra fails to insulate their own equipment against the Pyramid's effects – so how the hell will they conquer the world if they're powered down as well? The Fatal Fluffies instantly produce laser rifles when they shift from harmless plush critter-mode to their horned, fire-spouting demon forms. Destro flies his Cobra Rattler jet into a secret hanger in downtown Enterprise City – and apparently, nobody notices.

A few Joes – including Rock 'n Roll, Scarlett, Barbeque, Spirit and Dusty – are simultaneously captive on Space Station Delta and running about on various missions. For that matter, Quick Kick appears at Joe Headquarters before its destruction – indeed, before he even meets the team.

At the start of Part 2, why the hell does the Cobra security system acknowledge a voice print from Polly, who's a damn parrot? (It's possible he mimics a Cobra goon's voice, but it goes unspecified.) Also in Part 2, Mutt's black dog Junkyard sports Timber's gray coat at one point. In Part 3, Lady Jaye's spotted at one point wearing a brown jumper rather than her green combat fatigues.

During a frantic chase on a hand-pumped train trolley, Shipwreck turns aside to repair the engine and… ha-ha-ha… asks Timber, *the frickin' wolf*… HA-HA-HA!!… *to help Snake-Eyes pedal*… (Author wipes away tears). By the way, Snake-Eyes and Shipwreck conjure hitherto-unseen rifles for the last part of their pursuit.

Satin leaves Shipwreck and Snake-Eyes to their own devices in Part 4, then reappears in Part 5, having penetrated defenses aboard a Cobra rocket without a word of explanation.

Martial arts expert Quick Kick walks about shirtless and shoeless in arctic wastes, completely oblivious to the freezing temperatures and looking as if he's in Tahiti. Cobra ninja Storm Shadow, slightly better clad but hardly wearing an insulated jumper, similarly ignores what's probably a minus-50-degree wind chill. Alpine and Bazooka successfully hide from a heat stroke-inducing "Cobra Dragon" cannon, then appear among the Dragon's victims.

Atrocious plotting allows the Crimson Twins, having failed miserably with the "Pyramid of Darkness," to spontaneously unleash an "unstoppable" (and previously unmentioned) rocket ship at the end of Part 5. (Joes aboard Space Station Delta easily obliterate the twins' rocket, but man – talk about filler.)

G.I. JOE: THE MUSICAL Cobra prisoner Dusty decides to torment his captors (and the audience) with a hokey song about how he "loves" doing his work, "… to a boogie-woogie beat! Just let your feet tap and moo-o-o-o-ove …"

Memorably unable to fit in with Satin's dance troupe, Snake-Eyes resorts to a fit of breakdancing. Worse – oh, and trust us, this *is* worse – Satin deceives a Cobra border patrol by dressing up Shipwreck, Snake-Eyes and their animals as band members. As part of the disguise, Shipwreck struts about in a blue zoot suit, blonde wig and saxophone chattering something about "Agitation!" while Snake-Eyes almost mimics rocker Cyndi Lauper with a yellow dress, red wig and floppy hat. Adding to the mayhem, parrot Polly appears with a dinky beret and shiny glasses, while Timber the wolf hops about in a red wig, purple hat and something that vaguely looks like a stuck-on pink dragon tail. (Only the power of tequila helped us get through this scene.)

Martial arts expert Quick Kick regales Alpine and Bazooka with a Frozen Fudgie jingle: "Frozen Fudgies, quite a treat! Lots of chocolate, really sweet!" In part 5, Alpine, Bazooka and Quick Kick crank up their jeep's speakers and repeat their yodeling trick from Part 4 – bringing a rock outcropping down atop a Cobra cannon.

TV TIE-INS Captured a second time in "The Revenge of Cobra," Cobra Commander again opens this story walking about free without a word of explanation. Shipwreck and Snake-Eyes enter a disco joint playing the same music as "Danc-I-Tron" (Transformers: "Auto-Bop"). The music also crops up in "Cold Slither." Having only joined G.I. Joe in "The Revenge of Cobra," Shipwreck's moved through the ranks fast enough to here serve as a field commander. "The Revenge of Cobra" also provided glimpses of Cobra's Crimson Guardsmen, although Tomax and Xamot here lead the group.

Aircraft carrier leader Admiral Ledger appears as a member of the Pentagon brass in "The Synthoid Conspiracy."

CHARACTER PROFILE: JOES

• *Admiral Ledger:* Venerable seaman and commander of the *USS Flagg*, Ledger isn't overly respectful to women (Flint nicely puts Ledger in his place for slagging on Lady Jaye).

• *Airtight:* Essentially a nerd at heart, prone to running fuel consumption calculations for fun.

• *Airtight and Footloose:* Joe newcomers who've never been in charge of a mission.

• *Alpine and Bazooka:* Alpine thinks Frozen Fudgies are gross; Bazooka likes 'em.

• *Bazooka:* Decently lousy at hand-to-hand combat.

• *Dusty:* Used to repair refrigerators for a living. Dusty's a desert trooper, but gets assigned to Space Station Delta for some reason.

• *Lady Jaye:* One of her javelins projects a net.

• *Quick Kick:* Former movie stuntman and martial arts expert whose credits include *Last Jet to Killer Karate College* and a Robert Redford film. Quick Kick's movie work included pilot training. Despite a tendency to spout movie quotes every few minutes, Quick Kick possesses formidable martial arts skills and moves quick enough to parry Storm Shadow's throwing stars with his own. Encountering the Joes as a civilian, Quick Kick presumably joins the team soon after.

• *Shipwreck:* Among his many talents, Shipwreck plays the saxophone.

• *Wild Bill:* Not surprisingly, his father owns a ranch.

CHARACTER PROFILE: COBRA

• *Destro:* Among other things, he's an expert at robot design.

• *Tomax and Xamot:* Psionically connected twin brothers who routinely finish each other's sentences and, more strikingly, feel each other's pain (knocking one brother unconscious takes both of them out). The talent has its uses, however – by letting the Joes jostle him during a chase, Tomax enables Xamot to share in his trauma and thereby deduce his location.

The entrepreneurial brothers own the lucrative Extensive Enterprises Corp. (*see Places to Go*) and command the Crimson Guard, Cobra's elite band of shock troops. The two brothers are mirror images of each other, save for a scar on Xamot's face.

CHARACTER PROFILE: OTHER

Satin: Despises Cobra – and Cobra Commander in particular – for framing her father for unspecified crimes (it evidently left Pappa Satin a broken man). Her van's equipped with reinforced armor plating that deflects laser fire.

ORGANIZATIONS *Cobra:* Evidently pays its troopers in a currency named "gold fang shillings."

• *City of the Dead Guardians:* Essentially break down into two types: Large stone-cast samurai warriors and lightsaber-wielding skeletons.

PLACES TO GO *The City of the Dead:* Its radioactive mineral deposits interfere with scanning equipment (meaning the Joes can't detect Cobra's presence).

• *Space Station Delta:* Staffers include Duke, Scarlett, Clutch, Steeler, Rock 'n Roll, Doc, Breaker, Dusty and Mutt. The Joes rigged Delta with a proton beam powerful enough to obliterate the Extensive Enterprises rocket (*see Stuff You Need*).

STUFF YOU NEED *Cobra Dragon:* Main cannon that protects Cobra Headquarters from attack, capable of unleashing energy waves that instill a terminal case of heat stroke. Alpine, Bazooka and Quick Kick stymied the Dragon by amplifying their yodels (Author's Note: GROAN), bringing down rubble and squishing the device.

• *Cobra Rattler Jets:* Equipped with magnetic beams capable of moving metal.

• *Extensive Enterprises Corp.:* Tomax and Xamot-owned corporation that finances multiple Cobra projects. The main Extensive Enterprises towers, located in Enterprise City, contain a jet hanger and, as a weapon of last resort, a battle rocket and gantry. After the Pyramid of Darkness' failure, Tomax and Xamot briefly tried to unleash the rocket's power against the Joes, but Space Station Delta obliterated the attacking craft (the brothers escaped).

• *Fatal Fluffies:* Cobra-engineered shock troops, useful because they transform from harmless furry critters to fire-breathing, horned monstrosities with the blow of an ultra-frequency whistle. Less productively, the Fatal Fluffies are decently stupid, vulnerable to electricity and prone to infighting.

• *Starflies:* Cobra-used weapons that look like harmless glowing butterflies but release sleepy gas.

THE COMMAND DECISION Another step in the right direction, more entertaining, complex and adrenaline-laced than we'd remembered. We'll grant that where "The Pyramid of Darkness" bombs (the Fatal Fluffies, Shipwreck and Snake-Eyes dressing as rock singers, the Crimson Twins' gratuitous rocket etc.), it really bombs. Still, progress is progress, and – unlike some other Joe cartoons – we'd freely watch "The Pyramid of Darkness" again purely for fun.

1.6: "Countdown for Zartan"

US Transmission Date: Sept. 23, 1985
Writer: Christy Marx

BATTLE ROSTER *Joes:* Spirit, Lady Jaye, Gung Ho, Stalker, Doc, Recondo; *Cobra:* Zartan, the Dreadnoks, Cobra Commander, Destro.

MISSION BRIEF Hoping to pool information about Cobra's activities, renowned scientists and intelligence agents from several nations gather at the America's Worldwide Defense Center, an organization founded to end terrorism. Bristling at the Defense Center's potential to disrupt Cobra operations, Cobra Commander assigns disguise expert Zartan to eradicate the building and its occupants.

Aided by Cobra ninja Storm Shadow, disguise expert Zartan kidnaps Dr. Metier – a French terrorist expert – and infiltrates the Defense Center wearing Metier's identity. With Storm Shadow keeping watch, Zartan plants a sizeable bomb in the center's backup control room, setting the explosive with enough time for himself and Storm Shadow to escape. Fortunately, G.I. Joe tracker Spirit – assigned to guard the Defense Center's visitors – stumbles upon the Cobra goons and engages Storm Shadow in combat. Zartan knocks Spirit unconscious, allowing Storm Shadow to stealthily haul the unconscious Joe back to a Cobra outpost. But Spirit's eagle Freedom escapes and flies to Joe Headquarters, summoning Spirit's teammates.

Fearing for Spirit's safety, Lady Jaye, Gung Ho and various other Joes surge into the Defense Center just as the still-disguised Zartan attempts to "innocently" exit. Freedom tags "Dr. Metier" as a Cobra infiltrator, allowing the Joes to unmask Zartan and toss him into the Defense Center's holding cells. Itching to escape before the bomb detonates, Zartan makes Lady Jaye's team suspicious by begging to be incarcerated at Joe Headquarters. Further tipped off by the odd countdown ticking away on Zartan's watch, Lady Jaye's group fans out, feverishly searching the Defense Center for explosives.

As the countdown continues into its final minute, the captured Zartan – favoring survival over his Cobra loyalties – cracks like an egg and madly informs Gung Ho of the bomb's location. The Joes rush into the backup control room as the countdown expires – although the bomb oddly fails to explode – and dismantle the incendiary with little difficulty. When the Joes express surprise at their survival, Gung Ho confesses to advancing Zartan's digital watch by two minutes, figuring that Zartan wouldn't crack in time to properly disarm the bomb.

Learning of Zartan's failure, Cobra Commander abandons subtlety and orders a full frontal assault on the Defense Center. Zartan escapes in the resultant fracas, but by the same token, Spirit breaks out of the Cobra outpost with Dr. Metier and steals a Cobra jet. Lady Jaye's Joes expertly coordinate their efforts with the airborne Spirit, ultimately prevailing against superior Cobra firepower. With the Defense Center saved, Louisiana-born Gung Ho proposes celebrating with a round of homemade gumbo, eliciting various groans from his teammates while Dr. Metier rejoices, proclaiming the dish "an American delicacy."

MEMORABLE MOMENTS Recondo claims that the Joes once used Gung Ho's homemade gumbo as Skystriker fuel. Zartan hyperactively begs the Joes to save him from the bomb, then caps his pleas off with a sob of: "I'm doomed." In disarming Zartan's bomb, Recondo momentarily pulls the wrong wire and the countdown speeds up. The French Dr. Metier – and his stereotypically giant schnozz – make a memorable (if overly nasal) entrance.

LOVE AND WAR The ever-complimentary Dreadnok Ripper flatters Lady Jaye with: "What a nice bit of fluff you are..." (Little wonder why he spends Friday nights alone.)

ASS-WHUPPINGS Storm Shadow tosses Spirit about like a sack of potatoes. Purely for sport, the Dreadnoks flood Spirit and Metier's cell with laughing gas, intent on making them laugh themselves to death (Storm Shadow interrupts the grisly process, believing noble enemies such as Spirit shouldn't be treated in such a fashion).

NOW YOU KNOW If you're going to flame something, start with the foundation – it'll bring the rest of your target tumbling down.

PREPOSTEROUS PHYSICS Seeking to prove that "the ninja is a weapon" (i.e. that the human body, if properly honed, is more effective than a rifle), Storm Shadow leaps and prances about an old tank, randomly hitting and kicking its pressure points. Seconds later, the "weakened" tank falls apart like a bunch of Legos.

TV TIE-INS The Destro/Zartan rivalry begun in "The Revenge of Cobra" here continues full force, complete with lengthy bitching sessions. Spirit first tangled with Storm Shadow in "The Revenge of Cobra."

CHARACTER PROFILE: JOES

- *Gung Ho:* He's famed for his Cajun cooking and homemade gumbo (although his teammates – Stalker in particular – can't stand it), insisting that it builds muscles.
- *Gung Ho and Lady Jaye:* Gung Ho's a highly accurate

javelin thrower, but he's nowhere near Lady Jaye's league.

- *Lady Jaye:* Carries javelins with luminescent tips.
- *Spirit:* Keeps a small knife concealed in his headband.

CHARACTER PROFILE: COBRA

- *Destro, Zartan and the Dreadnoks:* Destro regards the Dreadnoks as useless air suckers, holding loyalty only to the gold that the "sniveling" Zartan feeds them.
- *Storm Shadow:* The ninja-trained Storm Shadow holds some honor, favoring fair fights and avoiding sneak-from-behind attacks when possible. He's a crack shot with a bow (although Spirit's eagle Freedom can intercept Storm Shadow's in-flight arrows).
- *Torch:* Dreadnok who's an expert at flame-throwing and arson.
- *Zartan:* Knows how to fool fingerprint-sensitive hand scanners.

ORGANIZATIONS *Dreadnoks:* Arrogant to the point of overconfidence. If anything should happen to Zartan (rendering him incapable of paying their salaries), Cobra promises to pay for their services.

STUFF YOU NEED *Dreadnok Weapons:* Torch's blowtorch, Ripper's bayonet and Buzzer's buzzsaw can cut and melt through tank steel.

THE COMMAND DECISION A paint-by-the-numbers story that's really two plots stapled together (with Cobra Commander resorting to the time-honored tradition of the air strike when Zartan fails). It's hardly painful – it's just not very moving either.

1.7: "Red Rocket's Glare"

US Transmission Date: *Sept. 24, 1985*
Writer: *Mary Skrenes*

BATTLE ROSTER *Joes:* Roadblock, Recondo, Flint, Lady Jaye, Blowtorch, Tollbooth; *Cobra:* Tomax and Xamot, Cobra Commander, Destro.

MISSION BRIEF Trying to kill two weeks of leave time, Joes Roadblock and Recondo travel up the California coast to visit Sarah and Caleb Bronson, Roadblock's aunt and uncle, at their new restaurant – a branch of the Red Rocket drive-in burger chain. But upon arrival, Roadblock finds motorcycle hoodlums chasing off his relatives' customers. After thrashing the cyclists (who're strangely armed with laser pistols), Roadblock and Recondo speculate why the punks would

MISCELLANEOUS STUFF!

NOW YOU KNOW MESSAGES

Let's face it... the *G.I. Joe* public service announcements – those nuggets of wisdom at the end of every episode, telling you useful stuff like how blind children can locate cats – often achieve a level of notoriety greater than the show itself. So here's a full list of the lessons, organized alphabetically by character, that ran throughout the Sunbow cartoons. Keep in mind that some characters appeared twice, and that only 34 of the messages were produced (there were a *lot* of repeat showings):

- **Airtight: Fainting first aid** – "Never lift the head of someone who's fainted. Keep him flat and brace his legs. Now loosen his clothes and use a wet cloth."
- **Alpine: What to do if you're lost** – "Stay calm. Think. Where did you see [your father/brother/whatever] last? Go back there. If he doesn't come back, ask a policeman for help."
- **Barbecue: False fire alarms just aren't funny** – "Remember, a firefighter's job is to fight fires – not answer false alarms."
- **Barbecue: What to do if your house catches on fire** – "If a fire breaks out in your home, always test the door first. If it's hot, find another exit or yell for help."
- **Blowtorch: What to do if your house catches on fire, pt. 2** – "If there's a real fire in your house, your first job is to escape immediately. Fire spreads quickly. Call the fire department from outside the house."
- **Cross-Country & Beach-Head: Helmets are your friends** – "These ATVs have as much power as a real motorcycle. You gotta respect them... and wear a helmet for protection."
- **Cutter: Fighting isn't the answer** – "When people disagree, sometimes they need someone who's not involved to settle things. Instead of fighting when you disagree, look for a better way."
- **Deep Six: How to avoid electrocution while swimming** – "At even the hint of a thunderstorm, get right out of the water."
- **Deep Six: Life jackets are your friends** – "A life jacket is good protection!"
- **Dial-Tone: Don't huff spray paint** – "All paints, and especially spray paints, have poisonous gases in

CONTINUED ON PAGE 27...

seek to run a Red Rocket burger joint out of business.

Meanwhile, Cobra moves forward plans to force dozens of Red Rockets across the nation out of business, acquiring them at bargain basement prices. By augmenting the rocket-shaped prop atop each Red Rocket with a real engine and Destro's newest invention – a "photon disintegrator" capable of wiping out entire cities upon impact – Cobra instantly creates 150 armed warheads ready for launch in the continental United States.

With the rocket modifications complete, Cobra Commander delivers a televised ultimatum, threatening to unleash hundreds of missiles upon North America unless the world's nations surrender to Cobra rule. But the crafty Joes, noticing a map of missile sites posted behind Cobra Commander's ranting form, matching the missile positions with known locations of the Red Rocket restaurants.

With half the battle behind them, frenzied Joe teams storm Red Rocket drive-ins across the country, tangling with Cobra skeleton crews and dismantling or destroying the augmented red rockets. With Cobra's plan ruined, Roadblock's relatives rename their restaurant "Joe's Place" and hold a celebratory barbecue for the victorious Joes.

MEMORABLE MOMENTS In a commentary on 1980s youth, a bunch of teenagers drive up to the Red Rocket inn owned by Roadblock's relatives. On the lookout for hooligans, Roadblock and Recondo prepare to crack the newcomers' heads, but Uncle Caleb shouts out: "No, they're the customers! It's those guys! The ones with the cycles and rayguns!" (some parents might argue there's not much difference). Oh, and years before the creation of Star Trek's Borg, one of the purple-haired geek customers asks during a firefight: "Can you like, really, assimilate this?"

Roadblock praises jungle trooper Recondo as expert enough to "find an eyelash you lost in the woods two years ago."

Just before the commercial break, Lady Jaye desperately clings to the undercarriage of Flint's helicopter, but a cackling Tomax and Xamot – portrayed in this story as total adrenaline freaks – grab Lady Jaye's legs and pull hard. The three of them plummet to certain doom – Lady Jaye screaming all the way – but survive thanks to some fancy gymnastics.

Cobra troops assault some Joes as they munch on Red Rocket burgers (rather like the telephone ringing after you've just stepped into the shower).

ASS-WHUPPINGS Roadblock stuffs a Cobra agent's head inside a trash can.

GOOFS We hardly need mention it's idiotic for Cobra to spend millions augmenting the Red Rocket rocket-shaped props into deadly missiles rather than simply building their own launch pads. (We're surmising that Cobra originally sold the Red Rockets as an investment scheme to swindle retired couples, later adapting it for the Red Rocket plot – but that's pure conjecture.)

The Crimson Twins over-zealously commit troops to capturing the single Red Rocket owned by Roadblock's relatives when they've already acquired 150 other drive-ins around the country. (Good grief, why bother?)

Cobra Commander's boobish enough to conveniently display a map of his missile locations to the whole world during his televised ultimatum.

Despite the events of "The Pyramid of Darkness," where the Extensive Enterprises towers converted into a Cobra battle rocket, the Joes only half-heartedly recognize the company's connection to Cobra. A test run of Destro's photon disintegrator completely atomizes a mock-up town – but strangely leaves an on-screen butterfly flapping about (must be a damnably tough butterfly).

PREPOSTEROUS PHYSICS When Joe member Blowtorch bursts into Destro's laboratory, Cobra goons topple some bookshelves toward the hapless Joe. Sensing the danger, Blowtorch responds by discharging his flame-thrower, entirely disintegrating the bookshelves when they should've more properly pancaked him beneath piles of flaming timber.

Too lazy to actually land their private jet, the Crimson Twins jump from their in-flight plane and land, sans parachute or other aid, atop an Extensive Enterprises tower.

Several Joes take out the photon disintegrator-laden rockets with laser cannons, when you'd think this would set it off (in fact, Lady Jaye causes a group of Cobras to hold their fire for fear of striking one of the photon devices). With the accuracy of James Bond, Flint uses a Skystriker missile to shear the nosecone – and its photon disintegrator – off an in-flight red rocket.

TV TIE-INS Once again proving that G.I. Joe has virtually no sense of continuity, Crimson Guard Commanders Tomax and Xamot continue to serve as thriving, legitimate businessmen despite having blackmailed the world in "The Pyramid of Darkness." The Extensive Enterprises Towers, stripped down to reveal a super-rocket and launch gantry in the same story, are here rebuilt without a word of explanation or comment.

Lady Jaye claims she's scared of heights, a fact that's reiterated in "Satellite Down."

CHARACTER PROFILE: JOES

- *Blowtorch:* Evidently one of the freshmen Joe members, as Roadblock dubs him "a kid."
- *Lady Jaye:* Carries a pistol that melts glass.

CHARACTER PROFILE: COBRA

• *Destro:* Worked on the photon disintegrator design for two years.

• *Tomax and Xamot:* Total adrenaline freaks, as evidenced by their grappling with Roadblock atop an in-flight red rocket (Roadblock wins, but the brothers deem their effort, "Worth it… just for the ride!"). The slimy Mr. Queeg handles some of the brothers' business matters.

THE COMMAND DECISION The subject (and rightfully so) of disdain from several corners of fandom, the rotten-at-the-core "Red Rocket's Glare" almost seems better suited as a ghastly Happy Days or Three's Company plot (so-and-so invests in a burger joint, loses their shirt to motorcycle thugs, etc.). Frankly, even for G.I. Joe, there's a line of ridiculousness that shouldn't be crossed – and this is it.

1.8: "Satellite Down"

US Transmission Date: *Sept. 25, 1985*
Writer: *Ted Pedersen*

BATTLE ROSTER *Joes:* Spirit, Lady Jaye, Dusty, Flint, Breaker; *Cobra:* Storm Shadow, Destro.

MISSION BRIEF When G.I. Joe launches an advanced surveillance satellite, Destro attempts to override the Joes' control and snare the device for Cobra's benefit. Left with little choice, the Joes scrub the mission and fire emergency boosters – bringing the satellite back to Earth rather than relinquishing it to Cobra. As the satellite crashes into an unexplored African region, both G.I. Joe and Cobra alert their agents to converge on the landing site.

In Africa, Flint and Lady Jaye's troops make progress through the thick foliage, but a scrap with a Cobra platoon separates Spirit and Lady Jaye from their fellows. Cobra ninja Storm Shadow follows and ambushes the two wayward Joes, but the trio finds themselves surrounded by a group of Primords – reclusive apelike proto-humans prone to killing outsiders.

Storm Shadow, Spirit and Lady Jaye quickly find themselves tied up in a Primord place of worship, where the savage Primords, taken with the satellite's "glowing eyes," regard it as a fallen god. As a sacrifice to their newfound deity, the Primords try to flatten Lady Jaye beneath a boulder, but Flint's troops thankfully mount a rescue attempt.

Spirit and Storm Shadow momentarily join forces, but the Cobra ninja snubs the Joes' innate mercy toward the Primords, setting off an explosion that threatens to flatten both Primords and Joes beneath falling boulders. While her teammates laser

MISCELLANEOUS STUFF!

CONTINUED ON PAGE 25...

them. If you breathe too much you can get very sick. Always read the label carefully and check for warnings before you start any job."

• **Doc: Don't take medicine without an adult present** – "Never take medicine without a grown-up present. You could do more harm then good. If you can, wait for your parents. Of if it's serious, ask a neighbor for help."

• **Dusty: Put reflectors on your bike** – "I couldn't see you! No wonder... you don't have reflectors. They tell drivers where you are. Remember, if you have to ride when it's getting dark, have the right equipment."

• **Flint: Work together to solve problems** – "Look, if you want to play your best, you've got to play like a team. Remember, you need teamwork to win, not arguments."

• **Flint: Don't blame others for your mistakes** – "Face up to what you've done. Don't take the easy way out. Remember, it's better to tell the truth."

• **Flint: Rely on your conscience** – "It's hard not to listen to the crowd, but sometimes, that path is just a dead end. Remember, listen to yourself."

• **Footloose: Nosebleed first aid** – "Pinch your nose closed and lean forward. If it doesn't stop in five minutes, pack your nose with gauze and pinch it closed for ten more minutes. If it's still bleeding, then see a doctor."

• **General Hawk: Be afraid of trains** – "Those gates are provided as a warning to let you know that it's not safe to cross [the tracks]."

• **Gung Ho: Don't judge girls by their cover** – "Don't judge people until you give them a chance."

• **Lady Jaye: Don't take stupid dares** – "There's nothing chicken about being smart. If you stop and think, there's almost always a better way."

• **Leatherneck: Use sunscreen** – "A bad sunburn can make you sick or even put you in the hospital."

• **Lifeline: Junk food is bad for you** – "A candy bar might give you a quick boost of energy, but after 20 minutes, you'll feel run down. So let's eat smart!"

• **Mutt: Strange dogs are not your friends** – "Don't run! Walk away slowly. Never try to pet an animal you don't know. He might be lost, sick or scared. If we don't

CONTINUED ON PAGE 29...

the incoming rocks into powder, Lady Jaye saves the life of the Primord chief's son – thereby winning the tribe's respect.

The Joes and Primords solidify their alliance, defending the satellite as Storm Shadow and a column of Cobra troops drive home another assault. During the fracas, Flint stops a Cobra helicopter pilot from hauling the satellite away, smashing the device to pieces. Run ragged, Storm Shadow flees, leaving the Joes to capture several of his soldiers. Standing down, the Joes gather the satellite's microchips – preserving its data contents – thank the Primords for their help and return to America.

MEMORABLE MOMENTS Spirit proposes an alliance with Storm Shadow against the Primords, but there's a delicious moment when Spirit – forced to fulfill on the deal by freeing the tied-up Storm Shadow – takes a knife and looks like he's having an internal debate. (Take our advice: Carve the damn ninja.) The thankful Joes gift the Primords with a TV as a "replacement" for the satellite, but the Primords smash the TV to pieces upon seeing a singing toothbrush commercial.

LOVE AND WAR Dusty impishly asks Flint if he likes "girls with guts," referring to Lady Jaye. Flint gruffly responds: "Professionally, yes. Personally, I'd like to see her [live] a while longer." Still, Flint dithers about the missing Lady Jaye a great deal – evidently not giving a toss about her fellow captive Spirit. Reunited with Flint, Lady Jaye learns about his concern, commenting: "That doesn't exactly make me unhappy, you know," giving him a very PG-rated, kid-safe hug.

ASS-WHUPPINGS A Primord bola brings down Spirit's eagle Freedom (who luckily recovers). Storm Shadow savagely tosses a young Primord against a rock face, also triggering a rockfall that presumably flattens some Primords like a pancake. Spirit shatters Storm Shadow's centuries-old sword.

GOOFS The Joe satellite survives a fall through the atmosphere – but a 100-foot drop from a helicopter ultimately does it in. Err, Storm Shadow raids the cabin of a reclusive explorer named McIntosh to find... what, exactly? (Stormy's presumably looking for maps of the region, but it's never stipulated.)

When Lady Jaye's tied up beneath a Primord sacrificial altar, moments away from being flattened by a falling boulder, Spirit's eagle Freedom tears away *one* of her bonds. But in the very next second, Lady Jaye's completely free and rolling out of the way.

PREPOSTEROUS PHYSICS Instinctually defending himself against large falling rocks, Spirit kicks a semi-boulder aside. (Lady Jaye adds: "Thanks, but you can't stop 'em all," to which we screeched, "He shouldn't have even been able to stop the one!")

TV TIE-INS Lady Jaye reiterates that she hates high places (first stated in "Red Rocket's Glare").

CHARACTER PROFILE: JOES

• *Lady Jaye:* Has seen Primords in museums and is highly adept with a bola. Mostly out of orneriness, Lady Jaye insults Storm Shadow by claiming he doesn't deserve an honorable end.

• *Spirit:* Knows a great deal about his American Indian heritage, including how his ancestors forged weapons. Spirit's quick enough to bat away Storm Shadow's throwing star with a makeshift club.

CHARACTER PROFILE: COBRA

Storm Shadow: Possesses extraordinary intuition that verges on a sixth sense (he manages to detect the Primords' presence). He's honorable, but sometimes leaves his opponents alive to further humiliate them in fair combat. His throwing stars can carve through rifle barrels. Storm Shadow's a talented fighter, but the Primords' natural strength and agility overwhelm him.

THE COMMAND DECISION Quite why animators too often insist on the obligatory "heroes meet primitive men" story, we're just not sure. But the barbaric Primords come off as dopey as they sound, leaving "Satellite Down" the sort of story that just barely attempts to do something interesting, then plummets to Earth before halftime.

1.9: "Cobra Stops the World"

***US Transmission Date:** Sept. 26, 1985*
***Writer:** Steve Gerber*

BATTLE ROSTER *Joes:* Duke, Ace, Scarlett, Sparks, Torpedo; *Cobra:* Cobra Commander, Destro, Major Bludd.

FIRST APPEARANCES *Joes:* Deep Six (SHARC driver), Grunt (infantry soldier).

MISSION BRIEF In a major offensive to cripple the world's energy supplies, Cobra attacks a number of North Sea drilling stations, Middle East oil fields and Alaskan pipeline links. As the world's nations quickly run out of power, they vest their hope in a major oil tanker convoy en route from South America. But that sneaky Cobra Commander uses a long-range cloaking device – newly invented by Destro – to enshroud and capture the convoy.

The Joes scour the globe for the nabbed oil tankers, trying to discern the location of Cobra's cloaking device. Meanwhile, as Cobra Commander calls on major powers across the globe to surrender, he proves his mettle by detonating two of the tankers via remote control. Thankfully, Joe communications expert Sparks backtracks the destruct signal to Pategonia Island, located 200 miles east of the Falklands. Mustering their forces, the Joes blister the remote Cobra base, allowing Scarlett to blow up Destro's cloaking device. Cobra Commander and Destro abandon their plans, fleeing as the oil tankers ease the world's energy crisis.

MEMORABLE MOMENTS There's a surreal moment when Scarlett disguises herself as a frail senior citizen, then bursts in on several Cobra troopers chatting over lunch.

LOVE AND WAR Scarlett cattily informs Duke that she "likes a man who knows what he wants." When Duke arrives in a stolen Cobra RATTLER jet, Scarlett wraps him in a big hug and comments: "I almost put a thermal arrow through one of your engines." (Kinky.) When all's said and done, Scarlett suggests she and Duke retire for dinner and a movie. (Duke agrees, although he spits out a clichéd "Now you're cooking with gas!")

ASS-WHUPPINGS Torpedo takes on a floating Cobra base, firing a harpoon into its gun port and wracking the entire outpost with explosions. Duke and Ace lose an aerial contest with a Cobra RATTLER. Scarlett kerwallops a team of Cobra troopers, crisping one goon's nosehairs with an incendiary crossbow bolt.

It goes completely unstated, but Cobra likely kills a whole mess of crewmen aboard the two detonated oil tankers.

PREPOSTEROUS PHYSICS A scuba-diving Torpedo somehow dodges a trio of Cobra missiles – presumably armed with state-of-the-art targeting systems.

GOOFS Errr... how does Destro's "cloaking" device capture the oil tankers? Force field? Telekinetic snare? Styrofoam?

Also, however crippling Cobra's initial assault, it's ludicrous to think that the entire world's energy reserves would hinge on a few South American tankers. Yet Colonel Sharpe insists: "Those tankers were the world's last hope. Every industrialized nation will be paralyzed," and Destro claims that "civilization will collapse into ruin." (Please. Credit us with some intelligence.)

TV TIE-INS Colonel Sharpe first appeared in "The Revenge of Cobra." Hasbro never produced Joe communications

MISCELLANEOUS STUFF!

CONTINUED ON PAGE 27...

know, we leave 'em alone."

- **Quick Kick: Don't rush through things without planning first** – "Remember, anything worth doing is worth planning. If you don't plan, you're out on a limb."
- **Recondo: Don't hide in the fridge or you'll suffocate** – "Remember, never get in anything that could close up and trap you."
- **Ripcord: Face your problems (and get glasses!)** – "Having your eyes tested may clear things up. Don't avoid a problem. Meet it... and beat it!"
- **Roadblock: Don't tell strangers where you live** – "Remember, never tell anyone you're home alone and never give anyone your address."
- **Roadblock: Downed power lines are not your friends** – "Remember, don't play around electric wires or you could be playing with fire."
- **Scarlett: Don't give up if you can't do something the first time** – "You'll never win if you give in."
- **Shipwreck: Stealing is bad** – "How would you like it if someone stole your bike? Remember, taking something that isn't yours just isn't right."
- **Shipwreck: Running away isn't the answer** – "Isn't it better to try to solve problems instead of running away from them? And remember, running away leads nowhere."
- **Snow Job: Don't skate on thin ice** – "Remember, frozen ponds and rivers may not be totally frozen."
- **Spirit: What to do if you catch on fire** – "Remember, running makes the fire worse. If your clothes catch on fire, wrap yourself in a rug or blanket."
- **Spirit: Don't discount people because of their disabilities** – "[Being] blind does not mean you cannot see how to solve problems. Remember, having a handicap doesn't mean you're helpless."
- **Torpedo: Learning how to swim** – "Open and close your legs like a scissor. Keep up a steady rhythm. Now cup your hands downward and move them in a figure-eight motion. Never play around water alone."
- **Will Bill: Say no to strangers** – "Just don't do what a stranger says. Check it out with an adult you know. Remember, a stranger can mean danger."

officer Sparks as an action figure, although he later appears – retired from the Joes and working for a TV station – in "Grey Hairs and Growing Pains."

CHARACTER PROFILE: JOES

• *Deep Six:* He's first and foremost a diver, more at home under the water than flying above it. Deep Six adores the quiet of the deep blue sea and detests loud music.

• *Scarlett:* One of her crossbow bolts fires a tow line, enabling Scarlett to haul herself to safety (although – alas! – she doesn't swing about the city like Batman).

CHARACTER PROFILE: COBRA

• *Cobra Commander:* His helmet sprays knockout gas that incapacitates people at close-range.

• *Destro:* For whatever reason, Destro thinks Cobra Commander's showing more intelligence than normal.

• *Major Bludd:* He's allied with the long-forgotten Yanomamo tribe – a society that's kept to itself for 1,000 years – in an unspecified South American jungle. Bludd negotiated with the Yanomamos to acquire the rare jewels needed to power Destro's cloaking device, but Duke and Ace's interference ruined the deal.

THE COMMAND DECISION An entirely worthless exercise that pulls you about bronco-style with a bunch of battles so irrelevant (Duke and Ace vs. Major Bludd and a bundle of tribesmen, etc.) that they're hardly worth mentioning. Plagued with clunky dialogue (a Cobra goon: "Attack! Open fire! Attack! Open fire!") and Cobra troopers who couldn't hit a barn at point blank range, "Cobra Stops the World" finishes as splintered as a shattered lump of peanut brittle.

1.10: "Jungle Trap"

***US Transmission Date:** Sept. 27, 1985*
***Writer:** Paul Dini*

BATTLE ROSTER *Joes:* Duke, Scarlett, Recondo, Rock 'n Roll, Snake-Eyes, Wild Bill, Ripcord; *Cobra:* Cobra Commander, Zartan and the Dreadnoks.

FIRST APPEARANCES *Cobra:* Copperhead (Water Moccasin pilot).

MISSION BRIEF In India, a geologist named Dr. Shakkor finishes design work on his Vulcan Machine, a geomagnetic device capable of re-routing lava flows from deep within the Earth's crust. But when Cobra offers Shakkor millions for the machine's specifications, Shakkor urgently contacts the Joes for protection. Led by Duke, a small Joe team arrives to take Shakkor into custody, but Cobra agents outwit the Joes and kidnap the geologist. Working from a temple deep in the jungle, Cobra Commander and Zartan enthrall Shakkor with a mind-control device – forcing the scientist to build a Vulcan Machine for them.

Meanwhile, the Joes hear rumors about a local "snake cult" and surmise (correctly) that Cobra's usurped control of an abandoned temple. The Joes make their way through the jungle, eluding a frightful amount of booby traps, but not before Shakkor completes his work on the Cobra Vulcan Machine. With Cobra Commander hopping at the chance to blackmail the world – threatening to roast any city that defies him in a geyser of hot lava – Duke's team overpowers a Cobra hovercraft crew, steals their uniforms and infiltrates the Cobra hideout.

Just as Cobra Commander attempts to demonstrate the Vulcan Machine's power by erasing Los Angeles from the face of the Earth, the Joes burst into the Cobra control chamber and liberate Shakkor. Cobra Commander hurriedly throws the Vulcan Machine into action, but the Joes blast the machine's support struts, re-directing its energies under their feet. As the Vulcan Machine obliterates the hidden temple with a localized lava flow, the Joes and Cobras separately escape and return to base.

ASS-WHUPPINGS A Cobra HISS tank volley buries the Dreadnoks in rubble (see Goofs). Recondo tricks a rhino into falling into a river (which naturally begs the question if rhinos can swim). Scarlett blasts a hole in the ceiling, making the darkness-loving Zartan squirm in direct sunlight.

PREPOSTEROUS PHYSICS Even allowing that he's a commando, Snake-Eyes miraculously kicks his way through a pack of striped hyenas. And… err… re-routing lava from the Earth's core would likely split the planet open like an overripe cantaloupe.

GOOFS Hotly pursuing Shakkor's kidnappers, the Joes accept directions from a "local" (actually Zartan in disguise) – who shouldn't have the slightest idea where they're going. Shortly afterward, Zartan and the Dreadnoks clumsily position themselves on a stairwell opposite from a Cobra HISS tank column, meaning that if the tanks open fire… err, yeah… the Dreadnoks just got shot.

Scarlett fires off one crossbow bolt, but two strike an approaching HISS tank. In the lava-filled climax, why do the Joes toss Cobra hovercraft pilot Copperhead overboard rather than forcing him to drive them to safety? And shouldn't the molten lava have fried Copperhead's hide?

TV TIE-INS Cobra dominates Shakkor with a mind-control headband, similar to those used in "The M.A.S.S. Device."

CHARACTER PROFILE: JOES

- *Rock 'n Roll:* He's a surfer from Los Angeles.
- *Scarlett:* Her crossbow fires flaming arrows.

THE COMMAND DECISION A very paint-by-the-numbers tale, entirely unworthy of writer Paul Dini, whose dazzling credits include Batman: The Animated Series, Batman Beyond and the outstanding Transformers episode "Dweller in the Depths." But whatever Dini's then-future resume, "Jungle Trap" amounts to little more than the Joes avoiding a string of lame booby traps. Whoo-hoo. Cigars, everyone.

1.11: "Cobra's Creatures"

***US Transmission Date:** Sept. 30, 1985*
***Writer:** Kimmer Ringwald*

BATTLE ROSTER *Joes:* Mutt, Junkyard, Scarlett, Ripcord, Flint, Spirit, Snake-Eyes; *Cobra:* Cobra Commander.

MISSION BRIEF Hoping to curry favor with Cobra Commander, a genius criminal scientist named Dr. Lucifer perfects "High Freak" – a high-frequency invention capable of mentally dominating any animal or insect on Earth. Lucifer offers High Freak to Cobra Cobra Commander in exchange for Cobra liberating Lucifer's beloved, the twisted Professor Attila, from the maximum-security Stonehall Prison. Cobra Commander provisionally agrees, first requiring a demonstration of Lucifer's device.

During a G.I. Joe parachute jump, Cobra troops sweep in and capture dog handler Mutt, his hound Junkyard and paratrooper Ripcord, dragging them to Dr. Lucifer's secluded castle. Lucifer gives Mutt a head start, then uses High Freak's ultrasonics to enflame Junkyard's killer instinct – compelling the dog to hunt his former master.

Satisfied with High Freak's efficiency, Cobra Commander enthralls herds of lions, whales, locusts, rhinos and more, seizing several oil refineries and world capitals with his animal armies. Giddy with success, Cobra Commander issues demands that several criminal scientists, including Professor Attila, be released into Cobra's care. But knowing Lucifer's feelings for Attila, the Joes authorize Scarlett to infiltrate infiltrate Lucifer's operation disguised as his beloved.

Escorted to Lucifer's castle by Cobra troops, Scarlett makes the mistake of showing Lucifer *too* much affection – failing to realize that Attila normally regards Lucifer with the warmth of a glacier. Lucifer sees through Scarlett's disguise, tossing her into the castle dungeon with Ripcord, leaving Scarlett to feverishly signal her position on a hidden communicator.

Outraged at Scarlett's deception, Lucifer sets hundreds of ravenous, High Freak-ed spiders upon the Joe prisoners, but Spirit and Snake-Eyes follow Scarlett's signal and rescue their teammates. In short order, Flint brings forward a massive Joe phalanx, capturing everyone in Lucifer's castle save Cobra Commander. The Joes destroy Lucifer's High Freak equipment, restoring the animal armies and Junkyard to normal. Again victorious, the Joes kindly fulfill Lucifer's dream of reuniting with Attila – by locking them in the same jail cell.

MEMORABLE MOMENTS Unable to harm his best friend Junkyard – no matter how psychotic he's become – Mutt wrestles a ravenous alligator off his his mind-controlled pooch.

LOVE AND WAR Dr. Lucifer's unswervingly in love with Professor Attila, but has never proposed to her (well, he's never proposed marriage, at any rate). Indeed, their sex life can't be too potent, as Lucifer dryly comments: "My Attila would never kiss me without insulting me." It's something of a goof, given the need to separate male and female prisoners, but Lucifer and Attila end this episode "happily" in the same prison cell.

ASS-WHUPPINGS Mutt smacks Junkyard around a few times to avoid the hound's deadly attacks, but stops short of lethal force. Locusts down Joe Sky Hawk fighters by gumming up their engines. Disguised as Professor Attila, Scarlett bitch-slaps some Cobra goons, later coming unglued when covered in High Freak-controlled spiders (mind, Ripcord suffers the same fate and screams just as loud).

GOOFS The Joes open spend a lot of time and effort to test the "Canine Corps Chute" – a prototype parachute for dogs – on Junkyard without explaining why the hell having masses of dogs parachute anywhere would be a good thing.

A herd of High-Freak-controlled rhinos, indigenous to Africa, are shown surrounding England's Parliament. (Did they *swim* the English Channel?) Snake-Eyes unconvincingly hang-glides with his wolf Timber. Also, Spirit and Snake-Eyes idiotically convince Timber and eagle Freedom to act as their "captors," thereby entering Lucifer's fortress.

CHARACTER PROFILE: JOES

- *Scarlett:* Disguises her identity with latex masks (*a la* the Baroness) and somehow duplicates other peoples' voices. Scarlett hates spiders, with her arachnid torment in Dr. Lucifer's dungeon only increases her loathing.
- *Spirit:* Somehow speaks directly to his eagle Freedom and Snake-Eyes' wolf Timber.

ORGANIZATIONS *Cobra:* Dr. Lucifer's gained a reputation as a long-standing, successful Cobra scientist. Noted criminal scientists – currently imprisoned – that Cobra wants to add to its ranks include: Dr. Lasco, "Victor the Hunn," "Accule the Mad Assassin" and Professor Attila.

• *G.I. Joe:* Has been tracking Dr. Lucifer's activities for some time.

STUFF YOU NEED Canine Corps Chute: Another instance of our tax dollars at work, the Canine Corps Chute is doggie-compatible and guaranteed to open at 1500 feet (see Goofs).

• *High Freak:* High Freak's capable of dominating any animal through ultrasonics (to give an order, simply speak into the main control center), but it's got limited range. Accordingly, Cobra Commander dispatches Cobra helicopter pilots to zap animal herds from close quarters, thereby drafting his animal armies.

• *Skystrikers:* Joe pilots can fly at least two other Skystrikers via remote control.

THE COMMAND DECISION Considering a few well-placed bullets and cans of mosquito dope could likely quell most of the animal armies (flocks of eagles capture Washington D.C., wolves surround the Kremlin, etc.), "Cobra's Creatures" fails to present much of a tangible threat. It starts out so-so, then peters out and eventually ends rather pathetically, with the animal corps playing second fiddle to some predictable Scarlett/Ripcord/Dr. Lucifer tension and Mutt's struggles to outrace Junkyard.

1.12: "The Funhouse"

***US Transmission Date:** Oct. 1, 1985*
***Writers:** Steve Mitchell and Barbara Petty*

BATTLE ROSTER *Joes:* Flint, Lady Jaye, Alpine, Bazooka, Airtight, Dusty, Gung Ho, Zap; *Cobra:* Cobra Commander, Zartan, the Baroness.

MISSION BRIEF Momentarily setting aside his insatiable quest for world domination, Cobra Commander re-prioritizes his need for cold-blooded revenge against G.I. Joe. Engineering the kidnapping of some notable scientists, Cobra Commander levels the Joes with a $60 billion ransom demand – knowing full well the Joes will track his transmission and blunder into a trap.

At a Cobra fortress in South America, G.I. Joe Skystrikers rip through a modest company of Cobra tanks and ground troops. Headed by Flint, a sextet of Joes penetrate the stronghold's outer wall, but blast doors suddenly crash down, isolating them from the main Joe force. Moments later, an overpowering magnetic field divests the captive Joes of their weapons, rendering them near-defenseless.

Using an internal TV system, Cobra Commander offers the Joes a sporting chance in his "funhouse." Drawing the Joes' attention to three passageways, Cobra Commander claims that two of the options lead to certain death while a third connects with the base's command center. As a further incentive to play the twisted game, Cobra Commander explains that the entire island is hotwired with an enormous bomb – which can only be disarmed from his command center.

Forced to play along, Flint separates his Joes into pairs and disperses them into the three passageways. In short order, Dusty, Airtight, Alpine and Bazooka variously endure a series of carnival-themed contests – including giant clowns and a killer roller-coaster ride – that ultimately render the four Joes unconscious.

Oblivious to their comrades' fate, Flint and Lady Jaye explore the middle passage and engage a battalion of robots that look like Cobra Commander. A surprise attack renders Lady Jaye dead to the world, but Flint desperately pushes past the robots and charges into a Cobra battle arena. Evading further assaults, Flint approaches the base's command center – prompting Cobra Commander to prime the island's bomb and flee in a private jet.

Unable to stop the countdown, Flint broadcasts a full retreat order, racing for his Skystriker and scooping up the unconscious Dusty along the way. Lady Jaye and the other Joes rouse themselves and locate their weapons, blowing a hole in the abandoned funhouse's perimeter and joining the evacuation. As the last Skystriker lifts off, Cobra Commander's bomb detonates and obliterates the island in a small mushroom cloud.

Left on surveillance duty, helicopter pilot Wild Bill shadows Cobra Commander's jet, radioing the true Cobra base's location back to his comrades. The Joes regroup and pummel the base's defenses, catching Cobra completely off-guard and liberating the captive scientists. Faced with insurmountable odds, Cobra Commander again flees with his tail between his legs.

MEMORABLE MOMENTS When Cobra Commander demands $60 billion in ransom money, Alpine whimsically suggests the Joes put it on his credit card, "G.I. Joe Express." (As if you couldn't guess, he "never leaves home without it.")

Bazooka gets *really* mad when a Cobra hit squad makes him accidentally swallow his gum, pummeling the goons into submission as retribution. Zartan encourages Cobra Commander to drag out the Joes' torture – because he's paid by the hour.

In one of the show's more shocking moments, hallucination gas deludes Dusty into thinking that teammate Airtight's become a nightmarish Cobra Commander – complete with snakes sprouting from his faceplate and hands. Airtight punches the manic Dusty's lights out, then vows: "Sleep tight, old pal. I'll be back for you after I've kicked some snake butt."

Cobra Commander knocks down Alpine in a giant bowling alley *(see Ass-Whuppings)* and crows: "Eleven! I got eleven!

That's even better than a strike!"

LOVE AND WAR Alpine asks the buffoonish, mustachioed Bazooka: "How come Flint always gets Lady Jaye to go with him and I always get you?" (Answer: Because Flint's a very, very smart man.)

At story's end, Lady Jaye suggests Flint take her for a moonlit beach walk. When Alpine and Bazooka brashly volunteer to take Flint's place, Flint threatens to make them scrub bathrooms for a week. Laughing, a whimsical Lady Jaye tells Flint: "You sure know how to keep a girl single."

ASS-WHUPPINGS The Joes fare poorly in Cobra's funhouse, with hallucination-inducing gas turning Dusty half-mad, a laser bolt grazing Bazooka's scalp during a killer roller coaster ride and Airtight getting struck unconscious by shrapnel during a giant clown attack. As a grand finale, Alpine finds himself lost down a corridor with a polished floor, complete with giant bowling pins. Unable to properly run, Alpine evades the Bowling Ball of Doom but gets half-crushed under a falling bowling pin. Oh, and a Cobra robot strikes Lady Jaye unconscious from behind – a scene that's gloriously depicted through use of shadows.

SAVE THEM! Cobra tanks hit by a Bazooka-fired shell gently tip over on their sides, enabling the drivers to easily jump to safety.

GOOFS Flint orders, in response to an incoming transmission: "If it's Cobra, trace it, Breaker." (What the hell else would Breaker do? "If it's Cobra, ignore them and turn on MTV, Breaker. It's time for The Tom Green Show.")

During a killer roller coaster ride, Bazooka – who's sensibly bent over to avoid a laser volley – looks up for apparently no other reason than getting shot. Flint fumbles for the unconscious Lady Jaye's pulse at commercial break and mysteriously can't find it (even barring the fact that Lady Jaye *isn't* dead, Flint might consider removing his combat gloves).

Never at a loss for hyperbole, Cobra Commander claims that killing *six* Joes in his funhouse will "rid him of G.I. Joe forever." (As if.)

PREPOSTEROUS PHYSICS Flint's laser pistol carves through a light tower – the industrial-strength sort you'd expect to find at Wrigley Field.

CHARACTER PROFILE: JOES

- *Bazooka:* His shoulder-mounted bazooka's capable of taking down Cobra tanks.
- *Gung Ho:* Is completely bald beneath his trademark beret.
- *Lady Jaye:* Carries explosive-loaded javelins.
- *Zap:* Used to sell insurance. The Zap toy claims his function is "bazooka soldier," but his TV incarnation serves as a munitions expert.

CHARACTER PROFILE: COBRA Zartan: In near-darkness, Zartan's camouflage power isn't just a color change – he actually turns invisible. Zartan's paid by the hour and charges extra for his acting services. He's usually the first out the door when a plan goes sour. Zartan sometimes bitches at the Baroness, but nowhere near the degree to which he despises Destro.

THE COMMAND DECISION Deceptively smart and strong, taking a seemingly goofy premise and turning it into a balls-to-the-wall fight for survival. "The Funhouse" triumphantly mixes comedy and malice (much like a twisted Batman vs. Joker story), keeping your eyes glued to the TV set until Flint's final gambit against his tormentors. Highly recommended.

1.13: "Twenty Questions"

US Transmission Date: *Oct. 2, 1985*
Writer: *Buzz Dixon*

BATTLE ROSTER *Joes:* Shipwreck, Flint, Alpine, Gung Ho, Cover Girl, Spirit, Duke; *Cobra:* The Baroness, Zartan and the Dreadnoks, Cobra Commander.

FIRST APPEARANCES *Joes:* Airborne (helicopter assault trooper); *Cobra:* Wild Weasel (RATTLER pilot).

MISSION BRIEF When the Joes commence a series of war games, pelting each other with fake laser beams and cannon-propelled flour bags, "Twenty Questions" talk show host Hector Ramirez unexpectedly shows up with a film crew. Ramirez and his associate – the ferret-like, slightly stubbled Arnold – ask a series of loaded questions, leveling the accusation that Cobra's merely an elaborate ruse intended to rip off the government. Afraid to throw Ramirez and Arnold out for fear of sparking a witch hunt, Flint pawns the TV crew off on Shipwreck until Duke returns to base.

Shipwreck gives the "Twenty Questions" group a guided tour of Joe Headquarters, but Arnold's increasingly wild conspiracy theories make the Joe sailor flip his lid. Desperate to shove proof of Cobra's existence down Arnold's throat, Shipwreck reads reports of Cobra scouts lurking near the Rocky Mountain Chemical Weapons Arsenal (RM Arsenal). In a completely unauthorized move, Shipwreck stuffs Ramirez, Arnold and their cameraman into a Dragonfly helicopter, departing for the Rockies to investigate.

Unfortunately, Shipwreck's snoopy group ventures close to a Cobra base secluded in an underground cavern – convincing the Dreadnoks to round up the hapless quartet. Shipwreck sweats over their predicament, but then gapes in astonishment when "Arnold" unmasks "himself" as the Baroness – assigned to infiltrate Ramirez's team and undermine Joe morale and public support. Worse, Cobra Commander embarks on a plan to raid the RM Arsenal, capturing a treasure trove of illicit gas canisters that include laughing gas, tear gas and – most dangerously – explosive gas.

Thankfully, a Joe quartet – consisting of Alpine, Gung Ho, Cover Girl and Spirit – set out to find Shipwreck and his guests, locating Cobra's underground cavern in the process. Alpine's group briefly tries to sneak in undetected, then defaults to the time-honored tradition of rushing in and shooting everyone.

Cobra Commander's jaw hits the floor as a maelstrom of lasers erupts in the underground cavern. Amid the brouhaha, Shipwreck escapes custody and reaches a Cobra drilling machine, bursting open non-lethal gas canisters and flooding the Cobra troops – plus the Joes – with laughing gas and tear gas.

Wracked with laughter, a string of Cobra hovercraft pilots lose control of their vehicles, crashing into the cavern's docks. The hovercrafts erupt in a string of fireballs, threatening to detonate the explosive gas stocks and collapse the entire cavern. Laughing harder than a pack of drunken hyenas, the assembled Joes, Cobras and TV media creatures crawl toward the cavern's exits – barely escaping as the explosive gas goes up and butchers the Cobra base. Afterward, the Joes depart for home as Ramirez – thrilled at gaining craploads of footage from the Joe/Cobra battle – promises the Joes a very flattering feature on "Twenty Questions."

MEMORABLE MOMENTS Flint looks so pistol-whipped after a session with the vulturish "Twenty Questions" crew that Alpine asks, "Now what, semi-fearless leader?" Slyly belying G.I. Joe's ties with Marvel, Cover Girl plays a Spider-Man video game.

In one of those moments that's funny but you can't really say why, Zartan disguises himself as a shepherd. (Curse those dastardly international terrorists who walk about disguised as shepherds!) When Cover Girl and Gung Ho recruit Alpine to hunt for Shipwreck, the Joe mountain climber understandably asks, "How does a sailor get himself into trouble in the Rockies?"

A juicy moment during the episode's climax features the laughing gas-induced Joes and Cobras cracking up as a series of explosions erupt around them. A giddy Gung Ho yells out, "Explosions!", followed by Spirit's cheerful, "There'll be a cave-in!", and Alpine cackling, "We'll all be crushed… to pulp!", with the entire mess climaxing as everyone yukks it up like a bunch of orangutans.

LOVE AND WAR In a double entendre, Shipwreck elaborates on the properties of a cue ball: "So round, so firm…" (Then again, Spirit squelches any air of naughtiness by sagely noting: "What the universe wills the ball to do, it shall do. There are no games of chance.")

ASS-WHUPPINGS During some war games, the Joes smear each other with flour bags. Alpine "blasts" Shipwreck with a fake laser. Trying to keep his wounded Dragonfly aloft, Shipwreck knuckle-punches the crowing Arnold (actually the Baroness) over his shoulder and cries out, "Shut up! I know what I'm doing!"

GOOFS The Joes seem woefully disorganized – when the main computer reports a Cobra presence in the Rockies, only Shipwreck and the "Twenty Questions" crew depart to check it out. Hell, when Spirit's team follows to save Shipwreck's ass, nobody logs a report to say, "By the way, we're flying into the jaws of peril. Please feed our goldfish."

Wild Weasel advises his pilots, "Don't let [the Joes] get behind you!", which seems pretty damn obvious (rather like shouting: "Don't let [the Joes] shoot you!").

We're baffled how the Baroness, when disguised as Arnold, flattens her mammaries to be totally flat-chested. Mind, the Baroness' gazongas *instantly* balloon into their proper shape when she removes her latex mask. Cobra Commander seems oddly immune to the laughing gas (of course, the commander's typical lunacy makes up for this).

TV TIE-INS Ramirez, viewing the Joes more favorably in future, helps the team expose a shady Cobra propaganda scheme in "Not a Ghost of a Chance." He's also glimpsed in "The Traitor."

Amusingly enough, *G.I. Joe* writer Flint Dille also used Ramirez over in the *Inhumanoids* cartoon series, where the "Twenty Questions" anchor cropped up in three episodes: "Primal Passions" and "The Masterson Team" concern an on-hand Ramirez covering the theft of the Statue of Liberty, while "Auger... For President?" sees a network momentarily cancelling Ramirez's show (although naturally, an Inhumanoid attack helps Ramierez get his job back).

CHARACTER PROFILE: JOES

- *Alpine:* His Uncle Oscar's a moocher.
- *Spirit:* He not only talks to pet eagle Freedom, but disgustingly holds foodstuffs in his mouth for Freedom to snitch.

CHARACTER PROFILE: COBRA

- *Buzzer:* He hasn't destroyed anything in two to three days and kinda misses it. His chainsaw cuts through walls.
- *Cobra Commander:* As you might expect, Cobra Com-

mander's extremely vain – ordering a stay of execution on his prisoners when Ramirez, desperately playing for time, agrees to interview the hooded Cobra dictator. Accordingly, Cobra Commander blathers to Ramirez about his past successes, claiming he once led a mutiny at his military academy. (*Side Note:* When Zartan returns to base and wonders why Cobra Commander's absent, the icy Baroness dribbles: "He's being interviewed for TV.")

ORGANIZATIONS *Cobra:* Entertains its troops with such movies as Amusement Park of Terror, described as "... mayhem on the merry go round and revenge on the roller coaster as the good guys try to beat the bad guys on the Ferris wheel."

THE COMMAND DECISION Sufficiently wacky and on-target, although Ramirez's deliberately annoying TV crew at times performs their roles too well. Still, the episode's second half redeems a clunky start, leaving this an above-average tale that's worth a once-over.

1.14: "The Greenhouse Effect"

US Transmission Date: *Oct. 3, 1985*
Writer: *Gordon Kent*

BATTLE ROSTER *Joes:* Alpine, Bazooka, Wild Bill, Barbecue; *Cobra:* Cobra Commander, Destro, Tomax and Xamot.

MISSION BRIEF When a brilliant scientist named Professor Bullock develops a ludicrously efficient nitrogen-based fuel variant, his lab janitor – secretly a Crimson Guardsman – steals a fuel sample for Cobra to analyze. Eluding various G.I. Joe members assigned to guard the nitrogen fuel, the Crimson Guardsman momentarily takes refuge in a greenhouse owned by the plump Harvey Lathrup. Thankfully, Harvey calls the police and reports the break-in – forcing the panicked Cobra trooper to hide his stolen canister in a potted tree before his arrest.

That evening, the illicit fuel canister sprouts a leak, dousing Harvey's plants with Bullock's nitrogen fuel. Overnight, the nitrogen-rich fuel makes Harvey's plants grow to massive proportions – generating a dizzying assortment of giant fruits and veggies. Giddy as a schoolgirl, Harvey attributes the plant growth to his secret (and worthless) "Super Grr-ow!" formula – exhibiting his big-ass produce at the country fair.

Unfortunately, just as Destro tracks down the Crimson Guardsman's secret fuel stash, Harvey's vegetables burst out of control and wreak havoc at the fair. Led by Wild Bill, a Joe team snitches the fuel canister back from Destro, but the steel-faced fiend escapes with a mutant bean pod. Forcing Cobra Commander to recognize the military potential of hyper-accelerated fruits and vegetables, Destro raids Harvey's greenhouse and stockpiles a huge amount of fuel-tainted seeds.

In a show of force, Destro and the Crimson Twins set about overrunning Chicago with their newest weapon, hammering the town with wrecking ball-sized oranges, berserk bean plants, towering celery stalks and more. Cobra Commander demands that Chicago surrender before the might of his mutant rutabagas, but thankfully, Joe hostile environment expert Airtight develops a fast-acting herbicide tailored to the plants' biochemistry. After crystallizing his super-plant killer, Airtight and his fellow Joes seed a bunch of storm clouds – dousing Chicago with plant-slaying rain and crushing Cobra's dreams of world conquest via titanic produce.

MEMORABLE MOMENTS Alpine jokes that they're at the top-secret research station because scientists just invented "the world's biggest Roman candle," to which the buffonish Bazooka replies, "Really?" Destro again wins an "Utterly Over-The-Top" citation with his declaration that: "With expendable fruits and vegetables replacing Cobra's ground troops, we can overrun the world!"

LOVE AND WAR As undercover Crimson Guardsmen fan out, trying to discover which greenhouse contains the stolen nitrogen fuel, one Cobra agent disguises himself as a vagabond and asks a local if he can sleep in his greenhouse. After kicking the "vagrant" out, the greenhouse owner comments: "Sleeping with banana plants... [he] must be from California."

ASS-WHUPPINGS Bazooka stumbles, knocking himself and Alpine down a hill after the Crimson Guardsman. The Crimson Guardsman overpowers some cops, but greenhouse owner Harvey nails him over the noggin with a potted plant.

Some assorted giant fruit/vegetable calamities: A massive banana swells, popping out of its peel and nailing Harvey in the gut. Exploding grapes pelt the audience at a county fair. Alpine missiles an out-of-control potato into spuds. Bean sprouts squash two Cobra troopers. The Crimson Twins plummet from a dizzying height – but cushion themselves with quick-growing cabbages (or maybe lettuce – we can never tell the difference).

PREPOSTEROUS PHYSICS The fuel-snitching Crimson Guardsman somehow epoxies a mop to Alpine's face like Crazy Glue. Soon after, Alpine's hind quarters get stuck in another bucket, but once he crashes through a window, it's on his head.

Super-growing sunflowers fire off seeds with enough force to puncture tires and dent trucks – but they miraculously fail to harm Harvey, who's sitting right in the line of fire. While chasing Destro, Wild Bill flies his Dragonfly helicopter through a giant celery stalk (err, it's a *helicopter,* not a tank).

GOOFS Barbecue consigns Wild Bill to the back seat of a Dragonfly helicopter and takes the stick himself – probably not the brightest move, since Wild Bill's a full-fledged pilot and firefighter Barbecue, to be fair, swings an axe and gets cats out of trees for a living.

Nestled atop their Extensive Enterprises branch in Chicago, the Crimson Twins proceed to pelt the city with hyper-growing vegetable seeds. Of course, you'd expect this would pose a problem by trapping their building with giant rhubarb and the like ("Comply with our demands, or we'll hem ourselves in!"), but it'd also make prosecution damnably easy. (A cop: "Your honor, you'll note footage of the twin brothers spraying giant pea pods all over Chicago.")

TV TIE-INS A chemist named Professor Molaney also develops a nitrogen fuel formula in "Joes' Night Out."

CHARACTER PROFILE: JOES Barbecue: Carries a foam-projecting pistol that shorts out electronic controls.

CHARACTER PROFILE: COBRA

- *Crimson Guardsman #9:* The janitor at the nitrogen fuel project – and proof that ugly people are invariably evil.
- *Destro:* He often accepts assignments purely to escape Cobra Commander's lunatic ravings. Destro's wrist rocket projectors also fire a tow line.
- *Harvey Lathrup:* He's filed 187 false alarms, so you can imagine the authorities' relief when he had a genuine intruder (the Crimson Guardsman). Oh, and he talks to his plants (telling them, once the cops haul off the Cobra thug, "The bad man is gone now, children").

THE COMMAND DECISION Forever claiming the dubious moniker of, "that G.I. Joe story with the giant vegetables," "The Greenhouse Effect" fails miserably as comedy, probably driving a stake through your heart before it's done. We barely know how to even explain this to someone ("You see, there's these vegetables, big enough to blot out the sun…") without feeling traumatized, let alone justify its existence, leaving this a G.I. Joe episode we'd love to retroactively wipe from history.

1.15: "Haul Down the Heavens"

US Transmission Date: *Oct. 30, 1985*
Writer: *Buzz Dixon*

BATTLE ROSTER *Joes:* Flint, Lady Jaye, Snow Job, Duke; *Cobra:* Cobra Commander, Destro, the Baroness, Firefly.

MISSION BRIEF When the Aurora Borealis – the electrical phenomenon that lights up skies in the Northern Hemisphere – suddenly goes haywire and looms closer to Earth, the Joes agree to escort a UN science team to the Arctic Circle to investigate. Flint, Lady Jaye and Snow Job find their expedition plagued by sabotage, but – more disturbingly – the aurora's electrical charge starts melting the polar icecaps, threatening to raise the world's oceans by 80 feet.

In short order, Flint's team stumbles upon a massive Cobra base in the Arctic. Unfortunately, UN geologist Dr. Inwizel unmasks herself as the Baroness – summoning Cobra battalions to surround the Joes. Snow Job escapes, but falls unconscious from battle wounds in the Arctic wastes. Simultaneously, the captive Flint and Lady Jaye discover that Cobra, having drawn the aurora closer to Earth with an "ion attractor," hopes to melt the Arctic regions enough to flood coastal cities around the globe. In the ensuing confusion, Cobra plans to stage a blitzkrieg strike and seize as much territory as possible.

Thankfully, a Ganoke Indian family rescues Snow Job, enabling him to radio Joe Headquarters for reinforcements. Unable to traverse the increasingly slushy Arctic planes with ATVs, the Joes break out their hovercrafts and storm the Cobra base. Flint and Lady Jaye escape and momentarily re-program the ion attractor, pulling the Aurora right atop the Cobra base and melting its icy foundation. As the enormous Cobra base sinks to a watery grave, the Joes escape in their hovercrafts and the Aurora returns to its normal distance from Earth.

MEMORABLE MOMENTS Lady Jaye turns a corner and screams out, "Gotcha!", intent on confronting a Cobra saboteur – then finds herself face to face with a roaring polar bear. We felt pangs of hysteria as Firefly wiped out the Joe Skystriker armada (see Ass-Whuppings). When Ripcord tears off a captive Wild Bill's mouth tape, Bill colorfully lets out a Texas whoop and hollers, "You idjit! No wonder they call you Ripcord!"

LOVE AND WAR Duke refers to the hotshot Lady Jaye as Flint's "flying fool girlfriend." While tied-up with Lady Jaye, Flint suggests a daring escape plan that requires her to,

"Push the button on my watch..." (Right. His "watch." Mm-hmm.)

ASS-WHUPPINGS Firefly taints the fuel at Joe Headquarters with a corrosive element, utterly annihilating the Joe Skystriker fleet. Lady Jaye slugs a posturing Destro through a window.

PREPOSTEROUS PHYSICS Err... that tiny bit about moving the Aurora Borealis closer to Earth.

GOOFS The Baroness concedes at one point that Flint "made a good guess" about Cobra's involvement in the Aurora Borealis. Of course, as she well knows, Flint had the advantage of spotting a gigantic Arctic base with a giant Cobra statue on it – so it wasn't much of a puzzler, was it?

A maid finds the real Dr. Inwizel tied up in her American motel room – and oddly wearing her Arctic parka. The real Inwizel seems decently pleasant, meaning none of her fellow UN scientists noticed when the Baroness spontaneously replaced her and "Inwizel" started acting like a frigid bitch monster from the depths of hell.

A Cobra goon's dumb enough to mistake a slumbering polar bear for two Joes huddling under a blanket (the trooper even kicks the bear's ass and grumbles, "You in there, Joe?"). For that matter, a single tranquilizer dart instantly pacifies the polar bear, but *three* such darts jab Snow Job and he somehow keeps walking. (Ah, the power of Wheaties...)

Duke dramatically turns and exhales "Oh no..." as if he's seeing the scrapped Joe Skystriker fleet for the first time – but he knew it was there. The Indian family breaks into a sudden rendition of the watusi, or possibly "The Funky Chicken" (we're not sure), to move and let Ripcord examine the fallen Snow Job.

When Cobra Commander pits the captive Flint and Lady Jaye against a polar bear for sport, he gives a Roman-style "thumbs down" at one point – as if the polar bear would stop to ask his approval. Later, the polar bear suddenly bares teeth sharp enough to *chew* through the Joes' shackles.

Finally, Cobra sloppily doesn't take into account that their own base might sink as the ice caps melt (morons).

G.I. JOE: THE MUSICAL A bound Flint and Lady Jaye draw their Cobra captors in closer by painfully singing "The Marine Hymn" (the one that goes: "From the halls of Montezuma / To the shores of Tripoli") badly enough to curdle milk. Mind, it's rather choice when the Cobras glance desperately at each other, wondering how to best gag their prisoners.

CHARACTER PROFILE: JOES

• *Flint:* His wrist-watch contains a short laser blade, useful for slicing through bonds.

• *Lady Jaye:* She cut short her furlough, giving up an African safari to participate in the Arctic mission.

CHARACTER PROFILE: COBRA *Destro:* He finally realizes that since he uses a standard design on the control panels of the equipment he makes for Cobra, the Joes constantly know how to push his buttons (err... so to speak). Destro vows to remove such a liability in future.

PLACES TO GO Joe Headquarters: It's available on the radio frequency J-O-E seventy-niner.

THE COMMAND DECISION Highly reminiscent of chop-suey – graced with a so-so beginning, an exciting bit in the middle (Firefly leveling the Skystriker fleet) and an overall blah effect. We appreciated "Haul Down the Heavens" for trying to keep our interest, but a couple of watered down elements (yet another arena fight – this time with a polar bear) make this story average at best.

1.16-1.17: "The Synthoid Conspiracy"

Episodes: *Two*
US Transmission Date: *Oct. 7-8, 1985*
Writer: *Christy Marx*

BATTLE ROSTER *Joes:* Duke, Deep Six, Torpedo, Ace, Ripcord, Flint, Scarlett, Rock n' Roll, Roadblock, Cover Girl, Quick Kick, General Franks, Colonel Sharpe, Admiral Ledger; *Cobra:* Cobra Commander, Destro, Zartan, the Dreadnoks, Copperhead.

FIRST APPEARANCES *Joes:* Frostbite (Snow Cat driver).

MISSION BRIEF ***Part 1:*** Hoping to erode G.I. Joe's command structure from within and collapse the organization, Cobra Commander and Zartan perfect a type of bio-engineered construct called "synthoids" – chemical imitations of human beings who're indistinguishable from the genuine article. Crafting synthoids of an impressive array of Pentagon officers – General Franks, General Howell, Admiral Ledger and Colonel Sharpe – Zartan disguises himself as a junior officer and infiltrates a series of G.I. Joe war games.

As the Joes commence various water maneuvers, the Dreadnoks spring from hiding and attack. In the resultant chaos, Zartan gasses the Pentagon brass unconscious, then radios a nearby Cobra submarine for pick-up and swaps the Pentagon leaders for synthoid duplicates. The Joes eventually rally and drive the Dreadnoks away, but the synthoid General Franks holds Duke and his team accountable for G.I. Joe's sloppy performance.

Programmed to obey Cobra's every whim, the synthoid Pentagon officers set about dicing G.I. Joe's funding – depriving the team of crucial equipment, ammunition and fuel. Various Joe members alert Duke to the supply problems, but Cobra stages a sweeping attack that butchers the fuel-depleted Joe Skystriker fleet. With the Joes reeling, Zartan and his Dreadnoks move under cover and kidnap Duke, replacing him with a synthoid copy to gain a mole within the Joe ranks.

The satisfied Cobra forces withdraw, allowing the false General Franks to further decry the Joes' lackluster combat abilities. Arguing that G.I. Joe's existence clearly draws Cobra's attention and incites further casualties, "Franks" stuns everyone present by ordering G.I. Joe to disband.

Sensing the General's duplicitous nature, Mutt's dog Junkyard jumps the general – leading to Franks ordering the pooch's termination. In a whirlwind of motion, Mutt and Junkyard flee while Quick Kick throws off Franks' aim, preventing him from shooting the fugitives in the back. Franks orders Quick Kick's arrest for attacking a senior officer, commanding still-loyal machine gunner Rock 'n Roll to capture Mutt. Reaching the base's perimeter, Mutt and Junkyard pause for lack of an escape route – even as Rock 'n Roll's gun-toting motorcycle bears down on them.

Part 2: Rock 'n Roll orders Mutt and Junkyard to hold still, then blasts a hole in the perimeter fence and allows his teammates to scamper to freedom. Hauling ass away from Joe Headquarters, Mutt and Junkyard are shocked to run into Destro, who gasses the two renegades unconscious. Greatly offended because Cobra Commander and Zartan impishly crafted a synthoid Destro purely for the purpose of kow-towing, Destro sets about gaining revenge by unraveling his associates' synthoid gambit. Accordingly, Destro drops Mutt and Junkyard near the Cobra base holding the captured Duke and Pentagon officers, putting Mutt in a position to rescue his missing leaders.

Meanwhile, the Joes find themselves reassigned to useless positions in the armed services branches, with Scarlett painfully serving as General Franks' coffee-fetching secretary. But when ex-Joe communications chief Breaker detects unauthorized transmissions emanating from the Pentagon (actually conversations between the Pentagon synthoids and Cobra Commander), the Joes become further convinced of a conspiracy tainting the Pentagon leadership.

Sneaking into Joe Headquarters with the intent of stealing their Skystrikers to investigate, the Joes confront Destro and learn the true nature of the synthoid conspiracy. Warning that a synthoid has infiltrated the Joe ranks – but unable to name the traitor – Destro programs his battle drones to hold off military forces sent to arrest the Joes for insubordination, urging the Joes to regroup aboard his aircraft carrier, the *Valkyrie.*

Aided by Destro's knowledge and fuel supplies, the Joes stage a blitzkrieg-style raid on Cobra Commander's base. In the confusion, Mutt helps the real Duke and Pentagon officers escape. The actual Duke indulges in fisticuffs with his doppelganger, but Junkyard identifies the real Duke and chases the imposter from the room.

The Duke double races into the base's command center, requesting further orders from Cobra Commander as the Joes pound home their attack. Wary that the "synthoid Duke" might be the genuine article, Cobra Commander plays it safe and uses his Neutralizer – a precautionary device made to destroy the synthoids with a simple signal – to melt the synthoid Duke into a pile of goo. Unfortunately, the rattled Cobra Commander fails to activate his Neutralizer at a low-level setting, inadvertently sending the Pentagon officer synthoids to their doom as well. Completely hamstrung, Cobra Commander and Zartan flee as the Joes overrun the base. Hailing the Joe's courage, the real General Franks reinstates G.I. Joe to active duty.

MEMORABLE MOMENTS Cobra Commander and Zartan humble Destro by creating a synthoid version of the metal-faced villain and making it kneel before them – a fun little mistake that costs them Destro's loyalty (and victory). Suddenly face-to-face with the shiny-faced Destro, Mutt claims that he's more likely to trust "a rabid weasel" than Destro. (Ah, Destro must feel so loved). It seems clichéd at first glance, but General Franks' announcement, "From this moment on, there is no G.I. Joe!", sends a shiver up the spine.

A Cobra hoverfoil pilot worries that Mutt – not his pooch Junkyard – might bite him. About 10 Joes surround Destro, who maintains the calm demeanor of someone waiting in line for a movie.

LOVE AND WAR Shipwreck tries to sweet-talk Scarlett into enjoying warm spaghetti and dim lighting with him at a port café – but gets slapped as a result. Scarlett evidently doesn't hold Shipwreck's come-on routine against him, promising to "sink one for him" during the upcoming war games (awww, how sweet). Ever the unattainable Joe female, Scarlett merely gives the real Duke a reassuring pat upon his return.

ASS-WHUPPINGS Shipwreck and Scarlett each blow up a Cobra moray with no sign of survivors. Zartan gasses the Pentagon brass unconscious. For what's probably the 182nd time, Duke gets pistol-whipped (this time by the Dreadnoks). Cover Girl pulls a "damsel in distress" routine to distract two guards while Recondo and Stalker slug their lights out.

GOOFS A Cobra submarine crew crashes through the observation battleship's window to retrieve Zartan and the unconscious Pentagon brass. (Err, wouldn't the Joes find the giant hole a bit suspicious?) Budget cuts imposed by the synthoid officers diminish G.I. Joe's ammo and fuel supplies so quickly, the real Duke doesn't even notice until his team's near-powerless. Plot requirements demand that Duke falls all-too-easily in hand-to-hand combat with the lumbering Dreadnoks. Cobra goons born with snail DNA can't run or shoot down the handcuffed Duke. Joe communications chief Breaker picks up a single errant transmission from the Pentagon, acting as if the Pentagon officials would never, ever talk with someone via radio.

TV TIE-INS Cobra's synthoids give Shipwreck an unbearable amount of headaches in "There's No Place Like Springfield."

Circa 2006 – and apparently years after Cobra's demise – a crime lord asks the homeless Cobra Commander (nicknamed "Old Snake") to revive his synthoid technology in a plot to funnel some troublesome Autobots (Rodimus Prime, Arcee, Ultra Magnus and Springer) into artificial human bodies (*Transformers*: "Only Human"). The Autobots ultimately prevail and regain their robotic forms, leaving Cobra Commander to shuffle back to the streets.

CHARACTER PROFILE: JOES

• *Duke:* Commands the G.I. Joe team, but oddly enough, he's only a sergeant. Mutt's mutt Junkyard is fond of Duke.

• *General Howell:* Serves as head of Pentagon budget committee with oversight on G.I. Joe.

CHARACTER PROFILE: COBRA

Cobra Commander and Destro: Cobra Commander presumably can't kill off Destro because he's too useful an ally. But by the same token, the Big Snake often keeps Destro at arm's reach and excludes him from some Cobra missions.

ORGANIZATIONS *G.I. Joe:* Scarlett sometimes serves as "Wingleader One" and Ace as "Wingleader Two" during Skystriker trial runs (and possibly real battles, for that matter).

STUFF YOU NEED *Synthoids:* Created by Zartan (although Cobra Commander refined the process) and using genetic engineering chemicals produced by Destro, synthoids are perfect imitations of human beings, programmed to obey Cobra's orders without question. Memory replication's a lot more difficult, however – synthoids frequently botch familiar names and places (the fake Duke calls Scarlett "Cover Girl" at one point)

THE COMMAND DECISION Excellent, and well worth watching because it machinistically grabs the Joes by the ankles, hoists 'em upside down and lets 'em dangle, arms flailing, for a while. There's a few criticisms, notably the predictable ending and a failure on the Joes' part to actually win the battle (rather, Cobra shoots itself in the head), but all in all, "The Synthoid Conspiracy" stays true to itself, nicely warranting its two-episode format.

1.18: "The Phantom Brigade"

US Transmission Date: *Oct. 9, 1985*
Writer: *Sharman DiVono*

BATTLE ROSTER *Joes:* Duke, Gung Ho, Scarlett, Wild Bill, Roadblock, Cover Girl, Snow Job, Quick Kick, Airborne; *Cobra:* Cobra Commander, the Baroness, Major Bludd.

MISSION BRIEF Tiring of fighting the Joes with conventional warfare, Cobra Commander travels to Trans-Carpathia, a nation famed for ghosts and vampires, for a supernatural solution. Although dismissive of fighting battles with spooks, the Baroness captures a gypsy queen attuned to the spirit realm. Accordingly, the gypsy queen explains that persons who die by accident or treachery don't fully cross into the afterlife, further claiming she can summon three such spirits.

Using objects important to the deceased in life – namely, an ancient coin, a wedding ring and a locket – the gypsy woman respectively calls forth the spirits of a Roman soldier, a female Mongolian warrior and a young American WW I fighter pilot. By possessing the three totems, Cobra Commander orders the spirits to assault Joe troop emplacements in Trans-Carpathia.

The Joes reel as the intangible ghosts swoop in, blitzing them with volley after volley of spectral firepower. Monitoring the battle, Cobra Commander gloats over his impending victory – then unknowingly blunders by questioning the value of his human operatives. Supremely miffed, the Baroness secretly contacts Duke, Scarlett and Roadblock – explaining the nature of the ghosts and the importance of the totems that bind them to our world.

Wild Bill gains the Joes a respite by flashing the American flag, netting the WW I pilot's attention and gaining his confidence. The pilot recognizes Cobra Commander's duplicitous nature, throwing in with the Joes and convincing the Roman and the Mongolian to aid an assault on Cobra Commander's citadel. As the Joes and their spectral allies near victory, Cobra Commander drops his totems and flees. The next morning, a solemn Duke buries the three objects in the Trans-Carpathian forest – allowing the spirits to pass to the great beyond.

MEMORABLE MOMENTS There's a crushing little moment, crumpling your heart like tinfoil, when the American pilot realizes he's snuffed it. Empathizing, Roadblock wonders what the afterlife feels like.

In an inexplicable, terrifying moment – likely generated by any variety of supernatural forces running about the place – a fleeing Cobra Commander comes face-to-face with an animated skeleton. The commander relents to the skeleton's demand that he, "release the [ghost] warriors or pay the price," but in a haunting afternote, the skeleton tells Cobra Commander: "One day, you will meet your fate, and we will be waiting," before collapsing into a heap of bone.

LOVE AND WAR Cover Girl uses her Skystriker radio to Scarlett that she shouldn't worry about Duke because, "he's right here beside me." So of course, Scarlett drips: "Yeah, I'll just bet he is."

The Mongolian warrior pines for her husband, who died soon after they married. The WWI pilot yearns to reunite with his girlfriend Jenny and, at story's end, Wild Bill catches a fleeting glimpse of the pilot's airplane – with Jenny aboard.

ASS-WHUPPINGS The Roman centurion buries Quick Kick in sheet metal, and the Mongolian's arrows blister the Joes with an ice attack. We don't know if you'd consider it an "ass-whupping," but the three spirits obviously pass on to the great hereafter.

GOOFS It's highly unlikely the Mongolians let females serve as warriors (hell, we still have trouble getting women enrolled at West Point).

COMIC TIE-INS Trans-Carpathia also crops up in the *G.I. Joe* comics (starting in *G.I. Joe* #21) as the home of the Silent Castle.

CHARACTER PROFILE: JOES Scarlett: Her jammer arrow disrupts holographic images.

CHARACTER PROFILE: COBRA

Cobra Commander: He's having trouble instilling order among his troops, most of whom aren't eager to die for money. As such, Cobra Commander finds supernatural troops all the more appealing – they don't tire and don't expect payment.

CHARACTER PROFILE: OTHER

• *The Roman Centurion:* He carried his gold coin for good luck before losing it gambling one night. He's far more telekinetic than the other ghosts, able to fling swords about like frisbees.

• *The Mongolian Warrior:* Her arrows freeze enemy tanks and buildings on impact.

• *The World War I Pilot:* He gave his commanding officer a locket for his girlfriend Jenny, but presumably died before the locket's delivery. His plane's Gatling guns shoot demonic laser fire.

ORGANIZATIONS *The ghosts:* As supernatural beings, the ghosts possess flight, intangibility and special abilities related to their backgrounds (see Character Profile).

THE COMMAND DECISION Sweetly effective, with less of a cracked premise than you might think. "The Phantom Brigade" avoids the obvious cop-out of simply going, "Boo! Ghosts!", mercifully humanizing Cobra Commander's three spirits and continually keeping its head in the game (the final scene, with a skeleton essentially condemning Cobra Commander to hell, holds up as one of the most underrated Joe scenes ever).

1.19: "Lights! Camera! Cobra!"

US Transmission Date: *Oct. 10, 1985*
Writer: *Buzz Dixon*

BATTLE ROSTER *Joes:* Shipwreck, Mutt, Blowtorch, Recondo, Dusty, Cover Girl; *Cobra:* Cobra Commander, Destro, Zartan, the Dreadnoks.

MISSION BRIEF When G.I. Joe captures a Cobra Firebat jet containing a prototype auto-pilot, Cobra Commander flips his hooded gourd to realize that the Joes now possess a craft capable of leading them automatically back to the newest Cobra Headquarters. Desperate to steal or destroy the Firebat in question, Cobra Commander hires Zartan and his Dreadnoks to handle the problem.

Meanwhile, Vehicle Motion Picture Studios starts production on a G.I. Joe-based blockbuster, requesting use of Joe equipment and specialists to increase the film's authenticity. Unaware of the Firebat's automatic recall device, the Joes lend the ship and other vehicles to the studio – assigning Shipwreck, Cover Girl and other Joes to serve as military advisors.

At the studio, Zartan and the Dreadnoks set about eliminating the on-site Joes, summoning the police to arrest Shipwreck and Cover Girl during a fortuitous bar riot – although Dreadnok Torch winds up tangling with a pool hall bruiser and also lands in the pokey.

Bailed out of prison, Shipwreck returns to the movie studio and catches Zartan approaching the Firebat. Knocking Shipwreck out cold, Zartan stuffs the Joe sailor into the Firebat and sends it back to Cobra HQ. Realizing the purpose of Zartan's mission, the Joes disguise Recondo as Dreadnok Torch, then radio Cobra Commander and threaten to torture Cobra HQ's location out of "Torch" unless Cobra surrenders Shipwreck. Favoring his base's safety over the doofus Joe sailor, Cobra Commander agrees to a swap.

Unaware of Cobra Commander's deal, Zartan breaks the real Torch out of prison. Simultaneously, Cobra Commander and a platoon of Firebats arrive with the tied-up Shipwreck at Vehicle Studios. Throwing himself away from the line of fire, Shipwreck gives Mutt's hound Junkyard the chance to jump Cobra Commander, instigating a major smackdown between Cobra Firebats and G.I. Joe Skystrikers. With movie director George filming every glorious minute, the Joes whip the enemy. Months after the fact, Shipwreck, Cover Girl and their teammates gather for the successful opening of *The G.I. Joe Story.*

MEMORABLE MOMENTS The opening of "Lights! Camera! Cobra!" makes you wonder if you've briefly popped into a parallel universe, with Snake-Eyes atypically hurling javelins at various Cobra soldiers, a Duke-like figure calling Cobra Commander "Snake Nose!" and other off-kilter incidents. (Seconds later, you realize you're watching a movie set.)

Dreadnok Torch displays some rare intelligence in phoning the police to arrest Shipwreck and Cover Girl, but a biker grabs him and hauls Torch into the fracas (the cops arrest him also).

After a high-octane Joe/Dreadnok clash, director George Lanceburg briefly glows over getting a crapload of battle-film – only to discover that a falling water tower, shrapnel and a runaway truck scrapped his cameras. Desperate to salvage even a snippet of film, George calls to his long-shot camera-man – wretchedly discovering that the boob wasn't even filming.

Shipwreck wakes up aboard a Cobra stronghold and, completely undaunted, punches Cobra Commander and announces to the assembled Cobra legion: "Okay, land lubbers, you're all my prisoners!"

LOVE AND WAR An airline attendant who can't wait to rid herself of the cloying Shipwreck groans: "That sailor's driving me crazy." Shipwreck's evidently spent too much time at sea, as he spots a group of babes and wonders, "When do we get shore leave?"

ASS-WHUPPINGS Dreadnok firepower puts Recondo and Dusty in the hospital. Shipwreck, Cover Girl and Dreadnok Torch wind up incarcerated for brawling in a pool hall. An explosion flings Blowtorch into Mutt. Joe dog Junkyard jumps Cobra Commander. Joe Skystrikers decimate a Cobra Firebat squadron.

PREPOSTEROUS PHYSICS Shipwreck flies over a group of coyotes in a captured Cobra Trouble Bubble, but a wolf clamps onto his leg cuff. After kicking the coyote into a vertigo-inducing gorge – complete with life-saving river at the 'Wreck utters a Road Runner-esque "Meep meep!"

GOOFS The Joes disguise Recondo as Dreadnok Torch to "torture" him, when it's much simpler to put the real Torch on the rack. Dusty wears camouflage paint on his face even when he's off duty and hanging around airport terminals. Recondo uses superhuman reflexes to toss aside a charging coyote. Cobra Commander explicitly orders Zartan to steal the captured Firebat, but Zartan completely ignores his instructions, trying to blow it up instead.

TV TIE-INS There's a telling moment when Destro happens upon a hoodless Cobra Commander eating lunch and requests: "Commander, your hood... put it on," suggesting that Cobra Commander's got a horribly disfigured mug. *G.I. Joe: The Movie* confirms this hint, explaining why the commander's less (or more, depending on your point of view) than human.

A movie maker similar to *The G.I. Joe Story* director helps Cobra Commander film a music video ("Cold Slither"), although it isn't concretely established as the same character.

CHARACTER PROFILE: JOES

Cover Girl: In a tidbit that'll make feminists groan, Cover Girl's painted as a stellar make-up expert.

CHARACTER PROFILE: COBRA

- *Cobra Commander and Destro:* Relations are presumably better (or perhaps merely more profitable) between them, as Destro rescues Cobra Commander's ass during the final firefight. By way of explanation, Destro shrugs off any sense of sentiment and claims he merely "...saved a customer."
- *Buzzer:* His buzzsaw's powerful enough to cut through a bank vault door.
- *Zartan and the Dreadnoks:* Cobra Commander offers them a fee of $4 million to deal with the Firebat problem.

STUFF YOU NEED Cobra Firebat Homing Device: Cost Cobra a cool $15 million to develop.

THE COMMAND DECISION Cornball, but self-consciously so, and another example of G.I. Joe episodes that favor comedy over gunplay. Braced with spiked cocoa and in the right mindset, we actually enjoyed the humorous bits of "Lights! Camera! Cobra!" – although we're fully aware that it'll probably shove bamboo under the fingernails of more serious-minded viewers.

1.20: "Cobra's Candidate"

US Transmission Date: *Oct. 11, 1985*
Writer: *Gordon Kent*

BATTLE ROSTER *Joes:* Scarlett, Lady Jaye, Snake-Eyes, Spirit, Zap; *Cobra:* Tomax and Xamot, the Dreadnoks, Cobra Commander, Zartan, Firefly, Storm Shadow.

MISSION BRIEF When a street gang named "the Rogues" starts terrorizing law-and-order mayoral candidate Robert Harper in favor of his rival Whittier Greenway, the President asks the Joes to step in and keep the peace. Accordingly, Scarlett, Lady Jaye and a handful of Joes hotly pursue the Rogues and their leader (a young woman named Pilar). But as the Joes near their quarry, the Dreadnoks – working in league with the Rogues – stage a sneak attack and make off with Snake-Eyes, Zap, Spirit and their respective animals.

Scarlett and Lady Jaye escape, wondering how to recover their comrades. Curious to learn more about Cobra's apparent interest in the election, the Joe women eavesdrop on a meeting between Harper and his "advisers" – turning stunned to discover that Harper directly reports to the Crimson Twins. Scarlett and Lady Jaye realize the twins, attempting to get their lackey-boy Harper elected mayor, hired the punkish Rogues to "trash" Harper's campaign – thereby portraying Harper as a champion of justice. As expected, the surge of support for the "defiant" Harper gives him a commanding lead in the polls.

Luckily, the male Joes alert Scarlett and Lady to their location, leading to a daring rescue and the capture of a Crimson Guardsman. By interrogating the Cobra goon, the Joes learn that Cobra plans for the Rogues to "ransack" Harper's final rally – swaying more voters and cementing Harper's victory.

Shortly before the rally, Cobra saboteur Firefly packs a series of nearby abandoned buildings with explosives as a safeguard against Joe interference. The rally swells into full swing, but to Pilar's dismay, her 10-year-old brother Tiho – struck with hero worship for his gang-leading sis – shows up to help the Rogues in their criminal endeavors. When Pilar futilely orders Tiho to go home, the Rogues mercilessly taunt the boy.

A bawling Tiho runs straight into a warehouse, failing to spot Firefly's incendiary devices. As Scarlett and Lady Jaye's team arrives to battle the Rogues, Firefly detonates his charges – triggering a series of explosions. Pilar races to save her screaming brother, but the Dreadnoks block her path, insisting that Pilar continue disrupting the rally. Finally enlightened as to Cobra's true colors, the Rogues – who aren't murderous by nature – abandon their employers.

In short order, the Joes force the Dreadnoks to retreat while Scarlett helps Pilar haul Tiho to safety. Panicking, Harper attempts to escape on a Cobra hovercraft with Firefly and Zartan, but the Cobras laughingly pitch Harper overboard, leaving him to face the authorities. As Pilar and her Rogues retire from street crime, news of Harper's association with Cobra sweeps Whittier Greenway into office.

MEMORABLE MOMENTS As proof of changing times, Pilar's brother Tiho struts into his mother's candy shop holding Lady Jaye's javelins and Scarlett's crossbow – and Mommy Tiho doesn't even flinch.

A rumble between Scarlett, Lady Jaye and the Rogues ends with a sweet cliffhanger at commercial break, as Pilar levels her gun at the trounced women and declares, "I'll finish this."

With 98 percent of the vote reporting, Greenway takes 2,104,938 votes while Harper gets a mere two. As the Joes scratch their heads, wondering who voted for Harper (Mama Pilar: "His mother?" Lady Jaye: "His wife?"), the fuming Crimson Twins rip up their voting stubs.

LOVE AND WAR Zartan examines Firefly's hand-held detonator device, but it sounds like he's... ahem... checking out something else. (Zartan: "Interesting little device, Firefly." Firefly: "There's nothing little about it, Swamp Breath.")

ASS-WHUPPINGS The Dreadnoks collapse a fire escape atop Spirit, Zap, Snake-Eyes and their animal companions. Later, the Rogues stun the Joes with a grenade, preventing their escape. Scarlett kicks Xamot from behind, making both him and brother Tomax fall into a dumpster. Later, a Rogue drops Lady Jaye and Scarlett through a window. In rescuing their comrades, Quick Kick, Lady Jaye and Scarlett pelt some Crimson Guardsmen with throwing stars, javelins and crossbow bolts. Spirit strangles a Crimson Guardsmen.

PREPOSTEROUS PHYSICS The motorcycle-clad Rogues whip some chains around a rally stand's support struts, then gun their engines and pull the whole structure down – when you'd think it'd simply haul the gang members off their cycles. For that matter, the falling timber erroneously seems to crush the crooked Harper to death (but he still wants your vote).

The Dreadnoks impossibly jump their ATVs from rooftop to rooftop. Bad timing during a skirmish at Extensive Enterprises allows Scarlett to run down several flights of stairs in maybe five seconds.

If we're to believe the Dreadnoks, merely shooting the top support strut of a fire escape will bring the entire apparatus down. Snake-Eyes, Spirit and Zap implausibly survive the falling fire escape with only a couple of bruises. The structure also fails to mush eagle Freedom and wolf Timber.

GOOFS Scarlett and Lady Jaye initially don't get suspicious – seriously, not a clue – when they drop off Harper for a meeting at the Crimson-twin-owned Extensive Enterprises. (Who the hell do they think he's chatting with? Sonny and Cher?) During the final act, Wild Bill and Quick Kick appear from nowhere in a helicopter to rescue Scarlett and Lady Jaye from a brawl with the Rogues. Shortly after, pilot Wild Bill comments, "I'm a-headin' that a-way, pardners," as if he's changing course – but Scarlett's shown doing the flying. Snake-Eyes' wolf Timber teleports from location to location, unless we're to assume he fits in a cramped helicopter cockpit (or somehow clings to the Joe helicopter's landing skids).

When one of Pilar's "Rogues" jumps over a fence, it looks like his jacket reads "Pogues." Why did Firefly think that blowing up some abandoned buildings would help ward off a Joe attack? Furthermore, why does Harper try to flee with Cobra at story's end – it's not like the Joes leveled any accusations against him, or indeed, collected any hard evidence (the Rogues genuinely believed their employers wanted Whittier Greenway to win). Finally, Pilar and her Rogues don't serve a drop of jail time, despite several obvious counts of public disorder, threatening behavior, etc.

TV TIE-INS Lady Jaye reiterates for the third time ("Satellite Down," "Red Rocket's Glare") that she's afraid of heights.

CHARACTER PROFILE: JOES *Scarlett:* Her crossbow fires suction cup arrows with tow lines, but the cords never seem long enough for the task at hand.

CHARACTER PROFILE: COBRA
- *Buzzer:* He can't read, the poor sap.
- *Storm Shadow:* His samurai sword makes a useful letter opener.

THE COMMAND DECISION Watchable, although the mercurial plot confusingly zips about with the randomness of an air hockey puck at points. Still, "Cobra's Candidate" keeps its moral center in the right place – notably through Pilar's reformation – even if its brain sometimes can't decide where to turn.

1.21: "Money to Burn"

US Transmission Date: *Oct. 14, 1985*
Writer: *Roger Slifer*

BATTLE ROSTER *Joes:* Lady Jaye, Flint, Roadblock, Alpine; *Cobra:* Tomax and Xamot, Cobra Commander, Destro.

MISSION BRIEF When Destro develops a "thermal molecular ignition transmitter" – a gadget capable of spontaneously combusting all American paper money by remote – Cobra Commander inwardly warms at the thought of gutting the American economy like a fish. As a prelude, Cobra agents steal a ferocious amount of jewelry, coinage, rare art and more – amassing the largest collection of tangible goods ever assembled. Soon after, Cobra Commander, the Crimson Twins and Destro relocate to a frosty Cobra base in the Rockies, watching as Destro's ignition device turns all American paper currency into ash.

Soon after, rioting and looting replace normal transactions, allowing the "magnanimous" Cobra Commander to "ease" America's suffering with gold-plated Cobra currency. Unable to otherwise barter, the American public rushes to the nearest Extensive Enterprises branch, trading their valuables for the evil money and further augmenting Cobra's coffers.

Momentarily left cross-eyed by Cobra's newest ploy, the Joes regroup and nab Madeline Henderhoff, a wealthy heiress scheduled to do business with Cobra. Lady Jaye disguises herself as Henderhoff, travelling aboard the twins' personal jet to Cobra's main vault and coinage manufacturing plant in the Rockies. With the Cobra stronghold invisible to radar, Joe paratroopers lock onto Lady Jaye's tracking signal and drop onto Cobra's doorstep *en masse.*

The Cobras give it their best, but fall to superior Joe firepower. As always, the Cobra leaders escape, but the Joes blow up the base, obliterating the ignition transmitter and thereby ruining Cobra's ability to further incinerate U.S. currency. With the American economy restored to normal, the Joes celebrate with a high-stakes poker game.

MEMORABLE MOMENTS As Destro flames all American paper money, a crooked car salesman tries to hide ill-begotten loot in his hat – only to have the spontaneously torched money set his toupee on fire. And it's probably horrible of us to laugh, but an old woman cries as her money-laden mattress erupts in a puff of smoke.

Tomax and Xamot interweave their sentences so fast, the Joes get cricks in their necks trying to keep up. Roadblock pacifies the captive Ms. Henderhoff by sharing an ultra-secret soufflé recipe.

ASS-WHUPPINGS A mob in front of Extensive Enterprises, desperate to trade tangible goods for food money, thump Lady Jaye and Ripcord for trying to cut in line. Heiress Henderhoff clobbers Gung Ho with a Gucci suitcase. Lady Jaye trips up a Polar Viper by shoving a javelin between his legs and upending the poor sap.

As per any story involving the Crimson Twins, Lady Jaye nails one brother but they both fall in agony (as Lady Jaye puts it, a "double play"). Tomax grapples with Lady Jaye, who activates her rocket javelin and sends him soaring into a chasm.

An inspired Ripcord takes out a Cobra soldier – by tying his shoelaces together.

PREPOSTEROUS PHYSICS It's never explained how the hell a "thermal molecular ignition transmitter" could possibly flame American currency from a distance. Firefly starts a tidal wave of Biblical proportions – strong enough to wash Joe tanks away – by melting snow with his hand-held blowtorch. Afterwards, the melted snow oddly turns to mud instead of ice.

GOOFS As the Crimson Twins barter for tangible goods, a Cobra driver maniacally drives around the corner and nearly runs the brothers down for no readily apparent reason.

Cobra's idiotic money-torching scheme wouldn't work for a number of reasons, partly because even in the event of an economic collapse, it's not as if vendors would fall all over themselves to honor Cobra currency. During the final firefight, Cobra troopers stop fighting when an explosion showers them with coinage and other goodies – a pretty stupid move, considering the loot's useless if you're stuck in the federal pokey, toiling away endless hours watching C-SPAN and playing ping-pong. After the fact, how does the American government reimburse the public for their lost cash?

Joe paratrooper Ripcord follows his intuition and swan-dives through a Cobra-projected mountain hologram – when he can't guarantee it's a radar malfunction (meaning Ripcord would've ended up very flat). Falling or walking through holograms somehow produces a slurpy noise. Flint's assault squad parachutes into position, but they're shown advancing on Cobra's Rockies base with assault vehicles. Tomax gives up a perfectly good chance to shoot Lady Jaye from a distance, preferring to wrestle with her instead.

Federal crime number 293 committed by the Crimson Twins with *no penalty:* Acting as brokers for Cobra, a known terrorist organization who's just destroyed America's paper currency. Finally, how does a Cobra guard say, "Make sure no unauthorized personnel get near the thermal molecular ignition transmitter!" without cracking up?

G.I. JOE: THE MUSICAL Ms. Henderhoff, gleeful for Roadblock's soufflé recipe, lets out a melodious "Yo, Jooooooee!" as the Joes scramble.

CHARACTER PROFILE: JOES *Flint:* He carries a TV watch (not for radio communication like Dick Tracy, but useful for catching the end of, say, a Lakers game).

ORGANIZATIONS *G.I. Joe:* Ace, Thunder, Roadblock, Alpine and Ripcord play poker together.

PLACES TO GO *Extensive Enterprises:* The main level's accessible through a false brick wall in the basement parking lot. The twins' office contains a hidden tunnel through a false bookshelf.

STUFF YOU NEED *Cobra Coins:* They're made from a gold-plated chemical polymer alloy.

THE COMMAND DECISION A story that makes even non-discerning G.I. Joe viewers gasp in horror, the absurd premise of "Money to Burn" pretty much rips out your giblets from the start. Granted, the work's rounded out with a couple of decent gags (Ms. Henderhoff and Roadblock bonding over soufflé, Ripcord tying a Cobra soldier's shoelaces together, etc.) and a worthy brawl at story's end – but none of that compensates for the sheer daftness of Cobra burning the world's money, leaving one to conclude that we could make G.I. Joe a lot more credible by pruning crap such as this.

1.22: "Operation Mind Menace"

US Transmission Date: *Oct. 15, 1985*
Writer: *Martin Pasko*

BATTLE ROSTER *Joes:* Airborne, Flash, Duke, Lady Jaye, Stalker; *Cobra:* Cobra Commander, Destro.

MISSION BRIEF Hoping to augment Cobra's forces with psionic shock troops – soldiers gifted with telekinesis, telepathy, teleportation, etc. – Cobra agents coordinate their efforts to kidnap several such psionics. Cobra operatives nab one such girl – an out-of-body traveler – in Honolulu, compelling Joes Airborne and Flash to trail the girl's abductors to Easter Island. But once there, the two Joes blunder straight into a massive Cobra training facility, leading to their capture.

Meanwhile, Duke and Lady Jaye oversee a battery of psychological tests for Airborne's brother: a budding telekinetic named Tommy Talltree. But almost on cue, Cobra agents burst in and seize Tommy, equipping him with a neural disrupter to guarantee obedience. Worse, the Cobra thugs fit Tommy with a psi-amplifier, exponentially increasing his telekinetic abilities.

Tommy's captors take the boy to Easter Island, but Cobra Commander becomes worried the Joes might track their missing comrades. Opting to eliminate Airborne and Flash, the whacked commander orders Tommy to telekinetically animate two of Easter Island's giant Moaib heads – complete with giant stone bodies – to squash the helpless Joes. As a final boast, Cobra Commander gloats about his destination – a remote

Cobra base atop mountain K12 – before withdrawing his personnel and enthralled captives from Easter Island.

The stone Moaib advance on Airborne and Flash, but Duke and Lady Jaye thankfully track down and rescue their teammates. As the Joes depart, Cobra's Easter Island base detonates on auto-destruct, flinging the Moaib into the ocean. Duke coordinates a massive strike on Cobra's K12 base, but Destro rallies a defense using Cobra's captive psionics. Thankfully, the psionics – lacking free-will thanks to Cobra's neural disrupters – fall to the Joes' superior strategy.

Cobra Commander plays Tommy as his trump card, but Airborne reaches his sibling and, in a show of brotherly love, gives Tommy the strength to short out his control tiara. Naturally, the Cobra leadership escapes, but the Joes liberate all of Cobra's captive psionics.

MEMORABLE MOMENTS When Tommy's diagnosed as a telekinetic, Lady Jaye understandably grimaces – sagely knowing the kid's troubles are only beginning.

ASS-WHUPPINGS Tommy telekinetically slices off a pair of Joe Sky Hawk engines.

PREPOSTEROUS PHYSICS A psychologist – likely Joe medic Doc – kicks an entire table through the air with enough force to skewer Storm Shadow. Mind, the Cobra ninja – just as implausibly – carves the table in half with his sword. Oh, and let's not even talk about the physics involved in telekinetically creating giant stone statues on Easter Island – not to mention the error that Tommy's "telekinesis" apparently endows the Moaib with independent life (they should require his constant presence and direction in order to move). Lady Jaye's crashing Sky Hawk merely scuffs the Washington Monument rather than breaking it like a giant toothpick. Joe Blowtorch unfreezes an ice-buried psionic with his flame-thrower – a risky gambit at best.

GOOFS A Cobra helicopter pilot lashes his kidnap victim to the chopper's landing skid when they could've just stuffed her in the back seat. Tommy, a powerful telekinetic, doesn't even try using his mental powers against his kidnappers.

Surrounded by a mentally projected ring of fire, Duke, Lady Jaye and a nameless federal agent escape "to the side" – except that, err… being a *ring*, it should toast them equally on all sides.

Cobra oddly forces its captive psionics to shed their civilian clothes and "uniformly" strut about in tattered rags for no reason. Cobra Commander's naïve enough to believe that "nobody will locate us atop K12," despite the fact that he apparently blathers about the base to anyone who'll listen.

Bad animation shows a stone giant on Easter Island kicking another giant head at Airborne – and apparently pulping him. A departing Cobra jet briefly distracts the towering Moaib, so of course, Flash and Airborne stupidly re-gain the giants' attention by uselessly shooting at them. The Moaib, who merely fall into the ocean, are probably still wandering about the place harassing tourists.

None of the captive psionics "want to hurt anyone," although you'd think one or two of them would actually enjoy the life.

CHARACTER PROFILE: JOES *Airborne:* He possesses a psionic link with his brother Tommy, but it's more empathic (i.e. the two brothers innately sense how each other's feeling) than physical (such as the Crimson Twins).

CHARACTER PROFILE: OTHER

Tommy: Tommy's a high-level telekinetic, powerful enough – with a sufficient psi-amplifier – to mold living and inorganic substances like clay. Tommy coined the code-name "Airborne" when his brother became an airman. Tommy idealizes his high-flying brother and owns some model planes.

ORGANIZATIONS *Cobra's Psionics:* Include a pyrokinetic named Carmody, capable of spontaneously creating fire and moving it with his mind, and a female Hawaiian out-of-body traveler, who projects an intangible astral body.

THE COMMAND DECISION Continually ill at ease with itself, and hailing from an early point in the series' production schedule, the amateurish "Operation Mind Menace" pretty much sucks the life from you with a high-powered vacuum hose. The characters sport about as much depth as our shotglasses, not to mention that Cobra's mesmerized psionics ultimately aren't worth spit. All this, plus the woeful Easter Island stone giants, make for a hugely lacking story.

1.23: "Battle for the Train of Gold"

US Transmission Date: *Oct. 16, 1985*
Writer: *David Carren*

BATTLE ROSTER *Joes:* Duke, Scarlett, Snake-Eyes, Cover Girl, Thunder, Gung Ho, Mutt and Junkyard, General Stack, Short-Fuze, Thunder; *Cobra:* Cobra Commander, Major Bludd, Destro, Zartan and the Dreadnoks.

MISSION BRIEF Duke marshals his Joes when Major Bludd's troops raid the U.S. Treasury Department, but to everyone's surprise, Major Bludd ignores the moolah pumping through the Treasury's presses and contents himself with stealing a video tape marked "A-4." The Joes briefly exchange high-fives over deflecting Bludd's attack, then turn chilled to realize that tape A-4 contained ultra-secret designs and schematics regarding the government's gold depository at Fort Knox.

Guessing that Cobra intends to steal Fort Knox's $60 billion of gold bouillon, the Joes beef up Knox's normal security contingent. Unfortunately, Cobra Commander and Zartan scour tape A-4, learning about a hitherto-forgotten tunnel that runs under the fort. Soon after, Zartan and the Dreadnoks take a small Cobra complement and infiltrate Fort Knox, capturing base commander General Stack. Disguising himself as Stack, Zartan orders the base's security personnel to leave the fort's main vault.

Duke, Scarlett and Snake-Eyes protest this turn of events to the General, only to charge into the main vault and find themselves captured by Cobra forces. Not expecting to find trouble *inside* Fort Knox, the Joes get caught flat-footed when Cobra troops open a firefight from within the base. Working at fever pitch, Zartan's men form a human chain, passing the fort's bouillon through the hidden tunnel and loading it onto an ultra-fast Cobra train – the high-powered "Cobra Bullet" – for transport to a waiting Cobra submarine.

The Cobra Bullet gets under way, but the Joes extrapolate the train's route and scurry like manic jackelope along a shortcut, pulling ahead of the train and blockading the tracks with transport trucks. Zartan tries to brake, but the Cobra Bullet plows through the truck barrier, losing enough velocity for several Joes to jump onboard.

As a massive slugfest breaks out in every train compartment, Duke's trio stages a jailbreak and storms the command car. Snake-Eyes and Scarlett mop up the Dreadnoks, allowing Duke to dive for Zartan's jugular, but Dreadnok Buzzer goes sprawling and accidentally slices the train's pressure regulator with his chainsaw. The smackdown rages on, but the Cobra Bullet's overheated engines rupture – derailing the train. Looking as if they've just gone five rounds with Mohammed Ali, the battered Joes and Cobras crawl from the train's wreckage and feebly hurl insults at one another. While Zartan and the Dreadnoks regrettably escape, the Joes return America's gold reserves.

MEMORABLE MOMENTS It's not deliberate, but we split our sides laughing when a Cobra trooper disguises himself as an aged male nun – part of a tour group at the Treasury Building – then screams out the Cobra battle cry and tries to shoot down everyone present (see Goofs).

At the U.S. Treasury, Cobra troopers shoot up a pallet of money and Scarlett remarks: "This is getting expensive." The Dreadnoks later remark that their Joe prisoners aren't much use because you "... can't eat 'em, can't drink 'em, can't spend 'em."

LOVE AND WAR Zartan and the Dreadnoks pull General Stack into a tunnel, where Zartan disturbingly announces: "Remove the General's uniform."

ASS-WHUPPINGS Duke walks straight into a bomb blast but emerges with only a headache. Snake-Eyes sharpshoots a catwalk support, crashing the whole apparatus and dropping a bunch of Cobra snipers to a lower level. Opportunist Cobra jets savage an entire fleet of parked Skystrikers. Scarlett, Gung Ho and Snake-Eyes thump the Dreadnoks. The Cobra Bullet derails, pounding everyone aboard worse than a raging mosh pit. The Joes capture a mess of Cobra troops at both Fort Knox and the wrecked Cobra Bullet.

PREPOSTEROUS PHYSICS When Duke, Scarlett and Snake-Eyes initially walk into the captured Fort Knox vault, they find themselves encircled by Cobra troops – who let loose a volley of bullets but miraculously miss the Joe trio. Even allowing that he's an expert commando, how can a tied-up Snake-Eyes flip himself upside down and snag a ladder rung with his foot when Cobra troopers toss him off the Cobra Bullet? The Cobra Bullet, probably clipping along at 100 or more miles per hour, fails to kill anyone when it derails in a hurricane of pent-up steam.

GOOFS Snake-Eyes "disguises" himself as a Treasury officer, but leaves his face visor showing (the effect's rather like Cobra Commander dressing up as a nurse but leaving his helmet on). Lowbrow Treasury guards fail to detect a tour group – actually a Cobra assault squad – wearing Cobra uniforms and carrying laser assault rifles beneath their civilian clothes. As part of the ruse, some Cobra troopers strut into the Bureau of Engraving disguised as nuns (albeit aged male nuns). Oh, and troopers wearing the standard Cobra soldier mouth coverings somehow don latex masks and make their lips move.

Even knowing that Major Bludd's priming a bomb, Duke methodically walks straight into the bomb's blast path. A vault full of American soldiers fail to notice when Zartan pulls General Stack through a floor grille in plain view.

With Cobra holding the central vault, Ace tells his team to "scramble the Skystrikers" – but what's he going to do? Missile Fort Knox into submission? (Oh, *that'll* make the White House turn cartwheels.)

The Joes, supposedly left vehicle-less after Cobra's assault on Fort Knox *(see Group Dynamics)*, somehow produce a jeep and several trucks out of thin air and blockade the Cobra Bullet.

CHARACTER PROFILE: JOES *Gung Ho:* Easily shrugs off Dreadnok Torch's punches.

ORGANIZATIONS *Joes:* Scrambling for a means of catching the Cobra Bullet, the vehicle-less Joes resort to riding thoroughbred horses owned by Thunder's friend Mr. Murphy. The Joes eventually learn the art of horseback riding – after a woeful amount of clumsy starts.

PLACES TO GO *Fort Knox:* The main vault's protected by 20-foot-thick titanium alloy.

HOT WHEELS *Cobra Bullet:* It's fully armed and armored, topping out at 200 miles per hour.

THE COMMAND DECISION Clearly above-average, although not without its detractors – which seems odd, considering the plot's mostly inspired, among other things, by the wildly loved Bond flick Goldfinger. Admittedly, there's a couple of rough edges, (the Joes trying to overtake the Cobra Bullet on a pack of thoroughbred horses, etc.), but for sheer bravo and a closer-to-Earth plot, "Battle for the Train of Gold" ultimately won us over.

1.24: "Cobra Soundwaves"

US Transmission Date: *Oct. 17, 1985*
Writer: *Ted Pedersen*

BATTLE ROSTER *Joes:* Ace, Gung Ho, Roadblock, Flint, Scarlett, Airborne, Wild Bill; *Cobra:* Cobra Commander, Destro, Major Bludd, Wild Weasel.

MISSION BRIEF In an unspecified country in the Middle East, Cobra raises hell with Destro's newest toy – a tower-mounted sonic cannon, capable of emitting soundwaves that shake, rattle 'n' roll approaching vehicles to pieces. Worried that Cobra will play its hand too soon, Destro advises caution – but Cobra Commander, lusting to capture some lucrative oil fields, spits on discretion and shakes apart a passing Skystriker squadron.

The Skystriker pilots – Ace, Gung Ho and Roadblock – quickly find themselves tossed in a Cobra battle arena and forced to spar with a giant robotic crab thing. Fortunately, after deducing that their crabby tormentor's tracking them with infrared scanners, Ace's trio starts a fire to draw the abomination's attention before escaping.

While Flint and a column of Joes defend the oil fields from Cobra's main assault, Ace leads a fresh Skystriker strike on Cobra's sonic cannon. The Joe pilots fall back as the sonic cannon dangerously vibrates their planes a second time, but Cobra Commander, over-eager to finish the Joes off, elevates the solar cannon beyond its recommended height. In a precarious move, a small group of hang-gliding Joes swoop under the precariously perched cannon, blasting away its support and dropping the cannon from a throat-lurching height. Cobra Commander and his supporters run for home, allowing the Joes to munch on a well-earned meal with the ruling Sheik Ali.

MEMORABLE MOMENTS When the sonic cannon plunges to its demise, Cobra Commander almost follows it. Momentarily thinking his commander's gone splat, a deeply sarcastic, stone-faced Destro merely utters: "Pity."

ASS-WHUPPINGS Cobra carves up a bunch of oil fields, seemingly without casualties on either side.

PREPOSTEROUS PHYSICS Ace miraculously starts a fire in a battle arena that's entirely bereft of wood. Oh, and he finds the time to accomplish this while dodging attacks from a giant robot crab. (Hell, he should've pitched a tent and roasted some marshmellows while he was at it).

The second Joe Skystriker attack successfully retreats, despite the sonic cannon dislodging a disturbing number of wing nuts and the like.

Destro insists that the sonic cannon can't shake apart the Joe hang-gliders, which lack moveable parts. That's possibly true – but you'd think the cannon's potent sonic booms would at least knock the gliders topsy-turvy. For that matter, it's likely that any vibration strong enough to rattle a Skystriker to pieces would also pulp the pilots.

GOOFS Cobra CLAW pilots swoop close enough to let the on-foot Roadblock, Gung Ho and Ace best them, when shooting the Joes from afar makes a lot more sense.

Yet again, Cobra spends an increasingly ridiculous amount of time and money crafting battle arenas with over-elaborate instruments of destruction, all for the purpose of tormenting prisoners (a bullet's so much more economical). During their escape, Ace and Roadblock repeatedly lose and regain their laser rifles.

Cobra Commander ruins everything by extending the sonic cannon beyond its proper elevation, leaving it vulnerable (you'd think Destro's engineers would build in some sort of failsafe).

Cobra Commander and Destro take the time to capture Sheik Ali – a splendid hostage – then sloppily let the Sheik go once they reach an escape helicopter.

TV TIE-INS Airborne's latent psionic abilities (previously mentioned in "Operation Mind Menace") let him intuitively sense the kidnapped Sheik Ali's distress.

CHARACTER PROFILE: JOES Gung Ho: Doesn't believe in luck.

THE COMMAND DECISION Did anything happen here? A clichéd episode that amounts to little more than Cobra collectively offering up its throat for the Joes to slit, "Cobra Soundwaves" drowns itself out with a lot of pointless running around and a shocking inability to provide a solid beginning, middle and end. As Jerry Seinfeld would put it, this story's "about nothing" – only not in a laudable fashion.

1.25: "Where the Reptiles Roam"

US Transmission Date: *Oct. 18, 1985*
Writer: *Gerry and Carla Conway*

BATTLE ROSTER *Joes:* Wild Bill, Lady Jaye, Alpine, Bazooka, Breaker, Snake-Eyes; *Cobra:* Cobra Commander, the Baroness, Destro, Zartan and the Dreadnoks.

MISSION BRIEF In an effort to shanghai a new NASA solar energy farm in West Texas, Cobra purchases a nearby dude ranch as a base of operations. But while hacking into their rivals' computer banks, the ever-nosy Joes learn about the oddball Cobra purchase. Curious to learn more, Flint sends Lady Jaye, Alpine, Bazooka and the whooping Wild Bill undercover to Cobra's Loco Toro guest ranch.

Wild Bill's troupe arrives at the ranch, masquerading as a cast of cowboys. Unfortunately, Cobra surveillance agents easily penetrate the Joes' disguises, keeping them distracted with a string of near-fatal "accidents." Finally, Cobra arranges a cattle stampede as a diversion – enabling Zartan to sneak into the neighboring solar farm and steal an ultra-secret control chip. Cobra technicians hotwire the solar farm's control chip into their own equipment, re-aligning the farm's solar collectors and satellite transmitters to form a destructive microwave beam.

Armed with the pulverizing energy beam – and able to direct it anywhere on Earth – Cobra Commander takes to the airwaves and demands a $1 billion pay-off from the world's governments. Meanwhile, Flint mounts up a Joe strike team to overrun Cobra's dude ranch. Cobra Commander tries to defend the Cobra camp with his satellite-directed microwave laser, but the Joes deny Cobra Commander a large enough target by advancing on foot.

As Cobra Commander reels – unable to pick off human-sized targets with his massive energy ray – Wild Bill sends the assembled Cobra troopers into utter chaos with a well-timed cattle stampede. Bested again, Cobra Commander and his officers retreat, leaving the Joes to savor their victory.

MEMORABLE MOMENTS A random Cobra trooper, voiced by the same actor who plays Autobot leader Optimus Prime in Transformers, sent shivers down our spines by telling the overconfident Joes, "Correction – we've got you!" Keeping Transformers in mind, you can imagine our geeky reaction when Lady Jaye comments that there's, "more to this than meets the eye."

Cornered, the dim-witted Bazooka simply declares: "Door!" and elegantly himself an opening with his hand-held bazooka.

LOVE AND WAR Wild Bill spends a great deal of time romancing the Loco Toro ranch manager's daughter – a sugar-sweet blonde named "Mary Belle" – who offers the Joe cowboy a private tour of the ranch. (A disgusted Lady Jaye on "Mary Belle": "Jezebel's more like it.") Although we doubt Wild Bill and Mary Belle – who's actually the Baroness in disguise – get much beyond first base, Bill's disappointed to discover that "Mary Belle" wasn't real. Of course, he kicks himself for not realizing that "Mary Belle" wasn't very convincing as a "Texas peach" – possessing far too much sweetness and not enough sass.

ASS-WHUPPINGS While flexing his particle beam's muscles, Cobra Commander atomizes San Francisco's Golden Gate Bridge – and God knows how many commuters. Wild Bill's diverted cattle herd overruns the Dreadnoks.

PREPOSTEROUS PHYSICS Bazooka uses his bazooka harmlessly in an enclosed room (you'd think the backblast would recoil and topple the Joes like dominoes). The Cobra outpost's metallic walls turn into rock rubble upon impact. Some artillery explosions cause a corn field to erupt into popcorn. Some hot-minded bulls muster enough strength to overturn Destro's jeep.

GOOFS Lady Jaye off-handedly comments that the solar power station, if used improperly, could fry a city, but Joes don't even consider that such destructive power might explain Cobra's presence in the area (the group initially thinks Cobra's using the ranch for an R&R center).

In another moment of Joe dim-wittedness, the Dreadnoks red-flag their true identities by riding away on RTVs and *cackling* precisely like the Dreadnoks – but the Joes still don't make the connection. (Alpine merely muses: "You know, I think those guys set us up…")

Lady Jaye "discreetly" shimmies down a ladder – in full view of everyone in the Cobra control center. She then dons a Cobra uniform for disguise purposes, only to clumsily let Destro and Cobra Commander see her face.

When the Baroness takes off her Mary Belle disguise, she conveniently shoots up two or three inches in height.

The diversionary cattle stampede supposedly prevented the

solar farm staff from noticing Zartan's theft of the control chip – even though Zartan lasers an extremely large hole in a control panel and you'd think they'd need the component to make things *work* properly.

Even if we're to believe that Cobra Commander couldn't pick off all the free-running Joes with his massive laser beam (which is doubtful), you'd think he could at least liquefy a few of them just for sport.

CHARACTER PROFILE: JOES

- *Lady Jaye:* Keeps a radio device in her belt buckle.
- *Wild Bill:* An expert helicopter pilot, adept horseman, top notch cattle herd and handy to have around if you're suddenly in need of a square dance caller.

ORGANIZATIONS *The Dreadnoks:* Like Zartan, they occasionally mask their identities with latex masks (although they're clearly less accomplished at the art of disguise).

PLACES TO GO *West Texas Solar Energy Farm:* Contains a series of microwave antennae that collect solar energy bounced from an orbiting satellite, relaying the energy gathered to electrical plants via standard power lines. It's a fairly secure process – presuming some hooded terrorist lunatic doesn't usurp control of the command center.

THE COMMAND DECISION A loopy tale that we strangely enjoyed watching once – but wouldn't flip on again. If there's a saving grace, it's that "Where the Reptiles Roam" avoids the temptation of wallowing in cowboy kitsch, allowing even country music-haters to yield to its madness for 23-odd minutes.

1.26: "The Gamesmaster"

US Transmission Date: *Oct. 21, 1985*
Writer: *Flint Dille*

BATTLE ROSTER *Joes:* Flint, Lady Jaye; *Cobra:* Cobra Commander, the Baroness, Destro, Zartan.

MISSION BRIEF Purely for fun, a whacked engineering genius named "the Gamesmaster" renovates his privately-owned island as a kids'-style killing ground and assassination center. Hungry to hone his skills, the Gamesmaster sends robotic agents to capture Flint, Lady Jaye, Cobra Commander and the Baroness, intending to pit the foursome against each other in a game of sport.

While Cobra and G.I. Joe trade blame for the kidnappings, the abducted quartet awakens on a candy mountain covered with butterscotch pools, licorice trees and the like. The Gamesmaster forces his prisoners to compete in a fight to the death, promising a one-man helicopter and ticket to freedom for the final survivor. But purely to keep things interesting, the Gamesmaster marshals his lethal robotic toy soldiers to dog the players at every turn.

After briefly slugging each other, Flint and Cobra Commander's duos finally come to their senses and team up against the Gamesmaster. Unfortunately, a giant robotic dragon – another of the Gamesmaster's toys – appears and apparently mauls Flint to death. While Cobra Commander, the Baroness and an anguished Lady Jaye struggle onward, the Gamesmaster's soldiers place Flint's body in a coffin.

Meanwhile, having realized the influence of a third party, Destro and Duke forge a short-term alliance to recover their missing comrades. Back on the Gamesmaster's isle, Flint luckily recovers from his injuries, pops out of his coffin and reaches the island's main communications array to send out a tracking signal. As the Gamesmaster assails his remaining players with a giant lawnmower, a joint Joe/Cobra task force hurries toward the lunatic Gamesmaster's stronghold.

The Gamesmaster's toy defenses – including a full array of mechanical rockets, battleships and airplanes – inflict heavy losses on the Joes and Cobras, but they finally rip their way through the Gamesmaster's armies. Defeated, the Gamesmaster escapes, leaving the Joes and Cobras to retrieve their comrades – and argue about who gets to leave the island first.

MEMORABLE MOMENTS While ingeniously capturing his Joe/Cobra players, the Gamesmaster drops Cobra Commander through a trap door in his own citadel. As a result, Destro confers with a dummy Cobra Commander until its head pops off.

During a punch-out on the candy mountain, Lady Jaye and Cobra Commander find themselves tossed into a gooey pond. Lady Jaye sensibly yells to Flint, "Get me out of here, I'm sinking in caramel!", but the disagreeable Cobra Commander – utterly insistent on having the last word – barks out: "Not caramel! Butterscotch!" To prevent the teams from ganging up on the other, the Baroness and Flint opt to rescue each others' teammates – a rare moment of cooperation in a series ostensibly about war.

"The Gamesmaster" contains some of the nuttiest Joe conversations ever. At one point, Cobra Commander crazily suggests to his fellow captives: "We find the helicopter and I fly it to safety. I will immediately dispatch troops to rescue you," although the scoffing Baroness replies: "Oh, even I cannot swallow that one."

Also, Cobra Commander, the Baroness and Lady Jaye happen upon the prized one-man helicopter – leading to a berserk race with the three of them continually tripping each other up and falling on their faces.

LOVE AND WAR The Gamesmaster's robots nab Lady Jaye as she's in a department store changing room, stripped to a blouse. Moreover, the Baroness is snatched up while lounging in a Jacuzzi. Although the Gamesmaster's mechanical soldiers replace Lady Jaye's clothes, the Baroness spends the entire episode running about in a bikini.

A pack of Gamesmaster robots – ultimately shot down by Destro and Duke – rather disturbingly shout, "Punish them! Punish them!" at their Joe and Cobra opponents. Most personally of all, Lady Jaye comes unglued after Flint's "death," laying bare their more-than-professional relationship.

ASS-WHUPPINGS A giant robotic dragon severely mangles Flint in its iron-toothed jaws, but he somehow survives. The stocky Gamesmaster flings Flint about the room with all the verve of a Sumo wrestler. Still, Flint tosses the hefty Gamesmaster aside at one point, squashing his cackling robotic assistant Cocoa.

GOOFS A caged Lady Jaye shouts out, "Put me down!" before any of the Gamesmaster's robot soldiers actually pick her up. Flint realistically shouldn't have survived the giant dragon's mastication (see Ass-Whuppings).

CHARACTER PROFILE: JOES

• *Ace:* Has lost three Skystriker jets this month.

• *Flint:* He's officially cited as the Joe second-in-command. Flint drives a red sports car, and lives in a waterfront apartment complex with underground parking.

• *Gung Ho:* His favorite rifle's named "Baby."

• *Lady Jaye:* She loves shopping for apparel. (As the Gamesmaster puts it: "Clothes are like candy to her.")

CHARACTER PROFILE: COBRA

• *Baroness:* She innately puts her own interests ahead of any regard for Cobra. Failing to escape from the Gamesmaster's isle on her own, the Baroness – in a display of gender loyalty – would rather Lady Jaye got away than Cobra Commander. We'll credit the Baroness for exceptional hand-to-hand combat skills – but she can't beat Flint.

• *Destro:* Far more practical than Cobra Commander, Destro fails to see the point of numerous Cobra-sponsored parades and processionals. Destro's more than happy to let Zartan rot in Joe custody – preferably in a dank, rat-infested cell.

• *Zartan:* He's carrying out experiments with deadly swamp flu.

CHARACTER PROFILE: OTHER

The Gamesmaster: A large, sharply dressed bald man with a beard – evidently an engineering genius but prone to childish fits. He's pretty adept at hand-to-hand combat, capable of knocking opponents aside with his blubbery gut.

PLACES TO GO The Gamesmaster's Isle: The entire island smells like candy, complete with bon-bon berry bushes and trees bearing liquorice, marshmallows and caramel apples (see Preposterous Physics).

THE COMMAND DECISION Easily (and wrongly) dismissed as tripe, "The Gamesmaster" goes about its "silly" business with intelligence, a sense of fun and precise implementation. A certain breed of viewer understandably won't tolerate a slugfest in a candy forest, no matter how well done, and we'd hardly call this an model Joe story – but it's a guilty pleasure that we laughed ourselves silly over it.

1.27: "Lasers in the Night"

US Transmission Date: *Oct. 22, 1985*
Writer: *Marv Wolfman*

BATTLE ROSTER *Joes:* Quick Kick, Lady Jaye, Duke, Gung Ho; *Cobra:* Cobra Commander, Destro, the Baroness.

MISSION BRIEF Endowed with fighting skills and gushing with hormones, a college student named Amber attends a G.I. Joe-hosted collegiate martial arts exhibition. Amber volunteers to spar with Joe silent weapons expert Quick Kick, losing the match but nonetheless snagging the shirtless Joe's attention. In short order, Quick Kick and Amber strike up a heated romance, jointly attending opera performances, baseball games and sweaty martial arts practice sessions.

Meanwhile, Cobra undertakes operations to steal a prototype long-range laser guidance system – only to find that the Joes have re-located the device to their headquarters. Switching tactics, the Baroness raids a Joe outpost and kerwallops Lady Jaye, allowing Cobra agents to spirit the female Joe away while the Baroness takes her place.

"Lady Jaye" returns to headquarters and bides her time, but Amber, desperate to prove her mettle to Quick Kick, decides that breaking into Joe Headquarters will demonstrate her prowess and net her Joe membership. The Joes easily apprehend the daft Amber, and, upon realizing she's harmless, allow Quick Kick to give her a guided tour of headquarters. Unfortunately, Amber takes it upon herself to run through the base like a five-year-old, inadvertently spying snippets of classified information.

Waiting for a choice moment, the Baroness secretly filches the laser guidance system. Minutes later, a Cobra RATTLER squadron strafes Joe Headquarters, nearly obliterating the Joes' main Skystriker fleet. Most of the Joes remain grounded, but "Lady Jaye" takes up a Skystriker and apparently falls to superior firepower, causing the Joes to mourn her loss.

With Amber missing, Duke yields to overwhelming evidence and pegs the blonde bimbo as traitorously aiding in the theft and Lady Jaye's subsequent death. Simultaneously, Cobra technicians hotwire the Joe guidance system into an enormous laser – preparing to carve Cobra Commander's likeness onto the moon's surface as a giant propaganda stunt.

Desperate to clear her name, Amber ventures out to single-handedly destroy Cobra Commander's base on the so-called Snake Island. But as expected, Cobra troops effortlessly capture the Joe wannabe, tossing her into jail with Lady Jaye. Quick Kick realizes Amber's plan and travels to Snake Island like a lovestruck puppy, but the Cobra troops also nab him. Cobra Commander completes his vainglorious self-portrait on the moon's surface, but the captive Joes thankfully escape and open up a hornet's nest of violence in the Cobra control center.

As Cobra Commander and Destro hurriedly evacuate, a Joe Skystriker squadron moves into position and secures the Cobra camp. In the aftermath, Quick Kick spares the world from forever gazing at Cobra Commander's puss by lasering the moon back into its normal shape. Admitting his error, Duke suggests recruiting the spunky Amber into G.I. Joe, but Amber opts to finish school first.

LOVE AND WAR As part of Quick Kick and Amber's romance, we're treated to shots of them watching ballet (well, Amber watches while Quick Kick snoozes), attending baseball games (where Quick Kick enjoys himself and Amber ponders the inside of her eyelids), breakdancing, martial arts practices and boat rides. Oh, and smooching. Lots of smooching. Even so, Amber's surprised when Quick Kick sticks his neck out to rescue her, although Quick Kick blows it off with: "Well, I had nothing else to do, there were no good movies playing...."

Attempting to locate Amber, a shirtless Quick Kick charges into a college sorority house, scattering scantily clad girls who're loitering about the place in their underwear. Impressed with Quick Kick's bulging muscles, Amber's roommate Brandy asks: "You wouldn't have a brother with shoulders like yours, would you?" – to which Quick Kick answers: "No, a sister."

ASS-WHUPPINGS Cobra troopers bring down Gung Ho with a laser whip.

GOOFS Quick Kick can't love Amber for her mind. He just can't. Rather than speaking to her local recruiter about joining the Joes, Amber opts to dazzle everyone with her skill at breaking into Joe Headquarters – but naturally, the Joes catch her in the first three seconds. After getting caught, Amber runs about Joe Headquarters like a little schoolgirl – purely because the plot requires her to barge into meeting rooms and glimpse classified information, later bringing her under suspicion of espionage.

It only gets worse from there. Amber's not even present during the guidance system theft and Lady Jaye's "death," but somehow realizes that Duke's pegged her for the crimes. Furthermore, she amazingly knows the location of Cobra Commander's base on Snake Island. Lacking explosives or anything even vaguely resembling a weapon, Amber nonetheless expects to "smash" the Cobra camp (With her bare hands? Is she mad?), but ends up aimlessly flitting about the Cobra base until she's captured. And for that matter, why would she bother leaving her hapless, mousy college roommate an answering machine message (*a la* "I'm off to Snake Island to blow it to bits – please don't tell Quick Kick") about her whereabouts?

Admittedly, nobody's big on brainpower this episode. Cobra technicians evidently equip the Snake Island base with zero early warning sensors, since both Amber and Quick Kick reach the main control chamber before getting spotted. Cobra guards toss Amber in a cell without tying her up, enabling her to enact a jailbreak (the *one* thing she gets right this story).

Quick Kick goes alone to rescue Amber rather than doing the sensible thing and alerting his teammates. His genius strategy for saving Amber's hide: Burst into the Snake Island control deck and scream out, "Amber! Are you in here?"

During the final fracas, three lightly armed Joes (Quick Kick, Lady Jaye and Gung Ho, who's totally irrelevant to the plot) miraculously overrun a heavily guarded Cobra base.

CHARACTER PROFILE: JOES

• *Quick Kick:* He's quick to point out that martial arts isn't about a lot of chopping – it requires well-honed discipline and total concentration. A total movie buff, Quick Kick's watched *Treasure of the Sierra Madre* and does (rather pathetic) imitations of Jimmy Stewart (from *It's a Wonderful Life*), Mae West and John Wayne.

• *Lady Jaye:* A technician named Alice services Lady Jaye's Skystriker.

CHARACTER PROFILE: COBRA *Destro:* A long-running contract mandates that Destro provide all of Cobra's weaponry.

CHARACTER PROFILE: OTHER *Amber:* Despite our reservations about her amazing capacity for screwing things up, Amber's decently good-hearted and believes in making a difference. Amber's a candy striper, expert swimmer and neat freak. She runs charity fairs, teaching karate to kids. She's advanced enough in her martial arts skills to chop through chains. She badly quotes Bette Davis from the movie Now, Voyager (a film so obscure, even Quick Kick's never heard of it).

ORGANIZATIONS *Cobra:* In close quarters, Cobra troopers sometimes use energy-charged laser whips invented by Cobra Commander.

STUFF YOU NEED *Joe Laser Guidance System:* Duke brags that the newly forged guidance system could "shoot a gnat off the rings of Saturn."

PLACES TO GO *Joe Headquarters:* The code "10-6-9" helps you slip past a number of early warning sensors.

THE COMMAND DECISION Eyes... rolling... back into... head... Achieving new heights of wretchedness, "Lasers in the Night" tortured us with the inept Amber's amazing and constant capacity for stupid behavior (see Goofs for a full laundry list). As if that's not enough, Cobra Commander's mad moon-carving scheme appalls even Destro ("You've wasted millions on this... this cosmic graffiti?"), plus there's oodles of excessive dramatic irony and Tonto-like dialogue. (Quick Kick picks up a weapon and declares: "Better hang onto this... I might need it.") Absolute hackwork.

1.28: "The Germ"

US Transmission Date: Oct. 23, 1985
Writer: Roger Slifer

BATTLE ROSTER *Joes:* Airtight, Ace, Lady Jaye, Flint, Shipwreck, Tollbooth, Dusty, Colonel Sharpe; *Cobra:* Tomax and Xamot, Destro.

MISSION BRIEF When hospital researchers accidentally create a new type of germ called "Bacteria X," a Cobra Crimson Guardsman steals the organism as a possible bioweapon, initially turning it over to Destro. Unfortunately, long-standing feuds amidst the Cobra leadership reach a new peak, compelling the Crimson Guardsman to steal back Bacteria X on the Crimson Twins' behalf. Just for kicks, the Guardsman also makes off with an experimental growth serum from Destro's laboratory.

The Crimson Guardsman attempts to depart, but Destro's troopers launch into a firefight with the Guardsman's support team. As the rival Cobra groups carve into each other, the Guardsman accidentally drops *both* vials – allowing Bacteria X to mingle with the growth serum. Within seconds, Bacteria X expands into a giant, gelatinous bio-blob, completely gobbling the research center along with a number of Cobra troopers.

Spotting the mobile bio-mass on recon satellites, G.I. Joe sends a Skystriker team to missile the lumbering blob. When that proves useless, Joe hostile environment expert Airtight recommends flying into the bio-blob with a hypodermic-shaped jet, bypassing the germ's defenses and dousing its nucleus with antibiotic-loaded canisters. Airtight succeeds in piloting the giant hypodermic into the mass, but fails to realize that the bio-blob stemmed from misuse of antibiotics. As a result, the monstrosity actually grows stronger from the antibiotic infusion.

To the Joes' horror, the blob undergoes mitosis, splitting into two identical entities. Struggling for a new strategy, the Joes collaborate with one of Bacteria X's creators for options. Favoring a toxin strike, Airtight and the hospital scientist propose dosing the bio-blobs with apple seeds, which naturally contain a tiny dose of cyanide. Ace's Skystriker team launches missiles to lure the first bio-blob into changing direction – convincing it to ingest two apple orchards. Fatally poisoned, the bio-blob shudders and explodes into a harmless splatter of goo.

Making their stand at the Hudson River, Flint's battalion pelts the second bio-blob with apples, but the monstrosity holds out against the fruity barrage. As Flint's Joes dive into the river for cover, Skystriker reinforcements arrive and airdrop hundreds of apples into the bio-blob's mass – starting a chain reaction that ruptures it. Completely soaked in bio-blob slime and applesauce, Flint's team returns to base for a hot shower.

MEMORABLE MOMENTS Ace grows concerned over Airtight's radio silence, but the geeky Airtight finally responds: "Ace, I can hear you perfectly well, I'm just ignoring you."

Finally, in a candid moment of seriousness while trapped in the original bio-blob, Airtight snaps at a stowaway Crimson Guardsman: "My [antibiotic] charges are set to go off in two minutes. Therefore, we have two alternatives – either you let me pilot the ship, or we die." Wisely, the stoic guardsman replies, "Then... we have no choice at all," and moves aside.

LOVE AND WAR Stuck in a held-up convoy of apple trucks, Shipwreck tries to "get cozy" with Cover Girl, but she dissuades him with a jab to the solar plexus.

Later, as Flint orders a retreat, a manic Shipwreck holds his ground, continually throwing apples into the advancing bio-germ's mass and insanely crowing, "This might be the one [that kills it]! This might be the one!" Unable to convince the loopy sailor to run for cover, Cover Girl hurriedly suggests: "If you leave now, I'll go out with you!", causing Shipwreck to immediately pick up his feet and scream: "Anchors away!"

Seconds later, Cover Girl whimsically suggests she and Shipwreck start their date right away by "Going swimming!", then dives with the Joe sailor into the Hudson River. Surfacing, a gleeful Shipwreck announces, "This is the best date I've had in weeks!"

ASS-WHUPPINGS Hotshot Joe pilot Ace crashes a Skystriker and a crop duster. The other Joes escape unscathed, save getting covered in apple-flavored blob goo when the bio-mass explodes. The first bio-blob gobbles a Crimson Guardsman and a number of Cobra divers but fails to digest them.

GOOFS Crimson Guardsman X99, working undercover in a hospital, stops to redon his proper Cobra uniform (conveniently kept in the closet for anyone to find) before stealing Bacteria X – pretty much guaranteeing that he'll be recognized as an intruder. Much later in the story, the swallowed guardsman swims through the bio-blob and sneaks aboard the Joe hypodermic vessel – a remarkable undertaking, considering he's not equipped with an air supply.

The bio-blob keeps several "eaten" Cobra missiles within its mass, but expels Joe-fired warheads back in their faces. The Joes never briefed a benevolent hospital scientist about their gambit with the antibiotics, but he somehow knows anyway. *G.I. Joe* animators render apple trees as bush-like plants with red dots on them. Most disturbing of all, Joe bazookas, tanks and jeep-mounted cannons are all evidently designed to fire apples in addition to heavy artillery.

ORGANIZATIONS *Cobra:* Lower-ranked Cobra soldiers regard the elite Crimson Guardsmen as snobs.

STUFF YOU NEED *Bacteria X:* The technical name for this organism is something like pseudo-monda U bacterius. (Author's Note: That's a rough transcription – our ancient Joe tapes lack closed captioning.)

THE COMMAND DECISION Hrrmmm. Ah, yes. "The Germ." Saddled with one of those wacky, "giant amoeba" premises (much like Star Trek's "The Immunity Syndrome"), it's near-impossible to make this story sound enticing. And that's a pity too, because the implementation includes a long-overdue clash between the Cobra officers, a ripping pace, and a well-honed sense of wackiness. Yet a large segment of fandom shrivels to hear about killing a giant bio-blob with appleseeds – and we can't blame 'em, leaving "The Germ" at best a curious oddity and more properly something that belongs on the rubbish heap.

1.29: "The Viper is Coming"

US Transmission Date: *Oct. 24, 1985*
Writer: *David Carren*

BATTLE ROSTER *Joes:* Barbecue, Scarlett, Roadblock, Lady Jaye, Gung Ho, Alpine, Footloose; *Cobra:* Destro, Major Bludd, Tomax and Xamot.

MISSION BRIEF When Barbecue throws a bash at his apartment, a refurbished firehouse, for his fellow Joes, a mysterious individual identifying himself only as "the Viper" phones to cryptically tell Barbecue: "The Viper is coming – 575." Presuming that the Viper's a hitherto unheard-of informant, the Joes dither over the meaning of "575," and – just for kicks – feed the number into their central computer as latitude and longitude coordinates. When the computer red-flags a remote location in Antarctica, the still-skeptical Joes dispatch a recon team to the icy continent. Once there, the Joes scour the area, turning surprised to discover a hidden Cobra R&R center. In the mayhem to follow, the Joes rout the enemy, capturing several dozen Cobra troopers.

Puzzled as to the Viper's identity, Barbecue hangs around his firehouse until the Viper calls and enigmatically whispers: "This is the Viper. I come on Friday, west corner." Quicker than a chihuahua on speed, the Joes take "west corner" to mean the U.S. military academy at West Point, rushing there to guard an in-progress ceremony. Almost on cue, Major Bludd arrives with a Cobra battalion to kidnap high-level West Point visitors Senator Roberts and General Grant as hostages. Scarlett and a Joe platoon stomp their opponents, apprehending a number of Cobra personnel.

Again, the Viper calls the flummoxed Joes, telling them: "The Viper is coming, tomorrow – top floor first." Accordingly, the Joes shift their attention to the tallest building in the world, the Crimson Twins' Extensive Enterprises headquarters, which houses the highest "top floor" on Earth. Scarlett and Barbecue take a Joe squadron and encircle the Crimson Twins' headquarters for good measure, putting pressure on in-residence Cobra officials, including the twins, Destro and Major Bludd.

While Snake-Eyes, Scarlett and Barbecue cautiously enter Extensive Enterprises, a Roadblock-led team trades bullets with a Cobra security force commanded by Zartan. Overwhelmed, the Cobra officers retreat, but the Joes again net truckloads of Cobra soldiers.

Happy but befuddled over their successes, the Joes perch at Barbecue's firehouse and await the Viper's next phone call. But when the Viper rings up to announce: "This is the Viper. I'll be there today. Be ready," the Joes feel ice running through their veins and heavily fortify the firehouse with tanks, blockades and massive troop deployments. The Joes clench their rifles like safety blankets – then raise a collective eyebrow as an old man appears down the street with a window wiper and bucket.

Possessing a slight speech impediment, the mustachioed man announces, "Mr. Barbecue, I'm the viper. I've come to vipe your vindows. Five seventy-five an hour. I start on West corner, top floor first." Giddy at the dreaded Viper's secret identity – and astonished to realize his clues were sheer coincidence – the relieved Joes erupt into hysterical laughter before heading home.

MEMORABLE MOMENTS At Barbecue's party, Gung Ho comically hops about like a skewered chicken while grooving with Lady Jaye (who notes: "I don't think I've ever seen this dance before."). Alpine and Footloose splinter Barbecue's upper gallery by rappelling from it. Oh, and Snake-Eyes serves as DJ.

By story's end, packs of Joes sweat blood while huddling in Barbecue's house, inwardly cringing and waiting for the dreaded Viper to call. The climactic revelation of the Viper's identity – an old man with a bucket and mop – shines as a top comedic moment for the entire series.

ASS-WHUPPINGS A high-octane basketball game inside Barbecue's firehouse entails Roadblock crashing through a window (mercifully, he makes his shot). Alpine and Footloose fall while rappelling and smash Barbecue's buffet table, covering Scarlett in edible glop.

Two Cobra tanks rotate to hit a Joe buggy, but shoot each other instead. Roadblock grenades a tank. Gym-prone Cobras at the Antarctic R&R center – understandably taken by surprise – pelt our heroes with billiard balls and barbells.

Destro "questions" Major Bludd and the Crimson Twins to determine the Viper's identity – but of course, Destro's idea of "interrogation" entails bashing his subjects about the room. A bit later, Snake-Eyes squarely punches Destro's lights out.

PREPOSTEROUS PHYSICS Wild Bill downs a Cobra helicopter near Extensive Enterprises, an edifice located in a thriving metropolis, but fails to harm even a hot dog vendor.

GOOFS Cobra troops lodging at the Antarctic R&R center play volleyball, swim and even eat with their masks on. For that matter, shorts-clad Cobra troopers working out at the gym change into winter parkas in the blink of an eye. Joe firefighter Barbecue variously does/doesn't wear his fire extinguishing backpack during the same battle.

Why didn't the Joes bother with attacking Extensive Enterprises before now? After all, they barge the door down on the Viper's word, suggesting they don't exactly need a search warrant.

CHARACTER PROFILE: JOES

- *Alpine:* He keeps a rock collection.
- *Footloose:* Alpine taught him the art of rappelling.

PLACES TO GO Cobra Recreation Center #3: Located in Antarctica, the R&R center contains "the Cobra Commander Gymnasium," "the Destro Dining Room" and "the Zartan Entertainment Center." The "Cobra Beauties" put on a spectacular floorshow. Sadly, skinny-dipping's verboten.

- *Extensive Enterprises:* The main Extensive Enterprises tower rises 80 stories tall, making it (in the Joe-niverse, that is) the tallest building in the world. It also incorporates helicopter hanger bays.

THE COMMAND DECISION Bravely putting its neck for the sake of a single jape, "The Viper is Coming" lovingly and hysterically gushes with gall. Although seemingly silly, the final joke with the window wiper only serves to pop the mounting, sweaty tension that permeates most of the episode. At the end of the day, this one's proof that writers can, should and must take risks in order to be worth their salt. Have fun with it.

1.30: "Spell of the Siren"

US Transmission Date: *Oct. 25, 1985*
Writers: *Gerry and Carla Conway*

BATTLE ROSTER *Joes:* Lady Jaye, Scarlett, Cover Girl, Flint, Duke, Roadblock; Cobras: The Baroness, Destro, Tomax and Xamot, Cobra Commander, Major Bludd.

MISSION BRIEF In the Adriatic Sea, Destro fortifies an enormous undersea Cobra base in an effort to find the Conch of the Sirens – a fabled seashell that, when blown into, creates ultrasonic waves capable of mesmerizing all males in earshot. Destro scours a string of undersea ruins, succeeding in his seemingly impossible task and unearthing the ancient artifact. But the Joes catch word of Destro's operation and ransack the Cobra base, apprehending Destro while the Baroness escapes with the conch.

Cobra Commander flies into a rage upon learning of the undersea debacle, vowing to let Destro rot in a Joe holding cell. Inwardly fuming for her lover's predicament, the Baroness travels to a Cobra operation on the Alaskan Pipeline, hoping to convince Major Bludd to help her bust Destro out of the pokey. But at that moment, the Joes assault the Cobra battalion – backing the Baroness into a corner and forcing her to blow into the conch in desperation.

Instantly, the conch's soundwaves radiate outward, rendering every male present completely passive. The female Joes load up their blank male allies and narrowly escape. But the newly empowered Baroness, outraged over Cobra Commander's abandonment of Destro, returns to Cobra Headquarters and uses the conch against Cobra Commander and Tomax – seizing leadership of Cobra.

Mustering some all-female Cobra assault teams, the Baroness prepares to storm Joe Headquarters. By electronically amplifying the conch's soundwaves, the Baroness instantly subverts even more male Joes. Scarlett, Lady Jaye, Cover Girl and a few other Joe women fight to the bitter end, but the Baroness orders her enraptured male slaves to turn on their female counterparts. Unable to hold their ground, Scarlett's trio unleashes a locker of paralyzing stun gas, rendering Joe Headquarters temporarily uninhabitable.

Satisfied upon freeing Destro, the Baroness retreats with her slave army. But to everyone's surprise, Xamot – angered at the Baroness for capturing his brother Tomax – approaches the few Joes at liberty and proposes a short-term alliance. More helpfully, Dr. Blackstone, a female audio scientist affiliated with the Joes, cobbles together a frequency gun designed to counter the conch's sonic pulse.

The Joes uneasily side with Xamot, using his intelligence information to breach the Baroness' security. Amid the firefight, the Joe women douse the Baroness' base with Dr. Blackstone's counter-pulse, freeing her captives. Ending his association with the Joes, Xamot liberates Tomax and Cobra Commander – even as Lady Jaye's javelin knocks the conch from the Baroness' hand. Judging the battle lost, the Baroness and Destro flee to fight another day. With everything back to normal, the Joes destroy the conch for good measure.

MEMORABLE MOMENTS With the Cobra troops blundering their way through the underwater battle, a testosterone-laded, rampaging Destro storms to the battlefront because "... someone has to show those fools how to fight!" Crimson Guard Commander Xamot saves Lady Jaye from a tight scrap, then laughs – in a truly hyena-worthy cackle – that she's been "rescued" by her mortal enemy.

LOVE AND WAR The lovestruck Baroness spends most of this story hauling Destro's worthless hide out of jail. Destro's content to let the Baroness keep control of Cobra, recognizing that he'll only benefit from her successes. The Baroness lets Destro keep his free will, recognizing the importance of sharing an empire with someone.

Lady Jaye's deeply upset when the Baroness' conch subverts Flint. Scarlett's similarly upset to lose Duke. During a minor scrap, Lady Jaye freaks after briefly losing consciousness and awakening to find Xamot looming over her in a "morning after" fashion.

ASS-WHUPPINGS A glass shard nails Lady Jaye's wrist, allowing the Baroness to strike her down (see Goofs). The Baroness' female troops gut Joe Headquarters. While helping Lady Jaye escape, an acrobatic Xamot bowls over a pack of Cobra women.

PREPOSTEROUS PHYSICS Admittedly propelled by an explosion, Xamot nonetheless turns into Hercules, knocking over a giant Cobra robot with his feet – when he should've more properly snapped his legs like dried-out twigs.

GOOFS The Baroness karate-chops Lady Jaye unconscious at one point, leaving the Joe in a puddle of rising water where she should've drowned.

Why isn't Destro affected by the Baroness' siren spell during her attack on Joe Headquarters? Scarlett, Cover Girl and Lady Jaye take down a number of their male counterparts with "paralyzing" stun gas, but some of the men – including Roadblock – get up and walk away a few minutes later. For that matter, how fast could the Baroness' crew possibly escape *on foot?*

The Baroness and her enthralled Joes clash with Scarlett's remaining forces in a tunnel – but in the blink of an eye, they're suddenly in an underground airline hanger. Newly restored by Blackstone's counter-pulse, the Joes busy themselves smashing Cobra vehicles and don't bother capturing the Baroness and Destro – who're standing maybe a few feet from them.

CHARACTER PROFILE: JOES

• *Deep Six:* Laser bolts only dent his diving suit.

• *Lady Jaye:* She's never ridden "rumble" seat on a Joe SHARC before now. Some of her javelins project a net or fire lasers.

CHARACTER PROFILE: COBRA

• *The Baroness:* Her family's been breeding rulers for centuries.

• *The Baroness and the Crimson Twins:* She respects the Crimson Twins' potential as powerful allies or dangerous foes (Destro's much more dismissive of them). Mind, the Baroness can't keep the brothers' names straight.

• *The Crimson Twins:* Regardless of the brothers' psionic link, the Conch of the Sirens fails to mesmerize Xamot when Tomax falls prey. Xamot speaks independently away from Tomax's company, later returning to their normal habit of interlacing sentences.

STUFF YOU NEED The Conch of the Sirens: The conch evidently works by producing a submissive effect on the male hormonal system. Eons ago, the conch lured 1,000 sailors to their doom.

HOT WHEELS Joe SHARCs: Additional Joe divers can ride on the SHARC's underbellies, magnetizing their oxygen tanks to the SHARC's hull.

THE COMMAND DECISION Well-polished, superbly bringing the Baroness to power while throwing the Joes into a hormonal wood chipper. "Spell of the Siren" packs an astounding amount of characterization into its 23-odd minutes (the Baroness' regard for Destro, the tenacity of the Joe women, Xamot switching sides, etc.), perfectly complimenting a lively amount of firefights.

1.31: "Cobra Quake"

***US Transmission Date:** Oct. 28, 1985*
***Writer:** Ted Pedersen*

BATTLE ROSTER *Joes:* Gung Ho, Flint, Lady Jaye, Quick Kick, Bazooka; *Cobra:* Cobra Commander, the Baroness, Storm Shadow, Scrap Iron, Wild Weasel.

MISSION BRIEF While Japanese officials prepare to host a Third World Economic Council, Cobra Commander, worried that too much international collaboration could upend Cobra's aims, looks for a means of wrecking the summit. In short order, Cobra Commander stumbles across Japanese seismology research indicating that carefully placed explosions could ward off earthquakes. Intensely studying the data, Cobra engineers find a way of doing the opposite – using detonations to unleash destructive earth tremors.

As a test, Cobra triggers a localized explosion that cascades into a major earthquake, leveling a Joe training camp in Hokkaido. Forming a theory about Cobra's involvement in the atypical earthquake, Flint dispatches Lady Jaye and Bazooka to meet with Dr. Morita, Japan's leading seismologist, at an ancient Shinto shrine. Unfortunately, Storm Shadow and a pack of Cobra ninjas kidnap the good doctor, needing his expertise to coordinate the far-more devastating earthquake tailored to level Tokyo.

Lady Jaye searches Dr. Morita's house for clues, but the Baroness' forces capture Lady Jaye and procure Morita's earthquake-related research. Cobra operatives plant explosives in three key locations on the Japanese isles, priming their bombs to trigger an unholy earthquake and wipe Tokyo off the planet.

Thankfully, Lady Jaye broadcasts a tracking signal, enabling Quick Kick and Bazooka to rescue her and Dr. Morita. Working with rapid speed, Dr. Morita identifies the location of Cobra's explosives, enabling Joe bomb disposal teams to de-activate the incendiaries and ruin Cobra's scheme. Having saved Tokyo, the Joes gather for some well-earned sake and octopus.

MEMORABLE MOMENTS At the Joe training camp, Bazooka sneaks up behind his waif-like trainee Teiko – so of course, Teiko hauls the football-jerseyed Joe about like a piece of pigskin.

There's a lively bit where the Joe trainees gather and Quick Kick – drawing his outline on a chalkboard to emulate Alfred Hitchcock – announces: "Good evening. Welcome to *Bomb Theatre*. In this episode, Bazooka, our bomb expert, must disarm the bomb in time… or we all die." Regrettably, Bazooka fumbles his way through the bomb simulation, failing to stop the device in time and triggering a flag that says, "Bang!" Afterward, Quick Kick eulogizes: "[Bazooka] was a good man. No bomb expert, but a good man."

Observing proper custom, Lady Jaye and Bazooka take off their boots before entering the Shinto shrine – meaning they consequently wear slippers while fighting Cobra ninjas. Seconds later, said Cobra ninjas push Bazooka and Lady Jaye off a balcony, then trade high fives.

LOVE AND WAR Some pent-up tension hovers between Bazooka and Joe ninja-in-training Teiko, but it's pretty harmless.

ASS-WHUPPINGS Cobra armorer Scrap Iron batters Quick Kick and Bazooka with evil samurai puppets. It's something of a goof, but Quick Kick offs some snakes with a fire extinguisher – that freezes them solid.

SAVE THEM! Cobra three-wheel drivers step out from under their wrecked vehicles, running away with balletic grace. A shot-down Cobra jet flips end-over-end, cracks its window and shaves off a wing – but its pilot nonetheless staggers clear (only to get whacked on the head by a falling red fruit). An explosion hurls Quick Kick and Bazooka out a window, then into a conveniently passing vegetable and fruit truck loaded with some kind of leafy green thing.

PREPOSTEROUS PHYSICS Flint performs maneuver that'd stagger even Evel Knievel, leaping his motorcycle into the air, then somehow stretching his arms to snag a Cobra goon's rifle and knock him to the ground. Ace flies his Skystriker jet through two close-quarters trees. Ninja tumble-and-roll training evidently lets you dodge giant, fast-moving boulders.

A motorcycle-riding Bazooka pops a wheelie, then hurls his motorcycle into the air – without an on-ramp – to nail Scrap Iron's helicopter.

GOOFS Cobra rather bizarrely spends this story worrying about a summit between Third World nations. (Do the impoverished, perpetually-starved nations of the world pose that much of a threat?)

Lady Jaye walks into Dr. Morita's house and finds his prized seismic information book – a treasure trove that Cobra, having ransacked the place, failed to discover – lying in the middle of the floor.

Cobra agents "hide" one of their explosive packets in plain sight around a giant Buddha's neck – and nobody notices. The ending's features Cobra armorer Scrap Iron spontaneously showing up in a helicopter to start shooting Bazooka and his assistant Teiko for no good reason.

CHARACTER PROFILE: JOES

• *Bazooka:* The lovingly oafish Bazooka prefers old-fashioned punching to the complexity of judo.

• *Bazooka, Flint and Gung Ho:* While Lady Jaye chomps away on her octopus, the Joe men turn green around the gills. (Flint: "I think it just grabbed my chopsticks!" Gung Ho: "Wait 'til it gets to your stomach.")

• *Gung Ho:* Turbulence bothers Gung Ho a hell of a lot more than emergency crash landings and getting shot at.

PLACES TO GO Japan: Cobra plants its explosive charges at a Toshobu shrine, at the Great Buddha in Kowakuda and on a precise part of Mt. Fuji.

HOT WHEELS Cobra RATTLER jets: Can clear an airplane runway through the forest by firing ATT rockets in carpet formation.

THE COMMAND DECISION Somewhat less than the some of its parts, holding a certain whimsy and character intimacy that works on a scene-to-scene basis. But combined as a whole, "Cobra Quake" collapses about as much as its title implies, winding up in a jumble of disconnected story elements.

1.32-1.33: "Captives of Cobra"

Episodes: *Two*
US Transmission Date: *Oct. 29-30, 1985*
Writer: *Christy Marx*

BATTLE ROSTER *Joes:* Duke, Gung Ho, Lady Jaye, Trip-Wire, Scarlett, Quick Kick, Shipwreck, Spirit, Thunder, Barbecue; Cobras: The Baroness, Tomax and Xamot.

MISSION BRIEF *Part 1:* At a remote laboratory, Cobra scientists futz up a chemical experiment involving "Piazo

MISCELLANEOUS STUFF!

FAMILY TIES

Unlike the *G.I. Joe* comic, the *G.I. Joe* cartoon frequently showed off the characters' relatives. What follows is a list of notable relatives (we've eliminated the obvious ones, such as Zartan's siblings, etc.):

• **Duke and Lt. Falcon (*G.I. Joe: The Movie*)** – A largely contrived relationship (they're half-brothers), cudgeled into the story to make Duke give a crap about Falcon's welfare.

• **Lady Jaye and Destro ("Skeletons in the Closet")** – Brace yourself for a shock: Destro and Lady Jaye are distant cousins. It's the sort of plot thread you'd *think* would turn bogus by story's end, although the Baroness confirms it as true.

• **Flint's cousin Ted Harris ("Flint's Vacation")** – Truth to tell, we never get a grip on Ted's character, since he spends most of the episode brainwashed by Cobra.

• **Airborne's brother Tommy ("Operation Mind Menace")** – A budding telekinetic who'd probably fit in better with the mutant X-Men than the Joes.

• **Roadblock's aunt Sarah and uncle Caleb Bronson ("Red Rocket's Glare")** – The owners of a Red Rocket burger joint, later renamed "Joe's Place."

• **Dusty's mother ("The Traitor")** – She comes off aged enough to be Dusty's *grandmother*, but the wheelchair-bound Mama Dusty clearly loves her boy.

• **Mainframe's ex-wife ("Computer Complications")** – She's only mentioned, but notable because it's hard to think of *any* of the clean-cut Joes getting divorced.

• **Low-Light's sister Una ("Glamour Girls")** – Quite the hottie, although she nearly loses her good looks in an evil face-swapping machine.

• **Lifeline's father and sister ("Second Hand Emotions")** – Lifeline's pacifist father smolders over his son's military occupation, but Lifeline gets along better with sis Stephanie.

• **Barbecue's father, Quick Kick's parents, Scarlett's father and three brothers, Shipwreck's nephew, Spirit's grandfather and cousin, Thunder's father, mother and sister, plus 137 members of Gung Ho's clan ("Captives of Cobra")** – A band of family members who're "fortunate" enough to get cited on a stolen Pentagon disc, thereby making them targets of a Cobra kidnap plot.

electric crystals" – unexpectedly leveling their base with a tremendous explosion. The Cobra personnel hurriedly withdraw, but as the dust settles, Duke and a small team of Joes arrive to investigate the accident site. Finding a strange lump of glowing crystals in the blast crater, Duke's squadron turns horrified to realize the hyper-sensitive crystals explode with unbelievable force upon the slightest impact. Worse, the crystals are steadily expanding outward, threatening to achieve critical mass and wipe out a nearby town.

Meanwhile, Cobra lusts to recover the newly birthed crystals as a weapon of war. With every hamster in her brain furiously turning its wheel, the Baroness concocts a plan to kidnap the Joes' family members, then brainwash them into Cobra service. Accordingly, Cobra ninja Storm Shadow raids the Pentagon, swiping a computer file containing the personal histories of Scarlett, Shipwreck, Quick Kick, Gung Ho, Thunder, Barbecue and Spirit.

Meanwhile, Duke's team modifies an ATV, hoping to transport the crystals to a barren part of the Mojave Desert and harmlessly detonate them. Needing a proper strike team to run defense, Duke recalls the aforementioned Joes from leave. But once Scarlett and her comrades depart to rendezvous with Duke, the Baroness and the Crimson Twins spearhead operations to kidnap the Joes' loved ones. Mission accomplished, the Cobra officers withdraw to an outpost near the accident site and place psycho-control discs on the Joe relatives' heads – linking their minds to a brainwashing machine and turning them into Cobra's thralls.

The Baroness and the Crimson Twins equip the Joe family members with protective battle suits and assault rifles, monitoring the situation from a flying Cobra dreadnought. Near the accident site, Duke's phalanx loads the crystals aboard the ATV and sets out for the desert. But as Scarlett's assault team scouts ahead, the Joes' blood runs cold to find their family members cocking their rifles and advancing on them in unison.

Part 2: Unable to return fire, Scarlett and her appalled teammates use every non-lethal means at their disposal to thwart their family members' approach. Unfortunately, the Joe relatives' battle suits make them impervious to anything less than lethal force. Duke's ATV team desperately scurries away, trying to put distance between the highly volatile crystals and the Cobra assault squad, but the danger of detonating the crystals slows the Joes' progress.

Rapidly losing maneuvering room, Duke frantically orders Scarlett to scour the nearby area for a Cobra control center. Scarlett's group complies and, thanks to Spirit's tracking skills, quickly locate a Cobra psycho-therapy center run by the fiendish Dr. Marx. With the enthralled Joe relatives only minutes from capturing Duke's ATV, Scarlett's crew desperately blows up Dr. Marx's brainwashing equipment. Mercifully, the Joe relatives snap back to normal, ending the immediate threat to Duke's ATV.

Outraged, the Baroness abandons subtlety and, accompanied by Cobra air support, moves her airborne carrier above the crystal-loaded ATV as a last-ditch effort. The Cobra carrier releases giant clamps, attempting to delicately – if such a thing is possible – pull the Joe ATV into its hanger. But the most fit of the Joe relatives reinforce their loved ones, bracing against Cobra's onslaught.

Amid the chaos, Spirit's grandfather nails a Cobra RATTLER jet, spiraling it out of control. The RATTLER accidentally severs one of the cables supporting the Joe ATV, forcing the Baroness to abandon her gambit and release the Joe ATV. As the Cobra carrier soars to freedom, the Joe ATV strikes the ground – causing the crystals to explode on impact. The Joes and their relatives take shelter during the ungodly explosion, blessedly emerging with zero casualties. In the battle's aftermath, Colonel Sharpe instigates strict security protocols to protect the Joe relatives' identities.

MEMORABLE MOMENTS Cajun Gung Ho vows to make Cobra pay for interrupting his vacation (his mama's making gumbo).

Detailing her kidnap scheme, the Baroness asks Cobra Commander, "Who in the world would you never let come to harm?", and the cowled lunatic instantly responds: "Me!"

The Joes' anguish at the end of Part One – terror-stricken to realize they're facing their rifle-totting family members – puts a lump in the throat.

At story's end, the defeated Baroness tries to revenge herself by raiding Gung Ho's Lefete family reunion. But the cast-iron Lefetes, born and bred in the Louisiana bayou, hog-tie the Baroness' men and cheerfully offer the terrorist vixen a bowl of gumbo. The Baroness promptly screams and runs off, almost falling into a reptile pit. (By way of finale, a random Lefete warns her not to step on his pet alligator, "Little Choo-Choo.")

ASS-WHUPPINGS Scarlett's father and three brothers, all martial arts experts, kick the shit out of some Crimson Guardsmen. Unfortunately, the O'Hara boys fall to Storm Shadow, forcing Papa O'Hara to surrender for the sake of his offspring. The other Joe family members endure brainwashing but otherwise escape unharmed.

GOOFS Storm Shadow downloads biographies on only seven Joes because security-prone Pentagon computers turn themselves off – so why didn't the failsafe cut in sooner? (Apparently, the failsafe shuts down the computer, but permits limited downloads – which seems kinda stupid.)

Duke's ATV pauses on a gravel road, but appears on pavement in the next shot. Firefighter Barbecue's doubly cautious – wearing a gas mask over his face-encompassing fireman's helmet.

When the mind-slaved Joe relatives catch up to the Joe ATV, the Baroness makes them laser their way inside – never mind that laserfire would surely set off the crystals.

Cobra evidently possesses an effective means of brainwashing even iron-willed individuals – and inexplicably refrains from using such machinery ever again.

CHARACTER PROFILE: JOES

• *Barbecue:* Firefighting's a tradition in Barbecue's family – his father's on active duty with the Boston Firefighter Department. As such, Barbecue holds reserve status with the Boston firefighters. His mother's also alive.

• *Gung Ho:* His relatives make up the 137 members of the Lefete Clan of Thurdelance, LA. His grandmother's still alive (but oddly sounds like an aged Lady Jaye).

• *Quick Kick:* His father and mother run a family grocery store in White's District, California. Mrs. Jackson, a family friend, remembers the studly Quick Kick being a "scrawny little thing." Quick Kick's dad knows some martial arts and is likely responsible for getting his son interested in the sport.

• *Scarlett:* The O'Hara clan, consisting of Scarlett's unnamed father and three brothers (Brian, Sean and Frank) live in Atlanta, GA. The family, all of 'em martial arts experts, makes a habit of routinely bushwhacking one another other (rather like Inspector Clouseau and his manservant Kato from *The Pink Panther* films). To keep Scarlett guessing, the brothers wear masks so Scarlett won't know who's who and adjust to their fighting style. (*Author's Note:* In other words, every time Scarlett goes home, her masked relatives jump her. Ah, the South…)

• *Shipwreck:* Shipwreck's adopted, but his aunt and uncle reside in San Diego, CA. His nephew Jesse just discovered that he's also adopted and went into something of an emotional tailspin, although Shipwreck helped Jesse talk through his trauma.

• *Spirit:* His grandfather and cousin Vena reside in Taos, NM. Cousin Vena's getting ready for her "ceremony of womanhood." But given the difference in age between her and Spirit, she calls him "Uncle Charlie."

• *Thunder:* His unnamed father, mother Flo and sister Chrissy reside in Louisville, KY.

STUFF YOU NEED *Cobra Battle Suits:* They're equipped with an independent air supply. The suits can release an electrical discharge powerful enough to burn through netting.

• *Cobra Brainwashing Device:* Essentially leaves your victims without independent thought – they'll obey your orders, but you gotta do *all* of their thinking for them. Strong-willed individuals – notably the men in Scarlett's family and especially Spirit's grandfather – can resist the device's effects, although psi-augmentors, placed on the victims' temples, intensify the effect and almost invariably curtail their will.

THE COMMAND DECISION Plodding, but suitably memorable for a personalized flavor that humanizes the Joes with rare form. It's a pity that G.I. Joe doesn't adhere to continuity more often, because some of these kick-ass characters (the O'Hara family, etc.) deserve a return appearance.

1.34: "Bazooka Saw a Sea Serpent"

US Transmission Date: *Oct. 31, 1985*
Writer: *Mary Skrenes*

BATTLE ROSTER *Joes:* Bazooka, Lady Jaye, Quick Kick, Alpine, Cutter, Duke, Shipwreck; *Cobra:* Cobra Commander, Tomax and Xamot.

MISSION BRIEF Collaborating with the Crimson Twins to push forward a highly lucrative extortion racket, Cobra Commander usurps a project instigated by noted engineer Professor Braxton to build a giant armored sea serpent. Braxton finishes refitting the serpent at gunpoint, allowing Cobra Commander to sink numerous ships with the mechanical abomination, then blackmail the major shipping companies to "prevent" more such disasters. Appalled, Braxton blows an escape attempt, apparently getting gulped to death down the serpent's gullet.

Assigned to investigate a possible connection between the ship sinkings and "monster" sightings on the isle of Mongo Pango, Lady Jaye and Quick Kick luckily stumble across Cobra Commander's personal sailing boat and sneak onboard. But regrettably for all concerned, a slugfest between the Joes and Cobra Commander's bodyguards ruins the hand-held control unit that restrains the sea serpent – switching it to permanent hunger mode.

Released from Cobra Commander's override circuit, the sea serpent munches on the Cobra ship, tossing Cobra Commander, his crew and Quick Kick into the serpent's internal sweatshop – where sailors from other devoured vessels sift through their ships' debris. Lady Jaye escapes into a side tunnel where she meets up with Professor Braxton, and together they reach the safety of an insulated room within the serpent's guts.

As the ravenous sea serpent continues its frenzied binge, Braxton voices worries that the serpent's self-repair circuits will use the raw materials it procures from digested ships to add onto the monster's frame, starting an unstoppable growth spurt. As if to concur, the sea serpent promptly makes mincemeat of a massive Joe contingent stationed aboard the *USS Flagg*, then rounds on a Joe WHALE hovercraft.

Flung about by the attack, Bazooka lands on the serpent's tail and pops off a bazooka shell at its head. The monster instinctively turns and stabs at Bazooka – inadvertently biting into its own tail and rupturing its hull integrity – allowing Bazooka to dive clear. As the serpent sinks, a pack of Cobra divers pull Cobra Commander to safety. Minutes later, a salvage vessel arrives to pull the shorted-out monstrosity back to the surface, rescuing the captive sailors and Joes within.

MEMORABLE MOMENTS When the sea serpent's automatic computer systems inquire as to whether its captives will perform manual labor, Cobra Commander prompts one of his troopers to say "No," just to see the result. After seething tentacles haul the hapless soldier away – presumably to his doom – Cobra Commander enthusiastically screams his consent.

With Cobra Commander missing, the top Cobra officers sit about casually chatting and eating fruit (Destro peels an banana, the Baroness scarfs an apple and the Crimson Twins down orange juice), then "toast" with their nibblies to a successful undertaking.

A vindictive Professor Braxton, outraged when a gun-toting Cobra Commander demands to be shown an escape pod, hollers: "It's *your* serpent! *You* stole it... *you* figure it out!"

LOVE AND WAR Lady Jaye and Quick Kick arrive at a beach setting to find a native girl fanning Shipwreck, who's dozing in a hammock. Duke, referring to his Skystriker's missiles, tells the sea serpent before commercial break: "Okay, pal... let's ram something hot down your throat!"

ASS-WHUPPINGS The sea serpent eats oodles of ships, but the crewmembers are saved thanks to super-dextrous tendrils lining the inside of the serpent's gullet. The serpent also batters New York City with its eye-beams, frying a Joe Mauler tank. Quick Kick mashes one Cobra trooper by simply opening a door.

GOOFS Cobra Commander's "master control" for the sea serpent amounts to a hand-held device with a single button labeled: "Devour On." A fantastically well-read reporter – also apparently gifted with the eyes of a hawk – rattles off the name of every Joe in a Dragonfly helicopter squadron.

It's established that Cobra *usurped* Professor Braxton's sea serpent project. So the question remains: Why on Earth would Braxton build such a monstrosity if not for terrorist purposes? Kiddie rides at the fair?

Destro, Baroness and the Crimson Twins plot like mad in Cobra Commander's absence – allegedly planning a major "strike" once the Joes run themselves haggard fighting the sea serpent. But when the Cobra officers ultimately enact their "master stroke," it's nothing more than sending divers to rescue Cobra Commander (which also seems implausible – do they *really* want Cobra Commander back that badly?). So what the hell was the big deal?

CHARACTER PROFILE: JOES

- *Alpine:* Claims he doesn't like Bazooka's cooked fish, even though he eats every bite.
- *Quick Kick:* Knows meditation techniques.

CHARACTER PROFILE: COBRA

Tomax and Xamot: They're highly skilled water-skiers as well as gymnasts. They didn't invest in Cobra Commander's wacky sea serpent scheme because he ran over budget and failed to properly oversee the project.

HOT WHEELS Dr. Braxton's Sea Serpent: Frightfully powerful, capable of shrugging off a Skystriker missile to the mouth without so much as a cracked tooth. Deprived of its override control, the sea serpent largely yields to its animalistic instincts to feed.

When the serpent swallows a ship, internal computer systems deploy tentacles to snag any crewmen or tangible goods aboard. The captured sailors then labor in a sweatshop fashion, sorting the stolen booty according to a droning computer voice. Every two hours, the captured sailors get a "coffee break," whereupon they basically collapse and get a meager amount of sleep.

Dr. Braxton crafted an immunized room that the serpent's bio-electrical systems couldn't reject. However, slender enforcer elements – looking like killer bean shoots – act like anti-bodies and continually assault Braxton's computer systems.

The serpent's occasionally referred to as "bio-electrical," but it's wholeheartedly made up of mechanical parts.

THE COMMAND DECISION Completely daft. The whole idea of a giant mechanical sea serpent pretty much rips out the story's heart and deposits it (still beating) on the table in front of you, with some extremely perplexing character behavior in parts finishing the job.

1.35: "Excalibur"

US Transmission Date: *Nov. 1, 1985*
Writer: *Dan Di Stefano*

BATTLE ROSTER *Joes:* Quick Kick, Footloose, Spirit, Mutt, Duke, Flint; *Cobra:* Storm Shadow, Cobra Commander, Destro, Major Bludd.

1.35, Excalibur

MISSION BRIEF Intent on delivering and setting up a new radar system to guard the United Kingdom against Cobra, the *USS Flagg* moves into position off the British coast. Unfortunately, a Cobra RATTLER squadron – anxious to wreck the radar system and further Cobra's insidious goals – dive-bombs the Joe aircraft carrier. In due course, the Joes win the day. Even better, one of Duke's missiles snags Storm Shadow's jet, dumping the Cobra ninja into a nearby lake.

Madly swimming for the surface, Storm Shadow spies a blonde woman casually lounging about the lakebed, keeping watch over an ancient sword. Recognizing the blade as King Arthur's fabled weapon Excalibur, Storm Shadow snatches the sword and returns to the surface. Almost immediately after the theft, storm clouds gather, preventing the *Flagg* from docking. Racing to complete their mission, a small team of Joes load the anti-radar system onto a WHALE hovercraft and reach the mainland.

The nigh-invulnerable Excalibur grants Storm Shadow unbelievable fighting prowess, but the Joes' sheer numbers halt the ninja from dicing the anti-Cobra radar system, forcing him to nab infantry trooper Footloose and flee. Meanwhile, the Joes scramble to fortify their position as the weather turns increasingly hostile. A knowledgeable Scotsman named Beamish approaches the Joes out of nowhere, warning that Excalibur's caretaker – the magical Lady of the Lake – will flood the British Isles unless the sword is returned. Duke ponders Beamish's words, but a renewed Cobra assault draws his attention. Amid vicious hand-to-hand fighting, Major Bludd launches a missile attack that obliterates a nearby dam, flooding the already deluged Joes and wiping out their anti-Cobra radar system.

Elsewhere, Joes Spirit and Quick Kick track the missing Footloose to Cobra Commander's temporary base of operations, leading to a one-on-one brawl between Quick Kick and Storm Shadow. As the storm whips itself into a further frenzy, Spirit's eagle Freedom rushes forward and snatches Excalibur from Storm Shadow's hands. Freedom flings the sword back into the lake – allowing the Lady of the Lake to reclaim her property. Storm Shadow and his Cobra associates quickly retreat, but the Lady of the Lake ends the freakish weather patterns, returning the British Isles to their normally drizzly selves.

MEMORABLE MOMENTS Ever adhering to his ninja code, Storm Shadow screams out, "Destiny, I await thy bidding!", while crashing his airplane.

In what's one of the most personal *G.I. Joe* moments, Destro lines up a distracted Storm Shadow in his crosshairs (*see Character Profile*) and turns deeply apologetic: "I'm sorry, my friend, but I must have Excalibur... no matter what the cost." It's a nicely emotive statement, considering that Cobra goons typically shoot each other in the back without mercy.

A wounded Quick Kick belts out an "owl" call to secretly draw Spirit's attention, but Spirit mistakes the noise for a wounded chicken. Soon after, Spirit mends Quick Kick's leg, making the restored, hyperactive Joe hop around the place and babble about "dancing in the rain!" In response, the stoic Spirit thinks to himself: "Next time, I'll fix his brain."

ASS-WHUPPINGS One of Destro's wayward missiles (see Character Profile) strikes a house, briefly knocking Mutt and Junkyard unconscious. Minutes later, Major Bludd reduces a local dam to pebbles, dashing the Joes with a resultant tidal wave and wrecking the radar guidance system. For an encore, a flood smacks aside the recovering Mutt and Junkyard, but at least they save a kitty in the process.

Storm Shadow knocks Quick Kick from a perilous height, thumping the Joe's ankle out of whack, but Spirit re-sets it. Later, in making his escape, Storm Shadow slyly dislocates Quick Kick's ankle a second time.

PREPOSTEROUS PHYSICS Storm Shadow stops Footloose from escaping by taking Excalibur and slicing through a stone column, dropping the whole damn thing onto Footloose's backside... a move which should've pulped the Joe like a grape.

GOOFS Put simply, we never find out the what's up with Beamish, nor how he knows so much about Excalibur.

TV TIE-INS Spirit still keeps a slender knife in his headband ("Countdown for Zartan").

CHARACTER PROFILE: JOES

- *Quick Kick:* Carries throwing stars that either explode or douse the immediate area with knockout gas.
- *Spirit:* Evidently possesses a form of shaman magic, giving him knowledge of ancient healing techniques.

CHARACTER PROFILE: COBRA

- *Destro and Storm Shadow:* Recognizing Excalibur's potency on the battlefield, Destro sets about acquiring the ancient blade before Cobra Commander recognizes its value. Accordingly, Destro uses an all-out assault on the Joes as a diversion – taking a hand-held missile launcher and aligning its crosshairs between Storm Shadow's shoulder blades. Destro actually laments his actions – whispering, "I'm sorry, my friend," – to indicate his shame over sacrificing Storm Shadow, but his greed wins out. Unfortunately for Destro, the ungodly English rain makes him sneeze, throwing off his aim and launching the missile heavenward, leaving Storm Shadow completely oblivious to his brush with death.

STUFF YOU NEED Excalibur: Virtually unstoppable, able to carve through rock and metal like butter.

THE COMMAND DECISION A well-tempered story, likeable despite the fact that Storm Shadow, potently armed with Excalibur, ironically accomplishes very little. Overall, "Excalibur" deliciously puts its good and evil characters to great use, befitting its Arthurian setting.

1.36-1.37: "Worlds Without End"

Episodes: *Two*
US Transmission Date: *Nov. 4-5, 1985*
Writer: *Martin Pasko*

BATTLE ROSTER *Joes:* Flint, Lady Jaye, Steeler, Clutch, Grunt, Barbecue, Airtight, Footloose; Cobras: The Baroness, Cobra Commander, Destro, Zartan and the Dreadnoks.

MISSION BRIEF ***Part 1:*** When the Dreadnoks steal a prototype matter transmuter – a device capable of instantly restructuring molecules and converting even the strongest armor plating into tissue paper – Zartan pockets the blueprints and hands off the device to Cobra hovercraft pilot Copperhead for safekeeping. Soon after, an eight-man Joe armor team finds and thrashes Zartan, relieving him of the transmuter schematics.

Traveling ahead of the armor team, Lady Jaye and Flint inspect a train concealing a mobile matter transmutation research lab. Unfortunately, the Joes unmask a pair of military researchers as the Baroness and Zartan – desperate to steal back the blueprints. As the train charges onward, the two Cobra hoods throw their opponents overboard, forcing Flint and Lady Jaye to cling to the side of a bridge for dear life.

Terrified for their teammates, the Joe armor team scampers up the bridge to help. But Copperhead, brashly hoping to recapture the transmuter blueprints himself, appears and levels the prototype transmuter at the Joes. Cornered, Joe tank driver Steeler lashes out with a kick – knocking Copperhead off balance and causing him to trigger the uncalibrated transmuter.

Instantly, the transmuter fires off a haywire energy wave that turns the bridge into crystal. Worse, the haywire transmuter beam rips open reality, tossing Flint's panic-stricken team through a nebulous vortex. Flint's Joes fall unconscious, awakening hours later on a desert plain. Finding no sign of Copperhead or the transmuter, Flint's baffled group heads towards town just as a disease-riddled wasp bites Steeler on his neck.

While a fever overtakes Steeler, the Joes struggle back to Joe Headquarters – devastated to find their base plundered, abandoned and condemned by order of Cobra Commander. Scanning the tattered remnants of the Headquarters' computer banks, the Joes find virtually all of their teammates listed as either dead or missing in action. Left without explanations, the team conjectures that the transmuter somehow put them into a lengthy sleep while Cobra slaughtered their comrades and conquered the world.

The anguished Joes dust off a few mothballed vehicles, splitting into recon teams to learn more. While Flint, Barbecue and Airtight depart to investigate Washington, D.C., Lady Jaye, Clutch and Footloose conduct an airborne sweep aboard Joe Sky Hawks. Joe infantryman Grunt remains behind to nurse the fever-stricken Steeler, but his delirious teammate leaps up and runs from Joe Headquarters – forcing Grunt to give chase.

In Washington, Flint's trio snags a newspaper, fixing the date as the same day that the transmuter rendered them unconscious. With this in mind, Flint's team theorizes that the transmuter has flung them into a parallel world – an alternate version of Earth populated by counterparts of "our" Joe and Cobra members. As if to confirm the Joes' theory, the parallel Earth versions of the Dreadnoks show up. Employed in this reality as policemen, the Cobra punks apprehend Flint's group for questioning.

High above Washington, Lady Jaye's Sky Hawk team cross-correlates their data, similarly concluding that they've arrived on a parallel world. But as the Joe Sky Hawk pilots continue their survey, a Cobra jet squadron appears – strafing the skies with missiles.

Part 2: Flint's team escapes custody, but a Cobra air patrol leader radios the alternate Destro to prepare a trap for Lady Jaye's squadron. Accordingly, Destro activates an energy web called "the Parasite Matrix," running Lady Jaye's Sky Hawks aground and capturing her trio.

Meanwhile, Grunt follows the increasingly distraught Steeler onto a weapons proving ground near Joe Headquarters, where they horrifyingly discover a resistance hideout containing the corpses of the parallel Grunt, Clutch and Steeler – evidently killed during a random Cobra weapons test. Steeler cries out in terror upon seeing "his" body, but to their surprise, agents of the alternate Baroness – who's secretly working for the Joes in this reality – shuttle him and Grunt to safety.

The Baroness cures Steeler's infection: a Strain-D virus that originated from Destro's ongoing biological experiments. Grunt and Steeler accept the alternate Baroness as an undercover Joe operative, but – more awkwardly – learn that Steeler's late counterpart and the Baroness were secret lovers. Tearful to learn about "her" Steeler's death, the Baroness agrees to help the Joes.

Aided by Grunt and Steeler, the Baroness plays this world's Cobra Commander and Destro against one another, convincing both leaders that the other plans to launch a devastating attack. As expected, long-running rivalries between Cobra Commander and Destro boil over, leading to a massive troop build-up that allows the Baroness to secure the release of Lady Jaye's team. Unsettled by the magnitude of what she's set in motion, the alternate Baroness helps Grunt and Steeler gather their missing comrades and head for their arrival point.

Reunited, Flint's group quickly pinpoints the transmuter-created vortex back to "our" reality. But Steeler, Grunt and Clutch – pained over the loss of their counterparts – volunteer to stay behind and re-create G.I. Joe on the parallel world. Flint's remaining Joes wish their friends the best of luck, then dive through the dimensional vortex just as it closes. Arriving home, the Joes bittersweetly imagine their three comrades fighting for survival on the Cobra-demolished Earth.

MEMORABLE MOMENTS When laser fire knocks a hang-gliding Zartan topsy-turvy, the cowled swamp urchin belts out a series of screams worthy of Homer Simpson.

During a sharply poignant moment, Steeler swings his main tank cannon to cover Zartan, brashly proclaiming, "I reckon I got you outgunned," but Zartan hauls up a fallen jeep missile assembly and blows Steeler's tank into paper clips. Although Steeler dives clear, he later laments on the hopelessness of the Joe/Cobra conflict, commenting, "Nothing changes. Cobra hits us, we hit them. Over and over…." – a rare instance of a Joe doubting the purpose of the war.

Some of the many gut-wrenching moments from "Worlds Without End": Lady Jaye gazes upon the plundered, parallel-reality Joe Headquarters and pines: "Breaks my heart… I don't recognize the place." Grunt starts weeping as Clutch taps the main Joe computer and reads off the casualty rolls. Finally, Steeler goes half-mad upon finding the bodies of the alternate Grunt, Clutch and himself – a turning point that stands as one of the most grotesque Joe moments.

LOVE AND WAR Steeler spends most of Part One bemoaning his lack of a girlfriend – so of course, he ends this story doing the wild thing with the alternate Baroness. At their first meeting, said Baroness mistakes "our" Steeler for her dead lover – and celebrates her shag-muffin's return by kissing his hand. (What, no lip massage?)

ASS-WHUPPINGS In the parallel reality, roughly 50 Joes, including Short-Fuze, Flash, Doc, Blowtorch, Duke, Bazooka, Breaker and Dusty, are listed as missing in action, presumably killed. The parallel universe's Dreadnoks suggest the alternate Flint, Airtight and Barbecue met a similar fate. Steeler and Grunt conclusively find the skeletons of the alternate Steeler, Clutch and Grunt on a Cobra weapons proving ground.

In our world, Steeler gloriously runs his tank over a Dreadnok jeep. In the parallel reality, a bite from one of Destro's virus-infected insects wracks Steeler with fever and delirium. Cobra RATTLER fire, attempting to hit Lady Jaye's Sky Hawks,

TV STORIES

1) **"Worlds Without End"** – About the closest the TV series can come to showing actual casualties of war, the parallel universe tale "Worlds Without End" conveys a striking amount of emotional timbre – turning Steeler, the Baroness and other familiar faces into full-fledged characters with internal lives.

2) **"Nightmare Assault"** – Arguably the most mature and empowering *G.I. Joe* tale, showing Low-Light channeling his tragic childhood as a source of incredible strength. For anyone who's overcome their own past, this one's a winner.

3) **"Skeletons in the Closet"** – Supremely and smartly scary, this story starts out as a rollicking farce, turning to gravely higher stakes as the Baroness nearly releases the supernatural abomination lurking beneath Destro's homestead.

4) **"The Most Dangerous Thing in the World"** – One of Cobra's more inspired ideas – promoting the hapless Shipwreck, Lifeline and Dial-Tone to the rank of colonel with continually hilarious results.

5) **"The Pyramid of Darkness"** – Hands-down the strongest *G.I. Joe* mini-series, sweetly complex and loaded with mayhem.

6) **"There's No Place Like Spring field"** – Certainly the most surreal Joe story, graciously giving Shipwreck a wife, child and happy home, purely for the purpose of screwing with his already mushy brain.

7) **"Computer Complications"** – Highly dramatic thanks to the fury-filled sinking of the *USS Flagg* (and no Leonardo de Caprio, thank God), but this episode also deserves points for convincing us that Mainframe and Zarana could seriously be getting it on.

8) **"The Viper is Coming"** – A hysterical G.I. Joe outing that makes the Joes frantically dance to the tune of a lisp-prone window wiper.

9) **"The Traitor"** – A intimate work, somewhat predictable but heavily enriched by some detailed implementation.

10) **"Raise the Flagg!"** – A gripping account that rushes at a breakneck pace, throwing three Joes and three Cobras (plus a mad chef) into an underwater meat grinder.

annihilates the Cobra Commander (formerly Lincoln) Memorial in Washington, D.C.

Flint, Barbecue and Airtight pummel the alternate Dreadnoks, crashing their police car. The parallel Cobra Commander briefly interrogates Lady Jaye, Clutch and Footloose, strapping them onto a "Centrifugal Persuader" – a sort of large Tilt-A-Whirl machine. Not believing the Joes' fantastic story about parallel worlds, Cobra Commander squeezes the three Joes with giant robotic boa constrictors, leading to Footloose flinging his mechanical snake in the commander's face. Cobra Commander consequently reels, shorting out a panel with his helmet and falling unconscious.

Flint drops a statue in front of the alternate Zartan, wrecking Zartan's ATV.

SAVE THEM! A poor animation overlay shows a hit Cobra helicopter pilot ejecting, then passing through the still-running helicopter blades. At the parallel Joe Headquarters, Flint's squad brings down a shocking load of rubble atop some Cobra guardsmen – enough to pancake them for good.

PREPOSTEROUS PHYSICS Much as we're impressed with the matter transmuter's abilities, it shouldn't be able – as a demonstration video suggests – to turn a rock into organic matter like an apple (in other words, the transmuter shouldn't just – voila! – create life).

GOOFS Cobra pilot Copperhead's standing at ground zero when the matter transmuter activates, but he's not transported to the parallel Earth with the Joes. For that matter, we're never told where Copperhead goes – nor the transmuter's ultimate fate. (Although if you count the DIC story "Operation Dragonfire" as canon, Copperhead reappears and gets promoted to Cobra's Python Patrol leader.)

The unconscious Joes lie in different positions before and after the commercial break (even allowing that they rolled over in their sleep, Flint's no longer in the middle of the circle). American currency's worthless in the alternate dimension, but a vendor doesn't notice the Joes peddling US dollars until after he closes his cash register. Clutch isn't wearing a helmet during an interrogation scene, but spontaneously gains one *after* tossing himself into the alternate Cobra Commander's control room.

At story's end, the Joes return to their arrival point in the parallel universe by locating a glowing black void that leads back to "our" reality. Of course, that begs the question as to why it wasn't evident in the first place. Why does the vortex suddenly close up when the Joes depart?

When Flint's Joes return home, Duke shouts, "You're back! But from where?", even though he's got no evidence that they actually went anywhere.

TV TIE-INS In the parallel reality, Cobra used a proving grounds near Joe Headquarters to test everything from new strains of bacteria (presumably Destro's biological experiments) to the Weather Dominator ("The Revenge of Cobra").

CHARACTER PROFILE: JOES

• *Flint:* His retinal scan confirms that he's not listed as a rebel in the alternate reality, suggesting the alternate Flint kicked the bucket.

• *Lady Jaye:* She's equipped with javelins that burst into flames on impact.

• *Steeler:* He's increasingly despondent about the futility of the G.I. Joe struggle and its cost to his social life – to the point where he's thinking of resigning. The parallel universe proves to Steeler the cost of losing the war against Cobra, compelling him to remain on the parallel Earth. Steeler has a tattoo on his left arm, but his alternate counterpart kept it on his right arm.

CHARACTER PROFILE: COBRA

• *The Baroness:* Her earrings contain gas capsules.

• *The alternate Baroness:* She doesn't appear to need glasses (or at the very least, wears contacts). Although she's secretly working for the forces of good, she remains in good standing with the Cobra leadership and commands her own Cobra battalion. A woman named Layla serves as her assistant.

ORGANIZATIONS *The Alternate Joes:* After the massive Cobra takeover, some of the surviving Joes took shelter on a Cobra weapons proving ground, evidently suspecting that Cobra wouldn't search for them there. The strategy backfired, killing off a few Joes and leaving some of their vehicles there unattended. In addition to the collapse of Joe Headquarters, the Joes' communications satellite has apparently fallen from orbit.

STUFF YOU NEED *"The Parasite Matrix":* Incorporated into the Washington Monument, Destro's newest toy sends out an energy-woven net to snag enemy aircraft passing over Washington. The Matrix derives its name from the fact that it drains energy from the webbed vehicles, even down to the pilots' laser pistol sidearms.

PLACES TO GO *The Alternate Earth:* Relative to its timeline, Cobra conquered the parallel Earth a number of years ago – instituting wave after wave of changes. Cobra brought virtually all the world governments under its banner, subjugating the entire United Nations. The Lincoln Memorial's been renovated into the Cobra Commander Memorial, Mount Rushmore sports Cobra Commander and Destro's heads, and the Statue of Liberty's been refashioned into a giant torch-wielding statue of the Baroness. American currency's utterly worthless, and Washington, D.C.'s largely a slave labor camp.

THE COMMAND DECISION A masterpiece among 1980s cartoons – unbelievably endowed with a sense of life and loss that puts the rest of 80's kids TV to shame. As geeky, post-pubescent kids, we shuddered at the sight of the alternate Joes' corpses, and Steeler's epiphany about why the Joe/Cobra conflict matters mirrored our struggles to give a crap about our teenage lives. At the end of the day, this story takes G.I. Joe to an entirely new and triumphant level.

1.38: "Eau de Cobra"

US Transmission Date: *Nov. 6, 1985*
Writer: *Flint Dille*

BATTLE ROSTER *Joes:* Flint, Lady Jaye, Snow Job, Shipwreck, Frostbite; *Cobra:* the Baroness, Cobra Commander, Destro, Firefly.

MISSION BRIEF At the British Museum, Cobra saboteur Firefly undertakes a new mission and steals an ancient Egyptian tablet. With tablet in tow, Firefly travels to an Arctic research base, intending to plunder recently discovered samples of a long-lost herb named "Jackal's Bane." Firefly makes off with the plants but accidentally glops himself with radioactive tracking dye used to track whale migrations, enabling Flint and Lady Jaye – who respond to the Arctic base's alarm – to tail Firefly to a Cobra base in Madagascar.

Cobra technicians decipher the Egyptian tablet, deriving the formula for an ancient love potion. Firefly's staff brews a batch of the aphrodisiac using the Jackal's Bane – dubbing the finished result "Eau de Cobra" – just as Flint and Lady Jaye assault the Cobra science lab. The Cobra personnel escape with Eau de Cobra, setting the base to self-destruct, but Flint and Lady Jaye snag the Egyptian tablet and flee just as the base becomes a raging inferno.

The blowout hurls the two Joes into a nearby river, forcing Lady Jaye to hurriedly translate the Egyptian tablet before Flint, unable to continually tread water, lets the heavy object sink to the bottom. Deducing that Cobra has successfully created a love potion, Flint and Lady Jaye call the trivia-minded Short-Fuze for information about the world's wealthiest bachelor. Short-Fuze immediately pegs Socrates Aertes, a shipping tycoon, further mentioning that the loaded bachelor's holding a yacht party to score a wife. Grimly, Flint and Lady Jaye conclude that if an Eau-de-Cobra-wearing Baroness snared Aertes, Cobra would gain possession of an immense shipping fleet.

Slipping into formal wear, Flint and Lady Jaye crash Aertes' yacht party. Simultaneously, the sultry Baroness zaps Aertes with her Eau de Cobra perfume, winning his undying love. Flint improvises by dancing with the Baroness, drawing her away from Aertes, but the female terrorist spritzes Flint with Eau de Cobra also, skewering him with Cupid's arrow.

In what quickly devolves into a sexual brouhaha, the Baroness asks the lovestruck Flint to eliminate Lady Jaye, but a jealous Destro, enraged to think of anyone else doing the horizontal mambo with the Baroness, arrives on Aertes' boat and brawls with Flint. Just as yacht guards throw Flint and Destro overboard, Lady Jaye snags the Baroness' Eau de Cobra bottle and sprays herself – thereby re-directing Aertes' attentions. Flint snaps out of his trance, but Aertes' other suitors sense the value of the perfume and squabble for it.

In desperation, Lady Jaye kicks the perfume overboard, sparking an underwater battle between Joe and Cobra retrieval teams. Blocking each other like a bunch of Dallas Cowboys linemen, the recovery squads gape in amazement as a crab playfully clutches the perfume and scuttles underground. Thwarted by a crab, Cobra Commander writhes in agony from a nearby boat as Eau de Cobra's effects wear off and the Baroness and Destro escape.

MEMORABLE MOMENTS A somewhat levelheaded first half soon gives way to an entirely loopy ending. Amid the mayhem: Flint dances with the Baroness but gets a faceful of Eau de Cobra for his trouble. Aertes' crewmen scoop up Destro in a giant net before flinging him into an on-deck pool (Cobra Commander, watching through his powerful binoculars, yuks it up at Destro's humiliation). Later, an indignant Destro, afloat in an inner-tube, threatens to shoot down Cobra Commander's boat unless the commander throws him a rope. (Rocking from Destro's warning shot, Cobra Commander screams out: "Of course, Destro! Welcome aboard!")

Preparing to make her escape, the Baroness – always the soul of discretion – karate-chops a duchess and takes the hapless woman's identity, letting Lady Jaye body-tackle the wrong woman before flinging herself overboard. Finally, Cobra Commander turns madder than a hatter when his troops fail to recover Eau de Cobra, screaming out: "A crab! They lost to a crab!"

LOVE AND WAR A swimming Flint butters up Lady Jaye by mentioning that she's so hot that she "doesn't need a love potion." When a fish slaps Flint in the face, Lady Jaye retorts: "Turn off the charm, Flint. You're likely to attract a whale."

Destro jealously flexes his trigger finger when the Baroness seduces Aertes, but that's nothing compared to Destro's wrath when she similarly entrances Flint (a binocular-peeping Destro chafes: "This mission is taking a most disastrous turn!", then rushes off to bash heads). Tossed overboard for his efforts, Destro comments that the Baroness is "Nothing but trouble," to which the vixen icily replies: "We will take up this conversation later, *Destro darling*."

At story's end, the Baroness escapes and hurls a last-minute flirtation: "It could have been wonderful, Flint!" Flint and Lady Jaye enjoy a final snog while the harassed Aertes decides to remain a bachelor.

ASS-WHUPPINGS In one of the series' most death-defying cliffhangers, an explosion serves up Flint and Lady Jaye like racquetballs just before commercial break. On Aertes' boat, Flint whaps Destro in the head with a serving platter, hurling the shiny fiend into a swimming pool. The Baroness makes her getaway by disguising herself as a duchess, leaping overboard while Lady Jaye body-tackles the wrong woman.

PREPOSTEROUS PHYSICS Destro, who's obviously enrolled in the "Body for Life" plan, shoves a piano at his enemies with enough force to knock it off Aertes' ship.

GOOFS When Firefly disguises himself as an Egyptian mummy to infiltrate the British Museum, his eyes open with a little electronic noise – odd, since he's not a robot. The Arctic base that Firefly raids contains an alarm button in an unlikely place – right in the middle of the floor (hell, you could trip it off just by fetching a doughnut).

Even given that they're leaving in a hurry, Cobra techs sloppily leave the Egyptian tablet behind for Flint and Lady Jaye to recover. The explosion that decimates Cobra's Madagascar base catches Flint and Lady Jaye in a closed room – but after a commercial break, they're flung outside the base and hit open waters.

Cobra scientists wear white lab coats one instant and the standard blue Cobra uniforms the next. Lady Jaye's spontaneously gifted with the ability to translate ancient Egyptian while half-concussed and treading water (oh, not to mention that she's befuddled reading Egyptian in "The Gods Below"). Plain-clothed Cobra operatives scream "Cobra!" before rushing Flint and Lady Jaye, giving them more than ample warning of the attack. Then again, Flint and Lady Jaye – *knowing* the Baroness possesses a love potion that affects males – should've sent Lady Jaye to deal with her (but then, it wouldn't be much fun if Flint *didn't* get zapped).

TV TIE-INS Shipwreck knows a lot about smugglers' hideouts, probably hearkening back to his freelance days ("The Revenge of Cobra").

CHARACTER PROFILE: JOES

- *Deep Six:* His battle suit contains powerful rockets.
- *Lady Jaye and the Baroness:* Keep radios in their necklace lockets.

CHARACTER PROFILE: COBRA Firefly: Highly acrobatic and fierce with a flame-thrower. Firefly gets paid into a Swiss bank account for successful hits. He takes great pains to conceal his identity, warding off his opponents with such terrifying warnings as: "to know my identity is to insure your doom." He even stops Cobra Commander from repeating his name over a coded transmission.

PLACES TO GO Pirate's Cove: A secluded location in Madagascar, used by smugglers for centuries and usurped by Cobra for its Eau de Cobra research lab.

STUFF YOU NEED Eau de *Cobra:* Composed of "two parts Jackal's Bane, crushed swamp moss" and other ingredients. When wafted into male nostrils, the love potion causes the man to fall hopelessly in love with the first woman he sees.

THE COMMAND DECISION Fluid and inspired, but certainly not for everyone. Writer Flint Dille's charm and boyish sense of fun will undoubtedly leave a bad aftertaste with G.I. Joe purists (i.e. comedy-haters), but we appreciated the sexual brouhaha and nearly burst our ribs with laughter.

1.39: "Cobra Claws are Coming to Town"

US Transmission Date: *Nov. 7, 1985*
Story: *Roy and Dann Thomas*
Script: *Gerry and Carla Conway*

BATTLE ROSTER *Joes:* Duke, Shipwreck and Polly, Cover Girl, Wild Bill, Blowtorch, Trip-Wire, Mutt and Junkyard, Roadblock, Dusty; Cobras: Cobra Commander, Destro, the Baroness, Wild Weasel, Firefly, Zartan and the Dreadnoks.

MISSION BRIEF Although most of the Joes return home for the Christmas holidays, Duke and a skeleton crew remain behind to man Joe Headquarters and collect toys for children's hospitals. Unfortunately, Destro simultaneously finishes work on a molecular reducer/enlargement pistol, crazily planning to reduce a battalion of Cobra vehicles to action-figure size and hide the tiny troopers among the hospital toys. While a Cobra phalanx assaults a Joe convoy as a diversion, Firefly scatters the gift-wrapped Cobra troopers among the Joes' presents.

Completely oblivious to their stowaways, the Joes drive their Cobra-riddled wares into Joe Headquarters, piling the "gifts" into a storage hanger. But as the Joes prepare to gobble a grease-dripping turkey dinner, the itty-bitty Cobra troopers break free, sabotaging the headquarters' automatic laser defense grid.

Duke's Joes recoil in surprise to find little Cobra jets and helicopters swarming around them like locusts. But seconds later, Firefly vaults over Joe Headquarters' defenseless perimeter, restoring the Cobra battalion to normal size with Destro's ray gun. Roadblock somewhat damages the molecular reducer/enlargement ray, but the Cobra troops quickly capture Joe Headquarters and its guardians.

Cobra Commander basks in his initial success, intending to capitalize on his win by ripping through Keystone City in the captured Joe vehicles – forever defaming the Joes as a public menace. Destro remains behind to repair his molecular reducer/enlarger, retaining a squad of robotic SNAKEs for protection. The Joes escape captivity and blow apart Destro's sentinels, but Destro pelts the Joes with reducing rays. Destro nails Shipwreck's parrot Polly, shrinking the bird down to insect size, but the Joes pile onto Destro and capture the fiend.

Trip-Wire apparently returns Polly to normal size, although he renders the bird unconscious in the process, allowing the Joes to quickly load into the left-behind Cobra vehicles and set out for Keystone City. But shortly after, an unexpected side effect from the enlargement ray enlarges Polly to a towering height, causing the mammoth parrot to burst through the roof of Joe Headquarters.

The Joes largely make mincemeat of the Cobra troops – scrapping their own vehicles for the sake of Keystone City – but Cobra Commander vows to fight to the bitter end. However, the sudden appearance of a gargantuan parrot makes Cobra Commander crap himself and order an immediate retreat. Having saved G.I. Joe's reputation, Duke's team celebrates the holidays and returns Polly to normal.

MISCELLANEOUS STUFF!

THE LOCATION OF JOE HEADQUARTERS

Although the cartoon continually cites "Joe Headquarters" as our heroes' happy homestead, the shows' creators never actually state where it's located. If we look at the clues scattered throughout the series, however, all roads lead to the East Coast.

To wit, the appearance of snow in "Cobra Claws are Coming to Town" eliminates California and the South as possibilities. More tellingly, Beach-Head comments in "Grey Hairs and Growing Pains" that the Joes have traveled "3,000 miles to California," which places Joe H.Q. along America's East Coast (unless we're boobish enough to think it's housed in Canada). Finally, "The Million Dollar Medic" confirms this theory when Lift-Ticket agrees to "buzz" Lifeline up to New York in a Tomahawk helicopter – and since the two of them don't go AWOL, one presumes it's a short distance (although Bree uses a stolen Tomahawk to reach Colorado in the same story, but that's neither here nor there).

MEMORABLE MOMENTS There's an extremely odd moment – as the itty-bitty Cobra vehicles emerge from the Joe's gifts – that your eyes pop out of your head in shock. The melodramatic Duke blathers some bravado about how the people will fight Cobra, and for once, Cobra Commander simply replies: "Then the people will be destroyed." Words can't describe the surrealness of seeing a giant parrot crashing through the roof of Joe Headquarters.

LOVE AND WAR Handcuffed and hanging from a hook in a meat locker, Shipwreck tries to wrest himself free by – and we're going by his words, folks – "having a meaningful relationship" with a side of beef (i.e. snagging it between his legs and wresting himself about, trying to gain some leverage). Duke seems to flirt with Cover Girl, but nothing transpires beyond a harmless Christmas peck.

ASS-WHUPPINGS Wasp-sized Cobra vehicles down Mutt with a gas attack, although Roadblock smashes one such Cobra jet with his elbow. Cover Girl walks away from a jet crash with only bruises. Duke shoots a SNAKE robot directly in the face. Blowtorch blasts apart several Dreadnok motorcycles. When Destro zaps Polly with his molecular reducer, the parrot turns into a fly-sized bird. In an utterly inspired moment, with Destro distracted, Cover Girl screams, "Smother 'em! Smother 'em!", just before Wild Bill, Roadblock, Blowtorch, Cover Girl and Shipwreck leap on Destro in a mountain of bodies.

Later, a colossal Polly crashes a hole through the roof of Joe Headquarters.

SAVE THEM! The Joes missile two of their commandeered tanks, but the Cobra troopers bail out after the missiles hit – when they'd surely be dead.

PREPOSTEROUS PHYSICS Wild Bill performs a rather impossible loop-de-loop in a Fang helicopter. Duke gives dog Junkyard an enormous drumstick that evidently originated from an ostrich (or Sesame Street's Big Bird).

GOOFS How do so many Joes take leave during the holidays? (Does Cobra cease hostilities for the last couple weeks of December?)

Duke and Flint evidently think it best to station Dusty, a desert trooper, at Joe Headquarters during the snowy winter months. Having captured the skeleton crew staffing Joe Headquarters, Cobra Commander imprisons the tied-up Joes in a meat locker without a single guard. Worse, he leaves the key to their handcuffs on a hook near the door to give them a "sporting chance."

Finally, a shrilling "little boy" ("Dad, aren't those the G.I. Joes?") sounds like a *lot* like Cover Girl.

CHARACTER PROFILE: JOES

• *Blowtorch:* As a boy, he always wanted a rocking horse.

• *Mutt:* Mutt always gets a left-out feeling at the holidays, recalling how his parents, swept up in a wave of holiday activities, never had time for him. Still, by story's end, Mutt learns to deal with it.

• *Shipwreck:* Regards a giant Polly as his worst nightmare come to life (he's not alone).

STUFF YOU NEED Destro's Molecular Reducer/Enlarger: Represents a decade of research.

THE COMMAND DECISION A straightforward tale, tailored for easy digestion. Mind, the giant Polly bird – which gave us flashbacks to the building-sized, moon-eyed Animal in The Muppet Movie – proves a bit hard to swallow, but even that oddly makes sense as part of the bigger picture.

1.40: "An Eye for an Eye"

US Transmission Date: *Nov. 8, 1985*
Writers: *Steve Mitchell and Barbara Petty*

BATTLE ROSTER *Joes:* Lady Jaye, Flint, Alpine, Bazooka, Recondo, Airtight, Shipwreck and Polly; Cobras: Cobra Commander, Major Bludd.

MISSION BRIEF When the Joes safeguard transport of a prototype jet fusion engine, Polar Vipers and a Cobra RATTLER jet squadron get the drop on the convoy near a mountain range. Desperate to repel the assault, Lady Jaye hurls a javelin that crashes a RATTLER straight into a nearby cabin. Although Lady Jaye and Bazooka fling themselves into the flames and save the cabin's occupants – a mother and two children – the home explodes into cinders. But thankfully, the Joes outlast Cobra's ammunition, winning the firefight and rushing injured civilians to a nearby hospital.

A short while later, computer programmer Charles Fairmont returns from a business trip, learning about his ruined cabin abode and injured loved ones. Thirsting for vengeance, Fairmont sneaks into Joe Headquarters' records center, hoping to track down a Cobra stronghold. Lady Jaye easily apprehends Fairmont, then begrudgingly agrees to help the tormented father out of guilt for aiding with his home's destruction.

Tapping government records, Lady Jaye identifies a Cobra depot located on an island northwest of San Francisco. Deeming the munitions dump a low-level target – but figuring that blowing it up might help Fairmont vent his spleen – Lady Jaye smuggles him aboard her Skystriker and jets off for the Cobra camp. Once there, the two shockingly discover that Cobra has recently refurbished their munitions dump into a major research lab.

Thrilled over the fortuitous arrival of Lady Jaye's Skystriker, Cobra techs test out their newly made "power destroyer" – a device that drains enemy vehicles of energy – and ground Lady Jaye's jet. Major Bludd apprehends Lady Jaye, but Fairmont eludes capture. Back at Joe Headquarters, Flint and other Joes track the missing Lady Jaye's whereabouts and ready an air assault to blitz the Cobra base. As the Joes zoom into the power destroyer's range, Fairmont frees Lady Jaye and helps her blow up the energy-draining device.

The Joes overrun the camp, but Cobra Commander seizes Fairmont as a hostage. Fairmont begs the Joes to ignore his safety and shoot Cobra Commander, but the noble heroes let Cobra Commander escape in exchange for Fairmont's release. When Lady Jaye reminds Fairmont that the Joes don't aid Cobra in destroying lives, Fairmont's quest for vengeance dissipates. Reassured, Fairmont returns to his family, leaving the ongoing Cobra conflict to the Joes.

MEMORABLE MOMENTS Lady Jaye whisks Fairmont's daughter out of her burning home – only to find the girl distraught and crying because when the Cobra jet hit the building: "I was eating all the cookies." When parrot Polly's less-than-forthcoming with information, Shipwreck asks Roadblock if he's got his recipe for "parrot under glass" handy. The final confrontation with Cobra Commander, while flawed, decidedly drives home the futility of obtaining vengeance.

ASS-WHUPPINGS Remarkably few, although Lady Jaye downs a RATTLER that levels Fairmont's home and singes his family.

GOOFS Cobra Commander orders his FANG helicopters to attack from three fronts – but they all dive at the Joes from the same direction.

Getting into Joe Headquarters, as Charlie Fairmont proves, entails nothing more than knocking the gate guard unconscious (granted, Lady Jaye catches him shortly afterward).

Fairmont holds some questionable philosophically to believe that blowing up a low-level Cobra munitions depot will even the score for his family's injuries (although it's hard to blame a kids' TV show for not resorting to greater extremes). Even more questionably, at story's end, Fairmont seems willing to stop Cobra Commander even if he dies in the process – an act that'd surely deprive the Fairmont family of a husband and father.

CHARACTER PROFILE: JOES

- *Alpine:* His great-grandmother died in 1957.
- *Bazooka:* Hails from Minnesota.

STUFF YOU NEED Cobra Interrogation Tiara: Deals out pain in proportion to the amount that you lie.

THE COMMAND DECISION Atypical among Joe stories for its weighty topic – the nature of vengeance – although everything's too surface-level for mature viewers. The final result's satisfactory but mostly bland, rather like eating plain yogurt, although it paves the way for more insightful efforts in Season 2.

1.41: "The Gods Below"

***US Transmission Date:** Nov. 11, 1985*
***Writer:** Gordon Kent*

BATTLE ROSTER *Joes:* Duke, Alpine, Bazooka, Lady Jaye, Barbecue; *Cobra:* Cobra Commander, the Baroness, Scrap Iron.

MISSION BRIEF After a noted archaeologist named Dr. Marsh locates a tomb dedicated to the ancient Egyptian god Osiris, Cobra Commander smacks his lips upon hearing rumors that the tomb contains a treasure trove of gold. Cobra kidnaps Dr. Marsh to discover the gold cache's location, but the Egyptian government, worried over Marsh's disappearance, asks G.I. Joe to find the missing American researcher.

Soon after, Duke and four other Joes arrive to scour Osiris' tomb for clues to Marsh's whereabouts. Cobra Commander tries to keep his troops hidden, but the Joes run afoul of a Crimson Guardsmen patrol. After overpowering the squad, Duke's team swipes the guardsmen's uniforms and masquerades as Cobra troops. When Cobra Commander approaches them, curious about the results of his Guardsmen's survey, the Joes frantically claim to know the treasure's location and leading Cobra Commander and a second Cobra patrol into the tomb's tunnel system.

The Joe-Cobra brigade reaches an elaborate throne room, where a gas trap luckily incapacitates the Cobra troopers. Duke's group grabs Marsh and heads for the surface, but the floor suddenly tilts downward, dropping the Joes to a lower level. The Joes find themselves in a cosmic viewing chamber, gazing at an impressive array of stars and nebulas. But seconds later – to everyone's shock – Osiris, Egyptian god of the dead, approaches the dumbstruck humans.

Osiris tests the Joes' mettle, promising eternal life in the underworld if they succeed – and torment by the monstrous Ammon if they fail. As members of Osiris' retinue sit in judgement, the Joes grapple with a destroyer god named Set-Ret. The Joes get tossed about like sacks of flour, but the humans' courage and camaraderie proves them worthy of Osiris' reward.

Meanwhile, Cobra Commander awakens to find himself face-to-face with a god of evil named Seth. Lying through his helmet, Cobra Commander slyly offers to raise an army and obliterate Seth's hated half-brother Osiris. Seth agrees, allowing Cobra Commander to take several bags of gold to fund the military recruitment. Unfortunately, Cobra Commander fails to realize that the gold magically binds Seth to his brother's tomb – and that removing it will loose the god of evil to consume the Earth.

In Osiris' domain, a dog-faced god named Anubis agrees to ferry the Joes to the eternal realm of the dead. But suddenly, the underworld quakes with Seth's newfound freedom, striking fear into Osiris and his allies. Cobra Commander jets off with his ill-gotten gold, but the Joes convince Anubis to let them help. Anubis shuttles the Joes to the surface in his flying boat, allowing the Joes to rifle Cobra Commander's RATTLER jet. Cobra Commander desperately ejects, giving Anubis the chance to retrieve the stolen gold and race toward Osiris' tomb.

En route, Anubis unexpectedly turns his boat over, dumping Duke's Joes in an oasis and setting them free among the living. Anubis returns the gold to its proper location, restoring Seth's bonds. As Cobra Commander escapes, the Joes ponder if Anubis let them go free because Osiris sensed they belonged among the living – or because Duke insulted Anubis by calling him "dog face."

LOVE AND WAR When the Crimson Guardsmen-disguised Joes prove less than forthcoming, the Baroness seductively cracks her whip and exclaims: "You know the penalty for withholding information is… severe!"

And in another double entendre, when Cobra Commander eavesdrops on the Joes, he overhears Lady Jaye cry out: "Careful, don't touch that!", followed by Alpine's: "I'm not touching anything!"

ASS-WHUPPINGS The monstrous Set-Ret seemingly incinerates Duke and Dr. Marsh, but it's only an illusion.

PREPOSTEROUS PHYSICS The Joes effortlessly heft a large stone slab like a piece of plywood.

GOOFS The Joes strip five Crimson Guardsmen down to their underwear and toss 'em in a pit – and presumably, they're still down there.

Lady Jaye, who adeptly translated Egyptian in "Eau de Cobra," now can't read it for spittle. Barbecue should fry like a poached egg, given that he struts about the desert heat wearing his insulated firefighter's outfit and helmet. Cobra Commander clairvoyantly knows that an approaching convoy contains hidden Joe members (then again, it's possible that he's operating under the "Who else could it be?" philosophy).

When the African-American Alpine's in a Crimson Guardsman outfit, his visible skin looks white. During the battle with Set-Ret, Alpine falls into a cosmic-spanning void – making us wonder what the self-sacrificing Bazooka hopes to accomplish by diving after his friend (the observing gods kindly save the Joes' asses).

ORGANIZATIONS *The Egyptian Gods:* According to Egyptian lore, Seth slew his brother Osiris, although Osiris' wife (and sister) Isis later brought her hubby/brother back to life. Afterward, Osiris became associated with resurrection, guiding people into immortality in the next life. Meanwhile, the dog-headed Anubis more properly ruled the underworld.

An unnamed hawk-faced god (probably Horus) serves as Osiris' advisor, with a winged snake named Butoh acting as his enforcer. Od, the guardian of universal law, and her father, Ammen-Ra, often sit in judgment over lesser beings. Ammen-Ra's other daughter, Set-Ret, a flying cat of sorts, tests humans' mettle by beating the snot out of them. The reptilian chop-shop creature named Ammon devours beings who're found unworthy in such trials.

THE COMMAND DECISION Tremendously befuddling, ironically not so much for the Egyptian gods' appearance, but because the story winds up so unbelievably far from where it started. As classical studies students, we probably enjoyed "The Gods Below" more than most, but we can't blame other viewers for feeling – at the story's conclusion – like they've been stuffed in a dryer and left on spin cycle for a while.

1.42: "Primordial Plot"

***US Transmission Date:** Nov. 12, 1985*
***Writer:** Donald F. Glut*

BATTLE ROSTER *Joes:* Gung Ho, Scarlett, Flint; *Cobra:* Cobra Commander, Destro, Tomax and Xamot.

MISSION BRIEF As part of a wacky scheme to raise dinosaurs for offensive purposes, Cobra agents steal 70-million-year-old dinosaur bones and kidnap Dr. Massey, a noted expert on cloning. Working from a secluded base on a South Pacific island, Cobra scientists adapt Massey's research and produce several cloned dinosaurs – including fully grown tyrannosaurs, triceratopses and stegosauruses – with a quick-grow catalyst.

Meanwhile, Flint, Scarlett and Gung Ho follow up on reports of heightened Cobra activity in the South Pacific, but Cobra rocket defenses shoot down the Joes' Skystrikers. Eager to test their new weapons, the Cobra officers douse the newborn dinos with radiation, making their brains receptive to Cobra Commander's cybernetic control disc.

Cobra Commander sends his rampaging dinos against Flint's trio. Unable to thwart the dinosaurs' advance, Flint's group attacks the Cobra laboratory, briefly seizing Cobra Commander's control disc and commanding the dinos to overrun the Cobra citadel. As ordered, the dinosaurs thrash the Cobra camp, forcing the Cobra officers to withdraw while Flint's team saves Dr. Massey. Leaving the dinosaurs to their jungle island environment, Flint's group departs for home.

LOVE AND WAR Gung Ho declares that he's got some "primal urges" to satisfy.

PREPOSTEROUS PHYSICS As with Donald F. Glut's script for Transformers: "Dinobot Island," dinosaurs are apparently invulnerable and superstrong, shrugging off laser bolts, crashing through walls, knocking over vehicles and defying electricity.

GOOFS Err, exactly how does one achieve cybernetic control over dinosaurs by dousing their brains with radioactive pink light? One oddball scene shows the Cobra officers submerging the dinos in an underwater tank (err... last time we checked, reptiles can't breathe underwater).

Scarlett claims: "Given a choice, animals always go for real food – humans always taste terrible." (That's not *entirely* true, and how would *she* know, hmm?)

Referring to Tomax and Xamot, Cobra Commander states: "Your Crimson guards are either incredibly brave or incredibly stupid, Destro," when they're actually *his* Crimson guards and more properly called Crimson Guard *commanders.*

At one point, a mini-dinosaur jumps on Flint – who'd certainly croak in the time it takes Scarlett to shoot the dino away. At story's end, it's a little naive to just leave the dinosaurs for anyone to find and exploit.

TV TIE-INS Writer Donald F. Glut also penned Transformers: "Dinosaur Island," although the dinos featured in that story and "Primordial Plot" are not the same.

CHARACTER PROFILE: JOES

• *Flint:* He's not Irish.

• *Gung Ho:* He grew up wrestling alligators in the Louisiana Bayou, although he tired of the life and couldn't wait to leave.

ORGANIZATIONS *The Crimson Guardsmen:* Are unionized.

STUFF YOU NEED *Cobra's Cloned Dinosaurs:* Most of Cobra's dinosaur DNA hails from the Upper Cretaceous Era. Cobra Commander's mental override can't squelch the dinosaurs' natural hunger instincts, meaning it's best to feed 'em every once in a while.

• *Destro's Wrist Rockets:* Grant Destro the power of flight. They're powerful enough to let him soar away with the Crimson Twins clinging to his ankles.

THE COMMAND DECISION Pray for your children. A lifeless dinosaur story that fails to even make its reptiles interesting, "Primordial Plot" tramples itself with a flavorless plot, tedious jungle action, wafer-thin characterization and heaps of clichéd dialogue. With a lobotomy, this might just seem tolerable.

1.43: "Flint's Vacation"

US Transmission Date: *Nov. 13, 1985*
Writer: *Beth Bornstein*

BATTLE ROSTER *Joes:* Flint, Lady Jaye, Breaker; *Cobra:* Zartan and the Dreadnoks, Cobra Commander, the Baroness.

MISSION BRIEF Always in the mood for cheap labor, Cobra Commander laces the local news broadcasts in a town named Pleasant Cove with subliminal messages, thereby enthralling the entire populace. Armed with an unquestioning work force, Cobra Commander sets about constructing an underwater domed city. Next, the cracked commander polishes work on a new missile that's capable of eradicating all vegetation on Earth. Chuckling like a mad fiend, Cobra Commander prepares to blackmail the world on pain of making Earth's surface uninhabitable, leaving the underwater settlement as the last remnant of humanity.

Meanwhile, Flint takes a leave of absence to visit his cousin Ted Harris' new residence in Pleasant Cove. But upon arrival, Flint finds the mesmerized Harris family following a rigid work routine. Flint initially shrugs off the Harris' stupor, but that evening, the Pleasant Cove townsfolk fall out en masse, reporting for a work detail run by Cobra troopers.

Flint tries to alert local authorities – only to unexpectedly find Zartan and the Dreadnoks running the Pleasant Cove Police Station. Shocked into action, Flint slugs everyone present and dashes for freedom, but Zartan nets Flint near the coast. Zartan shuttles Flint to the underwater Cobra dome, entrancing the Joe with the subliminal news broadcasts.

Cobra Commander announces his ultimatum to the world, demanding total control of Earth. Thankfully, Lady Jaye spots Flint in the background of Cobra Commander's broadcast, alerting Joe carrier command to coordinate a strike on Pleasant Cove. Parachuting into Pleasant Cove in advance of the main Joe operation, Lady Jaye and Breaker become suspicious when they find the local satellite dishes pointing down rather than up. Cracking Cobra's brainwashing scheme wide open, Breaker sets about engineering a counter-signal while the *USS Flagg* moves into position.

After capturing a Cobra submarine, Lady Jaye and a team of Joes wreak havoc in the Cobra city center. Cobra Commander responds by rousing his enslaved civilians to the attack, leaving the Joes in a pickle to defend themselves with non-lethal force. Thankfully, Breaker broadcasts a TV signal containing the subliminal message, "Ignore Cobra Commander! He's a jerk!", to the underwater base's monitors, freeing Flint and the Pleasant Cove populace from control.

Unable to deactivate Cobra's anti-vegetation bomb, Joe munitions expert Trip-Wire re-reroutes its guidance system to take the missile harmlessly into space. Beaten on every front, Cobra Commander retreats with his subordinates. Colonel Sharpe generously awards Flint an additional two weeks of leave, but Flint decides it'll be less stressful to simply return to active duty.

MEMORABLE MOMENTS There's an utterly surreal and delicious moment when a tormented Flint runs into the subjugated Pleasant Cove police station – feverishly trying to get the chief's attention – and entirely fails to notice the Dreadnoks playing poker behind him. In the psychotic car chase that follows, Flint pops a wheelie, thereby making the Dreadnoks crash into each other near a market – Buzzer lands in a fish stall, Torch gets pummeled by fruit and Ripper just spins hopelessly out of control (with whimsical background music to boot).

LOVE AND WAR Flint and Lady Jaye keep their respective things in their pants this episode, but clearly pine for one another.

ASS-WHUPPINGS Utterly surrounded, Flint makes a rabid burst for freedom by downing Zartan and the Dreadnoks with a fury of roundhouse punches, then flinging himself pell-mell through a window. Zartan, the Dreadnoks, Major Bludd and the Baroness all contest the Joes' sea supremacy – and wind up in the drink for their trouble.

PREPOSTEROUS PHYSICS Joe hovercraft come equipped with "Vertical Thrusters," which evidently enable the ship to somehow defy gravity, lifting into the air for a few split seconds while enemy torpedoes race past.

GOOFS The actor who voices Flint obviously pulls double-duty as a Pleasant Cove newscaster, meaning Flint eerily listens to his own voice on the evening news. While making his world-seizing ultimatum, Cobra Commander's foolish enough to let an enslaved Flint get seen in the background (hell, the camera pans to follow Flint) – allowing the Joes to locate the Cobra base.

An entranced Flint stops his murderous actions *before* hearing Breaker's mind-cleansing broadcast.

TV TIE-INS The Dreadnoks officially become policemen (well, in a parallel reality, anyway) in "Worlds Without End."

CHARACTER PROFILE: JOES Breaker: Much like his comic-book incarnation, he incessantly pops gum bubbles.

CHARACTER PROFILE: COBRA Dreadnoks: They often cheat at poker, sometimes producing six aces between them.

THE COMMAND DECISION Entirely run-of-the-mill, punctuated with one or two daring moments (Flint's mad dash from police headquarters, etc.). In short, "Flint's Vacation" tastes like that endlessly repetitive flavor of bagel and cream cheese you've gobbled every morning for three years – reliable and slightly comforting, but ultimately pretty passionless.

1.44: "Hearts and Cannons"

US Transmission Date: *Nov. 14, 1985*
Story: *Alfred A. Pegal*
Script: *Alfred A. Pegal and Larry Houston*

BATTLE ROSTER *Joes:* Footloose, Dusty; *Cobra:* Destro, Major Bludd.

MISSION BRIEF In an unspecified Middle East country, lightning strikes a Joe cargo plane, forcing the crew to pitch a massive Mauler tank overboard to reduce the weightload. Still needing to shed another 400 pounds, Dusty and Footloose bail out, allowing Wild Bill and Cover Girl to limp the plane back to base.

Left to their own devices, Dusty and Footloose wander through the desert and blunder across a Cobra weapons range, observing as Destro tests an immeasurably powerful, tank-mounted plasma cannon. Edging closer, the two Joes spot the plasma cannon's chief designer – the captive Dr. Nancy Winters – then risk their necks to liberate her from Cobra's clutches.

Dusty lingers behind to slow the pursuing Cobra troopers, but Footloose and Winters press on into the desert and bump into Jabal, a desert warrior desperate to liberate his enslaved countrymen from Cobra. Forging an alliance, Jabal helps his newfound allies locate the fallen Mauler tank. Footloose's oddball trio summons reinforcements with the Mauler's radio, then turns back for Dusty, all the while jousting with Destro's plasma cannon tank.

The plasma cannon's firepower quickly takes the advantage, but Dusty runs forward and immobilizes Destro's tank treads. Following Winters' guidance, Footloose nails a vulnerable spot on the plasma cannon's hide, blowing Destro's vehicle willy-nilly across the desert plains. Destro reaches a RATTLER jet and escapes with his troops, allowing Jabal to free his enslaved people. Afterward, Dusty and Footloose blink as Jabal – revealed as King Ahmed Razzuli Jabal – thanks the Joes for liberating his country, then seductively invites Winters to see his palace.

MEMORABLE MOMENTS Replete with stoner lingo, Footloose steals the best scenes, notably waking up in the desert, rolling over – and finding himself face-to-face with a scorpion. (Footloose feebly croaks: "Freakin' me out, man… help.")

When Dr. Winters steps on a landmine, she instantly freezes and asks for suggestions about defusing it. With their Cobra pursuers drawing closer – right before commercial break, mind you – Footloose sagely sits down Indian-style, telling Winter: "I'll tell you in a minute. I'm meditatin', man…"

Destro's Cobra soldiers understandably hesitate to follow the Joes and Winter across a minefield, but Destro orders his RATTLER jets to fire on any Cobra trooper who doesn't give chase. Hopelessly screwed either way, the Cobra goons give a weak "Cobraaaaa…" battle cry, then drive forward to their destiny (which involves a *lot* of explosions).

LOVE AND WAR Dusty and Footloose run about this episode acting like over-hormonal juvenile delinquents. For a start, Dusty mistakenly thinks Cover Girl likes him. Dusty also believes Dr. Winters wants to jump his bones, but Jabal, who calls Winters his "desert flower," wins over her heart (and, presumably, her other bits).

ASS-WHUPPINGS Dr. Winters nearly breaks her hand smacking Destro's faceplate. Dusty, Footloose and Winters bravely risk a Cobra minefield (lovingly named "the Death Zone") on foot, causing a bunch of Cobras to follow and rip their vehicles to shreds.

SAVE THEM! When a Cobra tank explodes, the driver doesn't so much "jump clear" as "get tossed onto a nearby roof." The overall effect looks like he's bouncing like a bunny, then jumping for cover.

PREPOSTEROUS PHYSICS The Joes drop a frickin' Mauler tank out of their transport plane, and it lands safely using only parachutes. Parachutes! For a tank!

Laser blasts tear off a Cobra Stinger jeep's missile rack without detonating a single missile. The same jeep jumps over the fence, but comes to a full stop upon landing *without skidding*.

A Cobra Trouble Bubble flies low enough – and shoots poorly enough – for Jabal to slash it with his sword. (Why, oh *why* can't Cobra troopers learn the value of shooting people from a distance?)

GOOFS After performing their emergency parachute jump, Dusty and Footloose somehow find blankets in the wide-open desert to cover them throughout the night. While freeing Dr. Winters, Dusty punches a Cobra guard – who conveniently falls across the hallway and smacks into an alarm switch.

The back of Destro's plasma cannon apparently isn't armored. For that matter, can't Cobra simply build more plasma cannons from the schematics?

STUFF YOU NEED The Plasma Cannon: It's powerful enough to blow up three Firebat jets all in one go.

THE COMMAND DECISION A story that'd completely sink into the quagmire but for the druggie-sounding Footloose's astounding ability to snatch scenes from certain doom. (He blathers at one point about a land mine: "I'm seein' something cosmic here. Everything is everything. To a landmine, you're just something heavy... ", etc.) But that aside, "Hearts and Cannons" emerges as a clichéd, mish-mash of a desert story. Not that we have any strong opinions.

1.45: "Memories of Mara"

***US Transmission Date:** Nov. 15, 1985*
***Writer:** Sharman DiVono*

BATTLE ROSTER *Joes:* Shipwreck, Lady Jaye, Duke, Deep Six; *Cobra:* Cobra Commander, Destro, Tomax and Xamot.

MISSION BRIEF A Cobra agent named Mara volunteers to let researchers tinker with her DNA as part of a Cobra experiment to create amphibious soldiers able to breathe both on land and underwater. Unfortunately, the experiment goes haywire, inadvertently turning Mara into a blue-skinned water-breather. Cobra scientists promise to reverse the procedure, but – sensing their inability to make her human again – Mara escapes into open waters.

Meanwhile, Cobra Commander captures the *USS Nerka* submarine and its crew, intending to dissect the vessel's advanced weaponry to make enormous profit. Unfortunately for Cobra, the *Nerka*'s disappearance mobilizes the Joes into an all-out manhunt. Aboard a Cobra submarine, Cobra Commander, Destro and the Crimson Twins stage a preemptive strike on Joes aboard the *USS Trogon* battleship. But as the firefight rages, Shipwreck spots an exhausted Mara and dives overboard to save her.

Shocked to discover Mara's gills, Shipwreck flails for a course of action as the *Trogon*/Cobra conflict continues. Luckily, the Cobra submarine takes a double beating from the *Trogon* and Deep Six's SHARC, making a full retreat. The Joes bring Mara aboard, rigging a water-breathing apparatus for her to survive on land for brief periods.

Shipwreck finds himself increasingly smitten with Mara, who ultimately spills her guts about the *Nerka*'s location. While Duke and Lady Jaye head up an underwater assault force, Destro heavily interrogates the *Nerka*'s captain, Commander Jordan, for the password to the *Nerka*'s central computer. With razor-sharp efficiency, the scuba-diving Joes draw Cobra's firepower while Mara plants a series of explosives and flees with the *Nerka*'s crew. Overrun, the Cobra officers withdraw as Mara's incendiaries rip the Cobra base apart. Afterward, Mara finds herself ill-suited to life on the surface world – despite her affection for Shipwreck – and departs for the open sea, leaving the Joe sailor heart-broken.

LOVE AND WAR Shipwreck shoves a medic aside to perform CPR on Mara. They later end up smooching (Shipwreck and Mara, that is... not the medic), enjoying a private little "prancing" scene on a beach while waiting for the Joes. Shipwreck and Mara clearly fall in love, but there's no evidence of nookie – an act that would, indeed, bring new meaning to the words "banging her blue."

ASS-WHUPPINGS Mara bashes Buzzer unconscious. The Crimson Twins double-punch Lady Jaye from behind.

GOOFS Yet again, we're baffled by some of the Joe mission assignments, especially when Alpine, a mountain climber, gets detailed to command a Joe diving mission. Wearing only her body suit, Mara mysteriously carries a large amount of plastic explosives that look like bread dough, evidently requiring her to "pat" them (one wonders if she previously worked in a pizza joint) into position all throughout the Cobra base. In the final battle, Destro and the Crimson Twins place Lady Jaye in their gill-granting device rather than more sensibly snapping her neck.

TV TIE-INS Mara returns as Shipwreck's "wife" in "There's No Place Like Springfield."

CHARACTER PROFILE: JOES *Shipwreck:* He's an expert seaman but knows little about diving.

CHARACTER PROFILE: OTHER *Mara:* Mara hails from a rough neighborhood, which initially made a home with Cobra seem all the more appealing. Her body spent weeks adjusting to its water-breathing state. She can only survive out of water for a few minutes. The Joes rig Mara a portable water-breather that lets her stay on land for 15-minute intervals, but even that dries out her skin.

ORGANIZATIONS *Cobra:* Mara suggests that Cobra "merhuman" researchers didn't lack for volunteers, suggesting Cobra troopers hold more loyalty to the organization than one might suspect.

HOT WHEELS *USS Trogon:* An American mine hunter, equipped with anti-torpedo missiles and an impregnable hull. Captain Hunt, whose authority supercedes even Duke's, serves as Trogon commander. It's a tough ship, but submarines nonetheless give it trouble.

THE COMMAND DECISION A so-so tale with a passable romance (we're not sure why Shipwreck and Mara fall in love, but we're not convinced they shouldn't either). As a pale Hunt for the Red October imitation – admittedly with a human-fish assignation thrown in – "Memories of Mara" just gets the job done, although Mara herself nets a better role in "There's No Place Like Springfield."

1.46-1.47: "The Traitor"

Episodes: *Two*
US Transmission Date: *Nov. 25-26, 1985*
Writer: *Buzz Dixon*

BATTLE ROSTER *Joes:* Dusty, Duke, Shipwreck, Flint, Deep Six; *Cobra:* Cobra Commander, Tomax and Xamot.

MISSION BRIEF ***Part 1:*** As military scientists perfect a new armor treatment that renders Joe vehicles immune to conventional bombs, missiles and lasers, the lump of coal that serves as Cobra Commander's heart lurches over the Joes' newfound invincibility. With the Joes spanking Cobra's legions left, right and center, Cobra Commander becomes desperate to acquire the Joes' armor-enhancing formula.

Meanwhile, Joe desert trooper Dusty takes leave to visit his ailing, asthmatic mother, worried about her ever-growing medical bills. Learning of Dusty's plight, the Crimson Twins approach the stressed-out Joe, offering to pay his mother's medical expenses in exchange for the new Joe armor formula. Dusty initially rebuffs the twins' proposition, unwilling to ruin the Joes' battlefield advantage, but finds himself without a better solution.

Later, Duke and Flint brief Dusty and other Joes on Cobra's intention to steal a load of Dialcon 98: a key ingredient needed to create mind-control gas. The Joes lay an ambush for Cobra at a Dialcon 98 stockpile, but Dusty, deeming the information a lesser sin than giving up the armor formula, phones the twins about the trap. The brothers happily pay a round of bills for Dusty's mother while their forewarned Cobra troopers run rings around the Joes, stealing several Dialcon 98 tankers.

Duke sweeps the Joe ranks for a traitor, then summons Flint for a secret conference and pegs Dusty as the turncoat. Needing proof, Duke and Flint bait Dusty by letting him overhear plans to raid a Cobra-controlled oil rig. Like clockwork, Dusty phones the twins, trading information on the oil rig assault for a further medical payment.

The twins agree, emptying the rig of Cobra personnel well before the Joes arrive. Outraged, Duke and Flint take the abandoned oil rig as further proof of Dusty's betrayal – then turn chilled to realize that Cobra also hotwired the rig with explosives. The Joes dive underwater with seconds to spare, escaping the blast, but Duke gets hammered with concussion and falls into a coma.

Already enraged to learn of Dusty's betrayal, the Joes return home and catch their friend photographing schematics for the Joe armor formula. With a heavy heart, Flint presides over a court-martial and finds Dusty guilty of treason, sentencing him to a life sentence at Ft. Wadsworth military prison. Dusty says nothing in his defense, allowing military police to lead him away. But Cobra Commander, assessing Dusty's potential as a Cobra agent, sends his troops to free the ex-Joe. Dusty escapes, making the Joes realize that, with their colleague fully on Cobra's side, none of their secrets are safe.

Part 2: With nowhere else to turn, Dusty fully throws in with Cobra, causing the Joes no end of trouble. In short order, Cobra Commander assigns Dusty to oversee production of Cobra's armor treatment formula, developing a compound that renders both Cobra attack vehicles and personnel uniforms invincible to attack. Armed with the formula – plus Dusty's knowledge of Joe protocols – Cobra Commander easily obtains the other ingredients needed for his mind-control gas. The Joes do their best, but Cobra wins a string of battles – capturing Flint, Lady Jaye and Shipwreck while netting the final mind-control element.

1.46-1.47, The Traitor

Innately suspicious, Cobra Commander orders Dusty to test the newly brewed mind-control gas by zombifying the captive Joes. Dusty pretends to comply – then spontaneously shifts sides and frees the Joes. In the ensuing mayhem, Dusty holes up in Cobra's gas manufacturing center with Flint and Lady Jaye, reprogramming the vats to create a compound that disintegrates anything treated with the armor formula. Released into the base, Dusty's new compound instantly shreds all armor-formula dosed vehicles and uniforms. Cobra Commander and his aides escape, but the Joes round up the base's troopers and score a major victory.

Afterward, Duke awakens from his coma, explaining that Dusty's "traitor" routine was a ploy from the very start. As the Joes learn, Dusty asked Duke for help when the twins first made their bribery offer. Knowing Cobra would eventually learn the armor formula's secrets, Duke opted to let Dusty turn renegade and "give" the formula to Cobra – turning it against them at a crucial juncture. But when a Cobra bomb put Duke into a coma, an alibi-less Dusty found himself forced to continue "working" for Cobra. Clearing Dusty's name, Duke happily restores the desert trooper to active service, allowing the Joes to celebrate their teammate's return.

MEMORABLE MOMENTS Dusty's initial meeting with the twins in the Western-themed "Stumble Inn" builds to a glorious brawl. The beginning of Part Two cleverly recaps Part One as a "Twenty Questions" broadcast (see TV Tie-Ins) rather than the usual "Last time on G.I. Joe…" bit.

LOVE AND WAR A blonde waitress flirts with Dusty, but he barely notices in his overwrought "How will we pay my croaking mother's bills?" state of mind. Xamot holds Dusty at gunpoint – by shoving a gun into his crotch under the table. As the anti-armor formula leaves Cobra troopers clad only in their underwear, Lady Jaye jumps a fleeing Cobra goon – and accidentally whisks off his boxers.

ASS-WHUPPINGS Duke spends most of this story in a coma. Trying to elude capture, Dusty breaks a chair over Shipwreck's head. Dusty brawls with Cobra Lt. Claymore (see Organizations) in a Cobra battle arena, winning the bout by forcing Claymore down into piranha-infested waters.

Dusty helps Cobra capture Flint, Lady Jaye and Shipwreck in a titanic pile-up of Joe vehicles. Later, Dusty kicks Tomax (and by extension his brother Xamot), although Tomax bowls the Joe over with a barrel. Shedding any loyalty for Cobra, Dusty hurls Cobra Commander into the twins. Shipwreck discovers the art of knocking Cobra troopers about with a pool cue.

SAVE THEM! Prison guards jump off a collapsing observation tower like they're leaping off the sofa. A Cobra helicopter grounds Dusty's prison truck with a massive missile strike – that fails to hurt anyone.

GOOFS During a bar brawl, a waitress paralyzes a customer by dumping beer on his head (good grief, it's beer, not morphine). Dusty's dumb enough to strut about Joe Headquarters with the Crimson Twins' Extensive Enterprises business card showing in his shirt pocket – mind, none of the Joes notice.

When Duke's group finds the rig laced with explosives, why not simply blow out the fuse? Furthermore, if Duke *asked* Dusty to betray their operation to Cobra, why is he asinine enough to waltz into an explosive-laden Cobra base?

Dusty never actually gets the Joe armor formula – the Joes certainly wouldn't let him keep photographs after his court-martial and he couldn't have *memorized* the damn thing (it's too complex) – but he inexplicably knows it at the beginning of Part Two.

Proving the invulnerability of armor formula-treated uniforms, Dusty allows a row of Cobra troopers to "shoot" him. Unfortunately, he's not wearing gloves and should've got his hands shot off (whoops).

Nobody stands guard in Cobra's chemical manufacturing center, presumably the most important part of the base. As Dusty frees his teammates, Duke, who's comatose at the time, appears with a pack of Joes jumping the Crimson Twins.

When the Joes lock themselves in Cobra's gasworks, Cobra tank drivers cannon their way inside (oh, *good move* – blow your way into the most volatile part of the complex).

TV TIE-INS Part Two opens up by recapping the Part One in the form of a "Twenty Questions" broadcast ("Twenty Questions"). Hector Ramirez, still the show's host, now has gray hair.

COMIC TIE-INS Ft. Wadsworth, here tagged as a military prison, appears in the G.I. Joe comics (starting with *G.I. Joe* #1) as a chaplain's assistants' school and the secret location of Joe Headquarters (a.k.a. The Pit).

CHARACTER PROFILE: JOES

• *Dusty:* "The Traitor" cites Dusty's real name as "Ronald Rudat," although his action figure filecard names him "Ronald Tadur." Avoiding such confusion, his mother just calls him "Dusty." His mother's essentially an invalid, confined to a wheelchair and oxygen tank. A Spanish housekeeper watches over her. The absence of Dusty's father goes unexplained.

CHARACTER PROFILE: COBRA

• *Cobra Commander:* He follows Stalin's policy of "Trust no one, even yourself."

• *Tomax and Xamot:* Strangely lounge about their offices balancing on their heads.

ORGANIZATIONS *Cobra:* Cobra soldiers routinely settle disputes and promotional issues in the battle arena. It's not terribly relevant, but for example, Cobra Lt. Claymore challenges Dusty for command of his unit – leading to the two of them dueling with rocket-powered nunchakus in a pit increasingly filled with water and man-eating piranha. Some clashes inevitably result in death, although the loser often winds up cleaning latrines or the like. Cobra also offers its soldiers medical plans.

• *G.I. Joe:* Operatives with Dusty's level of clearance have access to 6438 different security codes. Duke recovers in a building labeled "G.I. Joe Hospital," suggesting the Joes maintain their own medical center.

STUFF YOU NEED *The Armor Formula:* A highly effective means of insulating armor against laser and missile attacks. Unfortunately, the armor formula's vulnerable to certain counter-agents (as Dusty proves) and weakens in the presence of intense heat.

THE COMMAND DECISION Remarkably nourishing, making great use of its two-episode format and giving cause why Dusty could stab his comrades in the back (even if we rightly bet money that he wouldn't). Essentially, it's just about the closest you'll come – barring a totally balls-to-the-wall story such as "Worlds Without End" – to a Joe TV story that takes itself seriously. We cheered the finale.

1.48: "The Pit of Vipers"

US Transmission Date: Nov. 27, 1985
Story: Flint Dille
Script: James M. Ward

BATTLE ROSTER *Joes:* Scarlett, Breaker, Flint, Lady Jaye, Shipwreck, Frostbite, Colonel Sharpe, Admiral Ledger; *Cobra:* Cobra Commander, Destro, Tomax and Xamot, Zartan.

FIRST APPEARANCES *Joes:* Heavy Metal (Mauler M.B.T. tank driver).

MISSION BRIEF Embarking on a subterfuge designed to ruin Joe Headquarters, Cobra Commander assigns Zartan to mask himself as a scientist named "Dr. Hamler" and acquire U.S. funding for a new military computer system. In due course, Zartan/Hamler obtains Pentagon clearance to build a system called "Watchdog" as an "independent-thinking" computer brain, capable of assigning troop deployments in record time. But as the project's true designer, Destro builds Watchdog with overrides that enable Cobra to secretly direct its actions.

Soon after, the Pentagon names Watchdog as the Joes' top commander, overruling Duke and Colonel Sharpe's protests about the value of a human leader. The Joes inwardly despair but dutifully follow the Pentagon's whims, wearing Watchdog-linked communicators that enable the computer to issue orders at a moment's notice.

Over the next few days, Cobra sends the Joes – via Watchdog – on wild goose chases around the globe, tying up vast amounts of Joe manpower. As a means of distracting the *USS Flagg,* Cobra programs Watchdog to project a hologram of the *Cerebus,* a Cobra yacht, in the Indian Ocean. The *Flagg* easily rips apart the "*Cerebus,*" but Shipwreck turns suspicious when the *Cerebus* sinks and disappears without a trace. Shipwreck disregards Watchdog's orders to stand down, investigating further. In due course, the Joe sailor discovers Cobra Commander and Destro's underwater Cobra base, learning Watchdog's true nature but getting captured in the process.

Thanks to Watchdog, Cobra further whittles down the Joe Headquarters staff until only Breaker and Scarlett remain on base. Moving into the final phase of their operation, Cobra Commander and Destro ready the "Pit Viper" – a super-advanced drill – to run roughshod through Joe Headquarters. Again tapping Watchdog's control systems, Destro turns off Joe Headquarters' defenses in preparation for the Pit Viper's arrival. Thankfully, Shipwreck briefly escapes, radioing a warning to Joe Headquarters before getting overpowered again.

Breaker immediately contacts the American-based Joes, exposing Watchdog's scheme and ordering his teammates to hurry to Watchdog's computer core – housed in a remote desert mesa. Encountering heavy Cobra resistance at the Watchdog command center, the Joes are stymied in their efforts to crash the system. Thankfully, Breaker and Scarlett – forewarned about the Pit Viper's arrival – dodge its initial attack and bazooka their way inside.

Seizing manual control of the Pit Viper, Breaker and Scarlett pilot the powerful drill out to Watchdog's headquarters. While Cobra troops continue hamstringing the Joes' advance, Breaker and Scarlett tunnel under the mesa and drill straight up into Watchdog's brain. The two Joes bail out just as the Watchdog complex explodes, ending Cobra's scheme.

Noting their failure, Cobra Commander and Destro start throttling each other – failing to notice as Shipwreck escapes detention. Afterward, the Pentagon reassigns proper G.I. Joe command back to Duke, ending any and all thoughts of a computer-guided military.

MEMORABLE MOMENTS Shipwreck (a.k.a. Hector Delgado) launches his Watchdog communicator – which doubles as a tracking device – out a torpedo tube, causing the monotone Watchdog to warn: "Attention. Sensors indicate Delgado has evacuated craft. Action is unauthorized."

LOVE AND WAR When Lady Jaye asks Ace to join her on a bombing run, he cheekily suggests, "Blow in my headphones and I'll follow you anywhere."

ASS-WHUPPINGS Shipwreck gets knocked unconscious – twice. The Pit Viper punches holes in Joe Headquarters and mangles mass amounts of vehicles before Breaker and Scarlett stop it. The Watchdog command center goes up in a fountain of molten lava (See Preposterous Physics.)

PREPOSTEROUS PHYSICS The Joes easily parachute their attack jeeps and mini-tanks into a warzone, suggesting the vehicles are made from tin foil.

"The Pit of Vipers" ends in a spurt of volcanic action – which doesn't make much sense. Basically, Breaker and Scarlett tunnel underneath Watchdog's base with the Pit Viper, building enough steam to burst the Cobra drill into Watchdog's command center and somehow trigger a frickin' *lava burst* in the process. If you're following this, the Pit Viper carves through Watchdog with a ridiculous velocity – enough to launch the Cobra drill through Watchdog's roof and into the air. In fact, the Pit Viper flies so high, Breaker and Scarlett *parachute* to safety (and into said volcanic burst, one presumes).

CHARACTER PROFILE: COBRA

Zartan: Disguises himself as the impeccably credentialed "Dr. Hamler," who actually died in 1978.

HOT WHEELS Joe Skystrikers: They're equipped with Sidewinder missiles.

THE COMMAND DECISION Actually two storylines (the hogwild computer and Cobra Commander's drill scheme) stitched together, "The Pit of Vipers" ultimately gets the job done at the cost of some extremely noticeable seams.

1.49: "The Wrong Stuff"

US Transmission Date: *Nov. 29, 1985*
Story: *Flint Dille and Stanley Ralph Ross*
Script: *Stanley Ralph Ross*

BATTLE ROSTER *Joes:* Ace, Duke, Scarlett, Lady Jaye, Roadblock, Alpine, Bazooka, Flint, Colonel Sharpe; *Cobra:* Cobra Commander, Tomax and Xamot, Destro, the Baroness, Zartan and the Dreadnoks.

MISSION BRIEF Hoping to spark public unrest through propaganda, Cobra Commander dispatches a Cobra space shuttle to swallow Earth's entertainment and communications satellites. Deprived of broadcasting, Earth's airwaves fall hauntingly silent. But moments later, an unfettered Cobra space station starts transmitting the "Cobra Television Network" – featuring an array of society-corroding programming designed to make people fear Cobra's might.

While the Joes watch appalling Cobra-made shows such as *Father Knows Beast* and *The C-Team,* Cobra – snug in its position as the world's only television network – rakes in a fortune on inflated advertising rates. Desperate to put Cobra out of action, the Joes determine the Cobra space station's position and secure government help in upgrading their Skystriker jets with rocket boosters. Unfortunately, when the space station repels an initial assault by Ace, Alpine and Lady Jaye, the Joes reassess their need for space training.

Duke authorizes Ace to put the Joes through a hellish space training course, tagging Ace and his top five students as a strike force. The rocket-boosted Skystrikers renew their assault, but the space station's crew – composed of Destro, Zartan and the Dreadnoks – annihilate the Joe vehicles with a molecular disintegration ray.

The spacesuit-clad Joes bail to safety, crawling into the Cobra station through its gun ports. With no time to lose, the Joes rush their opponents and trigger a blistering firefight. In the process, the station's control room takes heavy damage – threatening to erupt and consume the entire station. While Destro and his associates evacuate in one Cobra shuttle, the Joes flee in a spare just as an explosion tears the station to shreds. Back on Earth, the Joes celebrate the return of normal television, with even the unemployed "Mr. C" shucking off his Cobra ties and applying for Joe membership.

MEMORABLE MOMENTS The Joes take a collective bucket of water to the face when they realize that the public will, in fact, believe anything they see on TV. The Baroness shows G.I. Joe's age by gushing about the "modern" wonders of CGI. The Joes enter the Cobra space station by crawling in through its gun ports (well, we were biting our nails).

LOVE AND WAR Some opening shots, which show the Joes working out in a gym, feature a tantalizingly sweaty Scarlett and Lady Jaye on exercise bikes.

ASS-WHUPPINGS Ace's Joe space training proves more debilitating than a Cobra attack. Shipwreck's tormented by endless push-ups; he later suffers nausea in anti-gravity. Everyone endures a torque rotation simulation, with Mutt growling, Bazooka covering his eyes and Alpine nervously chewing a thread. Oh, and that's before a re-entry scenario tries to knock the survivors flat on their ass.

A clash aboard the gravity-less Cobra space station entails Dreadnok Torch smacking his head on the ceiling while teammate Ripper misses on a swing and twirls head over heels.

Torch bashes Lady Jaye unconscious from behind while Alpine catches the fringe of an explosion.

PREPOSTEROUS PHYSICS Beaten during their initial assault on the Cobra space station, Ace, Alpine and Lady Jaye eject and swan dive into Earth's atmosphere, finally deploying their chutes and landing safely on the doorstep of Joe Headquarters – and completely violating several laws of atmospheric friction.

SAVE THEM! Destro's molecular destabilizer demolishes the Joe Skystrikers but somehow fails to harm the Joes or their spacesuits.

GOOFS In the Joe-niverse, local TV stations and other terrestrial broadcasts evidently don't exist – it's either satellite TV or nothing.

Cobra fortifies its space station with cannons that "can't be aimed straight up" – a pretty silly design flaw, considering the 3D nature of space warfare.

CHARACTER PROFILE: JOES

• *Alpine:* He's frantic to stop Cobra's broadcast scheme so he can watch *Bowling for Dollars* again.

• *Roadblock:* He's learned some French in the course of his cooking training.

CHARACTER PROFILE: COBRA

• *Buzzer:* A Dreadnok so lazy, he works missile control pads with his feet.

• *Cobra Commander:* Claims he decided, at age six, that he could run society "better than the morons who were in charge." (An interviewer responds: "That old, huh?")

ORGANIZATIONS *American Aeronautics and Space Committee:* Senator Flemm serves as its head, granting Joe requests for booster rockets in exchange for tickets to the annual Army/Navy football game.

• *Cobra Television Network:* Features a slew of TV programs designed to undermine trust in society, hopefully generating enough dissent to let Cobra one-up the American government. Granted, it doesn't hurt that, as the only TV station on the air, Cobra jacks its advertising rates to $5 million for a 30-second commercial.

Among the Cobra Network's shows, *Father Knows Beast* features a man who's a good citizen by day and werewolf by night – teaching its viewers not trust anyone. *The C-Team* sports "Mr. C," who – you guessed it – "pities the fool who don't join Cobra." A re-worked version of *King Kong* shows the big ape whipping everyone's rear, proof that, "You can never win if your enemy's bigger and smarter than you." Finally, *The Likeables* offers animated "pro-social fun," spotlighting a band of pixies who teach the importance of everyone looking and acting the same. ("Only when everyone looks alike... and acts alike... and thinks alike... and never, *ever* gets angry... can we achieve world peace!")

The Cobra Network accepts donations in the name of criminal enterprise (loosely clothed as "free speech") at: Cobra Network, c/o Extensive Enterprises, Box 22-22, Viper Beach, CA 90287.

• *G.I. Joe:* Roadblock, Scarlett, Lady Jaye, Wild Bill and Alpine ultimately qualify to join Ace's group of space-bound Skystrikers and learn a variety of zero-gee fighting techniques. Bazooka nearly made the cut, but faltered on the final stamina test. Other Joes eliminated from space duty include Duke, Flint, Mutt, Cover Girl, Gung Ho and Shipwreck.

STUFF YOU NEED Destro's Molecular Destabilizer: Incorporated into the Cobra space station, the solar-powered destabilizer snags enemy vessels in a tractor beam and rattles their atoms to bits.

THE COMMAND DECISION Highly schismed, with the first half offering wry satire like the Cobra Network's Likeables cartoon (a spoof almost worthy of Saturday Night Live), and the latter part squarely zeroing itself on standard space battles. The final effect's a watchable, laid-back 23-odd minutes, even if you can't tell which way it wants to go.

1.50: "The Invaders"

***US Transmission Date:** Nov. 29, 1985*
***Writer:** Dennis O'Neil*

BATTLE ROSTER *Joes:* Dusty, Duke, Barbecue, Gung Ho, Snake-Eyes, Colonel Sharpe; *Cobra:* Tomax and Xamot.

FIRST APPEARANCES *Other:* The Oktober Guard (Colonel Brekhov, Horrorshow, Stormavik, Daina, Wong).

MISSION BRIEF When Duke and a team of Joes to run down the Crimson Twins in a Middle Eastern desert, the Oktober Guard – the Soviet Union's elite commando force – compete with the Joes to capture the Cobra brothers for Mother Russia. The three factions trade lasers, but to everyone's bafflement, two flying saucers suddenly appear overhead, smearing the twins' outpost with laser beams. For an encore, a purple-headed alien from the planet Sirius steps forth, netting the twins in a tractor beam. As the Joes and Russians' jaws drop, the alien claims he's just kidnapped the twins as experimentation subjects, vowing to study humanity's nature and return to "inform Earth of its fate."

Soon after, the alien saucers unleash blistering laser attacks on America and the Soviet Union. As accusations of collaboration fly between the world powers, the President orders the Joes to eliminate the flying saucers at all cost. Trying to keep the peace between the two power blocs, Duke contacts Oktober Guard leader Colonel Brekhov and arranges a short-term Joe/Oktober Guard alliance.

Spurred onward, the aliens announce intentions to level San Francisco and Vladivostok, compelling the American and Russian militaries to beef up security at the targeted cities. Duke and Brekhov split their forces, searching for signs of the aliens in North America and Eastern Europe. Meanwhile, Snake-Eyes and guardsman Wong agree to scout out the missing Crimson Twins' Extensive Enterprises corporation.

Captured while snooping, Snake-Eyes and Wong find themselves face-to-face with their captors: the Crimson Twins. The brothers take their prisoners to one of the "flying saucers," where lead alien unmasks himself as Zartan, exposing the "alien saucer" as a modified Cobra airship. After grilling Snake-Eyes and Wong for information, Zartan confirms that Cobra's duped both the Americans and Russians. In return, Snake-Eyes and Wong learn that Cobra perpetuated the alien masquerade to draw attention to San Francisco and Vladivostok, leaving the White House and the Kremlin vulnerable.

Cobra forces surround both houses of leadership, intent on kidnapping American and Russian leaders and plundering the nations' military secrets. Thankfully, Snake-Eyes gets loose, overpowering Zartan and helping Wong to radio their respective forces. The Cobra troops roll toward their goals, but the Joes and Russians regroup and heatedly defend both targets. Cobra falls into full retreat, leaving Snake-Eyes to disable the secondary "alien saucer" with his own commandeered ship, ending Cobra's extraterrestrial career for good.

ASS-WHUPPINGS Gung Ho pops Russian Horrorshow one for calling him ugly. The Crimson Twins electro-shock Snake-Eyes and Wong unconscious.

GOOFS Goof #1A: Zartan dresses up as the purple-headed alien leader and then moronically broadcasts a worldwide ultimatum with his ungloved hand holding a carton of milk in the shot. It's such a dead giveaway that he might as well unmask and, in the fine tradition of Monty Python, wear a sign about his neck proclaiming: "I AM AN ALIEN."

Goof #1B: Of the millions watching the broadcast, only Snake-Eyes spots the milk carton, thereby recognizing the "aliens" as a Cobra conspiracy.

Goof #1C: Snake-Eyes' reasoning for this: The alien leader claims he's broadcasting from the moon, but he's holding an Earth milk carton. Ergo, he's not a real alien. That reasoning *might* hold water – except that the "alien" *was* spotted on Earth while "capturing" the Crimson Twins. Furthermore, if one has the power to traverse alien star systems, acquiring some Earth milk surely can't pose much of a problem. What if the aliens just *really* like milk?

Goof #1D: Snake-Eyes keeps the whole "Look! A milk carton!" thing to himself, only revealing the information when it's entirely worthless.

Goof #1E: When Snake-Eyes *finally* explains the milk carton discrepancy to Gung Ho, Snakes also makes mention of Zartan's ungloved hand. The problem being: During the first broadcast, the hand is nowhere to be seen. It only shows up on the replay!

All other non-milk-carton related goofs: A huge forested area has spontaneously replaced Pennsylvania Avenue in surrounding the White House. The Russians surely wouldn't let the Wild-West-loving Wong, supposedly a Communist military leader attached to the Oktober Guard through a Chinese exchange program, strut about in Cold War era Russia dressed like a cowboy. (It's just – dare we say it? – *wong.*) Zartan and the Dreadnoks follow the finest James Bond tradition in spilling their master plan instead of just carving the captive Snake-Eyes and Wong in half with a machete.

TV TIE-INS The Oktober Guard jousts with the Joes for control of Alaska in "The Great Alaskan Land Rush."

COMIC TIE-INS The Oktober Guard originally surface in *G.I. Joe* #6, making frequent re-appearances throughout the comic series, although only Colonel Brekhov, Horrorshow, Stormavik and Daina make it to the TV version. Side Note: The TV Daina has long dark hair, as opposed to her comic incarnation's short blonde locks.

CHARACTER PROFILE: JOES/OTHER

Gung Ho and Horrorshow: American born-and-bred Gung Ho nurses a healthy hatred for the Russians and is continually dismayed over working with Russian sergeant Horrorshow. Gung Ho revises his opinion later in this story, especially when Horrorshow saves his life during the White House battle. The two of them end the episode still insulting one another – but in a more brotherly fashion.

THE COMMAND DECISION Pretty damn silly however you slice it, crushed beneath a lifeless "alien" subterfuge and the unbearable Wong – a cowboy-loving Communist commando who hits the annoyance radar about as high as Jar-Jar Binks. We'd hoped for much more from writer Denny O'Neil – the DC editor responsible for the modern-day Batman – but even a warm regard for Denny can't save this story from the rubbish heap.

1.51: "Cold Slither"

US Transmission Date: Dec. 2, 1985
Writer: Michael Charles Hill

BATTLE ROSTER *Joes:* Duke, Scarlett, Lady Jaye, Cover Girl, Footloose, Breaker, Shipwreck, Rock 'n Roll; *Cobra:* Zartan and the Dreadnoks, Cobra Commander, the Baroness, Destro, Major Bludd, Firefly.

MISSION BRIEF When the Joes capture an outpost containing piles of Cobra's ill-gotten booty – enough to make Uncle Scrooge flush with envy – Cobra Commander finds himself facing the most dangerous foes of all: bankruptcy and an eternity of financial ruin. As Cobra's creditors bay for blood, the Crimson Twins inform Cobra Commander that he needs to cough up $200 million in 48 hours to keep Cobra afloat. In response, Cobra Commander embarks on a whacked get-rich-quick-scheme, ripping off a loan shark for $1 million and hiring Zartan and his Dreadnoks with the loot.

While Destro develops a subliminal message program that's compatible with the music industry, Cobra Commander and the Baroness dress up Zartan's crew as a punk rock band named "Cold Slither." Gifted with decent singing voices – as well as a talent for smashing their instruments – Cold Slither slithers up the charts in a mere three days after release. Atwitter about the new undertaking, the Crimson Twins cancel Cobra Commander's debt in exchange for a share of the Cold Slither profits.

With Destro's subliminals enthralling anyone who hears the Cold Slither theme song, thousands of people flock to a Cold Slither concert. With the concert arena bursting at its seams, Cobra Commander encircles the area with troops and takes to the airwaves – demanding a ransom of $100 billion in exchange for his hostages' lives.

Floundering for a course of attack, Duke sends the Joe women into action. Disguised as screaming rock groupies, Scarlett, Lady Jaye and Cover Girl sneak into the Cold Slither concert, making their way to the Dreadnoks' dressing room. When the Dreadnoks take a break, the girls beat the tar out of the swamp rats. Undaunted, the Joe females burst into the concert sound booth, tearing up the place and forcing Cobra Commander, the Baroness and Destro to run for the hills. Modifying Destro's subliminal sound system, the girls make the entranced crowd shout out "Cobra Commander is a clown!" before freeing everyone from Cobra's control and exposing Cold Slither as a Cobra front.

MEMORABLE MOMENTS With Cobra bankrupt, Ripcord, Bazooka and Torpedo grow devastatingly bored and convert the Joe training field into a golf course. (Torpedo: "You must admit, the obstacles are unique – especially the minefield.")

LOVE AND WAR/ASS-WHUPPINGS When Scarlett, Cover Girl and Lady Jaye disguise themselves as bubbly rock band groupies, the Dreadnoks think they're going to receive – well, what rock stars usually receive backstage at a concert. Instead, the female Joes bash the Dreadnoks senseless.

ASS-WHUPPINGS Cobra Commander, the Baroness and Destro escape by diving out of a sound booth, "gracefully" breaking their fall with a soft drink stand.

G.I. JOE: THE MUSICAL Nothing will prepare you for the sight of Zartan and the Dreadnoks decked out like KISS, screeching, "We're Cold Slither! You'll be joining us soon! We shall RULE!" The fact that the Dreadnoks chainsaw, cut and torch their instruments as a grand finale probably doesn't hurt. Less successfully, Scarlett, Cover Girl and Lady Jaye sing patriotic songs for the Cold Slither audience towards the end, even as Duke, Rock 'n Roll and Footloose play guitar and Shipwreck takes to the drums.

GOOFS In the opening battle, Cobra troops defend themselves with red lasers rather than the customary Cobra blue. Echoing Cobra Commander's financial woes, Cobra troops show up to claim unemployment benefits – in their Cobra uniforms (not very subtle, although it's really, really funny). Cobra Commander and Firefly enter a bar variously labeled "Stinky's" and "Sniky's."

TV TIE-INS The "Cold Slither" music video director looks suspiciously like the director behind The G.I. Joe Story ("Lights! Camera! Cobra!"). For that matter, he also resembles the movie director from Transformers: "Hoist Goes Hollywood," but there's no evidence that we're dealing with the same character. More likely, G.I. Joe and Transformers animators kept a standard "movie director" design, whipping it out as needed.

The "Cold Slither" music resurfaces in "Raise the Flagg!" and the *Transformers* episodes "Make Tracks" and "Auto-Bop."

COMIC TIE-INS As in the G.I. Joe comics (starting with *G.I. Joe* #25), the swamp shack exterior of Zartan's headquarters disguises a high-tech interior.

CHARACTER PROFILE: JOES

- *Cover Girl:* Her "scented perfume" spray bottle knocks people out.
- *Duke:* He's inept when it comes to pop culture.

CHARACTER PROFILE: COBRA

• *Cobra Commander:* His helmet's electrified to stop people sneaking a look at his face.

• *The Baroness:* Among her many talents, the Baroness is a mean make-up expert.

• *The Crimson Twins:* They don't normally dabble in real estate.

• *Zartan:* It's suggested that Zartan, who's paid a cool $1 million for the "Cold Slither" project, hires his Dreadnoks at a measly $5 per hour.

CHARACTER PROFILE: OTHER

The mispronouncing dwarf: Quite frankly, this has little to do with anything, but Cobra Commander does business with a midget loan shark who continually fumbles his words. To wit, the dwarf greets his guests with: "Glad to see you are punctuation. Time is a precious community, and I despise people who abstruse it. So, how many I be of abstinence to you?" Later, as Cobra Commander and Firefly pull a runner with the cash, the midget creams out: "Apprehended them!"

ORGANIZATIONS *Cobra:* The goodies captured in Cobra Commander's stockpile includes the Mona Lisa.

THE COMMAND DECISION We'd bet hard money that if long-past G.I. Joe viewers remember any episode from their childhood, it's probably "that one where the Dreadnoks dress up as rock stars." Mercifully, it's also a great story, pushing forth a completely ridiculous premise with near-perfect implementation. If there's a fault, it's that the final scene with the Joes singing nearly slit our collective jugular, but otherwise, it's completely mad – and we love it.

MISCELLANEOUS STUFF!

ONCE UPON A DREADNOK

Whereas most of the *G.I. Joe* action figure filecards stubbornly list "classified" when referring to the real names of the Cobra elite, the personnel profiles of the Dreadnoks rather conspicuously disclose their true identities. But frivolous we might think the *G.I. Joe* writers at times, that's hardly an accident. Believe it or not, the names of the three original Dreadnoks: Tom *Winken* (Torch), Dick *Blinken* (Buzzer), and Harry *Nod* (Ripper) stem from – drum roll, please – Mother Goose.

Don't believe us? The *Oxford Book of Children's Verse* notes the following kids' rhyme:

Winken, Blinken, and Nod one night
Sailed off in a wooden shoe --
Sailed off on a river of crystal light,
Into a sea of dew.

... and so forth. As if that weren't enough, the cheeky *G.I. Joe* creators continued the nursery-rhyme trend with Bill Winkie (a.k.a. Monkeywrench), evocative of "Wee Willie Winkie," a character purported by Mother Goose to: "... Run through the town, upstairs and downstairs, in his nightgown." Granted, it's hard to imagine one of the Dreadnoks dashing about in a *nightgown*, but it's an interesting jape nonetheless.

1.52: "The Great Alaskan Land Rush"

US Transmission Date: *Dec. 3, 1985*
Writer: *David Carren*

BATTLE ROSTER *Joes:* Duke, Scarlett, Gung Ho, Roadblock; *Cobra:* Tomax and Xamot, the Baroness; *Other:* The Oktober Guard.

MISSION BRIEF Instigating the real estate swindle of the century, Cobra loots the U.S. Archives and locates a long-forgotten record named "The Seward File." The Crimson Twins pore over the document, scrutinizing the purchase of Alaska as negotiated by Secretary of State William H. Seward in 1867. To the brothers' glee, Russia's sale of Alaska entailed the transfer of the Great Seal of Alaska – a relic allegedly lost in the Arctic aboard the Russian warship Romanov. Under the Seward File's provisions, however, anyone possessing the Great Seal technically owns Alaska.

Accordingly, Cobra strikes up a partnership with Sergei Potemkin, a New Jersey car salesman who claims that his family fled with the Great Seal in 1917. Aided by Potemkin's Great Seal, Cobra brings its legal might to bear and forces the courts to hand Potemkin ownership of Alaska. Figuring Potemkin almost certainly owns a counterfeit seal, Duke rallies his Joes to find the real artifact and thwart Cobra's land game.

As Duke's Joes set out for the *Romanov*'s last known location, the Soviet Union – lusting to draw Alaska back to the Russian fold – sends its Oktober Guard commandos to hunt for the Great Seal. But in the Arctic, the Joes and Russians turn startled when warriors dressed as 19th century Cossacks take them all prisoner.

The Cossacks march their captives to an isolated port city near the *Romanov*'s dock. Captain Lukrov, the Cossacks' leader, explains that the *Romanov*'s crew found a safe harbor in 1867, established an isolated settlement and abandoned the outside world. While Duke and the Russians fail to sweet-talk the Great Seal away from Lukrov, a Cobra tank squadron – having learned of the Joe/Russian missions – suddenly blitzes the Cossack city, bagging the Great Seal. Duke and Oktober Guard leader Colonel Brekhov agree to join forces and rescue the Great Seal, promising to return it to Lukrov after debunking Cobra's claims. Left with little choice, Lukrov agrees.

Lukrov's Arctic sleds let the Joe/Russian task force slip ahead of the Cobra tank column, lay an ambush and steal back the Great Seal. As expected, the Oktober Guard try to double-cross the Joes, but Duke's group gains the upper hand, obtaining Lukrov's permission to depart in the *Romanov*. Arriving in Juneau, the Joes undercut Potemkin's claim to Alaska, forcing Cobra to abandon the hapless car salesmen to his own devices.

MEMORABLE MOMENTS A regrettably timed Cobra assault forces the Joes to end a poker game – just as Gung Ho draws four aces. Having called the Oktober Guard's double-cross, Duke approaches Colonel Brekhov and icily asks for: "The Seal… comrade."

ASS-WHUPPINGS A Russian helicopter strike buries a bunch of Joe sleds in rubble. Scarlett and Daina double-team the Baroness, body-tackling her to nab the Great Seal.

GOOFS The Crimson Twins crash into the Alaskan governor's spartan office (which is only slightly more elaborate than a janitor's hovel), when walking through the door would've sufficed.

Even allowing for the Seward File's provisions, the American government surely wouldn't surrender Alaska to a whacked, plaid-wearing car salesman bearing "the Great Seal," a diamond-covered bell that could probably serve as a spittoon.

Generic Joe soldiers accompanying Duke's team to the Arctic disappear and reappear without warning.

The supposedly "separatist" Cossack colony possesses modern-day laser rifles. For that matter, it's never established just *why* the *Romanov* crew abandoned the outside world. Certainly, an ice blockade hemmed in the *Romanov*, but it's a startlingly *little* ice blockade, considering one shot from a HISS tank does it in.

Finally – and this is *really* weird – an Arctic plain seems to be dotted with lava vents.

TV TIE-INS The Oktober Guard previously appeared in "The Invaders." They join forces with the Joes in "Arise! Serpentor! Arise!" to defend Ivan the Terrible's tomb.

CHARACTER PROFILE: JOES Scarlett: She can fly the occasional Russian helicopter.

CHARACTER PROFILE: OTHER

Sergei Potemkin: Ends this story forever bankrupt, having ordered an incessant amount of caviar, diamond rings and even a *platinum bathtub* during his time as "owner" of Alaska.

ORGANIZATIONS *Oktober Guard:* Also refer to themselves as "Red Oktober."

STUFF YOU NEED *The Seward File:* Contains the terms behind Secretary of State William H. Seward's purchase of Alaska (on behalf of America) from Russia in 1867. Seward arranged to only pay 7 cents an acre, but to make the deal official, the Russians needed to send over the Great Seal of Alaska – a diamond studded, gold-plated bell-shaped thing. The Russian czar gave the Great Seal to Captain Ivan Lukrov of the Russian warship Romanov and sent him to America, but the vessel went missing in the Arctic. Presumably, the seal's loss wasn't enough to void the Alaskan land deal. The estimated value of Alaska (in the mid-1980s): one trillion dollars.

PLACES TO GO *The Cossack City:* Essentially a town out of time, still giving allegiance to the long-dead Czar Alexander II. Leadership's apparently hereditary, with the great-great grandson of Captain Lukrov serving as the head of state.

THE COMMAND DECISION One of those eyebrow-raising tales that catches you up in the moment, then topples like a string of dominoes once you apply a drop of analysis. Unfortunately, the overall tapestry – while questionable enough – gets overly tainted by some scenes ("Honest Sergei's" used-car style political broadcasts, etc.) that effectively put you on the rack and stretch your spine.

1.53: "Skeletons in the Closet"

***US Transmission Date:** Dec. 11, 1985*
***Writer:** Flint Dille*

BATTLE ROSTER *Joes:* Lady Jaye, Flint, Spirit, Snake-Eyes, Barbecue; *Cobra:* Destro, the Baroness, Firefly.

MISSION BRIEF When Destro gets overly flirtatious with a sexy female Cobra agent – who isn't the Baroness – the Baroness bristles over Destro's infidelity. Seething for revenge, the hot-tempered Baroness manipulates events to crush Destro's most prized possession: his family homestead in Scotland.

With the Destro family's annual gathering drawing nigh, the

1.53, Skeletons in the Closet

Baroness researches Destro's lineage and learns – to her pleasant surprise – that Destro and Lady Jaye are distant cousins. The Baroness secretly sends Lady Jaye a letter via a Scottish solicitor, informing the Joe that she's just inherited a place called "Doyle Manor" in Scotland and should travel there to claim her property. Lady Jaye elatedly sets out for the Scottish manor – setting her up, as the Baroness intended, for an inevitable clash with Destro.

In Scotland, Lady Jaye acclimates to the gloomy, torture-themed manor house, even as Destro's family starts gathering in the edifice's lower levels. To add to the creepiness, the Baroness projects ghostly holograms – whetting Lady Jaye's curiosity and baiting her to investigate the castle's underworkings. Minutes later, Lady Jaye's face drains of blood upon seeing Destro's relatives – all wearing animal-themed or metallic masks – conducting a pagan ritual for an ancient horror that resides underneath the castle.

Lady Jaye draws closer and observes the family members worshipping a monstrous octopid creature wallowing in a well of blood. Destro arrives soon after, but his kin capture Lady Jaye, preparing to sacrifice her to the abomination. Thankfully, Flint becomes suspicious about Lady Jaye's sudden "inheritance," traveling to Scotland and arriving just in time to haul his lover to safety.

Completely outnumbered, Flint summons a strike team from the *USS Flagg* to clash with Destro's contingent of Cobra soldiers. As the battle rolls through Destro's family homestead, Barbecue comes upon a modern-day control center and redirects the castle's holograms to scare the Cobra troops witless. The Cobras withdraw – with the Joes quickly following – but lingering fires from the battle burn the manor house to the ground.

Destro's family goes their separate ways, leaving an anguished Destro to pine for the loss of his homestead. Soon after, the Baroness reveals her role in bringing the manor to ruin, berating Destro for his unfaithfulness. In response, Destro ominously warns that in destroying the manor house, the Baroness may have unleashed forces beyond her comprehension. And in the ruins' lower levels, the abhorrent octopus – a supernatural remnant of a bygone era – starts salivating for human flesh.

MEMORABLE MOMENTS Destro auctions second-hand Cobra equipment to a bunch of foreign dignitaries, but the vehicles hysterically keep falling to pieces behind him. Flint spars with the Destro manor's fat housemaid (actually the Baroness in disguise) giving us the bizarre sight of a blubbery aproned woman performing a number of acrobatic stunts.

The first sight of Destro's family, all of 'em wearing animal heads, chills the blood, and it gets no better when the clan dangles a nightgown-clad Lady Jaye over the monstrous octopus' well. Oh, and it's completely over the top, but during the firefight, a crazed Firefly grabs Barbecue and screams a formidable battle cry of: "*Die,* fireman!"

MISCELLANEOUS STUFF!

HEARTS AND FLOWERS

Although made for younger viewers, the *G.I. Joe* cartoon occasionally endowed the Joe and Cobra agents with libidos. Here's a run-down of the more notable romances:

- **Duke/Scarlett –** Often a source of confusion, given the ongoing tryst between Scarlett and Snake-Eyes that runs steadfastly through the *G.I. Joe* comics. But on TV, Duke and Scarlett quietly romanced each other, as witnessed by "The M.A.S.S. Device," "Cobra Stops the World," *G.I. Joe: The Movie* and more. Granted, we can understand the need to make the Joe team leader seem more manly – and a romance with the mute Snake-Eyes probably wouldn't play very well on-screen – but the Duke/Scarlett pairing seemed so subtle at points, it's easily forgotten at times.
- **Flint/Lady Jaye –** About as genuine a relationship as one might hope for. Unlike Duke and Scarlett, Flint and Lady Jaye spent a great deal of time together, leading to heart-wrenching episodes such as "The Funhouse," "The Gamesmaster," "Not a Ghost of a Chance," etc.
- **Destro/the Baroness –** The only inter-Cobra lovefest worth mentioning, although it's certainly not without its difficulties ("Skeletons in the Closet," etc.). As Destro noted in "Last Hour to Doomsday," their relationship often worked better when they didn't get *too* cozy, but it nonetheless sparked memorable escapades such as "Spell of the Siren" and "Eau de Cobra."
- **Zarana/Mainframe –** A completely oddball pairing, although strong enough for Zarana to aid Mainframe in both "Computer Complications" and "Gray Hairs and Growing Pains." All in all, it's a love affair that makes you believe there's someone for everyone.
- **Shipwreck/Mara –** Ah, yes. The somewhat doomed affair between Shipwreck and Mara, an ex-Cobra agent who got turned into a blue-skinned water breather ("Memories of Mara"). Still, it supplied fodder for a massive Cobra deception in "There's No Place Like Springfield," leaving Shipwreck to bemoan the loss of his seemingly suburban life.

LOVE AND WAR Destro claims he wants to retire to a remote island with the Baroness, but he's been getting cozy with a blonde female Cobra operative on the side. If we had to guess, Destro's not doing the nasty with the blonde chick, but the Baroness has grounds for concern.

Just to get Destro's goat, the Baroness disguises herself as a fabled secret agent named "Coverta Fatale" and saves Destro from a near-scrape with the Joes. Over dinner with "Coverta," Destro unwisely describes the Baroness as "a confused creature with whom I have been erroneously linked." Destro probably doesn't get physical with "Coverta" either, but the encounter gives the Baroness plenty of ammunition to hurl in Destro's face later on. By story's end, the Baroness isn't Destro's favorite person, but he doesn't begrudge her for wanting retribution.

Lady Jaye wanders about the manor house in her sexy nightgown a *lot*. A secret admirer sends Roadblock a Chanel No.5-soaked love letter.

ASS-WHUPPINGS A nightie-clad Lady Jaye kicks several of Destro's relatives about the place. Flint follows suit, finally picking Lady Jaye up and racing for cover. Joe and Cobra teams outside the manor house tear into each other, with a missile strike inadvertently annihilating a homegrown giant mutant spider in the building's lower levels.

PREPOSTEROUS PHYSICS The Baroness masquerades as the manor's extremely plump, rotund housekeeper, forcing us to wonder again how the Baroness adds body mass to perpetrate her disguises. Destro assaults Flint and Lady Jaye with heat-seeking wrist rockets calibrated to 98.6 degrees – which you'd think would shred his similarly heated family members.

GOOFS Alpine's worked with Lady Jaye for at least a year now but doesn't know her real name. Destro brings Cobra troopers and Firefly to his family gathering – an event you'd think he'd want kept secret.

TV TIE-INS Cobra Commander attempts to awaken the octopoid abomination beneath the ruins of Destro's homestead in "Sins of the Father."

CHARACTER PROFILE: JOES

- *Gung Ho:* He has overdue car payments. Roadblock comments, during a frantic sewer chase, that their surroundings remind him of Gung Ho's apartment, except that "there's no TV."
- *Lady Jaye:* On road trips, she keeps her javelins in a golf club bag.

CHARACTER PROFILE: COBRA *Destro:* He doesn't believe in luck, only destiny.

ORGANIZATIONS *The Destro Family:* Centuries ago, one of Destro's ancestors was convicted of witchcraft, sentenced to wear a face mask for life. In the generations to follow, the affronted man's descendants vowed to forever fight law and order, donning distorted animal and metallic masks until, as Destro puts it, "Law is sacrificed upon the altar of history." Today, the individual Destro members carry out their own agendas, gathering on the longest night of the year (the winter solstice, December 21) to renew their vows and feed the horror underneath their family grounds.

PLACES TO GO *Destro's Homestead:* Although the Baroness almost certainly makes up the name "Doyle Manor," the house has stood in some fashion for 1,000 years. One painting in the manor house looks like Destro (presumably an ancestor), while another looks like Lady Jaye.

THE COMMAND DECISION An unbelievable tour de force for G.I. Joe "Skeletons in the Closet" smacked us in the chest with a gold brick, shedding the series' kiddie veneer and upending its foundation with a well-tempered trowel. Like most good drama, Destro suffers because of a personal failing (his fooling around on the Baroness), making his personal trauma alone worth the price of admission. Best of all, the chilling finale with the ravenous octopus-thing – which made our hair stand on end as kids – hasn't lost its punch after 17 years.

1.54-1.55: "There's No Place Like Springfield"

Episodes: *Two*
US Transmission Date: *Dec. 12-13, 1985*
Writer: *Steve Gerber*

BATTLE ROSTER *Joes:* Shipwreck, Lady Jaye; *Cobra:* Cobra Commander, Tomax and Xamot, Destro, the Baroness.

MISSION BRIEF When a chemist named Professor Molaney develops a formula that's capable of instantly converting ordinary water into a highly explosive substance, Cobra scientists at the ultra-secret "Temple Alpha" attempt to duplicate Molaney's work. But upon failing to identify one of the formula's crucial ingredients, Cobra researchers decide to simply kidnap Molaney instead. The hotly pursued chemist desperately seeks protection from the Joes, who schedule a pick-up rendezvous on a secluded island. Soon after, Lady

Jaye, Shipwreck and parrot Polly set out for the island, finding the half-starved Molaney and briefly resting around a campfire.

Wanting the Joes to have access to his water-exploding formula in case he kicks it, Molaney uses a neural link device to electro-chemically encode the formula directly into Shipwreck's brain. With Shipwreck unable to recall the data at will, Molaney tells Lady Jaye and Polly a secret code-phrase, designed to unlock Shipwreck's mental block in case of emergency.

As the trio prepares to depart, Cobra rolls forward a massive aerial assault. Shipwreck's team gets separated from Molaney during a heavy missile barrage, but they pile into their amphibious SHARC vehicle and make for the *USS Flagg*. Lady Jaye and Polly scramble to safety aboard the *Flagg*, but a secondary Cobra offensive plunges the SHARC underwater – with Shipwreck still aboard. With the distracted Joes defending the *Flagg*, Shipwreck falls unconscious as his vessel fills with water.

In the midst of the battle, Cobra scuba divers pull Shipwreck from the SHARC, taking him back to "Temple Alpha" – which masquerades as an island city named "Springfield" – for interrogation. Debating the best way to extract Molaney's formula from Shipwreck's head, the Cobra officers concoct an elaborate scheme designed to crack the Joe sailor like an egg.

Working quickly, Cobra constructs artificial synthoids that perfectly resemble Shipwreck's associates, then populates Springfield with the duplicates. Cobra programs the synthoids to convince Shipwreck that six years have passed since the *Flagg* attack. Accordingly, Shipwreck "awakens" in Lincoln Medical Center – only to be told that he "fell from his roof while installing a satellite dish" and developed selective amnesia as a result. Shipwreck's told that six years ago, the *Flagg* sank, but that the Joes later used Molaney's formula to wipe out Cobra for good. Shipwreck also learns that in the interim, he married his lost love Mara ("Memories of Mara") and sired a daughter named Althea.

Reeling, Shipwreck returns home with his "wife" and "daughter" to rest. Over the next few days, various Cobra agents drug Shipwreck's food and entrance him with mesmeric lights, trying to whittle down his mental defenses. Shipwreck becomes increasingly delusional, screaming in terror when former teammates – actually synthoids crafted to look like Flint, Scarlett, Torpedo and Deep Six – turn on him. Shipwreck fends off his "friends," turning horrified as each of them melts into puddles of synthetic goo.

With Shipwreck increasingly delusional, the Cobra officers put the sailor through a gauntlet of drug and hypnosis-induced questioning, threatening to destroy his "happy home" if he doesn't reveal Molaney's formula. Luckily, Shipwreck awakens after one such session and splashes water on his face – then turns puzzled when gray-colored dye (designed to make Shipwreck's facial hair look older) washes into his hands. Just then, the real Polly – who's been tirelessly scouting the islands for his master – arrives on the scene.

Seeing through Cobra's ruse, Shipwreck and Polly sneak into Springfield's top-secret research laboratories. Polly utters the secret code-phrase ("frogs in winter"), allowing Shipwreck to recite Molaney's formula. Cobra Commander, Destro and the Dreadnoks surround Shipwreck, but the Joe sailor hurriedly whips up a batch of Molaney's water-detonating formula and dumps it down a sink. Destro scoffs – explaining that the formula requires a trigger explosion to activate – but the buffonish Dreadnoks open fire. As Shipwreck and Polly dive aside, the Dreadnoks' laser bolts nail the sink and spark the water-detonating formula.

Instantly, Springfield's sewer system erupts in explosions, decimating every single building. Zeroing on the fireballs, Joes aboard the *Flagg* dispatch Skystrikers to overrun the Cobra hideout. While the Cobra leaders escape, Shipwreck turns back to his "home" to rescue Mara and Althea, failing to accept their existence as synthoids. Programmed to serve Cobra to the end, the false Mara and Althea take aim at Shipwreck with rifles. But mercifully, Polly uses a swiped Springfield gadget – preset by Cobra to neutralize its synthoids – to turn Mara and Althea into puddles of goo. Despairing over the loss of his "family," Shipwreck turns numb as the Joes shut down Springfield.

MEMORABLE MOMENTS Lady Jaye worries about Molaney zapping the water-detonating formula into Shipwreck's cranium, incredulously asking: "You put the formula in there?" In response, Shipwreck cries out: "Hey! It ain't like he flushed it down the sewer!"

The Springfield adventure includes the synthetic Joes melting before our eyes. "Roadblock" drives through a car wash, tells Shipwreck, "Sure was toasty… " – and melts. Soon after, Shipwreck finds himself attacked by Flint, Deep Six and Torpedo, who similarly dissolve into slime. Toward the finale, Shipwreck snags "Scarlett," begging her to not fight him, then wailing: "Scarlett! Don't go!" when she devolves into Jell-O.

Surreal *G.I. Joe* scene No. 239 shows a synthoid parrot Polly reporting to Cobra Commander. In one of the Springfield labs, the Dreadnoks play with the synthoids via remote control, using joysticks to make the little fake doughboys punch each other.

Best of all, Shipwreck crumples upon realizing that his "wife and daughter" were nothing more than synthoids. As Shipwreck stares at his burning home, Lady Jaye asks, "Was there something important in that house?" Unable to articulate his anguish, Shipwreck ends the episode by sadly replying, "Nah, nothing important," then walking away.

LOVE AND WAR Shipwreck never thought of himself as a suburban homemaker, but adapts to life with "Mara" pretty quickly. They share a bed, but probably don't get much nookie, considering the continual stress of Shipwreck's interrogation routine.

There's an *extremely* naughty conversation – if taken out of context – between a female Cobra interrogator named Demming and a synthoid of Joe medic Doc. Questioning Demming about her experience with a hallucinogenic interrogation chamber, Doc asks, "Your first time?" Demming: "I've run the simulator." Doc: "The real thing is considerably more demanding… "

The scene gets even *more* risqué when the sexy Demming straps the drug-addled Shipwreck to a table, barrages him with disco lights and straddles him while shouting questions. Indeed, the interrogation chamber gets so thick with whirling lights and sexual tension, both Shipwreck *and* Demming pass out. (*Author's Note:* If this technique had appeared on *The Prisoner,* No. 6 would surely have spilled the beans.)

Polly recalls a "night in Anapolis" when Shipwreck hugely embarrassed himself – presumably either with booze or women.

In Springfield's made-up "future," Duke and Scarlett got married. Since Lady Jaye supposedly died during the *Flagg* attack, "Flint" got engaged to an unspecified hot babe years later.

Cobra manufactures its synthoids from a material called "sudo-gasm," which sounds like something that'd make your mother blush.

ASS-WHUPPINGS Cobra RATTLERS pound the Flagg, annihilating an on-deck Skystriker squadron.

During Shipwreck's time in Springfield, Cobra operatives effectively remove his brains and back over them with a John Deere tractor. Shipwreck's made to think he's lost six years of his life, endures several drugged drinks, mind-numbing lights and spectral dreams of the Cobra officers haranguing him. Oh, and he's made to watch as several of his friends inexplicably melt into ooze.

Tomax and Xamot liquefy the synthoid Doc for questioning their orders. Cobra inquisitor Demming pushes an interrogation chamber's illusions too far, making herself pass out. Shipwreck dopes up a "hospital nurse" with drugged milk. Polly dissolves the fake Mara and Althea, plus a doppelganger of himself, with a synthoid "off" device.

PREPOSTEROUS PHYSICS Molaney claims that his formula makes water explosive by "weakening its oxygen-hydrogen bonds." Of course, if that were true, salting the driveway would smear you all over the garage.

GOOFS A recap at the start of Part 2 includes scenes that aren't in Part 1. While talking with the Crimson Twins, Cobra Commander spontaneously shifts between his casual hood and battle helmet. Where did Polly find the mind-bogglingly useful device that melts synthoids? An unconscious nurse's hair turns from black to blonde.

The name "Springfield" is variously shown as "Springfield" and "Spring Field." While evading some pursuers, Shipwreck and Polly run into a room that conveniently contains Cobra's notes on Molaney's formula – lying in the open by the sink – and all the necessary ingredients to make a batch. (All that's lacking is a cardboard sign proclaiming: "Mix water-exploding compound here.")

TV TIE-INS Shipwreck fell for Mara, an ex-Cobra agent turned amphibian, in "Memories of Mara." Cobra perfected its synthoid technology in "The Synthoid Conspiracy." They probably gleaned a wealth of information about Shipwreck's personal life from his military dossier, stolen by Storm Shadow in "Captives of Cobra."

An "Uncle Al" is touted as Shipwreck's only family, although "Captives of Cobra" also mentions an unnamed aunt and nephew Jesse. The haggard, half-dead Professor Molaney later recuperates, developing a nitrogen fuel formula that *again* gets him pursued by Cobra in "Joe's Night Out."

In Springfield, Shipwreck resides on 6 Village Drive, a reference to the 1960's TV series *The Prisoner* (wherein a secret agent is transported to a place called "The Village," renamed "No. 6," and subjected to various surreal interrogation techniques).

CHARACTER PROFILE: JOES

• *Lady Jaye:* Sometimes carries a crossbow as well as her usual javelin quiver.

• *Shipwreck:* Shipwreck grew up in Tuna Vista, CA, near the San Diego navy line. Inspired to become a sailor, he lied about his age and joined the Navy at 16. He traveled the world during his military service, encountering river pirates in Southeast Asia and smugglers off the Florida coast. Although usually on the side of angels, Shipwreck seemingly indulged in his own smuggling operations, departing the Navy and working as a freelancer until his first meeting with the Joes ("The Revenge of Cobra").

In the Springfield "future," an older Shipwreck supposedly runs "Marina del Shipwreck" – a dock and boat sales business – with ex-teammates Torpedo and Deep Six.

STUFF YOU NEED Professor Molaney's Water-Exploding Formula: Cobra scientists neatly duplicate Molaney's invention, although they fail to identify the crucial ingredient thulium isotope 185.

• *Synthoids:* Cobra's advanced its synthoid technology to the point that melted synthoids often get reconstituted into new models.

THE COMMAND DECISION A well-constructed framework that's marbled with scintillating detail, owes obvious influences to Patrick McGoohan's The Prisoner – and left us riveted in our seats. Part 1 in particular drags Shipwreck backward through a hedge like few other G.I. Joe stories (the anguished, unglued Joe cries out "Who's doing this to me?! What do you want?!"), leading to a heart-wrenching conclusion. Intoxicating.

2.1-2.5: "Arise, Serpentor, Arise!"

Episodes: *Five*
US Transmission Date: *Sept. 15-19, 1986*
Story: *Buzz Dixon*
Teleplay: *Ron Friedman*

BATTLE ROSTER *Joes:* Duke, Flint, Roadblock, Dusty, Recondo, Mutt and Junkyard, Shipwreck, Torpedo, Deep Six; *Cobra:* Cobra Commander, Tomax and Xamot, Scrap Iron, Zartan and the Dreadnoks.

FIRST APPEARANCES *Joes:* General Hawk (G.I. Joe commander), Sgt. Slaughter (drill instructor), Beach-Head (ranger), Lifeline (rescue trooper), Wet-Suit (SEAL), Leatherneck (marine), Sci-Fi (laser trooper), Low-Light (night spotter), Cross-Country (HAVOC driver), Lift-Ticket (Tomahawk pilot), Dial-Tone (communications), Slip-Stream (Conquest X-30 pilot), Mainframe (computer specialist), Iceberg (snow trooper); *Cobra:* Serpentor (Cobra Emperor), Dr. Mindbender (master of mind control), Zarana (Zartan's sister), Zandar (Zartan's brother), Monkeywrench (Dreadnok), Thrasher (Thunder Machine driver).

MISSION BRIEF ***Part 1:*** When Cobra Commander bungles yet another assault on Joe Headquarters, the Cobra officers begin to grow weary of their commander's continually inept performance. Simultaneously, top Cobra scientist Dr. Mindbender starts dreaming about the DNA helix, leading him to a sudden epiphany about new cloning techniques. Empowered by his findings, Mindbender secretly meets with Destro and the Crimson Twins, radically suggesting that they genetically create a new leader to lead Cobra to glory.

Confronted with raised eyebrows, Mindbender proposes raiding the tombs of history's greatest military leaders – masters of warfare such as Genghis Kahn, Napoleon, Ivan the Terrible, etc. – to acquire samples of the dead warlords' DNA. Mindbender then plans to combine the deceased rulers' genetic make-ups into a cloned human: a Cobra Emperor endowed with his sires' attributes.

Upon learning of Mindbender's designs, Cobra Commander attempts to arrest his disloyal subordinates, then gets a sinking feeling when the Crimson Guardsmen side with the Cobra officers. Under immanent threat of getting flushed as Cobra leader, Cobra Commander reluctantly authorizes Mindbender's endeavor – planning to either humiliate Mindbender if he fails or bend the newborn Cobra Emperor to his will.

Still wary of Cobra Commander's motives, Mindbender and his allies prepare to plunder famous tombs around the world. Mindbender radios Zartan to call in his siblings Zarana and Zandar as backup, motivating Zartan to hold open auditions for Dreadnok membership. Amid this flurry of heightened Cobra activity, top Joe commander General Hawk sends out Low-Light, Beach-Head and a drill sergeant named Sgt. Slaughter to infiltrate Zartan's camp.

In the Louisiana bayou, Sgt. Slaughter's trio watches as Zartan accepts an explosives expert named Monkeywrench into the Dreadnok fold. Springing into action, Sgt. Slaughter's trio surrounds Zartan's family and swipes a Cobra communiqué that lists several grave sites targeted for Cobra attack. Just as Sgt. Slaughter ponders breaking the Dreadnoks' noses for more information, a Dreadnok wannabe named Thrasher drives up in his Thunder Machine assault vehicle. Completely outgunned, Sgt. Slaughter's gang retreats into a nearby shack – sweating bullets as the unstoppable Thunder Machine bears down on them.

Parts 2-3: With seconds to spare, Sgt. Slaughter punches an escape route through the shack's back wall. The three Joes scurry to safety – just as the Thunder Machine collapses the entire building. Thinking Sgt. Slaughter's group pancaked beneath the rubble, Zartan and his Dreadnoks put themselves at Cobra's disposal. Meanwhile, Sgt. Slaughter's band returns to base with the list of Cobra's intended targets.

Confused over Cobra's new fixation with digging up corpses, Hawk nonetheless dispatches Joe teams around the globe to defend the various graves. Cobra agents repeatedly pummel the Joes, unearthing the military leaders' skeletons and using DNA extractors to digitize each man's genetic code. In Egypt, Zarana outwits a group of desert-trained Joes, fleeing with the ancient General Xanuth Amon-Toth's DNA signature. In Paris, the conniving Crimson Twins obtain Napoleon's genetic structure. Deep in the Yucatan jungle, Zartan and the Dreadnoks locate the dreaded Aztec leader Montezuma's corpse. Although the Joes give their best effort, Cobra successfully steals genetic samples from Ivan the Terrible, Vlad Tepes (a.k.a. Dracula), Alexander the Great and more.

Finally, Hawk concentrates his forces to protect the final two corpses on Cobra's list: the Chinese strategist Sun Tzu (best known for his treatise *The Art of War*) and Mongol warlord Genghis Khan. At the head of the Yang-Tse River, Dr. Mindbender and the Crimson Twins successfully reach Sun Tzu's burial mound, but Sgt. Slaughter muscles his way forward and destroys Mindbender's DNA extractor – keeping Sun Tzu's genetic code out of Cobra's hands.

The twins bemoan their failure, but Dr. Mindbender suggests they replace Sun Tzu's genetic make-up with DNA from the greatest soldier of the modern age: Sgt. Slaughter. Simultaneously, Joe medics Lifeline and Doc examine the damaged DNA extractor captured at Sun Tzu's burial mound, concluding that Cobra's embarked on a cloning operation.

With the Joes entrenched around Khan's mausoleum, an giant Cobra aircraft makes an attack run and pretends to take heavy damage. Thinking it's about to crash, the Joes hurriedly evacuate the imminent impact site – then look back as the faking Cobra ship snares Khan's sarcophagus with a giant gripper. Pulling an about-face, Sgt. Slaughter struggles to unlock the robot arm from Khan's sarcophagus, but the Cobra airship hauls *both* Khan's remains and the sergeant into its hanger bay. As an unstoppable horde of Battle Android Troopers (BATs) bring down Sgt. Slaughter, the Cobra vessel makes its getaway.

Part 4: At home on the sovereign nation of Cobra Island, Dr. Mindbender readies the final stage of his experiment. Implanting the DNA samples – including Sgt. Slaughter's – into a series of chemical vats, Dr. Mindbender prepares to infuse a lump of protoplasm with the genetic codes. Cobra Commander initially thwarts Dr. Mindbender's efforts by tainting one of the scientist's vats with a mutagen compound and turning the protoplasm into a raving monstrosity. Fortunately, the unstable abomination devolves back into goo, enabling Mindbender to learn of Cobra Commander's tinkering and start over.

Sick to death of fighting a defensive war, Hawk orders Beach-Head and a team of volunteers to hit the main Terror-Drome defense complex on Cobra Island. Beach-Head's team arrives on the isle, hoping to rescue Sgt. Slaughter and blow Cobra's cloning experiments wide open, but a shoot-out with the Dreadnoks wrecks the Joes' Tomahawk helicopter. Grounded, Beach-Head's team makes their way toward the main Terror-Drome.

In the Terror-Drome's main laboratory, Dr. Mindbender braces for his second attempt and throws his cloning machinery into high gear. As the warlords' DNA sequences surge into Mindbender's protoplasm, a half-mad Cobra Commander – desperate to stop the Cobra Emperor's birth – offers Sgt. Slaughter a short-term alliance. Out of options, Sgt. Slaughter agrees to thrash Mindbender's gang within an inch of their lives on Cobra Commander's behalf.

While Mindbender and his associates monitor the experiment, Cobra Commander frees Sgt. Slaughter. Swiftly, the Joe drill master smashes the genetic vat containing his DNA, depriving the Cobra Emperor blob of Slaughter's attributes. Sgt. Slaughter threshes Mindbender's companions like wheat and hauls Mindbender up by the scruff of his cape – then pauses as the ground trembles with a small earthquake. In keeping with the melodrama, the Cobra Emperor chooses to sit up at that very moment on the operating table – declaring himself "Serpentor."

Part 5: Cobra Commander immediately tries to bully Serpentor into serving him, but the new Cobra Emperor tosses the commander aside. Flush with newborn strength, Serpentor brawls with Sgt. Slaughter throughout the Cobra base. Beach-Head's Joes surge forward in the resultant mayhem, shooting up the Cobra command center and escaping with the sergeant.

Newly entrenched at Cobra's head, the over-confident Serpentor – lacking Sun Tzu's famed patience – orders an all-out invasion of America. The Crimson Twins plead for temperance, but Serpentor marshals his air, sea and ground forces to overrun Washington, D.C. As the Joes attempt to devise a means of dealing with the fledgling Cobra Emperor, Serpentor calls for America's total surrender.

Serpentor turns giddy when the president, vice-president and Congressmen agree to formally capitulate at the Washington Monument. But at the designated rendezvous, the "politicians" unmask themselves as Joe members and instigate a firefight. Swiftly learning that taking over the world requires long-term planning, Serpentor and his troops fall into complete disarray. The Cobra leaders escape, taking Cobra Commander along as a scapegoat and leaving the Joes to savor their victory in the name of freedom.

MEMORABLE MOMENTS Zartan establishes the rules of the Dreadnok "auditions" – essentially, beat each other silly – then crows out: "Start auditioning!" (Fight Club has nothing on this!) There's a juicy moment when Cobra Commander orders Dr. Mindbender's arrest and Destro wryly observes: "Everyone heard you, Cobra Commander, but nobody cares to obey..." – showing how far Cobra Commander's tumbled from power.

In Part 4, a string of Crimson Guardsmen emit lovely screams as a slobbering reptilian monstrosity – Mindbender's initial failed attempt to clone Serpentor – pitches them down a stairwell like flour bags. Beach-Head asks naïve pacifist Lifeline to approach a Cobra platoon and ask for a phone – using the distraction to punch the Cobra guards unconscious. In a rare moment of seriousness, a tied-up Cobra Commander tells Serpentor that he can't capture America in one fell swoop, desperately stressing: "I know... I've tried!"

LOVE AND WAR Shipwreck writes to a woman named Sally that she's wounding his heart. In Part 3, Shipwreck and other Joes get distracted watching some water-skiing chicks – brilliant decoys for Destro's impending offensive.

Finally, there's an extremely kinky scene in which the Crimson Twins each grab one of Sgt. Slaughter's wrists, drop the sergeant to his knees and kick his ribs while chanting: "You've been a *naughty* boy, Sgt. Slaughter!"

ASS-WHUPPINGS Foiling Cobra Commander's initial assault on Joe Headquarters, Sgt. Slaughter takes down an entire row of Battle Android Troopers (BATs), then grabs one of the faceless robots and beats its fellows with it. Later, Sgt. Slaughter "trains" some Joes by urging them to tackle him – whupping the trainees despite 6-to-1 odds.

When the Baroness collapses the castle of Vlad Tepes (a.k.a. Dracula), Mainframe and Beach-Head take shelter in Tepes' coffin. The Joes dig them out, but Mainframe despairs over spending 18 hours cooped up with a deodorant-less Beach-Head.

At Sun Tzu's burial mound, Sgt. Slaughter twirls Xamot, making his brother Tomax spin like a top. The battle for Genghis Khan's corpse results in 12 percent Joe casualties – none fatal, of course – and a 40 percent loss of Joe vehicles.

Dr. Mindbender's initial attempt to birth Serpentor results in a mindless reptilian hulk that tears through his lab. Sgt. Slaughter pummels the unstable monstrosity into submission, returning it to the goopy slime from whence it came.

On Cobra Island, Beach-Head's team crushes a number of Dreadnok swamp choppers but loses their Tomahawk helicopter in the process. Later, Beach-Head's team thumps the Dreadnoks within an inch of their lives. Beach-Head rolls during a firefight, scooping up a convenient bazooka that's just lying about and pasting an entire row of BATs.

During Serpentor's birth, Sgt. Slaughter head-butts Scrap Iron, smashes the Crimson Twins' faces together and dents Destro's scalp against a console. Serpentor and Sgt. Slaughter thrash each other like WWF wrestlers, but the duel mostly ends in a draw.

SAVE THEM! Several civilian workers safely jump off a burning oil tanker – when you'd think the ever-spreading oil fire would've toasted them. Thrasher and Zarana blow apart a dam, deluging Dusty's Joes with enough water to drown 'em several times over – but they all survive. (Indeed, the Joes' vehicles bob about like rubber duckies.)

PREPOSTEROUS PHYSICS Sgt. Slaughter escapes the Dreadnok swamp hideout by punching a hole through a stone wall. (Good grief, he's not the Hulk.)

In the Yucatan, Zartan gets the drop on Recondo at point-blank range. But in the next scene, when Zartan trips, his gun instantly discharges – so why wasn't Recondo ventilated? When the Joes jump into a pool for cover, Zartan decides to superheat the water with laser bolts – a dubious strategy at best. Giant spiders in Montezuma's lair weave webs large enough to momentarily immobilize Dreadnok Monkeywrench.

While battling for Julius Caesar's ashes, Destro blows up an oil tanker to keep the Joes busy – except that the flames, taking on a life of their own, *perfectly* circle the Joes and hold them hostage.

Shipwreck's parrot Polly evidently eats plutonium-laced crackers, since he can lift fallen tanker workers to safety with his beak alone. And even allowing that we're not wrestling fans, it seems ridiculous that Sgt. Slaughter head-butts Scrap Iron unconscious – *through Scrap Iron's helmet* – without a hint of a bruise.

GOOFS [Author's Note: Please pardon the following laundry list of goofs for "Arise, Serpentor, Arise!" The sheer number of episodes gave the story's creators a lot of chances to get things wrong. Of course, a glowing lack of attention to detail doesn't help.]

• ***Overall:*** At the risk of stating the obvious, the corpses of famous military leaders aren't just lying about the place for any boob to find. (When Montezuma died, for example, his followers evidently left his corpse sitting upright in his throne.) There's no tour guides, security staff or tourists at any of these sites – even public places like Napoleon's tomb – indeed, nothing to indicate these edifices' cultural and historical importance.

For that matter, skeletons and especially cremains should yield pretty shoddy DNA samples And the Joes strangely have authorization to operate in *any* country around the world.

• ***Part 1:*** Zartan "auditions" new Dreadnoks by making potential recruits beat the crap out of each other, awarding Dreadnok membership to whomever's left standing. That's fine, but when Monkeywrench wins by using explosives, Zandar accuses him of cheating. (So… err, are there rules or not?)

• ***Part 2:*** An Egyptian scene with Zarana stealing General Xanuth Amon-Toth's remains makes virtually no sense. In short, Zarana dresses up as a peasant girl, rushes forward and claims that Cobra "ransacked her village." Naturally, the brain-dead Joes instantly believe the desert waif's story, rushing off to the middle of nowhere and not leaving a *single* person behind to guard Amon-Toth's tomb.

Once inside the edifice, Zarana magically produces a crowbar from nowhere to open Amon-Toth's sarcophagus. She also evades a spiked ceiling trap that can't kill anyone without demolishing the sarcophagus it's designed to protect.

Later, in the Yucatan, Zarana's voice crops up among the Dreadnoks, even though we've just seen her in Egypt about three minutes previous.

In Paris, when the Crimson Twins knock Airtight down, his eyeballs literally vanish from his head. In Transylvania, Beach-Head stumbles into a torture rack that *padlocks* itself shut.

During the battle for Ivan the Terrible's tomb, Russian soldiers briefly appear alongside their enemies: the Cobra BATs.

• ***Part 3:*** In our favorite blunder of "Arise, Serpentor, Arise!", Hawk contacts Sgt. Slaughter by radio, listening as Slaughter screams to his men: "Take cover! It's Cobra!" It's pretty self-explanatory, but instead, Hawk has to ask: "Sgt. Slaughter! Are you under attack?" (*Author's Note:* What does he *think* Cobra's doing? Holding a sewing bee?)

Roadblock nails one of the Crimson Twins' FANG helicopters, but the next shot shows a Viper piloting the chopper instead. As Dr. Mindbender examines the DNA vats, his monocle oddly sprouts a glasses-like frame hooking over his ear.

Joe medic Doc examines a Cobra DNA extractors and deduces: "This one's the same as all the others," when the Joes only captured *one* of the devices. Before the giant aircraft stunt, Cobra stages an initial assault and withdrawal on Genghis Khan's tomb, which Dr. Mindbender states is only intended as a diversion – but for what?

Most painful of all, when the Cobra assault ship snares Khan's sarcophagus with an enormous gripper device, Sgt. Slaughter thinks he's capable of pulling the giant mechanical arm open – with his bare hands. For an encore, Sgt. Slaughter boobishly rides the stolen remains all the way into Cobra's airship rather than simply jumping off. (In other words, Cobra doesn't actually capture Sgt. Slaughter – he's just dumb enough to get caught.)

• ***Part 4:*** After Joe medics Lifeline and Doc detail Cobra's entire cloning scheme, Hawk reads reports about the theft of Julius Caesar's ashes and comments, "Heaven knows what Cobra wants with them."

As the Crimson Twins sample Sgt. Slaughter's DNA, a strap on the DNA extractor – designed to hook around Slaughter's chest – mysteriously disappears. The process admittedly knocks Slaughter unconscious, but the brothers then unchain the downed sergeant, foolishly thinking a locked cell door will keep him from escaping.

After Dr. Mindbender's initial attempt to create Serpentor turns to ooze, Sgt. Slaughter picks up the slushy creature and tosses it over the Crimson Twins (it's a puddle of ooze, not a blanket).

At one point, Beach-Head's group includes two Mainframes.

• ***Part 5:*** Bazooka, Alpine and Mainframe simultaneously appear on Cobra Island and at Joe Headquarters. Alpine, Bazooka, Breaker and *two* Airtights appear and disappear from the Cobra Island team.

The Joes draft up a computer simulation of Serpentor that's accurate down to his costume – which they haven't seen at that point. Scrap Iron conveniently loses his facial scar at a couple of points.

Graced with the military genius of Napoleon, Hannibal, Julius Caesar and the like, Serpentor begins his career as Cobra Emperor by ordering a completely unfeasible invasion of America. Essentially, Serpentor mandates an all-out assault with no strategy, subtlety or long-term planning. The Cookie Monster would fare just as well.

At story's end, Cobra troopers entirely fail to frisk the politician-disguised Joes, allowing them to waltz right up to Serpentor carrying briefcases with guns inside. Serpentor's lasers randomly shift from red to blue.

TV TIE-INS *G.I. Joe: The Movie* reveals that unseen operatives working from the time-lost nation of Cobra-La influenced Dr. Mindbender's dreams, granting him the technological know-how to create Serpentor. "My Favorite Things" further explores Serpentor's progenitors and compound personality. The Oktober Guard, here joining forces with the Joes to safeguard Ivan the Terrible's popsickled corpse, last appeared in "The Great Alaskan Gold Rush."

COMIC TIE-INS Unlike the G.I. Joe comic series, where Cobra manipulated the Joes into creating Cobra Island in the Gulf of Mexico (*G.I. Joe* #40-#41), there's no such corresponding TV origin story for Cobra Island – it just appears.

CHARACTER PROFILE: JOES

• *Hawk:* His belt comes equipped with mini-rockets, enough to blast him up to a Joe cargo jet.

• *Iceberg:* He's from Waco, Texas.

• *Leatherneck and Wet Suit:* They verbally spar with each other in a brotherly fashion.

• *Lifeline:* A Joe medic who holds steadfastly to pacifist beliefs.

• *Low-Light and Sci-Fi:* They're frightfully accurate sharpshooters, besting even Leatherneck and Wet-Suit.

• *Mainframe:* He formerly served in Vietnam and has children.

• *The U.S. President:* He's evidently brown-haired, with a moustache and glasses (and no, he's not Groucho Marx).

• *Roadblock:* His aunt lives in Peoria.

• *Sgt. Slaughter:* Slaughter's normally stationed at Bivouac, knocking recruits into shape. He's unfamiliar with numerous Joes, including Roadblock and Beach-Head. General Hawk, convinced the Joes need a further bout of training, asks Sgt. Slaughter to stay on as a drill instructor. Electro-chains can bind Slaughter despite his almost super-human strength. It takes at least three BATs to restrain him.

CHARACTER PROFILE: COBRA

• *Monkeywrench:* Dreadnok who specializes in "heavy metal, unprovoked mayhem and explosions." Even so, big spiders chill him to the core.

• *Scrap Iron:* His loyalty goes to the highest bidder, wavering between Cobra Commander and Dr. Mindbender's conspirators. Scrap Iron's an electronics expert, able to craft mechanical flies for surveillance purposes.

• *Serpentor:* Serpentor originated life as a blobby protoplasm armature – in layman's terms, a blank lump of goo – into which Dr. Mindbender encoded the various military leaders' genetic structures. Serpentor's attributes purportedly include Napoleon's military genius, Genghis Khan's ruthlessness, Alexander the Great's leadership skills and Ivan the Terrible's penchant for evil. Other genetic donors include Hannibal, Julius Caesar, Geronimo, Attila the Hun, Eric the Red and the mad monk Rasputin.

Serpentor's easily as strong as Sgt. Slaughter, if not more so. The Cobra Emperor lacks patience because he wasn't endowed with Sun Tzu's DNA.

• *Thrasher:* His fellow Dreadnoks despise him, mostly because he's impossibly arrogant and nuts.

ORGANIZATIONS *Cobra:* Conduct business with a currency called "gold serpentines." Beach-Head's team trashed all of Dr. Mindbender's DNA samples before exiting Cobra Island, thwarting any thoughts on Cobra's parts of further DNA tomfoolery.

• *G.I. Joe:* The top G.I. Joe commanders, in order of rank, are Hawk, Duke, Flint and Beach-Head. The Soviets sometimes allows the Joes to protect Russian property, such as Ivan the Terrible's tombs.

STUFF YOU NEED *Cobra BATS (a.k.a. Battle Android Troopers):* Robot automatons, difficult to drop with a single laser blast. The BATs possess limited intelligence, needing a human operator to think for them.

• *Cobra DNA Extractor:* A small box that somehow scans long-dead corpses and digitizes their genetic codes, disintegrating said body in the process. The extractor also works on living beings, sucking up their genetic code in a painful but harmless process.

HOT WHEELS *Cobra Night Raven jet:* Deploys a smaller hunting drone as needed.

• *Cobra STUNs:* Fast-moving ground assault vehicles, decently maneuverable but sorely lacking armor and firepower.

THE COMMAND DECISION Epic, and a real turn-on for some G.I. Joe fans due to its sizeable character debuts and wide-ranging story. Indeed, "Arise, Serpentor, Arise!" held the potential to become the top Joe story of all time, save that its implementation – its implementation – verges on the inexcusable, riddled with painful posturing, ungodly dialogue (Hawk: "We're in the dark now, but we've got to keep punching until we see the light..."), iceberg-sized plot holes and the birth of Serpentor, who's even – truth to tell – more inept than Cobra Commander. If beauty's in the details, then there's little that's beautiful in this mini-series – however much we applaud its ambition – leaving "Arise, Serpentor, Arise!" an extremely troubled season debut.

2.6: "Last Hour to Doomsday"

US Transmission Date: *Sept. 25, 1986*
Writer: *Tom Dagenais*

BATTLE ROSTER *Joes:* Flint, Lady Jaye, Deep Six, Wet-Suit, Duke, Hawk; *Cobra:* Cobra Commander, the Baroness, Destro.

MISSION BRIEF When a wiretap alerts the Joes to Cobra operations near the Panama Canal, the Joes round up a moray crew led by the Baroness. Preferring death to capture, the female Cobra agent dives overboard and apparently drowns. In turn, Lady Jaye costumes herself as the Baroness, proceeding onward to a South American Cobra base to infiltrate Cobra's operations.

Near Panama, Cobra Commander and Destro put the finishing touches on a "Vortex Cone" – an underwater dish designed to stir up the sea's electro-magnetic currents, producing tidal waves of unimaginable power. Lady Jaye swiftly copies the Vortex Cone's schematics to diskette, hiding the floppy disk in her bust. Unfortunately, a waterlogged, harping Baroness suddenly returns to base, blowing Lady Jaye's cover. Flint swoops in and saves Lady Jaye's curvaceous hide, but their frantic escape mangles Lady Jaye's diskette, leaving the Joes with preciously little information on Cobra's newest stratagem.

Meanwhile, Cobra Commander activates a low-level Vortex Cone near the Panama Canal, creating a fierce tidal wave to demonstrate his power. Mission complete, Cobra Commander takes to the airwaves, threatening to destroy America's East Coast with a more powerful Vortex Cone unless America surrenders.

Desperate to obliterate the ultra-lethal Vortex Cone, the Joes locate Cobra's "Undersea Base Delta" by tracking a Cobra reconnaissance plane. While a Flint and Lady Jaye-led task force draws Cobra's firepower, Joe SEAL Wet-Suit sloppily tries to disable the Vortex Cone. Destro and Cobra Commander breathe easy as Wet-Suit merely deactivates the Vortex Cone's back-up systems, but back at Joe Headquarters, Mainframe jury-rigs a disk drive to read Lady Jaye's crumpled diskette.

Hawk and Duke study the Vortex Cone schematics and transmit their findings to the Joe assault group, enabling Wet-Suit to correctly sabotage the Vortex Cone. As the shorted-out wave-maker explodes, Cobra Commander, Destro and the Baroness flee, allowing the Joes to victoriously return home.

MEMORABLE MOMENTS Highlighting the era that spawned G.I. Joe, a newly escaped Lady Jaye removes a crumpled 5-1/4" floppy disk from her bosom and presents it to Mainframe. Hawk wonders if it's possible to just "iron the disk out" or something, compelling Mainframe to spend most of the episode crafting a special disk drive to read the disk's files.

A Cobra trooper chuckles while reading the whimsically named *Cobra Life* magazine. Finally, after the undersea battle, Lifeline charges past some Joes with a hacksaw, determined to "... cut an arm off Shipwreck!" Flint and Lady Jaye pale, hearing Shipwreck's screams and imagining several flavors of agonizing battlewounds, then turn relieved to see Lifeline cutting a severed BAT arm off Shipwreck's ankle.

LOVE AND WAR Destro and the Baroness argue about an unspecified topic before the episode opens, compelling Destro to appease his lover (actually Lady Jaye in disguise). In fact, Destro offers to show "the Baroness" some "interesting hand-to-hand combat techniques" (Is that what kids are calling it these days?) in his quarters, but Lady Jaye plays the flirt and stalls for time. Destro buys Lady Jaye's act, citing "the Baroness" as "a playful little minx" – only to later discover that of course, she's an imposter. (A crushed Destro comments: "I knew it was too good to be true.")

As "the Baroness," Lady Jaye somewhat foolishly conceals her stolen disk in her bust – after all, Destro might search her there. Lady Jaye later agrees to have dinner with Flint.

ASS-WHUPPINGS Flint and Lady Jaye choose their escape vehicle poorly while fleeing from a Cobra base – unexpectedly finding themselves leading a Cobra RATTLER squadron back to "Undersea Base Delta." Decently panicked (and unable to stall forever), the two Joes daringly turn and catch the RATTLER pilots with their pants down – eliminating the entire attack group. Underwater forces commanded via remote by Destro and the Baroness scrap a lot of Joe attack walkers (think of a primitive version of the AT-ST "chicken walkers" from Star Wars).

PREPOSTEROUS PHYSICS Mainframe's obviously talking nonsense when he supposedly "rigs a free-floating head to read warped computer disks" – an invention that would surely make him a multi-millionaire. Lady Jaye takes out a heavily armored, hell-on-wheels Cobra BAT... by jabbing a hairpin in the back of its neck.

GOOFS Cobra apparently purchases its timing devices from the lowest bidder, as the Vortex Cone's "countdown" goes from 48:00:00 to 48:59:59. Hawk seemingly gives orders mere seconds after Cobra Commander's broadcast, but the clock suddenly jumps to 46:28:94 (a goof made even stranger by the fact that a clock should never read 94 seconds).

The Joes convince themselves pretty damn fast that the diving Baroness committed suicide. Cobra Commander yet *again* lets valued tactical information slip during a broadcast, informing the world: "Only Cobra will be safe [from destruction], located in the eye of the Vortex."

A Cobra robot tampers with a submerged Flint and Lady Jaye's air tanks to knock them out – so why didn't they suffocate? After a prolonged shoot-out, Destro and the Baroness think they've killed dozens of underwater Joes, despite a complete lack of bodies to show for it.

CHARACTER PROFILE: JOES Lady Jaye: She gave up a career in show business to join the Joes.

STUFF YOU NEED BATs: They're impervious to simple hitting and kicking. Indeed, you can sever a BAT in half and it'll still crawl forward to kill you – meaning complete dismemberment and destruction's your best bet. BATs also function underwater with little difficulty.

THE COMMAND DECISION Sensible enough, but entirely drained of drama, "Last Hour to Doomsday" probably started life as a Season 1 story that got hastily rewritten for the Season 2 cast (Torpedo = Wet Suit, Doc = Lifeline, etc.). The final effect's too generic and stuffed with filler (i.e. Flint and Lady Jaye's throwaway battle with a Cobra-fed giant octopus) to do much good.

2.7: "Computer Complications"

US Transmission Date: *Sept. 26, 1986*
Writer: *David Schwartz*

BATTLE ROSTER *Joes:* Mainframe, Beach-Head, Duke, Shipwreck, Wet-Suit, Deep Six, Admiral Ledger; *Cobra:* Zarana, Zandar, Zartan and the Dreadnoks.

MISSION BRIEF In deep space, an American space probe retrieves an immeasurably powerful lump of anti-matter and crashes into the ocean with its find. The Joes set up an offshore platform equipped with robot retrieval submarines to fetch the anti-matter pod from the ocean's depths. Cobra Commander assaults the platform, unwilling to cede the energy-laden anti-matter to the Joes, but Wet-Suit hurriedly reprograms the claw-armed submarine drones to carve up Cobra's underwater vehicles and force a retreat.

Desperate to override the Joes' computer access and put the robot subs under his control, Cobra Commander contacts the Zartan family for help. Accordingly, Zarana dresses up as "Sgt. Carol Wheedler," infiltrating Joe Headquarters as a computer specialist. Zarana successfully enters Joe Headquarters, but – to the lady Dreadnok's disgust – Joe computer expert Mainframe becomes increasingly attracted to her "Wheedler" persona.

Trying to eliminate the pesky nerd, Zarana upends a stack of heavy equipment boxes to squash the Joe. Unfortunately, the trap backfires, endangering Zarana until Mainframe body-tackles her to safety. Impressed by Mainframe's selfless act, Zarana finds herself returning Mainframe's affections despite her best efforts otherwise.

Zartan implores his distracted sibling to focus on her mission, forcing Zarana to get back to business. Thus, Zarana douses the lights during an intimate moment with Mainframe at Joe Headquarters – then electro-shocks Mainframe unconscious. Zarana puts the Joes' robot submarines under Cobra Commander's remote control, summoning Zartan and the Dreadnoks for a pick-up. But as a parting gift, Zartan pitches an explosive charge atop the insensate Mainframe. Unable to let Mainframe snuff it, Zarana electro-jolts her brother and turns back, pitching the bomb aside. Mainframe staggers to consciousness, compelling Zarana to confess her true identity. Inwardly torn, Mainframe lets Zarana flee before Joe security forces respond to the explosion.

Back at sea, the *USS Flagg* aircraft carrier moves into position as the Joes' offshore platform dredges up the fallen space probe. Unfortunately, Cobra sends its top airborne carrier and a fleet of Firebat jets to raid the *Flagg,* successfully making off with the anti-matter pod. The Joes wound the Cobra carrier, but as a *coup de grace,* Cobra Commander overrides the automatic submarines' control – ordering them to claw at the *Flagg*'s underbelly.

As the *Flagg* lists, Shipwreck programs a blistering missile attack that strikes the Cobra carrier dead-on. Cobra Commander and Dr. Mindbender try – and fail – to tap the anti-matter pod for the power needed to keep their ship aloft. With the *Flagg*'s hull integrity spoiled, Admiral Ledger orders his troops to abandon ship and swim for the offshore platform. Moments later, Cobra Commander's soldiers evacuate as their command carrier crashes into the *Flagg.*

Watching both the *Flagg* and Cobra's carrier – still holding the anti-matter pod – sink to the ocean depths, the Joes turn teary-eyed. The combatants return to base, considering the matter closed, leaving Mainframe and Zarana to separately lament their ill-fated relationship.

MEMORABLE MOMENTS In an amusing little romp, Zarana – still disguised as "Carol Wheedler" – moves to club Mainframe with a wrench. Mainframe cluelessly takes the tool from her to repair a circuit board, thanking "Carol" for her help. Next, Zarana tries stabbing Mainframe with a screwdriver, but again, he merely takes the instrument and keeps working. Overheating and out of tools, Zarana tries strangling Mainframe – but he mistakes the maneuver for an embrace and starts kissing her. (A perfect example of "Make love, not war.")

Admiral Ledger's scream of, "Abandon ship! Swim for the battle platform!" and the *Flagg*'s final demise left a knot in our throats.

LOVE AND WAR Mainframe starts flirting with "Carol Wheedler" the moment she arrives on base, suggesting he could "fill her in on the big picture." The disguised Zarana retorts that if Mainframe's 'help' "includes making a pass at me, I'll have you up on harassment charges faster than you can spit!" (Mainframe sputters in response: "Jeez! You sound just like my ex-wife!")

Mainframe later apologizes for his advances, but Zarana, grateful to Mainframe for saving her life, shares dinner with him. Mainframe and "Wheedler" try to enjoy a normal meal, but in the finest Joe tradition, Zartan arrives to goad his sibling – leading to a diner brawl between the Dreadnoks and several Joes. In the final act, Mainframe learns Zarana's true identity but lets her escape anyway. After the *Flagg*'s destruction, Mainframe recovers from his injuries and pines for the villainess. Conversely, the Dreadnoks taunt Zarana about her Joe boyfriend, but she silences them with a laser blast.

ASS-WHUPPINGS When a disguised Zartan gets pushy with Zarana at the "Eat at Joe's Diner," Zarana shoves her brother aside – leading to Leatherneck unexpectedly unmasking the Cobra agent. The resultant bar brawl between Zartan's Dreadnoks and several Joes wrecks the diner.

"Wheedler" cattily smooches with Mainframe (uttering: "I was told being on the Joe team was exciting, but I had no idea *how* exciting...") – then electro-zaps him unconscious and proceeds with her mission. She later jolts Zartan with a Taser stunner, turning back to save Mainframe's life.

Zartan's ATV nips Beach-Head as it races by. Cobra Firebats wipe out the *Flagg*'s Conquest X-30 squadron. This story largely ends in a draw, with a ferocious battle sinking both G.I. Joe and Cobra's main aircraft carriers.

GOOFS After Wet-Suit fires off some missiles, his uniform mysteriously shifts from blue to beige. An eyebrow-raising shot shows the Joe off-shore platform lowering the space probe instead of raising it.

TV TIE-INS The Joes and Cobras revisit the Flagg's remains in the appropriately named "Raise the Flagg!" Zarana affectionately aids Mainframe in "Gray Hairs and Growing Pains." Cobra Commander's still groveling to Serpentor, having lost the top Cobra leadership slot in "Arise, Serpentor, Arise!"

Beach-Head here fumes over the way Duke lets the Joes bend the rules, although Duke's shown as a stickler for discipline in *G.I. Joe: The Movie.*

CHARACTER PROFILE: JOES

• *Iceberg:* He can't wait to re-visit Antarctica's frigid temperatures.

• *Low-Light:* Gifted with unbelievable night vision, Low-Light's able to spot a camouflaged Zandar in almost total darkness.

• *Mainframe:* After serving in Vietnam, Mainframe "knocked around" until he wound up as a computer tech in Silicon Valley. He's authorized for "Top Secret" clearance.

STUFF YOU NEED Anti-Matter: A single anti-matter wafer could power California for a month.

HOT WHEELS Dreadnok ATV: Strong enough to plow through a wall.

• *Cobra Manta Subs:* As the title implies, they're shaped like manta rays. Hasbro never made toys of these subs, which sport names like *Anger, Revenge* and *Dagger.*

THE COMMAND DECISION One of the most striking G.I. Joe episodes, effortlessly shifting between the Flagg's disembowelment and miraculously making the oddball Mainframe/Zarana pairing seem believable. Luckily for us all, "Computer Complications" launches a noted maturing and progressiveness among the Season 2 stories that – if woefully inconsistent – gives rise to such gems as "Nightmare Assault," "Sink the Montana" and "Raise the Flagg!" Amen.

2.8: "Sink the Montana"

US Transmission Date: *Sept. 29, 1986*
Writer: *David Carren*

BATTLE ROSTER *Joes:* Hawk, Shipwreck, Deep Six; *Cobra:* Destro; *Other:* Admiral Latimer.

MISSION BRIEF Hawk travels to the Philadelphia Naval Yards for a solemn event: the decommissioning of the USS Montana, the world's largest battleship, after 45 years of service. Hawk lends personal support to his long-time friend, Admiral George Latimer, the Montana's commander. But Latimer, looking at the Montana as his only companion and protector, vows to save his ship from the scrapyard – even if it means allying with Cobra.

Latimer privately cuts a deal with Destro, putting his ship at Cobra's disposal. Accordingly, Destro and a platoon of Cobra Battle Android Troopers (BATs) overrun the *Montana,* seizing its control room. Hawk fails to make Latimer reconsider his actions, despairing as his friend defects from the U.S. military. Worse, as a show of loyalty to Cobra, Latimer fires the *Montana*'s weapons, decimating ships docked at the Philadelphia yard.

Destro orders Latimer to set sail for Northfolk, VA, intending to butcher the American seventh fleet and seize control of the Atlantic. To guarantee success, Destro equips the Montana with a newly invented "Pulse Modulator" – a device capable of neutralizing all electrical energy in a two-mile-wide radius. Hawk authorizes a Skystriker and hovercraft assault, hoping to stop the Montana before events get out of hand, but Destro's Pulse Modulator renders the Joe vessels and missiles completely useless.

With the seventh fleet on its way to futilely confront the *Montana,* Hawk's Joes set sail aboard the wind-powered *USS Constitution.* Hawk's team slips aboard the *Montana* as it passes by – destroying Destro's Pulse Modulator just as the seventh fleet comes into view.

Latimer advocates surrender, but Destro locks down the *Montana*'s automatic firing control and escapes. The *Montana* and the Atlantic fleet engage each other in a volley of titanic proportions, spreading carnage. Finally, Hawk's team retakes the *Montana*'s bridge, helping Latimer to reverse Destro's damage to the firing control.

The *Montana* falls silent, but fleet commander Admiral Overton, taking no chances, orders a continued bombardment. The fleet's volley fatally ruptures the *Montana,* forcing the Joes to dive overboard and swim for the *Constitution.* Latimer refuses to leave, preferring death to dishonor, but Hawk punches Latimer's lights out and hauls him to safety. As the Joes watch, the *Montana* sinks to the bottom – signaling the end of both a fine ship and Latimer's career.

MEMORABLE MOMENTS In a symbolic moment, BATs shoot away the Montana's American flag and replace it with a Cobra logo. Hawk lets out an anguished scream of: "George, no!" as the Montana levels the Philadelphia shipyard. In a groundswell of emotion, Hawk orders a Joe battalion to "... sink the Montana." And, during the finale, Latimer observes his drowning ship and mutters to Hawk: "It would have been more merciful to let me drown."

ASS-WHUPPINGS Hawk mows down reams of BATs with the Montana's anti-aircraft guns. The BATs triumph through sheer numbers, but they harmlessly toss Hawk overboard. Latimer ruins mothballed vessels docked at the Philadelphia shipyards. Destro's Pulse Modulator disables several Joe Conquest jets and WHALE hovercrafts. The seventh fleet's artillery, in addition to putting the Montana under, crisps a few Joes.

GOOFS Hawk depresses the Montana's anti-aircraft guns to fire at the ship's own deck and wipe out some BATs – when you'd think safety features would prevent such a self-destructive maneuver. Hawk's Joes insist on using the highly prized USS Constitution, the Navy's oldest vessel, when any sailing ship would have sufficed. For that matter, the Joes conveniently forget that one hit from the Montana's cannons would turn the Constitution and all aboard into the consistency of kelp.

CHARACTER PROFILE: OTHER
Admiral Latimer: Flashbacks indicate that Latimer's lived on the *Montana* for most of his life. Once, the *Montana* arrived in time to save Latimer from a helicopter wreck, causing him to regard the ship as a guardian. Although Latimer doubtlessly receives a court-martial and prison time, Hawk comments with regards to the *Montana*'s loss, "[Latimer's] already received the worst punishment imaginable."

HOT WHEELS USS Constitution: The Navy's oldest ship, lacking even an electric generator.

THE COMMAND DECISION Effectively using flashback scenes to generate sympathy for Latimer, however nutty his cause, "Sink the Montana" displays a sweet maturity. It's as much about Hawk grieving for his friend's misdeeds as Latimer's actual treachery – making this a rapid-fire tale of two men and a ship that served America well.

2.9: "Let's Play Soldier"

***US Transmission Date:** Sept. 30, 1986*
***Writer:** Sharman DiVono*

BATTLE ROSTER *Joes:* Leatherneck, Gung Ho, Roadblock, Beach-Head, Low-Light, Wet-Suit, Lift-Ticket, Lifeline, Dial-Tone, Slip-Stream; *Cobra:* Dr. Mindbender, Zarana, the Dreadnoks.

MISSION BRIEF In Thailand, Cobra researchers refine a process that turns sap from the Asian chaulmoogra tree into a potent mind-control chemical. In time, Cobra intends to mesmerize the world through a series of chaulmoogra-laced personal hygiene products such as mouthwash, toothpaste and deodorant. But needing to test the chaulmoogra's effectiveness, Cobra starts smuggling heaps of chaulmoogra-tainted bubble gum onto the Asian market.

Alerted to Cobra's presence in Thailand, a Joe marine and SEAL team ambushes river smugglers in Cobra's employ. The Joes capture and analyze a chaulmoogra sample, slowly forming theories as to Cobra's intent. Simultaneously, Joe marine Leatherneck befriends a group of Thai street urchins.

Shortly afterward, Leatherneck, Roadblock and Gung Ho get a tip-off about a favorite restaurant frequented by the Dreadnoks, instigating a massive brawl at the "Bangkok Inn." But the Dreadnoks get away, rounding up the trio with a pincer movement. Zarana hoodwinks the remaining Joes by leading them into a jungle and ditching them, but the street urchins bravely follow Zarana to save Leatherneck's rear.

While Dr. Mindbender loads huge stockpiles of refined chaulmoogra sap into a massive Cobra aircraft carrier, the urchins free Leatherneck's trio. At the last instant, Leatherneck jumps aboard Mindbender's ship, leading to a close-quarters firefight that starts the chaulmoogra stocks on fire. Leatherneck and Mindbender separately escape as the plane explodes, incinerating Cobra's chaulmoogra supplies. Soon after, the Joes assist in rebuilding the "Bangkok Inn," helping Leatherneck's street rats procure jobs and turn their lives around.

MEMORABLE MOMENTS Leatherneck correctly assesses that his young friends don't need to be Americanized; instead, they simply crave "a home and some love. What country they're in doesn't matter."

LOVE AND WAR Zarana monitors the Dreadnoks' rowdy activities disguised as a sexy Asian girl. There's a kinky bit when Dreadnok Ripper, failing to penetrate (so to speak) Zarana's disguise, suggests "How'z about joining us for a bit to eat, lovey?", to which even Dreadnok Torch adds "Riiiiight…", clearly thinking of a dish other than pad thai. Mercifully, Zarana puts the Dreadnoks in their place.

ASS-WHUPPINGS A river smuggler accidentally touches the refined chaulmoogra sap and gets mind-wiped. Roadblock clobbers Dreadnok Torch with a frying pan, then breaks a table over his head for good measure.

PREPOSTEROUS PHYSICS Leatherneck attacks the Dreadnoks by throwing dinner plates discus-style. Dressed as a chef, Roadblock impossibly deflects a burst from Torch's blowtorch with a heat-resistant frying pan. Leatherneck spontaneously turns into Spider-Man, clinging to the smooth exterior of an in-flight airplane.

GOOFS As the Joes "stealthily" sneak up on a smugglers' camp, Gung Ho erratically fires off a shot as if to announce: "Ready or not, here we come!" The Joes comment that Low-Light's conducting analysis on the chaulmoogra sap, but medic Lifeline's the one doing the work. And even allowing for Lifeline's findings, the Joes still make a leap in logic to determine that Cobra's lacing gum with their newfound narcotic.

Cross-Country spontaneously replaces Low-Light while Leatherneck's disciplining the street kids. As in "Arise, Serpentor, Arise!", the Joes moronically fall for a disguised Zarana's transparent "Help! Please! Raiders attacked my village!" ploy.

Sloppy editing shows Dr. Mindbender interrogating his captives one instant, then vanishing from view without actually leaving the scene, allowing one of Leatherneck's kids to slip their benefactor a pocket knife. Mind, a minute later, Dr. Mindbender turns to shockingly discover that his prisoners – who were in plain sight the whole time – have escaped.

How do Lifeline and Lift-Ticket know to show up with a Tomahawk helicopter *just in time* to save Leatherneck's sorry ass from Dr. Mindbender's flaming ship?

The Joe don't win this story, although they pretend otherwise. They don't wreck Cobra's chaulmoogra processing center, they barely handicap their supply lines and they certainly fail to prevent Cobra from pulling the same stunt elsewhere with chaulmoogra-laced deodorant or whatnot.

CHARACTER PROFILE: COBRA

• *Dr. Mindbender:* A brilliant biochemist – and a pretty damn good shot with a bazooka.

• *Dr. Mindbender, Zarana and the Dreadnoks:* The Dreadnoks continually violate orders, figuring that Dr. Mindbender will take the fall if they screw up, but Zarana's more inclined to follow the party line.

• *Zarana:* Disguised as an Asian beauty, Zarana wears exploding hairpins.

CHARACTER PROFILE: COBRA

• *Refined chaulmoogra sap:* It's flammable as hell, meaning a misplaced laser burst might make an barrelful of the stuff detonate.

THE COMMAND DECISION The premise, entailing Cobra seeking world domination through bubble gum, is so mind-bending (err... literally), it could actually work. But the numbing interplay of the chaulmoogra sap/street urchin storylines leaves "Let's Play Soldier" without much of an actual plot.

2.10: "Once Upon a Joe"

US Transmission Date: *Oct. 1, 1986*
Writer: *Buzz Dixon*

BATTLE ROSTER *Joes:* Shipwreck, Leatherneck, Wet-Suit, Duke, Beach-Head, Dial-Tone, Lifeline; *Cobra:* Zartan, Cobra Commander, the Dreadnoks.

MISSION BRIEF After raiding a think-tank named McGuffin Industries, a Cobra Firebat squadron makes off with a highly classified device named "The McGuffin Device." Moving to intercept, a Joe convoy led by Beach-Head locks lasers and scores several hits, unknowingly bringing the stolen McGuffin Device down to Earth. Unfortunately, Shipwreck lets off a second volley that downs one of the Firebats – hurling the flaming jet into an orphanage.

Beach-Head's crew scrambles like mad to save the orphans, but the building goes down in flames. The next morning, when the Joes show up to rebuild the orphanage from scratch, a little orphan girl begs the roguish Shipwreck to tell her a story. Somewhat reluctantly, Shipwreck incorporates his teammates into a wacky fairy tale.

As Shipwreck explains, a poor shoemaker (Duke) living in a giant combat boot once ran short of food. The shoemaker variously sent his sons – the oafish Leatherhead (Leatherneck) and the lumbering Frog-Face (Wet-Suit) – to buy hamburgers, but a giant cobra and an evil step-mother (Zarana) robbed the boys. Finally, the shoemaker sent his heroic son Shipshape (a.k.a. Shipwreck, naturally) to swipe food from an evil giant's hamburger mine.

Just as Shipwreck's tale spirals out of control, Leatherneck orders him to sweep the nearby forest for unexploded rockets, leaving the sailor's tale incomplete. Simultaneously, Cobra Commander hires Zartan to track down the missing McGuffin Device. Zartan quickly arrives on the scene, knocking Shipwreck unconscious just before locating the high-tech gadget.

Zartan goes to flee, but the Joes uncover his escape vehicle. Cut off, Zartan stalls by disguising himself as Shipwreck – only to find himself forced to guard the orphans. As "Shipwreck," Zartan finishes the kids' fairy tale, explaining that the evil cobra punished the shoemaker and his sons, proof that the strong (Cobra) will rule the earth.

The kids recoil in horror, but fortunately, one of the orphans happens across the real Shipwreck and unties him. Confronted by an underwear-clad sailor, Zartan summons a Cobra Night Raven assault to make his getaway, but Shipwreck swipes the McGuffin Device back and – in pure desperation – activates it.

Capable of altering reality to reflect its user's thoughts, the McGuffin Device literally brings the playful Joe-like characters from Shipwreck's fairy tale to life. Instantly, pie-wielding Shipshapes, Leatherheads and Frog-Faces assault the Night Raven crews, clinging to the Cobra jets and dismantling them. Traumatized by the *Looney-Tunes*-esque creations, Zartan and his rescuers fall into full retreat. Breathing a sigh of relief, Shipwreck deactivates the McGuffin Device, dissipating his creations. After turning the gadget over to authorities, Shipwreck thrills the kids by properly concluding his fairy tale.

MEMORABLE MOMENTS In one of the series' most outrageous and non-sequitor scenes, the Dreadnoks engage in, as Zartan puts it, a "weighty philosophical debate" – bashing each other silly with shovels and alligators over whether "candy mints" or "breath mints" are better. We have no clue what sparked the fight – or indeed, why the Dreadnoks give a damn about mints – but the sight of Zartan's brigade clubbing each other while shouting "Breath mint!" "Candy mint!" nearly made us snort milk through our noses.

Almost as amusingly, the Cobra pilots include a rather porky Strato-Viper (shades of Jeb Porkins from *Star Wars*).

In Shipwreck's fairy tale, shoemaker Duke remarks that his stew "tastes like laundry soap" – only to discover that he is, in fact, cooking laundry. A clever animator renders the fairy tale cow with sneakers and a sign blazoned with the word "Cow."

Lifeline provides the story's moral by claiming the Joes "accomplished a lot today." Beach-Head concurs, rattling off that the Joes' military accomplishments – leaving Lifeline to add: "I meant fixing the orphanage and making those kids happy."

LOVE AND WAR A little orphan finds Shipwreck – hogtied by Zartan – in the woods wearing nothing but his Fruit of the Looms. A tightie-whitie-clad Shipwreck then confronts his double (i.e. Zartan) at the orphanage (oh, the kids are gonna need therapy for years). The McGuffin Device generates cartoony, winged versions of Scarlett, Lady Jaye and Cover Girl, who happily smooch Leatherneck.

ASS-WHUPPINGS Beach-Head shoots off a BAT's head at point-blank range, but the headless robot tosses him aside and crashes a Joe HAVOC.

At the orphanage building site, Shipwreck deliberately spatters Wet-Suit and Beach-Head with cement mix, then nails Leatherneck with a wooden plank. Convinced that Shipwreck's an incompetent – as Shipwreck intended – Beach-Head's group toss the Joe sailor off the construction site, allowing him to snooze.

PREPOSTEROUS PHYSICS Cobra Strato-Vipers shatter a security screen around the McGuffin Device with a bazooka – running the risk of blowing the damn thing to smithereens. A canister housing a BAT mysteriously lifts up into nowhere (for all we know, it launches into orbit). Lift-Ticket's Tomahawk helicopter attaches a winch and tow-cable to the burning orphanage, tearing off the roof like a piece of aluminum foil.

GOOFS A Strato-Viper secures the McGuffin Device in a flimsy crate on his jet's underbelly – rather than stowing the gizmo more safely in his cockpit.

It's forgivable, but the fairy tale "hamburger mine" looks more like a "taco mine."

During Shipwreck's story, there's an extremely odd moment when two orphans shush a loudmouth kid, then inexplicably disappear in a pop. Mind, you can only see this goof by watching the scene in slow-motion – in real time, there's just a blur and a strange teleport noise.

Beach-Head loses/gains his battle vest and face mask in the same scene. The Joes rebuild the orphanage from the ground up in about 24 hours.

TV TIE-INS "Captives of Cobra" establishes that Shipwreck's also an orphan, allowing him to empathize with the kids' plight.

CHARACTER PROFILE: JOES *Leatherneck:* In Shipwreck's absence, Leatherneck badly tries to finish the fairy tale, relating a painful reworking of "The Three Little Piggies" (i.e. "The Three Little Joes") – and nearly killing the orphans with boredom.

CHARACTER PROFILE: COBRA *Zartan:* He's lethal with rocket-propelled homing darts, practicing this skill by torching dummies of Cobra Commander. Zartan's fee for grabbing the McGuffin Device: $300,000.

ORGANIZATIONS *The Dreadnoks:* Thrasher, Torch, Zarana and Buzzer favor "candy mints." Buzzer, Torch and Zandar prefer "breath mints." (See Memorable Moments.)

STUFF YOU NEED *Cobra BATs:* They're phenomenally strong, able to halt Joe mini-tanks in motion and hoist them above their heads.

THE COMMAND DECISION A daring experiment that almost should have fallen on its face, "Once Upon a Joe" steadfastly – aside from an extremely bow-tied ending – plays a beautiful hand. More than anything else, Shipwreck's talent for B.S. completely makes the episode – laying timber for some engrossing fairy tale scenes.

2.11: "The Million Dollar Medic"

US Transmission Date: *Oct. 2, 1986*
Writers: *Carla and Gerry Conway*

BATTLE ROSTER *Joes:* Lifeline, Duke, Lift-Ticket, Slip-Steam, Iceberg, Scarlett; *Cobra:* Tomax and Xamot, Serpentor, the Baroness, Zandar, Buzzer.

MISSION BRIEF Lusting after high-tech schematics from Defense Department contractor Van Mark Industries, Cobra sets about forcing Owen Van Mark to sell his business. In the Caribbean, a Cobra Night Raven phalanx missiles Van Mark's coconut milk bottling operation in a show of force, but a Joe Conquest X-30 jet team intercepts them. The skirmish makes a wounded Night Raven plow into Van Mark's personal yacht, compelling Joe medic Lifeline to haul Van Mark and his daughter Brittany ("Bree") to safety.

The 20-something Bree immediately swoons over Lifeline's rescue, falling desperately in love with the Joe medic. Soon after, the humble Lifeline despairs as the ludicrously wealthy Bree lavishes him with expensive gifts, including a platinum Swiss Army knife and a new wardrobe.

Regrettably, the Cobra officers learn about Bree's infatuation with Lifeline, hoping to capitalize on it and raid Joe Headquarters. Soon after, Lifeline inwardly shrivels as Bree rolls up to Joe Headquarters with a fleet of pink Rolls Royce ambulances for him. Fumbling for a response, Lifeline's interrupted when Cobra Battle Android Troopers (BATs), hidden in the ambulances without Bree's knowledge, emerge to start a firefight.

With the Joes' ground force in utter chaos, Cobra unleashes an immense air strike. The Joes staunchly drive away the intruders, but a shamed Bree steals a Joe Tomahawk to run away. Lifeline tries to stop her, leaping onto the Tomahawk's exterior in the last instant and absurdly clinging on for dear life. Needing to clear her head, Bree takes the Tomahawk – and Lifeline – to her family ski lodge in the Rockies.

Dismayed over the Joes' victory, Serpentor pops his nut, ordering the Baroness to kidnap Bree and thereby persuade Van Mark to sell his company. The Baroness rolls against the Van Mark abode with an armor column, but the Joes, tracking Lifeline's location, hit the Cobra troops with a Joe Conquest squadron. The Joes triumph again, forcing Cobra to end its costly attempts to blackmail Van Mark. Even better, Bree stops showering Lifeline with inappropriate gifts, allowing the two of them to happily suck face.

LOVE AND WAR Bree pretty much wants to jump Lifeline's thermometer from the instant he rescues them in the Caribbean, embracing him and pulling both of them underwater. Once Lifeline gets Bree to abandon her mad gift-giving routine, they apparently end this story as a couple. (In a bit of symbolism, a Joe Conquest patrol potently zooms by during their final embrace.)

ASS-WHUPPINGS Xamot badly aims a kick at Lifeline, bashing Zandar and Buzzer by mistake. Zandar soon recovers, slugging Lifeline and cracking a vase over his head. Seconds later, Joe Lift-Ticket waltzes into the fray, double-punching the twins and shattering a chair on Buzzer's noggin. The scene ends with rubble hitting the Cobra agents, who fall through the floor. (See Preposterous Physics.)

In a striking Joe battle shot, Scarlett empties her rifle into a crushing tidal wave of BATs. (The scene's gloriously – sniff – repeated during the final credits).

Bree's gold-plated helicopter *(see Preposterous Physics)* flails about, crashing into at least four Joe Conquest planes.

A Joe Dragonfly helicopter squadron and Cobra Night Raven jet division mutually annihilate each other, although the few Joe survivors rout a Cobra HISS tank column.

PREPOSTEROUS PHYSICS During a lighthearted battle at Van Mark Mansion, Buzzer drops his chainsaw – which circles about the room and cuts a sizeable hole in the floor. Simultaneously, Zandar swings a mace at Lift-Ticket, missing with enough force to shatter a marble ceiling support. (Side Note: The Zartan family sometimes displays superhuman strength, but it'd take an immeasurable force to fling the mace through a marble column). As a result, a collapsing column almost crushes the Crimson Twins, Buzzer and Zandar, who also fall through the gaping hole in the floor – and live.

As a gift for Lifeline, Brittany buys a 24K gold-plated, laser-proof helicopter. First off, we're not aware of gold *repelling lasers.* Second, the gold hopelessly weights the ship down – nearly killing Brittany and Lifeline on take-off. Of course, this begs the question: What aeronautics firm would build such a ship without *testing* it first? ("By the way, Ms. Van Mark, you know that this ship will never get off the ground.")

Lifeline ludicrously clings to the side of Bree's stolen helicopter – like a wet paper towel thrown against the wall – all the way from Joe Headquarters to the Rockies.

GOOFS Sweet mercy, where do we start? Lifeline's romance with Bree would surely get him court-martialed. No, really. Military regulations would never allow, as this episode suggests, a medic to strut about in a Tiffany's wardrobe. Bree gets off scot-free for stealing a Joe Tomahawk helicopter (let's not even mention that she instantly knows its access codes). Also, Lifeline goes AWOL, abandoning his post to enjoy roasted marshmallows and coffee at Bree's Rockies retreat. (Hate to say it, but the "I was kidnapped by my girlfriend" excuse shouldn't get him very far.)

In the first act, Owen Van Mark seems genuinely confused as to why Cobra's attacking his various businesses. So either: A) Van Mark really *doesn't* suspect that Cobra wants his weapons division, making him the biggest buffoon on the planet, or B) Van Mark *does* realize Cobra's goals and deliberately lies to the Joes – even though he's nothing to gain by that. Van Mark, supposedly a ruthless industrialist, considers handing out classified U.S. military schematics to any terrorist baboon who kidnaps his daughter.

The Crimson Twins insist they've devised a "failure-proof" means of dealing with Owen Van Mark and his daughter – which amounts to breaking into Van Mark Mansion and kidnapping them. Bree's pink Rolls Royce ambulances amuse the Joes so much that they apparently fail to search them (hell, you could spot the BATs inside just by glancing through the window). At the episode's climax, the Baroness and the Crimson Twins escape in a Night Raven jet – conveniently hidden in a shack near the Van Mark retreat – with a giant Cobra head logo blazoned on it.

CHARACTER PROFILE: JOES Lifeline: Lifeline considers himself a medic first and a Joe second, throwing life preservers to half-drowned Cobra Night Raven pilots. He sometimes doubles as a vet and patches up dog Junkyard. Shipwreck makes fun of Lifeline's woes with Bree, but Mainframe's more sympathetic.

HOT WHEELS Cobra Night Raven jets: Come equipped with a smaller jet drone that works on automatic pilot.

THE COMMAND DECISION About as appealing as listening to "Flight of the Bumblebee" for 40 hours straight, "Million Dollar Medic" commits exactly the same cardinal sin as "Lasers in the Night" – letting a dumb-ass guest character act completely brainless without penalty. A certain flavor of non-discerning viewer will probably appreciate this story, but Bree's continual antics – especially the bit with the gold-plated helicopter that can't fly – nearly put us in the grave.

2.12: "Cobrathon"

***US Transmission Date:** Oct. 6, 1986*
***Writers:** Martin Pasko and Rebecca Parr*

BATTLE ROSTER *Joes:* Duke, Mainframe, Lifeline, Sci-Fi, Beach-Head, Dial-Tone, Flint, Low-Light; *Cobra:* the Baroness, Dr. Mindbender, Destro, Tomax and Xamot, Serpentor.

MISSION BRIEF Serpentor grows pleased when Dr. Mindbender and the Crimson Twins propose the creation of a computer virus that's capable of obliterating the computer systems of all worldwide law enforcement agencies – but he chokes to hear the virus will cost a whopping $5 billion. Consequently, Dr. Mindbender and the twins hastily explain a fanciful scheme to let the world's criminals, who'd gladly pay to wreck Interpol and their criminal records, turn out their pockets to fund such an endeavor. With Serpentor's blessing, the Cobra officers prepare to hold a telethon, soliciting donations from felons and Mafia bosses across the globe.

Cobra broadcasts the telethon via a scrambled cable signal that's virtually undetectable without a compatible computer box. Thankfully, Duke, Mainframe and Beach-Head raid a Cobra computer station, obtaining a cable unscrambler and several print-outs of Cobra's virus programming code. The Joes tune in as the Baroness, Destro and other Cobra officers – all in fancy dress – continue their criminal pledge drive. To the Joes' horror, Cobra promises to activate its computer virus, housed at a remote location, the moment the Cobrathon rakes in $5 billion.

Joe communications chief Dial-Tone tracks the Cobrathon's cable signal to Nevada, allowing Joe teams to spread out and search Reno and Las Vegas. Simultaneously, Mainframe sets about deciphering the swiped print-outs, hoping to derive the logon code and learn the computer virus' location. With rapid-fire speed, Mainframe backtracks the virus to a group of abandoned Anasazi pueblos and hastens there with Duke and Beach-Head.

In Las Vegas, the Dreadnoks impulsively throw down the gauntlet against Flint, Low-Light and Dial-Tone. Flint's team fends off the Dreadnoks and drives forward into the Cobrathon's hotel, unleashing chaos amidst the Cobrathon phone banks. Meanwhile, Duke's trio locates the central computer housing Cobra's virus, allowing Mainframe to turn the virus back on itself with a specially tailored program. As the Cobra virus eradicates its own computer, ending the threat to the world's intelligence community, Flint's group forces the Cobra officers to abandon their telethon and flee.

MEMORABLE MOMENTS An utterly hysterical "Cobrathon" moment shows the punkish Thrasher and Zartan, decked out in dinner suits and lamenting the state of budding young criminals. While viewing footage of a police arrest, Thrasher moans, "Another budding criminal cut down in his prime by the authorities! What can we do about it, Zartan?" Zartan replies, "We can do a lot, Thrasher!", then turns to the audience and spits out: "Your dollars can stop this shameless waste of fresh, young talent..." Genius.

LOVE AND WAR The purring Baroness, decked out in a slinky evening dress, serves as Cobrathon hostess – telling the audience to "Keep the phones busy, darlings." A female casino customer, thrilled to meet a "real G.I. Joe," flirts with Dial-Tone until Flint tells his subordinate to "get a date on his own time."

ASS-WHUPPINGS Mainframe mashes some Vipers beneath a heap of boxes. Sci-Fi lasers a couple of piranha (Author's Note: After all, it's just not a proper G.I. Joe episode without flesh-eating piranha.) Cobra captures Sci-Fi and Lifeline, entertaining Cobrathon viewers by tossing the Joes about on giant roulette wheels of doom.

Three-member Joe Conquest and Cobra Night Raven patrols mutually wipe out each another's aircraft. Low-Light tears away an "O" from an enormous "Coconut Palm Hotel" sign (akin to the infamous "Hollywood" letters in LA), then bowls over the Dreadnoks with it. (In the immortal words of *Sesame Street:*

"Today's bloodsport has been sponsored by the letter 'O'!")

Low-Light also saves Lifeline's hide, dousing two cobras – no, actual *cobras* this time – with a fire extinguisher.

SAVE THEM! Low-Light drops enough stone rubble onto the Dreadnoks to pulp them.

PREPOSTEROUS PHYSICS A Cobra Night Raven jet dives at Duke's trio, expertly crashing into a cliff face (rather the equivalent of driving your car into a brick wall for the hell of it).

GOOFS The Baroness follows Cobra Commander's venerable tradition in letting slip a phrase during the Cobrathon broadcast that helps the Joes narrow their search to Reno and Las Vegas.

Lifeline, an absurdly staunch pacifist, won't *touch* a rifle – not even when it's offered as a club to haul him out of a piranha-infested water tank. (In other words, Lifeline foolishly prefers becoming a piranha snack to using a rifle as a stick.)

Joe laser trooper Sci-Fi says he doesn't read intelligence reports because they "get him riled up," ignoring the fact that they also "stop him from getting gutted and filleted."

Cobra entrusts a single BAT with guarding its hallowed computer virus at the remote Anasazi bluffs. For that matter, there's no computer techs around in case something goes wrong. The Cobrathon money counter keeps turning even when Flint, Low-Light and Dial-Tone tear up the place – making us wonder who's answering the phones.

CHARACTER PROFILE: COBRA *Destro:* He's conscripted to perform agonizing stand-up comedy for the Cobrathon. Highly degraded, Destro reaches critical mass and shoots his cue cards to pieces – immediately feeling relieved and carrying on as he sees fit.

ORGANIZATIONS *Cobrathon:* To make a donation, call in New Jersey or New York: 1-800-212-156; in Los Angeles: 1-800-213-555-8119; in San Francisco; 2-007-656-133-1958. (Side Note: This arguably belongs under Goofs, but we commend the show's producers for not giving out actual numbers – you know they'd get calls.)

THE COMMAND DECISION Something of a bi-polar effort, with joyous fits of absurdity fits of absurdity (Thrasher and Zartan stressing the importance of nurturing "the criminals of tomorrow," etc.) clashing with more wayward and random elements (Lifeline and Sci-Fi tangle with a piranha tank, then wind up on killer roulette wheels). With a couple of revisions to boil out the extraneous bits, this mid-range effort could've hit the A-level.

2.13: "The Rotten Egg"

US Transmission Date: *Oct. 7, 1986*
Writers: *Steve Mitchell and Barbara Petty*

BATTLE ROSTER *Joes:* Leatherneck, Wet-Suit, Low-Light, Beach-Head.

MISSION BRIEF Joe marine Leatherneck is pleasantly surprised when the CEC Military Academy invites him to serve as guest of honor for its graduation exercises. But on arrival, Leatherneck shockingly identifies the CEC academy leader as Buck McCann – Leatherneck's ex-trainee and a wanted criminal.

Leatherneck calls out McCann, demanding his arrest on a long-standing charge of desertion and hardware theft. Unfortunately, as Leatherneck realizes that the "CEC" is actually Cobra's elite training facility, a couple dozen Cobra cadets surround him. Nursing a personal grudge against Leatherneck (*see Character Profile*), McCann declares his plan to obliterate the military's Parris Island training facility – Leatherneck's former boot camp and a location dear to his heart.

McCann locks up Leatherneck, dresses his Cobra recruits as marching band members and heads for Parris Island. Even though Hawk, Beach-Head and other Joes serve as a Parris Island honor guard, the disguised Cobra troopers catch the Joes napping. McCann's soldiers capture some high-ranking military officials, then line several of the academy buildings with dynamite.

Thankfully, Leatherneck escapes and happens across a Dreadnok motorcycle brigade. Stealing Zandar's bike, Leatherneck makes tracks for Parris Island. Spitting mad, the Dreadnoks pursue. As Leatherneck charges up and thrashes McCann – desperate to stop his ex-trainee from throwing his detonator switch – the rabble-rousing Dreadnoks pursue the Joe into the academy. The Joes regain control during the mayhem, rounding up McCann and most of his soldiers, but the Dreadnoks escape. Leatherneck experiences mixed emotions as McCann goes off to jail, pleased for saving Parris Island but saddened over losing a good marine to his dark side.

MEMORABLE MOMENTS In a flashback, Leatherneck memorably informs Cadet McCann that, "The Marines Corps needs men for leaders, not bullies." (Sadly, the lesson doesn't take.)

ASS-WHUPPINGS Years ago, McCann unfairly bested Leatherneck by concealing a stick behind his back, then suddenly whipping it out and bludgeoning the future Joe member senseless. In the modern day, Leatherneck browbeats several of McCann's recruits, pummels some guard dogs and crashes an entire Dreadnok cycle patrol. In a final one-on-one duel, McCann nearly beats the toast out of his ex-superior officer, but Leatherneck's fighting experience wins the day.

GOOFS Leatherneck steals Zandar's bike, but Zandar gains another hog without explanation.

TV-TIE INS McCann's soldiers masquerade as "Gerberville" marching band members (possibly a nod to series writer Steve Gerber) rather than the more traditional Cobra hideout of "Springfield" (overrun in "There's No Place Like Springfield").

CHARACTER PROFILE: JOES

• *Leatherneck and Wild Bill:* Leatherneck deems Wild Bill a hotshot, but concedes that he gets the job done.

• *Leatherneck and McCann:* Years ago, Leatherneck served as McCann's drill sergeant. McCann showed enormous potential on the battlefield, breaking Leatherneck's personal endurance record and rifle accuracy scores. Leatherneck initially regarded McCann as one of the finest marines he'd ever met, but grew troubled by McCann's lack of responsibility and violent disposition.

Despite Leatherneck's efforts, McCann increasingly turned renegade – breaking a cadet's arm during a simple sparring match. The mean trick compelled Leatherneck to nix McCann's recommendation for the officer corps. Undaunted, McCann continued his walk to the dark side until Leatherneck caught McCann stealing military rocket launchers to sell on the black market. Leatherneck pummeled McCann's associates, but McCann brutalized Leatherneck (*see Ass-Whuppings*) and escaped as a wanted criminal.

• *Leatherneck and McCann's cadets:* Leatherneck's nobility (or more to the point, McCann's sadism) convinces Cadet Mike P. Randall to disavow his allegiance to Cobra. Unfortunately, Cadet Shelia McDermott solidly remains loyal to Cobra despite Leatherneck saving her from drowning when a chase goes awry.

ORGANIZATIONS *Joes:* They're supposed to check in with headquarters every 24 hours, even while on leave.

THE COMMAND DECISION Underrated, probably because it ignores the mainstay Cobra characters to focus on the well-crafted, evil seed Buck McCann. But to its credit, "The Rotten Egg" hatches as a deep-rooted personal dilemma for Leatherneck, laudably continuing the mature flavor of G.I. Joe Season 2.

2.14: "Glamour Girls"

US Transmission Date: Oct. 8, 1986
Writer: Beth Bornstein

BATTLE ROSTER *Joes:* Low-Light, Lady Jaye, Cover Girl, Dial-Tone, Mainframe, Flint, Lift-Ticket; *Cobra:* Dr. Mindbender, Zartan, Zarana, the Baroness, Serpentor, Cobra Commander.

MISSION BRIEF In an effort to upgrade Cobra's technological arsenal, Serpentor opens negotiations to acquire a makeshift "youth-granting" device from cosmetics tycoon Madame Veil. As Serpentor learns, Madame Veil's apparatus can "drain" a gorgeous woman of her good looks – literally stripping the beauty of her eyes, nose and mouth and leaving a smooth blank face behind. The device then transfers the blank woman's vitality to an old crone – stripping away the years and making the ancient biddy young, supple and beautiful again.

Madame Veil offers to share her gadget's secrets if Cobra will capture the world's most beautiful women for her to drain and discard. Serpentor agrees, fronting a magazine named *Glamour Girls* to lure models in for "photo sessions." Zartan and the Baroness disguise themselves as *Glamour Girls* agents, zapping the beauties with a modified camera flash laced with subliminal messages. Once "photographed," the mesmerized models make straight for a Cobra transport, heading for Madame Veil's secret island.

In due course, *Glamour Girls* hires Low-Light's sister Una and her roommate Satin – amateur models who easily fall prey to Zartan's camera flash. When Low-Light investigates his sister's disappearance days later, he learns about a number of missing models and convinces Flint to investigate *Glamour Girls.* Disguising Lady Jaye and Cover Girl as models, Flint sends them to scope out *Glamour Girls,* but the Joe women fall prey to Zartan's subliminal camera.

Simultaneously, Zarana's bullying of the lazy Dreadnoks reaches titanic proportions, inciting them catch her with the camera flash. When Zartan learns that the Dreadnoks sent his sister to Madame Veil's face-stripping base, he systematically kicks each Dreadnok in the face. Royally pissed, Zartan contacts Dr. Mindbender for help – but the despicable doctor prioritizes Cobra's deal with Madame Veil over Zarana's safety.

Contacting the Joes for help, Zartan offers information about Madame Veil's headquarters in exchange for his sister's safe return. Without a second's hesitation, Flint takes a strike team and runs roughshod through Madame Veil's island. As the Joes press home their assault, Madame Veil straps Low-Light's sister Una into her face-swapping machine, intending to revitalize her own aged face. But as the machine activates, Low-Light bursts into the room and frees Una. Left without a "youth donor," the machine continues on automatic, erasing Madame Veil's facial features completely. Horrified at Madame Veil's fate, the Joes effectively end Cobra's face-blanking scheme.

LOVE AND WAR Dial-Tone yuks it up when a modeling agent comments that Low-Light wouldn't look too good in a string bikini. During the final break-out, a Viper mistakes a Joe-crewed hovercraft for a Cobra ship and screams, in a stunning imitation of a frat boy: "You've got here just in time! The women are escaping!"

ASS-WHUPPINGS When he learns that the Dreadnoks sent Zarana to Madame Veil, Zartan skillfully kicks each and every one of his lackey-toads in the face (the viewer gets a glimpse of Buzzer's quivering mug before Zartan's boot comes into view). Later, Low-Light thumps Zartan unconscious. Falling crates squash a few Joes, although the Joe-affiliated women even the score by thrashing a Viper squad.

PREPOSTEROUS PHYSICS Captive actress Tara Dawset overrides the cell control for Veil's prisoners with a lockpick, shorting out the entire Cobra base's power supply in the process. Indeed, the bubbly Dawset comments on her lock-picking skill, "Just like in one of my pictures! Gee!", suggesting she can barely pick her nose.

GOOFS Madame Veil's face-blanking device simply defies all principles of logic. If, as the story implies, it restores youth by stripping the face off of a beautiful woman and slapping it onto an old ugly woman: A) This would hardly improve the old biddy's social relations; if she wears an entirely new face, how would her friends and family recognize her? B) We also might add that simply gaining a new face would do nothing to correct the sagging effects of gravity on other parts of the crone's body.

If, however, the device restores youth by draining the model of her youth and vitality and pumping it like caffeine or collagen into Grandma: A) With the model's youth being drained (and Grandma looking more like a Maybelline commercial by the second), why doesn't the young woman shrivel up into an aged prune? B) Why does the model lose her face? If the device only transfers the girl's "youth essence," *where does the face go?*

Speaking of which, how do Madame Veil's faceless victims breathe? For that matter, how does the blank-faced Madame Veil *talk* at story's end? And how the hell does Serpentor expect to profit from Veil's face-switcher device anyway? ("Mwa-ha! I shall rampantly switch world leaders' faces and send the globe into political chaos! Old crotchety women shall rule Hollywood and send me cookies! This I command!")

The Joes apparently follow Lady Jaye thanks to a tracer in her purse – but she isn't carrying one.

TV TIE-INS Una's roommate Satin bears no resemblance to the blonde singer of the same name in "The Pyramid of Darkness."

CHARACTER PROFILE: COBRA The Baroness: Her busy work schedule doesn't let her keep up with current magazines (she fails to realize that Fashion World ceased publication years ago).

STUFF YOU NEED Cobra's Hypnotic Camera: Capable of plunging its victims into a dream world (in which its victims "see" the Dreadnoks as well-dressed gentlemen). For whatever reason, the hypnotic suggestion wears off at the stroke of midnight.

- *Glamour Girls:* Extensive Enterprises technically owns the magazine, but Serpentor authorizes the endeavor.
- *Madame Veil's Youth Machine:* It doesn't literally swap faces, meaning that the revitalized old hags don't wind up looking like their victims. But through a completely baffling process, the machine seems to steal the young women's' "youth essence," restoring senior citizens to their bouncy 20s (*see Goofs*).

THE COMMAND DECISION Arrggh! Braced with strong pacing, on-target characterization and a choice moment when Zartan and Low-Light find common ground in their endangered sisters, "Glamour Girls" holds a lot more merit than one might expect. But the agonizing premise, saddled with Madame Veil's imbecilic face-erasing machine, holed us like a fast-moving torpedo.

2.15: "Iceberg Goes South"

US Transmission Date: *Oct. 15, 1986*
Writer: *Mary Skrenes*

BATTLE ROSTER *Joes:* Iceberg, Lady Jaye, Snow Job, Wet-Suit, Beach-Head; *Cobra:* Dr. Mindbender.

MISSION BRIEF Hoping to grow soldiers with enhanced physical abilities, Cobra funds experiments – conducted by a genetic scientist named Dr. Wendigos – to create a series of half-human, half-animal creatures. Under Dr. Mindbender's supervision, Wendigos constructs a tropo-dome – a small tropical habitat shielded from sub-zero temperatures – in the Arctic wastes for privacy. Next, Wendigos splices several Cobra troopers' DNA with various animals, creating a variety of human-animal hybrids with wolves, walruses, bears, weasels and more. Dr. Mindbender's initially pleased, but soon learns, to his frustration, that the hybrids must routinely consume a synthetic protein to stabilize their condition.

Some miles away, Iceberg sets out from a Joe Arctic research base, hoping to test some survival equipment. By happenstance, Iceberg bumps into an old acquaintance: Dr. Wendigos' niece and assistant, a young Jamaican woman named Mahia. Admittedly happy to see Iceberg, Mahia collects animal tissue samples for her uncle's research. But as Mahia returns to the tropo-dome, she discards a valuable test tube of seal DNA.

Curious, Iceberg pockets the seal sample and travels to Wendigos' tropo-dome, where he's captured by Cobra wolf-men. Dr. Mindbender overrides Mahia's pleas for mercy, overdosing the hapless Iceberg with whale DNA and turning him into a full-blown killer whale. (*Author's Note:* That's not a misprint.)

Meanwhile, Wet-Suit, Snow Job and other Joes search for the missing Iceberg, arriving at the Cobra-controlled tropo-dome. Wet-Suit detonates several explosive charges as a precaution. Unfortunately, the tropo-dome fractures, hurling the whale-ish Iceberg into the open waters. After shutting down Dr. Mindbender's operation, the Joes scramble to recover their missing teammate.

Using Wet-Suit as bait, the Joes lure the Iceberg whale to a stable ice floe and nail him with tranquilizer darts. With Iceberg doped up, Mahia runs forward and makes her oceanic friend munch down on a raw steak. The influx of organic protein destabilizes Iceberg's whale DNA, returning him to normal and ending Cobra's hybrid experiments.

MEMORABLE MOMENTS It's completely irrelevant, but Snow Job's inflatable suit hysterically blows him up like a sumo wrestler.

LOVE AND WAR Iceberg and Mahia share a fair amount of sexual tension, although they certainly don't act on it in this story. (You know what they say about whale members...) Still, Mahia catches a glimpse of Iceberg's naughty bits when he reverts – sans clothing – back to normal from being a whale.

P.S. A picture of an attractive blonde woman off-handedly appears on Beach-Head's desk.

ASS-WHUPPINGS Cobra wolf-men knock Iceberg out in about three seconds flat. Lady Jaye gases a quartet of terrorist wolverines unconscious.

PREPOSTEROUS PHYSICS Wet-Suit somehow conceals his cast-iron diving helmet in his parka. Also, he dons the helmet underwater, meaning it should've filled with water before he put it on. How does the human-sized Iceberg spontaneously gain mass to achieve killer whale size?

GOOFS The title reads "Iceberg Goes South," but the Joes work from an Arctic research center. It's never clear why Mahia discards her seal DNA, motivating Iceberg to travel to the tropo-dome.

Snow Job's goggles disappear and reappear. The whale Iceberg turns from pursuing a pack of seals to eat Wet-Suit, who shouldn't taste, look or smell right to a whale.

Mahia convinces the whale Iceberg to chew down on raw meat – despite the fact that they've doped him unconscious. Dr. Wendigos, who willingly aided and abetted with Cobra's plans to get funding, presumably walks free.

TV TIE-INS Mahia later resurfaces as Iceberg's date in "Nightmare Assault."

CHARACTER PROFILE: JOES

• *Iceberg:* He hails from Brownsville, TX, although he's also visited Galveston. Iceberg detests his native climate and relishes cold temperatures. He joked that he wouldn't mind gaining a polar bear's strength – so of course, he gets turned into killer whale.

• *Snow Job:* Snow Job's insulated suit inflates like a giant beach ball (useful, if you're ever knocked into freezing waters by walrus-people).

• *Wet-Suit:* He's conducting diving suit performance tests for the Navy SEALs. Wet-Suit's boots sprout diving flippers. He wears a backpack with small propellers for underwater work.

CHARACTER PROFILE: OTHER *Dr. Wendigos:* His name's obviously a play on "wendigo," the half-human/half-animal creature rumored to roam the Canadian woods. Cobra's moolah allowed Wendigos to bypass 10 years of red tape and start his experiments immediately.

ORGANIZATIONS *Cobra Animal-Humans Hybrids:* They require synthetic protein to retain their animal characteristics, but the carnal sides of their nature lust for real meat.

THE COMMAND DECISION Completely absurd, Iceberg Goes South" only gets more banal and ridiculous as it goes along. The final half – because glory knows, it wouldn't be a human-animal hybrid story without turning one of the Joes into a killer whale – made us cradle our heads and weep.

2.16: "The Spy Who Rooked Me"

US Transmission Date: Oct. 13, 1986
Writer: Susan K. Williams

BATTLE ROSTER *Joes:* Flint, Lady Jaye, Cross-Country, Dial-Tone; *Cobra:* Dr. Mindbender, Zarana, the Dreadnoks.

MISSION BRIEF Dr. Mindbender negotiates on Cobra's behalf with a black market dealer, hoping to purchase an innocuous vial of liquid that transforms into a deadly nerve gas cloud on contact with air. Thankfully, British super-agent Matthew Burke foils Dr. Mindbender's deal – crashing the Cobra scientist's car, swiping the nerve toxin vial and running for the hills.

Soon after, Burke collaborates with Hawk on how to safely transport the vial to the Rocky Mountain Chemical Weapons Arsenal. Favoring a small Joe team over a massive convoy, Hawk assigns Flint, Lady Jaye, Cross-Country and Dial-Tone to ferry the vial to safety. Unfortunately, a disguised Zarana eavesdrops on Hawk and Burke, tipping off Cobra to the Joes' plans.

Flint's team sets off in an Armadillo mini-tank, but Zartan and the Dreadnoks continually dog them. Burke appears and saves the Joes' hides, but a higgledy-piggledy chase involving numerous Cobra operatives ultimately leads to the heroes' capture. Dr. Mindbender swipes the nerve toxin vial, letting the Joes and Burke live to prove Cobra's supremacy. But when Mindbender's crew makes for a nearby airstrip, the Joes escape and pursue their foes. Flint, Lady Jaye and Burke draw first blood – crippling Dr. Mindbender's still-grounded Night Raven squadron – while Cross-Country and Dial-Tone summon massive reinforcements.

Defeated on all sides, Dr. Mindbender throws the nerve toxin vial at Flint's trio to cover his escape. Flint valiantly smothers the shattered vial with his own body – shouting at his teammates to run – but Burke reveals that the vial contains harmless cream soda. As a dripping Flint and the other Joes gape in astonishment, Burke explains that Hawk knew of Zarana's breach of security from the very beginning. Flint's team served as a decoy, drawing Cobra's attention while the real nerve toxin vial reached the weapons arsenal 24 hours ago. The beleaguered Joes return home, fuming when the media credits Burke – an international man of mystery – with "single-handedly" thwarting the Cobra plot.

MEMORABLE MOMENTS An impassioned moment features Dr. Mindbender tossing the "nerve toxin vial" – and Flint, trying to selflessly save his comrades, belly-flopping onto the shattered vial while screaming out: "Run! I'll smother it!" Of course, a second later, Burke clears his throat and confesses that Flint's just hurled himself onto a puddle of cream soda.

LOVE AND WAR When Lady Jaye comments: "No more picking scorpions out of my boots," it sounds more like she's saying: "No more picking scorpions out of my boobs."

Flint smolders while the elegant Burke flirts incessantly with Lady Jaye – offering her a ride in his air-conditioned car and wiping smudges from her nose, commenting: "On you, a dab of grease looks as good as rouge." (Later, Flint nearly hits the boiling point when Lady Jaye over-affectionately calls Burke "Matt.")

The jealousy gestates in Flint's gut, erupting when Burke takes the "nerve toxin" and seemingly abandons the Joes. Trailing Burke to his motel, Flint leaves his credit card with the front desk – paying off, in advance, any damages he might incur while cleaning Burke's clock. By story's end, Flint dismisses Burke's threat to his manhood, especially when Lady Jaye decries the British agent for hogging the limelight.

ASS-WHUPPINGS Joe artillery fire blasts apart Zartan and Buzzer's motorcycles, but a retaliatory strike hamstrings the Joe Armadillo mini-tank. The Dreadnoks literally dismantle Burke's car to find the nerve toxin (Zartan humorously finds it in the glove compartment). Burke's benefactor, mysteriously named "Auntie," supplies another car – which Burke blows up while trying to stop Dr. Mindbender's getaway. Lady Jaye angrily tosses a TV across the room, enraged when Burke hogs the credit for their mission.

SAVE THEM! A Joe Armadillo mini-tank scores a direct hit on Zartan's motorcycle – ripping it to pieces but leaving the Dreadnok leader unharmed.

PREPOSTEROUS PHYSICS Flint, Dial-Tone and Cross-Country push a rock that's multiple times their body mass.

GOOFS Cross-Country throws a wrench that evidently turns phases in and out of existence, somehow nailing Dreadnok Thrasher without breaking the windshield on his Thunder Machine.

This is a *lot* of hoopla over *one* nerve toxin vial – which, let's face it, would suck as a long-range weapon. Indeed, Dr. Mindbender tosses the "toxin" at Flint, Lady Jaye and Burke without fearing for his own life.

TV TIE-INS Flint carries a G.I. Joe credit card that's similar to one that Alpine flashes ("The Funhouse"). Cobra previously assaulted the Rocky Mountain Chemical Weapons Arsenal in "Twenty Questions."

CHARACTER PROFILE: OTHER

Matthew Burke and "Auntie": A mysterious benefactor named "Auntie" (possibly a take-off of a British nickname for the BBC – "Auntie Beeb") supplies Burke with his Bond-like array of vehicles and weaponry. "Auntie" also arranges for various supplies – even new cars – to reach Burke while he's in the field.

Burke typically carries a laser pistol and laser-equipped cufflinks. He's graced with stellar acrobatic skills.

PLACES TO GO Ft. Watucka: Its engineering staff sometimes performs repairs and maintenance on G.I. Joe HAVOCs.

HOT WHEELS Burke's Sports Car: Features the usual assortment of secret agent gadgets, including smoke emitters, spikes to derail cycle-riding enemies and an ejector seat. Supplied by "Auntie," it's got enough horsepower to tow a G.I. Joe Armadillo mini-tank.

THE COMMAND DECISION Above average, and almost achieving a smooth synthesis of G.I. Joe and "James Bond." Susan Williams, who wrote the keynote Transformers episode "Only Human," keeps her characters on target, propelling this story through the finish line with a pleasing – if not particularly Top 10-worthy – effort.

2.17: "Grey Hairs and Growing Pains"

***US Transmission Date:** Oct. 14, 1986*
***Writers:** Dave Marconi and Flint Dille*

BATTLE ROSTER *Joes:* Beach-Head, Low-Light, Dial-Tone, Flint, Lady Jaye, Sci-Fi, Mainframe; Cobras: Dr. Mindbender, Zarana, the Dreadnoks, Serpentor.

MISSION BRIEF The Joes raise a collective eyebrow when Cobra steals a famed "youth treatment" formula from the venerable Versailles family – a means of making people vastly younger or older in a matter of minutes. Pondering the possible uses for such a formula, Flint and Lady Jaye consult with ex-Joe communications expert Sparks. Now working in the television industry, Sparks tips off his colleagues to commercials with actress Donna Dasher hawking ads for the "Ageless Care Spa" – a subsidiary of the Crimson Twins' Extensive Enterprises.

Curious, a six-pack of Joes investigates the Ageless Care Spa in Beverly Hills. Dressed in sweats, the Joes sign up for a gym session, but Dr. Mindbender, scanning the spa's security system, easily penetrates the Joes' disguises. To eliminate his competition, Dr. Mindbender's staff escorts the "undercover" Joes into the spa's sun and steam rooms. But once inside, the Joes find themselves zapped with Versailles' aging/de-aging formula. In the steam room, Lady Jaye, Dial-Tone and Mainframe revert to seven-year-old bodies. Simultaneously, Flint, Gung Ho and Sci-Fi find themselves aged into senior citizens in the sun room.

Thankfully, the kid Joes retain their fighting edge, battering their way past a troupe of Cobra Vipers and escaping with the aged Joes. Fearing a full-blown Joe investigation, Dr. Mindbender's staff evacuates the Ageless Care Spa. While pondering their next move, the age-zapped Joes learn that Cobra punished the money-hungry Donna Dasher by advancing her to old age. With Dasher's help, the Joes learn about a desert-based Ageless Care research station and cobble together makeshift weapons.

At the desert site, Serpentor gapes as a troupe of senior citizens and skateboard-racing kids run his Vipers ragged. But amid the firefight, Zarana – still pining for Mainframe – pulls the pee-wee Joe aside and gives him the Versailles formula. Mainframe returns himself to normal in the base's prototype sun room, then bluffs the Cobra troops into thinking he's activated the base's self-destruct. The Cobra troopers quickly retreat, allowing the Joes to shed their gained/lost years and summon reinforcements from Joe Headquarters.

MEMORABLE MOMENTS As Lady Jaye turns into a child, she shouts Sentence No. 239 we thought we'd never hear in G.I. Joe: "The steam is shrinking us!" Almost as amusingly, the kiddie Lady Jaye, Dial-Tone and Mainframe race about on skateboards, upending various Vipers.

LOVE AND WAR A couple years before Tom Hanks' Big, Mainframe – reduced to boyhood – re-encounters his lost love Zarana. She helps Mainframe out, but they otherwise part company.

Sci-Fi's attracted to actress Donna Dasher (well, when she's young, anyway). The child-size Lady Jaye sheds her oversized sweatpants and runs about in a giant sweatshirt – which means she's pantless when she's returned to normal size. (Blushing, she hurriedly covers up her derriere.)

ASS-WHUPPINGS At Madame Versailles' estate, Dial-Tone blasts some Dreadnoks with a high-powered hose. Actress Donna Dasher, hoping to avoid questions about her alleged ties to Cobra, starts an elephant rampage during a safari film shoot – nearly flattening Flint and Sci-Fi beneath a pile of pachyderms. Similarly, NFL player Brett Tinker – also an Ageless Care spokesperson – convinces his teammates to trample Mainframe and Dial-Tone during a practice session. The end tally for both Joe groups: 27 minor cuts and abrasions, but no serious injuries.

GOOFS Madame Versailles supposedly only keeps one copy of her family's "priceless" youth formula around. Of course, we never learn how the formula works. (For that matter, the older Versailles is hardly a come-hither-yonder beauty.)

How does Cobra expect to make money from the Ageless Care process? They could try charging through the nose to "youthenize" wealthy clients, but Cobra seems to keep its "ageless" capabilities secret from everyone.

The "Ageless Care Spa" strangely lets men and women share steam rooms, although that might explain why Mainframe, Dial-Tone and Lady Jaye enjoy their steam bath decked out in workout sweats.

Mainframe says the age-zapped Joes can't contact Joe Headquarters for help because it'd be "too embarrassing" – but that's *surely* preferable to getting shot. Serpentor, depicted as an impetuous military conqueror in every other *G.I. Joe* story, seems atypically scared to engage the age-inappropriate Joes in battle.

TV TIE-INS Zarana and Mainframe previously shared a meaningful flirtation in "Computer Complications." Sparks, cited as Joe communications chief in "Cobra Stops the World," retired from active service at an unspecified point and currently works for TV station ABN.

Beach-Head provides the most concrete proof of Joe Headquarters being located along the East Coast, off-handedly remarking that the Joes have traveled "3000 miles" to California (*see "Joe Headquarters' Location" sidebar*).

CHARACTER PROFILE: JOES

Flint, Gung Ho and Sci-Fi: Flint keeps his hair as he ages, but Sci-Fi and Gung Ho can't say the same.

THE COMMAND DECISION Largely off-kilter, given that the first half (chock full of irrelevant elephant rampages, football practices, etc.) barely resembles the latter part (with the Joe geriatrics and chilluns) at all. Still, as with most Flint Dille scripts, there's a sense of fun that's hard to unearth – even with a supremely sharpened trowel – elsewhere, meaning "Grey Hairs and Growing Pains" holds payoff if you're in the right mood.

2.18: "My Brother's Keeper"

US Transmission Date: *Oct. 15, 1986*
Writer: *Buzz Dixon*

BATTLE ROSTER *Joes:* Sgt. Slaughter, Sci-Fi, Low-Light, Dial-Tone, Hawk; *Cobra:* Dr. Mindbender, Zarana and the Dreadnoks.

MISSION BRIEF Moving forward with his scientific efforts, Serpentor authorizes experiments to create a "Voltronic Galaxator" – an energy weapon capable of altering a substance's polarity and turning it into hyper-explosive anti-matter. Unfortunately, Dr. Mindbender's attempts to fine-tune the device fail, causing the prototype Galaxator to shred itself on every test run. At his wits' end, Dr. Mindbender proposes recruiting the handicapped Dr. Jeremy Penser – one of the greatest minds in quantum physics – to tinker with the Galaxator's design.

Having eavesdropped on Dr. Mindbender's plans, a Joe surveillance team alerts Hawk to the danger. With the arrogant, unlikable Penser signing copies of his newest book at the World Science Fiction Convention, Hawk details Sgt. Slaughter and Sci-Fi to keep tabs on the wheelchair-bound physicist. Regrettably, Dr. Mindbender and the Dreadnoks reach Penser first, offering to surgically restore Penser's mobility in exchange for his scientific know-how. Penser initially rejects Dr. Mindbender's offer, but finds the prospect of walking again too tempting and agrees.

Penser moves to depart with Dr. Mindbender, unceremoniously leaving his young brother, Timothy Penser, behind in the convention hall. Sgt. Slaughter mashes the Dreadnoks' faces, but Penser and the Cobra goons all escape. The two Joes pursue in a HAVOC, reluctantly taking Timothy along to reason with his sibling.

Sgt. Slaughter's trio trails Dr. Mindbender's crew to a secluded Cobra base, where Penser completes modifications to the Cobra Galaxator. Once discovered, Sgt. Slaughter's trio tangles with the Dreadnoks. When Dr. Mindbender zealously orders the Galaxator into action, Penser selfishly complies by firing on the Joes and his brother. But shortly after, Penser recants his misdeeds – fearing for Timothy's safety – and shorts out the Galaxator's main power source. Infuriated, Dr. Mindbender leaves Penser to die in the impending chain reaction, but the Joes save Penser and race away. The Galaxator detonates, obliterating the entire Cobra base and leaving the normally smug Penser to view his brother in a better light.

MEMORABLE MOMENTS Sci-Fi correctly judges that his futuristic Joe uniform will blend right in with the World Sci-Fi convention-goers. The convention mirrors real-life sci-fi gatherings a little more closely than we'd like to admit, with attendees blathering about such life-altering topics as, "Where'd you get your Fantastic Four #28?" and "The sequel to Attack of the Turnips will be out next month!" Best of all, the fans rapturously watch the Slaughter/Dreadnok slugfest, thinking it's a staged performance.

ASS-WHUPPINGS By way of a diversion, Sgt. Slaughter "gets Cobra's attention" by beating the crap out of every villain in sight. At the sci-fi convention, Sci-Fi drops a giant robot model atop the Dreadnok Thunder Machine. Later, young Timothy offs the Thunder Machine with one of Dreadnok Monkeywrench's own explosives (see Goofs). Sgt. Slaughter takes out a Dreadnok Swampfire squadron by shooting 'em from behind.

PREPOSTEROUS PHYSICS There's an extremely odd bit of direction when Sgt. Slaughter, fighting the hapless Dreadnok Buzzer – who's standing still – keeps whiffing his punches through thin air. (For pity's sake, hit 'im!)

GOOFS Sci-Fi evidently lounges around his living quarters in his laser trooper outfit (hmmm... kinky). A sizeable firefight at the sci-fi convention doesn't hit any innocent bystanders with a stray shot. Dreadnok Monkeywrench makes the absurd mistake of throwing a ludicrous amount of dynamite with a lengthy fuse, allowing the Joes to throw it back.

TV TIE-INS Slaughter's itching to give Dr. Mindbender some payback after serving as his guinea pig ("Arise, Serpentor, Arise!").

CHARACTER PROFILE: COBRA

Zarana: Her lipstick conceals a secret communications device.

CHARACTER PROFILE: OTHER

Dr. Jeremy Penser: He's one of the world's foremost physics experts, also writing science-fiction on the side. Penser's one of the most unlikable jerk-weeds you've ever met – extremely self-righteous and verging on callous. By story's end, Penser displays some compassion for his younger brother Timothy – i.e. Penser shows enough humanity to not want his sibling spread across a battlefield like Smucker's strawberry jam. But even then, Penser's hardly what we'd call a warm individual.

STUFF YOU NEED Voltronic Galaxator: Cone-shaped, it's able to reverse an object's structural polarity and turn it into an anti-matter bomb.

HOT WHEELS Dreadnok Thunder Machine: The exterior's electrified.

THE COMMAND DECISION A potential Galaxy Quest in the making, regrettably watered down by too many chases and the handicapped Jeremy Penser – who reforms after trying to vaporize his younger brother.

2.19: "My Favorite Things"

US Transmission Date: *Oct. 16, 1986*
Writer: *Doug Booth*

BATTLE ROSTER *Joes:* Wet-Suit, Leatherneck, Lifeline, Flint, Lady Jaye, Low-Light, Dial-Tone, Mainframe; *Cobra:* Serpentor, Destro, Cobra Commander.

MISSION BRIEF Turning nostalgic for the military conquerors who contributed to his DNA ("Arise, Serpentor, Arise!"), Serpentor sets about locating his progenitors' favorite possessions. Serpentor quickly learns that each acquisition triggers a different sector of his genetic code, supercharging the Cobra Emperor with the original owner's attributes. With his DNA in flux, Serpentor's face rapidly morphs to resemble the different leaders who spawned him.

In the Netherlands, Serpentor itches to retrieve "Skullsplitter" – a battleaxe belonging to one of his forefathers, a feared Norse warrior named Ulric the Batterer. The Joes and NATO, holding joint war games in the area, sputter when Serpentor's troops obliterate a local dike. The resultant tidal wave tears through Amsterdam, allowing Cobra morays to assault a weapons museum and seize the battleaxe. Serpentor flails Skullsplitter about with remarkable proficiency, but a one-on-one bout with Leatherneck leaves the weapon sliced in half.

As the Cobra troops withdraw, Serpentor vows vengeance against Leatherneck. Serpentor's face again shifts to another of his successors, allowing Leatherneck to identify the mug in question as Vlad the Impaler (a.k.a. Count Dracula). Accordingly, the Joes travel to Dracula's Transylvanian castle, where they encounter a squad of Cobra troopers. While Serpentor salivates over the possibility of re-possessing Dracula's interrogation devices, the Joes press home their assault. Upset over the Joes' continued interference, Serpentor coats a dart with his venom-laced blood and nails Leatherneck. Serpentor then withdraws in a huff – leaving Dracula's keepsakes behind – while Wet-Suit hastily pulls his friend to safety.

Leatherneck becomes grievously ill and falls into a coma, making Joe medic Lifeline wish for a sample of Serpentor's blood to make an anti-toxin. Thankfully, the Joes detect Serpentor's group heading for Southern India, allowing Wet-Suit and Lifeline to give chase in a Conquest X-30.

In a Southern Indian temple, Serpentor's face takes on reptilian features – a mirror image of King Tashaka, the self-proclaimed "ruler of all serpents." Serpentor summons forth a 5000-year-old, room-sized female serpent, the nexus of Tashaka's power. Per Tashaka's traditions, Serpentor nourishes himself by drinking the serpent's venom: a purified form of the toxin already inherent in Serpentor's blood. Simultaneously, Lifeline and Wet-Suit quietly arrive, determining that a sample of the serpent's venom could generate an anti-toxin for Leatherneck.

Pressed for time, Wet-Suit hurriedly binds his forearm with a piece of cloth. Wet-Suit encourages the big-ass snake to bite his arm, thereby soaking his wrist cloth with venom. The effort also leaves Wet-Suit poisoned, but Lifeline wrings out the venom needed to make anti-toxin for his fallen friends.

As Lifeline helps a dying Wet-Suit limp back to their Conquest, the ailing Joe hurls a grenade as a parting gift – igniting the weapons arsenal aboard Serpentor's mothership. As the two Joes flee, the mothership erupts in a fireball, triggering a localized avalanche. The Cobra officers survive, but the rockfall opens a chasm, pulling Serpentor's colossal serpent into its depths. Back at base, Lifeline saves Leatherneck and Wet-Suit's lives – while Serpentor, abandoning his acquisition scheme, grow pleased for saving one of the gigantic serpent's newly hatched babies.

MEMORABLE MOMENTS Sick to death of Wet-Suit's selfishness, Joe medic Lifeline strafes his teammate: "So. It's okay to risk your life for revenge, but to save Leatherneck's life, you won't square up against a snake?! Some guys make fun of me because I don't carry weapons, but saving lives takes courage too. And if you're too scared to help, I'm going after that snake alone." Suitably flailed, Wet-Suit follows Lifeline and risks venom poisoning to save Leatherneck's hide.

LOVE AND WAR Admit it – there's still something decidedly kinky about the name "Vlad the Impaler."

ASS-WHUPPINGS A Cobra Battle Android Trooper (BAT) hands off a prized picture of Rasputin (more fodder for Serpentor's collection), then swan-dives off a cliff. The BAT crashes through a shack and takes a bit of damage but finds the strength to walk home.

Leatherneck skewers a BAT on a spiked pole. Serpentor then poisons the Joe marine, rendering him comatose for half the story. Wet-Suit fries a BAT with a cup of the colossal serpent's acidic venom, then gets poisoned himself.

G.I. JOE: THE MUSICAL Okay, so there aren't really any musical moments in "My Favorite Things," but the title conjures up images of Serpentor prancing about like Julie Andrews in The Sound of Music and singing: "Pics of Rasputin and torture devices / Giant girl snakes and an big axe that slices / Statues of Ceasar and a dart that stings / These are a few of my favorite things!" Sigh. (We need help.)

PREPOSTEROUS PHYSICS A dueling Serpentor and Leatherneck completely disregard the fact that they're underwater and effortlessly swing weapons about the place. For that matter, one wonders if a museum guillotine, hampered by water pressure, could slice Serpentor's axe like a carrot.

Serpentor has ample time to nail a fleeing Leatherneck's backside, but moments later, Serpentor's dart is shown impaling Leatherneck *through* a door, meaning Serpentor hurled it with impossible force. For that matter, if Serpentor's blood lives up to its title of, "the most powerful poison in the world," shouldn't Leatherneck have died instantly?

Wet-Suit superhumanly rips off the left side of his shirt – one-handed, mind you – without even removing it.

Worst of all, Wet-Suit somehow sets an Olympic record by hurling a grenade *hundreds of yards away* to destroy Serpentor's parked mothership. Never mind that the ship's so flimsy, a simple grenade brings the whole damn thing to ruin.

GOOFS A Joe/Cobra conflict previously collapsed another of Dracula's castles in "Arise, Serpentor, Arise!" Once again ("The M.A.S.S. Device," etc.), the underwater Joes and Cobras talk through a mouth-full of scuba gear.

Hawk dubiously lets Lifeline and Wet-Suit venture off to Southern Africa alone, babbling some feeble excuse that the Joes "need time to plan this mission!"

Wet-Suit scorches a BAT with a cupful of the giant serpent's venom – without any proof that the venom was acidic. Also, Wet-Suit spends this entire story in civilian clothes (the better to tear his shirt when needed) rather than his customary uniform.

TV TIE-INS "My Favorite Things" further details the military geniuses who contributed to Serpentor's genetic makeup ("Arise, Serpentor, Arise!").

CHARACTER PROFILE: JOES

• *Leatherneck:* He's not much of a gourmet diner, prone to eating – as Wet-Suit puts it – the equivalent of "sea rations sautéed with dog food."

• *Wet-Suit:* He hates snakes, but braves Serpentor's monster serpent to save Leatherneck's skin.

CHARACTER PROFILE: COBRA

Serpentor: Serpentor's relics include various tanks, a painting of Rasputin and statues of Julius Caesar, Ivan the Terrible and Genghis Khan. Serpentor's ousted Cobra Commander from his quarters on Cobra Island, filling it with his progenitors' possessions instead.

Thanks to King Tashaka's genetic inheritance, Serpentor gains strength by drinking the giant serpent's venom. In the serpent's presence, Serpentor can empathetically summon a wide variety of serpents (rather like "the Pied Piper" – only with snakes).

STUFF YOU NEED Cobra BATs: They're strong enough to keep functioning even if you drive a massive spike through their center mass.

THE COMMAND DECISION Excelling as an iron-willed story, "My Favorite Things" goes to the unexpected, astonishing lengths – only 19 episodes into the season – of actually molding Serpentor into a credible threat. Granted, it's also a bit piecemeal, but the serious tone of the work both nourishes science-fiction lovers and even makes Serpentor's relation to the reptilian King Tashaka seem credible. We gobbled it up.

2.20: "Raise the Flagg!"

US Transmission Date: Oct. 20, 1986
Writer: David Carren

BATTLE ROSTER *Joes:* Roadblock, Wet-Suit, Leatherneck, Hawk, Admiral Ledger; *Cobra:* Zartan, Zarana, Zandar, Cobra Commander, Serpentor.

MISSION BRIEF Learning that the sunken *USS Flagg* and a Cobra heli-carrier have descended to a reachable deep sea shelf ("Computer Complications"), Serpentor dispatches the Zartan family to salvage the deep-space anti-matter pod, still snug aboard the Cobra carrier. But when intelligence satellites alert the Joes to Cobra activity near the sunken Flagg's position, Hawk takes a squadron and assaults the Zartan clan's off-shore rig.

Zartan and his siblings flee, but Hawk's team scours their computer banks and discovers Cobra's intent. Panicked at the thought of Cobra acquiring the fiercely powerful anti-matter, Hawk sends Roadblock, Leatherneck and Wet-Suit to survey the *Flagg*'s remains while the Joes consider how to surface the venerable aircraft carrier.

Meanwhile, Zartan, Zarana and Zandar attempt to steal the anti-matter pod before the Joes can act. Zartan's group follows Roadblock's SHARC in a Cobra manta sub, but a close shave mangles both ships. After struggling to reach an air pocket aboard the *Flagg*, the Joe and Cobra trios discover that after the ship went down, someone tapped the anti-matter pod to generate electricity, purify the air and germinate kelp for food.

Suddenly, a legion of Cobra Battle Android Troopers (BATs) surrounds the intruders, taking everyone prisoner. To everyone's surprise, a Cobra mess hall cook named B.A. La Carre – lost aboard the Cobra carrier when it went down – steps forth. Driven utterly mad in his solitude, La Carre orders the BATs – reprogrammed serve the cracked chef – to make the captive Joe and Cobra trios help harvest the kelp beds.

Back on the surface, Serpentor turns dismayed at Hawk's progress, sending Cobra Commander to obliterate the sunken ships and prevent the Joes from nabbing the anti-matter. Hawk's Joes drive away Cobra Commander's flotilla, but not before the Cobra fleet launches several depth charges, pushing the *Flagg* closer to a deep sea trench. La Carre bumps his head in the process, regaining his sanity. But regrettably, the Joe and Cobra teams realize that the *Flagg*, further fractured by Cobra's assault, is filling with water.

As time runs out, Roadblock proposes reactivating the Cobra heli-carrier's main rotors. With the Cobra ship still impaling the *Flagg,* Roadblock conjectures that the carrier's blades might lift both ships. La Carre and Zartan's group assist their makeshift allies, tapping the anti-matter pod to charge the Cobra ship with power. Galvanized into action, the Cobra heli-carrier hauls itself and the *Flagg* back to the surface.

La Carre forswears his allegiance to Cobra, but Zartan's troupe – true to type – tries to turn around and thieve the anti-matter pod. But suddenly, the assembled Joes and Cobras, having risen to the surface too quickly, collapse from the bends. A Cobra moray extracts Zartan's group, allowing the Joes to secure the anti-matter pod and toss Roadblock's crew into a decompression chamber. As the Joes put the *Flagg* into a dry dock in Norfolk and send the anti-matter pod to Washington, Hawk offers the repentant La Carre a position as a Joe chef.

MEMORABLE MOMENTS Holding a kangaroo court, the wigged-out, lunatic B.A. La Carre converses with himself as judge and district attorney.

Also, La Carre decides to execute Roadblock and Zarana as an example, ordering his BATs to "Play the death march!" – i.e. the soundtrack from "Cold Slither." (Luckily, Cobra interrupts the proceedings by firing depth charges.)

ASS-WHUPPINGS Shockingly few, although a case of the bends takes out Roadblock's trio, La Carre and the Zartan family.

PREPOSTEROUS PHYSICS Hawk's Joes concoct a nutty scheme to raise the Flagg and the Cobra heli-carrier with inflatable cushions.

GOOFS When Roadblock, Wet-Suit and Leatherneck ditch their crumpled SHARC and reach the Flagg's air pocket, they seem oblivious to the fact that Zartan's manta ship just hit them.

TV TIE-INS The Joes thought the sunken Flagg ("Computer Complications") was lost forever in deep waters, but Cobra somehow discovered that the vessel was salvageable. La Carre enjoys listening to the "Cold Slither" soundtrack ("Cold Slither"). The refitted *USS Flagg* sees service in "G.I. Joe and the Golden Fleece."

CHARACTER PROFILE: COBRA B.A. La Carre: The initials "B.A." stand for bon appetite – a nickname bestowed upon La Carre when a few Strato-Vipers got food poisoning from eating his dinner slop.

STUFF YOU NEED The Anti-Matter Pod: It could likely power America's eastern seaboard for a month.

HOT WHEELS *USS Flagg*: It's a quarter-mile long and 20 stories high.

• *Joe SHARC:* Holds about 12-plus hours of air.

THE COMMAND DECISION Superbly constructed, the intoxicating "Raise the Flagg!" makes good use of its continual twists, shifting loyalties (the Joes allying with Zartan's folk against La Carre, etc.) and high-caliber battles (Cobra Commander: "How many times must I retreat in one day?"). It's also aged well, meaning that if G.I. Joe ever returns to the airwaves, its creators would do worse than to look at this story and "Computer Complications" for guidance.

2.21: "Ninja Holiday"

US Transmission Date: *Oct. 22, 1986*
Writer: *Michael Charles Hill*

BATTLE ROSTER *Joes:* Sgt. Slaughter, Wet-Suit, Leatherneck, Beach-Head, Sci-Fi, Low-Light; *Cobra:* Cobra Commander, Storm Shadow.

MISSION BRIEF In the South Pacific, Cobra hires local mercenaries to attack remote Joe outposts, spurring Sgt. Slaughter and a well-honed team of Joes to bust up the goons' base of operations. Relaxing at a hotel afterward, Sgt. Slaughter angrily learns that Joe SEAL Wet-Suit intends to participate in a martial arts competition – a smackdown sponsored by Pierre La Fonte, an international criminal. Citing Joe regulations, Sgt. Slaughter forbids Wet-Suit from taking part in the illicit event. But as the Joes get ready to return home, the sergeant takes a phone call intended for Wet-Suit – leading to La Fonte's agents mistaking Sgt. Slaughter for the Joe SEAL.

Suddenly, ninjas burst from hiding, gassing the sergeant unconscious. With Cobra operatives fooling Beach-Head and the other Joes into returning home, La Fonte's agents ferry the slumbering sergeant to a remote jungle base. There, Cobra goon La Fonte introduces "Wet-Suit" to a variety of polished killers and rogues from across the world – pitting his "contestants" against each other in a last-man-standing fight, with the winner serving as an assassin for Cobra.

Sgt. Slaughter faces a seemingly endless wave of opponents, besting every enemy tossed his way. Meanwhile, Hawk vents his spleen over Sgt. Slaughter's prolonged absence, ordering Beach-Head's Joes to return and find their missing colleague. Beach-Head's team tracks Sgt. Slaughter's whereabouts, just as the sergeant ass-whips his last contestant, emerging as the winner.

Suddenly, Cobra Commander arrives to meet his "master assassin." But Cobra Commander pops a nut to see Sgt. Slaughter, condemning La Fonte for letting such a high-ranking Joe infiltrate his secret operation. Thankfully, Beach-Head's group arrives onhand, carving through La Fonte's bodyguards. Cobra Commander escapes in the mayhem, but the Joes capture La Fonte and his men. Shortly afterward, Sgt. Slaughter smacks his head when he learns that Cobra Commander wanted an assassin to kill Serpentor – meaning he missed his chance to severely cripple the Cobra leadership.

MEMORABLE MOMENTS As two Cobra ninjas flail their nunchuks, Beach-Head's Joes discharge their rifles – obliterating an entire wall around their attackers. The ninjas look back – startled to see daylight save for two ninja-shaped pieces of wall – and wisely surrender.

ASS-WHUPPINGS Sgt. Slaughter whips dozens of La Fonte's guards as an initiation test, then defeats a string of would-be assassins including wrestler Osi Bisa and a boxing chef named Andre Velocite. La Fonte's ninjas kick the snot out of Sci-Fi, Low-Light, Wet-Suit and Leatherneck, although the Joes ultimately win through superior firepower.

PREPOSTEROUS PHYSICS Once again, Sgt. Slaughter cracks concrete with his bare fists.

GOOFS Two ninjas in La Fonte's employ lounge about in the "Green Monkey Cantina," kicking back and downing some brewskies – in their ninja fighting togs (that's stealth for ya). A close-quarters fight makes it look like Beach-Head's emptying his rifle into a thug's stomach (and that can't be right – sweet mercy, this is G.I. Joe we're talking about).

TV TIE-INS Sgt. Slaughter uses a G.I. Joe credit card (a la Alpine in "The Funhouse," Flint in "The Spy Who Rooked Me," etc.).

CHARACTER PROFILE: JOES

• *Leatherneck:* He once saw the movie *The Heart is a Lonely Hunter.*

• *Low-Light:* The jungle reminds Low-Light of Joseph Conrad's novel *Heart of Darkness.*

• *Wet-Suit::* Wet-Suit's an accomplished martial-arts expert, highly skilled at the Japanese art of *kendo* (a form of combat entailing wooden swords) – but he can't beat Sgt. Slaughter.

CHARACTER PROFILE: COBRA

• *Cobra Commander:* Storm Shadow serves as the commander's aide and confidant, helping the commander conspire against Serpentor.

• *Major Pierre LaFonte:* He often uses the "Green Monkey Cantina" bar in Manilla as a mail-drop and safehouse.

THE COMMAND DECISION The WWF-compatible G.I. Joe episode, "Ninja Holiday" throws its characters into an oddball – but strangely enthralling – smackdown. The title's a bit dippy (and somewhat erroneous) but otherwise, we appreciated this story's whirlwind nature and sense of bravado – not to mention Sgt. Slaughter's well-implemented bouts with virtually everyone.

2.22: "G.I. Joe and the Golden Fleece"

US Transmission Date: *Oct. 27, 1986*
Story: *Flint Dille;* ***Teleplay:*** *Rick Merwin*

BATTLE ROSTER *Joes:* Beach-Head, Lady Jaye, Lift-Ticket, Sgt. Slaughter, Leatherneck, Wet-Suit; *Cobra:* Dr. Mindbender, the Baroness.

MISSION BRIEF The Joes stand their ground when Cobra blockades the Suez Canal, leading to a massive firefight in Greece. But as the laser bolts fly, an alien airship – curious to learn more about Earth culture – ventures into the area. The Joes hold their fire, but a Cobra legion adopts a "shoot first, clean up the bodies later" policy, striking the alien ship's underbelly and ominously dislodging a golden hyperdrive coil.

Worried about Cobra obtaining advanced technology, Hawk asks Sgt. Slaughter and Beach-Head to head up a retrieval team. Sgt. Slaughter's brigade reaches the coil first but immediately takes fire from the Baroness' troops. But as the firefight continues, a poorly-aimed laser bolt strikes the temporally active hyperdrive – making it malfunction, hurling the assembled combatants thousands of years into the past of ancient Greece.

While Lady Jaye snags the golden coil, getting separated from her comrades in the process, the Joes and Cobras disengage to conserve their strength. Thankfully, the local population befriends the Joes after mistaking Lifeline for Aesclepius, the fabled Greek god of healing. With the Joes' Tomahawk low on fuel, the locals agree to float the helicopter downriver on pontoons. The Joes set out to recover Lady Jaye and the alien coil, unnervingly discovering a boy named Jason – who mispronounces the word "Tomahawk" as "Argonaut" – among their crew.

Elsewhere, Dr. Mindbender and the Baroness capture a nearby city, refining the Greeks' kerosene into a compatible fuel source. Unfortunately, Sgt. Slaughter falls overboard while repelling a follow-up Cobra assault, washing ashore and making the acquaintance of King Aegeus. Bargaining to obtain Aegeus's help, Sgt. Slaughter takes up the challenge of cleaning the king's unbelievably filthy stables in a single day. As you might expect, Sgt. Slaughter dams up a local river with a rock slide, diverting the water to flush out Aegeus' stables. Having cemented himself in history as the mythical Hercules, Sgt. Slaughter conscripts Aegeus to aid the other Joes.

Beach-Head's group finally meets up with Lady Jaye on the isle of Limnos. Minutes later, Cobra blitzes the ammunition-depleted Joes, who resort to a savage amount of hand-to-hand combat. Thankfully, Sgt. Slaughter arrives with Aegeus' troops, overwhelming the Cobra Vipers through sheer numbers.

Finally, Lady Jaye snags the Baroness' laser rifle and shoots the alien hyperdrive unit – re-activating its temporal field and flinging the Joes and Cobra troopers back to the present. While the Baroness' battered Cobra soldiers retreat, the Joes reach the refitted *USS Flagg.* Shortly after, the alien ship returns, snares the missing hyperdrive with a tractor beam and heads back into space.

MEMORABLE MOMENTS Spotting the alien ship, Hawk sensibly tells his Joes to stand down rather than "shoot first and ask questions later." Simultaneously, in a neat little contrast, Dr. Mindbender barks at his troops: "Shoot first and ask questions later!"

ASS-WHUPPINGS A gaggle of Cobra Trouble Bubbles ground the Joe Tomahawk. Some Greeks attack Dr. Mindbender and the Baroness' troops with flaming bolas and spears, but the Cobra soldiers prevail. At story's end, the Joes and Aegeus' honed soldiers roughhouse the Cobra goons into submission.

PREPOSTEROUS PHYSICS It's unclear, but Aegeus' soldiers carry polished, laser-refractive shields – useful for dodging Cobra's laser bolts, but not very convincing.

GOOFS Sigh. We probably don't need to mention the extreme contrivance of an alien ship just showing up in

Greece, nor the highly convenient happenstance of the alien ship losing only its time-travelling hyperdrive unit. How exactly does the coil move objects through time? And at story's end, why doesn't it teleport Aegeus' Greek soldiers to the present day?

Lady Jaye's seen standing by Sgt. Slaughter *after* she gets separated from the main Joe group. The legends of "Jason and the Argonauts" don't parallel the Tomahawk crew's journey all *that* much, although one could allow for several centuries of language corruption. Sgt. Slaughter's river-based solution to the stable problem wouldn't so much *clean* Aegeus' stables as it would just make them very, very soggy.

Lady Jaye correctly guesses that a second laser bolt will reactivate the alien coil, but there's no clue *how* she comes by that conclusion.

TV TIE-INS The *USS Flagg*'s back in service – a rather remarkable recovery, considering Cobra sank the noble vessel in "Computer Complications" and it sat on the ocean bottom, severely holed, until last episode ("Raise the Flagg!").

CHARACTER PROFILE: JOES

• *Leatherneck:* He once enjoyed a drunken night in Hong Kong, complete with hangover.

• *Sgt. Slaughter:* Ironically, the muscle-clad Sgt. Slaughter's took a year of ancient Greek in college. (The sergeant tells a startled Lifeline: "What's the matter? Can't believe I went to college?")

ORGANIZATIONS *G.I. Joe/Cobra:* To summarize how the Joes and Cobras impact history, medic Lifeline gets mistaken for Aesclepius, the Greek god of healing. Sgt. Slaughter turns into Hercules, the name "Tomahawk" gets corrupted into "Argonaut" and Cobra's one-man, airborne CLAW fighters get taken for harpies. The golden alien hyperdrive obviously becomes the "golden fleece" of Greek myth.

STUFF YOU NEED *The Alien Hyperdrive:* A real odd duck, it perfectly teleports people, vehicles and equipment into the past, also immobilizing Cobra's BAT robots into statues. (Then again, perhaps the materials composing the BATs make them vulnerable to the transfer process.)

THE COMMAND DECISION Monstrously contrived, with an out-of-left-field alien ship instigating a flatline adventure in ancient Greece. Historical pieces are notoriously hard to do well (although Transformers: "A Decepticon Raider in King Arthur's Court" springs to mind as a superior effort), with the witless "G.I. Joe and the Golden Fleece" proving no exception – and barely recognizable as G.I. Joe.

2.23: "The Most Dangerous Thing in the World"

US Transmission Date: *Oct. 29, 1986*
Writer: *Buzz Dixon*

BATTLE ROSTER *Joes:* Shipwreck, Lifeline, Dial-Tone, Hawk, Leatherneck, Wet-Suit, Beach-Head, Cross-Country, Lift-Ticket; *Cobra:* Serpentor, Dr. Mindbender.

MISSION BRIEF Utterly haggard from military operations, Serpentor and Dr. Mindbender search for a means of seeding G.I. Joe's destruction from within. While General Hawk departs for a trip to Europe, Dr. Mindbender hacks into the Defense Department's personnel records. Mindbender promptly promotes the three Joes most likely to botch a leadership position – the pacifist Lifeline, the bumbling Dial-Tone and the hopelessly disaster-prone Shipwreck – to the rank of colonel.

Aghast to learn of their teammates' promotions, Beach-Head and Mainframe agonizingly inform Lifeline, Dial-Tone and Shipwreck of their "good fortune." The three hopelessly incompetent "colonels" proceed to rework the Joes' duty and workout rosters in apocalyptic ways. Knowing the chaos will only last until Hawk returns, Serpentor takes his submarine/tank hybrids to attack the Bio-Research Institute.

Shipwreck, Dial-Tone and Lifeline sloppily try to mount a defense, but Serpentor's well-oiled machines overwhelm Dial-Tone's overcomplicated stratagems, Lifeline's pacifist tendencies and Shipwreck's ability to ruin everything he touches. Serpentor's armada runs circles around the Joe ranks, then turns to assault Joe Headquarters.

As the Joes fall into total disarray, Hawk airdrops into Joe Headquarters. Hawk pulls the Joes together, mounting a decisive counter-strike against the overconfident Cobra troops. Serpentor gapes as the tables turn, ordering an immediate withdrawal. Breathing a sigh of relief, Hawk strikes down Lifeline, Dial-Tone and Shipwreck's unauthorized promotions.

MEMORABLE MOMENTS With Serpentor knocking on Joe Headquarters' doorstep, Shipwreck completely flips his noodle and fires off the HQ's main particle beam. Never designed as a short-range weapon, the particle beam recoils, crashing through several levels of Joe Headquarters and burying Shipwreck in rubble. After the battle, Leatherneck and Wet-Suit decide to cut the Joe sailor loose... after their coffee break.

Leatherneck provides the story's title: We got a saying in the Marines. The most dangerous in the world is a green officer in the dark with a book of matches."

ASS-WHUPPINGS Before Lifeline's "promotion," a brawling Leatherneck and Wet-Suit bat the Joe medic aside. Later, the "colonels" botch a training exercise, leading to friendly fire nearly charbroiling Leatherneck and Wet-Suit.

During a disastrous outing against Serpentor, Dial-Tone orders a ridiculously complex maneuver that crashes the Joe HAVOCs into one another (naturally, the Cobra troops obliterate the crumpled Joe vehicles). Cobra BATs kneel, ripping apart the floatation skirts on Shipwreck's hovercrafts. Serpentor's men easily down a fleet of Joe Tomahawk helicopters, given that Lifeline's pacifist tendencies won't let him fire back.

Shipwreck's stunt with the particle beam demolishes multiple levels of Joe Headquarters. Upon Hawk's return, the Joes rally and smear Cobra's submarine tanks with dynamite packs.

TV TIE-INS As in "Arise, Serpentor, Arise!", this story also ranks Hawk, Duke, Flint and Beach-Head as the top Joe officers, although Sgt. Slaughter's also mentioned among the Joe elite.

CHARACTER PROFILE: JOES

• *Beach-Head:* He judges Roadblock and Slip-Stream – and himself for that matter – as far better officer material than the Cobra-made "colonels."

• *Dial-Tone:* Dial-Tone's a perfect example of someone who wildly dreams about becoming a military officer but just doesn't have the raw leadership talent to achieve promotion. He's not a bad person – he just can't properly boss people around. He's currently working on a new satellite tracking system that keeps falling apart due to a lack of proper research.

• *Hawk:* He clears all Joe promotion requests.

• *Lifeline:* Hawk thinks that Lifeline actually holds the ability to become an effective officer, but simply lacks the desire. Lifeline agrees, preferring to remain a humble medic.

• *Shipwreck:* As Hawk puts it, Shipwreck has "neither the [proper] desire nor the ability" to command – he's drunk with power and about as capable as a dead tortoise to lead a military unit.

HOT WHEELS Cobra Submarine Tanks: They're not so much "tanks" as amphibious smooth-rolling ground assault vehicles that double as submarines. (Hasbro mercifully never made these vessels into toys.) Although the tanks' ability to function in two environments comes in handy, they're vulnerable because their guns can't depress in close quarters.

THE COMMAND DECISION Unbridled brilliance, "The Most Dangerous Game in the World" features a smarter-than-average Cobra hacking the Joes off at the knees. The fact that the entire episode revolves around Lifeline, Dial-Tone and Shipwreck's personality quirks makes it all the juicier, endowing this work with a ripping pace that left us in stitches. In the infamous words of Bill and Ted: Ex-cellent.

2.24: "Nightmare Assault"

US Transmission Date: *Oct. 30, 1986*
Writer: *Marv Wolfman*

BATTLE ROSTER *Joes:* Low-Light, Hawk, Lifeline, Iceberg, Lady Jaye, Mainframe; *Cobra:* Serpentor, Dr. Mindbender, Zartan and the Dreadnoks.

MISSION BRIEF In an attempt at psychological warfare, Dr. Mindbender crafts a "Sound-U-Lator" – a fiendish device capable of instilling ungodly nightmares in its victims by remote. Over the next few days, dozens of Joes experience hellish nightmares, sleep depravation and dementia. Hawk tries to rally his team, but the excruciating dreams whittle down the Joes' battle proficiency.

Meanwhile, night sniper Low-Light, who gained a high tolerance for nightmares due to abuse he suffered as a child, resists the Sound-U-Lator's effects. Dr. Mindbender throws his device into high gear, tormenting the sleeping Low-Light with visions of giant serpents and rat-shaped cars. In turn, an enraged Low-Light stands his ground, blasting the nightmare constructs into oblivion.

The next morning, the haggard Joes clutch mugs of coffee – only to find Low-Light fresh as a daisy. Comparing notes, the Joes start identifying similarities between their nightmares, coming to the conclusion that Cobra's interfering with their sleep. Using Low-Light's immunity to the Joes' advantage, Lifeline modifies an EKG machine to route the Joes' dreams through Low-Light's mind. The following night, the Joes share an interactive dreamscape, calling on Low-Light's guidance to combat their nightmares.

Under pressure to show results, Dr. Mindbender uses the Sound-U-Lator to mentally enter the Joes' dreams. Able to directly intervene, Dr. Mindbender pummels the dreaming Joes with a pack of nightmarish snakes. Thankfully, Low-Light focuses his inner resolve like a laser, bringing up metallic mongooses to crush Dr. Mindbender's creations. The experience unhinges Mindbender, who awakens on Cobra Island in a state of terror. Finding the device too evil even for him, Mindbender eradicates the Sound-U-Lator, allowing the Joes – and Low-Light – to enjoy some well-earned sleep.

MEMORABLE MOMENTS "Nightmare Assault" immediately gets down to business, opening with a dreaming Lifeline finding Iceberg half-frozen. The tormented medic tries to save his friend, but Iceberg hands him a laser pistol

– then plunges into icy waters. Seconds later, Lifeline's gun turns into a snake, shocking him into screaming wakefulness.

Serpentor praises Dr. Mindbender's Sound-U-Lator project by stating that "this isn't one of Cobra Commander's pathetic little schemes." (Gracious, no – it's one of Dr. Mindbender's pathetic little schemes.) A series of shots show the Joes desperately trying to avoid sleep – with Mainframe tinkering with his computer, Leatherneck and Wet-Suit playing cards and Quick Kick karate-chopping his pillow.

Best of all, Low-Light shows unbelievable resolve while resisting the Sound-U-Lator. Directing the frustration of his abused childhood at Dr. Mindbender's giant serpents, Low-Light unloads his laser rifle and screams: "You gotta be tougher than me! And these days, they don't *make* anyone tougher! *You hear me, Dad*?!" Unforgettable.

LOVE AND WAR Lady Jaye experiences a nightmare in which she's singing the national anthem at the Super Bowl – in her skivvies. A wiped Iceberg falls asleep during a drive-in movie date.

ASS-WHUPPINGS Virtually nothing happens in the real world, but there's loads of dream violence in this episode: Iceberg falls to his death (twice, actually), Mainframe turns into metal and Dial-Tone goes mute. Thankfully, Low-Light's resistance helps the Joes cure themselves and rally against Dr. Mindbender. The counter-assault shocks the Cobra scientist awake, more unhinged than ever, making him blow up his own Sound-U-Lator device.

GOOFS When Low-Light happily bursts into the cafeteria, he's already been seen inside chatting with Mainframe.

TV TIE-INS A sleep-deprived Iceberg here snoozes on a date with zoologist Mahia ("Cobra's Creatures").

CHARACTER PROFILE: JOES

• *Lady Jaye:* As a Joe intelligence officer, Lady Jaye presents Hawk with the morning security reports.

• *Low-Light:* The precise nature of Low-Light's childhood abuse goes unspecified, although it's clearly more mental abuse than sexual. If we piece together the puzzle, Low-Light's overly dictatorial father wanted to "strengthen" his son – by verbally degrading him. Worse, Low-Light's dad repeatedly locked him in the cellar, forcing young him to kill rats in the dark as a show of manhood. Presumably, this went on for years, endowing Low-Light with continual nightmares – but also the resolve to fight them.

STUFF YOU NEED Dr. Mindbender's Sound-U-Lator: It emanates "psychic waves," generating nightmares by remote and potentially driving its victims mad. Failing that, the continued nightmare trauma triggers dementia and poor judgment during the waking hours. For instance, Hawk convinces himself that a giant inflatable snake deployed by the Dreadnoks is real.

THE COMMAND DECISION The story that grabbed us with an iron fist and refused to unclench, "Nightmare Assault" stands unique among G.I. Joe for deftly examining a truly gut-wrenching tragedy (Low-Light's childhood trauma) and turning it to a better purpose (his inner resolve). Not that we'd wish for intensely personal trauma every episode, but if more stories molded themselves as well as "Nightmare Assault," G.I. Joe could've launched itself to greater heights of glory. If there's a single Joe tale you must watch, this is it.

2.25: "Second Hand Emotions"

US Transmission Date: *Oct. 31, 1986*
Writers: *Gerry and Carla Conway*

BATTLE ROSTER *Joes:* Lifeline, Roadblock, Shipwreck, Lift-Ticket, Iceberg, Hawk, Scarlett, Sci-Fi; *Cobra:* Serpentor, Dr. Mindbender, Zartan, Zarana, the Dreadnoks.

MISSION BRIEF While Hawk, Scarlett and Sci-Fi test new Joe armor at a Pittsburgh weapons range, a handful of Joes attend the nearby wedding of Lifeline's sister Stephanie. Unfortunately, Zartan and the Dreadnoks peg Lifeline and Hawk's groups in the back of the neck with tiny electro-receivers. Once in place, the receivers transmit signals from Dr. Mindbender's newest invention: a device capable of instilling uncontrollable emotions – including fear, anger and jealousy – into its victims.

The wedding proceeds, but Dr. Mindbender plays havoc with the Joes' emotional control, making Lifeline blow his top and decry his sister for marrying too young, Simultaneously, Lift-Ticket, Shipwreck and Iceberg brawl with one another, tearing up the church in the process. Lifeline and Hawk's unhinged groups eventually meet up, nearly causing a trolley accident, but they finally assert enough control over their emotions to prevent fatalities.

Hawk tries to pull his emotionally wrecked team together, but sporadic bouts with the warmongering Dreadnoks only expose the Joes' inability to focus. Granted a respite from the battle, the Joes finally come to their senses enough to pin the blame for their mercurial feelings on Cobra. Mustering inner reserves of calm, the Joes dredge up the focus needed to pound Zartan's motley crew. As the Dreadnoks escape, Serpentor deems Dr. Mindbender's mood machine a failure and wrecks it. Convinced that Cobra actually helped them defeat their inner weaknesses, Hawk's team settles down to watch Stephanie get married.

ASS-WHUPPINGS Zartan and Zarana capture Roadblock early in the story, enabling Dr. Mindbender and Serpentor to hammer the Joe with the emotion machine at close range. Roadblock experiences every shade of fear, anger, jealousy, despair and the like – collapsing into tears – but later bursts free.

The over-emotional Joes fall apart during a skirmish with the Dreadnoks, leading to a collapsed truck partly squishing Iceberg. Lift-Ticket erratically flies his helicopter right into Zartan's line of fire and crashes. Zartan and Zarana karate-chop Sci-Fi and Iceberg while they're laughing over Lift-Ticket's sprawled carcass. Hawk and Scarlett also get blasted unconscious in the crossfire.

Shipwreck drops a bundle of ice and snow on Buzzer and Torch's heads.

SAVE THEM! Lift-Ticket downs a Night Raven jet over an obviously populated area, evidently without casualties.

PREPOSTEROUS PHYSICS Roadblock's strong enough to snap metal chains.

GOOFS Do the Joes even know Lifeline's sister, or have they avid A Wedding Story viewers? In the final act, the Joes miraculously identify Cobra's base of operations without any evidence.

CHARACTER PROFILE: JOES Lifeline: Lifeline's family left Seattle three years ago, moving to a pacifist community in Pennsylvania. Papa Lifeline preaches at a local church, although most of the congregants shun Lifeline for his military career. Indeed, Lifeline's father never forgave his son for joining the Joes, disowning him for a number of years. But by story's end, Lifeline's dad grows to accept his son's identity, welcoming him back into the fold.

Lifeline wishes his sister Stephanie wasn't marrying so young, but only mentions this when Cobra chips away at his emotional control. Still, Stephanie forgives the outburst, asking Lifeline to walk her down the aisle (her father's officiating).

CHARACTER PROFILE: COBRA Zarana: She carries a bottle of "perfume spray" that incapacitates her victims.

STUFF YOU NEED Dr. Mindbender's Emotion Machine: Mostly for kicks, Dr. Mindbender's rigged the control panel of his emotion-generating device to resemble an organ. Playing different keys sends out different harmonics that converge in anyone wearing a electro-receiver, upsetting their emotional balance.

Presuming your parents give you permission to use such a device, remember the following color codes: Red, pain; yellow, fear; green, envy; purple, vanity; orange, anger; blue, despair.

THE COMMAND DECISION Polished, though slightly draining since the Joes act like freakish lunatics most of the time. Still, the conflict between Lifeline and his stoic father contains a great deal of depth, pushing "Second Hand Emotions" forward as a story needing to be told.

2.26: "Joe's Night Out"

***US Transmission Date:** Nov. 10, 1986*
***Writer:** David Schwartz*

BATTLE ROSTER *Joes:* Dial-Tone, Leatherneck, Wet-Suit, Hawk, Mainframe.

MISSION BRIEF Eager to check out a new dance club named "Open Air," Leatherneck and Wet-Suit convince Dial-Tone to call up his sometimes-girlfriend Holly and arrange dates for them. Wet-Suit becomes thrilled when Holly shows up with his date, a blonde bombshell named Cindy. But Leatherneck groans upon spotting his escort – a mousy girl in a plaid skirt.

Meanwhile, Dr. Molaney, a Joe colleague, conscripts Mainframe's help to refine his new fuel formula, which modifies planes to draw limitless power from the nitrogen in the air. But to Molaney and Mainframe's chagrin, the nitrogen fuel formula runs too hot, obliterating every engine it touches. Nonetheless, in an effort to obtain the nitrogen fuel formula, Serpentor takes to the airwaves – revealing that Cobra secretly constructed the "Open Air" dance club as a weapon of terror.

Just as Serpentor makes his proclamation, booster rockets hidden in the "Open Air" tower ignite, launching the club and everyone in it into space. Serpentor threatens to obliterate the club unless Molaney surrenders to Cobra, compelling the scientist to capitulate. Molaney reaches Cobra Island as agreed, but Serpentor, never intending to keep his word, moves to detonate plastic explosives lining the dance club. Thankfully, Dial-Tone and his allies rig up a space survival suit and airlock for Wet-Suit, enabling him to venture into space on a tow-line and deactivate the explosives.

Meanwhile, on Cobra Island, Molaney begins adapting a fleet of Cobra Firebats to run on nitrogen fuel – neglecting to mention that his fuel formula doesn't actually work. Simultaneously, Cobra blocks the Joes' rescue attempt, leaving them unable to reach the in-orbit dance club. As a last-ditch effort, the Joes radio Molaney's formula to Dial-Tone's group. Dial-Tone's team modifies the club's rocket engines to run on nitrogen fuel and – although Molaney's formula burns out the engines in the process – propelling the club back to earth.

Unaware of this, the modified Cobra Firebat squadron sets out on a test run, taking Molaney along as an advisor. But in short order, the unstable nitrogen fuel formula wrecks the Firebats' engines, allowing the Joes to round up the whole armada and rescue Molaney. With both the club-goers and Molaney safe, an enraged Serpentor abandons his attempts to acquire the nitrogen fuel formula.

MEMORABLE MOMENTS Wet-Suit propels himself through outer space by opening pressurized soda cans – a 1980s move if ever we've heard one.

LOVE AND WAR Holly's a little plain-looking, but she's hardly an unattractive match for Dial-Tone. (Indeed, after the "Open Air" debacle, she stops accusing Dial-Tone of taking her on boring dates.)

Wet-Suit's date, a gorgeous blonde named Cindy, credits the quick construction of "Open Air" as "proof of what big, strong men can do with a little encouragement."

As you've probably guessed, Leatherneck romantically belly-flops in this story, as he's paired with a nerdy redhead. The Joe marine doesn't even bother dancing with his date, fervently hoping that "Open Air" has a video arcade because he "wants to shoot something." Later, when the redhead hugs Leatherneck after a successful rescue, he cries out in anguish: "Which way's the airlock?"

ASS-WHUPPINGS Total casualties from the "Open Air" debacle: Several fish, killed when the gravity loss lets them float out of their aquarium. Molaney's botched fuel formula eradicates a fleet of Firebats. Mainframe's computer virus (see TV Tie-Ins) takes out a Cobra computer bank, covering Serpentor and Dr. Mindbender in rubble.

G.I. JOE: THE MUSICAL The "Open Air" dance club plays a remix of singer Satin's song about Cobra ("The Pyramid of Darkness").

PREPOSTEROUS PHYSICS If Molaney's formula doesn't work, why doesn't the Joe-modified "Open Air" club explode? For that matter, Dial-Tone, Wet-Suit and Leatherneck don't have a drop of engineering skill between them, making it highly unlikely they could adapt the unstable formula well enough to bring the club safely back down to earth.

GOOFS Dial-Tone, Leatherneck and Wet-Suit wear their uniforms and military gear on dates. The Joes implausibly rig Wet-Suit a "space suit" from garbage bags and an aquarium tank that fits over his head. Wet-Suit's supposedly "holding his breath" during his outer space excursion, but he somehow keeps talking to Dial-Tone. An animation glitch shows Wet-Suit's tow line floating into space before the commercial break when in fact, it's never severed.

TV TIE-INS Mainframe claims this story takes place a few months after "Cobrathon." It's irrelevant to the plot, but in addition to Molaney, Cobra acquires a data disk containing Molaney's fuel conversion formula. Fearing that Cobra might someday perfect Molaney's formula, Mainframe taints the disk with the computer-wrecking "Cobrathon" virus ("Cobrathon").

Shipwreck and Lady Jaye previously saved Molaney from Cobra in "There's No Place Like Springfield."

CHARACTER PROFILE: JOES Lift-Ticket and Slip-Stream: Their piloting skills evidently include space shuttle training.

CHARACTER PROFILE: COBRA Serpentor: Serpentor never engineered the "Open Air" club to return to Earth, suggesting he planned to welch on his trade for Molaney whatever the outcome.

THE COMMAND DECISION Completely ludicrous, although it ends decently well. By itself, the action's decently fun (Wet-Suit flying about in space via carbonated soda cans, etc.) – it's just that one can't even talk about a rocket-propelled dance club without smacking one's forehead against a handy wall.

2.27: "Not a Ghost of a Chance"

***US Transmission Date:** Nov. 13, 1986*
***Writer:** Sharman DiVono*

BATTLE ROSTER *Joes:* Lady Jaye, Flint, Hawk, Beach-Head, Lift-Ticket, Slip-Stream; *Cobra:* Cobra Commander, Serpentor, Dr. Mindbender.

MISSION BRIEF Near the Aleutian Islands, the sudden destruction of the military's prototype AR90-A Ghost stealth jet makes the American government suspicious of sneaky wrongdoing on Cobra's part. But Serpentor denies shooting down the Ghost, accusing the Joes instead of unjustly painting Cobra as villains. Amid the squabbling, both organizations fan out to find the Ghost's missing pilots, Frank Sullivan and Ron Michaels, as key witnesses to explain the jet's destruction.

2.27, Not a Ghost of a Chance

Meanwhile, Sullivan and Michaels take shelter on a barren island, desperately trying to avoid Cobra patrols. Flint chafes over having to search for Michaels – Lady Jaye's former flight school classmate and possible snuggle-bunny – but nevertheless heads up a retrieval team. After blasting a series of BATs, Flint's team brings Sullivan and Michaels into protective custody, while Serpentor and Cobra Commander keep decrying the Joes' assault on Cobra's character.

Wanting to leave zero doubt about Cobra's evil intent, the Joes coordinate with "Twenty Questions" host Hector Ramirez to catch Cobra with its serpentine mitts in the cookie jar. The Joes schedule a test flight of the Ghost's sister ship, providing Cobra with a juicy, technology-laden target. As expected, Serpentor sends a fleet of Night Raven jets to capture the Ghost, allowing Ramirez's team to broadcast the Cobra ambush in full color. A Joe Conquest squadron shreds the Night Ravens, allowing the Ghost to return to base. As a happy footnote, Michaels concedes Lady Jaye's love for Flint, quelling Flint's errant jealousy.

MEMORABLE MOMENTS Hardly a cool cucumber at the best of times, Serpentor tries to stay calm during an interview on the talk show "Twenty Questions." But reverting to type, Serpentor loses it and shouts at host Hector Ramirez: "You insignificant piece of shriveled-up shoe leather! I'll see you staked out on an African ant hill at high noon!"

LOVE AND WAR Flint thinks Lady Jaye and Major Michaels – old flight school chums – are doing the horizontal mambo after overhearing Michaels inviting Lady Jaye to his apartment and telling her to "wear something casual." Flint storms off, unaware that Michaels is actually conscripting his friends for a wallpaper party. Luckily, Michaels later admits Lady Jaye's love for Flint of his own volition, curbing the Joe warrant officer's jealousy.

ASS-WHUPPINGS Flint squashes some BATs flat beneath a boulder. Everyone else gets by unscathed – except Michaels, who busts an ankle.

GOOFS We don't normally index color goofs, but Michaels' uniform annoyingly keeps changing from dark blue to light blue. Co-pilot Sullivan's hair similarly keeps shifting from red to black.

TV TIE-INS To debunk the Joes' claims that Cobra shot down the Ghost, Serpentor and Cobra Commander appear as guests on Hector Ramirez's "Twenty Questions" ("Twenty Questions").

In a choice moment, the Cobra leaders argue that the Joes are unjustly smearing Cobra's character. In turn, Ramirez reminds the audience that Cobra previously sponsored an invasion of Washington, D.C. ("Arise, Serpentor, Arise!"), a robotic sea serpent attack on New York ("Bazooka Saw a Sea Serpent"), a scheme to melt the polar ice caps ("Haul Down the Heavens"), destroyed the world's currency ("Money to Burn"), raided the Rocky Mountain Chemicals Weapons Arsenal ("Twenty Questions"), created a bogus heavy metal band named "Cold Slither" ("Cold Slither"), participated in sinking the *USS Montana* ("Sink the Montana!") and the *USS Flagg* ("Computer Complications"), staged a telethon for criminals ("Cobrathon") and tried to swindle Alaska from the United States ("The Great Alaskan Land Rush"). Undaunted, Cobra Commander brushes off this laundry list of crimes and misdemeanors with, "Picky, picky, picky..."

Dr. Mindbender regrets not cloning Serpentor with a better sense of humor ("Arise, Serpentor, Arise!").

The snakes that make up Serpentor's shoulder pads are, in fact, alive, foreshadowing his use of them as weapons in *G.I. Joe: The Movie*.

CHARACTER PROFILE: JOES

- *Hawk:* Touted as one of G.I. Joe's founders.
- *Lady Jaye:* She's college-educated, hailed as one of the world's foremost intelligence experts.

CHARACTER PROFILE: COBRA

Strato-Vipers: They're physically augmented to withstand higher G-forces than the average pilot.

HOT WHEELS Ghost AR90-A: A prototype reconnaissance aircraft, so named because it's invisible to radar. (Lady Jaye sloppily claims the ghost only appears as a "radar ghost," which seems to imply some sort of detection, but let's move on.) The Ghost, capable of Mach 4, flies at 93,000 feet and can scan 200,000 square miles per hour. The military hopes to have 20 Ghosts in service by the end of the decade, monitoring the United States and maybe oversea countries. The Ghost features voice-activated controls.

THE COMMAND DECISION Thankfully level-headed, "Not a Ghost of a Chance" sweetly balances its action scenes with a tasty Flint/Lady Jaye/Major Michaels romantic triangle. Hector Ramirez's interview with Cobra Commander and Serpentor drags a bit, but at least whimsically illustrates Cobra's myriad of crimes throughout the series (see TV-Tie Ins). The final result's hardly Shakespeare, but deserves kudos for favoring military-driven themes over rampant silliness.

2.28: "Sins of Our Fathers"

US Transmission Date: *Nov. 18, 1986*
Story: *Steve Gerber;* ***Teleplay:*** *Buzz Dixon*

BATTLE ROSTER *Joes:* Dial-Tone, Flint, Hawk, Lift-Ticket; *Cobra:* Serpentor, Cobra Commander, Destro.

MISSION BRIEF Searching out a mystical solution for dealing with Serpentor, Cobra Commander returns to the remains of Destro's Scottish homestead ("Skeletons in the Closet"). Once there, a Cobra Tele-Viper team rigs up a communications laser, hoping to awaken the octopoid abomination – worshiped throughout the centuries by Destro's family – from its peaceful slumber. But the Tele-Vipers' laser shorts out from excessive feedback, convincing Cobra Commander to seek outside technical expertise.

Meanwhile, Joe communications chief Dial-Tone inwardly shrivels when Flint submits an unfavorable recommendation, denying Dial-Tone's re-enlistment. Booted out of the Joes, Dial-Tone returns to his seedy apartment and ponders his future. But soon after, a businesswoman named "Chipper Dugan" – actually Zarana in disguise – approaches Dial-Tone with an offer of gainful employment building a communications array.

Oblivious to the fact that he's working for Cobra, Dial-Tone leaps at the offer and travels to Scotland. Having dismissed Dial-Tone from Joe service purely learn more about Cobra's plans, Flint follows, but a Cobra SWAT team captures the Joe warrant officer. Zarana tries faking Flint's reports to Joe Headquarters, but Hawk figures out the gambit and sends a fleet of Joe Tomahawks to crush the Cobra troopers.

Aided by plain-clothed Cobra techs, Dial-Tone finishes constructing the communications laser. Instantly, the laser travels into the monster's lair, translating its ancient language. To everyone's horror, the beast erupts from beneath the earth as a giant dragon-like thing, flailing a pair of mandibles and crying out for tribute. Cobra Commander bargains with the monstrosity, promising it unspeakable riches if it will gobble Serpentor whole. The abomination agrees, effortlessly repelling the Tomahawks' missiles and swimming toward Cobra Island.

Hawk extracts Flint and Dial-Tone, restoring the communications officer to full Joe service. Meanwhile, the abhorrence reaches Cobra Island, tearing through several Cobra columns and reaching Serpentor's command center. In an uncharacteristically honorable moment, Serpentor desperately leads the monster away to preserve Cobra's seat of power.

In the meantime, Destro hurriedly contacts Hawk, gravely concerned about his family's enraged creature running amok. Destro explains that in times past, his ancestors summoned the horror with a secret chant. Reciting the incantation for the Joes, Destro proposes using the mantra to lure the creature into a deep-sea trench near Cobra Island. Left with little choice, the Joes boost Destro's chant on maximum volume through a loudspeaker. The enormous serpent/dragon follows the summons, even as the Joes ditch their amplified speaker into the water over the deep-sea trench. As the monster follows, the Joes unleash a massive depth charge volley – forever burying the freak of nature beneath tons of rubble.

MEMORABLE MOMENTS The giant serpentine creature sent chills up our spines, hungrily belting out the name of its prey – "Serpentor!!"

MISCELLANEOUS STUFF!

DESTRO'S SUBLIMINAL MESSAGE

Ah, the 1980s. Home to "Transformers," *Footloose*, Madonna – and a lot of paranoid fears about Satannic messages getting seeded into childrens' entertainment. With rumors about the dangers of subversive – and even subliminal – messages at an all-time high, parents increasingly scrutinized children's programming and hobbies like never before, looking slantways at little Tommy's robot truck, taking *Dungeons and Dragons* players to task, etc.

All this occult furor didn't escape the *G.I. Joe* writers, and as a tongue-in-cheek answer to the often-hyper-sensitive 1980s, they included a little something special in the ancient chant that Destro uses to control his sorcery-spawned family monster in "Sins of the Fathers." On screen, the chant sounds like magical mumbo-jumbo, but if you play it backwards, the following "subliminal message" – spoken by Destro actor Arthur Burghardt – unspools :

"Anybody listening to this backwards for a secret occult message is a real dweeb!"

[*Author's Note:* To experience this phenomenon in its full auditory glory, head to http://www.yojoe.com/cartoons/index.shtml#destro to listen to the chant in MP3 form.]

ASS-WHUPPINGS Masquerading as a stable hand, Flint makes his horse kick two Cobra Tele-Vipers. Still, a mess of Cobra troopers beat the snot out of him, tying Flint up and depositing him in a laundry hamper.

TV TIE-INS A Joe/Cobra slugfest previously leveled Destro's ancestral home in "Skeletons in the Closet." The reptilian creature that Cobra Commander here summons to munch Serpentor appeared as a mutant octopoid in the same story, although the summoner's nature (Cobra Commander vs. Destro's family) might affect the supernatural creature's appearance.

"Twenty Questions" host Hector Ramirez ("Twenty Questions") delivers a news broadcast about Dial-Tone's dismissal from the Joes.

CHARACTER PROFILE: JOES

• *Dial-Tone:* Dial-Tone badly lacks a personal life, living in squalor and eating meals straight out of the can.

• *Flint and Hawk:* An undercover Flint uses the code-name "Checkmate." Hawk is "Bird One."

CHARACTER PROFILE: OTHER

The Destro Family Monster: Since the unnamed creature hails from a bygone era of sorcery and magic, it heals wounds caused by conventional weapons almost instantly. The monster's immeasurably strong, hefting vehicles with little trouble. It easily withstands the jolt from a Terror-Drome's electrified exterior. The creature claims it's slept for "ten times 10,000 years," awakening only to nibble sacrifices like Cheetos before returning to sleep.

ORGANIZATIONS *G.I. Joe:* Cobra possesses a device capable of mimicking Flint's voice (and presumably that of other Joes), but a voice modulator attached to the Joe's communication gear can uncover such deception.

THE COMMAND DECISION Enormously scary, shedding the subtlety inherent in the preceding "Skeletons in the Closet" (rather like the complete and total tone shift between Alien to Aliens). Overall, "Sins of Our Fathers" superbly wraps up the dangling plot thread of the monstrosity lurking beneath the Destro household, crafting an admirable slugfest.

2.29: "In the Presence of Mine Enemies"

US Transmission Date: *Nov. 19, 1986*
Writers: *Chris Weber and Karen Willson*

BATTLE ROSTER *Joes:* Slip-Stream; *Cobra:* a Night Raven pilot ("Raven").

MISSION BRIEF On a bombing run, Joe Conquest pilot Slip-Stream records an ultra-secret Cobra command code, pocketing the tape and making all speed toward the *USS Flagg*. Unfortunately, a Cobra Night Raven jet intercepts Slip-Stream's Conquest, sparking a dogfight that grounds both airships on a remote isle. Slip-Stream benevolently hauls his opponent, a Cobra pilot named "Raven," out of her burning vessel. But in turn, Raven spits on Slip-Stream's help, viewing him as a mortal enemy.

Suddenly, a Cobra BAT platoon shows up to eliminate any intruders (including Raven) on the isle, forcing the two pilots to reach an abandoned Cobra research center. Gradually, Raven confesses that the isle once housed one of Dr. Mindbender's bioengineering labs, abandoned by Cobra techs after an unspecified accident. But to the Raven and Slip-Stream's horror, the freakish result of the Cobra bio-experiments – a tentacled, gooey reptilian mass dubbed a "bio-annihilator" – bursts into the room.

The two pilots pound down a corridor, reaching the base's control center. Slip-Stream contacts the *USS Flagg* for an immediate pick-up, but Raven communicates with Dr. Mindbender – appalled when the Cobra scientist won't spare the expense to rescue her. As the bio-annihilator draws closer, Raven helps Slip-Stream reach the base's control center and initiate a self-destruct program.

With seconds to spare, Slip-Stream and Raven reach the safety of a Joe Tomahawk, looking back as explosions tear Dr. Mindbender's base – and the ooze-covered bio-annihilator – to shreds. While Slip-Stream returns to the *Flagg* with the Cobra command code, Raven – opening her eyes to Cobra's turncoat nature – forswears her loyalty to the group.

LOVE AND WAR Although trapped on a remote isle, Slip-Stream and Raven don't make like it's The Blue Lagoon – spending the vast bulk of this story bitching at each other and dodging bullets.

ASS-WHUPPINGS An airborne Slip-Stream slyly downs a Night Raven jet by deploying his Conquest's emergency chute – completely blinding the Night Raven pilot beneath a giant piece of canvas. Slip-Stream mostly accounts for a Night

Raven patrol, but a duel between himself and "Raven" downs both their fighters. Slip-Stream douses one BAT with acid, although the bio-annihilator munches most of the offending robots.

GOOFS An oddball scene shows a group of BATs bursting through a door into the base's communications center – except that the wall behind the robots has no hallway. When the bio-annihilator munches on a BAT, it also chomps on its own tentacle. Slip-Stream thinks the Joes might "recruit" Raven, although that seems hopelessly optimistic. (Would they really admit a former Strato-Viper, solely on Slip-Stream's word?)

CHARACTER PROFILE: COBRA Raven: Like all Cobra Strato-Vipers, she's got surgically enhanced reflexes.

THE COMMAND DECISION Worthy, but nothing worth watching multiple times. The writers score points for upending Raven from her unswerving loyalty to Cobra – but it's mostly a one-trick pony.

2.30: "Into Your Tent I Will Silently Creep"

US Transmission Date: *Nov. 20, 1986*
Writers: *Buzz Dixon and Michael Charles Hill*

BATTLE ROSTER *Joes:* Cross-Country, Mainframe, Hawk, Sgt. Slaughter, Sci-Fi, Low-Light; *Cobra:* Cobra Commander, Serpentor, Dr. Mindbender, the Dreadnoks, Storm Shadow, Firefly.

MISSION BRIEF Intent on sabotage, Destro crafts a pack of scaly, fast-moving armadillo-like robots named "Ratillos," programming the droids to steal valuable equipment and datafiles from Joe Headquarters. Unfortunately, the in-development Ratillos – while sufficiently sleathy – erroneously make off with useless gadgets such as the Joes' blow dryers, calculators and rifle scopes. Perhaps worst of all, the Ratillos bag HAVOC driver Cross-Country's tape deck, depriving the Southern Joe of his fighting music.

Fuming, Cross-Country sets out a shiny, new tape deck as bait – lying in wait to bushwhack the unidentified thief. Staggered to spot the Ratillos filching his music player, Cross-Country follows the critters out of Joe Headquarters and into a nearby Chinatown. Before long, Cross-Country trails the scurrying robots to a vast underground cavern, finding it inhabited by a secret brotherhood named "the Coil."

As Cross-Country observes the Coil's rituals, he learns that Cobra Commander founded the organization for the express purpose of eliminating Serpentor, Dr. Mindbender and the Joes. Aided by the Dreadnoks, Firefly, Storm Shadow and a reluctant Destro, Cobra Commander uses a slave labor force to mine gold and fund the Coil's activities. The Dreadnoks briefly spy Cross-Country, leading to a whirlwind chase, but the Joe driver escapes and summons his teammates.

Hawk and a team of Joes rush the Coil-controlled caverns en masse, spurring a slave revolt with frightening ease. Cross-Country recovers his tape deck in the melee, only to bust the gadget during a slugfest with Storm Shadow. While the Cobra officers yield to their adversaries' combined and flee into the night, the Joes return to base and Cross-Country requisitions a new tape player.

LOVE AND WAR Err. Umm. Dare we mention this story's title?

ASS-WHUPPINGS Cross-Country tortures some Tele-Vipers by broadcasting country music over their headsets. Storm Shadow assails Cross-Country with a whirlwind of punches and kicks, although Cross-Country gets in a lucky shot by slugging the ninja with a tape deck-heavy pouch.

PREPOSTEROUS PHYSICS Cross-Country's underground excursion entails his gaining several Spider-Man-like superpowers, including super-strength (Cross-Country pushes a dragon statue weighing several tons), invulnerability (he survives atop said statue's neck when it plummets from a purchase and crashes through a stone wall), super-leaping and the ability to stick to walls. Cross-Country seemingly holds his breath underwater for 15 minutes, and discourages a hungry shark with an overly simple kick to its snout.

GOOFS Why would Cobra Commander build an elaborate underground settlement within walking distance of Joe Headquarters? For that matter, how on Earth would a bunch of cowled brethren take out Serpentor and G.I. Joe? And how could Cobra Commander possibly keep his "secret" brotherhood meetings secret? (Hell, at one point, Serpentor conspicuously wonders: "Where oh where have all my Vipers gone?")

Joe Headquarters is evidently located within walking distance of such cross-cultural pleasures as a Chinatown, a deserted lighthouse, vast underground caverns and – best of all – hitherto undiscovered gold mines.

When the Ratillos tap the central Joe computer, the machine registers their access as "unauthorized," but permits a download anyway. The computer then displays: "Datas appear in succession." ("Data" is already a plural word, unless you're referring to multiple copies of the pasty-faced android aboard the *USS Enterprise-D*).

An animation glitch makes sewer water stop flowing when the Ratillos run across it. A group of slaves' hair turns from gray to brown in the blink of an eye.

The baddies leave Cross-Country handcuffed in a cell – but forget to lock the door. Cross-Country runs through one of Cobra's most useless booby traps – a blade-throwing device that couldn't hit an elephant stuck in glue.

Cross-Country stops during a raging Joe/Cobra battle to search through a junkpile for his tape deck (*and* Lady Jaye's hairdryer, let's not forget).

CHARACTER PROFILE: JOES

- *Cross-Country:* His Aunt Hazel's kitchen "hasn't been cleaned in a coon's age."
- *Roadblock:* He doesn't like country music.

CHARACTER PROFILE: COBRA

Cobra Commander: Destro thinks Cobra Commander's totally gone off the deep end with regards to the Coil, but Firefly better accommodates to the commander's ideas (and money, one presumes).

THE COMMAND DECISION Not a bad try – if it were written by a 10 year old. But much like a child's grasp on reality, "Into Your Tent..." moves from one absurdity to the next, morphing Cross-Country into a superhero and spouting some truly atrocious dialogue. Totally brainless.

"G.I. Joe: The Movie"

US Transmission Date: *Apr. 25, 1987*
Writer: *Ron Friedman*
Order: *Intended as a theatrical release, this was actually screened as TV movie. It was later re-shown as a five-part mini-series.*
Starring: *Don Johnson as Lt. Falcon, Burgess Meredith as Golobulus, Sgt. Slaughter as himself.*

BATTLE ROSTER *Joes:* Duke, Hawk, Roadblock, Sgt. Slaughter, Scarlett, Flint, Lady Jaye, Mainframe, Dial-Tone, Quick Kick, Snow Job, Cross-Country, Sgt. Slaughter, Shipwreck, Snake-Eyes, Dusty; *Cobra:* Cobra Commander, Serpentor, Destro, the Crimson Twins, Dr. Mindbender, the Baroness, Zartan, Zarana, the Dreadnoks.

FIRST APPEARANCES *Joes:* Lt. Falcon (Green Beret), Law and Order (M.P. and K-9), Jinx (ninja/intelligence), Tunnel Rat (explosive ordnance disposal), Chuckles (undercover), Big Lob (unspecified), Mercer, Red Dog and Taurus (Sgt. Slaughter's Renegades); Cobra-La: Golobulus, Nemesis Enforcer, Pythona.

MISSION BRIEF At Cobra Island's main Terror-Drome, Serpentor and his subordinates despair over Cobra Commander's continued bungling, further threatening the commander's already precarious standing with his own organization. Suddenly, a lithe, cloaked intruder breaches the Terror-Drome's perimeter and makes for Serpentor's war room. Easily dispatching of all opposition, the intruder stands before Serpentor and introduces herself as "Pythona." Vaguely recalling Pythona's face – as well as other memories of a lost world – from the murky depths of his subconscious, Serpentor refrains from attacking the newcomer. Consequently, Pythona persuades Serpentor to steal a device called the "Broadcast Energy Transmitter" (BET) – a contraption capable of re-directing almost limitless power across the globe via an energy beam – from G.I. Joe's custody.

In a remote part of the Himalayas, the Joes prepare to give the BET a test run. Several Cobra columns bear down on the Joe encampment, but the Joes stand firm, capturing Serpentor and driving off his legions. Most of the Joes stay behind to guard the BET, but Roadblock mounts up a small unit to pick off the fleeing Cobra forces. Under Cobra Commander's promise of a safe haven, the haggard Cobra brigades head deeper into the Himalayan mountain range. Finally, Cobra Commander directs his troops to an ancient, forgotten city named Cobra-La – a time-lost settlement whose very buildings, bridges and walkways are entirely composed of organic creatures. The Cobra troopers balk at their bizarre setting, but Cobra Commander celebrates a return to his homeland.

Moments later, Roadblock's group rolls up, scattering the Cobra soldiers and inciting a response from Cobra-La's defenders. Led by a superstrong winged humanoid named Nemesis Enforcer, a band of soldiers in insectoid armor easily take Roadblock's team captive. Nemesis Enforcer and the returning Pythona then clap a sputtering Cobra Commander in shackles, readying Cobra-La's prodigal son for a trial. While the Cobra leaders stagger in stock, overwhelmed by the setting and their hosts' considerable power, Pythona offers Zartan and the Dreadnoks an enormous ruby, taking them into Cobra-La's employ.

Meanwhile, Hawk locks up Serpentor at Joe Headquarters, securing the BET at a separate site. Worried about Roadblock's team's continued absence, Hawk reluctantly speeds up training for a group of freshmen Joes – collectively named "the Rawhides" – to bolster the Joes' ranks. Unfortunately, an undisciplined Rawhide named Lt. Falcon proves a continual disappointment to his trainers. Worse, the libidinous Lt. Falcon abandons his guard duty watch in an attempt to seduce a Joe ninja named Jinx.

Simultaneously, a team composed of a few Cobra-La agents

and the Dreadnoks capitalizes on Falcon's negligence, slipping past Joe Headquarters' early warning systems. The villains trounce multiple Joes and easily escape with Serpentor. Outraged, Hawk court-martials the reckless Falcon, but Duke steps forward and pleads for clemency. Conceding that Falcon is his half-brother, Duke argues that his wayward sibling nonetheless has the makings of a fine officer. Adequately swayed, Hawk orders Falcon to take remedial training at the "Slaughter House" boot camp.

Back at Cobra-La, Serpentor and the Cobra officers convene with Golobulus, the supreme Cobra-La leader. Golobulus explains how 40,000 years ago, the Cobra-La nation dominated the Earth with a culture based on organic technology. But when a sudden Ice Age struck, Cobra-La retreated into the Himalayan wastes, yielding their territory to primitive man. Humanity evolved in the centuries to follow, leaving the displaced Cobra-La with a burning obsession to reclaim the planet. Emboldened in the modern day, the machinistic Golobulus hand-picked a Cobra-La nobleman – the future Cobra Commander – to go forth, raise a human army and conquer Earth in Cobra-La's name.

Moved by this revelation, the Cobra leadership pledges loyalty to Cobra-La, convincing Golobulus to detail his newest master plan. Golobulus reveals a forest of towering fungoid pods, all of them hyper-engineered to launch seed pods into space. Once in orbit, the pods will shower Earth with mutagenic spores, devolving the whole of mankind into incompetent barbarians. Golobulus speculates that only Cobra-La, snug beneath its protective ice dome, will escape the transformation. However, Golobulus stresses that since the spores cannot ripen in the cold of space, they require the BET's energy beams to warm them to maturity.

With his master plan in full swing, Golobulus sets about putting the disgraced Cobra Commander on trial for his multiple failures. Finding Cobra Commander guilty of mass incompetence, Golobulus exposes the dethroned commander to a dose of the mutagenic spores. To the Cobra officers' horror, Cobra Commander sprouts scales – signaling the start of his transformation into a serpent. Purely to prove the futility of escape, Golobulus tosses the tormented Cobra Commander in prison with the captive Joes.

Elsewhere, Sgt. Slaughter and his "Renegades" – a trio of headstrong Joes – put Falcon through a grueling degree of training, teaching him the value of teamwork. Soon after, Cobra-La and Serpentor combine forces, unleashing a multi-pronged assault on the BET storage facility. The Renegades reinforce the on-site Joes, sparking a fever-pitched battle. Serpentor batters Falcon near-senseless, then readies a killing blow with his staff – but Duke dashes forward, interposing himself between Serpentor and his brother. Serpentor's staff stabs into Duke's chest, downing the Joe hero as Serpentor and his army make off with the BET. The grievously wounded Duke slips into a coma, making Falcon thirst for vengeance.

Back in Cobra-La, Serpentor victoriously brings the BET before Golobulus, radiating the device's energy waves into space. The spores bask in the BET's heat, ticking down humanity's control of Earth. Thankfully, the Joes triangulate Cobra-La's position from the BET transmissions, compelling Hawk to muster his troops for war.

The Joes burst into Cobra-La, but Golobulus rouses the city's component organic creatures to arms. While dozens of Joes grapple with Serpentor's troops and the Cobra-La abominations, Falcon, Sgt. Slaughter and Jinx penetrate Golobulus' central chamber. Sgt. Slaughter and Jinx engage Nemesis Enforcer and Pythona, but Serpentor starts strangling Falcon with a large snake. Thankfully, Cobra Commander – having fully devolved into a giant serpent – rouses enough of his former personality to spar with Serpentor's pet. Falcon recovers enough to blast Serpentor's battle sled, hurling the Cobra Emperor out of Golobulus' chamber and allowing a hissing Cobra Commander to slither out of sight.

Supercharging himself with Cobra-La's lifeforce, Golobulus telekinetically opens up a protective chasm around the BET, trapping Falcon on the opposite side of the gap from his teammates. Falcon bravely engages Golobulus, stabbing a rod into the Cobra-La leader's eye. Finally, Golobulus flies off, confident because the spores have reached maturity.

In desperation, Falcon revs the BET up to maximum output and jumps across the chasm, sweeping destructive energy through Earth's stratosphere and incinerating the spores into ash. The BET overloads in the process, prompting the Joes to flee the ancient city. The Joes take cover in the Himalayas just as the BET erupts, decimating Cobra-La and its populace. Celebrating their survival, the Joes cheer to learn that Duke's recovered from his coma. Falcon and Jinx romantically watch the torched spores trickle down to Earth, then depart with their comrades for home.

MEMORABLE MOMENTS In a nice bit of surrealism, Pythona leaps upon some Cobra engineers, looking like an inhuman wraith. The first sight of the Cobra-La defenders – strange insectoid warriors who leap from the ground – chilled us to the core.

When Golobulus details how primitive man evolved, the Baroness looks at the Dreadnoks – spotting Ripper scratching his chest, Buzzer cleaning his ear with a finger and Torch picking his nose – then remarks: "If you ask me, some of them did *not* evolve." Cobra Commander's origin makes for some seriously intoxicating viewing. And when Serpentor skewered Duke like a tomato – almost certainly the most visceral moment in *G.I. Joe* history – our hearts skipped a beat.

LOVE AND WAR Lt. Falcon debuts while sweet-talking a babe named Heather (actually Zarana in disguise), setting himself up as a playboy. Falcon and Jinx loosely share a romantic history when the movie opens (Jinx claims they previously "kind of had a date"), but Heather's presence makes Jinx jealous anyway. Later, Dreadnok Thrasher gets fresh with "Heather" – failing to identify her as Zarana – so she slam-dunks him into a pond.

Later, Falcon makes advances on Jinx, claiming she's got "nice legs for a grease monkey." (Ah, the silver-tongued devil.) When Jinx bops her head, Falcon offers to "kiss and make it better," but she rebuffs him. The two of them gradually warm to each other, smooching and walking away hand-in-hand by story's end.

A heart-broken Scarlett weeps over the fallen Duke (*see Sidebar*). Pythona's subtly slinky toward Serpentor. Tunnel Rat irreverently calls Beach-Head "sweetheart."

ASS-WHUPPINGS Cobra initially catches the Joes napping in the Himalayas, obliterating several HAVOCs. The Joes retaliate, however, crashing several Cobra STUNs.

A Dreadnok laser bolt singes Duke's arm. Duke flings Serpentor against the electrified BET dish, crisping the Cobra Emperor. Cobra-La's defenders smear the Joe intruders, with a royal guardsman viciously grabbing Quick Kick's leg, then hurling him face-first into a stone wall. Nemesis Enforcer personally bests Roadblock in a fist-fight. Snow Job tries to wreak havoc in a HAVOC, but Nemesis Enforcer hauls the vehicle up, tossing the Joe Arctic trooper aside. One of Nemesis Enforcer's weapons sprays a gas cloud that blinds Roadblock.

In freeing Serpentor, Nemesis Enforcer roughhouses Gung Ho, Alpine and Bazooka, putting them into the hospital. Pythona tosses combustible Cobra-La slugs, taking out a Joe patrol.

During a covert operation to Cobra Island, Taurus wraps a Viper's head in his powerful thighs. Taurus' teammate Red Dog shoots down a number of Trubble Bubbles and STUNS. All in all, Sgt. Slaughter's Renegades savage most of Serpentor's defenders, eradicating the main Cobra Island Terror-Drome by detonating its armory.

A Rawhide-filled Joe Tomahawk crashes through several layers of a building. Serpentor's grenade launcher takes out Sgt. Slaughter's tank, knocking him unconscious. Duke takes a blow from Serpentor meant for Falcon – standing out, in our minds, as the bloodiest *G.I. Joe* injury.

In Cobra-La, an admirable extended fight scene shows the Joes punching everyone's lights out. Sgt. Slaughter rifle-butts a bridge – actually a giant mantis-type creature – insensate, then gives some big-ass spiders the same treatment. A giant pupa thing eats Tunnel Rat, but he lasers his way out of the creature's side.

Pythona mis-aims a strike at Jinx, killing a giant clam-thing by accident. Jinx and Sgt. Slaughter hurl Pythona and Nemesis Enforcer into a yawning abyss. Serpentor drags Falcon under his flying sled, but Falcon hurls the Cobra Emperor out of Golobulus' sanctum sanctorum. Falcon also stabs out Golobulus' eye, although it happens off-screen. Cobra-La winds up grievously butchered – if not outright destroyed.

MISCELLANEOUS STUFF!

THE (EXAGGERATED) DEATH OF DUKE

It's fairly well documented at this point, but *G.I. Joe: The Movie* – in an glorious swath of drama – initially planned to leave Duke pushing up daisies.

We can well believe it. Certainly, Serpentor's lance bloodily rips open Duke's chest beyond all hope of recovery, and the clash's aftermath is clearly configured as a death scene. In short, Duke utters some memorable words and "expires," followed by Scarlett, Falcon and Hawk crying their eyes out – which seems, at the risk of being unkind, like a lot of overdone hullabaloo if he's not dead. Also, Falcon cradles Duke's body in precisely the fashion you'd expect someone to hold a dead relative – not a grievously ventilated person in need of medical attention.

But for reasons somewhat lost to the mists of time (it's possible that test audiences balked at Duke's death, or that backlash against Optimus Prime's demise in *Transformers: The Movie* influenced the as-yet unreleased Joe flick), *G.I. Joe: The Movie* creators hastily re-engineered the film's dialogue to make Duke survive. Accordingly, when Duke "kicks it" on the battlefield, Scarlett suddenly acquires a doctorate and declares: "He's gone into a coma!" (A fairly absurd claim, by the way, since comas usually result from head trauma, not chest wounds.) Also, Hawk makes the awkwardly dubbed statement: "Falcon, don't worry – we'll do everything we can for Duke."

Later, just as the Joes wipe out Cobra-La, Doc awkwardly radios in: "Duke's come out of his coma!" The Joes hoot and holler in celebration, seemingly for Duke's revival – but you can pretty much tell they were originally hooting and hollering for having survived the arduous struggle against Cobra-La.

Overall, the tweaks convince you that Duke pulled through – which is something of a pity. Considering the cartoon didn't continue (except for the enormously wretched DIC series), his demise could've added some dramatic punch to a supposedly "epic" movie, leaving it all the more memorable.

PREPOSTEROUS PHYSICS Sgt. Slaughter hefts what seems like an impossibly large crate at some Vipers.

GOOFS Cobra Commander seems unclear as to where he stands with Cobra-La – he thinks it offers safe haven until Pythona walks onto the scene, making the commander instantly freak and try to get the hell out of Dodge. Since he clearly knows Pythona, why didn't he anticipate her presence?

Dusty, a desert trooper, pulls BET guard duty in the Arctic. The ice age that butchered Cobra-La evidently entailed giant ice shards spontaneously erupting from the ground – a hell of a lot stranger than any ice age we're familiar with.

Golobulus couldn't have anticipated the BET's creation, so why spend decades breeding fungii that can't mature in space? (It's rather like building a car without a gas tank.)

Duke's "fatal" wound (*see Sidebar*) teleports from his left to right side. Given that snakes are cold-blooded, the fully serpentine Cobra Commander should've become a snakesicle while wandering through the snowy region outside Cobra-La.

COMIC TIE-INS Jinx's claim of tutoring under a "blind ninja master" most likely refers to the Blind Master (first seen in *G.I. Joe* #59). A prologue to this story, depicting Destro's initial attempts to capture the BET, appears in *G.I. Joe European Missions* #6.

TV TIE-INS *G.I. Joe: The Movie* claims Golobulus secretly arranged Serpentor's creation ("Arise, Serpentor, Arise!"), using a psychic motivator (a small spider-like Cobra-La bug) to infuse Dr. Mindbender's brain with revolutionary genetic manipulation techniques. Retroactively, this explains Dr. Mindbender's DNA-themed dreams in "Arise, Serpentor, Arise!" Additionally, Golobulus' psychic motivator secretly compelled Dr. Mindbender to encode subtle memories of Pythona, Nemesis Enforcer, Cobra-La and Golobulus himself into Serpentor's subconscious, preparing for their future meeting.

Steeler and Clutch pop up as extras in this story's background, most likely selected at random by animators to fill space. However, *G.I. Joe* fandom at large interprets this to mean that these two Joes returned at an unspecified point from the parallel universe in "Worlds Without End." Grunt's appearance in DIC's *G.I. Joe* series confirms this theory.

Beach-Head formerly criticized Duke for too often turning a blind eye ("Computer Complications"), but Duke now seems a stickler for detail.

G.I. Joe: The Movie confirms that Cobra Commander was facially disfigured even before he turned into a snake, as hinted in "Lights! Camera! Cobra!" and other stories.

G.I. Joe: The Movie effectively finishes the cartoon universe for Joe purists (i.e. viewers who only accept the Sunbow stories as canon), although the Joes and Cobra renew their conflict in two seasons of *G.I. Joe* cartoons produced by DIC. Indeed, Cobra Commander finishes *G.I. Joe: The Movie* as a snake, but regains a humanoid (albeit still reptilian) form in the DIC G.I. Joe mini-series "Operation Dragonfire."

CHARACTER PROFILE: JOES

• *Beach-Head:* He's a grueling drill instructor, dismissing Falcon as a goof-off but deeming a fellow Rawhide named Law as a true soldier.

• *Big Lob, Tunnel Rat and Lift-Ticket:* They're hoping Falcon gets justifiably punished for neglecting his post.

• *Chuckles:* Since he's no good at firing a rocket launcher by the proper method, he resorts to throwing missiles at enemy tanks by hand.

• *Duke and Lt. Falcon:* Lt. Falcon technically outranks Duke (who's a first sergeant), although Duke holds jurisdiction over Joe operations and bases. Duke promised his mother that he'd look after Falcon, although Falcon often resents Duke's overly protective eye.

• *Jinx:* Although she's rumored to bring her teammates bad luck, it's usually the opposite. Educated under a blind ninja master, Jinx fights best when she's blindfolded. She's something of a grease monkey, capable of hotwiring helicopters.

• *Lt. Falcon:* Hawk describes Falcon's military record as a "shameful parade of insubordination and gross dereliction of duty." But for Duke's intervention, Hawk likely would've bounced Falcon out of the military. Still, Falcon's a dead-on shot with a laser pistol.

• *Mercer:* He's an ex-Cobra Viper who defected to the Joes. As such, Mercer knows the Terror-Drome's layout and a few Cobra command codes.

• *Order:* Law's dog, trained to sniff out bombs. Beware that if you pitch a a stick of dynamite away, Order might well think you're playing – and fetch it back.

• *Red Dog:* A former pro football player, booted out for continued unnecessary roughness. Red Dog carries a fighting staff, but, as a remnant of his failed pro football career, has teamwork issues.

• *Roadblock:* He's strong enough to give Nemesis Enforcer pause.

• *Taurus:* A scimitar-wielding, ex-circus acrobat who's none too bright. As his name implies, Taurus pays special attention to the horoscope.

CHARACTER PROFILE: COBRA

• *Cobra Commander:* Like most Cobra-La residents, Cobra Commander – who was actually quite handsome back in the day – previously sported a striking bald head and blue skin. Unfortunately, a laboratory accident involving some type of mutagenic seeds disfigured the future Cobra leader, horrifically mottling his head with sores and generating multiple eyes on his forehead. The deformity – and the fact that Cobra Commander was never fully human – explains his fetish for battle helmets and masks.

Previous to *G.I. Joe: The Movie*, Cobra Commander botched a desert campaign by countermanding one of Destro's orders. The commander's taken to wearing a black cape and strutting about with a ceremonial staff. He's familiar with Cobra-La's layout. Pythona strikes the fear of God into him.

By now, the Cobra leadership barely tolerates Cobra Commander's presence even as a scapegoat. Destro deems the commander a world-class "buffoon," Dr. Mindbender cites his cowardice and the Twins and the Baroness make general insults. Cobra Commander's too neutered to actively plot Serpentor's death at this point, but he clearly wouldn't object if someone else rubbed out the Cobra Emperor.

• *Serpentor:* The snakes that adorn Serpentor's costume can stiffen – when he commands – into venom-tipped "serpent javelins." (If Serpentor misses his target, the "serpent javelin" becomes an ordinary snake). Alternatively, Serpentor's snakes can remain pliable, constricting around his foes.

• *Zarana:* She keeps a camera hidden in her earring.

CHARACTER PROFILE: COBRA-LA

• *Cobra-La Royal Guard:* Elite Cobra-La soldiers are armed with laser-deflecting schimitars and handguns that fire immobilizing plants (*see Hot Wheels*). Oh, and they usually charge into battle with a rather painful "Cobra La-la-la-la-la-la-la-la-la!" battle cry – which yes, sounds a great deal like *Xena: Warrior Princess*.

• *Golobulus:* Golobulus maintains an empathic relationship with the organisms that compose Cobra-La, motivating them telepathically to defend the city. By integrating himself with Cobra-La's life force, Golobulus can perform localized telekinetic effects. His right eye (at least, until Falcon stabbed it out) appears augmented, expanding and contracting like an advanced iris.

Golobulus levitates atop a bulbous, green bio-mass, although it's merely a protective casing. The bottom half of his body – wrapped up in the bobble – is actually serpentine, enhancing his fighting speed and agility when needed.

• *Nemesis Enforcer:* He's basically the Cobra-La equivalent of Superman, strong enough to pick up a HAVOC and graced with invulnerable wings. Nemesis Enforcer doesn't speak, preferring to communicate with almost avian grunts. Blades attached to his wrists cut through high-density metal that Dreadnok weapons can't scorch. He sometimes wields other Cobra-La weapons, such as throwing starfish.

• *Nemesis Enforcer and Pythona:* Nemesis Enforcer can't punch through one of the Joes' rubbery "peneplastic shields," but Pythona's acidic claws can tear the screens to ribbons.

• *Pythona:* An extremely tactile fighter, blessed with incredible stamina and agility. Pythona's retractable claws, laced with

MISCELLANEOUS STUFF!

THE SUNBOW SERIES BY THE NUMBERS

Watching the "G.I. Joe" cartoons often makes you feel like you're wrapped in a temporal paradox. Just how often *does* the Baroness wear a latex mask and covertly flatten her boobs, anyway? So purely in the interests of science, Mad Norwegian Press conscripted top-notch researchers to slog through the episodes and uncover the following "by the numbers" information.

Keep in mind that this list *only* refers to the Sunbow cartoons. Also, we're counting multi-part stories (the mini-series, "The Traitor," etc.) as one each, leaving each category with a possible score of 75. So here's the number of episodes in which...

• The Baroness wears a disguise: **10**
• Zartan wears a disguise: **16**
• Cobra invents/steals a device or gadget: **38**
• The Joes get thrown into a battle arena: **7**
• Cobra employs some type of brainwashing technique: **8**
• Cobra blackmails and/or holds the world hostage with the finesse of Dr. Evil: **8**
• Cobra reveals something terribly obvious in their threatening broadcasts, thus ruining their plans: **6**
• Something (vegetables, parrots, etc.) becomes preternaturally large: **19**
• The Crimson Twins commit an obvious felony or even treason, but somehow keep operating as legitimate businessmen: **7**
• Cobra agents kidnap or impersonate a scientist: **11**
• An animal saves the day: **7**
• The Joes and Cobra unite against a common enemy: **5**
• The Joe/Cobra women triumph over all: **4**
• Everything revolves around a silly pun: **1** ("The Viper is Coming")

As a footnote, the series also contains:

• **13** fleeting pointless romances (plus 5-6 random smittings in "Eau de Cobra")
• **172** Joe/Cobra relatives (including the 137 members of Gung Ho's LaFitte clan, seen in "Captives of Cobra)

acid, cut through stone and enable her to touch an electrified fence. Her fingernails also emit hallucinogenic gas.

Pythona keeps many Cobra-La beasts in her cape's folds, including a four-headed, hydra-like creature that eats through electrical fencing, a small green spongy creature that sprays sleepy gas, a green globe-shaped creature that wraps up attackers in high-velocity fronds, and a squid-like thing that latches onto yer head and won't let go. Also at her disposal: clams that project holograms and exploding crustaceans – perfect for bowling over your pursuers.

Like many high-ranking Cobra-La agents, Pythona knows detailed information about the Cobra elite.

PLACES TO GO Cobra-La: Cobra-La is entirely composed of organic creatures, down to every building, sidewalk and appliance. In short, every single device in Cobra-La is an organism of some sort. A worm crawling up a rod keeps time. Padlocks require an organic key. A giant clam binds prisoners. A regal carpet walkway, is composed of crabs. Golobulus' "Web of Remembrance" casts historical images of superior quality to modern-day television.

Your standard Cobra-La citizen is blue-skinned and bald, with the royal guard (*see Character Profile*) serving as the city's elite defenders. The people of Cobra-La consider themselves civilized, adhering to ancient laws spawned when primitive man couldn't make fire and scratched himself a lot. Thinking themselves the true heirs of Earth, the Cobra-La inhabitants think of mankind's reliance on inorganic technology as a travesty and perversion of the natural order.

• *Cobra Island Terror-Drome:* In case of total annihilation, a reinforced dome in the Terror-Drome's interior shields the Cobra elite.

STUFF YOU NEED Broadcast Energy Transmitter (BET): It cost a billion dollars (in 1980s currency) to produce. The BET's useful for energizing the Joes' weaponry by remote.

• *Cobra-La Marauders:* Giant centipoid creatures with stubby legs, capable of eating through metal. They're super-strong and laser-proof but vulnerable to a bazooka attack on their underbelly.

HOT WHEELS Cobra-La Vehicles: Although never produced as toys, Cobra-La vehicles come in several varieties. A bio-organic bubble acts like a personal submarine, melting away upon completion of its mission. Inflatable, bug-eyed creatures serve as fast-moving Cobra-La dirigibles. Sleek-shaped Cobra-La airships pelt their enemies with "plant bolts" (that's our wording) that sprout into immobilizing fronds strong enough to stop vehicles. A flying crab-like creature hauls heavy cargo.

THE COMMAND DECISION A love it or leave it proposition, greatly contingent on your point-of-view. We're the first to admit – and let's be clear about this distinction – that the movie makes for an atrocious G.I. Joe story (the Cobra-La elements understandably go over like a lead balloon with military lovers). But from a science-fiction point-of-view, there's a lot to love (the animation's striking, the characterization's on target, the theme song's outstanding, etc.). Is the movie misguided? Given Cobra-La's presence, unquestionably. Does it digress too much? Without a doubt (the Joe training camp scenes waste everyone's time). But truth to tell, we watched the movie straight through and didn't glance at our watches once – leading one to suspect that various sectors of fandom erroneously wrong G.I. Joe: The Movie, making it worthy of a re-evaluation.

DIC mini-series: "Operation Dragonfire"

US Transmission Date: *Sept. 1989*
Writer: *Doug Booth*
Order: *DIC Mini-Series #1*

Note: The scant amount of information available on the DIC stories suggests that (for whatever oddball reason) the scant amount of people who care spittle about them place the stories in production, not broadcast. Thus, you'll have to pardon if the broadcast dates seem hopelessly randomized; we're here bowing to the majority will.

BATTLE ROSTER *Joes:* Sgt. Slaughter, Rock 'n Roll, Spirit, Barbecue, Low-Light, Stalker, Lady Jaye, Footloose, Mutt; *Cobra:* Serpentor, Cobra Commander, Destro, the Baroness, Copperhead.

FIRST APPEARANCES *Joes:* Scoop (combat information specialist), Recoil (long range recon patrol), Backblast (anti-aircraft soldier), Downtown (mortar man); *Cobra:* Gnawgahyde (Dreadnok poacher).

MISSION BRIEF In the Himalayas, Serpentor's forces attack a secluded monastery, hoping to seize control of the "dragonfire": an electro-magnetic energy source hidden deep within the Earth. Cobra troops round up the monks – the dragonfire's custodians – and decipher ancient writings explaining how to gain mastery of dragonfire caches around the world. Gradually, Cobra learns how to technologically tap the dragonfire, transmitting it around the globe as immense laser beams and force shields.

Meanwhile, the Baroness seethes with rage when Destro

dumps her in favor of Zarana. Spiteful towards the Cobra elite, the Baroness conscripts Dreadnok Gnawgahyde to help restore the fallen Cobra Commander to power. Quietly spiriting away the commander – still trapped in the body of a serpent after the Cobra-La debacle (*G.I. Joe: The Movie*) – the Baroness and Gnawgahyde join a Cobra excursion to tap a dragonfire pool in France. Once there, the Baroness supercharges a DNA converter with the dragonfire's molecular-reconstructing energies and turns Cobra Commander back into a reptilian approximation of a human form.

The Joes spar with Cobra across the globe, but Serpentor's forces route more and more dragonfire energy through a "Dragonstar" satellite, networking their resources with the dragonfire motherload in the Himalayas. But unfortunately for Serpentor, Cobra Commander and Destro – convinced to dump Zarana and side with the Baroness once more – stage a successful coup. Newly returned to power, Cobra Commander reprograms his dragonfire-powered machinery to molecularly fuse Serpentor with Gnawgahyde's lizard pet – devolving Serpentor into a demented lizard-beast.

In due course, the Joes discover the command frequency that allows Cobra to modify the dragonfire. Creating a backlash through the entire dragonfire network, the Joes best their rivals and secure Cobra's dragonfire bases. Cobra Commander and his officers escape, abandoning their newest scheme but promising future battles.

STUFF YOU SHOULD KNOW Cobra Commander got turned into a snake in *G.I. Joe: The Movie*. Serpentor, here converted into a sort of lizard-thing, runs off into the forest and is never heard from again. As part of his return to power, Cobra Commander dons the battle armor chiefly worn in the G.I. Joe comic series by Cobra Commander II.

"Operation Dragonfire" opens with United News journalist Leonard Michaels supposedly accompanying the Joes as an independent observer. Michaels quickly joins the Joes' ranks as a data specialist named "Scoop" – but we quickly learn that he's an undercover Crimson Guardsman. Initially tricked into thinking that the Joes murdered his parents (a deception on Destro's part to gain Michael's loyalty), Scoop finally learns the truth and disavows his Cobra allegiance. Properly convinced of Scoop's change of heart, Sgt. Slaughter lets him remain with the team.

Destro dons his gold-plated helmet, also seen in the comics from *G.I. Joe* #69 onward. Several veteran Joes such as Low-Light, Stalker, Footloose, Spirit and Mutt make an appearance in re-colored costumes, matching their re-released 1989 action figures. (Most of the toys were cited as part of "Sgt. Slaughter's Marauders," although the DIC series blessedly doesn't mention this appellation.)

It doesn't make much sense, but among other things, Cobra Commander uses his dragonfire-powered machinery to "fuse" several Cobra vehicles and uniforms with the "stealth and strength" of a snake. To wit, the dragonfire literally dissolves some snakes, embedding their atoms into the Cobra equipment. As such, the toughened Cobra gear proves invisible to radar (don't ask us how), giving birth to the "Python Patrol" (which also debuts in *G.I. Joe* #88). Copperhead, formerly a Cobra hovercraft pilot, is named here to lead the Python Patrol.

DIC Season 1

UNITED WE STAND

US Transmission Date: *Sept. 25, 1990*
Writer: *Tony Zalewski*
Order: *DIC Season 1 #1*

• ***Battle Roster:*** *Joes:* Lady Jaye; *Cobra:* Cobra Commander II, Gnawgahyde.

• ***First Appearances:*** *Joes:* Capt. Grid-Iron (hand-to-hand combat specialist), Salvo (anti-armor trooper), Pathfinder (jungle assault specialist), Ambush (concealment specialist), Stretcher (medical specialist), Bullhorn (intervention specialist), Rampart (shoreline defender); *Cobra:* Metal-Head (Destro's anti-tank specialist).

• ***Mission Brief:*** Cobra Commander tries to bluff the world with a $50 billion blackmail scheme (he's got some behavior modification gas, but only one aged missile with which to deploy it).

REVENGE OF THE PHAROAHS

US Transmission Date: *Sept. 27, 1990*
Writer: *Ted Pedersen*
Order: *DIC Season 1 #2*

• ***Battle Roster:*** *Joes:* Hawk, Lady Jaye, Bullhorn, Salvo, Rampart, Capt. Grid-Iron; *Cobra:* Cobra Commander, Destro.

• ***First Appearances:*** *Cobra:* The Night Creepers (ninjas), and the Night Creeper leader.

• ***Mission Brief:*** Cobra's Night Creeper leader bonks his head during a raid in Egypt – making him think he's the reincarnation of a 3,000-year-old pharaoh.

• ***Stuff You Should Know:*** This story introduces the Night Creepers – freelance, technologically savvy ninjas in Cobra's employ. General Hawk surfaces in the DIC series, complete with revamped costume.

GRANNY DEAREST

US Transmission Date: *Sept. 27, 1990*
Writer: *Chris Weber and Karen Willson*
Order: *DIC Season 1 #3*

• ***Battle Roster:*** *Joes:* Pathfinder, Capt. Grid-Iron; *Cobra:* Metal-Head, Gnawgahyde, Cobra Commander, Destro.

• ***First Appearances:*** *Joes:* Free-Fall (paratrooper).

• ***Mission Brief:*** Metal-Head's grandmother, mistakenly believing Cobra's an on-the-level security force, volunteers to help Cobra snatch a prototype magnetic turbine – capable of powering battleships or levitating office buildings – from the Joes.

VICTORY AT VOLCANIA

Episodes: *Two*
US Transmission Date: *Oct. 1-2, 1990*
Writer: *David B. Carren and J. Larry Carroll*
Order: *DIC Season 1 #4-#5*

• ***Battle Roster:*** *Joes:* Hawk, Salvo, Bullhorn, Duke, Lady Jaye, Capt. Grid-Iron; *Cobra:* Cobra Commander, Destro, Metal-Head, the Baroness.

• ***First Appearances:*** Topside (Navy assault seaman).

• ***Mission Brief:*** Some Joes whoop it up at a R & R facility on the Pacific island of Volcania, but Cobra Commander invades the locale to stuff a "space gun" inside a dormant volcano.

THE NOZONE CONSPIRACY

US Transmission Date: *Oct. 4, 1990*
Writer: *Eric Early*
Order: *DIC Season 1 #6*

• ***Battle Roster:*** *Joes:* Sgt. Slaughter, Bullhorn, Salvo, Ambush; *Cobra:* Cobra Commander, Metal-Head, Gnawgahyde, Zarana.

• ***First Appearances:*** *Joes:* Sub-Zero (winter operations specialist).

• ***Mission Brief:*** Cobra steals 40 million gallons of shaving cream, hoping to use its CFC emissions to slice up the ozone layer, then make a fortune selling $500 tubes of ultra-sturdy sunblock.

I FOUND YOU... EVY

US Transmission Date: *Oct. 22, 1990*
Writer: *Sharman DiVono*
Order: *DIC Season 1 #7*

• ***Battle Roster:*** *Joes:* Ambush, Sgt. Slaughter, Scoop, Dusty, Hawk, Stretcher, Sci-Fi (directed energy expert).

• ***First Appearances:*** *Joes:* Sandstorm (Dusty's coyote).

• ***Mission Brief:*** Joe concealment specialist Ambush discovers that Evy, his childhood friend and the only person capable of locating him while hidden, has joined Cobra's ranks as a Range-Viper.

• ***Stuff You Should Know:*** Wholeheartedly one of the more watchable stories from DIC Season 1. Ambush ends this story troubled because Evy's genuinely converted to Cobra's cause – greatly compromising his effectiveness in the field.

NIGHT OF THE CREEPERS

US Transmission Date: *Oct. 16, 1990*
Writer: *Rick Merwin*
Order: *DIC Season 1 #8*

• ***Battle Roster:*** *Joes:* Low-Light, Scoop, Bullhorn, Rampart; *Cobra:* Night Creeper leader, Cobra Commander, Destro.

• ***First Appearances:*** *Joes:* Heavy Duty (heavy ordnance trooper), Skydive (Sky Patrol leader), Red Star (a.k.a. Captain Krimov, Oktober Guard officer).

• ***Mission Brief:*** In Thailand, Destro uses a "life force regenerator" to bring a long-dead emperor's personal retinue – the forefathers of the Night Creepers – to life as mummified warriors.

• ***Stuff You Should Know:*** In wake of the Soviet Union's demise, the Oktober Guard remodeled itself as a G.I. Joe division. As such, Red Star's attached to the American military.

GENERAL CONFUSION

US Transmission Date: *Oct. 15, 1990*
Writer: *Steven Greene*
Order: *DIC Season 1 #9*

• ***Battle Roster:*** *Joes:* Heavy Duty, Low-Light, Sci-Fi, Red Star; *Cobra:* Zarana, Destro, Cobra Commander, Metal-Head.

• ***First Appearances:*** *Joes:* Big Ben (SAS trooper).

• ***Mission Brief:*** A disguised Zarana pulls official military strings to question the Joes' funding, leaving the team without proper supplies during a Cobra attack.

STUCK ON YOU

US Transmission Date: *Feb 13, 1991*
Writer: *Steve Mitchell and Barbara Petty*
Order: *DIC Season 1 #10*

• ***Battle Roster:*** *Joes:* Pathfinder, Lady Jaye, Duke, Big Ben; *Cobra:* Cobra Commander, Night Creeper leader.

• ***Mission Brief:*** Cobra Commander and Joe member Pathfinder wind up stranded in the jungle, forced to rely on each other to survive. All this, plus a slinky female gorilla lusts after Cobra Commander – weeping her eyes out when he goes home.

PIGSKIN COMMANDOS

US Transmission Date: *Oct. 8, 1990*
Writer: *Roger Slifer*
Order: *DIC Season 1 #11*

• ***Battle Roster:*** *Joes:* Sgt. Slaughter, Capt. Grid-Iron, Lady Jaye; *Cobra:* Cobra Commander, Metal-Head.

• ***Mission Brief:*** Cobra Commander kidnaps Sgt. Slaughter, leading to the first Joe/Cobra football game to decide the sergeant's fate. Led by Capt. Grid-Iron, the Joes fare well – until an over-heated Cobra Commander rolls several tanks onto the football field.

• ***Stuff You Should Know:*** Sgt. Slaughter's beefy, unnamed and camouflage-pajama wearing sister makes a cameo.

COLD SHOULDER

US Transmission Date: *Oct. 10, 1990*
Writer: *Craig Miller and Mark Nelson*
Order: *DIC Season 1 #12*

• ***Battle Roster:*** *Joes:* Rampart, Red Star, Sgt. Slaughter, Sci-Fi, Low-Light, Sub-Zero, Stretcher; *Cobra:* Cobra Commander, Gnawgahyde.

• ***Mission Brief:*** The Night Creeper leader sabotages the first combined G.I. Joe/Oktober Guard space mission, paving the way for Cobra to acquire the Joes' "Starsmasher Satellite." Red Star and Rampart crash in the process and narrowly escape getting eaten by a salivating polar bear.

INJUSTICE AND THE COBRA WAY

US Transmission Date: *Oct. 11, 1990*
Writer: *Flint Dille and Meg McLaughlin*
Order: *DIC Season 1 #13*

• ***Battle Roster:*** *Joes:* Capt. Grid-Iron, Duke, Pathfinder, Rampart, Bullhorn, Salvo, Stretcher, Dusty and Sandstorm, Scoop, Rock 'n Roll, Ambush; *Cobra:* Cobra Commander.

• ***Mission Brief:*** Cobra Commander dresses up as a superhero named "Serpent Man," completing a series of "heroic acts" designed to upstage the Joes. As part of the hoax, "Serpent Man" rescues the female President Mason, allowing a disguised Zarana to take her place.

• ***Stuff You Should Know:*** Journalist "José Riviera" crops up as a Geraldo Rivera rip-off – somewhat confusing, given that the Sunbow series already spawned a Rivera clone in the form of "Twenty Questions" host Hector Ramirez.

THE MIND MANGLER

US Transmission Date: *Nov. 8, 1990*
Writer: *Christy Marx*
Order: *DIC Season 1 #14*

• ***Battle Roster:*** *Joes:* Duke, Skydive; *Cobra:* Zarana, Gnawgahyde.

• ***First Appearances:*** *Joes:* Airborne (Sky Patrol parachute assembler), Drop Zone (Sky Patrol weapons specialist), Altitude (Sky Patrol recon scout), Airwave (Sky Patrol audible frequency specialist), Static-Line (Sky Patrol demolitions expert).

• ***Mission Brief:*** A Cobra scientist named "the Mind Mangler" brainwashes Duke, enabling a masked Zarana to "rescue" him and infiltrate Joe Headquarters.

• ***Stuff You Should Know:*** Confusingly, Sky Patrol member Airborne isn't the same as the Joe helicopter assault trooper from the Sunbow cartoons – Hasbro simply recycled the name for its action figure line.

D-DAY AT ALCATRAZ

Episodes: *Two*
US Transmission Date: *Nov. 5-6, 1990*
Writer: *David B. Carren and J. Larry Carroll*
Order: *DIC Season 1 #15-#16*

• ***Battle Roster:*** *Joes:* Pathfinder, Topside, Capt. Grid-Iron; *Cobra:* Cobra Commander, Destro, Metal-Head, the Baroness.

• ***Mission Brief:*** The Cobra elite let themselves get imprisoned on a renovated Alcatraz Island, hoping to procure a deluxe submarine from the nearby San Francisco Harbor.

AN OFFICER AND A VIPERMAN

US Transmission Date: *Oct. 24, 1990*
Writer: *Michael Hill*
Order: *DIC Season 1 #17*

• ***Battle Roster:*** *Joes:* Pathfinder, Topside, Ambush, Hawk, Sgt. Slaughter; *Cobra:* Cobra Commander, Destro.

• ***Mission Brief:*** An undercover Ambush, Pathfinder and Topside infiltrate a Cobra Viper training facility, hoping to identify a mole within the Joes' ranks. Unfortunately, they unwittingly draw attention from Cobra Commander, who orders his "recruits" to lead a mission against the Joes.

• ***Stuff You Should Know:*** Hawk's officially cited as a "brigadier general."

THAT'S ENTERTAINMENT

US Transmission Date: *Oct. 18, 1990*
Writer: *George Carangonne*
Order: *DIC Season 1 #18*

• ***Battle Roster:*** *Joes:* Hawk, Sgt. Slaughter, Rock 'n Roll, Red Star, Heavy Duty, Low-Light, Stretcher; *Cobra:* Cobra Commander, the Baroness, Metal-Head.

• ***Mission Brief:*** Cobra Commander and the Baroness dress up as military entertainers (shades of movie stars Bob Hope and Dorothy Lamour), conspiring to steal a fusion generator from Joe Headquarters.

BIOK

US Transmission Date: *Feb. 11, 1991*
Writer: *Christy Marx*
Order: *DIC Season 1 #19*

• ***Battle Roster:*** *Joes:* Skydive, Lady Jaye, Airwave, Airborne, Altitude, Static-Line, Drop Zone; *Cobra:* Cobra Commander, Destro.

• ***Mission Brief:*** Cobra Commander and Destro craft an artificial intelligence named BIOK to dominate computer systems around the globe.

DIC Season 2

INFESTED ISLAND

US Transmission Date: *Sept. 23, 1991*
Writer: *Martha Moran*
Order: *DIC Season 2 #1*

• ***Battle Roster:*** *Joes:* Flint (Eco-Warrior commander); *Cobra:* Cobra Commander.

• ***First Appearances:*** *Joes:* Ozone (ozone replentisher trooper), Clean Sweep (anti-tox trooper), Skymate (glider trooper); *Cobra:* Cesspool (chief environmental operative).

• ***Mission Brief:*** A Cobra toxic sludge expert named Cesspool develops a means of creating giant insects. A team of Joe environmental guardians dubbed the Eco-Warriors try to stop the fiend, but Cesspool mutates Joe member Ozone into a toxic-waste-spitting human/insect hybrid.

CHUNNEL

US Transmission Date: *Sept. 24, 1991*
Writer: *Tony Zalewski*
Order: *DIC Season 2 #2*

• ***Battle Roster:*** *Joes:* Duke, Scarlett, Big Ben, Wet-Suit; *Cobra:* Cobra Commander, Major Bludd, the Baroness.

• ***First Appearances:*** *Joes:* Big Bear (Oktober Guard anti-armor specialist); *Cobra:* Road Pig (Dreadnok).

• ***Mission Brief:*** Cobra Commander tries to kidnap the Queen of England, swipe Britain's Crown Jewels and set himself up as the new British monarch.

• ***Stuff You Should Know:*** In a non-kiddie moment, Big Ben enjoys beer with his fish and chips. Also, the Queen's dog Foo-Foo takes a whiz on Major Bludd's shoes.

EL DORADO – THE LOST CITY OF GOLD

US Transmission Date: *Sept. 30, 1991*
Writer: *Phil Harnage*
Order: *DIC Season 2 #3*

• ***Battle Roster:*** *Joes:* Grunt (infantry squad leader), Duke, Low-Light, Pathfinder, Roadblock; *Cobra:* Cobra Commander, BATs.

• ***First Appearances:*** *Cobra:* Overkill (BAT leader).

• ***Mission Brief:*** Cobra finds the legendary, gold-filled city of El Dorado and forges an alliance with the ghosts of conquistador Pizarro and his men.

• ***Stuff You Should Know:*** Grunt's obviously come back from the parallel universe in "Worlds Without End," nicely complimenting viewers who point to Steeler and Clutch's appearance in *G.I. Joe: The Movie* as proof that the dimensionally-dislocated Joes returned home.

THE SWORD

US Transmission Date: *Sept. 23, 1991*
Writer: *Ted Pederson and Steve Hayes*
Order: *DIC Season 2 #4*

• ***Battle Roster:*** *Joes:* Snake-Eyes, Storm Shadow, Hawk, Scarlett; *Cobra:* Cobra Commander, the Night Creeper leader, Overkill.

• ***First Appearances:*** *Joes:* T'Jbang (ninja swordsman), Nunchuk (nunchaku ninja), Dojo (silent weapons ninja); *Cobra:* Slice (ninja swordsman), Dice (bo-staff ninja).

• ***Mission Brief:*** Snake-Eyes, Storm Shadow and other Joe ninjas try to stop the Night Creeper leader from acquiring "The Sword of Destiny," an immeasurably powerful ninja weapon.

• ***Stuff You Should Know:*** "Shadow of a Doubt" explains, after-the-fact, Storm Shadow's sudden defection to the Joes.

LONG LIVE ROCK & ROLL

Episodes: *Two*
US Transmission Date: *Oct. 2-3, 1991*
Writer: *Doug Booth*
Order: *DIC Season 2 #5-6*

• ***Battle Roster:*** *Joes:* Rock 'n Roll, Lt. Falcon, Hawk, Scarlett, Snake-Eyes, Skymate; *Cobra:* Cobra Commander, Major Bludd, Metal-head, Road Pig.

• ***First Appearances:*** *Joes:* Psyche-Out (deceptive warfare), Tracker (Navy SEAL).

• ***Mission Brief:*** Cobra kidnaps several audio experts, forcing them to convert a skyscraper into a sonic weapon capable of obliterating New York.

• ***Stuff You Should Know:*** Cobra here modifies an old Extensive Enterprises building, although there's no word on the Crimson Twins' fate. Still, it's suggested that the company fell on hard times years ago.

KINDERGARTEN COMMANDOS

US Transmission Date: *Sept. 24, 1991*
Writer: *Doug Booth*
Order: *DIC Season 2 #7*

• ***Battle Roster:*** *Joes:* Duke, Mercer (mercenary), Tracker; *Cobra:* Cobra Commander, Overkill, Road Pig, Metal-Head, Slice, Dice.

• ***Mission Brief:*** Cobra tries subverting America's social fabric with pro-Cobra history classes and books for youngsters, but some kindergartners take on the Cobra officers. And win.

KEYBOARD WARRIORS

US Transmission Date: *Nov. 12, 1991*
Writer: *Misty Taggart*
Order: *DIC Season 2 #8*

• ***Battle Roster:*** *Joes:* Duke, Wet-Suit, Grunt; *Cobra:* Cobra Commander, Destro, Metal-Head, Overkill.

• ***Mission Brief:*** A video game scientist inadvertently develops a souped-up war computer for Cobra, causing two kids to inadvertently launch a major offensive against the Joes. (*Author's Note:* Can anyone say… *WarGames*?)

THE GREATEST EVIL

Episodes: *Two*
US Transmission Date: *Oct. 21-22, 1991*
Writer: *Bob Forward and Eve Forward*
Order: *DIC Season 2 #9-10*

• ***Battle Roster:*** *Joes:* Lt. Falcon, Duke, Mutt; Cobras: Cobra Commander, the Baroness, Metal-Head.

• ***First Appearances:*** *Joes:* Bullet-Proof (DEF leader), Shockwave (SWAT specialist); *Other:* The Headman (drug kingpin).

• ***Mission Brief:*** Duke flies off the handle when his half-brother, Lt. Falcon, gets addicted to a new drug named "Spark." With too many of their members succumbing to the drug, Joe and Cobra forces unite against a major Spark distributor named "the Headman."

• ***Stuff You Should Know:*** This story's written by Bob Forward, later to become one of the brain trusts behind *Transformers: Beast Wars* (rather ironic, considering *Beast Wars* develops the idea of the "spark" – the lifeforce that animates every Transformer). "The Greatest Evil" also re-affirms the sibling relationship between Duke and Lt. Falcon, first established in *G.I. Joe: The Movie.*

Some critics theorize that the Joes' "Bullet-Proof" and a similarly named character from the futuristic cartoon COPS are one and the same, but it's unclear. At story's end, the Headman apparently kicks it from a Spark overdose, making him one of the only characters in *G.I. Joe* TV history who actually *dies.*

A IS FOR ANDROID

US Transmission Date: *Sept. 26, 1991*
Writer: *Sandra Ryan*
Order: *DIC Season 2 #11*

• ***Battle Roster:*** *Joes:* Hawk, Psyche-Out, Ambush, Pathfinder; *Cobra:* Cobra Commander, Destro.

• ***Mission Brief:*** Cobra agents replace General Hawk with an android double, programming the ersatz Hawk to scrap Joe Headquarters' security system.

THE SLUDGE FACTOR

Episodes: *Two*
US Transmission Date: *Oct. 7, 1991*
Writer: *Phil Harnage*
Order: *DIC Season 2 #12-#13*

• ***Battle Roster:*** *Joes:* Flint, Clean Sweep, Hawk, Bullhorn, Rock 'n Roll; *Cobra:* Cobra Commander, Cesspool.

• ***First Appearances:*** *Joes:* Major Altitude (battle copter pilot).

• ***Mission Brief:*** Cobra Commander plans to hack off major arteries of the world's food supply, then rake in heaps of loot by opening extremely overpriced "Cobra Mart" stores.

Meanwhile, the deranged Cesspool embarks on his own agenda, plotting to cover the Earth with lethal volcanic dust.

• ***Stuff You Should Know:*** In a flashback story, it's established that during a firefight between Flint, Clean Sweep and some BAT's, the CEO of a chemical company fell into a vat of chemically-laced fertilizer. The incident left the CEO – later to become Cesspool – heavily disfigured and aching for revenge against Flint and Clean Sweep. "The Sludge Factor" bizarrely ends with a volcanic eruption destroying Cobra's hoarded food stocks – which would surely push an already famished Earth into complete starvation levels.

Purely to confuse us further, "Major Altitude" isn't the same character as Sky Patrol member "Altitude" (DIC Season 1).

COBRA WORLD

US Transmission Date: *Nov. 14, 1991*
Writer: *Tony Zalewski*
Order: *DIC Season 2 #14*

• ***Battle Roster:*** *Joes:* Dusty, Duke, Grunt; *Cobra:* Cobra Commander, Road Pig, Metal-Head.

• ***Mission Brief:*** Trying to convince the public that Cobra's gone legitimate, Cobra Commander opens an amusement park named "Cobra World." The Joes spit on Cobra's "turn-of-heart," exposing a scheme to tunnel from "Cobra World" into a nearby gold repository.

MESSENGER FROM THE DEEP

US Transmission Date: *Oct. 14, 1991*
Writer: *Marv Wolfman and Noel Watkins*
Order: *DIC Season 2 #15*

• ***Battle Roster:*** *Joes:* Flint, Duke, Wet-Suit, Heavy Duty, Scarlett, Cutter, Red Star; *Cobra:* Cobra Commander, Destro.

• ***Mission Brief:*** The Joes intercept Cobra agents intent on plundering an underwater city – actually a disused alien colony – leading to a clash with the city's serpentine guardians.

• ***Stuff You Should Know:*** A DIC Season 2 episode that's actually somewhat watchable – although that's not saying much.

THE ELIMINATOR

US Transmission Date: *Sept. 23, 1991*
Writer: *Sandra Ryan*
Order: *DIC Season 2 #16*

• ***Battle Roster:*** *Joes:* Mercer, Duke, Roadblock; *Cobra:* Cobra Commander, Destro.

• ***Mission Brief:*** Cobra android Overkill gets rebuilt into a more lethal variant named "the Eliminator." Meanwhile, Cobra Commander snitches information from G.I. Joe mercenary Mercer, thereby raiding a peace conference and discrediting Mercer as a traitor.

• ***Stuff You Should Know:*** In *G.I. Joe: The Movie,* it's established that Mercer previously defected from Cobra to become part of Sgt. Slaughter's Renegades.

METAL-HEAD'S REUNION

US Transmission Date: *Nov. 19, 1991*
Writer: *Steve Weiss and Paul Dell*
Order: *DIC Season 2 #17*

• ***Battle Roster:*** *Joes:* Capt. Grid-Iron, Grunt, Wet-Suit; *Cobra:* Metal-Head, Cobra Commander.

• ***Mission Brief:*** Metal-Head takes over his high school reunion to nab an armor-enhancing formula.

• ***Stuff You Should Know:*** It's established that Metal-Head, Capt. Grid-Iron and Suzanna Winters – the armor formula inventor – attended the same high school. Metal-Head's grandmother (from "Granny Dearest") logs a return appearance.

SHADOW OF A DOUBT

US Transmission Date: *Nov. 6, 1991*
Writer: *Michael Charles Hill*
Order: *DIC Season 2 #18*

• ***Battle Roster:*** *Joes:* Storm Shadow, Snake-Eyes, Hawk, Scarlett, Nunchuk, Tracker, Major Altitude; *Cobra:* Cobra Commander, the Baroness, Major Bludd, the Night Creeper leader.

• ***Mission Brief:*** An offer of returning to Cobra service tempts Storm Shadow.

• ***Stuff You Should Know:*** Stormy claims that he joined Cobra long enough to "discover who dishonored his ninja clan" – a likely allusion to his quest to find the Hard Master's killer in the *G.I. Joe* comic series. "Shadow of a Doubt" also debuts a new Joe Headquarters.

BASIC TRAINING

US Transmission Date: *Jan. 7, 1992*
Writer: *Phil Harnage*
Order: *DIC Season 2 #19*

• ***Battle Roster:*** *Joes:* Hawk.

• ***Mission Brief:*** Hawk grills a bunch of Joe recruits on the nitty-gritty about becoming a full-blooded Joe member.

• ***Stuff You Should Know:*** Most of this episode consists of flashback scenes from previous stories. Indeed, Hawk's "recruitment speech" to his trainees stems from his android double's appearance in "A is for Android."

THE LEGEND OF METAL-HEAD

***US Transmission Date:** Jan. 20, 1991*
***Writer:** Phil Harnage*
***Order:** DIC Season 2 #20*

• ***Battle Roster:*** *Cobra:* Metal-Head.
• ***Mission Brief:*** Metal-Head breaks the fourth wall and blathers about his greatness.
• ***Stuff You Should Know:*** Yet *another* flashback-loaded tale, this one focuses on Metal-Head's exploits throughout the DIC series. This story's sometimes referred to as "The Ballad of Metal-Head," although our video copy more properly cites it as "The Legend of Metal-Head."

Transformers: "Only Human"

***US Transmission Date:** Nov. 13, 1986*
***Order:** Transformers Season 3 #23*
***Writer:** Susan K. Williams*

BATTLE ROSTER Autobots: Rodimus Prime, Ultra Magnus, Springer, Arcee; *Cobra:* Cobra Commander.

NOTES Set in 2006, "Only Human" debuted in Transformers Season 3, which dealt with the continued war between the heroic "Autobots" and evil "Decepticons" – robots from the planet Cybertron who transform into various vehicles and useful gadgets. (Author's Note: Trust us, if you're unfamiliar with Transformers continuity, it's too complicated to explain here. We can only refer you to that brilliant and breathtaking tome, Prime Targets: The Unauthorized Guide to Transformers, Beast Wars and Beast Machines, available from yer friends at Mad Norwegian Press.)

As part of an unofficial *G.I. Joe/Transformers* crossover, Cobra Commander – although never acknowledged by name – appears in "Only Human" as a vagrant named "Old Snake," who's sought out by criminal elements to develop a synthoid project (*a la* "The Synthoid Conspiracy," "There's No Place Like Springfield," etc.). Granted, the *G.I. Joe* and *Transformers* TV series don't perfectly match continuity-wise, but Joe fandom by-and-large views "Only Human" as canon. And given the lack of a modern-day *G.I. Joe* series to contradict "Only Human," we're content to accept it as such.

MISSION BRIEF When the heroic Autobots co-ordinate with Earth authorities to thwart a number of terrorist attacks and shipments, crime lord Victor Drath decides the Autobots have thwarted his business for the last time and begins working toward their destruction. Drath seeks out a helmeted, demented drifter named "Old Snake," the former leader of a terrorist organization [obviously Cobra].

Snake confirms that his organization formerly used synthoid-based technology capable of transferring minds into synthetic bodies. Under Snake's guidance, Drath's men set up a processing laboratory, then plant a fake tip of terrorist activity. Autobots Rodimus Prime, Ultra Magnus, Springer and Arcee respond, but as they enter the facility, electro-harnesses restrain them. Snake activates the equipment, transferring the helpless Autobots' minds into synthetic humanoid bodies. Although Snake convinces Drath to keep the Autobots' robot bodies as weapons, Drath orders their new humanoid forms melted down.

Drath's men place Rodimus' quartet into a lethal trash compressor, but the humanoid Autobots recover just in time to escape. Shocked to find themselves in human bodies, Ultra

MISCELLANEOUS STUFF!

FLINT'S TRANSFORMERS APPEARANCE

Chatting about G.I. Joe characters cropping up in *Transformers* would be remiss without mentioning an older Flint's cameo in *Transformers*: "The Killing Jar." Also set in 2006, a gray-haired Flint shows up for a surprise visit with his daughter, Earth Defense Command Captain Marissa Faireborn. But it's actually not Flint himself, but rather a hologram crafted by the fiendish Quintessons and... well, this gets a trifle complicated.

Marissa's father goes unnamed onscreen, but "Flint" voice actor Bill Ratner provides his voice – Ratner's *only* appearance in *Transformers*. More to the point, Marissa and Flint share the same last name and, as if there were much doubt, the episode's cast list formally acknowledges the character as "Flint." Given writer/producer Flint Dille's ties to both *G.I. Joe* and *Transformers*, it's easy to see how such a connection came about, and as with Cobra Commander surfacing in *Transformers*: "Only Human," we're content to let Flint's appearance stand as canon until someone makes *G.I. Joe* cartoons to prove otherwise. Marissa Fairbourne, it should be noted, emerges as one of the most striking human characters from *Transformers* Season 3, making *G.I. Joe*'s connection with *Transformers* a bit more solid than most people suspected.

Magnus and Arcee leave to contact Autobot City for aid while Rodimus and Springer investigate the synthetic transfer process. Drath's men capture Ultra Magnus while Arcee desperately runs for Autobot City (a.k.a. the giant robot Metroplex). Unfortunately, Metroplex's security guards don't recognize the raving, human-looking Arcee and lock her away.

Meanwhile, Rodimus and Springer get spotted infiltrating Drath's home, forcing Rodimus to draw the guards away while Springer escapes. Nearby, Drath's thugs encounter difficulty handling the Autobot bodies, allowing Springer to offer his engineering expertise as a driver. Not recognizing the humanoid Autobot, the thugs agree, assigning Springer to pilot his own robotic body.

Wounded by gunfire, Rodimus briefly takes refuge with Michelle, Drath's paramour, but she betrays him to Drath. Snake suggests that if Ultra Magnus and Arcee survived to escape and warn Autobot City, their Autobot compatriots will seek unholy retribution. Knowing he couldn't withstand an all-out Autobot attack, Drath orders the captive Autobot robot bodies loaded with explosives, plotting to roll them toward Autobot City and level it completely.

Springer switches his robot body to helicopter mode, rescuing the humanoid Ultra Magnus and making a break for freedom just as the explosive-laden bodies of Rodimus Prime, Ultra Magnus and Arcee roll toward Metroplex. Unable to radio ahead, Springer and Ultra Magnus improvise by firing their weapons at Metroplex, forcing him to transform into battle station mode before the explosive-laden robot shells arrive. Metroplex's retaliatory strike grounds the Autobot shells at a safe distance until the explosives are disarmed.

Rodimus escapes just as Metroplex' denizens contact Earth authorities to arrest Victor Drath. Autobot scientist Perceptor deduces how to reverse Old Snake's equipment, restoring the humanoid Autobots' minds to their robotic forms. With Drath incarcerated, Snake wanders off to his homeless existence, muttering that "They simply don't make terrorists like they used to."

MEMORABLE MOMENTS Robotic Rodimus Prime lazily scratches his ear with a canister, not realizing it's filled with explosives. A human hand reaching out of the trash compressor right before commercial break – our first sign of what's happened to the Autobots – comes off as utterly macabre. Springer and Ultra Magnus inspiringly fire on Metroplex, knowing they could be ripped to bits in the crossfire. Best of all, Old Snake tries to give the Cobra battle cry at story's end but starts coughing and doesn't quite complete it.

LOVE AND WAR There's potential for nookie between Rodimus Prime and Victor Drath's paramour Michelle, but she betrays him to Drath first.

ASS-WHUPPINGS Robotic Rodimus Prime takes an exploding canister in the face. Human Rodimus takes some gunshot wounds.

GOOFS Helicopter mode Springer catches a falling pedestrian who dives right onto him – but it's hard to see how his blades didn't slice up the human like a tomato. The newly humanoid Autobots miraculously find coveralls that perfectly co-ordinate with their robotic colors.

TV TIE-INS In terms of TV continuity, Cobra Commander became homeless after the final defeat of Cobra (which presumably occurred sometime after the DIC cartoons). Synthoid technology debuted in "The Synthoid Conspiracy," although we've never seen it used for mind transference before now.

THE COMMAND DECISION Ahhhhhh. Exceptional and bold, proof why *Transformers* is more than just big robots hitting each other. "Only Human" smartly shows four Autobots out of their element and out of luck, completing an unofficial crossover with *G.I. Joe* (when we realized Old Snake was Cobra Commander, we nearly leapt out of our G.I. Joe Underoos). In short, if you need a story to serve as an epilogue to the *G.I. Joe* cartoon, this is the one.

The Comics

G.I. Joe #1 to #5

Titles: *"Operation: Lady Doomsday" and "... Hot Potato!" (#1), "Panic at the North Pole!" (#2), "The Trojan Gambit" (#3), "Operation: Wingfield!" (#4), "Tanks for the Memories" (#5)*
Release Dates: *July 1982 to Nov. 1982*
Art: *Herb Trimpe ("Operation: Lady Doomsday," #1; #3, #4), Don Perlin ("... Hot Potato!", #1; #2, #5)*

BATTLE ROSTER/FIRST APPEARANCES *Joes:* Snake-Eyes (commando, #1), Hawk (missile commander/G.I. Joe field commander, #1), Scarlett (counter intelligence, #1), Stalker (ranger, #1), Breaker (communications officer, #1), Grunt (infantry trooper, #1), Rock 'n Roll (machine gunner, #1), Flash (laser rifle trooper, #1), Short-Fuze (mortar soldier, #1), Clutch (VAMP driver, #1), Steeler (tank commander, #1), Zap (bazooka soldier, #1), Grand Slam (laser artillery soldier, #1), Brigadier General Flagg (top G.I. Joe commander, #1), Major General Austin (Pentagon officer, #1); *Cobra:* Cobra Commander (Cobra commander, #1), the Baroness (intelligence officer, #1); *Other:* Dr. Adele Burkhart (#1), Kwinn (special ops, #2).

MISSION BRIEF ***Issue #1 (main story, "Operation: Lady Doomsday"):*** When a leading nuclear physicist named Dr. Adele Burkhart publicly vilifies her involvement in America's "Doomsday Project" – a retaliatory weapons array capable of annihilating all life on Earth – Pentagon officials steel themselves for a series of potentially humiliating Congressional hearings. But before the hearings commence, a ruthless, subversive terrorist group named Cobra kidnaps Burkhart to comb her brain for nuclear secrets.

Unable to leave Burkhart in Cobra's clutches (and fearing the political fallout from simply terminating her) Brigadier General Flagg and Major General Austin call upon G.I. Joe, the military's special counter-terrorist group, to rescue Burkhart. Led by General Clayton Abernathy (a.k.a. Hawk) and operating from a secret headquarters (a.k.a. the Pit) beneath the army chaplains' assistant school at Fort Wadsworth, a dozen code-named G.I. Joe specialists track Burkhart to a Cobra stronghold in the Caribbean.

The Joes besiege the Cobra fortress, engaging hundreds of troops led by Cobra's head honcho, Cobra Commander, and his chief lieutenant the Baroness. Unfortunately, the Joes soon discover that Cobra Commander merely kidnapped Burkhart as a feint to draw the Joes in closer, hoping to detonate the Cobra base and thereby wipe out Cobra's main opposition.

Thankfully, the Joes' superior fighting skills prevail, forcing Cobra Commander to escape via a hidden passage while the Joes and Burkhart escape in a Cobra helicopter. Safe from harm, Burkhart adheres to her anti-warfare views but at least acknowledges the Joes' heroism.

Issue #1 (back-up story, "... Hot Potato!"): As Middle East violence escalates, Cobra worsens hostilities by bankrolling a dictator named Colonel Sharif and his "Guardians of Paradise" terrorist cell. Learning of a video tape in Sharif's possession that could defuse the situation, the Pentagon orders Joe members Scarlett, Rock 'n Roll and the mute Snake-Eyes to infiltrate Sharif's territory and steal the tape – strenuously insisting that the Joes prioritize the tape's recovery ahead of all else.

Snake-Eyes' team snitches the tape, but Scarlett takes a bullet in the leg while fleeing from Sharif's soldiers. As senior officer, the hobbled Scarlett orders Rock 'n Roll and Snake-Eyes to run for the border while she delays their pursuers. Snake-Eyes forces Rock 'n Roll to sprint to safety, then violates orders by returning for Scarlett. Rock 'n Roll passes off the tape to a Joe pick-up crew, then follows suit and rejoins his surrounded teammates. Scarlett's trio finds their options increasingly bleak, but General Hawk, taking a broad interpretation of the Pentagon orders, obliterates their pursuers with a heavy jeep cannon.

Issue #2: When unidentified commandos butcher a team of American researchers at the North Polar Ice Cap, a Joe ranger named Stalker takes Breaker, Scarlett and Snake-Eyes to investigate a nearby Russian research station. Finding the Russian scientists dead from exposure, Stalker's group suspiciously spots a freelance special ops agent named Kwinn operating in the area.

The Joes try to apprehend Kwinn for questioning, but the crafty mercenary captures the Joes instead. Kwinn details how the dead Russians researchers developed a long-range, low-frequency transmission device capable of dousing the human brain with uncontrollable fear and paranoia. Intending to target America with the fear ray, the Russian scientists mistakenly believed that the American researchers were spying on them and wiped them out, perishing soon after when the Russian base's heater malfunctioned.

Hired by Russian officials to retrieve the fear-inducing Frequency Modulator, Kwinn increasingly finds his employers' goals abhorrent but feels duty-bound to honor his contract. Seeking a loophole, Kwinn "abandons" the Joes to the Arctic elements, depositing the firing pins to their rifles four miles away. Traveling a mile further, Kwinn turns over the Frequency Modulator to his Russian contacts, who validate the completion of his contract. Kwinn rides away satisfied, but soon after – as Kwinn predicted – the Joes expertly locate their missing firing pins, eliminate the Russians and take the Frequency Modulator into custody.

Issue #3: As Hawk and Scarlett keep up appearances at a social tea event for Fort Wadsworth's chaplain's assistants, Cobra Commander undertakes a grand scheme to locate Joe Headquarters (a.k.a. the Pit, nested beneath Fort Wadsworth). Accordingly, Cobra Commander allows the Joes to capture a Cobra battle-robot and take it to the Pit for further study. Unfortunately, the "inert" 'bot, preprogrammed to fight past the Pit's shielding and transmit a homing signal, suddenly reactivates and embarks on a rampage.

The mechanical abomination runs the Joes run ragged, but Steeler, Breaker and Clutch finally trick the robot into falling down the Pit's six-story-tall hydraulic lift. The robot shatters on impact, but a dozen tiny spider robots – each equipped with a homing transmitter – emerge from the robot's head and scurry through the Pit's air ducts. The Joes madly squash, laser and blow up 11 of the drones, but the final one emerges into Fort Wadsworth and prepares to send its homing signal. Thankfully, Scarlett off-handedly grinds the spiderbot into itty-bitty pieces with her heel – inadvertently keeping the Pit's location secret.

Issue #4: Disturbed when a rogue officer named Commander Wingfield uses Cobra funding to create a reclusive, anti-government training camp in Montana, Hawk and Joe infantry trooper Grunt infiltrate Wingfield's operation as a pair of green recruits. But while eavesdropping on Wingfield's planning sessions, Hawk and Grunt horrifyingly learn that Cobra also provided Wingfield with two nuclear devices.

Wingfield swiftly makes plans to drop one of his warheads on Vladivostok in Russia, hoping to trigger a United States-Soviet Union nuclear exchange and pave the way for Cobra to dominate the world. As backup if the Vladivostok gambit fails, Wingfield plans to detonate the second warhead in Montana – fanatically committing suicide to achieve the same results.

Wingfield's second-in-command lifts off in a B-29 bomber to drop the Vladivostok warhead, but Hawk follows in one of Wingfield's spare jets and guns the plane down into the Pacific – thankfully preventing a detonation. Utterly deranged, Wingfield primes the second warhead, but his wife Shary, convinced of her husband's insanity, shoots Wingfield in the back. The Joes overrun Wingfield's camp, enabling munitions expert Zap to defuse the nuclear bomb and spare the world from a nuclear holocaust.

Issue #5: Seeking to ease Pentagon concerns that the Joe team's advanced MOBAT tank might prove too tempting a target for Cobra, General Flagg arranges to include the MOBAT in Manhattan's Armed Forces Day Parade – hoping to show the Joint Chiefs of Staff that the MOBAT's indistinguishable from other tanks. Unfortunately, Cobra Commander learns of Flagg's decision and sends a platoon of Cobra troopers, disguised as the "Springfield Drum and Bugle Corps," to capture the MOBAT and make off with its technology.

During the parade, a MOBAT crew of Steeler, Clutch and Breaker nearly pee in terror when the Springfield band suddenly produces anti-tank weapons and a "Nautilus at the North Pole" float simultaneously attempts to swallow the MOBAT whole. Turbo-charged with adrenaline, Clutch guns the MOBAT's accelerator, leading to a wild chase through Manhattan's crowded streets.

Believing the Joes aren't carrying live ammunition, the emboldened "Springfield Corps" members converge on MOBAT in Central Park. But moments later, the Cobra foot soldiers turn white as a sheet when the MOBAT fires a "warning shot," then brings its main cannon to bear on them. Staring down the MOBAT's barrel, the Cobra soldiers surrender, unaware that Breaker merely simulated a "cannon shot" by cranking up the MOBAT's speaker system and popping his gum.

MEMORABLE MOMENTS Hawk advises his troops: "Don't turn your back on the Baroness unless she's dead... even then, I'd search her for grenades." In a nice bit of camaraderie, Rock 'n Roll practically begs to return for the wounded Scarlett, offering to let Snake-Eyes finish their mission (Snake-Eyes solves the problem by going back himself).

Issue #5 steals the best moments, especially when the fugitive MOBAT – accompanied by Breaker hollering, "Clear the sidewalk! Runaway tank!" – forces New York hot dog vendors and civilians to scatter like terrified ducks. During the New York melee, a Cobra lieutenant advises proceeding "with caution," prompting an outraged Cobra Commander to scream: "Fool! How long do you think you can run around the streets of midtown Manhattan with machine guns and rocket launchers before the authorities start reacting?!"

It's irrelevant to the plot, but General Flagg unexpectedly gets the chance to plug Cobra Commander in issue #5 – until the fiend takes shelter amid a Girl Scout troupe. Flagg understandably hesitates, but Cobra Commander – questioning Flagg's courage – singes the general's scalp with a bullet and retreats. Questioned later as to why he didn't even release the safety on his sidearm, the noble Flagg simply responds: "... because we're the good guys."

LOVE AND WAR Rock 'n Roll provides the first hint of a romance between Snake-Eyes and Scarlett, airing suspicions that the two have feelings for one another. We never get confirmation of Rock 'n Roll's observation, but the wounded Scarlett, normally tough enough to wrestle a rhino, weeps when Snake-Eyes returns for her.

Breaker misses the opportunity for coffee (and potential nookie) with an MIT worker when he's summoned for a mission in issue #2.

The Springfield "band" includes some curvaceous majorettes (yes, there's *women* in the Cobra army). Before the hostilities break out, Steeler zeroes the MOBAT's viewer on a majorette's posterior and brings it into *full* magnification – the better, he insists, "to keep abreast of the rear-guard situation!"

ASS-WHUPPINGS Cobra wipes out the entire population of a Caribbean village to prevent them from aiding the Joes (issue #1). Dr. Burkhart rushes Cobra Commander, taking a bullet in the arm for her trouble, but Scarlett retaliates by burying a throwing star in Cobra Commander's wrist. Snake-Eyes takes down a six-pack of Cobra troops with, as one of his teammates puts it, "... something in his boot that's gotta be against the Geneva Convention." Snake-Eyes and Scarlett annihilate waves of Colonel Sharif's soldiers until their guns run dry.

Scarlett thumps a nameless opponent in a martial arts competition. Steeler, Clutch and Breaker drop an elevator on Cobra's biggie robot (#3) then arrange a more-permanently damaging six-story drop. Hawk gives Wingfield's second-in-command, Captain Carruthers, a chance to jump to safety, but Carruthers goes down with his plane. The craven Girl Scout-encircled Cobra Commander grazes General Flagg's temple with a bullet.

GOOFS Grunt "doesn't like a look that Snake-Eyes flashes him" – which is an odd comment, considering Snake-Eyes never removes his mask.

COMIC TIE-INS Hawk assigns Stalker and a group of Joes to rescue Dr. Burkhart – again – from trigger-happy rebels in *G.I. Joe* #38-#39. Cobra operates from "Cobra Island" in issue #1, which bears no relation to the "Cobra Island" nation established in #41.

Kwinn returns in *G.I. Joe* #12, working for whacked Cobra scientist Dr. Venom. The Joes success secure the Russian Frequency Modulator in #2, but Cobra somehow obtains the technology anyway, later adapting it as part of a money-making Terror-Drome scheme (#54-#68).

In issue #2, an army officer reacts with horror upon seeing Snake-Eyes' unmasked face, suggesting it's deformed (*G.I. Joe* #10 and #27 further detail his disfigurement). Snake-Eyes occasionally travels to Columbia University, supposedly to immerse himself in the college's total sensory deprivation unit, although *G.I. Joe* #108 shows that Snakes actually keeps a secret den there.

G.I. Joe #5 debuts Cobra Commander's long-running fetish for gunning down cardboard cutouts of the Joes as target practice. Stalker thinks the black-suited Snake-Eyes will abandon his wounded teammates at the first available opportunity, but later stories (notably #26-#27) retroactively upgrade Stalker's opinion of Snakes. The Joes engage Colonel Sharif's Middle Eastern troopers again in *G.I. Joe* #58 and *Special Missions* #3.

CHARACTER PROFILE: JOES

• *Breaker:* Breaker sometimes refines MIT's computer system while he's off-duty. He's always chewing gum and blowing his trademark bubbles.

• *Major General Austin:* Also known as "Old Iron Butt."

• *General Flagg:* Flagg serves as the Joes' direct link to the Pentagon. He's a former Army Pistol team captain and typically carries a .45 sidearm.

• *Hawk:* Hawk doesn't agree with Dr. Burkhart's anti-war views, but declines to brand her a traitor, strenuously informing his troops to defend her Constitution-given right to disagree with the government.

• *Rock 'n Roll:* Fires 7.62 NATO armaments.

• *Scarlett:* During the Middle East operation (#1), Scarlett contemplates suicide over capture. She easily wins martial arts tournaments.

• *"Shooter":* Joe member randomly included on the team roll call – although he's not a Hasbro toy, and we never see him in action.

• *Snake-Eyes:* Completely mute, Snake-Eyes sometimes communicates with Scarlett via sign language. Snake-Eyes insists on checking everyone's weapons before battle, fearing his teammates' guns might jam while covering his back.

• *Stalker:* An amateur photographer among other things, Stalker's known to take pictures of wildlife in Wisconsin.

• *Steeler:* Strong enough to lift 200 pounds.

• *Zap:* Hasn't flown a helicopter in two years (but remembers how in a panic).

CHARACTER PROFILE: COBRA

Cobra Commander: American intelligence knows virtually nothing about him. His firing aim's a bit high and to the left.

CHARACTER PROFILE: OTHER

Kwinn: Highly effective special ops freelancer who's worked for CIA, MOSSASD, KGB, MI-6 and other security agencies. The name "Kwinn" likely designates an alias; his real name's unknown. Kwinn's presumably of Inuit origin, stands 6'10" high, weighs 260 pounds and typically carries a .30 caliber belt-fed machine gun. Despite his line of work, Kwinn never lies and fulfills contractual obligations to the letter, preferably without senseless violence. He'll never betray an employer, but might manipulate events to guarantee justice.

PLACES TO GO The Pit (a.k.a. "Joe Headquarters"): Hidden beneath the army chaplains' assistant school at Fort Wadsworth, the five-level Pit's protected by steel-reinforced, radiation-shielded concrete and alloy armor. The complex can seal off its various levels to minimize damage. It's built to withstand a direct hit from a five-megaton warhead. The bottom two levels, containing living quarters, computer banks and generators, can function as a self-sustained environment for six months. The Pit sometimes stores aluminum foil designed to "chaff" enemy radar. A massive hydraulic lift, located in the Fort Wadsworth motor pool, allows the Joes to transport vehicles to different Pit levels. Most importantly, the canteen's located on level five.

HOT WHEELS ***G.I. Joe Multi-Ordinance Battle Tank (MOBAT):*** The MOBAT features state-of-the-art technology, including two gas turbines, fewer moving parts, more horsepower and minimal vibration and noise when compared to your average tank. A centrally located computer speeds up the operator's reaction time. The MOBAT's waterproof hatches and retractable snorkels allow it to function underwater for an hour.

THE COMMAND DECISION One of the most important comic debuts of the 1980s – but also inherently clunky – *G.I. Joe* #1 can't help but read like a toy catalog, given its mandate of introducing a staggering 17 characters in the 28 pages that compose "Operation: Lady Doomsday." The backup story, "… Hot Potato," at least highlights the Joes' camaraderie – but even that's like looking at a murky thumbnail sketch rather than a finished painting. In short, G.I. Joe fans point to the premiere issue as the greatness from which the series spawned – but if we're being entirely honest, it's too wooden and clunky to give much satisfaction.

Issue #2's so-so Arctic plot decidedly improves with the introduction the multi-faceted (albeit dopey-looking) Kwinn, who ironically contains more character shading than everyone else combined. Unfortunately, issues #3-#4 devolve back into easily-ignored, cliched military plots – somewhat forgivable since Cobra – with only two recognizable characters at this point (Cobra Commander and the Baroness) – regrettably can't carry every issue.

The best of the entire bunch, "Tanks for the Memories" (#5) sports a painful title but triumphs in a raucous romp through New York City. Even if you skip the early *G.I. Joe* stuff, fish this one out of a back-issue bin, because it's worth a re-read.

G.I. Joe #6 to #7

Titles: *"To Fail is to Conquer... to Succeed is to Die!" (#6), "Walls of Death!" (#7)*
Release Dates: *Dec. 1982 to Mar. 1983*
Writers: *Larry Hama and Herb Trimpe (co-plotter)*
Art: *Herb Trimpe*

BATTLE ROSTER *Joes:* Stalker, Hawk, Scarlett, Clutch, Steeler, Flash, Breaker; *Cobra:* Cobra Commander, the Baroness.

FIRST APPEARANCES *Other:* The Oktober Guard (Colonel Brekhov, Scharage, Daina, Horrorshow, Stromavik, all #6).

MISSION BRIEF ***Issue #6:*** When a prototype Russian spycraft, loaded with advanced surveillance equipment and an anti-gravity device, crashes in Afghanistan, the Pentagon assigns Hawk to retrieve the airship's technology for the United States. Volunteering for the mission, Stalker, Scarlett, Clutch and three other Joes parachute into Afghanistan with a Rough Terrain Vehicle (RTV) and Clutch's VAMP jeep. However, Russia's top-notch commando team, named "the Oktober Guard," and Cobra operatives separately dog the Joes, setting up a three-way contest for the downed spyplane.

The Joes net the spycraft first, but a frenzied, close-quarters battle with the Oktober Guard batters both teams. Pouncing at an opportune moment, Cobra Commander's troopers easily take both the Joes and Russians prisoner – threatening to execute both teams.

Issue #7: Unwilling to delay moving the Russian spyplane, Cobra Commander leaves his top torture experts – Rattler and Copperhead – to execute the prisoners while the main Cobra force heads for a Cobra stronghold in Iran. Rattler and Copperhead salivate at the chance to torment the Joes and Russians, but Clutch secretly maneuvers his VAMP jeep's cannons with a remote-control device – eradicating the Cobra hitmen in a hailstorm of machine gun fire.

Greatly outnumbered by Cobra Commander's troops, the Joes and Oktober Guard agree to jointly liberate the downed spyplane, then shoot each other up afterward. At Cobra's camp in Iran, the Oktober Guard tries to double-cross the Joes, but the Americans nonetheless sweep through Cobra's opposition and drive off with the spyplane. Safe upon reaching a Joe base in Pakistan, Stalker's group accepts Hawk's congratulations for a successful assignment, then pales to learn they were a decoy from the very start – risking their necks while another extraction team effortlessly escorted the real spyplane out of Afghanistan.

MEMORABLE MOMENTS Afghan rebel fighter Ahmed intrinsically trusts Stalker because Stalker's a plain-spoken fighting man – not a silver-tongued CIA operative or politician. There's a delicious, Cold War-reminiscent moment when Oktober Guard member Horrorshow screams at the Joes: "Amerikanski fools! The Oktober Guard will teach you the error of your capitalist ways!" The top moment of all comes when the Joes arrive home and learn their entire operation was a decoy – making Stalker feel like putting his fist through Hawk's face.

LOVE AND WAR Clutch suggests to Scarlett that the two of them deliberately "run out of gas somewhere." Referring to the film Every Which Way But Loose, Scarlett venomously responds: "I'd sooner have a date with Clint Eastwood's baboon." (Author's Note: Actually, the critter in question was an orangutan – I can't believe I know that).

ASS-WHUPPINGS The Joes lay waste to an Iranian border patrol (Breaker takes a bullet during the fracas), with the Oktober Guard running behind and mopping up the enemy. A Cobra booby trap half-electrocutes Steeler, Breaker and Stalker. Flash literally encounters a nest of cobras, lasering the snakes to death and eliciting a "Disgusting!" from Scarlett.

GOOFS The **Battle Roster** in issue #6 lists Grand Slam as part of the Afghanistan insertion team, but Flash inexplicably goes in his place. (Then again, the two of them wear the same costume.)

Cobras Rattler and Copperhead do little by way of pain and torture to their prisoners, but Rattler nonetheless asks his partner: "Have you seen them sweat enough yet?" After killing some Iranian border guards, Russian Horrorshow judges a similar slaughter on the Joes' part as, "Another example of American imperialist aggression!" (Commie hypocrites!)

CHARACTER PROFILE: JOES

- *Hawk:* Sometimes feeds Cobra false information as an informant named "Songbird."
- *Scarlett:* Grows outraged, more so than her fellow Joes, at the thought of collaborating with the Oktober Guard.
- *Stalker:* Carries C-4 plastic explosives.

CHARACTER PROFILE: OTHER

Colonel Brekhov: Combat's a tradition in his family – Brekhov's father fought at Stalingrad and his grandfather saw duty on the Eastern front.

ORGANIZATIONS *The Oktober Guard:* As you might expect from a Cold War, KGB-run culture, the Oktober Guard faces stiff penalties for failure. The Oktober Guardsmen normally carry AK-47 assault rifles.

HOT WHEELS *G.I. Joe Rough Terrain Vehicle (RTV):* Extremely portable Joe vehicle, mostly composed of plastic aluminum and foam composite, dropped via parachute and assembled in hostile territory (the Joes complete the task in 23 minutes). The RTV's designed for structural strength but sucks for acceleration. The upper turret rotates to give the Joes a higher firing point.

THE COMMAND DECISION Somewhat notable for introducing the Oktober Guard and the final twist of Stalker's team risking their lives as bait. But otherwise, issues #6 and #7 only offer up meaningless brawls and the extreme awkwardness that punctuates *G.I. Joe*'s first year (Cobra Commander's mind-bogglingly dumb, "We'll just walk away and leave our two stupidest troopers to torture and shoot you," routine at the start of #7).

G.I. Joe #8 to #9

***Titles:** "Code Name: Sea-Strike" (#8), "The Diplomat" (#9)*
***Release Dates:** Feb. to Mar. 1983*
***Writers:** Herb Trimpe (#8), Steven Grant (#9)*
***Art:** Herb Trimpe (#8), Mike Vosburg (#9)*

BATTLE ROSTER *Joes:* Hawk, Stalker, Clutch, Scarlett, Snake-Eyes, Zap, Short-Fuze, Breaker, Flash, Grunt, Steeler, Rock 'n Roll, Grand Slam; Cobras: Cobra Commander, the Baroness.

MISSION BRIEF ***Issue #8:*** When Cobra constructs a number of underwater launch sites, the Joes oversee security on a Kennedy Space Center satellite designed to knock out Cobra's missiles. Cobra mobilizes to destroy the entire space complex, but the Joes succeed in launching the satellite into orbit. Failing to eliminate the satellite, Cobra Commander self-destructs his network's central complex, allowing the victorious Joes to return to base.

Issue #9: After capturing a Cobra safehouse in Nebraska, the Joes learn of a Cobra plot to assassinate U.S. diplomat Brian Hassell. Needing Hassell to bring the Persian Gulf nation of Al-Alawi under America's sphere of influence, the Pentagon orders Scarlett and Clutch to serve as Hassell's personal bodyguards.

Heading for a negotiation site in the Italian Alps, Scarlett and Clutch help Hassell evade several Cobra attackers, but upon arrival, they shockingly discover that Hassell's actually a Cobra assassin who intends to murder an Al-Alawi ambassador. Fortunately, the ambassador's bulletproof vest stops Hassell's bullets, enabling Scarlett to kerwallop Hassell and take him into custody.

LOVE AND WAR Scarlett struts about the French Riviera in a bikini. She later lounges about her hotel room in a bathrobe, swiftly changing into fighting togs in the car during a battle (Scarlett to Clutch: "You keep your eyes on the road!").

ASS-WHUPPINGS A Joe MOBAT tank falls to a Cobra land torpedo. The Joes eradicate several Cobra SEA Legs transports (see Hot Wheels).

PREPOSTEROUS PHYSICS Flash presumes that since space is a vacuum, his personal jet pack can match a missile's speed (err, no, but thanks for playing). Crazily, he pushes the missile off-trajectory.

Cobra Commander and the Baroness own a helicopter that doubles as a submersible vessel. They also drive an airplane that starts up while completely submerged.

Breaker chews his gum (and presumably pops his trademark bubbles) inside a space helmet – which could be messy if not near-fatal.

GOOFS Hawk happily struts about the Arctic in a short-sleeved shirt. The Baroness accuses some Cobra traitors of being "capitalist lackeys" – when Cobra clearly strives for monetary gain.

Cobra Commander kindly gloats before self-destructing one of his bases, allowing the Joes to escape unharmed. The Joes let Ambassador Hassell, who's supposedly marked for death, lollygag on a beach where any passing gunman could pick him off. A lackey tells Stalker and Snake-Eyes only that Amsterdam holds a Cobra safehouse – and they somehow conjure an exact location and contact name from that tip.

CHARACTER profile: JOES

- *Clutch:* An expert road driver, but terrible with planes. He lost a game of Chicken – once.
- *Clutch and Scarlett:* Scarlett considers Clutch a scruffy rogue and doesn't like teaming with him.
- *Hawk:* Remarks that he's spent 30 years in military service.
- *Scarlett:* One of her crossbow arrows fires a tow cable.

PLACES TO GO Cobra's Underwater Launch Sites: Maintain an underwater depth of at least 12,500 meters, putting them too deep for a surface attack.

HOT WHEELS Cobra Surprise, Engage and Attack (SEA Legs): Amphibious walkers that aren't based on any Hasbro toy and, it must be said, look idiotic.

THE COMMAND DECISION A wet loaf of bread, issue #8 just demonstrates how appallingly generic *G.I. Joe* gets when non-military writers take the helm. Mind, writer/artist Herb Trimpe's efforts seem almost Shakespearean when compared to Steven Grant's atrocious plotting and dialogue (Cobra Commander: "Greetings, you pathetic clod!") in #9, making for a horrendously painful story with outrageously cliched characterization (a captured Hassell to his enemies: "You'll pay for this! You'll pay!")

G.I. Joe #10 to #15

Titles: *"A Nice Little Town Like Ours..." (#10), "The Pipeline Ploy!" (#11), "Three Strikes for Snake-Eyes" (#12), "Last Plane from Rio Londo" (#13), "Destro Attacks" (#14), "Red-Eye to Miami!" (#15)*
Release Dates: *Apr. to Sept. 1983*
Art: *Mike Vosburg*

BATTLE ROSTER *Joes:* Snake-Eyes, Scarlett, Hawk, Zap, Stalker, Breaker, Rock 'n Roll; *Cobra:* Cobra Commander, the Baroness; *Other:* Kwinn.

FIRST APPEARANCES *Joes:* Gung Ho (marine, #11), Doc (medic, #11), Snow Job (Arctic trooper, #11), Wild Bill (helicopter pilot, #11), Airborne (helicopter assault trooper, #11), Torpedo (SEAL, #13), Ace (Skystriker pilot, #14); *Cobra:* Destro (weapons supplier/Cobra field commander, #14), Dr. Venom (mad scientist, #10), Scar Face (courier, #12), Major Bludd (mercenary, #15); *Other:* Billy (#10).

MISSION BRIEF ***Issue #10:*** Mobilizing against a Cobra safehouse in midtown Manhattan, Hawk readies his forces for a ground assault while Snake-Eyes, Scarlett and Zap break in through the roof. Unfortunately, the Baroness incapacitates Snake-Eyes' trio and spirits them away to Cobra's main base of operations – an innocent-looking town, named Springfield, located somewhere in the continental United States.

With expert precision, a ruthless Cobra scientist named Dr. Venom straps Snake-Eyes into a brainwave scanner, attempting to loot Snakes' mind for the Pit's location. Nearby, a locked-up Scarlett and Zap ally themselves with a young boy named Billy, a member of Springfield's anti-Cobra resistance movement, and escape with his help.

Unable to resist the brainwave scanner indefinitely, the ninja-trained Snake-Eyes fakes his death with a self-induced coma. Dr. Venom unstraps the "dead" Snake-Eyes, allowing the mute Joe to recover, slug Venom unconscious and flee. Reunited, Snake-Eyes, Scarlett and Zap hijack an aircraft from the Springfield airport, leaving Billy behind to rejoin the Springfield underground movement. Forced to fly blind through a tremendous storm on the East Coast, Snake-Eyes' team arrives back at New York City hours later – with no clue as to Springfield's whereabouts.

Issue #11: Seeking to improve Cobra's efficiency, Cobra Commander employs a military strategist and arms supplier named Destro to lead Cobra troops on the battlefield. Meanwhile, the Joes investigate reports of Cobra interference with the Trans-Alaskan Pipeline, despairing to find Cobra troopers contaminating the pipeline oil with a lethal plague toxin. The Joes capture the Cobra goons, but the shootout tears open the toxin canisters, contaminating all concerned and leaving them with six hours to live.

Using the plague as a distraction, a second Cobra team embarks on the true objective of the Alaskan operation, stealing enough plutonium from a nuclear power plant to grant Cobra nuclear capabilities. As the troopers send their plutonium-filled canister down the pipeline to a waiting Cobra helicopter squad, Destro surprises some Joes and holds them at gunpoint. For motives known only to him (i.e. for reasons we can't quite figure out), Destro spills the beans about Cobra's strategy in Alaska, bragging that he holds the only supply of plague antidote. Fighting for their lives, the Joes overpower Destro and nab his antidote, forcing him to retreat.

Working at a fevered pace, Joe medic Doc injects his teammates with the antidote, then bluffs the Cobra helicopter team into thinking they're also contaminated by the plague toxin. By exchanging the "antidote" (actually simple tetanus shots) for the plundered plutonium, Doc foils Cobra's nuclear aspirations.

Issue #12: Embarking on a yet another cracked master plan to wipe out G.I. Joe Headquarters, Cobra Commander sets about obtaining a virus strain (housed at independent labs in San Francisco) that, when combined with a Dr. Venom-made serum, produces a deadly plague. Accordingly, Cobra courier Scar-Face steals the virus strain from San Francisco and travels to Dr. Venom's island bunker in Sierra Gordo.

Meanwhile, a quartet of Joes (Stalker, Snake-Eyes, Gung Ho and Breaker) track illicit shipments of missile guidance chips – actually a side business to finance Dr. Venom's operations – and arrive in the South American banana republic of Sierra Gordo. There, Snake-Eyes' party infiltrates Dr. Venom's missile chip warehouse, but the Inuit mercenary Kwinn (*G.I. Joe #2*), hired by Cobra to guarantee missile chip deliveries, easily captures the Joes.

Soon after, the Baroness arrives to transport both the virus strain and Dr. Venom's serum back to Cobra Headquarters. The Baroness and Scar-Face board a Cobra jet, but the Joes burst loose and wreak havoc. Amid the chaos, Dr. Venom finds Kwinn's loyalty tenuous at best and unwisely tries to shoot the mercenary in the back – compelling Snake-Eyes, who recalls his previous torment at Venom's hands (#10), to thrash the Cobra scientist and save Kwinn's life.

Stalker, Gung Ho and Breaker try to escape, but the Baroness dive-bombs them, tossing the three Joes into a river. As Stalker's trio flounders, the Baroness deems Dr. Venom expendable and drops a bomb onto the good scientist's lair – apparently leveling Venom's bunker along with Dr. Venom, Kwinn and Snake-Eyes.

Issue #13-#14: Stranded in the volatile Sierra Gordo, Stalker, Gung Ho and Breaker mourn for the lost Snake-Eyes and scour the remainder of Dr. Venom's Sierra Gordo project, locating a dot-sized microchip amid the ruins. Summoning their teammates for a pick-up, Stalker's group returns to Joe Headquarters and examines the microchip – staggered to find it contains the location of the Cobra-controlled city of Springfield.

Meanwhile, the Baroness and Scar-Face return to base with the stolen virus and Dr. Venom's serum, allowing a gleeful Cobra Commander to continue machinations to locate Joe Headquarters. Collaborating with the Baroness, Cobra Commander intends to inject both the virus and serum into a random Cobra trooper, allowing the deadly disease to gestate within the trooper's body until his very touch turns lethal.

Furthermore, Cobra Commander details how he encoded the Joe-captured microchip with a *false* location for Springfield, hoping to spur a Joe attack on a decoy site. If all follows as planned, the Joes will "capture" the diseased trooper and incarcerate him at Joe Headquarters – then quarantine the base when the plague comes to term. By directing his spy satellites to detect unusual quarantine activity at military bases, Cobra Commander hopes to pinpoint the Joes' center of operations, then marshal his forces against it. (*Author's Note:* Good grief, I hope you're following all of this. Have a bourbon, if it helps.)

Back in Sierra Gordo, Snake-Eyes, Kwinn and Dr. Venom awaken in the remains of Dr. Venom's island bunker, shunted underwater by the Baroness' bomb. Distrustful of Dr. Venom, Snake-Eyes and Kwinn nonetheless combine efforts with the Cobra scientist and escape, emerging into a war-torn country without support or allies.

Cobra Commander journeys to a Vermont-based Cobra research facility to oversee the final phase of his master plan, blissfully unaware that Destro, intending to usurp Cobra leadership for himself, actually encoded Cobra Commander's microchip with the location for Cobra Commander's laboratory in Vermont. Basking in the thought of the Joes catching Cobra Commander flat-footed, Destro turns outraged to learn his ex-lover, the Baroness, accompanied Cobra Commander to the Vermont lab. Still harboring feelings for the Baroness in the lump of coal that serves as his heart, Destro scraps his intended betrayal and leads a Cobra assault squad to the Vermont base. Destro's forces fend off the Joes until Cobra Commander and the Baroness jet to safety. As the battle ends and Destro retreats, both the Joes and Cobra realize they've got preciously little to show for all their war efforts.

Issue #15: Back at Cobra Headquarters, Cobra Commander smells treachery by discovering that Dr. Venom, hoping to guarantee his continued importance to Cobra, never provided him with the final, crucial catalyst to the plague toxin. More dangerously, Cobra Commander comes to suspect Destro's involvement in the Vermont debacle and hires a mercenary named Major Bludd to plot Destro's elimination.

In war-torn Sierra Gordo, Snake-Eyes and Kwinn flirt with the rather pleasant idea of plugging Dr. Venom, but keep him alive to due to the Cobra scientist's piloting skills. Accordingly, the motley trio steals a World War II British Avro Lancaster bomber from the Sierra Gordo airport. After a harrowing take-off, Snake-Eyes and his companions reach the Gulf of Mexico.

Worried about ending this little escapade in jail, Dr. Venom secretly radios Cobra with promises to provide the plague toxin catalyst. Unfortunately, a skirmish with sea smugglers forces Dr. Venom to crash-land the stolen bomber onto Miami Beach, where local authorities arrest Dr. Venom, Snake-Eyes and Kwinn for unauthorized air travel and reckless endangerment. Moments later, a Cobra-hired lawyer shows up to secure Dr. Venom's release – allowing the cracked scientist to depart while the police book Snake-Eyes and Kwinn as Class A felons.

MEMORABLE MOMENTS In one of the series' more surreal moments, Dr. Venom's hallucination gas makes Scarlett think that Zap's melting like a candle. Ironically, a similarly zapped Zap believes he's an upended turtle frying in the sun, begging for someone to turn him over.

Doc tries to lift up Snake-Eyes' mask to check for frostbite, but Snake-Eyes discourages the good doctor – with his Uzi – from seeing his facial disfigurement.

Dr. Venom "kindly" offers to hold Kwinn's guns while he shifts a heavy door, but Kwinn deadpans: "It's no bother, Dr. Venom. Really."

Memorable for its sheer preposterousness, Dr. Venom announces that his base is protected by: "Three crack Cobra commandos, a missile firing sea-plane, an armored bunker surrounded by concertina wire… and a pair of vicious Dobermans!"

Racing on foot to Springfield, Destro sees one of his men falling behind and orders: "Shoot him, Scar-Face. Then fall back to the last position and administer the same to any other laggard." Issue #15 peaks when the ever-disloyal Dr. Venom opens the plane's bomb bay doors, causing Kwinn to cling for dear life by his fingertips while Snake-Eyes dangles from the Inuit's leg. The syrupy Dr. Venom advises: "Kick him loose, Kwinn. He will only weigh you down and make you fall!", but Kwinn resolutely crawls back into the plane – despite Dr. Venom braining him with a wrench – and saves both their lives.

Perhaps most memorable of all, the reluctant Baroness calls her ex-lover by his newly adopted name, breathlessly uttering the word "Destro."

LOVE AND WAR The Baroness and Destro obviously shared a failed romance before their reunion as Cobra operatives. Rather than rush back into Destro's arms, the Baroness insists, "Things are different now. It can't be like it was before," but Destro loves the Baroness to the point of saving her – at the cost of letting Cobra Commander live.

Snow Job pranks Rock 'n Roll by arranging a date with Gung Ho's "fashion model" sister, neglecting to mention that she's nine years old.

ASS-WHUPPINGS Snake-Eyes blows away a Cobra pilot at point-blank range (accompanied by "Punch! Punch! Punch!" sound-effects) and later downs a Cobra heavy machine gun team. (The lesson: It's very, very unwise to even think of pissing off Snake-Eyes). Snake-Eyes also kills two Cobra hanggliders with a rocket-propelled grenade (seems like overkill, but whatever works). He also shoots or strangles the Dr. Venom's Dobermans (puppy killer).

In the finest *High Noon* tradition, Wild Bill outdraws three Cobra goons and shoots 'em dead. Destro mercilessly beats Doc's face with his boots. San Francisco gang members randomly beat the tar out of Breaker. The Joes spike a Cobra trooper to death in a pre-set Burmese tiger trap.

Swimming to a riverbank, Stalker finds himself wrestling with a crocodile and buries his knife in the animal's head. Granted, he falls over from the effort and contracts a vicious fever. Buffoonish smugglers insanely fire on Dr. Venom's plane while it leaks fuel all over their boat (#15), sparking an explosion with their guns' muzzle flash.

It just occurred to us, but a great chunk of these issues feature Snake-Eyes, Dr. Venom and Kwinn relentlessly hitting each other (a "Three Stooges" knock-off, perhaps?). Snake-Eyes rifle-butts Dr. Venom in the face (#10), but Dr. Venom later pistol-whips Snake-Eyes and sets him afire in a burning Cobra warehouse (#12), then clubs Kwinn in the head with a wrench (#12). Snake-Eyes in turn stomps Dr. Venom's hide (#12) and throttles him underwater for a bit (#15). When all's said and done, Venom arguably gets the final word by *again* bashing Kwinn with the wrench in #15. (Our final insight: Dr. Venom... in an airplane bomb bay... with the wrench.)

PREPOSTEROUS PHYSICS During a frantic car chase, Scar-Face tears a stationary car in half with his commandeered van – without causing any harm to the other driver. More believably, Scar-Face blows up his van by colliding with the back of a Pinto (ah, remember those halcyon "exploding cars" of yesteryear?).

GOOFS Destro spills the beans about Cobra's Alaskan undertaking (#11) for no readily apparent reason (perhaps overconfidence or simply that he doesn't want Cobra to win?). Billy fools his cell guards into thinking that he's attending a resistance meeting... when he's in the slammer.

Issues #10-#14 are chock full of willful blindness – or errant stupidity, take your pick. Having previously met Kwinn in *G.I. Joe* #2, Scarlett doesn't get suspicious upon seeing a contraband shipment addressed to a "K. Winn." Snake-Eyes fools Dr. Venom not once but *twice* with a death-like coma. Stalker deduces that "Arbco" is an amalgam of "Cobra" – revealing "Arbco" as a Cobra business front – but the Joes entirely forget the discovery in future. Finally, Scar-Face is a blithering idiot for not realizing that Destro magically decides that Cobra Commander is in danger – because Destro put threw the commander into the frying pan in the first place.

Why did the Baroness' missile knock aside the entire Cobra bunker rather than blow it to pebbles? Errant art in issue #12 shows Stalker's leg *inside* the mouth of a crocodile he's wrestling.

Issue #14 ends with Cobra troops binding Snake-Eyes and Dr. Venom, then leading them through the forest, but #15 starts with the captives untied, back where they started and Venom begging for mercy.

NOW YOU KNOW... British Avro Lancaster bombers need all four of their Rolls-Royce Merlin engines revving up to 2500 RPMs before they get an inch off the ground. If the Lancaster's engines stall during take-off, try building up speed with the working engines and injecting extra fuel, essentially push-starting the monster.

COMIC TIE-INS Freelance mercenary Kwinn, here working for Cobra, first appeared in *G.I. Joe* #2. Snake-Eyes and Kwinn free themselves in #17, attaining revenge on Dr. Venom in #19.

The Baroness and Major Bludd later conscript Cobra resistance member Billy to assassinate Cobra Commander (*G.I. Joe* #30). In issue #10, the brainwave scanner provides some images of Snake-Eyes' ninja training and the helicopter accident that disfigured him – events further detailed in #26-#27. Cobra next uses Dr. Venom's brainwave scanner in *G.I. Joe* #38.

In addition to taking nature photos for a hobby (*G.I. Joe* #2), Stalker's extensively studied animal biology (he rattles off a crocodile's attributes in #14). In issues #10 and #12, Snake-Eyes fakes his death using a self-induced coma called "The Way of the Inner Anvil." Cobra ninja Storm Shadow later pulls the same stunt, alternately calling the technique "The Sleeping Phoenix," in *G.I. Joe* #47.

The Baroness suggests that Destro's recently adopted the name "Destro," when future issues (notably #57, #96 and more) better denote "Destro" as a family name.

CHARACTER PROFILE: JOES

• *Airborne:* He's a Native American.

• *Gung Ho:* A Cajun from New Orleans with an out-*rageous* French accent.

• *Snake-Eyes:* Snake-Eyes confuses Dr. Venom's brainwave scanner by concentrating on trivial memories from his youth, such as his teen-aged tenure as a gas station mechanic and his high school prom. Years later, during a military mission in a Middle Eastern desert, a helicopter fuel line exploded and grievously disfigured Snake-Eyes' face (he's now so hideous, Sierra Gordo natives take him for a river demon). Snake-Eyes has traveled to Berlin, Cuba, Cypress, Chile, Laos and Cambodia. In a poignant touch (*a la Miss Saigon*), he was apparently on the last helicopter out of Saigon.

• *Zap:* He's good at rigging mechanical ambushes, such as claymore mines with trip-wires.

CHARACTER PROFILE: COBRA

• *The Baroness:* She possesses expert flying skills, typically serving as Cobra Commander's personal pilot. She deems Snake-Eyes, Kwinn and Dr. Venom the most cunning and dangerous men she's ever met (which is saying a lot, really).

• *Cobra Commander:* His battle helmet and uniform are airtight, recycling his air supply. Unlike the Baroness (and his TV incarnation), Cobra Commander's not a stickler for formality.

• *Destro:* As his Hasbro toy suggests, Destro often fires wrist rockets.

• *The Baroness, Destro and Cobra Commander:* Destro and the Baroness know each others' history. The Baroness insists that she owes Cobra Commander too much to outright betray him, but by the same token, she doesn't blab Destro's plans to kill the Cobra leader.

• *Dr. Venom:* Keeps millions of dollars salted away in Zurich. He's a fully qualified fixed wing pilot with single and multi-engine certifications.

• *Scar-Face:* Not the hacked-up monstrosity you might suspect, with a single scar running down each side of his otherwise-pleasant looking visage. Scar-Face ultimately cedes loyalty to Destro, who knows unsavory details about Scar-Face's past.

CHARACTER PROFILE: OTHER

Kwinn: He's a good enough shot to disarm opponents with well-placed bullets (a remarkable trick, considering Kwinn wields a .30 caliber air-cooled Browning machine gun). Kwinn appeals to Inuit animal spirits such as the otter, the bear and the weasel. He's qualified to pilot single-engine aircraft, making him little more than a glorified instrument reader on more complex vessels.

ORGANIZATIONS *Cobra:* Cobra Commander serves as the Cobra counterpart to the Joes' top-ranking General Flagg. Using the same analogy, Destro's the top Cobra leader on the battlefield – the rough equivalent of Hawk.

PLACES TO GO *Fort Wadsworth:* Has a baseball field (up to bat this week: the Chaplain's Assistants vs. Permanent Latrine Orderlies).

• *Springfield:* A "perfectly boring" American town – concealing the biggest Cobra support network in the continental United States. Years ago, Cobra gained a toehold in Springfield through a household-cleaning pyramid sales scheme that slowly dominated the town and advocated an authoritarian way of life. Today, Springfield's garages house Cobra tanks, a pizza parlor stores poison gas and the town's teenagers serve as junior Cobra officers. Billy's probably accurate about the existence of a resistance movement against Cobra – but we never see its members.

STUFF YOU NEED Dr. Venom's Brainwave Scanner: Works by feeding your brain a series of simple images (an apple, etc.) to gauge your brainwaves' response pattern. Soon after, the brainwave scanner attunes itself to your thoughts and extracts whatever information it pleases.

THE COMMAND DECISION Admittedly a cornerstone of continuity, *G.I. Joe* #10 rather woodenly lays the foundation for Springfield, Billy and Snake-Eyes' past. The action's all too convenient (the sudden tsunami-level thunderstorm that prevents the Joes from backtracking to Springfield, etc.), but you're probably better off reading it as a harbinger of what's to come.

Issue #11's another goof-riddled throwaway story, slathered with Mike Vosburg's increasingly tiresome, silly Golden Age-reminiscent art. But with issues #12-#15, *G.I. Joe* definitely gains momentum – basing storylines on triads of characters (Snake-Eyes, Kwinn and Dr. Venom; plus Cobra Commander, Destro and the Baroness) with continually shifting alliances and motives. You can sense the quality gradually increasing, with the aircraft-based, continually suspenseful issue #15 in particular shining as a hell of a ride.

G.I. Joe #16 to #19

Titles: *"Night Attack!" (#16), "Loose Ends" (#17), "Destro Returns!" (#18), "Joe Triumphs!" (#19)*
Release Dates: *Oct. to Jan. 1984*
Art: *Mike Vosburg*

BATTLE ROSTER *Joes:* Hawk, Scarlett, Snake-Eyes, Doc, Gung Ho, Ace, Stalker, Grand Slam, Rock 'n Roll; *Cobra:* Cobra Commander, Destro, the Baroness, Major Bludd, Dr. Venom, Scar-Face; *Other:* Kwinn.

FIRST APPEARANCES Cover Girl (Wolverine driver, #16), Tripwire (mine detector, #16).

DEATHS *Joes:* General Flagg; *Cobra:* Dr. Venom, Scar-Face; *Other:* Kwinn (all #19).

MISSION BRIEF ***Issue #16:*** Ransacking Cobra's laboratory in Vermont, the Joes find test samples of printer's ink and biological containers. In short order, the Joes conclude that Cobra intends to assault the US Bureau of Printing and Engraving and lace American currency with a plague toxin – thereby disrupting the country as a prelude to an invasion.

Planning to complete the Treasury operation and eliminate Destro in a single blow, Cobra Commander draws the Pentagon's attention by threatening to blow up the U.S. Capitol. With Pentagon officials protecting the wrong target, Dr. Venom, Scar-Face and a small Cobra patrol sneak inside the Treasury. Thankfully, a vanguard of Joes spot the villains and alert Hawk. Amid a massive firefight, Dr. Venom adopts the "every man for himself" policy and leaves Scar-Face behind to die. Overwhelmed by superior Joe firepower, Cobra Commander orders a retreat – fleeing with Destro and Dr. Venom in one HISS tank while Major Bludd and the Baroness ride in another.

As battle rages, Major Bludd rotates his gun turrets – per Cobra Commander's orders – to eliminate Destro at a critical juncture. Realizing Bludd means to kill her ex-lover, the Baroness jackknifes the HISS tank in desperation, throwing off Bludd's aim but crashing the tank into a parked truck and dousing the area with gasoline. Major Bludd stumbles free and runs for cover, ignoring the pinned Baroness' pleas. Seconds later, the gasoline explodes, annihilating the tank.

The Joes rally, but Hawk jumps onboard the remaining HISS tank to duke it out with Destro. To cover up his failed assassination attempt, Cobra Commander shoots Hawk three times. Scarlett and Clutch race to assist their fallen leader, even as the surviving Cobra leaders escape and Scar-Face eludes capture on an outgoing bus.

Issue #17: Scarlett and Clutch find that although Hawk's ballistic nylon vest stopped Cobra Commander's bullets, it failed to soften the projectiles' impact. Consequently, the two fly Hawk out to Bethesda Naval Hospital to stop his internal bleeding. Simultaneously, the Joes recover the severely maimed Baroness from her wrecked HISS tank, transporting her to the naval hospital's burn unit.

Upon returning to Springfield, Cobra Commander lies through his helmeted face to Destro, claiming that Major

Bludd, infatuated with the Baroness, tried to kill Destro in a fit of jealousy. Cobra Commander's falsehoods renew Destro' vigor to hunt down Bludd and kill him.

Major Bludd tries to flee Washington, but Stalker and Grand Slam pursue and pummel the mercenary into submission. Upon learning of this, Destro theorizes that the Joes will imprison Bludd at their headquarters. Hoping to score a Cobra victory and eliminate Bludd in one fell swoop, Destro proposes carrying through with Cobra's initial plan to contaminate Joe Headquarters with a slow-acting plague. Deeming Scar-Face a suitable plague carrier, Destro gains Cobra Commander's permission to ferret out the courier from his hideout on Coney Island.

In Miami, the still-incarcerated Kwinn pulls a hidden saw blade from his boot heel, hacking himself and Snake-Eyes to freedom. After winning a car in a gambling match, Kwinn and Snake-Eyes set off to locate Scar-Face and beat Dr. Venom's location out of him – obsessed with punishing Dr. Venom for his various misdeeds.

Issue #18: Snake-Eyes summons Joe reinforcements to Scar-Face's hideout on Coney Island, but Kwinn grows impatient and breaks through the door. Scar-Face details the extent of his knowledge about Dr. Venom's laboratories and warehouses, thereby gaining Kwinn's gratitude.

Meanwhile, Destro arrives at Coney Island, sparing with the Joes while Kwinn graciously tells Scar-Face to flee. Unfortunately, Destro nabs Scar-Face first and sweet-talks the courier into hijacking an airplane from Kennedy Airport, then traveling to a Cobra safehouse in Libya. Once there, Destro turns Scar-Face over to Dr. Venom, who – as threatened – injects Scar-Face with the plague toxin.

As Destro expected, the Joes track the hijacked airliner and assault the Cobra stronghold. Deciding that Cobra will exterminate him no matter the outcome, the plague-infested Scar-Face gives himself up to the Joes – who victoriously return to the Pit with their prize.

Issue #19: Scar-Face details Cobra Commander's plan to ferret out the Pit's location, providing the Joes with a plague toxin antidote that he stole from Dr. Venom. General Flagg and a recovered Hawk concur that Cobra Commander intended to make the Joes initiate quarantine protocols, thereby giving away the Pit's location as a prelude to a massive Cobra strike.

With this in mind, the Joes deliberately instigate quarantine procedures around the Fort Wadsworth motor pool, enticing Cobra to level a pre-fabricated "Joe fortress" inside the motor pool, thereby concealing the Pit underneath. To enhance the illusion, Hawk authorizes Major Bludd and the still-wounded Baroness to be transported from Washington to Fort Wadsworth.

Simultaneously, Snake-Eyes and Kwinn burst into one of Dr. Venom's warehouses at the Old Brooklyn Navy Yard, preparing to rearrange the good doctor's face. Unfortunately, Cobra troopers subdue the rogues, encasing them in remote-controlled, humanoid SNAKE-brand armor. Cobra Commander and Destro amass their forces – including the SNAKE-encased

MISCELLANEOUS STUFF!

COMIC/TV DIFFERENCES (JOES)

Since the differing worlds of the *G.I. Joe* comics and TV aren't all that easy to reconcile, here's a quick-and-dirty rundown of notable Joe comic characters – and how they differ from their TV incarnations:

• **Snake-Eyes** – Considering Snake-Eyes barely existed at times in the Sunbow cartoon, it's ironic that he serves as the heart and soul of the *G.I. Joe* comics. One supposes TV creators could only accomplish so much with a mute character, leaving Snake-Eyes to play a largely irrelevant role in the TV series (save for a few exceptions: "The M.A.S.S. Device," "Battle for the Train of Gold," etc.). By contrast, the comic book staked out Snake-Eyes' Vietnam service and ninja training as its core, with keynote stories such as *G.I. Joe* #26-#27, #85, #93-#96 and #144 fleshing out everything you could ever possibly need to know about the silent ninja.

• **Scarlett** – On TV, Scarlett admittedly had a stronger TV presence than Snake-Eyes, although Lady Jaye routinely usurped her position as the Joes' most prominent female. Still, Scarlett's comic-spawned romance with Snake-Eyes kept her around even after most of the original Joes retired from active duty, positioning her to take a field command role in the Image series.

• **Duke** – Let's call a spade a spade. On TV, Duke was a bit of a patsy. He certainly wasn't *ineffective*, although like Superman or *Transformers*' Optimus Prime, Duke often seemed too wholesome for his own good. But in the comics, writer Larry Hama re-cast Duke as a bad-ass, endowing the top sergeant with a formidableness and inner steel that made you think he could flatten tanks simply by grimacing at them.

• **Hawk** – Hawk served as the top Joe leader in TV and comics, but he failed to surface in the cartoon until Season 2, leaving Duke as the Joes' default field leader. Other than that, Hawk's TV and comic incarnations are virtually identical.

Snake-Eyes and Kwinn – against the Joes' pre-fabricated fortress, but the Joes heatedly "defend" their base.

Amid a fury of bullets, a Cobra helicopter pilot trooper lands on the Joe-made fortress' roof, lining it with explosives. Upon hearing the helicopter's arrival, Major Bludd breaks free, guns down General Flagg and spirits away the wounded Baroness to hopefully curry favor with Destro – leaving the still-shackled Scar-Face behind. As General Flagg dies from massive blood loss, Major Bludd kills the Cobra pilot, loads the Baroness aboard the helicopter and escapes.

In the heat of battle, Snake-Eyes overrides his SNAKE's motor control and frees Kwinn, allowing the Inuit mercenary to grab Dr. Venom and wave a de-pinned grenade in his face. But perceiving that Dr. Venom harbors a despicable Inuit weasel spirit, Kwinn opts not to sully his own honor with Venom's blood, instead letting the weaselly doctor "to go squander his miserable life." Outraged at the moral slight, Dr. Venom pulls his pistol and shoots Kwinn in the back. Dying, Kwinn makes peace with his maker and pitches forward – causing the grenade to roll out of his lifeless fingers. The grenade explodes, obliterating Dr. Venom and Snake-Eyes to bemoan the loss of Kwinn.

Seconds later, the Cobra-planted charges detonate, leveling the fabricated Joe Headquarters and slaughtering Scar-Face. Hawk celebrates the completion of a "successful" operation, only to learn about General Flagg and Kwinn's deaths.

MEMORABLE MOMENTS The pinned Baroness implores Major Bludd to help her get loose before her HISS tank explodes, but Bludd vanishes like a frightened goose. Seconds later, the Baroness' tank goes up – forcing the reader to wonder if any Joe/Cobra character is safe from harm.

Scarlett notes that a dead skunk has more charm than Clutch. An injured Hawk makes Bethesda doctors nervous when he refuses to surrender his shoulder holster and .45 sidearm. Snake-Eyes ridiculously struts about in his full-body black commando gear and a cowboy hat, having won it in a Miami card game. Just as bizarrely, Destro makes his escape from Coney Island by hijacking an ice cream truck.

Kwinn's idea of simultaneously playing good cop and bad cop to Scar-Face entails mentioning, "Nice day, isn't it?", then threatening to tear the Cobra agent apart. Most gut-wrenching of all, the mute Snake-Eyes writhes in silent anger and grief when Dr. Venom shoots Kwinn in the back.

LOVE AND WAR Destro goes near-catatonic when the Baroness "dies." (An unsympathetic Dr. Venom comments: "Doesn't [Destro] realize that love is simply overestimating the difference between any one given woman and another?")

Snake-Eyes alerts the Joes to his location with a postcard containing a note for Scarlett's eyes only. (We're unclear on the details, but Scarlett sheds a tear.)

Torpedo and Rock 'n Roll land their MANTA water glider on the beach, drawing some attention from bikini-clad women. When Torpedo returns for the MANTA, Rock 'n Roll speculates that Torpedo's "... probably getting down to some heavy maneuvers in the sand right now!"

ASS-WHUPPINGS An exploding HISS tank severely maims the Baroness, but she somehow lives with third-degree burns covering 80 percent of her body. Fearing betrayal on Cobra Commander's part, Dr. Venom kills his own Cobra troopers in the U.S. Treasury building. Cobra Commander pumps three bullets into Hawk's back, but he survives (ah, the miracle of Kevlar).

In a gymnastic move worthy of Mary Lou Retton, Grand Slam dives through a bus window and nails Major Bludd with his feet. (A doctor later looks at Bludd and comments: "What happened to this man? Looks like somebody used his face for a trampoline!") Rock 'n Roll's machine gun takes out Scar-Face's escape vehicle – a perfectly serviceable pink Cadillac.

PREPOSTEROUS PHYSICS Irked when a snob in a (regrettably named) Shelby GT Cobra car blocks traffic, Gung Ho rips off a car door and smashes the vehicle to pieces.

GOOFS Hawk's fists somehow clean Cobra Commander's clock – through his protective helmet. Having only met Scar-Face briefly in Sierra Gordo, Kwinn somehow knows the location of his private hideout. Mind, Dr. Venom illogically knows that Cobra Commander ordered Destro killed (but keeps the knowledge to himself).

Why does Cobra insist on infecting Scar-Face (and not just any Cobra goon) with the toxin? For that matter, why did Scar-Face accurately forecast that Cobra would jab him full of plague?

Destro orders his RATTLER pilot to discretely land near Coney Island so Scar-Face can't hear the jet's arrival – so of course, the pilot drops Destro atop the nearest roller coaster (which might not be that out of place – after all, it is New York).

Badly rendered art makes Destro's leg seem as large as an entire fence (issue #18). Speaking of scale, Cobra's fooled into thinking the entirety of Joe Headquarters isn't any larger than the Fort Wadsworth motor pool (perhaps the Joes employ a lot of midgets).

The Joes tie up Major Bludd and Scar-Face in the false Joe fortress but sloppily leave an arm free on each of them – allowing Major Bludd to kill General Flagg and escape during the battle. Hawk thinks the hulking SNAKE armor covering Snake-Eyes has a "familiar walk." (How can Hawk pick out Snake-Eyes' walk when he's controlled by Dr. Venom and encased in armor like the Pillsbury dough boy? And err... why has Hawk studied Snake-Eyes' walk in such detail?)

Most agonizing of all, how the bloody hell does Cobra fake out the Joes in issue #16 by "assaulting" the US Capitol with radio-controlled toy-sized airplanes? (God save us, even the most moronic of the Joes can't be *that* blind or stupid.)

COMIC TIE-INS Although the Pit wasn't destroyed as such in *G.I. Joe* #19, Hawk here diverts massive manpower to rebuilding the Fort Wadsworth motor pool and augmenting the Pit. As such, the Pit virtually becomes a newly created structure, so we'll call it the Pit II from here out.

After fleeing Fort Wadsworth, Major Bludd briefly hides out in Montreal, then takes the bandaged Baroness to Switzerland for reconstructive surgery (*G.I. Joe* #22-#23). The Baroness informs Destro of Cobra Commander's attempt on his life in #24. The Joes properly lay General Flagg and Kwinn to rest, but toss Dr. Venom's body into a pauper's grave in *G.I. Joe* #22.

A helmeted Cobra Commander somehow drinks a goblet of wine, although issue #24 suggests the commander sucks liquid, using a straw, through a small slit in his helmet. Also, a helmeted woman on #19's cover is a rendering of *G.I. Joe* Assistant Editor Linda Grant (a marketing gimmick that was part of Marvel's "Assistant Editor's Month" promotion back in 1984).

CHARACTER PROFILE: JOES

• *Cover Girl:* One of the best-looking (and for that matter, one of the only) Joe females – and she knows it. There's little love lost between Scarlett and the extremely vain Cover Girl, who verbally spar like wildcats.

• *Gung Ho:* Turns his thick Cajun accent on and off when he feels like it.

• *Hawk:* Sometimes wears ballistic layered SWAT vests, strong enough to stop a 9mm hardball round.

• *Snake-Eyes:* Keeps a collection of spike-knuckled trench knives.

• *Trip-Wire:* Joe explosive ordnance expert, specializing in de-fusings, excavations, pyrotechnics and light removals. Tripwire's extremely clumsy, falling on his face an average of once per issue, and carries O-shaped explosive mines.

• *Torpedo:* Hasn't met Snake-Eyes before.

CHARACTER PROFILE: COBRA

• *Destro:* His face plate's made from polished beryllium steel.

• *Destro, Cobra Commander and the Baroness:* Destro's trying to keep his former relationship with the Baroness secret, but Cobra Commander clearly suspects something is up between them.

• *Major Bludd:* A despicable bootlicker, albeit a master tactician. He writes poetry so painful, it'll strip the flesh from your bones.

STUFF YOU NEED Cobra SNAKE armor: Humanoid armor that's too heavy to move without assistance from its internal systems. As a safety precaution, the pre-programmed SNAKES won't fire on anything wearing Cobra blue.

HOT WHEELS Cobra HISS Tanks: Resist firepower from Joe VAMP jeeps.

• *G.I. Joe PAC/RATS:* Automated weapons droids that fire either missiles, machine guns or flame-throwers.

• *Joe Wolverine:* Armed with Stinger missiles.

THE COMMAND DECISION Issue #16's largely enthralling as the series' first use of vicious, down-and-dirty combat between the Joes and Cobra. In particular, the Baroness' method of saving Destro – jackknifing her own HISS tank – is nicely inspired, and her sudden "demise," even today, makes one's eyes bulge in surprise.

The so-so #17 and #18 merely form the bits that fall in-between the major firefights, burdened with sloppy motives and more of Vosburg's uninspiring art. More laudably, issue #19 ("Joe Triumphs!") memorably offs several cast members, establishing how the comic series, to its credit, realistically portrays the consequences of war. The final effect needs some polish, making you wince and cry out "Oof!" in several places, but the overall story progression – and especially the ongoing feud between Snake-Eyes, Kwinn and Dr. Venom – lets one walk away satisfied.

G.I. Joe #20

Title: *"Home is Where the War Is ..."*
Release Date: *Feb. 1984*
Writer: *Steven Grant*
Art: *Geof Isherwood*

BATTLE ROSTER *Joes:* Clutch, Scarlett, Flash, Gung Ho, Breaker.

MISSION BRIEF Granted leave, a gleeful Clutch returns to his hometown in New Jersey and bumps into his childhood friend Billy Kline. Employed by Watash Automotive to build experimental engines for the federal government, Kline feels out Clutch's interest in test-driving prototype cars. Clutch finds himself interested enough to learn more, but a quick investigation of the Watash plant uncovers a covert Cobra operation to build compact, waist-worn jetpacks. Clutch helps rescue Kline's family – held hostage to guarantee Kline's cooperation with the Cobra undertaking – then radios the other Joes to bust up the Cobra lab. After capturing or eliminating the Cobra engineers, the Joes find Clutch eager to end his "relaxing" vacation and return to duty.

ASS-WHUPPINGS Clutch clobbers one Cobra goon with a wrench, then drops huge steel beams on three more. Another Cobra trooper outrageously bites it by falling into an exploding gas tank.

PREPOSTEROUS PHYSICS Gung Ho takes a hint from the cartoon series, shooting down a plane with his odd-looking machine gun. Clutch nebulously comments that Kline used "unstable fuel" when crafting his flying belts, but we've no idea what that means (save that the belts instantly explode upon impact with large gas tankers).

GOOFS During a training simulation, a cardboard cutout of Hawk fools Clutch. Despite the need for subterfuge, Cobra workers strut about in a Watash "top security" area wearing Cobra garb.

COMIC TIE-INS Clutch's hometown goes unnamed, but issue #23 pegs it as Asbury Park.

CHARACTER PROFILE: JOES

Clutch: Hasn't had a vacation in six months. His high school classmates branded him with the "Clutch" nickname, probably due to his skills as a mechanic. Mr. Vilsky taught him in shop class. A youthful Clutch once had an accident with a speeding car, knocking a house off its foundation.

THE COMMAND DECISION Unbearably pointless, obviously crafted as a low-expectation fill-in issue, and further proof that non-military men should think – really think – about what they're doing before scripting war stories.

G.I. Joe #21

Title: *"Silent Interlude"*
Release Date: *Mar. 1984*
Art: *Larry Hama*

BATTLE ROSTER *Joes:* Snake-Eyes, Scarlett; *Cobra:* Cobra Commander, Destro.

FIRST APPEARANCES *Cobra:* Storm Shadow (ninja); *Other:* the red ninjas.

NOTE We probably don't have to tell most of you that #21's known for its lack of word balloons, relying solely on art to convey its story.

MISSION BRIEF At a remote Cobra castle, a Cobra-employed ninja named Storm Shadow arrives with Scarlett as his captive. Storm Shadow locks Scarlett up in the castle's dungeons, but Snake-Eyes, embarking on a one-man mission to rescue his teammate, secretly parachutes into the castle's compound.

Snake-Eyes efficiently kills a heap of Cobra soldiers and subordinate ninjas, finally coming face-to-face with Storm Shadow. Luckily, Scarlett frees herself, stealing a Cobra rocket glider just as Snake-Eyes races onto the castle's upper level. Simultaneously, Storm Shadow rears back to fling his sword at the Joe commando.

With an instant to spare, Scarlett lands her glider between the two foes, intending to intercept Storm Shadow's sword with her own body. Luckily, Snake-Eyes reaches over Scarlett, catches the blade between his palms and flings it away. Scarlett rockets herself and Snake-Eyes to freedom, unaware that Snake-Eyes and Storm Shadow mysteriously bear identical wrist tattoos.

MEMORABLE MOMENTS Destro ponders a chess board with various Joe and Cobra members rendered as the pieces – taking a moment of silence for the "captured" (i.e. "deceased") royalty such as the Baroness. Destro first senses his castle's been invaded when a Cobra trooper – tossed over the side by Snake-Eyes – plummets past Destro's office window.

Confronted by a sai-wielding ninja, Snake-Eyes makes like Indiana Jones and eliminates his fast-moving foe with a casually tossed grenade.

At story's end, Scarlett's move to sacrifice her life for Snake-Eyes landmarks itself as one of the most dramatic moments in Joe history. Mind, it's trumped a few seconds later by the disclosure that Snake-Eyes and Storm Shadow bear similar tattoos – an announcement, so far as Joe fans are concerned, on par with the revelation that Darth Vader is Luke's father.

ASS-WHUPPINGS Storm Shadow roughs up Scarlett in the course of her capture, but Scarlett at least bites Storm Shadow's thumb. Scarlett chain-chokes two Cobra goons in making her escape. Snake-Eyes knifes two Cobra troopers and viciously tosses another over a castle wall. He also thumps a ninja with a manhole cover, obliterates a sai-wielding ninja with a grenade and tricks Storm Shadow into slicing a ninja comrade in half.

COMIC TIE-INS *G.I. Joe* #26-#27 explains why Snake-Eyes and Storm Shadow possess similar tattoos, detailing their long-running friendship (and current feud).

Issue #22 explains how Storm Shadow nabbed Scarlett in the first place. *G.I. Joe Yearbook* #3 and *G.I. Joe* #85 take after "Silent Interlude" by crafting themselves as wordless stories.

THE COMMAND DECISION The visceral story that single-handedly put *G.I. Joe* on the map, "Silent

Interlude" reboots the entire series' tenor and (for once) deserves every drop of hype. It's almost regrettable that its "silent" nature has spawned some second-rate copycats over the years (#85, Marvel's "Nuff Said crossover in 2001), but that doesn't stop this tale – deftly rendered by Hama's cut-throat pencils – from reading every bit as strong 18 years after the fact.

MISCELLANEOUS STUFF!

THE SILENT CASTLE

Given the sprawl of *G.I. Joe*'s whopping 12-year run, the comic creators deserve kudos for avoiding an obscene amount of continuity errors. However complex his time-lines could get at times, writer Larry Hama thankfully refrained from generating blatant continuity *conflicts*.

That said, one of the more prominent oddities occurs in regards to the infamous castle setting of "Silent Interlude" (#21). Destro's major role in the story leads us to think it's his abode (not to mention the fact that in *G.I. Joe #31,* Destro himself berates Snake-Eyes for humiliating him while Cobra Commander was "a guest" in "his castle"). It's therefore easy to see how some readers confused said castle with Castle Destro, first seen in issue #57.

But in a dazzling display of retcon, *G.I. Joe* #121 comes along and makes the castle from #21 into a separate edifice named "the Silent Castle." Indeed, Cobra Commander – who let the place fall into disuse after Snake-Eyes' humiliating rescue of Scarlett – signs the property *over* to Destro as repayment for having turned Castle Destro to pebbles in *G.I. Joe* #116. From that point, the Silent Castle – graced with an amusing/baffling ability to transform itself into a *replica* of the flattened Castle Destro – serves as Destro's base of operations, with Cobra forces showing up about every five minutes to wrest control of the joint. As such, it's a hotbed of treachery, and ninja action (but then, that should surprise nobody).

G.I. Joe #22 to #24

Titles: *"Like Chimney Sweepers Come to Dust..." (#22), "Cobra Commander Captured at Last!" (#23), "The Commander Escapes!" (#24)*
Release Dates: *Apr. to June 1984*
Art: *Mike Vosburg (#22-#23), Russ Heath (#24)*

BATTLE ROSTER *Joes:* Snow Job, Gung Ho, Cover Girl, Clutch, Rock 'n Roll, Grunt; *Cobra:* Cobra Commander, Destro, the Baroness, Major Bludd, Storm Shadow.

FIRST APPEARANCES *Joes:* Duke (first sergeant, #22), Roadblock (heavy machine gunner, #22); *Cobra:* Firefly (saboteur, #24), Wild Weasel (RATTLER pilot, #24), Zartan (cameo, #24).

MISSION BRIEF ***Issue #22:*** Having preserved the Pit's secret location, Hawk rallies his Joes to repair the battle damage to the Joe headquarters and augment it into an impregnable, six-story complex built entirely beneath Fort Wadsworth.

In a private ceremony, Snake-Eyes sets Kwinn's body adrift, per Inuit tradition, in a raft near Montauk Point, watching the waters carry his friend's remains toward the Arctic. Meanwhile, the military dress-clad Joes gather to bury General Flagg in Arlington National Cemetery.

Without a shred of decency, Cobra Commander authorizes a prototype Cobra RATTLER jet to level the funeral service. The unarmed Joes gape in horror as the RATTLER dives straight at them, but suddenly, a pair of hitherto-unseen Joes appear on a nearby hill and dice the RATTLER with machine gun fire, crashing it nearby.

The Joes turn and greet their saviors, a heavy machine gunner named Roadblock and first sergeant Duke – both of them newly assigned to the Joe team. While Hawk assumes General Flagg's position as the Joe/Pentagon liaison, Duke takes charge as the Joes' top field commander – promising to apply a hard-boiled leadership style in the fight against Cobra.

Issue #23: Having narrowly rescued the maimed Baroness from the battle at Fort Wadsworth (#19), Major Bludd takes his charge to Bern, Switzerland for reconstructive surgery. But using a tracer device planted in the Baroness' ear during her hospital stay, Duke, Roadblock and a covert Joe team track the villainess, hoping she'll lead them to high-ranking Cobra officials.

Surgeons restore the Baroness' face to normal, allowing Major Bludd to contact Cobra Commander and demand a $2 million payoff in exchange for the Baroness keeping quiet about the commander's attempt on Destro's life (#16). Fearing Destro's wrath, an annoyed Cobra Commander agrees and schedules a rendezvous with the renegades in Lucca, Italy.

Duke's team follows the villains to Lucca, but a stalemate quickly erupts when Cobra ninja Storm Shadow captures Major Bludd while the Baroness similarly apprehends Cobra Commander. Disgusted with everyone present, the Baroness deserts Bludd and spirits away the Commander – and the $2 million in his Gucci briefcase – at gunpoint. Storm Shadow and

Major Bludd put aside their differences to pursue, but the Joe surveillance team springs into action, sparking a frantic and peril-filled chase at the Italian-Swiss border. Ultimately, the Baroness escapes with Bludd – begging him to save her one last time – but the Joes take Cobra Commander into custody.

Issue #24: Storm Shadow immediately departs to rescue Cobra Commander from the Joes, but Major Bludd, hoping to keep tabs on the commander, slips a tracking device into Storm Shadow's sword handle.

Soon after, Major Bludd and the Baroness return to Cobra Headquarters, informing Destro that Cobra Commander authorized the hit on his life – thereby quelling Destro's impulse to plug Bludd between the eyes. Destro agrees to jointly seize control of Cobra with the Baroness and Major Bludd, further conceding that, even imprisoned, Cobra Commander remains a liability and must be rubbed out. Accordingly, the usurpers conscript Cobra's best pilot, named Wild Weasel, and an internationally-renowned saboteur named Firefly to follow Major Bludd's tracer and locate Storm Shadow – hopefully finding and butchering Cobra Commander as a result.

Storm Shadow finds Major Bludd's homing device and mails it to an unknown location near Chokoloskee, FL, then continues tracking the captive Cobra Commander to a makeshift Joe base in the Rockies. The ninja approaches the Joes' position with a low-flying Cobra rocket glider (CLAW), grabbing Cobra Commander and making a fast getaway. However, Roadblock's bullets damage one of the CLAW's rockets, leaving the glider unable to carry two people. Cobra Commander uses the CLAW's remaining fuel to reach a pick-up plane and escape, but Roadblock beats Storm Shadow to a bloody pulp and discovers his shipping receipt for the tracer device.

Meanwhile, Wild Weasel and Firefly follow the tracer to a deserted shack in the Florida Everglades. The two Cobra agents contact Destro and his fellow conspirators for further instructions, but seconds later, a cowled figure named Zartan leaps from the shadows, taking them prisoner.

MEMORABLE MOMENTS Unable to find a hammer before a wooden strut collapses and flattens several Joes, Gung Ho pounds the support back into place – with his fists. Spotting the incoming RATTLER during General Flagg's funeral, Stalker grabs the American flag from the coffin and resolutely announces, "He's not shooting holes in my flag." Dining in a Lucca restaurant, Duke and Roadblock flip when Cobra Commander seemingly strolls in through the door – only to discover that Lucca's hosting an annual International Fantasy Convention.

LOVE AND WAR Snow Job foolishly tries to ingratiate himself to Cover Girl by praising "women's liberation" – because it means guys no longer have to pay for everything (she's not impressed). Clutch suggests that he and Cover Girl pretend to be make out as a cover identity, compelling Cover Girl to counter-suggest, "Let's take our chances in the open."

ASS-WHUPPINGS Clutch and Cover Girl crash while trailing Major Bludd, but the Lucca fantasy convention-goers think it's a well-staged stunt. Years before Speed, Duke does a 180 in his Sky Hawk and missiles two Cobra FANG helicopters.

Storm Shadow slices up some Italian Mafia goons like a beef brisket, then cuts a chandelier's supports, dropping it onto Roadblock. Later, Storm Shadow sword-splits Gung Ho's back open, but the Bayou-born marine shrugs it off, insisting he's had worse from bowie-knife wielding Creoles. Even so, an *extremely pissed* Roadblock body-tackles Storm Shadow and whales on him, causing Rock 'n Roll to later ask, "What happened to [Storm Shadow]? Looks like somebody *la machined* his face!" (Roadblock's comment: "I dunno. Dude kept fallin' down. Wasn't my fault.")

GOOFS Snow Job sports white-colored hair and beard (#22) rather than his customary red. Roadblock nails a low-flying RATTLER with his heavy machine gun (reasonable), but Duke also hits it with his sidearm (which seems a lot like tossing spitballs). Roadblock struts about a frigid Rockies peak wearing a loose-fitting camouflage shirt; mind, Gung Ho only dons a marine vest. (Can't the army even afford T-shirts?)

NOW YOU KNOW... "Nap-of-the-Earth" flying, i.e. hugging the Earth in a low-level aircraft, helps you sneak under radar.

COMIC TIE-INS Hawk now fills General Flagg's position as the Joes' Pentagon liaison, answering to Major General Austin (*G.I. Joe* #1).

The Joes disseminate multiple cover stories to explain the destruction of the Fort Wadsworth motor pool (*G.I. Joe* #19). Indeed, Clutch tells the Fort Wadsworth chaplains' assistants, "A boiler exploded," prompting Breaker to add, "All the boilers exploded. All the propane tanks too. In fact, everything in the motor pool that could possibly explode, exploded!"

Major Bludd rescued the Baroness in #19, failing to realize that the Joes previously (#17) planted a tracking device behind her ear. The Joes honorably lay General Flagg and Kwinn (killed in #19) to rest, but Dr. Venom's corpse (ditto) gets unceremonially dumped in Potter's Field, City Island, New York – a designated burial spot for paupers, winos and other "John Does."

Cobra captured Scarlett (*G.I. Joe* #21) while she was getting her parachute certification (she passed through a cloudbank but never came out). Snake-Eyes' highly unauthorized mission to get her back goes unpunished.

Sierra Gordo resumed a full-fledged civil war after the Joes left (#15). Cobra Commander's still using cardboard cutouts of various Joe members (particularly Cover Girl) for target practice (*G.I. Joe* #5, #14, etc.).

Storm Shadow holds unquestionable loyalty to Cobra Commander for reasons revealed in *G.I. Joe* #32. The ninja here demonstrates his ability to mysteriously escape from in-flight aircraft, a trick the Soft Master duplicates in #35.

Schematics for the Pit II in issue #22 make note of an escape route through a false water tower (used by Hawk in *G.I. Joe* #53) and a 12-foot diameter tunnel-boring machine (#55).

Major Bludd suggests the Baroness uses "Baroness DeCobray" as a cover identity, although *G.I. Joe* #94 pegs her real name as "Anastasia DeCobray." Storm Shadow's shipping receipt prompts the Joes to converge on Zartan's Everglades shack in issue #25.

CHARACTER PROFILE: JOES

• *Clutch:* Joe VAMP driver who scoffs at driving a Porsche, preferring a '57 Chevy or classic Detroit Iron.

• *Duke:* A bundle of concentrated meanness, Duke's tough as titanium and carries a 1911 sidearm.

• *Gung Ho:* Unlike Roadblock, Gung Ho's an eating machine, guzzling mess-hall fruit punch and atrociously bland C-ration ham and limas.

• *Roadblock:* One of the most formidable Joes in terms of raw strength and firepower, although he'd much rather be cooking. Roadblock's extremely cultured palate distinguishes between fresh and tinned raspberries. He finds Bern's cuisine appalling ("Waiter, this *pâte de maison* is a disgrace to the cheese it shares board with. If you throw it far enough North, they'll call it liverwurst."), but loves Lucca's fare. He's normally armed with a .50 caliber Browning machine gun.

• *Rock 'n Roll:* He's in awe of fellow machine gunner Roadblock's heft and firepower.

• *Snake-Eyes and Kwinn:* Per tradition, Snake-Eyes included Kwinn's machine gun and Dr. Venom's pistol in Kwinn's burial raft – so that Venom's spirit will serve Kwinn in the next world.

CHARACTER PROFILE: COBRA

• *Cobra Commander:* Cobra Commander keeps offices below Springfield but can walk about the town freely with the populace saluting him.

• *Cobra Commander and Major Bludd:* Cobra Commander can't stand Major Bludd's poetry, deeming the major mad.

• *Destro, the Baroness and Major Bludd:* Destro and the Baroness uneasily allow Major Bludd to participate in their plot to overthrow Cobra Commander, likely planning to bump Bludd off later.

MISCELLANEOUS STUFF!

COMIC/TV DIFFERENCES (COBRAS)

Just to play fair, here's a summary of how the comic-based Cobra brass differs from their TV counterparts:

• **Cobra Commander** – The TV show took great pains to neuter Cobra Commander, characterizing him as a lunatic oddball with all the subtlety of the Joker or the Penguin from the Adam West *Batman* series. But mercifully for us all, comic writer Larry Hama used Cobra Commander for a more intellectual effect. To that end, the comic Cobra Commander leans more towards corrupting the American way of life from within. Only when Billy's revealed as Cobra Commander's son in *G.I. Joe* #33 does the commander suddenly gain humanity and a genuineness that his TV counterpart never possessed. Indeed, just before his "death" (#61), Cobra Commander tries to surrender a lifetime of power purely for Billy's sake, but renegades within Cobra shoot him instead. It's a pity, too, because once the commander "returns," he's far more prototypical and far less interesting.

• **Destro/The Baroness** – The comic-based Destro and Baroness achieve an iron-clad relationship that their romantically challenged TV versions never attain. Especially after *G.I. Joe* #76, they prove inseparable, double-teaming their adversaries with a frightening efficiency.

• **Storm Shadow** – The TV Storm Shadow merely howled a lot and kicked things, but the comics actually give Storm Shadow depth and personality (far too much to explain here, although *G.I. Joe* #26-#27, #38, #45-#50 are a good place to start).

• **Serpentor** – Egads. Serpentor. Supposedly spawned from the DNA of "military geniuses," the TV Serpentor comes off as savvy as a tree stump. But despite admitting to a great loathing for Serpentor, comics writer Larry Hama put him to far better use. While certainly not the most popular character, the comic Serpentor gives everyone a run for their money – only perishing due to a well-timed arrow on Zartan's part.

• **Zartan and Firefly** – Although largely similar to their TV versions, the comic Zartan and Firefly play respective roles in the death of the Hard Master (*G.I. Joe* #26). As a result, Zartan routinely employs ninja-like skills, while Firefly ultimately leads an entire ninja cell to ruin.

• *Wild Weasel:* Cobra's best pilot, even more skilled than the Baroness.

PLACES TO GO *G.I. Joe Makeshift Rockies Base:* Holding pen for Cobra Commander, armed with a radar-guided 30 mm Gatling gun to knock down troop-carrying aircraft and a .50 caliber to deploy tracers and burn holes through enemy parachutes (Duke notes: "It plays havoc with the morale").

• *The Pit II:* Hawk's envisioning the new Pit as a six-story office building equivalent, entirely constructed underground. He's hoping to build the new structure in six months, tapping manpower from the remainder of General Flagg's Pentagon staff. Issue #22 contains blueprints for the Pit II, noting its reinforced, nuclear-blast-proof buffer concrete, ICBM missile silo and nuclear electric generator *(see Comic Tie-Ins)*.

STUFF YOU NEED *Cobra Commander's Helmet:* Plastic explosives line Cobra Commander's helmet, ready to detonate without the proper code sequence. (Duke tells the captive Cobra Commander, "When the time comes, we'll just pull your face out without opening the helmet. I suspect it'll hurt some.") The helmet also contains a short-range radio receiver and has a slit that lets Cobra Commander drink through a straw.

THE COMMAND DECISION What deceptively starts out as a simple farewell to fond friends (General Flagg and Kwinn) emerges as *G.I. Joe*'s first sustained burst of solid storytelling, pushing the comic series' envelope beyond the kid-prone TV series and exploring such mature issues as mourning and loss (a three-page depiction of General Flagg's funeral procession, etc.). There's a notable shift in tone – much for the better – whetting the appetite for a superb run of stories.

Markedly contrasting the solemn #22, issue #23 instigates an utterly insane, glorious romp through the Swiss Alps – complete with Storm Shadow and Major Bludd commandeering a dragon float – that gets your juices flowing. Climaxing the previous two issues, issue #24 dazzled us with a heated mountain battle – this time wonderfully displayed by Russ Heath's fluid pencils – that's superior to a number of today's comics.

G.I. Joe #25 to #27

Titles: *"Zartan!" (#25), "Snake-Eyes: The Origin" (#26-#27)*
Release Dates: *July to Sept. 1984*
Art: *Frank Springer (#25, #27), Larry Hama (#26)*

BATTLE ROSTER *Joes:* Snake-Eyes, Scarlett, Hawk, Stalker, Roadblock, Tripwire, Torpedo; *Cobra:* Storm Shadow, Destro, the Baroness, Cobra Commander, Firefly, Wild Weasel.

FIRST APPEARANCES *Joes:* Mutt (dog handler, #25), Junkyard (dog, #25), Cutter (hovercraft pilot, #25), Deep Six (SHARC driver, #25), G.I. Jane (freighter, #25); *Cobra:* Zartan (master of disguise, #25), Buzzer, Ripper and Torch (Dreadnoks, #25); *Other:* The Soft Master, the Hard Master (ninja senseis, #26).

DEATHS *Other:* Snake-Eyes' family, the Hard Master (both in flashback, #26).

MISSION BRIEF ***Issue #25:*** The Joes imprison Storm Shadow on Alcatraz Island in San Francisco Bay, but against all odds, the sneaky Storm Shadow vanishes from his cell – and the island – without a trace.

Meanwhile, Cobra Commander triumphantly returns to Springfield and tosses the backstabbing Major Bludd into a dungeon cell for betraying him in Switzerland (#23), deeming the Baroness too charming to warrant the same treatment. Destro and the Baroness accompany Cobra Commander to pick up Firefly and Wild Weasel in Chokoloskee, FL., running into a disguise expert named Zartan – an old associate of Cobra Commander – and his punkish trio of Dreadnoks.

The Joes track down the location specified on Storm Shadow's mailing receipt (#24), converging on Zartan's Everglades shack. Torpedo, Tripwire and a Joe dog handler named Mutt (plus his dog Junkyard) move closer to reconnoiter the area. But unexpectedly, Junkyard runs off and starts panting on Zartan's doorstep. Raising his eyebrow to find a "stray" loose in the swamp, Zartan unholsters his pistol to "mercy-kill" the beast.

Issue #26-#27: Destro halts Zartan from offing Junkyard, curious about the dog's presence and his strange fixation with a nearby group of Cypress groves. Destro takes Zartan, the Baroness and Cobra Commander to sweep the area for Joes, but the crafty Junkyard maneuvers the villains into a quicksand pit. Enraged at being outmaneuvered by a dog, Destro fires off a wrist rocket and downs a nearby tree, enabling the Cobra foursome to climb to safety. Destro's group briefly trades bullets with Torpedo, Mutt and Tripwire, but the Joes return to the *G.I. Jane* freighter.

Back at the Pit II, Hawk, Scarlett and Stalker decide it behooves them to learn the connection between Snake-Eyes and Storm Shadow, comparing notes about Snake-Eye's service in Vietnam with Stalker, the death of Snake-Eyes' family and his horrific disfigurement in a helicopter accident *(see Sidebar)*.

Simultaneously, Snake-Eyes arrives in Spanish Harlem to visit his former ninja master, a kindly old man called the Soft Master. The two of them reflect on Snake-Eyes' training at the Soft Master's complex in Japan, a period spent with the Soft

Snake-Eyes: Unmasked!

UNPACKING SNAKE-EYES' ORIGIN

Nobody saw it coming at the time, but it's astounding, with hindsight, how much Snake-Eyes' origin story solidified a fan base for Snakes and Storm Shadow, rocketing them over time to become the most iconic Joe characters.

Indeed, by sketching out Snake-Eyes and Storm Shadow's ill-fated brotherhood and mutual sense of loss in *G.I. Joe* #26-#27, comic writer Larry Hama turbocharged the entire *G.I. Joe* property, and to large degree supplied timber for the modern-day *G.I. Joe* renaissance. Unfortunately, Hama couldn't resist the urge to revisit the successful tale time after time, retconning Snake-Eyes' origin – and not in an exceptionally satisfying way – to include Cobra Commander, Zartan (both #84), the Baroness (#93-#96) and Firefly (#126) – bastardizing continuity that was far better left alone. None of that detracts from the impact of Snake-Eyes' original origin tale – but it cumulatively makes things a hell of a lot more complicated.

Rather than drive everyone nuts by piece-mealing out Snake-Eyes' history, the following section sketches out the entirety of Snake-Eyes' past – including his relationships with Storm Shadow, Scarlett, Cobra Commander, etc. – in one go. It effectively spills the collective guts of the *G.I. Joe* series, but trust us: You're better off, as with a shot of whisky, downing it all at once.

SNAKE-EYES: THE VIETNAM YEARS

During the Vietnam era, Snake-Eyes served on a long-range recon patrol with Stalker, Ramon Escobedo, Dick Saperstein, Wade Collins and a Japanese-American named Thomas Arashikage (who later became Storm Shadow). Snake-Eyes formed a bond with Tommy, making Stalker feel a bit excluded, and learned a great deal about Tommy's "family business" (obviously the Japanese Mafia, a.k.a. the Yakuza) (*G.I. Joe* #26). The tour of duty included a stop in Taiwan, where a shoot-out with VeitCong soldiers regrettably killed the Baroness' philanthropist brother Eugen (*G.I. Joe* #94).

On a particularly fateful day, Snake-Eyes' cell tangled with a group of North Vietnamese troopers – a battle that killed Ramon and Dick and left Wade heavily wounded (*G.I. Joe* #42). Mistakenly believing Wade dead, Stalker, Snake-Eyes and Tommy retreated and radioed for a helicopter evacuation, but Vietnamese tracer bullets felled Snake-Eyes at the designated landing zone. Stalker ordered Tommy to leave Snake-Eyes behind, but Tommy waded through enemy firepower and miraculously saved his friend, pausing long enough to retrieve Snake-Eyes' prized picture of his twin sister (*G.I. Joe* #26).

Left for dead, Wade spent two years recovering in a Vietnamese prison, finally returning home to an America seemingly filled with bile for the Vietnam vets. Finding a new purpose with Cobra, Wade rose through the ranks and underwent plastic surgery to alter his facial features (*G.I. Joe* #43), emerging as one of several identical-looking Crimson Guardsmen code-named "Fred Smith" (first seen in *G.I. Joe* #29).

Meanwhile, the man who would become Cobra Commander grew to idolize his older brother Dan, who extended his Vietnam tour of duty to keep his brother out of the war. (*Author's Note:* A Department of Defense rule prohibits two members of the same family from serving simultaneously in a war zone, probably to avoid a familial massacre *a la* the ill-fated Sullivans, five brothers who died aboard the U.S.S. *Juneau* during World War II.) Dan returned home but increasingly became a daredevil, hot-rodding his way through traffic.

On the day that Snake-Eyes flew back from Vietnam, his parents and twin sister left to pick him up from the airport, but a stoned-out Dan crashed into the family car – killing everyone involved, including himself (*G.I. Joe* #84). As a colonel, Hawk informed Snake-Eyes of his loss, marking their first meeting (*G.I. Joe* #26).

SNAKE-EYES: THE NINJA YEARS

With his family's demise, Snake-Eyes accepted Tommy's offer of joining the "family business." Under the tutelage of Tommy's uncles, the Hard Master and the Soft Master, Snake-Eyes spent three years training to become a ninja (*G.I. Joe* #26), becoming wrist-branded with the Arashikage family tattoo (first seen in *G.I. Joe* #21).

Eventually, Snake-Eyes learned to best Tommy, now

CONTINUED ON PAGE 155

Master's brother – named the Hard Master – and nephew, the Cobra agent known as Storm Shadow. Sadly, the Soft Master also recalls the Hard Master's apparent murder at Storm Shadow's hands (*see Sidebar*).

In a blinding flash of coincidence, Storm Shadow raids the Soft Master's restaurant, stealing the arrow that slew the Hard Master. Snake-Eyes corners Storm Shadow on a New York train, but Storm Shadow claims he was framed for the Hard Master's murder, later joining Cobra's ranks to expose the true killer. Acknowledging his former friend's words, Snake-Eyes lets Storm Shadow escape to avenge the Hard Master.

MEMORABLE MOMENTS Roadblock encourages Storm Shadow to break out of his Alcatraz cell – so that Roadblock can rough him up again.

A gun-totting street punk tries to rob the glib Soft Master ("Oh, my good gracious me! Is this a robbery? Am I being threatened with wanton violence by a feral youth?"), but the Soft Master expertly disarms the kid and offers him $50 for his pistol. (Snake-Eyes watches the whole exchange with a newspaper covering his Uzi – just in case.)

A child mistakes Storm Shadow for another white-clad Marvel character, shouting out: "Moon Knight!"

In various flashbacks, Storm Shadow displays an ultimate show of camaraderie by turning back for the fallen Snake-Eyes against orders. The Soft Master realizes that the superior Snake-Eyes keeps throwing practice matches to Storm Shadow, not wanting him to lose face. The Hard Master's murder forms the crux of years of *G.I. Joe* stories to come.

LOVE AND WAR Snake-Eyes and Scarlett flirted with the idea of a romance some time before *G.I. Joe* #1, but his disfigurement (see Sidebar) greatly distanced them. Scarlett wishes Snake-Eyes would confide in her more, but nevertheless maintains a great friendship with him.

GOOFS Snake-Eyes rolls up his sleeve in #25 for no other reason than fulfilling a plot thread by "accidentally" letting Gung Ho see his wrist tattoo. If Storm Shadow wanted to ditch Major Bludd's tracking device, why the hell did he mail it to Zartan, with whom he has no association?

NOW YOU KNOW... When the Japanese conquered Okinawa and banned the natives from using knives, the Okinawans invented some of the deadliest forms of unarmed combat. As the Soft Master notes, anti-weapons legislation won't necessarily deter humanity from creating more efficient forms of destruction.

Rifle silencers mask your gun's discharge report, but won't quiet the bullet's sonic boom. As Storm Shadow demonstrates, it's much preferable – if you're going for stealth – to fight with a bow and arrow.

COMIC TIE-INS Storm Shadow didn't immediately recognize the leather-covered Snake-Eyes at the Silent Castle (#21). The Soft Master visits Snake-Eyes in *G.I. Joe* #32. In the same issue, Storm Shadow re-enters Cobra Commander's service on the condition of learning who killed the Hard Master (a mystery revealed in #45).

G.I. Joe #84 and #126 retroactively augment (although not in a good way) the tale of the Hard Master's murder (*see Sidebar*). Issue #144 fleshes out the helicopter accident that savaged Snake-Eyes' face and ruined his voice. Snake-Eyes doesn't resent Stalker for trying to leave him behind in Vietnam (*see Sidebar*), understanding that Storm Shadow's rescue was ill-advised.

First seen here, Snake-Eyes' cabin comes under attack from Destro, Firefly and Cobra Crimson Guardsman Fred Smith in *G.I. Joe* #31-#32. Snake-Eyes, Stalker and Storm Shadow endured a bloody Vietnam mission (*see Sidebar*) that included a soldier named Wade Collins, who surfaces in #32 as Fred Smith's replacement. Storm Shadow's last name goes unspecified (it's actually "Arashikage") until issue #84.

Snake-Eyes doesn't harbor a grudge against Stalker for trying to leave him behind in Vietnam (*see Sidebar*), but Stalker's guilt overwhelms him in *G.I. Joe* #55.

CHARACTER PROFILE: JOES

• *Deep Six:* Unlike his TV incarnation, the comic book Deep Six operates in his own little world – to the point of looking glazed as a doughnut.

• *Junkyard:* An extremely playful dog, difficult to control.

• *Snake-Eyes:* Snake-Eyes holds the equivalent of a high-ranking black belt and proficiently used an M-60 in Vietnam. He's kept tabs on the Soft Master for years, probably out of fondness for his former mentor. Snake-Eyes sometimes hunts rabbits without a gun and tries, out of regard, to avoid killing Storm Shadow. In Vietnam, a battered picture of Snake-Eyes' twin sister served as his good luck charm (the Soft Master guarded the photo for a time). He's friends with a wolf named Timber, who stays near Snake-Eyes' cabin in the High Sierras.

CHARACTER PROFILE: COBRA

• *Storm Shadow:* Storm Shadow's originally from Fresno, California, and knows Snake-Eyes can best him with a blade. As the only son of the Hard and Soft Masters' dead younger brother, Storm Shadow held full voting rights on the "family" board.

• *Zartan:* He absorbs camouflage patterns with a simple touch, able to blend into his background.

CHARACTER PROFILE: OTHER

• *The Hard Master:* Storm Shadow's late Mafia uncle and chairman of his family board. Among other things, the Hard Master knew a technique called "the Blind Sword" – a particu-

Snake-Eyes: Unmasked!

CONTINUED FROM PAGE 153

known as "Storm Shadow" or "the Young Master," with a sword or knife, but Storm Shadow outmatched Snake-Eyes in the field of archery. In particular, Storm Shadow possessed "The Ear That Sees" – a sense of hearing so acute, it allows the archer to hear his target behind obstacles and even shoot through walls (*G.I. Joe* #26).

Needing someone to blame for his brother's death, the future Cobra Commander funneled his hatred onto Snake-Eyes – the son of the family who "killed" Dan. Flush with cash from his growing pyramid sales scheme (a pre-cursor to Cobra), Cobra Commander contracted the man who would become Firefly to assassinate Snake-Eyes. Already an assistant to the sword-maker Onihashi, Firefly entered the Hard Master's house as a budding ninja expert named "the Faceless Master" (first seen in *G.I. Joe* #62) to scope out Snake-Eyes' fighting techniques. But chilled to witness Snake-Eyes' formidable skill, Firefly convinced Cobra Commander to hire an outside contractor for the actual hit (*G.I. Joe* #126).

Cobra Commander turned his attention to a freelance operative and pool hall rogue named Zartan, who followed in Firefly's footsteps by apprenticing himself to the sword-maker Onihashi. As such, Zartan gained access to the Hard Master's compound, stealing one of Storm Shadow's arrows to frame him for the Hard Master's impending murder (*G.I. Joe* #84). To duplicate Storm Shadow's "Ear That Sees," Zartan used sound-amplification equipment provided by Firefly (*G.I. Joe* #126).

Favoring Snake-Eyes over Storm Shadow, the Hard Master asked Snake-Eyes about the possibility of naming him heir to the family business. Snake-Eyes declined, not wanting to take steal Storm Shadow's inheritance, but the Hard Master continued the discussion by demonstrating "The Chameleon's Mantle" – a means of fooling "The Ear That Sees" by imitating another's breathing, movement patterns and heartbeat. Purely as an example, the Hard Master assumed Snake-Eyes' biorhythms. Unfortunately, a ninja-disguised Zartan chose that moment to fire his arrow through a wall at "Snake-Eyes" – skewering the Hard Master by mistake (*G.I. Joe* #26).

Storm Shadow pursued the disguised Zartan, watching him flee aboard the Cobra helicopter (*G.I. Joe* #126) piloted by Firefly. Joining Cobra's ranks, Storm Shadow tried to accrue enough clout to learn the true killer's identity (*G.I. Joe* #27).

SNAKE-EYES: THE SCARLETT YEARS

With the Hard Master's death, the Arashikage "business" dispersed and Snake-Eyes returned to his cabin in the High Sierras. Six years after his initial meeting with Snake-Eyes, Hawk began forming the original G.I. Joe team. Hawk tracked down Snake-Eyes on Stalker's recommendation, convincing him to sign up. By far the most accomplished Joe candidate, Snake-Eyes first met Scarlett at a training camp – allowing her to "defeat" him on the wrestling mat to preserve her pride.

Scarlett found herself fascinated with the seemingly hard-boiled Snake-Eyes, thinking him inwardly compassionate and lonely. However, her romantic intentions got somewhat drenched when Snake-Eyes mentioned that Scarlett reminded him of his late sister.

Months later, Snake-Eyes, Scarlett, Rock 'n Roll and Grunt departed on a "simple" hostage rescue mission to the Middle East. When their helicopter unexpectedly collided with another, Rock 'n Roll and Grunt jumped out, but Scarlett's gear became entangled and pinned her. Snake-Eyes paused to pull Scarlett clear just as their vessel struck another American helicopter. In the resultant collision, aviation gas detonated – hitting Snake-Eyes square in the face. Rock 'n Roll and Grunt scrambled to the crash site, finding a tremendously disfigured – and now mute – Snake-Eyes caring for an unconscious Scarlett. (*G.I. Joe* #27) Horribly maimed, Snake-Eyes insisted on completing the mission and rescued his would-be brother-in-law George Strawhacker (*G.I. Joe* #144).

Military surgeons did their best, but nothing could make Snake-Eyes look normal again. Snake-Eyes pushed Scarlett away – probably not wanting her to feel responsible for the accident, leading to their on-and-off relationship (*G.I. Joe* #27).

means of extending one's sword with a scabbard.

• *The Soft Master:* Served his family as vice-president of finance, later travelling widely under a variety of aliases. Today, he runs the "Comidas Chinas Y Criollas" restaurant in Spanish Harlem as a cover.

PLACES TO GO Snake-Eyes' Cabin: Located on Iron Knife Ridge in the High Sierras.

• *Zartan's Everglades Base:* The interior's loaded with high-level technology hidden behind a hologram.

STUFF YOU NEED Storm Shadow's ninja tattoo: The brand worn by Storm Shadow's family (and Snake-Eyes) forms a hexagram that hails from the I-Ching.

THE COMMAND DECISION Gifted with a potent playing card (the introduction of Zartan), issue #25's surprisingly bogged down with Frank Springer's murky art and because nobody does much beyond run about the swamp a lot. Zartan displays little of his trademark roguishness at this point, and you could easily dice out a lot of this issue with little penalty.

The heart and soul of *G.I. Joe*, "Snake-Eyes: The Origin" (#26-#27) stands as Larry Hama's greatest gift to comicdom, layering Snake-Eyes and Storm Shadow with some unforgettable character shading. The only regret is that the Everglades-based action seems pedestrian against the unfolding saga of Snake-Eyes' history, but even that fails to stop this two-parter from forming the backbone of *G.I. Joe* – and completely rebooting the series' focus – for years to come. Treasure it.

G.I. Joe #28 to #29

Titles: *"Swampfire!" (#28), "Beached Whale" (#29)*
Release Dates: *Oct. to Nov. 1984*
Art: *Marie Severin (#28), Frank Springer (#29)*

BATTLE ROSTER *Joes:* Steeler, Breaker, Clutch, Roadblock, Deep Six, Duke, Cutter; *Cobra:* Destro, Firefly, Cobra Commander, The Baroness, Wild Weasel.

FIRST APPEARANCES *Cobra:* Cobra Crimson Guard (#29), Fred Smith (Crimson Guardsman, #29).

MISSION BRIEF ***Issue #28:*** Torpedo's recon team informs Duke of the precise location of Zartan's hideout, leading the Joe commander to ready his heavy artillery. Rightfully concerned about a Joe attack, Zartan puts his Everglades camp at Cobra Commander's disposal and departs with his Dreadnoks for points north.

As part of evacuation protocol, the Baroness, Destro and Wild Weasel retrieve three Cobra RATTLER jets from a Cobra equipment store. While the Baroness heads off to prepare Springfield for Cobra Commander's return, Wild Weasel and Destro depart to pick up Cobra Commander and Firefly at Zartan's abode. But unknown to all, the Baroness secretly frees Major Bludd from the Springfield detention block, gaining his support for a plan to assassinate Cobra Commander.

Duke deploys a three-pronged land, air and sea attack on Zartan's base, mowing through a series of robotic Cobra tanks and infantry troopers constructed by Zartan. Wild Weasel liberates Cobra Commander moments before the Joes overrun Zartan's base, but Destro turns aside to strafe the Joe WHALE hovercraft. The Joes down Destro's jet, but Destro ejects and forges an alliance with the fuming Firefly, promising to punish Cobra Commander for abandoning them.

Issue #29: Snugly back in Springfield, Cobra Commander unveils "the Crimson Guardsmen," an elite breed of covert Cobra agents designed to infiltrate America's social structure as respected family members, businessmen and community leaders. The first of these Crimson Guardsmen, code-named "Fred Smith," leaves Springfield with his wife and two children to purchase a home on Staten Island and expand Cobra's spy network.

Meanwhile, Duke puts the bullet-peppered WHALE hovercraft in for repairs at Ehrlinger's Cove, even as Destro and Firefly hunt for a way to escape the battle scene. The two hijack the WHALE late at night, insanely trying to reach the Atlantic's open waters, but the Joes eventually corner the WHALE with the *G.I. Jane* freighter.

The *Jane* swallows the WHALE into its main docking bay, but a squadron of well-armed Joes find the hovercraft deserted – realizing after the fact that Destro and Firefly scraped plastic explosive out of two depth charge barrels, hopped in and fired themselves overboard, easily slipping past the *Jane*. The Joes try to pursue the fugitive barrels, but the local shrimp fleet, having deployed at dawn, impedes the *Jane*'s progress. While Duke smolders over losing the Cobra goons, Destro and Firefly hijack a fishing boat and make for home.

MEMORABLE MOMENTS During a nail-biting helicopter landing, Wild Bill rattles a sweating Duke by offering: "You wanna try [landing this bird] yourself, Duke? Here. Take the stick...." After abandoning Firefly in the Everglades, Cobra Commander notes to himself: "I must remember to re-stock my supply of lackeys when I get back to Springfield."

Firefly takes aim at Roadblock and Duke with the WHALE's Gatling gun, but a desperately improvising Roadblock deflects the vicious blast by hauling up a giant piece of armored plating. Cutter notes, after a slugfest with Destro: "Feels like I been stopping bowling balls with my face."

Tripwire hysterically informs pilot Cutter that the *Jane* is losing hull integrity and Cutter, who really should switch to decaf, hollers back: "Details! Why bother me with details? I've got a ship to steer!"

NOW YOU KNOW... When Trip-Wire tries to selflessly smother one of Firefly's bombs with his own body, Roadblock kicks Trip-Wire off the incendiary and hurls the explosive away – impressing on Trip-Wire that clear thought's preferable to recklessly throwing your life away.

ASS-WHUPPINGS Destro's bullets spray Cutter, Duke and Deep Six. (Duke barks at his crew: "Everybody's hit! That's no excuse to stop firing!") Destro and Firefly hijack a poacher's boat, then drown the hapless fool upon reaching their destination. Cutter bashes his hand punching the steel-plated Destro in the face. Destro's powerful wrist-rockets take out Duke and Wild Bill's helicopter.

PREPOSTEROUS PHYSICS The G.I. Jane's hydrofoils surely couldn't support the freighter enough for it to hover on top of the water's surface.

GOOFS Destro and Firefly vow, on no uncertain terms, to make Cobra Commander pay for his misdeeds – but they never carry out the threat (indeed, Destro saves Cobra Commander's hooded ass in #33).

COMIC TIE-INS Torpedo, Trip-Wire, Mutt and Junkyard return to the G.I. Jane, having tangled with Cobra leaders in *G.I. Joe* #25-#27. Destro's still smarting from Cobra Commander's attempt to bump him off (#16).

Issue #29 introduces Fred Smith as the first of several Crimson Guardsmen bearing identical names and facial features. Fred Smith I joins Destro and Firefly on a Joe hunt in #31, but an identical Fred Smith II shows up in *G.I. Joe* #32. If this makes sense, all of Cobra's "Fred Smith" agents are Crimson Guardsmen, but not all Crimson Guardsmen are "Fred Smiths" (as evidenced by Professor Appel in #38).

CHARACTER PROFILE: JOES Cutter: Cutter's one of the most accomplished Joe sea drivers – and an utter maniac when the need calls. He has implicit trust in Wild Bill's helicopter skills.

CHARACTER PROFILE: COBRA Fred Smith: A golden boy among the Crimson Guardsmen, cited as young, intelligent, good-looking – in short, promotion material. Like the best of the Crimson Guardsmen (see **Organizations**), Fred carries himself as a trusted businessman, concerned citizen and loving husband and father, but his household – including his wife, son and daughter – is armed to the teeth with nasty Cobra equipment.

MISCELLANEOUS STUFF!

THE YEARBOOKS

Playing off the Marvel tradition of releasing "Annual" comics (extra-length stories that complimented ongoing series), the *G.I. Joe Yearbooks* went a step further and presented themselves as guides to the series.

Each *Yearbook* contained a recap of the series up to that point, essentially a massive "Last time on *G.I. Joe*"-style feature to aid newcomers. The *Yearbooks* also featured information about the *G.I. Joe* cartoon and a wealth of pin-ups and personnel profiles.

G.I. Joe Yearbook #1 contains the aforementioned features, plus a reprint of *G.I. Joe* #1. *G.I. Joe Yearbooks* #2-#4, on the other hand, include the following original stories:

- **"Triple Play" (*Yearbook* #2)** – When the Oktober Guard field-tests a prototype laser cannon in Afghanistan, Cobra forces led by Destro and the Baroness move to swipe the weapon. The two sides bash each other silly until a Joe contingent swoops in and ferrets the laser away. Duke gloats that the laser – crafted by Soviet engineers with American laser technology – will allow the Joes to eliminate various Russian moles in the States.

NOTE: This story introduces Oktober Guard member Dragonsky.

- **"Hush Job" (*Yearbook* #3)** – See *G.I. Joe* #54-#56 for the low-down on this tie-in tale.
- **"My Dinner With Serpentor" (*Yearbook* #3)** – Dr. Mindbender is steamed when the Dreadnoks serve Serpentor paltry microwaved pizza for dinner. But in response, Serpentor wistfully recalls how one of his progenitors witnessed Roman troops inventing pizza as a morale booster during the Roman siege of Alesia in 52 B.C. Pizza gave the Romans the fortitude to help slaughter the Gauls, making it a fitting dish for an Emperor.

CONTINUED ON PAGE 159

ORGANIZATIONS *Cobra:* Cobra Commander's household cleaning product pyramid scheme continues to generate gobs of money. In order to indoctrinate civilians to its totalitarian views, Cobra holds nationwide "Greed is Good for You" seminars. The Cobra media department's succeeded in green-lighting "10 more mindless sitcoms" – intended to lower America's intelligence and deter free thinkers. Armies of Cobra accountants annually advise Americans to cheat on their taxes, prompting defense spending cuts.

• *Cobra Crimson Guardsmen:* Cobra's elite troops, mostly composed of long-term undercover agents who infiltrate America's infrastructure and social fabric disguised as upstanding family people, i.e. concerned citizens, lawyers, doctors, etc. We've no idea why Cobra wants its "Fred Smiths" to look identical, beyond Cobra Commander's standard obsession with conformity.

PLACES TO GO Springfield: The detention section's accessible through the "Fresh as a Daisy" Car Wash.

HOT WHEELS Cobra RATTLER jets: Equipped for vertical take-off and landing. Although the RATTLERs possess infrared targeting systems, they don't have lock-on memories (meaning you can sometimes disappear from a RATTLER's systems by dousing your tank engine with water).

• *G.I. Jane:* As a desperation ploy, the Jane can deploy hydrofoils and, given sufficient velocity, "surf" over land for a limited period (however, you need a whacked driver like Cutter to even attempt such a maneuver).

THE COMMAND DECISION Arguably generic, although the story's ripping pace, as Socrates used to say, "makes for a damn good ride." There's some decent turnabouts (i.e. Destro and Firefly triumphing through sheer gall), and the introduction of Crimson Guardsman Fred Smith – while seemingly irrelevant at times – nicely marbles Cobra with Nazi overtones.

G.I. Joe #30

Title: *"Darkness"*
Release Date: *Dec. 1984*
Art: *Frank Springer*

BATTLE ROSTER *Joes:* Hawk, Wild Bill, Scarlett, Clutch, Steeler, Ace; *Cobra:* The Dreadnoks, Cobra Commander, Zartan, the Baroness, Major Bludd; *Other:* Billy.

MISSION BRIEF ***Issue #30:*** While plotting to make Cobra Commander bite the big one, the Baroness and Major Bludd find Cobra resistance member Billy snooping through Cobra's shipping records. Using Billy's hatred for Cobra to their advantage, the Baroness and Major Bludd sway the youngster to their cause.

On Staten Island, Crimson Guardsman Fred Smith purchases a rural home on the doorstep of Fort Wadsworth, expanding Cobra's intelligence operation to find Joe Headquarters. Meanwhile, Zartan notices a high number of Joe vehicles routing through New Jersey's McGuire Air Force Base, erroneously suspecting McGuire of housing the Joe base of operations. Cobra Commander acts on Zartan's information by readying an assault squadron, ordering the Dreadnoks to cut open McGuire's outer fence prior to the main assault.

Although Cobra Commander commands the Dreadnoks to take no further action, the rabble-rousing Dreadnoks – never overly endowed with gray matter – hack through the McGuire fence and proceed to start sawing, torching and mangling McGuire's parked military vehicles. Eventually, Dreadnok Buzzer accidentally topples a Joe Skystriker, exploding the plane and alerting McGuire personnel to a perimeter breach.

The McGuire staff alerts the Pit II, just as Cobra Commander – severely miffed at the Dreadnoks' disobedience – rolls forward his assault. Cobra Commander escapes as the Joes butcher his soldiers, foiling yet another Cobra strike.

MEMORABLE MOMENTS At the Pit II, Clutch advocates getting a wounded Wild Bill to the medical bay ASAP because: "We just laid down all this new floor tile and don't want you bleeding all over it." Chased by an entire phalanx of Joe tanks and jeeps, a panicked Buzzer crows: "Ride, Dreadnoks! Ride!!"

ASS-WHUPPINGS Clutch nails a FANG; Steeler takes out two HISS tanks (a sub-par day, really).

PREPOSTEROUS PHYSICS Buzzer accidentally topples a Joe Skystriker by cutting through its main support strut – meaning he was directly under the thing – but magically avoids getting squished or blown up.

GOOFS "Espionage" expert Fred Smith drives around town with a Cobra logo as his hood ornament (no, that's not conspicuous). Cobra Commander takes a ludicrously small force to capture "Joe Headquarters."

COMIC TIE-INS Cobra resistance member Billy first appeared in *G.I. Joe* #10. The Baroness here comments that Billy resents "what Cobra did to his father," but we never learn what the hell that means, and issue #33's revelation of Billy as Cobra Commander's son makes the source of Billy's supposed vendetta all the more baffling.

McGuire Air Force Base often serves as a departure point for Joe vehicles (notably *G.I. Joe* #24 and more).

Zartan here disguises himself with holograms by instantly turning into "Hawk," foreshadowing his multiple identity shifts in *G.I. Joe* #48. The Dreadnoks get their rocks off again, smashing jeeps, helicopters and more, in #35.

Fred Smith (*G.I. Joe* #29) here purchases a Staten Island house near Fort Wadsworth, unknowingly putting himself right on the Pit II's doorstep. Low-ranking soldiers suggest Hawk once turned down a full general's star to stay with the Joes, but he gets promoted in *G.I. Joe* #45.

PLACES TO GO McGuire Air Force Base: Their air traffic controllers have Joe-level security clearance and a direct hotline to the Pit II.

THE COMMAND DECISION A decent little action-packed issue, comically highlighting the Dreadnoks' mania (well, we certainly laughed), but it's almost too detached from the main Joe plotlines to matter much.

G.I. Joe #31 to #32

Titles: *"All Fall Down!" (#31), "The Mountain!" (#32)*
Release Dates: *Jan. to Feb. 1985*
Art: *Rod Whigham (#31), Frank Springer (#32)*

BATTLE ROSTER *Joes:* Snake-Eyes, Airborne; *Cobra:* Destro, Firefly, Fred Smith I; *Other:* The Soft Master.

FIRST APPEARANCES *Joes:* Spirit (tracker, #31), Lady Jaye (covert operations, #32), Ripcord (HALO jumper, #32), Blowtorch (flame-thrower, #32), Recondo (jungle trooper, #32); *Cobra:* Fred Smith II (Crimson Guardsman, #32).

DEATHS *Cobra:* Fred Smith I (#32).

MISSION BRIEF ***Issue #31:*** Destro and Firefly return to Springfield and report for duty as normal, keeping quiet their desire to tie Cobra Commander's neck into a knot for abandoning them. Meanwhile, the Baroness and Major Bludd make plans to include Billy in a Cobra Youth troupe at an upcoming Springfield rally, giving the lad the opportunity to do in Cobra Commander with a .357 Magnum at point-blank range.

Meanwhile, Zartan monitors the Joes' movements by planting a homing device aboard a C-130 transport plane. Soon after, Hawk schedules a training flight with the C-130, graciously turning a blind eye as Snake-Eyes parachutes out over the High Sierras to visit his private cabin. But worried for his friend's safety, Hawk assigns Joes Spirit and Airborne to secretly keep watch on Snake-Eyes for a few days.

Curious as to why the C-130 briefly circled in the High Sierras, Destro and Firefly link up with Crimson Guardsman Fred Smith and scour the area for a Joe hideout. Destro's trio quickly happens upon Snake-Eyes' cabin, instigating a shoot-out with Snake-Eyes, Spirit and Airborne.

Spirit grievously wounds Fred, but Firefly grows impatient for a quick victory and lobs a satchel charge inside Snake-Eyes' cabin. With combatants on both sides severely wounded and Snake-Eyes briefly incapacitated, Firefly's charge detonates and blows the cabin to smithereens.

MISCELLANEOUS STUFF!

CONTINUED FROM PAGE 157

• **"Trade-Offs" (*Yearbook* #4)** – Serpentor and Dr. Mindbender knock Cobra Commander II unconscious, dressing up a BAT in the commander's armor for the purpose of humiliating him. Unfortunately, a covert Oktober Guard team infiltrates Cobra Island and kidnaps the disguised BAT. A shoot-out scraps the BAT, allowing Cobra Commander II to don his spare armor and reassert his authority.

NOTE: Serpentor and Dr. Mindbender learn Cobra Commander II's an imposter in this story, but they refrain from killing him, probably fearing a backlash from Cobra troops loyal to the commander. Serpentor never again mentions knowing the commander's secret, although Dr. Mindbender uses the information to his advantage in *G.I. Joe* #77.

• **"Bystander" (*Yearbook* #4)** – While on the road, Snake-Eyes and Scarlett stop to get talcum powder when Snake-Eyes' rubber mask starts chafing him. Unexpectedly finding himself thwarting a convenience store robbery, Snakey sets the place on fire to evacuate the joint and save lives. Scarlett, deciding she can't take Snake-Eyes anywhere, hands over his talcum powder and drives onward.

Issue #32: Astonished when Storm Shadow re-surfaces in Springfield, Cobra Commander entrusts the ninja to safeguard his life until an upcoming Springfield rally. As enticement, he offers to tell Storm Shadow the name of the Hard Master's killer (#26) at the rally's conclusion

Back in the Sierras, the Soft Master visits his former pupil Snake-Eyes, finding a variety of unconscious Joes and Cobras scattered around Snake-Eyes' destroyed cabin. Destro recovers enough to fire two wrist rockets, but the ninja-trained Soft Master effortlessly bats the rockets away with his pick-axe. Knowing when he's outmatched, Destro beats a retreat with Firefly and the bleeding Fred.

The Soft Master tends to Airborne's wounds, then gains Spirit's help in clearing wood away from Snake-Eyes' fallen cabin. The Soft Master discovers that Snake-Eyes took shelter before the blast in a secret bolt-hole, finding him alive but half-asphyxiated.

After Spirit departs to gather firewood, the still-bleeding Fred, thirsting for vengeance, violates Destro's orders by sneaking off to wantonly slaughter the Joes. Fred cocks his rifle to blow away Airborne and Snake-Eyes, but the Soft Master informs Fred that his actions amount to despicable murder, not an honorable kill. Finding his "revenge" extremely unsatisfying, Fred loses his will to live and succumbs to his wounds, dying in the snow.

Nearby, a brief tangle with Spirit leaves Destro and Firefly adrift in a river, but the two of them ultimately make it back to Springfield. A few days later, another Crimson Guardsman identical to the "late" Fred Smith returns home to Staten Island, greeting "his" children and taking his place as head of household.

MEMORABLE MOMENTS Destro pauses to savor his supremacy over the incapacitated Snake-Eyes: "Ahhh, there's more than a glimmer of life left in you! You think that you might be fast enough to raise your Uzi for one final burst, eh? I think not. I think you will die like a dog."

Gunning for the wounded Joes, Fred Smith kindly offers to let the Soft Master leave. In one of the series' most dramatic moments, the Soft Master resolutely informs Fred: "To turn your back on evil is to be a part of it. If you want to shoot these men, you'll have to shoot me first." (Thankfully, Fred dies first.)

ASS-WHUPPINGS In a round robin of bullets, Fred shoots Airborne, Airborne nails Firefly, Snake-Eyes nicks Destro and Spirit hits Fred (giving him a festering wound that ultimately kills the Cobra operative). All of the assembled Joes and Cobras fall down when Snake-Eyes' cabin explodes (hence the issue's title), and Snake-Eyes and his pet wolf Timber suffer from concussion and lack of oxygen while hiding in a bolt-hole. Firefly and Destro hang on for dear life when a toppling tree hurls them into a river.

PREPOSTEROUS PHYSICS Snake-Eyes somehow spies Spirit, who's hidden 10 miles away in thick branches (even allowing for Snake-Eyes' almost magical ninja veneer, it's a preposterous idea). Spirit and Airborne run the 10 miles to Snake-Eyes' cabin in about five minutes when it more reasonably should've taken them at least 40.

NOW YOU KNOW... In a nugget of wisdom worthy of the NRA, the Soft Master points out that guns don't "covet wealth, seek revenge or try to justify their actions," suggesting that it's better to fear men rather than the weapons they carry.

By the way, if you're cornered up a tree by a bear, don't drop a satchel-full of TNT atop the bear – you might also topple the tree. It's far more sensible to loop the charge around the bear's neck, then lure him away from the tree (keep running until it starts raining bear bits).

COMIC TIE-INS Previously seen in *G.I. Joe* #26-#27, the Soft Master confers here with Snake-Eyes and embarks on a quest to find the Hard Master's killer in #35-#43. In an issue #32 cameo, Storm Shadow similarly continues his quest for his uncle's murderer (started in #27).

We learn that Storm Shadow escaped from Alcatraz (*G.I. Joe* #25) by fashioning a mattress spring into a lengthy lock-pick, then clinging to the bottom of Duke and Roadblock's Coast Guard launch – breathing via a length of rubber hose stolen from the laundry room – and returning to San Francisco.

In #31, Destro and Firefly finally make it back to Springfield after their Florida escapade (*G.I. Joe* #28-#29). Destro claims that he owns the Silent Castle (#21), but *G.I. Joe* #120-#122 unswervingly establishes that it belongs to Cobra Commander.

The late Fred Smith's replaced here by a lookalike who later reveals his true identity as an associate of Snake-Eyes and Stalker in *G.I. Joe* #42. Fred Smith II leads a pack of Cobra goons against Snake-Eyes and Scarlett in #36.

At the end of issue #32, newcomers Lady Jaye and Ripcord shockingly show up to replace Scarlett and Grunt as Joe members – hailing a massive team restructuring in *G.I. Joe* #33.

CHARACTER PROFILE: JOES

Scarlett: Apparently can't get along with any female Joe member, trading verbal barbs with Lady Jaye. (Mind, the uppity Lady Jaye lights the fuse by announcing: "I don't like this tawdry redhead's attitude.")

CHARACTER PROFILE: COBRA

Cobra Commander and the Cobra leadership: He's fully aware that the Baroness released Major Bludd, but finds her amusing nonetheless. Cobra Commander also knows that Zartan and his Dreadnoks only work for themselves and that Destro holds good reason to hate him. That leaves Storm Shadow as the only operative who will faithfully safeguard Cobra Commander's life – and even that's only to learn the name of the Hard Master's killer.

CHARACTER PROFILE: OTHER

The Soft Master: Clearly possesses a sixth sense – enabling him to bat away mini-rockets fired at his back. The Soft Master's adept enough to remove bullets buried in Airborne's leg by simply applying pressure.

THE COMMAND DECISION Tight-knit, and shrewdly contrasting the majority of the G.I. Joe comics as the story of a few well-armed men desperate to survive. Mind, Rod Whigham's highly textured art in issue #31 somewhat diffuses when you hit Frank Springer's rudimentary pencils in #32, but that still leaves this two-parter an unsung hero and G.I. Joe comics.

G.I. Joe #33

Title: "Celebration!" (#33)
Release Date: Mar. 1985
Art: Frank Springer

BATTLE ROSTER *Joes:* Major General Austin, Hawk, Duke, Spirit, Ripcord, Blowtorch; *Cobra:* Cobra Commander, Destro, the Baroness, Major Bludd; *Other:* Billy.

FIRST APPEARANCES *Other:* Candy (a.k.a. Bongo the Balloon Bear, #33).

MISSION BRIEF *Issue #33:* On Staten Island, Fred Smith II makes efforts to acclimate "his" family to the fact that he's a doppelganger of their late husband and father, taking the Smith clan on a visit to a local mall. Unfortunately, freshmen Joes Ripcord and Blowtorch escort Spirit, who's still recovering from the firefight at Snake-Eyes' cabin, to the same mall to purchase restorative herbs.

Spirit turns shocked to see the "deceased" Fred Smith casually strolling about eating ice cream, but Fred's family pounds the Joe tracker and flees. As the fracas moves to the mall parking lot, a party entertainer named "Bongo the Balloon Bear" – a woman named Candy wearing a bear costume – pulls her van over to lend the Joes assistance. The Joes quickly commandeer Bongo's van but lose the Smiths' trail.

Meanwhile, Major General Austin formally commemorates the Pit's restoration (begun in #22) and official re-opening, surprisingly rotating eight of the original Joes (including Scarlett, Stalker, Breaker and Rock 'n Roll) off active duty to serve as the new Pit II's administrative arm. Accordingly, Hawk expands Duke's duties as the Joes' top field commander, freeing Hawk to better manage the Pit II's operations.

Back in Springfield, Destro morally questions the Baroness' decision to arm a young boy to murder Cobra Commander (#31). As the long-anticipated Springfield rally begins and Cobra Commander hawks his Crimson Guardsman program to Springfield's populace, Destro steels himself to watch events unfold.

Destro scans the Cobra Youth for a sign of the Baroness' assassin, then feels his guts churn to spot Billy in the front row – recognizing him as a key figure from Cobra Commander's past. Unable to cross a certain moral line, Destro throws off Billy's aim and halts Storm Shadow from eviscerating the lad.

Cobra Commander impulsively orders Billy's execution, but Destro encourages Cobra Commander to look at the boy. With complete astonishment, Cobra Commander finally identifies Billy – as his son.

MISCELLANEOUS STUFF!

RETIRING THE ORIGINAL JOES

In a move that reflects the ever-growing number of Joes, *G.I. Joe* #33 sees eight of the team's original members (Breaker, Zap, Grunt, Short-Fuse, Stalker, Rock 'n Roll, Flash and Scarlett) promoted up a rank and taken off the active duty roster – assigned to serve as the new Pit's administrative staff. (*Side Note:* Snake-Eyes remains on active duty, probably considered too lethal to deserve a desk job.)

However, the move's little more than symbolic, as it certainly doesn't reduce the characters' presence in the series. Indeed, writer Larry Hama, showing an obvious affection for many of the originals, pits Rock 'n Roll and Breaker against the Dreadnoks in issue #35, lets Scarlett brawl with Fred Smith II in #36 and Stalker undertake a commando mission in #39-#40. For that matter, *all* of the originals are recalled to active duty in #49 and... well, you get the idea. However poignant the "duty rotation" ceremony in *G.I. Joe* #33 might seem, it ultimately changes little.

MEMORABLE MOMENTS The retirement of the original Joes, even though they're not as sidelined as you might suspect, brings a lump to the throat. Cobra Commander acknowledging Billy as his son paves the way for a whole lotta unanswered questions.

LOVE AND WAR Clutch and Breaker try (and fail) to convince Scarlett and Cover Girl to embark on a lucrative career as a mud wrestling team, generously offering to split the proceeds in half. Ripcord shows enough romantic interest in Candy (a.k.a. "Bongo the Balloon Bear") to invite her out to dinner.

GOOFS Why does Spirit visit a mall florist, of all things, to purchase special herbs? Fred Smith II's heat-seeking missiles lock onto Bongo's van engine amid a flurry of traffic.

COMIC TIE-INS Billy first appeared in *G.I. Joe* #10 as a throw-away character, but stands revealed here as Cobra Commander's son. The Baroness and Major Bludd conscripted Billy to blow away dear ol' Dad in #30.

The Joes commemorate the re-opening of the Pit, completing the reconstruction started in #22. The Pit's original opening (pre-*G.I. Joe* #1) hit a small snag when they couldn't find catering personnel with sufficient security clearance to staff the event. As a result, the Pentagon brass who attended the event ate "cold C-rations and bug juice." The Pit II's opening supposedly relegates Hawk to a desk job, but he's promoted in #45 and returns to active duty in #46.

Ripcord here meets Candy (a.k.a. Bongo the Balloon Bear) and continues attempts to romance her in *G.I. Joe* #37.

Spirit buried the original Fred Smith in the High Sierras (*G.I. Joe* #32), although *G.I. Joe* #91 revisits his corpse. Fred II next stalks Snake-Eyes and Scarlett in #36.

The Baroness faints here when Destro, purely to foster trust between them, shows her his true face. *G.I. Joe* #55, however, suggests that Destro isn't disfigured, so the Baroness likely passes out from the import of the gesture itself.

CHARACTER PROFILE: COBRA *Fred Smith II:* His wife carries a purse full of grenades. His car's armed with heat-guided missiles.

ORGANIZATIONS *G.I. Joe:* The Pentagon houses any presidential citations or medals awarded to the Joes, awaiting the day when Congress declassifies the team.

THE COMMAND DECISION An eyebrow-raising story that generates as many questions as it answers, "Celebration!" rocket-fuels the series' momentum and makes you salivate for whatever's coming next. Granted, Springer's stilted pencils stifle a lot of this story's heartbeat, but the entire package keeps you suitably hooked.

G.I. Joe #34

Title: *"Shakedown!"*
Release Date: *April 1985*
Art: *Rod Whigham*

BATTLE ROSTER *Joes:* Ace, Lady Jaye; *Cobra:* the Baroness, Wild Weasel.

MISSION BRIEF At McGuire Air Force Base, American military techs augment a Joe Skystriker jet with new control systems and electronic counter-measure pods, asking Ace and Lady Jaye to give the newly fitted vessel a test flight. Simultaneously, Cobra engineers outfit a RATTLER with state-of-the-art computer banks and tactical capabilities, compelling Cobra pilot Wild Weasel and the Baroness to take the jet up for a shakedown course.

Both crews run their ships through their paces, stumbling upon one another over the continental United States. Ace and Wild Weasel engage each other in aerial chess, respectively relying on Lady Jaye and the Baroness for tactical support. Using top-level radar systems and a lot of gall, both crews dodge their adversaries' missiles – leaving both teams reliant on Gatling guns. Although Ace and Wild Weasel proceed to tear each other apart, they exhaust their ammunition in the process. Unable to battle further, Ace and Wild Weasel make a final pass, saluting each other as honorable opponents. Silently, the two pilots return to base – leaving Lady Jaye and the Baroness baffled as to why the men broke off hostilities.

MEMORABLE MOMENTS Toward the end, Ace and Wild Weasel perform gun checks, realize their weapons are empty and salute each other – a moment that stands as one of the most empowering in *G.I. Joe* history. Failing to understand the pilots' code of honor, the Baroness and Lady Jaye nearly tear their hair out wondering why their partners are returning to base. (Lady Jaye to a silent Ace: "You're going to just let them fly away... so we can go back to McGuire and eat breakfast?")

ASS-WHUPPINGS Ace's Skystriker and Wild Weasel's RATTLER return home looking about as tortured as that VW bug you drove in college. (You know, the one that had a resale value of two cheesecakes.) A potshot from the Baroness dices the Joe aircraft enough to crack Ace's helmet. The finale features both ships tearing each other to ribbons with 20 mm and 30 mm electric cannons.

NOW YOU KNOW... When zooming along at low altitudes, it's easiest to navigate by following highways. Air-to-air combat often ends more simply than you think – whomever spots the enemy and obtains a targeting lock first typically wins. If you're spotted first, pray to Heaven that you can pop a turn faster than your adversary – banking a tight circle's your best bet to avoid getting a missile up your ass.

A desperate ploy for avoiding radar-directed missiles entails firing your ordnance into a junkyard. If you're lucky, you'll stir up a hornet's nest of scrap-metal and confuse the missiles' sensors.

CHARACTER PROFILE: JOES

Lady Jaye: Lady Jaye's already passed a Class II physical and altitude chamber training, so she's not prone to passing out at high altitudes. She's qualified to run multi-mode pulse Doppler radar – a useful trick when you're up in a fast-moving jet mapping objects on the ground.

HOT WHEELS Cobra souped-up RATTLER: Ah, paradise. You could almost catch up on the latest Tom Clancy novel while your RATTLER's flying low to the ground – the jet's radar and autopilot will automatically dodge anything in your path. The cockpit's lined with a titanium steel-armored "bathtub," so Gatling gun fire might not even trim the pilot's toenails.

Bad news for any Joes reading this: If you're targeting a RATTLER, be sure to fire *before* they slam on the speed brakes – otherwise, you run the risk of sailing right past your target. The good news: RATTLERs can only fire radar-directed missiles head-on. If you're targeted, try to pitch yourself into a hard turn – the missiles' servos will likely futz up trying to follow you.

• *Joe souped-up Skystriker:* Ace's Skystriker possesses the most advanced radar system ever built. An onboard 92K memory computer automatically registers civilian aircraft as "safe," alerting Ace as a precaution when one draws near. The radar system's also clever enough to distinguish low-flying planes from ground objects. If there's a flaw, it's that anyone with even a crappy radar detector can backtrack *your* radar signal and zero in on your Skystriker's position. (Of course, simply turning off your radar off nips *that* problem in the bud.) Also, be forewarned that your computer might get fooled during a 90 degree turn, as you're no longer moving consistently against the earth.

The Skystriker contains the usual assortment of electronic counter-measures, radar-reflective Rapid Blooming Chaff (RBC) and decoy heat-seekers. It's capable of three gees of stress.

THE COMMAND DECISION As geeky teenagers, we despised this issue, deeming it one of the most drawn-out G.I. Joe comics ever written and nearly flinging it underneath our school bus' tires. But as adults... well, it impressed us as being very, very clever. It's an aerial chess match between Ace and Wild Weasel that masquerades as a ruthless shootout, and truth to tell, we can't do its nuances justice in a cut-and-dried story summary. Suffice to say, "Shakedown!" evolves beyond a simple aerial battle – and works.

G.I. Joe #35 to #37

Titles: *"Dreadnoks on the Loose" (#35), "All the Ships at Sea!" (#36), "Twin Brothers" (#37)*
Release Dates: *May to July 1985*
Art: *Rod Whigham, Mark Bright, Bob Camp, Larry Hama (all #35-#36), Frank Springer (#37)*

BATTLE ROSTER *Joes:* Snake-Eyes, Scarlett, Ripcord, Rock 'n Roll, Breaker, Clutch, Lady Jaye, Gung Ho, Wild Bill, Doc, Cutter, Deep Six, Snow Job, Torpedo, Trip-Wire, Blowtorch; *Cobra:* the Dreadnoks, Fred Smith II, Zartan, Major Bludd, the Baroness; *Other:* the Soft Master, Billy, Candy.

FIRST APPEARANCES *Joes:* Barbecue (firefighter, #36), Flint (warrant officer, #37), Footloose (infantry trooper, #37), *USS Flagg* (aircraft carrier, #36); *Cobra:* Tomax and Xamot (Crimson Guard commanders, #37).

MISSION BRIEF ***Issue #35:*** Hanging out in Zartan's lair under Springfield, Dreadnok Buzzer impishly swipes Zartan's souped-up motorcycle, equipped with a series of hologram projectors, and leads fellow Dreadnoks Ripper and Torch on a wrecking spree.

Meanwhile, an on-leave Breaker, Rock 'n Roll and Clutch depart New York in Rock 'n Roll's '56 Bel Air Nomad, intending to enjoy surfing, sand and chicks in California. But the Dreadnoks, randomly vandalizing cars like a bunch of rowdy high schoolers, zoom by and dice a lengthy cut in Rock 'n Roll's car. The Joes give chase, but Buzzer uses his motorcycle's hologram projectors to cast the illusion of a giant skull-laden semi. Rock 'n Roll swerves to avoid a collision and crashes into a hillside, noting the license plate on Buzzer's "semi" (ZTN-123) before he passes out.

Miffed to find his motorcycle stolen, Zartan disguises his back-up transport (ZTN-456) as a bus and rolls down the highway searching for his missing property. For some unknown reason, Zartan picks up an old woman (actually the Soft Master in disguise), then continues on his way.

Tanked on adrenaline, the Dreadnoks start hacking up berthed airplanes at a local Air Force Base. Unfortunately, Torch accidentally blows up an aircraft, putting the base on a security alert. Buzzer holographically disguises the Dreadnoks as military police, quietly leading his team onto the highway, but Rock 'n Roll, riding by in an ambulance with Breaker and Clutch, spots the license plate number ZTN-123 on Buzzer's "jeep."

Rock 'n Roll commandeers the ambulance and gives chase, flinging an oxygen bottle that knocks Buzzer off his motorcycle. Buzzer's bike explodes, but Zartan arrives, scoops up Torch and Ripper, shifts his vehicle into helicopter mode and flies away. Whining up a storm, Buzzer finds himself Rock 'n Roll's prisoner. Zartan lands in Springfield, but the cross-dressing Soft Master, appreciative of the lift, adeptly eludes capture and continues his mission to find the Hard Master's killer.

Issue #36: Scarlett and a rubber-masked Snake-Eyes share a romantic ride on the Staten Island Ferry, but Fred Smith II takes a Crimson Guard contingent to kidnap Scarlett for interrogation. Snake-Eyes thumps Fred's companions, then brawls with Fred, nearly knocking the two of them off the ferry. Fred lunges for Snake-Eyes in desperation and accidentally peels off his mask, exposing Snake-Eyes' ruined face. Horrified, Fred screams and falls into the Hudson River, swimming to shore while Snake-Eyes re-covers his face.

Meanwhile, a team of Joes aboard the *G.I. Jane* freighter and the WHALE hovercraft investigate reports of Cobra activity in the South Atlantic. The Joes find a Cobra platoon fortified on a small island, then set about whittling down the opposition thanks to the WHALE's superior maneuverability. Cobra's cumulative firepower sinks the *Jane,* but the Joes ultimately prevail and await pick-up from the *USS Flagg* aircraft carrier – entirely clueless about Cobra's intent in the Atlantic.

Issue #37: Seeking to repay party performer Candy for borrowing her van (#33), Ripcord and a small group of Joes help Candy set up a balloon show at an Arbco Bros. circus ground – completely unaware that the circus serves as a front for Cobra operations. Stationed at the circus to work on Cobra's newest master stroke, the Crimson Guard Commanders – a pair of psionically linked twin brothers named Tomax and Xamot – send their troopers to eliminate Ripcord and Candy. Simultaneously, the twins personally assault a roller-coaster-riding Gung Ho and Blowtorch.

Innocently passing by the circus in a helicopter, a newly assigned Joe warrant officer named Flint spots the roller coaster commotion and throws himself into the melee. Flint bashes Xamot, forcing Tomax to save his brother, even as Ripcord and Candy escape their pursuers. With the Joes still befuddled about Cobra's newest scheme, Tomax and Xamot withdraw. But Candy, while appreciative of Ripcord's romantic intentions, grows increasingly frustrated at the secretive nature of his work and storms off.

MEMORABLE MOMENTS Rock 'n Roll madly chases the Dreadnoks down the interstate at a speed which frightens even the combat-prone Clutch and Breaker (Clutch screams out: "The gauge stops at 85! We're still accelerating!"). Fred Smith II unleashes a wail of pure terror upon seeing Snake-Eyes' face – reminding us all that it's not easy being Snakes.

LOVE AND WAR A delusional Clutch fanaticizes about California girls drooling all over him. In other news, Ripcord fails to score with Candy, who drives off in a huff. Finally, Scarlett and Snake-Eyes share a "romantic" ride on the Staten Island Ferry. But really, how romantic can a night out with Snake-Eyes really be?

Scarlett: Isn't it a beautiful night, sweetums?

Snake-Eyes: ...

Scarlett: The moon glitters so beautifully on the water, don't you think?

Snake-Eyes: ...

Scarlett: Hold me, Snakey. Tell me you love me.

Snake-Eyes: ...

ASS-WHUPPINGS The Dreadnoks drive Rock 'n Roll to crash his Nomad, then proceed to saw, rip up and torch parked Air Force jets. Rock 'n Roll nails Buzzer with an oxygen bottle.

Fred Smith II accidentally shoots one of his Crimson Guard associates while trying to kill Snake-Eyes. Snake-Eyes happily whips the crap out of Smith's lackeys.

Torpedo's nutty driving allows the Joe WHALE to pick off Cobra hydrofoils. Doc and Trip-Wire, two of the more passive Joes, combine efforts to repair the *Jane*'s Gatling gun and pulp a Cobra jet. Joe firefighter Barbecue also downs a Cobra RATTLER plane, but it crashes into the *G.I. Jane* and hastens the freighter's demise.

PREPOSTEROUS PHYSICS Rock 'n Roll performs a miraculous, one-handed throw that hurtles an oxygen bottle through the air and catches up to Buzzer's racing motorcycle, nailing the Dreadnok dead-on. When some of Candy's balloons escape out of her van, Ripcord achieves superhuman speed by racing out of the vehicle, pouncing on a trampoline and netting the balloons with a circus cape before they fly away.

GOOFS Dreadnok Torch blows up a grounded plane – but doesn't even singe his nose hairs in the process. For reasons which completely elude us, a Cobra Crimson Guardsman – supposedly one of Cobra's elite troops – fails to release his safety, missing his chance to shred Snake-Eyes. The G.I. Jane freighter seems frightfully understaffed with its crew of four.

There's an extremely confusing bit in a circus mirror hall, when suit-wearing Cobra goons physically surround Ripcord and Candy. In the very next scene, the Cobra troopers have magically teleported behind the mirrors and spontaneously morph into their Crimson Guardsmen uniforms (hologram projectors, maybe?). As if that weren't enough, the encircled Crimson Guardsmen somehow shoot at Ripcord and Candy *through* the mirrors without shattering a single one (or, for that matter, nailing each other). Oh, and they spontaneously turn blind, failing to realize that their quarry have, in fact, long since hoofed it.

NOW YOU KNOW... Rock 'n Roll doesn't advocate signing up for the Army (or getting married, for that matter) purely as a means of "escaping" from home. Too often, you're just running away from yourself.

The Joe WHALE's armor is concentrated up front, so for pity's sake, don't veer from your target. P.S. Beware cresting waves that wash out your boat's Gatling guns.

COMIC TIE-INS Cobra Commander locks himself in his office, likely sorting out conflicting emotions regarding his son Billy's attempt on his life (*G.I. Joe* #33), leading to Billy's trial in #38. The Commander allows Major Bludd, illicitly released by the Baroness in #28, to run free on some feeble excuse of Bludd "picking up the administrative slack."

Bludd vanishes from the series – largely because there's too many characters competing for stage time – finally reappearing in #57.

Issue #35 essentially contains a repeat of the Dreadnoks' vehicle-carving rampage at McGuire Air Force Base (*G.I. Joe* #30).

Ripcord's girlfriend Candy (a.k.a. Bongo the Balloon Bear) first appeared in *G.I. Joe* #33. She returns in #38, utterly floored to learn her father's a Cobra Crimson Guardsman. Cobra's grand undertaking in the South Atlantic comes to fruition in #40-#41. Fred Smith II further menaces Snake-Eyes and Stalker in #42.

CHARACTER PROFILE: JOES

• *Deep Six:* He (sadly) never touches hot cocoa.

• *Flint:* He previously worked with Duke, who recommended Flint's transfer to the Joes. Roadblock considers Flint "mean in a firefight."

• *Footloose:* Freaks at Wild Bill's wild flying.

• *Rock 'n Roll:* Hasn't been home to Malibu in three years.

• *Scarlett:* Kindly keeps a spare rubber mask for Snake-Eyes in her purse (some women have lipstick, others mascara, others rubber masks for their hideously disfigured boyfriends…).

CHARACTER PROFILE: COBRA

• *Ripper:* Once got run off the road by a Chevy – and therefore can't stand 'em.

• *Tomax and Xamot:* Like their TV counterparts, the comic book Crimson Twins are highly gymnastic. Unlike their TV selves, who were merely empathic, the comic twins share a blatantly telepathic bond and can see through each others' eyes.

• *Zartan:* Evidently a genius with laser optics, incorporating large holographic projectors into his prized bike and smaller ones into his costume.

HOT WHEELS G.I. Jane: Its defensive radar-directed 30 mm Gatling guns intercept missiles.

• *Cobra HISS Tanks:* Designed for a single operator. Logically enough, your right foot controls the tank's right track and your left foot controls the left track – leaving your hands free to shoot stuff.

• *Zartan's Bike:* Possesses advanced hologram-casting devices, although the range is limited.

THE COMMAND DECISION "Dreadnoks on the Loose!" (#35) deserves merit for indulging in a surprisingly runamuck road spree, with the Dreadnoks showing about as much restraint as Animal from "The Muppet Show." Enjoy the ride.

Unfortunately, the subsequent two issues lack #35's sense of balance, diving into a quagmire of mindless fighting. The sub-plot with Fred Smith vs. Snake-Eyes and Scarlett briefly snags interest, but overall issues #36 and #37 merely fill in the gap between two major storyarcs. Toss 'em.

G.I. Joe #38 to #43

Titles: *"Judgments" (#38), "Walk Through the Jungle" (#39), "Hydrofoil" (#40), "Strategic Diplomacy" (#41), "Ties That Bind" (#42), "Crossroads" (#43)*
Release Dates: *Aug. 1985 to Jan. 1986*
Art: *Rod Whigham*

BATTLE ROSTER *Joes:* Snake-Eyes, Stalker, Ripcord, Gung Ho, Roadblock, Recondo, Duke, Lady Jaye, Blowtorch, Mutt, Cover Girl, Barbecue, Doc, Tripwire, Major General Austin; *Cobra:* Cobra Commander, Storm Shadow, Destro, Fred Smith II, Zartan, the Dreadnoks, Tomax and Xamot, the Baroness, Major Bludd, Firefly; *Other:* Billy, the Soft Master, Candy, Dr. Burkhart.

FIRST APPEARANCES *Joes:* Shipwreck (sailor, #40); *Cobra:* Professor Appel (Crimson Guardsman, #38), Scrap Iron (armament expert, #43).

DEATHS *Other:* Billy (apparent, #43), the Soft Master, Candy (#43).

MISSION BRIEF ***Issue #38:*** Cobra Commander hauls his would-be assassin son Billy before a Cobra board of inquiry, hoping to learn the names of Billy's accomplices. When Billy refuses to squeal on the Baroness and Major Bludd, Cobra Commander authorizes use of the late Dr. Venom's brainwave scanner. Unfortunately, Billy's memories start revealing too much information about his father's past, forcing Cobra Commander to end the experiment. But Storm Shadow commends Billy for refusing to betray his partners, acknowledging the boy's integrity and honor.

While Cobra Commander pauses to re-think his strategy, Storm Shadow – having abandoned all hope of identifying the Hard Master's killer while in Cobra's employ – breaks Billy out of a detention block. Working together, Storm Shadow and Billy flawlessly escape from Springfield.

Meanwhile, Hawk prepares a Stalker-led quartet of Joes to enter the war-torn country of Sierra Gordo and rescue the sole survivor of a massacred negotiation team – Dr. Adele Burkhart (previously saved by the Joes in issue #1). Accordingly, Stalker's group airdrops into Sierra Gordo, meeting up with Joe jungle trooper Recondo.

Finally, the Joes backtrack clues at the Cobra-run Arbco Bros. Circus (#37) to a pedestrian Staten Island house. But when a pack of Joes besiege the dwelling, Crimson Guard Commanders Tomax and Xamot roar to freedom on a Cobra ATV, accompanied by a Crimson Guardsman named Professor Appel. Seconds later, Ripcord's pseudo-girlfriend Candy (a.k.a. Bongo the Balloon Bear) drives up to the house – staggered to learn that her father, Professor Appel, is a Cobra agent.

Issue #39: Stalker's group swiftly rescues Dr. Burkhart from a Cobra-funded revolutionary camp in Sierra Gordo. Meanwhile, working from a hideout concealed in a disused Manhattan water tank, Storm Shadow begins teaching young Billy ninja skills. And last but not least, Duke turns gravely concerned by Coast Guard charts, tidal tables and military survey maps of New Orleans found in Professor Appel's house, dispatching several Joes to the Big Easy to uncover Cobra's newest plan.

Issue #40: Pentagon officials grow concerned about preserving the Constitutional rights of Candy (who's still being held for Joe questioning about her father's activities) and keeping captive Dreadnok Buzzer secure. Accordingly, Hawk smolders – but complies – when his superiors force him to relinquish Buzzer and Candy to military police. But once outside the Pit II, Buzzer kills his police escort – fleeing with Candy as his hostage.

In the Gulf of Mexico near New Orleans, the Joes set up an offshore portable headquarters, unaware that Cobra deliberately leaked Professor Appel's files to lure the Joes into the region. Monitoring events from a submarine, the Cobra leadership and Professor Appel enter the final phase of their grand scheme. Using automated systems embedded in a fortified bunker on the Gulf floor, Cobra unleashes a ultrasonic attack that wipes out all marine life in the region, threatening to make the entire Gulf a dead zone.

Needing a nuclear-level explosive to breach the bunker's defenses – but unwilling to risk radiation fallout – the Joes annihilate the bunker with a 200-ton high explosive charge. But as Professor Appel predicted, the Joes' detonation triggers a major faultline – causing a massive upheaval on the Gulf floor.

Issue #41: Bracing themselves, the assembled Joes and Cobras ride out a series of tidal waves and tremors as the detonated fault line hauls up a large landmass in the Gulf of Mexico. As the newborn island is located in international waters, well beyond the three-mile limit of any sovereign state, Cobra immediately overruns the island with troops. Minutes later, Cobra representatives arrive in Washington D.C., Mexico City and Havana, lobbying to get the island recognized as a Cobra-run nation-state.

The Joes bring the combined might of their organization to bear, hoping to tear Cobra off the island before it gains nationhood. But just as the Joes come within a whisker's hair of a makeshift Cobra headquarters, American, Cuban and Mexican officials grant the Cobra nation official status as "Cobra Island." The Joes leave with their tails between their legs, forced to withdraw beyond Cobra Island's three-mile limit, leaving Cobra Commander to chortle about what one can accomplish with lawyers and money.

Issue #42: Major General Austin blows his top over the Cobra Island debacle, but suddenly suffers a massive heart attack and is rushed to a hospital. Snake-Eyes and Stalker drive Hawk into Washington to visit the general, but Fred Smith II passes the Joes along the way and tags their vehicle with a tracking device.

While Hawk attends to General Austin, Snake-Eyes and Stalker decide to pay respects to fallen comrades at the Vietnam Memorial. Stalker recalls a fateful recon patrol (mentioned in #26) involving himself, Snake-Eyes and Storm Shadow. On that occasion, three of their comrades – Ramon Escobedo, Dick Saperstein and Wade Collins – perished, but Snake-Eyes oddly fails to locate Collins' name on the deceased roster. Suddenly, Fred Smith II steps from cover and reveals himself as the "lost" Wade Collins, holding his former colleagues at gunpoint.

Meanwhile, having hitching a ride with Zartan to Springfield (#35), the ninja-trained Soft Master struts into the Cobra-run Springfield Police Department. Bashing the crooked cops within an inch of their lives, the Soft Master hacks into Springfield's main computer network to uncover the identity of the Hard Master's killer.

Elsewhere, the fugitive Buzzer steals a pick-up truck, attempting to return to Cobra Headquarters with Candy as his captive. Fortunately, Candy finds a shotgun in the stolen truck and shoves the weapon in Buzzer's face. Buzzer wisely bails out of the truck, enabling Candy to drive off.

Finally, with Storm Shadow away purchasing groceries, Billy departs to confront his father. Returning home, Storm Shadow finds an apologetic note from Billy and wishes his young charge well.

Issue #43: When Candy's stolen pick-up breaks down, she accepts a lift from a passing car. After also picking up a hitchhiking Billy, the benevolent driver continues on toward Springfield.

Meanwhile, Buzzer returns to Springfield on a train, meeting up with a patrol composed of Firefly and a Cobra armament expert named Scrap Iron. In the Springfield Police Station, the Soft Master discovers the name of his brother's killer and hastily transmits the information to Snake-Eyes. Mission complete, the Soft Master attempts to escape as Springfield's police officers regroup.

Shocked to see the Soft Master whipping the police about like Tickle Me Elmo dolls, Firefly's band tries to intercept, but the ninja master steals a police car and runs rings around them. The Soft Master nearly escapes, but a near-collision crashes the car bearing Candy, Billy and their unnamed driver, rendering them unconscious. The Soft Master lingers to help the injured party, but Scrap-Iron shimmies up a telephone pole and fires his portable missile launcher. Unwilling to let innocents perish for his deeds, the Soft Master flings himself in front of Scrap Iron's missile – perishing instantly.

Seconds later, Firefly signals to Scrap Iron to eliminate all witnesses, authorizing a second missile that eradicates the car containing Billy, Candy and their driver.

Back in Washington, Wade Collins explains how he survived and spent two years in a Vietnam prison when Snake-Eyes and Stalker left him for dead (#26). Angered at his colleagues for leaving him, Collins finally returned home to an American that viewed the Vietnam vets as an embarrassment. Virtually unemployable, Wade found purpose in Cobra, studying its philosophies and undergoing the plastic surgery to become one of the identical "Fred Smith"-series Crimson Guardsmen.

Stalker slowly convinces Wade to abandon his hatred and appreciate the gift he's been given in the late Fred Smith's family. Wade returns to Fred's wife and children, ashamedly conceding that he'll never be more than a shadow of the real thing. However, the family embraces Wade as their own, abandoning their Cobra affiliation and setting off to find a new, happier life together.

MEMORABLE MOMENTS Stalker insists that Dr. Burkhardt's uppity, self-centered and pretentious – but he admires her inner steel. He doesn't agree with Burkhardt's anti-military views, stressing that the Joes must fight for the Constitution's guarantee of free speech.

On streets of New York City, martial arts novice Billy frightens away three muggers – with a hungry look.

Shipwreck cries out during an assault: "Those blasted Cobras are tearing my base apart!", compelling axe-wielding firefighter Barbecue to reply: "No, they're shooting holes in it and setting it on fire... *I'm* the one who's tearing it apart!"

Scarlet comments that, "Certain Joes who will remain unnamed, like Clutch, have all the sensitivity of a rabid hyena."

An infantry soldier plants the Cobra flag on Cobra Island – signaling an unending political storm for the Joes.

The kind-hearted (albeit highly lethal) Soft Master warns Springfield police that if they persist in giving him trouble, "... it will hurt!" After properly thumping the cops, the Soft Master pauses and notes, "Tsk tsk tsk... violence only brings violence back on itself. I've broken a fingernail..."

During the fracas to stop the Soft Master, Firefly's troupe fires a missile barrage that nails a Tom Turkey truck, showering the Cobra agents with uncooked turkeys.

The Soft Master sacrifices his life to save innocents. A few pages later, the "lost" Wade Collins regains a family (proving that in the midst of death, there's life).

LOVE AND WAR The captive Buzzer regales Candy with one of the Top Ten Worst Pick-Up Lines of All Time: "I'm Buzzer and I love you! Ride with me on my pan-head Harley and I shall sweep you away to... New South Wales!" Later, Candy discourages Buzzer's advances in the traditional fashion (with a shotgun).

ASS-WHUPPINGS Storm Shadow kills two guards to free Billy – a pretty dramatic way of tendering his Cobra resignation. The Crimson Twins spray Duke and Lady Jaye with bullets, but Kevlar vests save the Joes' lives.

Dreadnok Buzzer strangles one military policeman with his handcuffs, then hits the brakes and slams another through a windshield. Candy frees herself by smashing Buzzer's glasses and firing a shotgun burst near his head. (Buzzer: "Whoa, girl! That was close! Those double-ought pellets went by so close I could count them!")

Recondo brings three of his friends, all Tucaro Indians, along as back-up to rescue Dr. Burkhart, but they're killed in the crossfire. Somewhat balancing the scales, Recondo takes out Burkhart's interrogator, two guards and two snipers in an unspecified (but obviously brutal) fashion.

Joe sailor Shipwreck guts a Cobra hydrofoil pilot with his tow cable hook. In similar fashion, Joe firefighter Barbecue does in a HISS tank pilot with an axe. A tidal wave hammers Joes aboard the WHALE and the *USS Flagg*, eliminating a stand-by squadron of Skystrikers.

Cobra hydrofoil pilots singe Snow Job and Ripcord with bullets. Joe pilot Ace pursues a RATTLER jet, forcing Cobra troops to annihilate their own plane rather than give Ace an opening to level their position. Gung Ho and Roadblock hoist a piece of timber to thump the Crimson Twins. The Soft Master tosses about members of the Springfield Police Department.

In a Vietnam flashback, Stalker, Snake-Eyes and Storm Shadow escape harm while AK-47 fire kills their partner Ramon. Another colleague, Dickie, dies stepping on a land-mine. Wade Collins also takes some bullets but ultimately lives.

The death of the Soft Master makes for one of the series' most notable kills. Although less extraordinary, Candy's demise spurs the next half-year of comics. Billy survives Scrap-Iron's assault, we later learn, but loses an eye and a leg.

GOOFS With Buzzer presumably right behind her, Candy tells the driver who offers her a lift that she's in "no hurry" to flee from Springfield. Incoming *G.I. Joe* artist Rod Whigham draws Candy with shoulder-length hair, but his predecessor, Frank Springer, rendered her with short hair. (Author's Note: Actually, Springer made Candy's hair look like a dollop of cottage cheese, but let's not quibble.)

A pre-plastic surgery Wade Collins doesn't look all that much different from his post-op (Fred Smith II) self.

NOW YOU KNOW... Storm Shadow imparts to Billy that acquiring martial arts means using it less. By mastering violence, one can abolish it. Don't freak out if your overheated Gatling gun barrels glow red. It's not unheard of for the barrels to turn white-hot or even translucent (you'll see the bullets zipping through like black hornets).

COMIC TIE-INS For details on the history of Wade Collins (a.k.a. Fred Smith II), see *G.I. Joe* #26 sidebar, "Snake-Eyes: The Vietnam Years." Wade replaced the late Fred Smith in *G.I. Joe* #32 and here sports a fever, recovering from his dip into the Hudson River in #36. Wade finally leaves with the original Fred Smith's family but reappears to help Snake-Eyes in *G.I. Joe* #95. It's suggested that the family's true surname is "Broca," although it seems too coincidental that it's also the name of Cobra's base of operations in Broca Beach, NJ (*G.I. Joe* #81 and onward).

Cobra Commander opens this story arc putting his son Billy on trial for his failed assassination attempt (*G.I. Joe* #33). Billy tried to off Daddy with a .357 Magnum loaded with mercury-tipped explosive bullets. Billy's presumed dead here at Scrap Iron's hands, but turns up, comatose, in #55.

The Soft Master hitched a lift from Zartan in *G.I. Joe* #35, reaching Springfield to find the murderer of his brother, the Hard Master (detailed in #26). Snake-Eyes receives the Soft Master's message – which names Zartan as the killer – in #45.

Rock 'n Roll caught Buzzer in *G.I. Joe* #35, but the Dreadnok here escapes.

The Joes previously rescued Dr. Burkhart's ass in *G.I. Joe* #1. A fugitive Roadblock seeks the good doctor's help in #77.

General Austin's heart attack forces him to resign as the Joes' Pentagon-level supervisor, prompting Hawk's promotion to Brigadier General in *G.I. Joe* #45. Ripcord searches for Candy in the same issue, unaware of her death.

Sierra Gordo's puppet military dictatorship collapsed after the Joes first left in *G.I. Joe* #15, with extremists, crackpots and "plain vanilla" psychos jousting for control.

Used on Billy in #38, Dr. Venom's brainwave scanner first appeared in *G.I. Joe* #10. Dr. Mindbender acquires it for the Serpentor project in #49. Newbie Joe jungle trooper Recondo only stayed at the Pit II for a week (*G.I. Joe* #33) before shipping out to reconnoiter Sierra Gordo.

CHARACTER PROFILE: COBRA

• *Cobra Commander:* He's trying to show strong leadership by not letting Billy off the hook despite their familial ties.

• *Firefly:* He's astonished by the level of Dreadnok Buzzer's repulsiveness.

• *Zartan:* Has extensive connections in the criminal world, enough to learn about Cobra's classified brainwave scanner.

CHARACTER PROFILE: OTHER

• *Billy:* Storm Shadow teaches Billy a sixth sense called "the inner eye" (which might explain how Billy forecasts his fiery injuries in #43). Billy wishes Storm Shadow, rather than Cobra Commander, were his father. He can sometimes defeat Storm Shadow at "mental chess," a game played exactly like normal chess except that you have to remember the piece positions.

• *Candy:* Candy's full name is (groan, agony) "Candy Appel." She was genuinely clueless about her father's Cobra activities, thinking he meekly ran the "balloon bear" business.

ORGANIZATIONS *Cobra:* Cobra Commander began his business career by developing a cover company named "Arbco." Refusing to knuckle to government pressure, Cobra Commander instigated a pyramid sales scheme, using it to bypass government restrictions and thereby expand his terrorist and extortion activities. He likely chose the name "Cobra" out of a desire to wrap the world in his organization's "coils." Cobra uniforms mask the individuality of Cobra troopers.

• *Snake-Eyes' Vietnam Platoon:* Wade Collins often took point with the suppressed Swedish K (Karl Gustav 9mm Machine Gun). Snake-Eyes wielded an M-60 while Stalker possessed a starlight scope on his Mike-one-six.

PLACES TO GO Cobra Island: Functions like a legitimate country, with diplomatic immunities, tax shelters, printed money and import duties.

• *Fort Wadsworth:* The Joes sometimes enter and exit through a false wall at Fort Wadsworth's rear, afraid to attract too much attention by using the main gate.

• *Sierra Gordo:* The CIA, Russians, Cubans and Chinese all sponsor various revolutionary groups in Sierra Gordo (some revolutionary cells have multiple benefactors).

THE COMMAND DECISION Both a departure point and a story that won't let you up for air until it's finished, "Judgments" (#38) readily hits high gear, crystallizing Storm Shadow's defection – a plot thread more than a year in the making – and taking Billy's character to new heights.

Moreso the stuff of filler, issue #39 features the Joes *again* rescuing Dr. Burkhart after a drawn-out escape (whoopie). Thankfully, issues #40-#41, pick up the slack, helping polish the diplomacy minded Cobra into more than just a bunch of trigger-happy thugs.

Finally, "Ties that Bind" (#42) and "Crossroads" (#43) provide some of the series' most unpredictable reading, redeeming a villain (Fred Smith II) while offing the extremely honorable Soft Master. The fact that "Crossroads" stands as a personal drama shows how far *G.I. Joe's* progressed from the pap of its early issues and the story remains, thanks to its emotional outcome, among the top Joe stories to love.

G.I. Joe #44

Titles: "Improvisation on a Theme" (#44)
Release Dates: Feb. 1986
Art: Rod Whigham

BATTLE ROSTER *Joes:* Lady Jaye; *Cobra:* Destro, the Baroness.

FIRST APPEARANCES *Joes:* Bazooka (bazooka soldier), Airtight (hostile environment), Heavy Metal (MAULER tank driver), Crankcase (AWE striker driver); *Cobra:* Dr. Mindbender (master of mind control).

MISSION BRIEF Having developed a new type of biological warfare – a "creeper bomb" that ensnares enemies with quick-growing vines – a vastly intelligent (but decently mad) scientist named Dr. Mindbender approaches Destro and the Baroness about putting his prototype weapons system into full production. Accordingly, Destro's trio proposes testing their creeper offensive by ambushing Lady Jaye and a quartet of freshmen Joes on maneuvers.

Dr. Mindbender's initial creeper bomb attack completely catches Lady Jaye's group unaware, leading to their capture. But needing to guarantee that the creepers aren't a one-trick pony, Destro's trio deposits the Joes into a junkyard. Lady Jaye's squad recovers quickly, dodging attacks from robotic Battle Android Troopers (BATs) bearing more creeper bombs. Finally, Lady Jaye's quintet comes up with the inspired idea of sizzling the creeper vines with battery acid.

The Joes take to the offensive, forcing Destro's trio to abandon their dreams of invading America with fast-growing weeds. The villains take flight aboard a FANG helicopter, leaving Lady Jaye thrilled over her recruits' unexpected field performance.

MEMORABLE MOMENTS Amid the junkyard fracas, Lady Jaye reaches an electro-magnetic crane, hauls a truck into the air and tells her fellows: "I've covering you with a whole crane! Anybody gives you trouble, I'll drop this truck on 'em!" Newbie Joe Airtight scrounges the desert for some scorpions, piles 'em into a first aid kit and hurls it as his opponents – forcing Dr. Mindbender and Destro to turn tail and run from the sudden scorpion attack.

ASS-WHUPPINGS The fall-guy BATs get run over in mass droves. Oh, and Airtight flattens a HISS tank in a car crusher.

PREPOSTEROUS PHYSICS Bazooka gains enough strength to throw a big recoil-less rifle, decapitating an android trooper.

TV TIE-INS Dr. Mindbender's creeper plants strikingly (and not in a good way) resemble the rampant creeper vines from "The Revenge of Cobra."

CHARACTER PROFILE: JOES

• *Airtight:* Despite habitually wading through hostile environments, Airtight doesn't carry herbicides because they're bad for the environment.

• *Heavy Metal:* He once attended a "Twisted Sister" concert.

STUFF YOU NEED *Dr. Mindbender's Creeper Bombs:* In theory, the creepers seem like a sensible idea (but then, in theory, communism works). They're more cost-effective than you might think, completely derived from natural ingredients. They also emit pollen that renders enemy soldiers unconscious. A single BAT can carry a creeper bomb, allowing for easy delivery in cities or battlefields. However, in practice, the creepers aren't terribly effective once you discover that simple gas masks block their pollen and fire or acid burns 'em to a crisp. Dr. Mindbender hoped Destro might license the creeper bomb design for production in his weapons factories while the Baroness convinced Cobra Commander to purchase it for Cobra, but it came to naught.

• *Cobra BATs:* They're programmed not to hit each other, meaning you're often better off running between them.

THE COMMAND DECISION Entertaining despite a goofball premise ("Oh, no! It's attack of the killer creeper vines!"), "Improvisation on a Theme" makes for a sweet little interlude, expertly introducing four Joes and Dr. Mindbender along the way.

G.I. Joe #45 to #50

Titles: "In Search of Candy" (#45), "Who's Who on Cobra Island" (#46), "Sea Duel" (#47), "Slaughter" (#48), "Serpentor" (#49), "The Battle of Springfield" (#50)
Release Dates: Mar. to Aug. 1986
Art: Rod Whigham

BATTLE ROSTER *Joes:* Ripcord, Snake-Eyes, Storm Shadow, Hawk, Flint, Gung Ho, Scarlett, Duke, Stalker, Spirit, Beach-Head, Wet Suit, Major General Austin; *Cobra:* Zartan, Cobra Commander, Destro, Dr. Mindbender, the Baroness, the Dreadnoks, Tomax and Xamot, Professor Appel.

FIRST APPEARANCES *Joes:* Quick Kick (silent weapons, #45), Alpine (mountain trooper, #45), Sgt. Slaughter (drill instructor, #48), Leatherneck (marine, #49), Lift-Ticket and Slip-Stream (both pilots, #49); *Cobra:* Serpentor (Cobra emperor, #49), Zarana (Zartan's sister, #50).

DEATHS *Joes:* Storm Shadow (apparent, #47); *Cobra:* Professor Appel (#46).

MISSION BRIEF ***Issue #45:*** Desperately needing intelligence on Cobra Island – but unable to blatantly violate its newfound sovereignty – Hawk authorizes Ripcord and Ace to race by Cobra Island on a Skystriker reconnaissance flight. But as Hawk predicted, Ripcord – concluding that Dreadnok Buzzer took Candy back to Cobra Island after his escape from the Pit II (*G.I. Joe* #40) – stuns Ace by bailing out to search for her.

In the hospital, Major General Austin questions Hawk's choice of assigning the emotionally charged Ripcord to serve as Ace's co-pilot. Hawk merely shrugs, slyly commenting that the Joes now "have no choice" but to send a team and forcibly grab the wayward Joe. Realizing that such a team could return from a Cobra Island "rescue mission" with covert information, General Austin congratulates Hawk for his craftiness.

Still recovering from his heart attack, Austin resigns as G.I. Joe's top leader. At Austin's recommendation, the President and Joint Chiefs of Staff promote Hawk to Brigadier General, expanding his authority as G.I. Joe's commander-in-chief.

Back at the Pit II, Snake-Eyes receives the Soft Master's last transmission from Springfield – an eye-popping communiqué that pegs Zartan as the Hard Master's murderer. Snake-Eyes swiftly travels to New York City and shares his findings with Storm Shadow, motivating the two bloodthirsty ninjas to salivate for vengeance. After stealing a RATTLER jet from a Cobra safehouse, Snake-Eyes and Storm Shadow depart to hunt down Zartan.

On Cobra Island, Zartan and Professor Appel examine radar reports, curious to know why a Joe Skystriker wobbled as if ejecting something. Worried that a ninja's stalking him, Zartan takes a bow and arrow to search the Cobra Island beach. There, Zartan comes across Ripcord, leading to a lengthy firefight. Finally, Zartan uses his camouflage talent to approach Ripcord and thrash the Joe paratrooper unconscious.

Issue #46: Relishing his victory, Zartan hurriedly exchanges clothes with Ripcord – leaving "Zartan" unconscious and bleeding in the sand while "Ripcord" awaits rescue. Hoping to discover Joe Headquarters' location, Zartan holographically changes his face to resemble Ripcord and looks for signs of a Joe pick-up squad. Nearby, a Joe quartet led by Flint makes a covert beach landing, taking several photographs of Cobra Island's fortifications. Mission accomplished, the four Joes locate "Ripcord" and head out to sea.

Meanwhile, Professor Appel searches for Zartan and finds Ripcord dressed in the Cobra shape-changer's clothes. Suitably fooled, Appel takes "Zartan" for treatment at a "Terror-Drome" – a mini-fortress built around a Cobra Firebat jet launch facility. Simultaneously, Snake-Eyes and Storm Shadow covertly land at the airport, spotting "Zartan" on Appel's transport and marking the shape-changer for death.

In the Terror-Drome, Professor Appel turns shocked to realize that "Zartan" is actually a Joe member Ripcord awakens and compares notes with Appel, but Snake-Eyes and Storm Shadow instigate a killing spree, trying to murder their way to Zartan.

Deeming Ripcord the best chance of finding his missing daughter – and fearing the ninjas can't be stopped in their slash fest – Appel loads Ripcord into the Firebat and programs it for automated take-off. Storm Shadow bursts into the launch bay, preparing to hack "Zartan" to pieces, but Appel unwisely blocks the ninja's trajectory with his own body. As Storm Shadow cuts Appel in half, the Firebat roars upward and Ripcord escapes.

Issue #47: In Springfield, Ripcord's Firebat lands on automatic, compelling the Dreadnoks to mistake the Joe for Zartan and take their "fallen leader" to a local hospital.

Near the international waters that mark Cobra Island's territory, a Joe WHALE hovercraft picks up Flint's group. However, an incoming helicopter containing Destro and the Baroness happens to spot the Joes. Cutter nails the 'copter with heat-seeking missiles, forcing Destro's crew to perform a terror-stricken landing. Destro's cadre lands safely but crumples every parked vessel on the Cobra Island airfield, crushing Snake-Eyes and Storm Shadow's hope of escaping in a stolen aircraft.

General Hawk arrives to personally supervise the situation, allowing Doc to drug "Ripcord" and send him to the Pit II for medical treatment. On the Cobra Island beachfront, Snake-Eyes and Storm Shadow hijack a hydrofoil, but Cobra torpedo transports damage the stolen vessel, tossing the ninjas into shark-infested waters. Hawk's team pulls Snake-Eyes to safety, but after hacking his way through a school of sharks, Storm Shadow finds himself alone on the beach.

Suddenly, the Baroness rolls up in a HISS tank and confronts the tattered, exhausted ninja. Taking no chances, the Baroness empties her pistol into Storm Shadow's chest. Snake-Eyes despairs to see Storm Shadow pitch forward dead, but unable to help their fallen ally, the Joes withdraw from Cobra waters.

Issue #48: On Cobra Island, Dr. Mindbender places Storm Shadow's corpse in cold storage while a mourning Snake-Eyes and crew return to the Pit II. But to everyone's confusion, "Ripcord" (a.k.a. Zartan) awakens in the Joe infirmary and hurriedly adopts several disguises, attempting to bluff his way out with the Pit II's location. But as Duke puts the Pit II on full security alert, Sgt. Slaughter, a new Joe training officer, reports for duty.

Zartan nearly escapes up an air vent, but Gung Ho pursues the Cobra goon and brawls with him through the Ft. Wadsworth reading room. To heighten the confusion, Zartan holographically disguises himself as a mirror image of Gung Ho. Sgt. Slaughter solves the problem by randomly grabbing a "Gung Ho" and punching his lights out. Thankfully, Slaughter guesses correctly and renders Zartan unconscious.

While the Joes stand down, Cobra makes the veiled threat of allying itself with America's mortal enemies. Faced with the possibility of a foreign power constructing a missile system on Cobra Island – within hair-raising striking distance of the American heartland – the U.S. government formalizes diplomatic ties with Cobra Island. As a result, the Pentagon's top policy makers – a machinistic panel of generals known only as "the Jugglers" – order Hawk to cease and desist all Joe operations concerning Cobra Island.

Issue #49: Hoping to generate a military genius capable of crushing the Joes, Cobra steals the corpses of 10 famed military leaders, intending to combine their DNA into an "ultimate soldier." Working from Springfield's Museum of Antiquities, Dr. Mindbender places the leaders' cadavers into genetic solution tanks, intending to combine their attributes and bring a faceless, humanoid simulacrum to life. Purely for the sake of adding "fresh meat," Dr. Mindbender adds Storm Shadow's frozen body to the genetic stew.

Elsewhere in Springfield, Ripcord – still mistaken for Zartan – phones Joe Headquarters and hurriedly relays Springfield's location. Unfortunately, Cobra telecommunications experts detect Ripcord's phone call and alert the Dreadnoks, leading to Ripcord's capture.

Armed with the location of Cobra's main domestic base, Hawk marshals his organization and restores all desk-bound Joes to active status. Back in Springfield, Dr. Mindbender throws his machinery into high gear, coaxing the simulacrum to reshape into a humanoid form. As the simulacrum continues its development, the Dreadnoks arrive at the Museum to interrogate Ripcord with the late Dr. Venom's brainwave scanner – confirming that the Joes are aware of Springfield's position.

The Joes send a strike team to blow up Springfield's power station while massive strike and security teams prepare to carve their way through the Cobra-dominated town. With Cobra Commander stationed on Cobra Island, Destro and the Baroness collaborate on how to evacuate Springfield before the Joes arrive in force. But to everyone's shock, the simulacrum rises from his genetic bath – fully encoded via a historical program with recent events – and outlines the Joes' most probable battle-plan in breathtaking detail.

Adopting the name of "Serpentor," the newborn military strategist volunteers to stem the Joe advance while Destro and the Baroness evacuate Springfield's populace. Destro agrees, putting a bare minimum of Cobra troopers and vehicles at Serpentor's command just as G.I. Joe security and strike teams flood into Springfield. Serpentor rallies his small force, intending to win the day despite the odds – and emerge from the conflict as the emperor of Cobra.

Issue #50 ("The Battle of Springfield"): Led by Stalker, a Joe assault team tears a bloody path through Springfield, leaving the security and strike teams to seal off the city and

MISCELLANEOUS STUFF!

THE SPECIAL MISSIONS PREVIEW

To preview the new *G.I. Joe Special Missions* spin-off series, the Marvel creative team split *G.I. Joe* #50 between the finale of the Springfield invasion story arc ("The Battle of Springfield") and a *Special Missions* back-up story named "Best Defense." Written by Larry Hama and drawn by Herb Trimpe, "Best Defense" quickly establishes the flair of *Special Missions* – with Flint, Beach-Head and Lady Jaye using extreme cleverness to paste a trio of airplane hijackers – although it somewhat jarrs readers (ourselves included) wound up by the epic clash for Springfield. Read in modern times, "Best Defense" grows on you, although Trimpe's sketchy, undefined art waters down the mix.

• **"Best Defense," G.I. Joe #50** – Government officials are flummoxed when three hijackers commandeer a Russian airliner containing the American chess team, then mysteriously fail to make any demands. While Hawk and his Joes quickly pin the crime on followers of the late Leon Trotsky, a Soviet Union co-founder later exiled and murdered by Joseph Stalin, Flint, Lady Jaye and Beach-Head sneak onto the hijacked plane when it stops to refuel in Anchorage.

Regrettably, Hawk and Stalker discover that the hijackers – hoping to revenge Trotsky's disgrace and murder upon "Stalin's heirs" – intend to plow the plane into a Soviet chemical weapons depot in Beringovsky, creating a lethal gas cloud that will kill millions of Russians. Flint and Beach-Head neutralize two of the hijackers, leaving Lady Jaye to blow the third – a terminal lunatic named Roger, who's strapped to 50 pounds of C-4 explosive – out the plane's hatch. As the C-4 explosive ignites and smears Roger across the open sky, the hungry Joes return to San Francisco for a steak dinner.

capture its airport. However, Serpentor's stratagems block all of Stalker's moves, forcing the team to run for its life.

Back at the Museum of Antiquities, the genetic solution tanks used to create Serpentor start knitting Storm Shadow's body back together – resurrecting the ex-Cobra ninja to confront the Dreadnoks. Zartan's lackeys just about crap themselves in surprise, but a well-timed Joe attack forces the Dreadnoks – along with Storm Shadow – to flee Springfield.

After the Joes rescue Ripcord, Serpentor's force makes a diversionary charge for the airport – allowing the Destro and the Baroness to coordinate the real evacuation from Springfield High School. Having already destroyed all Cobra-related documents, the Springfield townsfolk load themselves into massive transport helicopters – hidden in underground tunnels beneath Springfield – and depart for the safety of Cobra Island.

To the Baroness' surprise, Destro takes the last two helicopters and rescues Serpentor's forces. As the Cobra leadership escapes, the Joes can only watch helplessly as pre-set charges detonate Springfield's underground tunnel network – erasing all proof that Cobra ever inhabited the city.

Hawk's victory sours when it dawns on him that thanks to Cobra's quick thinking, the Joes have just demolished a seemingly "innocent" town. Hawk congratulates the Joes for a fine performance, but inwardly steels himself for the inevitable inquiry from the Pentagon.

Meanwhile, Cobra Commander studies reports of Serpentor's battle prowess – growing disquieted to realize that Serpentor, who more truly embodies the "ultimate military leader" than "the ultimate soldier," will almost certainly try to hack Cobra Commander to pieces once he lands on Cobra Island.

MEMORABLE MOMENTS Issue #45 seemingly ends with Ripcord stumbling up after his tussle with Zartan, raving about how he's heading off to infiltrate the enemy's headquarters. But in one of the series' greatest japes, the reader learns on the first page of #46 that the fight's victor is actually Zartan – who's cleverly disguised as Ripcord (number of Mad Norwegian Press editors who fell for this gag back in the day: 3-2).

Storm Shadow and Snake-Eyes butcher their way into Cobra Commander's central chamber, leading to Storm Shadow's ice-cold demand: "I want [Zartan]. Give him to me." Later, during a tussle in shark-infested waters, Storm Shadow tells Cobra divers: "Fight hard! Even if you live through the sharks… you'll still have me to contend with!"

The smelly Dreadnoks hang out at "the Tiki Lounge," where Torch munches on little paper cocktail umbrellas. Ripcord's escape from Springfield is cut short when a little girl – Cobra-brainwashed from an early age – shoves a .357 Magnum into Ripcord's face. The child explains that the Magnum makes an entry wound like an extra navel and an exit wound like a pot pie, then turns Ripcord over to his pursuers with a cheerful: "You're welcome, Mr. Dreadnok, Sir!"

In a top dramatic moment, Serpentor motivates his small task force to embark on their "holding action" (i.e. suicide mission) against the Joes, rhetorically whipping his crew into a battle frenzy. And amid the cheering Cobra troops, a satiated Serpentor mutters to himself: "Soldiers never change… they love to hear the same speeches."

LOVE AND WAR As Gung Ho brawls with Zartan and tears up the Ft. Wadsworth reading room, an exceptionally geeky chaplain's assistant cries out in surprise: "Well, I never!", to which a biting Gung Ho replies: "I'll bet you haven't!"

Destro's acting rather frosty toward the Baroness (*see Character Development*).

ASS-WHUPPINGS Zartan fires off an arrow that holes a Cobra trooper through the chest (whoops) and impales Ripcord's right arm. Ripcord in turn shoots up Zartan's right thigh and left shoulder, although a second arrow volley singes Ripcord's scalp. Zartan finally pounds Ripcord into submission, silencing the Joe's final protests with a few swift kicks.

Storm Shadow and Snake-Eyes slice through Cobra Island troops and bathe in blood like *Mortal Kombat* contestants. Some hapless Cobra techs throw up a blast shield, but Storm Shadow simply leaps over it and chops the fools to pieces.

Cutter gets lucky when his heat seeker missiles plow into Destro's helicopter, forcing the Cobra ship to sloppily land and take out rows of parked RATTLERs and FANGs.

Snake-Eyes grotesquely knifes a shark. Joe mountaineer Alpine empties his carbine into a Cobra search-and-retrieval squad.

With the Pit II on security alert, Heavy Metal, Clutch and Steeler haze the newly arrived Sgt. Slaughter as a potential infiltrator, threatening to search his duffle bag. In turn, Sgt. Slaughter rough-houses his fellows – convincing Heavy Metal's group through sheer force that he's legit.

Destro zaps members of a Mid-Eastern constabulary with his wrist rockets. The Springfield firefight wounds Recondo and Scarlett (although she regains enough strength to shout: "Just give me a rifle and point me in the right direction!"). Serpentor also takes a bullet in the shoulder and, just to prove he's a man (albeit one made from reconstituted DNA), cauterizes the wound with a red-hot knife.

PREPOSTEROUS PHYSICS The Dreadnoks steal an ambulance at one point, burning rubber down a highway. Discouraging a police pursuit, Buzzer opens the ambulance's back door and dices the policemen's car engine with his chainsaw. The problem being: Buzzer must have arms like Plastic Man to reach that far.

GOOFS It's pretty obvious why Zartan steals Ripcord's identity, but moreso puzzling why Zartan gives the unconscious Ripcord his identity rather than just plugging Ripcord between the eyes. It's somewhat forgivable that Professor Appel doesn't immediately recognize Ripcord under a coat of grime and face paint, but it's ridiculous to think that the Dreadnoks wouldn't spot the disguise.

NOW YOU KNOW... If your rifle scope is off-center, simply correct it "by eye" (i.e. If it's shooting to the left, aim to the right a bit.)

Torpedoes have inertial fusing systems, meaning they won't arm until they're a safe distance from their launcher. As a result, you can detonate an incoming torpedo with small-arms fire – if your timing and aim are perfect.

COMIC TIE-INS Ripcord falsely assumes that when Buzzer escaped detention in *G.I. Joe* #40, he kidnapped Candy and returned to Cobra Island. Actually, Candy bit the big one at the hands of Cobra armaments expert Scrap Iron in #43. Billy finally informs Ripcord of Candy's fate in #63.

Zartan is revealed here as the Hard Master's killer, ending a mystery started in *G.I. Joe* #26. Cobra Commander also pegs Zartan as the assassin during the Cobra Island melee, foreshadowing the shape-changer's origin story in #84. To virtually nobody's surprise, Storm Shadow continues stalking Zartan in #85.

The Joes reel from the legal ramifications of Cobra becoming a legitimate nation (*G.I. Joe* #41). Major General Austin resigns after suffering a heart attack in #43, although he helped formulate "Plan Alpha," a contingency arrangement crafted since the Joe team's formation (before *G.I. Joe* #1), that allowed for Hawk's rapid-fire promotion

Hawk preps for the Springfield operation by reinstating the original Joes (mostly relegated to desk jobs in *G.I. Joe* #33) to active service. The Pentagon brigade of generals known as "the Jugglers" view the Joe invasion of Springfield with about as much fondness as changing the taste of Coke, ultimately shutting down the Joes in #52.

After fleeing Springfield in this story arc's climax, the Dreadnoks and Storm Shadow arrive at their New Jersey gas station hideout (first seen in *G.I. Joe* #30) and meet Zartan's sister Zarana. Upon learning of her brother's capture, Zarana rescues her hapless sibling in #51. Issue #52 better explains how Storm Shadow survived his "death" at the Baroness' hand (#47). Cobra Commander fails to assassinate Serpentor in *G.I. Joe* #52, sparking a long-running feud that later erupts into full-fledged civil war between Serpentor and Cobra Commander II in #73.

Dr. Mindbender adapted the late Dr. Venom's brainwave scanner (*G.I. Joe* #10) to aid in Serpentor's creation. Issue #97 suggests that Dr. Mindbender's gizmos can also clone people. Indeed, a carbon copy of Mindbender himself awakens in #140.

MISCELLANEOUS STUFF!

THE INVASION OF SPRINGFIELD

Sharpening the whole of G.I. Joe as a well-tuned weapon against Springfield (issue #49), Hawk splits his forces into an assault team, a strike team and a security team.

The assault team includes the sneakiest and nastiest Joe members (i.e. the ones you least want to meet in an alley), assigned to cut off Springfield's power, communications and water supplies – and shred anyone who tries to stop them. While the assault team wreaks havoc, the strike and security teams jointly capture the Springfield airport. Afterward, the security team covers the airport and cordons off all roads out of Springfield, while the strike team moves to capture the main Cobra headquarters.

- **Assault Team Members:** Stalker, Snake-Eyes, Scarlett, Quick Kick, Recondo, Spirit, Torpedo, Beach-Head and Leatherneck.
- **Security Team Members:** Duke, Steeler, Grunt, Rock 'n Roll, Flash, Gung Ho, Trip-Wire, Short-Fuse, Breaker, Mutt and Junkyard, Snow Job, Zap, Doc, Cover Girl, Roadblock.
- **Strike Team Members:** Hawk, Lady Jaye, Barbecue, Heavy Metal, Flint, Deep Six, Airtight, Footloose, Bazooka, Alpine, Crankcase, Blowtorch and Shipwreck.

CHARACTER PROFILE: JOES

- *Beach-Head and Wet-Suit:* Among the newest Joes and the most qualified for water missions.
- *Ripcord:* His rifle's armed with 7.62 mm NATO ammunition.
- *Shipwreck:* Carries "willy-pete" (a white phosphorous flare).

CHARACTER PROFILE: COBRA

- *Destro and the Baroness:* Honorable Destro somewhat begrudges the Baroness for killing the exhausted, unarmed Storm Shadow, but acknowledges the Baroness' counter-claim that your average ninja is simply too dangerous to take prisoner.

During the Springfield evacuation, the Baroness wonders why Destro's risking his life to protect Cobra for Cobra Commander's benefit. In turn, Destro claims that although he doesn't respect Cobra Commander much, he won't discard his loyalty out-of-hand (which clashes with Destro's attempt on Cobra Commander's life in #14, but let's move on).

• *Major Bludd:* The Baroness thinks fondly of Major Bludd's poetry, but Cobra Commander dubs Bludd a clod who thinks "Proust" rhymes with "Faust."

• *Serpentor:* Serpentor began life as an inert simulacrum of a human being, saturated with the genetic inheritance of multiple military leaders, including Napoleon, Hannibal, Xerxes, William the Conqueror, Genghis Khan, King Sargon (or certainly someone from Sumer, possibly Hammurabi) and Pygmalion. Presumably, World War I British General Haig was also included in the mix. Somewhat for kicks – or possibly to improve Serpentor's combat skills – Dr. Mindbender also tossed Storm Shadow into his genetic broth.

Dr. Mindbender's mega-computers extrapolated the working model of a brain in Serpentor's developing form, then seeded his noggin with a historical catalog of his progenitors' achievements. As such, Serpentor doesn't possess his progenitors' memories but remains acutely aware of their battle tactics. To guarantee Serpentor's allegiance to Cobra, Dr. Mindbender used the brainwave scanner to confer his scientific knowledge and loyalties into the newborn Cobra Emperor. Mindbender coined the name "Serpentor."

Unlike the craven Cobra Commander, Serpentor motivates his troops by dodging bullets with them on the battlefield. Just as importantly, Serpentor endows his troops with loyalty to their comrades – demanding that they can't abandon their brothers-in-arms.

• *Storm Shadow and Serpentor:* Storm Shadow's short-lived bath in Dr. Mindbender's genetic vats allows the ninja to share in the computer program that encoded Serpentor with his historical knowledge. As such, Storm Shadow experiences flashes of various battles fought by Serpentor's progenitors.

• *Zartan:* Zartan used sound amplification equipment to mimic Storm Shadow's "ear that sees" – allowing him to shoot through obstacles. Also, Zartan's high standing with Cobra merited his use of a helicopter.

Zartan's personal hologram emitters allow him to simulate invisibility. There's some disagreement about how much Zartan has to concentrate to maintain his illusions – he dons Ripcord's clothes because it leaves him with "less [hologram space] to concentrate on," but Zartan retains Ripcord's face even while unconscious. Zartan's hologram projectors allow him to instantly disguise himself as Snake-Eyes, Doc, Trip-Wire or Duke. He possesses almost inhuman strength.

ORGANIZATIONS *The Jugglers:* A secret committee of Pentagon generals, dedicated to shifting the inevitable blame for disastrous military operations onto others. In other words, the Jugglers decide which troops to throw into the meat grinder, then create scapegoats to preserve the image of various politicians and military leaders.

STUFF YOU NEED *Cobra Terror-Drome:* An aerial attack defense station able to house and vertically launch a highly maneuverable Firebat jet. The Firebat contains advanced servo-controls and largely operates on automatic – capable of making high-G turns that'd pulp a pilot.

HOT WHEELS *Joe Devil Fish:* Damnably fast three-man sea skimmers. Beware that dropping a Devil Fish into the water from a transport might damage its missile-compressed air launch system.

• *Joe Skystrikers:* Capable of at least Mach 2.

• *Joe WHALE hovercraft:* Armed with electronic counter measures and jamming equipment.

THE COMMAND DECISION A tour de force among G.I. Joe comics, dripping with bloodlust and blessed with an ever-shifting emotional temperature scale that includes compassion (Ripcord's quest to find Candy), sheer ruthlessness (Storm Shadow and Snake-Eyes dismembering everyone in sight) and craftiness (Zartan running the Joes haggard). Hama even makes Serpentor seem appealing, topping the entire mix with the Joes' climactic siege of Springfield. Back in the day, this story kept us salivating for the next installment, and even by today's standards, it's a chunk of comics that makes you feel good to be alive.

G.I. Joe #51 to #53

Titles: *"Thunder Machine" (#51), "Snap Decisions" (#52), "Pit-Fall" (#53)*
Release Dates: *Mar. to Aug. 1986*
Art: *Rod Whigham*

BATTLE ROSTER *Joes:* Sgt. Slaughter, Snake-Eyes, Scarlett, Quick Kick, Flint, Lady Jaye, Hawk; *Cobra:* Serpentor, Cobra Commander, Destro, Zartan, Zarana, Zandar, the Dreadnoks, Tomax and Xamot; *Other:* Storm Shadow.

FIRST APPEARANCES *Joes:* Cross-Country (HAVOC driver, #51), Thunder (self-propelled gun artilleryman, #51), General Hollingsworth (#53), General Ryan (#53), Admiral Dyson (#53); *Cobra:* Zandar (Zartan's brother, #51), Thrasher (Dreadnok, #51).

G.I. Joe #51 to #53

DEATHS *Joes:* General Ryan, Admiral Dyson (#53).

MISSION BRIEF ***Issue #51:*** At Zartan's gas station hideout in New Jersey, the Dreadnoks unexpectedly bump into Zartan's brother Zandar and pink-haired sister Zarana, who grow dismayed to learn of Zartan's incarceration. Thanks to Buzzer's knowledge of the Pit II's location, Zarana and Zandar infiltrate Joe Headquarters and easily free their wayward brother. But unknown to everyone, Storm Shadow secretly enters the Pit II on his own to speak with Snake-Eyes.

Zartan's group steals a top-level Joe communications module on their way out the door, but a new Joe named Cross-Country spots the crooks, giving chase with Sgt. Slaughter in a Joe HAVOC attack vehicle. Zartan's trio rendezvous with an unhinged, strangulation-prone Dreadnok named Thrasher, climbing aboard his rolling Thunder Machine and sparring with the HAVOC through New Jersey.

Cross-Country and Thrasher continually one-up each other, forcing their passengers' hearts up into their throats, but Thrasher finally opens up his Gatling guns and blasts his way through a moving train car – hurling the Thunder Machine through the gap and escaping into the New Jersey swamps.

Issue #52: As Serpentor prepares to land triumphantly on Cobra Island after the Springfield battle, Cobra Commander engages in sweaty panic and rings the airfield with sniper teams – determined to plug Serpentor between the eyes and thwart any further aspirations to power. Easily anticipating the Commander's ploy, Serpentor rolls his helicopter forward and brakes mere inches from Cobra Commander's nose hairs, then leaps out and embraces Cobra Commander like a long-lost puppy.

With the sniper teams unable to fire without shredding Cobra Commander, Serpentor delivers a moving speech to the Springfield refugees – stressing that the noble Cobra Commander would never, *ever* stoop to assassination tactics. As Serpentor's popularity soars, an exasperated Cobra Commander realizes he can't blow away Serpentor without risking a full-scale revolt.

Soon after, Cobra Commander orders Zartan to dress the Dreadnoks as various G.I. Joe members and disembowel Serpentor, hoping to pin the crime on the Joes. Zartan's "Joes" storm Serpentor's quarters, but the Baroness rushes to protect the newfound Cobra emperor's life. Destro intervenes, rounding up the Dreadnoks to keep the Baroness from harm, but Serpentor uses the incident to whip the island's residents into an anti-Joe frenzy. With Zartan providing the Pit II's location, Serpentor advocates an immediate assault on the Joe headquarters.

Meanwhile, Storm Shadow contacts Snake-Eyes and disavows his lifetime of revenge. Putting faith in his long-lost brother, Snake-Eyes allows Storm Shadow use of his High Sierras cabin and lets the ex-Cobra ninja depart. But disturbingly, the Pentagon demands that the Joes account for their botched invasion of Springfield, orders the Pit II sealed and confines all Joe personnel to base.

Issue #53: Hawk uneasily escorts Pentagon officials General Ryan, General Hollingsworth and Admiral Dyson through the emptied Pit II, answering Ryan's charges about the Joes' rampage through the seemingly innocent town of Springfield. General Hollingsworth seems to accept Hawk's story, but the two of them fail to convince Ryan that Cobra represents a legitimate threat.

Meanwhile, Serpentor, Cobra Commander and Destro coordinate a multi-pronged ground assault on the Pit II. While Cobra sniper teams assault the confined Joes within Ft. Wadsworth, Hawk's quartet finds themselves cut off and overrun by Cobra Battle Android Troopers (BATs). Admiral Dyson dies while prematurely detonating a BAT with 20 pounds of C-4 explosive, but Hawk, Hollingsworth and Ryan break open weapons lockers and stand their ground.

Unwilling to let Serpentor grab all the glory, Cobra Commander and Destro volunteer to lead an attack squadron into the Pit II's bowels. Faced with a chance to eliminate Cobra's high command, Hawk's trio seeds the Pit II's central support pillar with explosives. Hawk and Hollingsworth flee down an escape tunnel, but Ryan, his legs crushed by a Cobra grenade, stays behind to trigger the charges.

The resultant explosion collapses the Pit II, killing Ryan and convincing Serpentor to write off Cobra Commander and Destro as a lost cause. While Serpentor's remaining lieutenants gun their way to freedom in the Dreadnok Thunder Machine, Hollingsworth – supplied with ample proof of Cobra's ongoing threat – reinstates the Joes as a mobile battle unit.

MEMORABLE MOMENTS Storm Shadow acknowledges wasting his life on vengeance and appeals to Snake-Eyes for an alternative: "Revenge is the dream of the weak. A soldier knows that no enemy is forever. Help me. Forgive me." Snake-Eyes replies by giving Storm Shadow access to the remains of his High Sierras cabin – forgiving Stormy by remaining his friend.

During a tumultuous game of Chicken between the Thunder Machine and the HAVOC, Thrasher evades the oncoming Joe vehicle by ordering the Dreadnoks to shift their weight, popping the Thunder Machine onto its side two wheels (Thrasher cries out to the nauseous Buzzer: "Don't lose yer cookies yet! The weight loss will throw us off balance!") The Dreadnoks start to sweat when Thrasher announces his main advantage over Cross-Country – "I'm completely nuts!" – then proceeds to hurl the Thunder Machine at a moving train.

Cobra Commander orders Zartan's family to disguise themselves as Joes, so Zartan, Zandar and Zarana respectively burst into the commander's offices dressed as Flint, Stalker and Lady Jaye. But the boobish Dreadnoks – hardly adept at disguise (or much of anything else) – flop onto the scene like the sorriest-looking Joes you've ever seen.

While off-duty Joes amuse themselves playing "darts" with knives and axes in the Ft. Wadsworth tea room, the perturbed, geeky chaplains' assistants storm off and vow to never mend the Joes' torn doilies again.

Finally, the Pit II's destruction closes a chapter in *G.I. Joe* history, opening a new era of grit and determination for America's heroes.

LOVE AND WAR Zartan once commented that his sister Zarana was "extremely cheap" – referring to her financial pettiness – but Buzzer presumed it meant… err, something else.

A brash Flint tries to finagle Lady Jaye into bed, mentioning how he's "good looking, dashing and intelligent." Lady Jaye doesn't fall for it, not even when he dangles the ultimate bait: "I've got the standard [insurance] policy from Uncle Sugar. Interested in being my beneficiary?"

ASS-WHUPPINGS Thrasher unloads the Thunder Machine's twin Gatling guns, making Swiss cheese out of a Joe tank and toppling an AWE Striker jeep. The Joes object to Storm Shadow's infiltration of the Pit II, so Stormy bats Stalker and Barbecue aside and knocks Quick Kick unconscious. Once the dust settles, Barbecue questions Snake-Eyes' motives for letting Storm Shadow escape – so an infuriated Scarlett slugs Barbecue for good measure.

Hawk and the trio of generals scrap a lot of BATs, notably dropping a squadron of the robots down a 50-foot shaft. Flint "distracts" some Cobra frogmen, getting beat up for his trouble while Lady Jaye escapes. Issue #53's titanic battle ends with the Pit II's destruction and the deaths of General Ryan and Admiral Dyson.

GOOFS The Joes comply with Pentagon demands to close the Pit II, but it doesn't occur to anyone that Zartan's escape with the Pit II's location spells a likely Cobra attack in the next five minutes. Then again, Serpentor takes a shockingly small number of troopers to overrun Joe Headquarters (had the Pit II been active, the Cobras would've been dog meat).

Storm Shadow's explanation of his "resurrection" (*see Comic Tie-Ins*) doesn't make any sense – a self-induced ninja coma won't save your life if your heart gets shot out.

An incarcerated Zartan's shown in his proper uniform even though he was captured wearing a hospital gown (#48). General Ryan's nuts to think that Cobra's not a threat at this point (the Treasury raid, #16; and the formation of Cobra Island, #40 alone should be proof).

COMIC TIE-INS Snake-Eyes learns here that when the Baroness' bullets razed Storm Shadow's chest (*G.I. Joe* #47), Storm Shadow forced himself into a self-induced coma called "The Sleeping Phoenix." Storm Shadow's vital signs slowed to a death-like state, compelling Dr. Mindbender to freeze the ninja's "corpse" (#48) for use in experiments to create Serpentor (#49). Thankfully, Dr. Mindbender's machines repaired Storm Shadow's body – allowing his return to life in #50.

Storm Shadow travels to the remains of Snake-Eyes' cabin (leveled in *G.I. Joe* #31), having heard Snake-Eyes mention it during their Vietnam service (#26). Stormy attains some peace, although Scarlett later summons him (*G.I. Joe Yearbook* #3) to save Snake-Eyes' ass.

The Dreadnoks return to Zartan's gas station hideout in *G.I. Joe* #60. Thrasher and his Thunder Machine again fight Cross-Country and his HAVOC in #79. Dreadnok Monkeywrech appears on the cover of *G.I. Joe* #51 (curiously looking a lot like artist John Byrne), even though the character doesn't officially debut until #60.

The Pentagon shuts down the Pit II, pending an investigation for the Joes' wayward invasion of Springfield (*G.I. Joe* #49-#50), but Hollingsworth restores the Joes to active service. Hollingsworth reappears in #73, and the Joes begin construction on the Pit III in Utah in #59.

Issue #53 spotlights a mug shot of Snake-Eyes – one of several "face covers" featured on Marvel titles to celebrate the company's 25th anniversary.

CHARACTER PROFILE: JOES

- *Barbecue:* The Joe firefighter's lethal with an axe, considering Cobra troopers nothing more than "doors with rifles."
- *Cross-Country:* A redneck "and proud of it."
- *Quick Kick:* A silent weapons expert who prefers going for a direct kill when possible.
- *Scarlett:* Recognizes that Snake-Eyes loves Storm Shadow like a brother and won't betray him.
- *Snake-Eyes:* Disgustingly efficient with a "subtle cut" – a sword stroke that's so quick, the target doesn't recognize it's been hit until it splits in two.

CHARACTER PROFILE: COBRA

- *Cobra Commander:* Holds some regard for the Baroness, but remains, to Destro's annoyance, overly prone to sacrificing his troopers' lives.
- *The Baroness:* For reasons known only to herself, the Baroness seems somewhat taken with Serpentor and aids his cause.
- *Destro:* Destro doesn't plan on shucking his loyalty for Cobra Commander, suggesting the commander waste Serpentor and pin the crime on the Joes. Still, Destro squelches the assassination attempt when it threatens the Baroness' safety.

• *Dr. Mindbender:* He's playing toady to both Serpentor and Cobra Commander right now, waiting until one of them emerges victorious.

• *Serpentor:* Engenders loyalty and battle fervor among his troops by sharing in their manual labor, emphasizing that he's one of them. Reflecting his toy incarnation, Serpentor gains his proper battle armor and flying personal attack sled here.

• *Thrasher:* A Dreadnok alumni who terrifies his teammates. Zartan found Thrasher in the swamps, then got sick of the goon's sadistic tendencies and dumped him. Thrasher spent some time killing stuff, but pollution sadly decimated the local wildlife and left him without anything to strangle. He ultimately resigned himself to fixing up old vehicles and maximizing their destructive force – crafting the Dreadnok Thunder Machine.

• *Zandar:* Zartan's brother innately blends into furniture and other inanimate objects – it's a not camouflage talent, just that nobody notices him.

• *Zarana:* Zartan's petty sister helps her incarcerated sibling only because she lusts after a gold cache that Zartan swiped from a South American dictator and hid in the swamp. Zarana doesn't possess her brother's holographic talent, but she wears many disguises.

• *Zartan:* The Joes possess electronic handcuffs that neutralize Zartan's hologram-casting abilities. Quid pro quo, Zartan only gets his siblings out of trouble if it suits his interests.

CHARACTER PROFILE: OTHER *Storm Shadow:* Fast enough to catch Scarlett's crossbow bolt in mid-air. He bests Quick Kick in one-to-one combat because Quick Kick, although highly skilled, doesn't have Stormy's inner coldness and killer's edge.

ORGANIZATIONS *G.I. Joe:* When communications are compromised, the Joes switch to using prearranged code over police bands.

• *The Ft. Wadsworth Chaplains' Assistants:* Typically entertain themselves with "crazy" stunts such as whist tournaments. The assistants are sore because some paper pusher's been ignoring their long-running requests for new tea cozies.

STUFF YOU NEED *BATs:* Resolute, but typically need on-the-spot leadership to win battles.

HOT WHEELS *Dreadnok Thunder Machine and Joe HAVOC:* Their main guns point forward and don't track, so if an enemy approaches you from the side, pop out your rifle and spray them with bullets. The HAVOC's equipped with a short-range one-man utility flyer.

THE COMMAND DECISION An electric aftermath to the "Springfield invasion" plotline, giving the Joes maybe five minutes to rest before utterly annihilating their headquarters. Hama thankfully mixes a number of old threads (Storm Shadow begging Snake-Eyes for forgiveness) with new elements (the mad, mad Thrasher and his Thunder Machine) marking the must-read end of an era.

G.I. Joe Special Missions #1 to #5

Titles: *"That Sinking Feeling" (#1), "Words of Honor" (#2), "Burn-Out" (#3), "No Holds Barred" (#4), "Showdown!" (#5)*
Release Dates: *Bi-monthly from Oct. 1986 to June 1987*
Art: *Herb Trimpe*

BATTLE ROSTER *Joes:* Deep Six, Shipwreck, Cutter, Torpedo, Wet-Suit, Stalker, Snow-Job, Airtight, Clutch, Recondo, Roadblock, Alpine, Breaker, Lift-Ticket, Ace, Crankcase, Slip-Stream, Leatherneck, Wild Bill, Cobras: The Baroness, Firefly, Destro, unnamed Strato-Viper; *Other:* The Oktober Guard.

FIRST APPEARANCES *Joes:* Dial-Tone (communications, #2), Lifeline (rescue trooper, #4).

MISSION BRIEF ***Issue #1:*** When a Los Angeles-class attack submarine apparently crashes in the Baltic, Cobra and Russia's Oktober Guard – believing that the submarine contains advanced sound-dampening gear – race to loot the sub's technology. Led by Colonel Brekhov and a harbor master named Captain Bulgakov, the Oktober Guard spots several Joe members secretly manning the Swedish trawler Christina, but Cobra deems the Oktober Guard the greater threat and raids their frigate.

In the midst of the battle, Destro arrives with new intelligence information. According to Destro, the Joes aboard the *Christina* faked the submarine crash from the start – hoping to trick the Russians into bringing Captain Bulgakov, a soon-to-be defector, to their pick-up point in the Baltic. In response to Destro's accusations, Bulgakov details how the Communist Party shoddily treated his late Jewish wife, thereby spurring his desire to join the West.

Already strapped into a STABO extraction harness (*see Stuff You Need*), Bulgakov braces himself as a low-flying Joe transport swoops in, easily snatching him from the deck of the Russian frigate. Bested, the Cobras and Russians return home while the Joes celebrate winning a victory without firing a shot.

Issue #2: In Greenland, a routine patrol happens upon a World War II German Condor bomber frozen half-in, half out of a wall of ice. Combing their files, the Joes discover that the bomber went missing 40 years ago, after originally setting out from German-occupied Spitsbergen to bomb New York City.

As the Condor's discovery makes worldwide headlines, an aged Nazi poison expert named Otto Totenschadel contacts the American government from Brazil, warning that the bomber contains eight metric tons of nerve toxin, enough to wipe out Greenland – as well as most of America's Eastern seaboard. Continually hunted by Israeli commandos intent on slitting his throat, Totenschadel offers to neutralize the nerve toxin in exchange for protection. Totenschadel additionally requests the Americans keep their pact quiet from his neo-Nazi buddies, a group called the SS Elite that are currently shielding him from the vengeful Israelis.

Although he sends Recondo and other Joes to "kidnap" Totenschadel from the SS Elite, Hawk hedges his bets by dispatching a Snow Job-led team to Greenland to try and remove the Condor's two toxin canisters. In Brazil, Recondo's party scopes out the SS Elite stronghold – but suddenly find themselves surrounded by a group of Israeli Mossad commandos. Left with little option, the Joes form a short-term pact with the Israelis to eliminate the SS Elite men, planning to grab Totenschadel and run afterward.

In Greenland, Snow Job's team rappels into the ice-encased Condor, but Cobra troops arrive to steal the two nerve toxin canisters. Cobra bullets rupture one toxin canister, but Airtight discovers that the nerve toxin is only fatal when *both* canisters' elements combine. With one canister already released, the Joes trick Cobra into blowing up the Condor – burning off the already-released toxin component and ending the nerve gas threat.

From the Condor's retrieved flight logs, Alpine deduces that a second Condor was assigned to transport gold stolen by the New Reich to a safe location in Argentina. But Totenschadel, a member of the Condor crew, faked a hydraulic line failure, tricking both planes into landing in Greenland. After killing his comrades, Totenschadel made off with the Fuhrer's gold to Brazil, living a life of luxury until the Israeli commandos came hunting for him.

Totenschadel crumples upon learning the Americans defused the nerve toxin without his help, demanding they honor their pledge to protect him from the Israelis. Agreeing, the Joes and Israelis depart the SS Elite compound – leaving the SS troops, outraged at Totenschadel for betraying the Reich, to shoot the aged Nazi in the head.

Issue #3: In an undisclosed Middle Eastern country, Stalker, Slip-Stream and Leatherneck explore ways to cripple the bloodthirsty Colonel Sharif's operations and steal one of his prized planes: a Russian YAK-36 plane. The Joes collaborate with a double agent named Deke, one of several American mercenaries who fly jet-fighters for Colonel Sharif, to learn the precise location of the surface-to-air missiles (SAMs) protecting Sharif's air base.

Unfortunately, Sharif discovers the Joe snoopers, putting Stalker's crew on the run in a heavily armored van. Worse, Sharif's interrogators capture and torture Deke, forcing a confession from him. In the process, the interrogators reveal the existence of an undisclosed SAM site that's virtually guaranteed to annihilate any Joe air support.

Stalker's group crashes through defenses at Sharif's airfield, even as a Joe Skystriker squadron begins a bombing run to eliminate the Colonel's SAM launch pads. As the Skystrikers pummel the airfield to smithereens, Stalker's group loads the YAK-36 into a Russian transport plane and takes off. Sharif's men target the commandeered Joe ship with their hidden SAM system, but Deke escapes, vowing not to let American servicemen die. Out of time, Deke steals one of Sharif's MIG planes and plows it into the hidden SAM site, sacrificing himself to save the Joes.

Issue #4: Along the Malay Peninsula, an airborne Joe team composed of Leatherneck, Lifeline, Wild Bill and Roadblock hurriedly dissect a captured Cobra Firebat to retrieve its "black boxes" (i.e. the aircraft's most crucial electronic components). But the Oktober Guard, hoping to nab the black boxes for Mother Russia, shoot down the Joe transport plane and its Firebat cargo.

Leatherneck's squad abandons the Firebat and skedaddles with its black boxes, engaging in a sniper melee with the Russians. But out of nowhere, a group of smugglers led by a haridan called Sarawak Sally round up the Joe/Russian combatants and amuse themselves by having the prisoners punch each others' lights out.

Disturbingly, Joe medic Lifeline finds himself facing goliath Russian Horrorshow, but using defensive *akido* skills, Lifeline mops the floor with his opponent. Sally orders the pacifist medic to slay Horrorshow, but he instead offers to help Sally sell the Firebat black boxes back to Cobra in exchange for the Russians' lives. Leatherneck bristles to hear Lifeline giving up the black boxes, but Sally applauds the strength of Lifeline's convictions. After dumping the black boxes into a tributary of the South China Sea – an offering to various river spirits in celebration of Lifeline's valor – Sally releases her captives to go their separate ways.

Issue #5: On Cobra Island, a thuggish Strato-Viper degrades the "low-lifes" that compose his pit crew, then boards his Night Raven jet. The hotshot Strato-Viper lifts off to reconnoiter an Air Force base in Florida, but Hawk, sick to death of Cobra pilots skirting the boundary waters between America and Cobra Island, assigns Ace and Slip-Stream to fly near enough to the Strato-Viper to jostle his nerves.

Ace and Slip-Stream receive a warm reception from their pit crews, exchanging high-fives before jetting into the air. The Joe pilots sabre-rattle the Night Raven, but the Strato-Viper impulsively pops a missile onto Ace's tail. Ace's Skystriker plummets into the Gulf of Mexico, but Joe rescue teams scramble and extract their teammate with blazing speed.

Meanwhile, the Strato-Viper finds his aircraft's systems out of alignment due to poor maintenance. Cleared to fire, Slip-Stream unleashes a frenzy of Sidewinder missiles and swats the blind-running Night Raven from the sky. As Slip-Stream returns to base and acknowledges respect for his ground team, the plummeting Strato-Viper finds that Slip-Stream's missile has damaged his ejection system. The Strato-Viper radios for pick-up upon hitting the ocean, but the Cobra rescue teams, disinclined to hurry for the brash Strato-Viper, proceed at the slowest speed possible.

Trapped, the panicked Strato-Viper fails to locate his break-out crowbar and quickly drowns as the Night Raven sinks. Finally arriving at the Strato-Viper's watery grave, the pit crew shrugs and disposes of the Night Raven's crowbar – deliberately swiped before the Strato-Viper took off – and returns to base.

MEMORABLE MOMENTS When the Baroness belts out the standard, "For Cobraaaa!" battle cry, Firefly candidly seconds her with: "For personal survival and the promise of riches!"

When Leatherneck airs his disdain for Lifeline's pacifist beliefs, Roadblock reminds him that he might require Lifeline to patch him up someday. In response, Leatherneck deadpans with a Klingon's stoicism: "I'd rather bleed."

ASS-WHUPPINGS The Oktober Guard and Cobra dice each other to pieces in issue #1, with Daina grenading some Cobra frogmen, then pot-shooting two more Cobras with her Dragunov sniper rifle. By comparison, Deep Six merely beans Horrorshow with a No. 6 pipe-wrench, then tosses him overboard. (Horrorshow cries out: "Horrorshow is not forgetting this!")

Totenschadel apparently killed thousands in his Reich-sponsored nerve toxin experiments. Joe communications chief Breaker tosses a grenade that makes a HISS tank – and its driver – skid into a chasm.

Leatherneck grenades a BTR (Russian-built 8X8 armored personnel carrier). One of Colonel Sharif's captains blows away American mercenaries who refuse to shoot down their fellow countrymen. Fighter pilot Deke dies saving the Joes' asses from a hidden missile system.

When Daina gets a head wound in issue #4, Colonel Brekhov kindly wants her patched up – so she can keep shooting. Leeches slurp blood from Lifeline's group of Joes in Malaysia, but they burn 'em off. A showdown between the Joes and the Oktober Guard criss-crosses Leatherneck and Wild Bill, plus Russians Stormavik and Schrage, with bullet wounds.

MISCELLANEOUS STUFF!

LAUNCHING THE SPECIAL MISSIONS

During *G.I. Joe's* heyday in 1986 (appropriately enough, the same year that spawned *Top Gun* as its top-grossing film), Marvel decided to bleed the fans for a greater share of their milk money by unleashing a second *Joe* title onto the market. But faced with the problem of making sure the two *Joe* titles didn't contradict each other into a sloppy, sauerkraut-laden mess of continuity – not to mention insuring that the creative teams didn't collapse trying to make double deadlines – Marvel editors wisely kept the newfound *G.I. Joe Special Missions* separate from the main *G.I. Joe* title.

As such, *Special Missions* serves as a departure from the typical "Joe vs. Cobra" storylines, with each issue focusing on an tight-knit crew of Joe military specialists covertly dealing with operations so secretive, even most of the Joes are kept in the dark. Although Cobra sporadically shows up to cause mayhem (notably in issues #1, #5 and #7), *Special Missions* mostly squares the Joes off against fascist dictators, radical nationalists and Communist wanna-bes – and therein lies the problem.

Fandom tends to slag on the *Special Missions* series, largely because it doesn't seem as relevant to watch the Joes throw themselves into the meat grinder against Dictator X or "Him with the Toxic Gas Bomb" rather than Cobra. It also doesn't help that *Special Missions* relies heavily on stand-alone stories, forcing each 22-page issue to reboot itself with an entirely new premise.

It's a real pity, too, because if read in rapid succession while you're loafing in front of the TV, *Special Missions* offers a lot in the way of tasty moral dilemmas (issue #5's discussion of camaraderie, a hostage drama in #22 that continually keeps you guessing, etc.) – but it's the sort of appreciation that comes from fishing a *Special Missions* set out of the 50 cent bins and consuming them all in one go, not from reading the series on a month-to-month basis. Still, we appreciate the stronger *Special Missions* tales for their grit – making this spin-off, in our opinion, an underrated cache of good reading.

GOOFS Slip-Stream says he's purchased a "Jetfire" Transformer toy for a pit crew member's son, but its actually a "Megatron" figure. (Author's Note: A part of me wishes I didn't know stuff like that.)

NOW YOU KNOW... The next time you're covered in leeches, flame them off with matches – if you rip 'em off, the parasites' heads get stuck in your wound and make it fester. Tigers are often scaredy-cats – if you keep from making sudden moves, they'll often go away.

COMIC TIE-INS The Oktober Guard debuted in #6-#7 and last appeared in *G.I. Joe Yearbook* #2. The Cobra Night Raven jet formally debuts in *Special Missions* #5, although Flint's reconnaissance team spotted a tarp-covered prototype in *G.I. Joe* #46. Destro and the Baroness evacuate the Silent Castle (#138) with a STABO device (see Stuff You Need) similar to Captain Bulgakov's apparatus in *Special Missions* #1.

CHARACTER PROFILE: JOES

• *Alpine:* He speaks German, having climbed lots of mountains in Germany and Switzerland.

• *Clutch:* Clutch's grandmother, a concentration camp survivor, lived with his family when he was a child. One day, as Clutch was innocently watching *Hogan's Heroes*, Grandma Clutch wandered in and – upset to see a prisoner-of-war camp comedy – started screaming.

• *Leatherneck:* Leatherneck's handy with a grenade launcher. He thinks Lifeline's near-worthless because he won't fight.

• *Lifeline:* He can't stand combat, but holds a black belt in akido, a Zen martial art that directs an opponent's violent energy back onto himself.

• *Slip-Stream:* He can't read Russian or Farsi.

CHARACTER PROFILE: OTHER

• *Daina:* She's armed with a Dragunov sniper rifle that's based on the AK-47.

• *Herr Doktor Otto Totenschadel:* As an ex-head of poison gas research for the Third Reich, Totenschadel ran experiments on prisoners at Sachsenhausen and Natzweiller-Struthof. After making off with the Fuhrer's bouillon, Totenschadel lived quite handsomely in Buenos Aires while his fellow neo-Nazis assumed he toiled in poverty.

ORGANIZATIONS *Cobra:* Keeps spies in Scandinavia.

• *Cobra Strato-Vipers:* They're surgically altered to resist altitude sickness and G-forces.

• *G.I. Joe:* They're allied with various Middle East royalists, but typically don't patrol the Baltic.

• *The Oktober Guard:* They typically fly about in Hind-E attack helicopters rather than the Soviet navy's Helixes and Hormones. The Oktober Guard possesses extensive dossiers on individual Joes from intelligence operatives. Among other things, they're pissed because some tin-pot Southeast Asian dictator's installing Cobra Terror-Dromes near a Soviet naval base in Cam Ranh Bay.

STUFF YOU NEED *Sarin-Plus:* Nerve agent developed by Totenschadel, so potent that 0.01 mg can kill a grown man by neutralizing the actions of cholinesterase – an enzyme essential to the transmission of nerve impulses. Apparently, it's a particularly excruciating and vicious way to die.

• *STABO (STAbilized BOdy extraction harness):* A rather bizarre means of extracting someone from a danger zone, requiring you to cinch the person in question into a harness tethered to a low-flying hot air balloon. The harnessed person holds still while an airplane swoops down and snags the tether with an extended support strut – zinging the person into the air until the airplane crew can safely haul him aboard.

HOT WHEELS Cobra Night Raven: Designed for stealth, fast and slippery with radar-elusive body panels.

• *Joe Skystrikers:* Carry electronic counter-measures (ECM) to jam frequencies, infrared flares to confuse heat-seeking missiles and all-weather air control (AWACS) to spot incoming aircraft.

• *Joe Conquest X-30:* Uses an infrared threat detection system, plus flares that fry enemy sensors. The X-30's armed with 20 mike-mike depleted uranium armor piercing rounds and Sidewinder missiles.

THE COMMAND DECISION Five issues that make for a sizeable departure from typical *G.I. Joe* fare, lacking the immediate gratification of a Joe/Cobra slugfest but offering their own rewards, especially when read in bulk. *Special Missions* #1 provides an interesting dynamic, maneuvering the Russians and Cobra into blowing holes in one another while the crafty Joes win without resorting to violence. The intricate issue #2 relies on traditional "mad Nazi" themes, quickly driving itself toward a gritty ending (the Joes don't paste the wholeheartedly evil Totenschadel – they just don't bother saving him).

Issue #3 makes for the weakest of the bunch, tossing out a passable Middle East drama that arguably puts too much emphasis on one-off pilot Deke. Issue #4 also drags its feet a bit, although the pacifist Lifeline – and the timbre of his beliefs – shine through. Finally, the somewhat drawn-out issue #5 rose up to rock our world as a story about camaraderie, deftly drawing the distinction between the Joes' brotherhood and Cobra's mercenary nature. In the end, we walked away fulfilled.

G.I. Joe #54 to #56, Yearbook #3

Titles: "Launch Base" (#54), "Unmaskings" (#55), "Jungle Moves" (#56), "Hush Job" (Yearbook #3)
Release Dates: *Dec. 1986 to Mar. 1987*
Art: *Rod Whigham (#54-#56), Ron Wagner ("Hush Job," Yearbook #3)*

BATTLE ROSTER *Joes:* Snake-Eyes, Slip-Stream, Flint, Stalker, Beach-Head, Leatherneck, Scarlett, Grunt, Recondo, Dial-Tone, Trip-Wire, Roadblock; *Cobra:* Cobra Commander, Destro, Serpentor, Tomax and Xamot, the Baroness, Dr. Mindbender, Zartan, the Dreadnoks.

FIRST APPEARANCES *Joes:* Low-Light (sniper, #55); *Cobra:* Cobra Consulate Building (#55); *Other:* Lola (student and future love muffin, #56).

MISSION BRIEF ***Issue #54:*** On Cobra Island, Serpentor fortifies his position as Cobra Emperor, embarking on a lucrative scheme to sell Cobra Terror-Drome launch bases to prominent terrorists and dictators around the world. Serpentor enjoys some early success, but the Joes grow curious when intelligence reports locate a Terror-Drome in the chaos-torn country of Sierra Gordo.

Lusting to examine a Terror-Drome without violating Cobra Island's sovereignty, Hawk suggests that Snake-Eyes let himself get captured in Sierra Gordo, then use his ninja training to escape and examine the Terror-Drome's technical specs. But worried that Cobra might instigate extra security protocols while detaining a commando such as Snake-Eyes, Hawk recommends that Snake-Eyes disguise himself as the less-threatening Flint.

Accordingly, Joe fighter pilot Slip-Stream zips by the Sierra Gordo Terror-Drome in his Conquest X-30, drawing firepower as an excuse to eject "Flint." The Crimson Twins apprehend "Flint" like clockwork, but to Snake-Eyes' horror, the twins and Dr. Mindbender strap him into the late Dr. Venom's brainwave scanner – intending to run roughshod through their captive's memory.

Issue #55: Near the Sierra Gordo Terror-Drome, Stalker, Low-Light and other Joe snipers coordinate with local counter-revolutionaries, preparing to rush the Cobra fortress and liberate Snake-Eyes upon the completion of his mission. Amidst a flurry of fighting, Stalker's team infiltrates the Terror-Drome and frees their comrade from the clutches of Mindbender and friends. Unfortunately, a sudden gunfire volley gravely wounds Stalker.

Recalling a similar situation in Vietnam, Stalker orders the

MISCELLANEOUS STUFF!

G.I. JOE AND THE TRANSFORMERS

Titles: "Blood on the Tracks" (#1), "Power Struggle" (#2), "Ashes, Ashes..." (#3), "...All Fall Down!" (#4). Release Dates: Monthly from January to April 1987. Writer: Michael Higgins. Art: Herb Trimpe.

CONTINUITY NOTES: Back in 1987, Marvel collaborated to bring Transformers and G.I. Joe into a single story. The result was the four-issue *G.I. Joe and the Transformers* mini-series – a dubious, continuity-wrecking bastard child to the established *Transformers* storyline. It fits better with *G.I. Joe* continuity, but it's too problematic to count as anything other than apocrypha.

MISSION BRIEF: Under Hawk's command, G.I. Joe oversees security protocols on Power Station Alpha – the world's first mobile nuclear power station. Unfortunately, Cobra and a team of energy-hungry Decepticon robots forge simultaneous plans to steal the device. Autobot leader Optimus Prime sends Bumblebee to scope out their Decepticon rivals, but Bumblebee stops to save youngster Anthony Duranti from getting mashed by the power station. In turn, the Joes mistake Bumblebee for an attacker, cannon-shelling him into mangled metal.

The Decepticons and Cobra briefly forge an alliance to seize the power station, but Cobra subsequently learns that the Decepticons plan to beam Power Station's Alpha's energy into the Earth's crust – erupting the planet into a giant fireball – then using the power station to beam the resultant energy to Cybertron. The Decepticons successfully launch Power Station Alpha into space, but Cobra hastily allies itself with the Autobots and the Joes in an effort to save Earth. Working in concert, the Autobots, Joes and Cobra blow up Power Station Alpha, ending the threat – while Autobot medic Ratchet rebuilds Bumblebee into a new robot named Goldbug.

THE COMMAND DECISION: Once in a blue moon, a story comes along so heinous, it's hard to even make fun of it. A bad idea from the start, *G.I. Joe and the Transformers* is complete hack work, compressing the worst comic books have to offer – bad plotting, absurd characterization, crackpot scientific principles, atrocious dialogue and more – into a single story. Completely unspeakable.

Joes to leave him and make tracks with Snake-Eyes. However, Snake-Eyes relieves the blood-soaked Stalker of command, ordering Low-Light's group to take their leader and run while Snake-Eyes stymies their Cobra pursuers.

Meanwhile, Destro and Cobra Commander find themselves entombed in the collapsed Pit II, hopelessly cut off from reaching the surface. Luckily, Destro locates a Joe drilling machine – a fail-safe vehicle intended to help trapped Joes burrow out of the Pit II.

Working together, Destro and Cobra Commander tunnel into a Staten Island mall closed for renovation and raid a clothing shop to travel incognito. Calling upon his former career as a used car salesman, Cobra Commander forges dealership papers and steals a yellow Corvette. However, a cop pulls over Cobra Commander and Destro for a minor traffic offense, compelling Cobra Commander to show his genuine driver's license.

When the police officer finds Cobra Commander's last name strangely familiar, he matches it with a young man left comatose by a car accident – a boy named Billy. Cobra Commander hurriedly visits his hospitalized son and, discovering that Billy lost his right eye and left leg in the accident, bemoans his failure as a father. While Cobra Commander attempts to salvage his family life, Destro leaves the commander's company to return to his Scottish homestead.

Issue #56: Although Low-Light's team reaches the *USS Flagg* safely with Stalker in tow, Cobra stun grenades incapacitate Snake-Eyes. The Joes storm the Terror-Drome, but Dr. Mindbender and the Baroness fly the battered ninja to the newly erected Cobra Consulate Building in New York.

With the Joes on the brink of discovering Cobra's ulterior motive behind the accelerated Terror-Drome sales, Tomax and Xamot line the Sierra Gordo Terror-Drome with explosives and flee. However, the Joes employ the time-honored art of snipping the explosives' detonating wire, then collapse the Terror-Drome into its various components for transport.

Tomax and Xamot indulge in brotherly panic, radioing Serpentor for an airstrike. Luckily, the Joes load decoy Terror-Drome components onto a train – letting Serpentor missile the train to pieces while the Joes casually float the real Terror-Drome fragments downriver to the *USS Flagg*.

Yearbook #3: Dr. Mindbender and the Baroness practically salivate at the chance to work over Snake-Eyes, but Scarlett contacts Storm Shadow for help in liberating their loved one. While Scarlett infiltrates the Cobra Consulate Building disguised as an aged cleaning woman, Storm Shadow shimmies through the Consulate's sewer system and hacks his way through several Cobra ninjas.

Re-strapped into Cobra's brainwave scanner for the umpteenth time, Snake-Eyes marshals his inner calm into a Zen trance that overloads the brainwave scanner's circuits. Reunited, Storm Shadow and Snake-Eyes disembowel a number of Cobra goons, but ultimately find themselves heavily outnumbered and facing a Cobra firing squad. Thankfully, Scarlett bitch-slaps the Baroness unconscious and steals her identity, taking Snake-Eyes and Storm Shadow away at gunpoint – then simply walking the two ninjas out of the building to freedom.

MEMORABLE MOMENTS In an odd juxtaposition, Snake-Eyes and Scarlett pause by the Pit II's remains to honor Destro's memory – a mark of respect for a fallen adversary. Touchingly, the weeping Baroness flies her RATTLER jet over the Pit II's ruins and drops a wreath for her lost love.

A trapped Cobra Commander has a conniption fit in the Pit II's remains, wailing about his past failures (he really should switch to decaf): "I had such magnificent plans! Everything was going smoothly! All those years of sacrifice and denial! Arrrrrrgh! We have to get out of here!" Once freed, Destro pokes fun at Cobra Commander's wardrobe and the commander fires back: "Hrmph! Fashion snobbery from someone who wears a gold chain with an open shirt!"

In one of the series' most dramatic moments, Cobra Commander, the man who imprisoned, outlawed and subjected Billy to the brainwave scanner, humbles himself before his son's hospital bed. As Cobra Commander puts it, "True villainy lies not in the commission of evil but the denial of it," finally acknowledging that he should have loved Billy better. Showing a decent bit of empathy for the commander's predicament, Destro consoles his colleague with: "You can't change the past. Let it go. Do something about the future."

LOVE AND WAR Thank God for college co-eds – a Georgia Tech-based Grunt quickly strikes up a romance with Lola, another engineering student and former army mechanic. Scarlett remains continually terrified for Snake-Eyes' safety on away missions, although she's getting better at covering her fear. A Corvette-driving Cobra Commander and Destro race cute girls and wave at them. Flint sacrifices his shirt and beret for a decoy operation, although Scarlett thinks it's just an excuse to flaunt his muscles.

ASS-WHUPPINGS Billy survived his catastrophic run-in with a missile (#43) at the cost of his right eye, his left leg, third degree burns, a concussion, five cracked ribs and a long-running coma. Snake-Eyes squirms under Cobra's fiendish brainwave scanner but finally blows up the device, showering Dr. Mindbender with shrapnel.

GOOFS The Joes idiotically continue making use of Ft. Wadsworth's facilities – which seems damnably risky, given Cobra twice-over knows the base housed the Pit II.

G.I. Joe #54 to #56, Yearbook #3

COMIC TIE-INS Grunt leaves active Joe service to enroll at Georgia Tech's engineering program. He later volunteers for a rescue mission in *G.I. Joe* #62, but the Joes decline his offer. Grunt and his newfound squeeze Lola finally get some action (so to speak) by helping to free the captive Hawk and General Hollingsworth in #78.

Snake-Eyes formerly writhed in agony under Cobra's brainwave scanner in *G.I. Joe* #10, but develops a tolerance for the machine's effects.

Cobra Commander and Destro were trapped in the collapsing Pit II in *G.I. Joe* #53. The two of them flee the Pit II in a Joe tunneling machine, formerly rendered on blueprints in #22. Billy survived Scrap Iron's missile (#43) but remains comatose. Cobra Commander takes Billy to Denver in #58 to obtain a prosthetic leg for the lad.

Destro departs for Scotland only to find an imposter enjoying high tea in his family castle in *G.I. Joe* #57. We're treated to glimpses of Destro's face, which seems quite normal, suggesting the Baroness fainted in #33 over the unmasked Destro's show of trust, not from some hideous disfigurement. Issue #97, in fact, shows Destro's whole kisser.

Stalker recalls an occasion in Vietnam when he ordered his men to leave a wounded Snake-Eyes behind (*G.I. Joe* #26) – making Snake-Eyes' modern-day sacrifice to save the wounded Stalker all the more abrasive.

Strom Shadow traveled to the remains of Snake-Eyes' cabin in *G.I. Joe* #52, but Scarlett here retrieves him. Stormy reunites with Billy in #63.

CHARACTER PROFILE: JOES

- *Airtight:* Is a demon at basketball.
- *Grunt:* Steadfast friends with Clutch.
- *Flint:* It's sometimes hard to tell if he's truly fearless – or just genuinely stupid.
- *Leatherneck:* Carries an M-203 (a 40 mm grenade launcher mounted on an M-16 rifle).
- *Low-Light:* His rifle fires hypodermic darts, aimed with a starlight scope.
- *Slip-Stream:* His piloting skills make him a fiend at video games. (A word to the wise: Don't challenge Slip-Stream to play "Defender").
- *Snake-Eyes:* His face remains about as attractive as a train accident – Dr. Mindbender hurriedly tosses a towel over Snake-Eyes' face so none of the assembled Cobras get sick.

CHARACTER PROFILE: COBRA

- *Cobra Commander:* Evidently used to work as a car salesman, noting that, "Forming Cobra was a step toward honesty for me!" He's able to forge registration and cardboard plates, but keeps his actual driver's license as a legitimate form of ID in case of an emergency.
- *Destro:* Destro hasn't seen Cobra Commander's unmasked mug until this point.

CHARACTER PROFILE: OTHER *Lola:* Grunt's hot bit of stuff paid for college by serving four years as an air-cavalry helicopter mechanic. She likes Grunt because, despite his army training, he isn't saddled with macho neuroses.

ORGANIZATIONS *Cobra:* Keeps secret bases in the Everglades, the Carolina Sea Islands and the Jersey marshes. Serpentor's increasing Cobra's business operations, making headway into the arms market, off-shore investments and high-level graft.

PLACES TO GO *Cobra Consulate Building:* The Manhattan-based consulate building's 50-stories tall, made from steel and reinforced concrete. It houses oodles of Cobra surveillance and satellite communications gear, functioning as an extension of Cobra Island and therefore protected by diplomatic immunity.

STUFF YOU NEED *Cobra Terror-Drome:* The Terror-Drome's Firebat jet makes it extremely useful as an air defense installation, but it fares poorly at thwarting ground attacks. Cobra constructs the Terror-Dromes from three standard segments that repeat themselves in a circle.

HOT WHEELS *Joe Conquest X-30 jet:* Contains guidance systems and sensors so accurate, it can fly at Mach One at less than 100 feet above the ground and avoid radar completely. The Conquest's got computer-enhanced control systems, so if computers go down, you go splat.

THE COMMAND DECISION Issue #54 gets the job done, but curiously makes a mystery out of the doppelganger Flint's identity – when it's blatantly obvious that it's Snake-Eyes. Still, the pivotal #55 gloriously alternates between the loud (Snake-Eyes' liberation) and the quiet (Cobra Commander and Destro on a juicy little road trip). It also sports one of the most memorable Joe covers: a jaw-dropping shot of Snake-Eyes, Cobra Commander and Destro unmasking (back in the day, we elbowed Boy Scouts aside to snatch this issue off the newsstand). The rollicking effort falls flat in #56, though, by focusing on a lackluster Terror-Drome conspiracy. If all that sounds fairly damning, keep in mind: It's unfair to expect unabashed brilliance every issue, leaving #54-#56 a necessary – if average at times – effort with an outstanding middle.

G.I. Joe #57

Title: *"Strange Bedfellows"*
Release Date: *Mar. 1987*
Art: *Ron Wagner*

BATTLE ROSTER *Joes:* Flint, Lady Jaye; *Cobra:* Major Bludd; *Other:* Destro.

FIRST APPEARANCES *Joes:* Mainframe (computer specialist, #57).

MISSION BRIEF G.I. Joe technical advisers aboard the *USS Flagg* joyfully dissect the Terror-Drome components seized in Sierra Gordo, but several of the pieces defy analysis. Desperate to learn more, Hawk hears reports of the supposedly "late" Destro travelling through Kennedy Airport en route to Scotland. Accordingly, Flint and Lady Jaye agree to quietly track Destro and hopefully obtain his Terror-Drome blueprints.

Returning to his family castle, the normally reserved Destro pees himself in surprise to discover his personal retinue taking high tea with a doppelganger of himself. Forewarned about the imminent arrival of an "imposter," local authorities arrest the *real* Destro, leaving the duplicate free to plunder the castle's store of technical specifications and hardware blueprints.

Observing this whirlwind change of events, Flint and Lady Jaye peg the arrested Destro as the genuine article and break him out of jail. The two Joes offer to liberate Destro's castle in exchange for Terror-Drome schematics and Destro, who nearly tosses his cookies at the thought of ever working for Cobra again, agrees.

Leery about Castle Destro's multitude of defenses, the Joes and Destro favor a sledgehammer approach, plowing a requisitioned British airship into the castle's greenhouse. The castle's guards muster a defense, but the authentic Destro beats up his rival. Finally, Destro conks the intruder unconscious and unmasks him as Major Bludd – sent to steal Destro's technical schematics for Serpentor. Newly restored as the lord of the castle, Destro honors his agreement with the Joes by presenting Lady Jaye with the Terror-Drome blueprints.

MEMORABLE MOMENTS During the double-Destro slugfest, Destro's castle guards hold themselves back – knowing that the true Destro will inevitably clobber his opponent. The final act, with Destro completing his deal with the Joes (Destro to Lady Jaye: "The problem with making a pact with a pretty lady... is that one is obligated to honor it.") sets the stage for dozens of stories with a slightly reformed Destro.

ASS-WHUPPINGS Destro enjoyably mops the floor with Major Bludd, smashing his face into a concrete pillar.

GOOFS It's never clear why Serpentor orders Major Bludd to steal Destro's Terror-Drome schematics (it's possible – although never stated – that Serpentor's merely disposing of evidence that could expose his Terror-Drome conspiracy). For that matter, if Serpentor thinks Destro's dead, why were the local authorities warned about the arrival of an imposter?

COMIC TIE-INS Destro here returns home after departing Cobra Commander's company in *G.I. Joe* #55. He takes a breather from the business of killing his rivals, then shows up in #69. The Joes find themselves unable to read Destro's Terror-Drome schematics without a proper Terror-Drome central computer and send Mainframe and Dusty to find one in #58.

Cobra Commander II brings his troops to bear against Castle Destro in *G.I. Joe* #87 and gets his ass whipped. The castle serves Destro well for a number of years but meets its end in #116.

CHARACTER PROFILE: DESTRO

Destro: Destro hails from old money – his family's owned the weapons-dealing MARS (*see Group Dynamics*) for generations (his father has crafted highly durable goods for the British government). Castle Destro employs private troops dressed in traditional Scottish uniforms (his grandfather fancied them). Tragically, Destro hasn't found time for a decent high tea in ages.

ORGANIZATIONS *Military Armaments Research Syndicate (MARS):* Destro's family firm, an international weapons corporation headquartered in Scotland. James McCullen Destro, a forefather of the current Destro and the "Fifteenth Earl of something or the other," originally founded MARS in 1752 as a naval gun foundry.

STUFF YOU NEED *Cobra Terror-Dromes:* Destro's company only supplied some parts for the Terror-Dromes – a security feature implemented so that nobody save the top Cobra brass would know the dromes' final makeup. As the project's major contractor and primary consultant, however, Destro's entitled to a full set of blueprints.

PLACES TO GO *Castle Destro:* Equipped with radar, infrared detectors, motion sensors, passive listening devices and – a bit less threateningly – an arboretum. The castle staff wisely follows protocol and never, never serves high tea unless Destro's in residence.

THE COMMAND DECISION A juicy little side-story, upending our notions of Destro as a black-hearted villain and laying pavement for his strengthened relationship with the Joes.

G.I. Joe #58 to #59

Titles: *"Desperate Moves" (#58), "Divergent Paths" (#59)*
Release Dates: *Apr. to May 1987*
Art: *Rod Whigham (#58), Ron Wagner (#59)*

BATTLE ROSTER *Joes:* Mainframe, Crankcase, Clutch; *Cobra:* Cobra Commander; *Other:* Billy.

FIRST APPEARANCES *Joes:* Dusty (desert soldier, #58), Tunnel Rat (explosive ordnance disposal, #59), Outback (survivalist, #59), Jinx (ninja/ intelligence, #59); *Cobra:* Raptor (falconer, #59), Fred Smith VII (Crimson Guardsman, #58); *Other:* the Blind Master (ninja sensei, #59).

MISSION BRIEF ***Issue #58-#59:*** Finding Destro's Terror-Drome schematics useless without a genuine Terror-Drome computer to process the information, Hawk dispatches desert trooper Dusty and computer specialist Mainframe to a possible Terror-Drome location in the Middle East. Together with revolutionaries fighting the oppressive Colonel Sharif, Dusty and Mainframe locate a bricked-up Terror-Drome hidden inside a giant oil tank. By rigging a simple phone connection, Mainframe provides access to the Terror-Drome's central computer – enabling the Staten Island-based Joes to read Destro's files.

Meanwhile, Cobra Commander withdraws his comatose son Billy from the hospital and drives to Denver. There, Cobra Commander arrives at an auto repair shop run by Fred Smith VII, a Crimson Guardsman and master engineer, to obtain Fred's help in crafting a prosthetic replacement for Billy's missing leg. Acknowledging Cobra Commander's position, Fred VII also offers his leader a newly forged, super-strong and bullet-proof battle suit. Cobra Commander bristles with his new-found prowess, then turns tearful as Billy awakens from his coma.

Stricken with amnesia, Billy allows Fred VII to equip him with an artificial leg. While Billy acclimates to his new situation, Fred VII's associate Raptor – a Cobra falconer and master accountant – offers to hack into government pay records and track the nomadic Joes. Raptor uncovers evidence of Joe activity in central Utah, prompting Cobra Commander to test his new body armor and another of Fred's inventions – a high-velocity, bouncing battle vehicle named the POGO.

In Central Utah, Cobra Commander engages a Joe convoy en route from Jerkwater Flats to Ft. Carson, bouncing the POGO about faster than a kangaroo on crack. Unfortunately, the POGO malfunctions and causes a near-collision in a tunnel, turning Cobra Commander white as a sheet and forcing him to retreat.

Left alone, Billy feels drawn to a ninja school located near Fred's garage, making the acquaintance of a sightless sensei named the Blind Master and a slinky female ninja named Jinx. The Blind Master and Jinx confess to keeping Fred under surveillance, hoping for the chance to find Cobra Commander and thereby meet Billy. Slowly regaining his memory, Billy is stunned to find Jinx possesses the same wrist brand as his former teacher – the ninja named Storm Shadow.

MEMORABLE MOMENTS Mainframe's surprised to see 13-year-old boys among the revolutionaries, but Dusty notes: "There were drummer boys younger than him at Gettysburg, Mainframe!"

Mainframe shrugs off young Rashid's favoritism toward the hardened Dusty – who's admittedly a man's man – and insists that thinking's always preferable to fighting. Rashid still doesn't get the hint, decrying Mainframe with, "Have you no honor?", but Mainframe remains cool as a pickle. (Rashid later acknowledges his ignorance for thinking Mainframe impotent.)

Cobra Commander accurately thinks the feather-covered Raptor looks completely absurd, asking Fred, "What's [Raptor] doing running loose without a strait-jacket?" Later, Cobra Commander zings Raptor with, "What do you sleep in? A nest?", and pretty much sums up our sentiments with: "I'm sick and tired of wackos in funny suits!"

ASS-WHUPPINGS Four of Sharif's soldiers lie in ambush for Mainframe's group, but Dusty smells the troopers' tobacco and wipes them out ("Nasty habit, smoking," he notes, "... can be downright lethal.") Under Mainframe's remote direction, a Firebat jet blasts apart several desert platoons.

GOOFS Scarlett shares credit with Flint for acquiring the Terror-Dome schematics from Destro, when it was actually Flint and Lady Jaye who brought home the bacon.

NOW YOU KNOW... As Dusty points out, a soldier wins simply by surviving.

COMIC TIE-INS Baseless since the Pit II's destruction (*G.I. Joe* #53), the Joes here begin operations in Utah to create the Pit III (which officially debuts in #65). Cobra Commander located his comatose son Billy in #55. Upon awakening, Billy remembers his ninja skills (taught to him by Storm Shadow in #39-#42). Fred Smith VII's part of the ever-growing "Fred Smith" classification of Crimson Guardsmen, first seen in issue #29.

The Joes last entered Sierra Gordo in an effort to rescue Dr. Adele Burkhart (*G.I Joe* #38-#39). Dusty and Mainframe work here with a young Sierra Gordo revolutionary named Rashid, who grows up to become one of Destro's computer techs in #118.

The Joes formerly tangled with Colonel Sharif's forces in *G.I. Joe* #1. Sharif later shows up on Cobra Island as a visiting dignitary in #97.

Jinx wears the same ninja tattoo as Snake-Eyes and Storm Shadow (first seen in *G.I. Joe* #21).

CHARACTER PROFILE: JOES

• *Mainframe:* Now a computer specialist, Mainframe saw service in Vietnam and sports a wealth of battlefield experience. As a veteran campaigner, Mainframe's developed the art of falling asleep in rickety vehicles. He wisely stays out of Dusty's way when it comes to desert commando-style killing, but doesn't feel the need to prove himself to anyone.

• *Outback:* He's been roughing it in the Rockies for a month, testing new equipment and freeze-dried foods. Outback says the "crummy" equipment fell apart after the first week and the freeze-dried vittles was inedible, meaning he's been living off the land instead. As you might expect, Outback's smart about animals and their natural habitat. He fires 7.62 NATO bullets.

CHARACTER PROFILE: COBRA

• *Cobra Commander:* Reveals his identity to undercover Crimson Guardsmen with a secret handshake and the password: "Greed, ambition and ruthlessness!"

• *Fred VII:* Fred's primarily a movement enhancement expert, meaning he lives in a world of servos and articulated robot arms.

• *Raptor:* Destro initially caught Raptor poaching on Cobra property with specially bred and mutated hawks, but later thought the loopy Raptor's accounting skills might come in handy. Raptor served Destro for a time, later becoming Fred VII's accountant. Raptor's bred a number of super-intelligent falcons that respond to his voice commands. He wears a heinous bird costume, claiming that it "makes his falcons more comfortable" (we think he just likes running around in it). Raptor's broken speech patterns – along with everything about the character, for that matter – suggest that he's decently mad.

CHARACTER PROFILE: OTHER

• *Billy:* His numerous martial arts maneuvers include a specialized flip called a "modified low iron horse."

• *The Blind Master:* His students refer to him as "Sensei Moore."

ORGANIZATIONS *G.I. Joe:* Since the Pit II's destruction, the Pentagon funnels many of the Joes' paychecks and files through Ft. Leonard Wood and Ft. Carson. Some Joes such as Tunnel Rat use G.I. Joe credit cards, presumably similar to ones used on TV by Alpine ("The Funhouse") and Flint ("The Spy Who Rooked Me").

On paper, several Joes were assigned to the Ft. Wadsworth motor pool – even despite a complete lack of mechanical skills – suggesting it was technically the best-staffed motor pool in the nation.

PLACES TO GO *Cobra Terror-Dromes:* Cobra designed the Terror-Drome's command systems with easily-understood graphic symbols for the benefit of its international clientele. To boot up the central system, input the access code: "Greed, ambition and ruthlessness."

STUFF YOU NEED *Billy's Prosthetic Leg:* Fred VII masterfully designs it as self-actuating, internally-powered, gyro-stabilized and tactile-responsive. It doesn't impede Billy's ninja skills in the slightest.

• *Cobra Commander's Armor:* Fred VII requisitioned Cobra Commander's measurements from Cobra Central. The armor responds to Cobra Commander's movements and enhances them – negating the need for controls. The armor makes Cobra Commander bulletproof and super-strong and comes equipped with infra-red scanners.

HOT WHEELS *POGO:* Designed by Fred VII, it's a giant bubble that flops out on bouncy legs, supposedly to avoid getting shot.

• *Joe SLAM attack vehicle:* Capable of target acquisition and firing while in motion.

THE COMMAND DECISION Showcasing an armored Cobra Commander that bears only a drop of his previous incarnation's charm, #58 makes us wonder if a time-delayed narcotic made Hasbro toy designers increasingly nutty as time went on. Granted, the central Terror-Drome storyline with Dusty and Mainframe holds more merit – but even that's pretty forgettable.

Saddled with some of the most unbearable Hasbro creations in history, #59 spotlights the feathered, hopeless Raptor and the equally silly POGO attack bubble. We'll credit Hama for giving this tale his best – making the POGO look pretty damn fierce and having Cobra Commander take the piss out of Raptor – but back in 1987, this book made us severely question the future of the Joe toy line.

G.I. Joe #60

Title: "Cross Purposes"
Release Date: June 1987
Art: Todd McFarlane

BATTLE ROSTER *Joes:* Hawk; Cobras: Zarana, Buzzer.

FIRST APPEARANCES *Joes:* Chuckles (undercover), Lt. Falcon (Green Beret), Law and Order (MP and K-9), Fastdraw (mobile missile specialist); *Cobra:* Monkeywrench (Dreadnok), Zanzibar (Dreadnok pirate).

STORY SUMMARY When Hawk arrives at Newark Airport on a routine flight, a band of U.S. military men named Lt. Falcon, Chuckles, Fastdraw and Law forcibly whisk the general away to a failed beach resort on the New Jersey shore. There, Chuckles explains that a band of maverick Pentagon officials – wanting to hide a potent missile system away from prying eyes – called up Chuckles' team, telling them that they were reassigned to G.I. Joe and ordering them to babysit the missile. With their dirty laundry tucked away in the defunct resort, the rogues then doctored official paperwork to make the missile system conveniently "disappear." Realizing the scam, Chuckles' foursome conspired to bring Hawk to the resort – knowing that he would have the authority to expose the racket.

Meanwhile, at Zartan's New Jersey gas station hideout, Zarana and Buzzer bitch-slap Dreadnok outcasts Zanzibar and Monkeywrench for trying to steal Zartan's fuel. Tongue loosened, Zanzibar rattles off intelligence information about the hidden missile system. Curious to learn more, Zarana disguises herself as an aged bimbo tourist and enters the disused resort – just as Hawk and Chuckles discover the missile's aimed at Cobra Island.

Nervous that Hawk's involvement will crack their conspiracy wide open, the Pentagon mavericks remotely arm the missile system and prep it for liftoff. While Buzzer summons assistance from the Cobra Consulate Building in New York, Zarana takes Monkeywrench and Zanzibar to attack the missile site. Chuckles' Joes try to destroy the missile themselves, but the resultant Dreadnok/Joe brouhaha distracts them away and the missile takes off. Thankfully, a Cobra Consulate helicopter blows up the missile just above its launch pad – sparing Cobra Island and preventing an international incident. In the aftermath, Hawk formally admits Chuckles' team into G.I. Joe, leaving Chuckles to compile evidence on the "lost" missile and force the renegade Pentagon officials to resign.

ASS-WHUPPINGS Law's dog Order chomps on Monkeywrench's leg. Monkeywrench and Zarana upend Chuckles, then proceed to grind the tropical-shirted Joe's face into the sand (Chuckles gets by with bruises and some sand up his nose).

PREPOSTEROUS PHYSICS An extremely odd panel shows Buzzer bashing Monkeywrench with his chainsaw – an act that should've grievously wounded the unfortunate Dreadnok... if not killing him outright.

COMIC TIE-INS Chuckles' little band of Joes formally reports to the Pit III in *G.I. Joe #64*.

CHARACTER PROFILE: JOES

• *Fastdraw:* Fastdraw's slightly more than just a missile *specialist* – his blast-proof suit fires mobile missiles.

• *Order:* Faithful dog who's good at sniffing out iron objects (such as pistols).

CHARACTER PROFILE: COBRA

• *Zarana:* She's not above thieving from brother Zartan, but she'll thump anyone who beats her to it.

• *Zanzibar:* Habitually sells bootleg gasoline to Zartan, steals it back and sells it to him again.

• *Monkeywrench:* He formerly rode with the Dreadnoks in Australia. As an explosives expert, Monkeywrench likes to hear things go bang.

THE COMMAND DECISION Absurdly hyped up because it's drawn by legendary Spawn artist Todd McFarlane, "Crossed Purposes" is so sloppy, it can't bother to mention its villains' names. The whole thing's rushed, off-kilter, full of careless characterization – and entirely overrated.

G.I. Joe #61 to #62, Special Missions #6

Titles: "Beginnings... and Endings" (#61), "Evasion" (Special Missions #6), "Transit" (#62)
Release Dates: July to Aug. 1987
Art: Marshall Rogers (#61), Herb Trimpe (Special Missions #6), William Johnson and Arvell Jones (#62)

BATTLE ROSTER *Joes:* Stalker, Outback, Snow Job, Quick Kick, Hawk, Jinx, Leatherneck; *Cobra:* Cobra Commander, Fred Smith VII, Raptor; *Other:* Billy, the Blind Master.

FIRST APPEARANCES *Other:* Tyrone (ninja-in-training, #61).

DEATHS *Cobra:* Cobra Commander (apparent).

MISSION BRIEF ***Issue #61:*** While talking to Jinx and the Blind Master, Billy slowly regains his memory, then returns to Fred VII's garage to confront Cobra Commander. Unable to betray his father to the authorities, Billy nonetheless disavows Cobra Commander's legacy of crime and departs in a huff to start a new life. Billy meets up with Jinx and, correctly suspecting her to have G.I. Joe ties, asks for help in renewing his ninja training.

Left to contemplate Billy's defection, Cobra Commander decides to resign from his lifelong pursuit of terrorism, carnage and suffering. Cobra Commander removes his battle armor, intending to follow Billy and win back his son's respect, but Fred VII goes mad at the thought of Cobra collapsing. Shockingly, Fred VII produces a handgun and plugs Cobra Commander in the back – killing the former Cobra leader. Standing over Cobra Commander's body, Fred VII ponders the stark simplicity of donning the battle armor and taking his place among the Cobra leadership.

Meanwhile, the Defense Department asks G.I. Joe to intervene when the socialist country Borovia imprisons a hack reporter named Devlin Winchell, falsely accusing him of espionage. Worried that Winchell might end up drawn and quartered purely to humiliate the United States, Hawk sends Stalker, Outback, Snow Job and Quick Kick to rescue him – stressing that the government will, if necessary, disavow all knowledge of Stalker's operation.

In Borovia, Stalker's pack masquerades as trade emissaries, hooking up with an underground agent named Spigou. In due course, the Joes charge into Borovia's state security building, guns at the ready – only to find its prison cells empty. With a sinking feeling, they learn that the American State Department negotiated Winchell's release and neglected to mention it to the Defense Department – leaving Stalker's Joes with their pants down in a hostile country.

Seconds later, Borovian security officers discover the intrusion and sound the alarm – forcing Stalker's troop to flee amid a hail of lead. The Joes reach Spigou's truck, but Borovian bullets wound Quick Kick and Snow Job. Failing to find an escape path, Spigou orders the Joes to dismount while he delays the opposition.

With moments to spare, Stalker decides to stay behind with the wounded Quick Kick and Snow Job – giving Outback a direct order to escape and inform Hawk of their fate. Agonized at leaving his comrades, Outback scurries into Borovia's sewer system, just as a Borovian artillery shell blows up Spigou's truck and kills him. Borovian soldiers led by the harsh Colonel Ratnikov quickly surround Stalker, Quick Kick and Snow Job – forcing an immediate surrender.

Back in America, the Joes listen to newscasts about Stalker's "unauthorized" Borovian mission, making preparations to mount a rescue mission. But to everyone's dismay, Hawk hands down Pentagon orders writing off the captive Joes – and threatening to disavow anyone who breaks rank to save their buddies.

Special Missions #6: Borovian Colonel Ratnikov, eyes looming like bloated goldfish behind his inch-thick spectacles, takes Stalker, Quick Kick and Snow Job into custody – then concludes that Outback fled into the sewers. Ratnikov douses the sewer system with gasoline, turning it into a raging inferno, but Outback escapes into the Borovian countryside.

With Ratnikov's troops sealing off Borovia's Western border, Outback drops some forged Borovian rubles to buy a chicken farmer's truck and heads north toward Austria. Unfortunately, Ratnikov's men track Outback, giving chase in a helicopter.

Knowing Ratnikov will surely run him aground, Outback deliberately crashes his truck and slaughters a chicken – trailing its blood into the woods – then removes his clothes and stuffs them with snow. A short while later, Ratnikov and his aide lands their helicopter and gives chase on foot, following the blood trail and discovering Outback's "corpse." Ratnikov realizes Outback's deception, but the underwear-clad Joe steps out from his cover and takes the colonel captive.

Commandeering Ratnikov's helicopter, Outback forces the colonel and his pilot to fly to the Austrian border. Outback tells the Borovians to return home and parachutes out, but the enraged Ratnikov turns the helicopter about to perforate the Joe with bullets. Thankfully, an Austrian border patrol doesn't take kindly to the Borovians' incursion of their airspace, firing off a missile that obliterates Ratnikov's helicopter. Moments later, the Austrian commander heeds Outback's ramblings about speaking with the American consul.

Issue #62: In a palpable display of injustice, a kangaroo court in Borovia sentences Stalker, Snow Job and Quick Kick to five consecutive life terms of "socially corrective hard labor." Almost immediately, Borovian authorities transport the Joe prisoners to a detention gulag – a work camp with appalling conditions, turncoat inmates and a disastrously high "accident" rate.

Back in the States, the Joes give the returning Outback a damnably frigid reception – openly blaming him for leaving Stalker and company behind. Unable to discuss the matter without clearance, Outback cagily warns his most vocal critics to nix thoughts of threatening him with violence.

Finally, in Denver, Billy continues his training with Jinx and the Blind Master, trying to renew his spirit after recent events. Billy learns more details about Storm Shadow's clan, but eventually, the Blind Master leaves for parts unknown and Billy and Jinx depart for a Joe hideout in San Francisco's Defense Language Center.

MEMORABLE MOMENTS During interrogation, Stalker provokes Ratnikov into punching him unconscious by goading the Borovian: "Is that the best you can do, Sissy-boy? That was chump. You want me to talk, you gotta start hitting like the big boys do!" Holed up in the sewers, Outback feels Stalker's blood leak onto his face – symbolically showing Outback's guilt for leaving his teammates.

While searching for Outback, a leery trooper asks "What if he shoots first?", prompting Ratnikov to fire back: "Then you'll know where he is, won't you?"

A Borovian security agent decides a pedestrian isn't decrying the American prisoners enough and the hapless civilian replies: "Ulp! I'm decrying as hard as I can!"

In the gulag, Stalker takes charge of the prisoners and forces them to distribute food equally – helping the captives to regain their self-respect. Best of all, Leatherneck angrily strafes Outback for leaving his friends behind, but Outback calmly whips a hunting knife from under his pillow and levels Leatherneck with: "Don't even *start* to threaten me. You hear?"

ASS-WHUPPINGS Fred VII tries to stop Billy from leaving, but the ninja-trained teen thumps him. Still, Fred VII at least gets the pleasure of emptying his pistol into Cobra Commander's chest. Snow Job and Quick Kick take hits while escaping in Borovia, although Colonel Ratnikov also knocks Stalker unconscious (ah, equality).

A hitch-hiker tries to steal Outback's truck, but the Joe survivalist, running short on patience, slams on the brakes and cracks the hitch-hiker's head against windscreen, then grabs his noodle and rams it again for good measure.

The Joes' contact Spigou favors death over a trip to the Borovian gulags – and gets his wish. Colonel Ratnikov gets a missile up his exhaust.

GOOFS Stalker's group all wear black commando garb in issue #61 but magically transform into their individual uniforms in *Special Missions* #6. Even more absurdly, the temperature in Borovia evidently accommodates both the shirtless Quick Kick and the parka-wearing Snow Job. A Borovian trooper claims Outback has a "brown beard," and he's depicted that way on the cover of *Special Missions* #6, but he's red-haired the rest of the time. Although Raptor threatens to sell the location of the Joe camp in San Francisco (located at the Defense Language Center) to Cobra in #62's cliffhanger, he inexplicably never follows through with the threat.

COMIC TIE-INS Cobra Commander apparently shuffles off this mortal coil, but reappears – more hammy than ever – in *G.I. Joe* #98.

Billy met the Blind Master and Jinx in *G.I. Joe* #59. The Blind Master shows Billy a photograph here containing mem-

MISCELLANEOUS STUFF!

THE ARASHIKAGE FAMILY TREE

They not only kick ass, they seem to multiply like rabbits. So if you have trouble keeping track of Storm Shadow's family – ninjas and the like affiliated with the Arashikage household – here's a rundown of the relevant relatives:

- **Snake-Eyes (a.k.a. the Silent Master, first seen in *G.I. Joe* #1) and Storm Shadow (a.k.a. the Young Master, *G.I. Joe* #21)** – Storm Shadow's the one connected with the Arashikages by blood, although he invited Snake-Eyes into the family business after Vietnam (#26). Storm Shadow lost his standing with the family after the Hard Master's death (also #26), although Snake-Eyes still endeavors to maintain Arashikage traditions – assuming the mantle of "the Silent Master" in *G.I. Joe* (vol. 2) #1.
- **The Hard Master and the Soft Master (*G.I. Joe* #26)** – Storm Shadow's uncles and the family patriarchs. Although the Hard Master's murder (#26) arguably influenced events more than his life, the Soft Master provided Snake-Eyes with invaluable support until his own demise in *G.I. Joe* #43.
- **Jinx (*G.I. Joe* #59)** – Storm Shadow's second cousin on his mother's side – a fierce ninja and an intelligence expert to boot.
- **Billy (*G.I. Joe* #10)** – Never a formal member of the Arashikage house, although Storm Shadow extensively mentored Billy in #39-#42.
- **The Blind Master (*G.I. Joe* #59)** – Another Arashikage master who owed the Hard Master a life debt. The Blind Master aided Snake-Eyes' cause until he died in battle with Zartan in *G.I. Joe* #91.
- **Onihashi (first mentioned in *G.I. Joe* #62)** – Fabled sword-master to the Arashikage household. Firefly and Zartan both served as Onihashi's assistants, with Onihashi later committing suicide (#85) over Zartan's misdeeds.
- **Firefly (a.k.a. the Faceless Master, mentioned in *G.I. Joe* #62, revealed in #126) and Zartan (revealed in #24)** – Notable as the first non-Japanese person to master a ninja skill, Firefly originally trained with the Koga clan but allied with the Arashikages. Although he served

CONTINUED ON PAGE 191

bers of the Hard Master's household – including a curiously blurred shot of an assistant to Professor Onihashi, the mystic sword-smith. Although #84 suggests the unnamed assistant is Zartan, who later murdered the Hard Master while trying to kill Snake-Eyes (#26), #126 correctly identifies the faceless assistant as Firefly (a.k.a. the Faceless Master) – originally pegged to carry out Zartan's assignment.

Grunt's still attending Georgia Tech as an engineering student (he left Joe service in #55), but phones Joe Headquarters to volunteer for a rescue mission to save Stalker's bunch. The Joes decline, but Snake-Eyes, Scarlett and the Blind Master take matters into their own hands in #63.

Issue #62 gives us our first glimpse of the Pit III in Utah, although the structure isn't formally put into use until #65.

Leatherneck recalls an occasion (#55) when Snake-Eyes refused to obey Stalker's orders and leave him behind. However, Roadblock's quick to point out that Snake-Eyes rightfully relieved the wounded Stalker of command – Outback wasn't given such an option.

CHARACTER PROFILE: JOES

• *Jinx:* Storm Shadow's second cousin on his mother's side. Jinx drives a Ford GT40 Mark V and apparently listens to Bach and Coltrane. She's 23 years old.

• *Outback:* Outback normally carries a P-08 9mm parabellum.

CHARACTER PROFILE: COBRA Raptor: He'd likely serve jail time for tax fraud without Cobra to cover his illicit activities. Raptor possesses a whistle that, when blown, incites his birdies to tear his opponents apart.

CHARACTER PROFILE: OTHER

• *Billy:* He flunked French twice, failing to see the point of learning a language spoken by people who hate America's guts (although Jinx reminds Billy that the French, in point of fact, hate everybody).

• *The Blind Master:* Jinx claims the Blind Master drives her Ford… at night... while listening to the Beastie-Boys, Kill Me and the Thugs.

• *Professor Onihashi's Assistant:* The Blind Master makes mention of Professor Onihashi, an expert sword-smith who sometimes forged weapons for the Hard Master. However, Onihashi's assistant – whose face always appears blurred in photographs – practiced a ninjutsu style belonging to the extinct Koga Clan.

PLACES TO GO Borovia: Borovia shares an eastern border (and a chronic abundance of vowels) with Siberia and Russia. Its northern neighbor is Austria, but a tangled mountain range blocks easy access. "Decadent democracies" lie to the West. Borovia's capital is the city of Krogdnsz. Religious fanatics inhabit Borovia's southern region.

THE COMMAND DECISION One of the most inspired and triumphant *G.I. Joe* stories, structured as a morality play (Outback's face getting literally covered with Stalker's blood, Stalker helping the prisoners to regain their humanity, etc.) but full of action. For once, it's compelling to see the Joes as the underdogs, completely screwed over and disowned by the State Department, proving that no good deed goes unpunished.

G.I. Joe #63 to #66, Special Missions #7

Titles: *"Going Under" (#63), "The Old Switcheroo" (Special Missions #7), "Shuttle Complex" (#65), "The Tenth Letter" (#66)*
Release Dates: *Sept. to Dec. 1987*
Art: *Ron Wagner (#63-#65), Herb Trimpe (Special Missions #7)*

BATTLE ROSTER *Joes:* Snake-Eyes, Scarlett, Storm Shadow, Stalker, Snow Job, Quick Kick, Jinx, Outback, Flint, Lady Jaye, Chuckles, Dial-Tone; *Cobra:* Cobra Commander II, the Baroness, Serpentor, Zarana, Zartan, Dr. Mindbender; *Other:* Billy, the Blind Master.

FIRST APPEARANCES *Joes:* Psyche-Out (deceptive warfare, SM #7), Payload (Defiant pilot, #64), Hardtop (Crawler driver, #64), Back-Stop (Persuader driver, #64), Sci-Fi (laser trooper, #65); *Other:* Captain Minh (#63), the White Clown (#65).

MISSION BRIEF ***Issue #63:*** While Stalker, Quick Kick and Snow Job endure hell in the Borovian gulag, Billy and Jinx arrive at the Joe hideout in San Francisco and joyously reunite with Storm Shadow – Billy's former mentor and Jinx's second cousin.

Meanwhile, Fred Smith VII leaves Raptor to his own devices, loading his POGO battle vehicle and the late Cobra Commander's body armor into a pick-up truck and departing for Galveston. Once there, Fred hires a fisher named Captain Minh to ferry him out to Cobra Island, intending to impersonate Cobra Commander by donning his armor.

Unable to rescue Stalker's team without risking court-martial, Flint and Lady Jaye go on a double-date vacation with Snake-Eyes and Scarlett to Grenada. But while taking a stroll before dinner, Snake-Eyes and Scarlett stop to help a blind black man – actually the Blind Master – across a grassy field. Seconds later, Flint suddenly discovers torn-down signs with the words "Danger – landmines." Heart pounding, Flint screams out for his teammates to take cover, but a massive explosion seemingly obliterates Snake-Eyes, Scarlett and their blind charge.

Lady Jaye and Flint summon minesweepers and search for their teammates' pulped corpses, but fail to find so much as a fingernail. Decently baffled, Flint calls Hawk at the San Francisco base for further orders. Skeptical that the ninja-trained Snake-Eyes would blithely tap-dance onto a landmine, Storm Shadow questions Flint and becomes convinced that the Joe lovers faked their deaths. Moreover, Storm Shadow identifies their accomplice as the Blind Master – a ninja sensei who supposedly died years ago.

Special Missions #7: Assigned to wiretap the Cobra Consulate's main communications network – enabling the Joes to monitor all messages between the Consulate and Cobra Island – Chuckles, Psyche-Out, Lady Jaye and Dial-Tone concoct a complex plot to distract the Consulate personnel and enter the building unnoticed.

Accordingly, Chuckles disguises himself as a freelance military adviser and sells "C-4 explosive" to the Menshevikistas – a group of yuppie counter-revolutionaries seeking to debunk Cobra's support of Sierra Gordo's puppet government. A short while later, the revolutionaries plow a truck into the Consulate's lobby, besieging Cobra forces led by the Baroness. The suicidal revolutionaries lock themselves in the Consulate's boiler room, threatening to collapse the structure with Chuckles' C-4 explosives unless their demands are met.

The Baroness favors caution and evacuating the Consulate save for a skeleton crew. With the Consulate staff focused on the Menshevikistas, Chuckles' team quietly hang-glides onto the Consulate roof, letting their gliders fly on and crash into the Hudson River. With rapid-fire speed, the Joes complete their mission and wiretap the Consulate communications net.

Moving into the operation's final phase, Lady Jaye disguises herself as the Baroness and contacts the revolutionaries – calling their bluff and pushing them to trigger the C-4 detonator. Unfortunately, the "C-4 explosives," actually tear gas packets devised by Chuckles, unleash a billowing cloud that blinds everyone present. Wearing protective masks, Chuckles' group casually struts past the weeping Cobras and revolutionaries – departing the Consulate without leaving a hint of their presence.

Issue #64: Miffed about the Baroness' lousy performance against the revolutionaries, Serpentor relieves the terrorist harridan of command and orders her back to Cobra Island. Simultaneously, Captain Minh's boat, bearing Fred Smith VII, enters Cobra Island's waters and draws the attention of a MAMBA helicopter patrol. As Fred expected, the MAMBAs missile Captain Minh and his boat to shreds, but Fred dons the late Cobra Commander's armor, escaping in his POGO attack vehicle.

On Cobra Island, Fred tries to pass himself off as the original Cobra Commander – making Serpentor's testicles shrivel at the thought of yielding Cobra leadership. As a mass of Cobra troops thirst to see Serpentor and "Cobra Commander" bash each other's brains out, the Baroness' helicopter lands nearby. Convinced that "Cobra Commander" must be an imposter, Serpentor suggests letting the Baroness – the only officer present who knows Cobra Commander's true face – identify the newcomer in private.

In a sealed helicopter, Fred VII nervously admits his scheme to the Baroness, lying through his teeth that the real Cobra Commander departed for a new life with his son Billy. But unexpectedly, the Baroness returns to the assembled Cobra legions and validates Fred's identity as "Cobra Commander"

CONTINUED FROM PAGE 189

as Onihashi's first assistant (Zartan was the second), Cobra Commander later contracted Firefly to kill Snake-Eyes. Fearful of failure, Firefly sub-contracted the hit to Zartan, fleeing when Zartan botched the hit and slew the Hard Master by mistake. The error left Zartan hunted for years, although Firefly later resurfaced – purely for evil's sake – to lead the red ninjas to glory.

- **The Red Ninjas (*G.I. Joe* #21)** – A lesser breed of Arashikage ninjas that're just damn annoying in their ubiquity. After the Hard Master's murder, the red ninjas pooled their resources against his alleged killer – Storm Shadow – but largely got threshed like wheat in subsequent *G.I. Joe* issues.
- **Slice and Dice (*G.I. Joe* #120)** – Slice and Dice run around with the red ninjas, but they're not specifically identified with Storm Shadow's family biz (although heaven knows you can't be a ninja in the G.I. Joe comics without eventually unveiling a tie to the Arashikages).
- **Nunchuk, T'jbang and Dojo (*G.I. Joe* #117)** – The three ninjas who – along with Snake-Eyes and Storm Shadow – compose the core of the often-lambasted "Joe Ninja Force." Although never Arashikage masters, they respectively tutored under the Blind Master, Onihashi and the Soft Master.
- **Kamakura (*G.I. Joe* vol. 2 #1)** – Snake-Eyes' current pupil. He bears the Arashikage brand, but we know virtually nothing about him.

– forcibly making Fred a silent partner to gain her more authority within Cobra.

Issue #65: Having faked their deaths in Grenada, Snake-Eyes, Scarlett and the Blind Master journey deeper into Europe, hoping to rescue Stalker, Quick Kick and Snow Job without putting the other Joes at risk. Eventually, a circus owner named the White Clown hires Snake-Eyes' motley crew as knife-throwers, enabling the Joes to tour through Borovia with the carnival.

Meanwhile, Cobra officials freak when the U.S. Air Force upgrades its spy satellites, putting Cobra's ultra-secret Terror-Drome under threat of discovery. In response, the Baroness takes Cobra Commander II to jointly lead a Cobra space shuttle launch – hoping to blast various satellites out of orbit and hamstring the American surveillance network.

At the newly constructed Pit III, built under a few simple-looking huts in the Utah desert, the Joes detect the Cobra launch and ready their own space shuttle, the *Defiant*, for lift-off. High above Earth, the *Defiant* and the Cobra shuttle pepper each other with laser fire, causing the Baroness to hit her head and fall unconscious.

Deprived of the Baroness' battle experience, Cobra Commander II momentarily freezes, then barks out a series of decisive orders and reasserts himself as the alpha male. Galvanized into action, the Cobra shuttle singes the *Defiant* and wipes out a series of American spy satellites, guaranteeing the completion of the Terror-Drome operation on schedule. Damaged and unable to pursue the fleeing Cobra ship, the *Defiant* limps back to Earth.

Issue #66: At Storm Shadow's urging, Jinx compiles US intelligence information on Borovia and tags Gulag 23 near Pvnsk as the labor camp holding Stalker, Quick Kick and Snow Job. Jinx also locates a newspaper photo of the White Clown's circus – with a tiny Scarlett in the background.

In Borovia, the White Clown continues touring near various gulags, hoping to locate his lost lover Magda – a horseback rider and prominent government dissenter who disappeared into the gulag system. Storm Shadow, Jinx and Billy travel to Borovia to assist Snake-Eyes' group, but the White Clown learns the Joes' identities and ponders betraying them for information about Magda.

The Joe ninja force enters Gulag 23 under cover of a thunderstorm, slitting most of the guards' throats without raising an alarm. Swiftly dispatching the remaining resistance, the ninjas arm the prisoners and help them scurry into a nearby forest. Snake-Eyes' party reunites with Stalker's trio and makes for a river bordering Borovia, only to find themselves sandwiched between guard towers and Borovian troops commanded by the bloodthirsty Sgt. Mosiev.

The Joes flounder for a course of action, but the White Clown, unable to let the heroes perish, drives up with a circus cannon. In short order, the White Clown fires the Joes across the river and over the Borovian border like human cannonballs, putting them beyond the Borovians' jurisdiction. With the Joes safe, the resourceful White Clown makes his own departure, pleased for upholding Magda's belief in justice.

MEMORABLE MOMENTS The Cobra Consulate siege turns hysterical as the Baroness analyzes her Sierra Gordo foes and concludes: "We're being blackmailed by radical yuppie terrorists!" As the Baroness preps her troops for slaughter, Zarana non-chalantly eats grapes and frivolously slices the Baroness' judgement to ribbons.

Soon after, the Baroness follows the No. 1 rule of a terrorist negotiation, namely, "Storm the enemy's hideout and find out if they've got any fire in their bellies!" As a result, the revolutionaries shoot a *lot* of Cobra Vipers, escalating the bitching between the Baroness and Zarana to new heights (the Baroness scalds her rival with: "That pink hair-dye is shriveling what's left of your brains...")

Rowdy troopers on Cobra Island suggest that Serpentor and Cobra Commander II settle their dispute in the traditional manner – by emulating *Fight Club* and thrashing each other silly (Zartan laments: "Alas, Serpentor... you allowed your troops to get bored... and bored troops are bloodthirsty!")

Questioning what possessed her to aid with Fred's mad scheme to assume Cobra leadership, the Baroness criticizes Fred for even attempting such a ruse. In turn, a somewhat-manic Fred hysterically concedes: "I must have been having a sugar imbalance!"

There's a completely off-the-wall moment during circus auditions as the Blind Master balances atop an inflated green ball and juggles chainsaws while Snake-Eyes stands on his shoulders and tosses knives at a strapped-down Scarlett (the White Clown finally announces: "You're hired! You'll go on after the dancing bears!")

LOVE AND WAR Lady Jaye formerly resisted Flint's charms (#55), but evidently caved into his slobbering desires, traveling with him to Grenada with Snake-Eyes and Scarlett (presumably, the couples enjoy bikinis and nookie all around).

ASS-WHUPPINGS Chuckles' team didn't intend wanton death and mayhem at the Cobra Consulate Building – but hardly shed tears when the revolutionaries hole a pack of Cobra Consulate Vipers. Infuriated at Zarana's constant whining, the Baroness loses restraint and jumps the pink-haired bitch. Seconds later, the revolutionaries' "C-4 explosive" (i.e. tear gas) douses everyone except the Joes.

Cobra patrol helicopters splinter Captain Minh's boat, but Fred Smith VII devastates a Cobra MAMBA helicopter with his

POGO attack bubble (not exactly the best way to ingratiate oneself to Cobra, but nobody holds it against him). Mind, Cobra ground troops smear another MAMBA while trying to recapture Fred's POGO.

Smugglers accost the Blind Master's troupe in France, but the sensei performs a hair-raising leap and tosses a grenade into the smugglers' car. In Borovia, Storm Shadow's ninja cadre knives, garrotes and flattens the gulag guardsmen. Scarlett nails one with a throwing star in the neck.

During the final escape, Sgt. Mosiev challenges Stalker to a long-distance rifle duel. Thankfully, the Joe ranger easily zips a bullet through Mosiev's heart, then flees with his comrades.

GOOFS Someone – and we seriously don't know who – keeps re-clothing the gulag-trapped Joes. In short, #62 showed Quick Kick entirely shirtless, but he oddly regains his red chest wrap in #63.

Fred VII's seemingly unconcerned that Raptor knows the location of Cobra Commander's body and could blow his cover, but for whatever reason, Raptor doesn't.

Issue #64 shows *Defiant* commander Payload with black skin, but he's white in #65.

Finally, how did White Clown know to magically appear at precisely the right moment *with a circus cannon in tow*, thus helping the Joes escape? (If only he'd brought along a trampoline to make sure our heroes landed safely on the other side!)

COMIC TIE-INS *G.I. Joe* #59 hinted that the Joes were undertaking operations in Utah (here revealed as the Pit III), but the original Cobra Commander, who made the discovery, "died" in #61 and didn't investigate further (CC's co-conspirators, Fred and Raptor, busied themselves with other concerns). Still, Serpentor and Dr. Mindbender grow increasingly suspicious of Cobra satellite photos marking Joe activity in Utah and finally dispatch the Star Viper (#72) to learn more.

Storm Shadow previously trained Billy as a ninja in *G.I. Joe* #39-#42 and was last seen helping Scarlett extract Snake-Eyes from the Cobra Consulate Building (*G.I. Joe Yearbook* #3). Billy here informs Storm Shadow and Ripcord about the deaths of their loved ones, the Soft Master and Candy (killed in *G.I. Joe* #43).

Cobra MAMBA helicopters missile Captain Minh's boat to pieces, but Minh survives and roughs it on Cobra Island for nearly a year, turning up in *G.I. Joe* #72.

The Baroness assumed Consulate command upon fleeing Sierra Gordo in *G.I. Joe* #56. Serpentor here demotes the Baroness and awards the post to Zarana, who spontaneously cedes the position to Zartan in #79. In the same issue, Cobra uncovers Chuckles' wiretap on the Consulate's communications web.

Like his predecessor, Cobra Commander II wears a helmet lined with anti-tamper explosive (#24). A scar on the Blind Master's arm suggests he wore the brand of Storm Shadow's family (first seen in #21) but later removed it.

Snake-Eyes later returns to Borovia and – among other things – liberates the White Clown's lover Magda in *G.I. Joe* #103-#106.

CHARACTER PROFILE: JOES

- *Flint:* Appears slightly callous to the missing Joes' plight, arguing they knew the dangers of venturing to Borovia.
- *Hardtop:* Not very talkative, he typically delivering answers in sentences of one syllable.

CHARACTER PROFILE: OTHER

- *The Blind Master:* He's apparently skilled at faking his death. Although sightless, the Blind Master possesses almost superhuman senses – performing a stunning number of acrobatic stunts.
- *The White Clown and Magda:* By allying himself with the Joes, the White Clown fails to learn that the vicious Sgt. Mosiev wounded Magda during an escape attempt from a different Borovian gulag. Thankfully, Magda survived. The White Clown's often accompanied by a human cannonball, a dwarf named Orlovsky.

PLACES TO GO The Pit III: Designed for stealth and efficiency, lacking even hydraulic lifts. A single ramp provides Pit access for a number of Joe vehicles, including the Defiant.

STUFF YOU NEED Katas and Kuji-No-In: Storm Shadow and his fellow ninjas sometimes indulge in katas, formal martial arts exercises that explore different aspects of reason and the intellectual mind. One such exercise, called kuji-no-in, involves finger-knitting various symbols that represent different facets of one's intuition, supposedly channeling one's ki (a.k.a. life force) as a result. The tenth kuji-no-in symbol represents "the void," a mental state of nothingness that clears the ninjas' minds before battle.

HOT WHEELS Joe Hang-Gliders: Built for stealth, they employ ceramic rotary engines with high-efficiency sound mufflers.

THE COMMAND DECISION A fantastic array of character shading, gelling Snake-Eyes, Scarlett and their ninja associates into a family unit like never before. The bookend chapters in Borovia (issues #63 and #66) mostly focus on the depths of friendship, echoing the army's code of never leaving its boys behind. Issue #64's also a gem, allowing the Baroness' defection of Serpentor to further Fred Smith's madcap quest. If there's a fault, it's that issue #65 drags the entire project down like a lead weight (repeat the following:

G.I. Joe never works as space opera), although even that black eye merely pulls back on the reins a bit, leaving the bulk of these issues a story arc to savor.

G.I. Joe Special Missions #8 to #10

Titles: *"Ambush" (#8), "Plausible Denial" (#9), "Turnabout" (#10)*
Release Dates: *Bi-monthly from Dec. to Apr. 1988*
Art: *Herb Trimpe*

BATTLE ROSTER *Joes:* Low-Light, Flint, Wild Bill, Psyche-Out, Slip-Stream, Lt. Falcon, Chuckles, Roadblock.

MISSION BRIEF ***Issue #8:*** In Southeast Asia, a CIA agent named Anderson conscripts Flint, Low-Light, Beach-Head and other Joe members to perform a manhunt for Theron Portland – an American defector making his way via armored convoy to Russia. Claiming that Portland stole a top-secret computer chip, Anderson authorizes sniper Low-Light to assassinate Portland if they fail to capture him alive. Curious as to why the CIA didn't conduct the operation in-house, Flint and Low-Light start to suspect Anderson of setting them up to fail.

Flint's team lies in wait, only to discover that Anderson deliberately underestimated the size and strength of Portland's convoy. Worse, a microchip siren, concealed by Anderson in the Joes' radio, starts wailing and blows their cover. Seriously outgunned, Flint's team abandons their mission, racing like mad for an extraction zone. Simultaneously, Low-Light gives chase as Portland panics and runs off into the jungle.

Unable to kill an unarmed man, Low-Light contents himself with knocking Portland unconscious and stealing his computer chip. A few minutes later, Low-Light arrives at the rendezvous point, escaping aboard a Joe Tomahawk 'copter with his friends. Aboard the Tomahawk, the Joes work Anderson over, learning that the CIA *wanted* Portland to give Russia his chip – secretly tainted with a virus – in order to wreck the Soviets' key computer systems. Having gone to all this trouble to make the Joes fail, Anderson is suitably upset to learn Low-Light inadvertently ruined the scheme by bagging Portland's microchip.

Issue #9: Assigned to rescue CIA chief Chip Toler from an Iranian prison, Lt. Falcon, Psyche-Out and Slip-Stream look for a way to fulfill their mission with a minimum of effort. Consequently, the three Joes disguise themselves as Russian officers and liberate three Russian Spetsnaz commandos from an Afghan holding cell. Claiming that Soviet officials want Toler for questioning, Falcon's trio orders the Russian commandos to rescue the CIA man.

Having penetrated the Joes' flimsy disguises, the three commandos nonetheless play along, butchering their way through Toler's guards and snagging the CIA chief. The Russians send Toler on his way to the Joes' escape plane – with a horde of Iranian soldiers on his tail. Panicking, the Joes pull Toler aboard and fly South toward an American submarine. Reveling in their little distraction, the Soviets head north toward Mother Russia.

Issue #10: In the equatorial country of Kalingaland, a communist regime falls from power, leading the American government to call for the ousted Prince Ngoto's restoration to power. Accordingly, Chuckles and Roadblock travel to England – where the prince currently works as an Oxford lecturer – and shield him from Kalingan communist assassins.

The Joes dodge bullets and missiles all the way to Kalingaland, finally returning Ngoto safely to the capitol building. Secure in his power, the prince magnanimously calls for a fair election, encouraging the people to choose between a democratic or socialist government. But to help the Kalingans learn self-reliance, Ngoto expels *both* the American and Russian ambassadors. Having expected the prince to be a little more grateful, the American ambassador bemoans his expulsion, but Chuckles and Roadblock deem Ngoto an honest and upright man.

MEMORABLE MOMENTS In issue #8, Low-Light teases spineless CIA agent Anderson for using terms such as "render operational" instead of the more accurate "shoot with extreme prejudice" or "kill so-and-so in cold blood."

In the same issue, Portland's convoy finds itself unable to pass a local kid and his buffalo on a narrow jungle road. The kid begs the Russian officers that his family needs the buffalo to cultivate rice and survive, but a nameless Soviet officer callously blows the buffalo away – proof positive that innocents often suffer most in war.

ASS-WHUPPINGS Low-Light unflinchingly plugs a Soviet officer who's about to unjustly kill a local boy for perceived treachery. Psyche-Out, Lt. Falcon and Slip-Stream manipulate Russian commandos into committing wholesale slaughter on their behalf.

Chuckles pumps a Kalingan communist full of lead, letting the man's corpse fall down a well. Roadblock fatally dissuades some pursuers with a .50 caliber machine gun burst.

GOOFS Leatherneck's moustache disappears while he's sweating in the jungle (#8). Issue #9's a bit goofy in that Psyche-Out's concerned about shifting potential blame for the Iranian undertaking onto the Russians – so why dress the

Russkie commandos up as Americans?

COMIC TIE-INS Oily CIA agent Anderson returns in *Special Missions* #14-#15.

CHARACTER PROFILE: JOES

- *Roadblock:* He detests violence – because it plays havoc with one's digestive system.
- *Lt. Falcon and Psyche-Out:* Psyche-Out wonders if Lt. Falcon's preference for direct violence stems from an unfortunate relationship with his mother (Falcon rebuffs this as nonsense).
- *Low-Light and Agent Anderson:* In order to make the "retrieval operation" believable, Anderson ordered Low-Light to assassinate Portland – knowing that the moralistic Joe wouldn't shoot down a man in cold blood.

CHARACTER PROFILE: OTHER

Prince Ngoto: Even though he's middle-aged, he's acknowledged as "Prince Ngoto the Younger." His brother, Prince Ngoto the Elder, tragically perished in polo accident in 1953.

HOT WHEELS Joe Black C-47 Dakota: A top-of-the-line stealth ship, built for espionage and equipped with virtually every anti-detection device imaginable: radar-resistant paint, electronic counter measures pods, radar blisters, engine noise mufflers, chopped-tip wooden blades to mask rotor sound and infra-red baffles to reduce the ship's heat signature.

THE COMMAND DECISION Admittedly long-winded, issue #8 exists to glowingly spotlight Low-Light's character (he unswervingly executes a would-be child killer, but stops from offing unarmed traitor Portland). It's also a classic example of government agencies failing to comprehend a soldier's purpose in life (CIA stooge Anderson can't even utter the word "kill"), highlighting the need for soldiers who're more than zombified gunmen.

Special Missions #9 is an interesting experiment of some Russians outwitting the Joes, although the story's murky twists leave you scratching your head at points. Finally, issue #10 climaxes with the delicious twist of the Americans and Russians *both* failing to win Prince Ngoto's loyalty, but a string of run-of-the-mill chases water down the story, making it average at best.

G.I. Joe #67 to #68

Titles: *"Cold Snap" (#67), "Cut and Freeze Dried" (#68)*
Release Dates: *Jan. to Feb. 1988*
Art: *Ron Wagner*

BATTLE ROSTER *Joes:* Stalker, Quick Kick, Snow Job, Outback, Snake-Eyes, Scarlett, Flint, Lady Jaye, Storm Shadow, Jinx, Hawk; *Cobra:* Cobra Commander II, The Baroness, Dr. Mindbender; *Other:* The Blind Master, Billy.

FIRST APPEARANCES *Joes:* Frostbite (Snow Cat driver, #68), Iceberg (snow trooper, #68), Battle Force 2000: Blaster (Vindicator pilot, #68), Maverick (Vector pilot, #68), Blocker (Eliminator driver, #68), Avalanche (Dominator driver, #68), Dodger (Marauder driver, #68), Knockdown (Sky-Sweeper anti-aircraft driver, #68)

MISSION BRIEF As Stalker's party lands at the Pit III in Utah, a remorseful Outback melts in shame for abandoning his teammates in Borovia. In turn, Stalker praises Outback for following orders – leaving several Joes sheepish for accusing Outback of cowardice. Thankfully, Outback fails to mention the Joes' bullying, taking his rescued comrades out for drinks.

Meanwhile, in the Nordic country of Frusenland, Prime Minister Volff abandons his predecessor's reactionary policies and solidifies ties with America – firing Cobra as the country's primary weapons supplier. In response, Cobra waits for the beginning of Frusenland's reindeer festival and initiates the final phase of its ultra-secret Terror-Drome scheme. With the flip of a switch, Cobra Commander II, the Baroness and Dr. Mindbender activate paranoia ray devices (#2) secretly installed in Frusenland's Terror-Dromes – dousing the entire country with fear-inducing radio waves.

As Cobra expected, Frusenland plunges into near-anarchy, leaving Volff little choice but to sign a new Cobra weapons pact in order to to restore order through heavily armed riot-control troopers. Unwilling to abandon US-Frusenland relations, the Americans dispatch a Joe battalion, including a state-of-the-art Joe task force named Battle Force 2000, to Frusenland to "protect" an imaginary American research team "already stationed there." The paranoia ray makes the Joes angrily flare their nostrils at one another, but Battle Force 2000 member Blaster – having noticed Cobra troops wearing protective headphones – makes his teammates wear sound mufflers.

Restored, the Joes whip several Cobra squadrons, eventually discovering that Cobra sold its Terror-Dromes worldwide at a loss, purely as a means of entrenching its paranoia-rays. Cobra intended the paranoia rays to generate civil unrest, thereby setting the stage for a record number of arms sales, but the Joes publicly reveal Cobra's scheme. With political leaders across the globe decrying Cobra's plot, Volff expels Cobra from Frusenland and returns his country to normal.

MEMORABLE MOMENTS Stalker shows disbelief at the mere suggestion that the Joes would haze Outback for obeying orders and fleeing Borovia. But as the guilt-stricken Joes fall silent, Outback rises above the occasion by declaring: "Not in a million years, Stalker! The Joes are made of better stuff than that!"

Also, Storm Shadow speculates that the Blind Master, who's gushing with pearls of wisdom, secretly reads Braille fortune cookies.

LOVE AND WAR Flint berates Snake-Eyes and Scarlett for concealing their plans to infiltrate Borovia (#63), but an irked Lady Jaye slugs him for being so insensitive. Lady Jaye stresses that Snake-Eyes and Scarlett didn't want her and Flint implicated out of compassion – then lets slip her own feelings for the Joe warrant officer. Flint immediately downshifts, admitting his error, and wraps Lady Jaye in a hug.

ASS-WHUPPINGS Fear-inducing soundwaves make Battle Force 2000 members Dodger, Avalanche and Blocker roughhouse each other. Lady Jaye topples an entire row of HISS tanks with a single laser cannon shot. Iceberg empties his anti-tank weapon into a Cobra MAGGOT driver's face at point-blank range.

GOOFS Snow Job's still wearing his winter parka – even in Utah's heat. Cobra Commander II's seen toasting with a champagne glass – but Heaven only knows how he's drinking it.

Jinx, a highly trained ninja, "lets her concentration wander" and allows a street punk to snatch her purse (yeah, right). Reversed word balloons on page 16 of issue #68 show Hawk saving Iceberg but oddly shouting, "I got you, Hawk!"

The Joes fail to actually prove that Cobra's indulging in illicit fear broadcasts, but Volff believes the Joes' accusations anyway (then again, it's not like Cobra's got a squeaky-clean record).

COMIC TIE-INS Stalker, Snow Job and Quick Kick finally return to base, five months after their capture (#61) and imprisonment in a Borovian gulag (#62). The Joes (unjustly) tormented Outback for abandoning his teammates in #62. Joe psychologist Psyche-Out covers for the prodigal Snake-Eyes and Scarlett's absence, reporting that the Grenada mine blast (*G.I. Joe* #63) left them momentarily "deranged" and unable to realize the consequences of their Borovian expedition (#64-#66).

In *G.I. Joe* #2, Inuit mercenary Kwinn helped the Joes obtain a fear-inducing ultra-frequency wave transmitter from the Russians. But at an unspecified point, Cobra Commander acquired the transmitter's blueprints and asked the late Dr. Venom (first seen in #10, killed in #19) to modify the gizmo. Cobra finally launched its Terror-Drome project, designed to spur arms sales through these mass-inducing fear rays, in #54.

The Blind Master accepts a street punk named Tyrone, who re-appears in *G.I. Joe* #91 as his newest pupil.

Storm Shadow's trying to quell his thoughts of revenge against Zartan (revealed as the Hard Master's killer in *G.I. Joe* #45-#47), but finds himself at odds with the Cobra shapeshifter in #85.

CHARACTER PROFILE: JOES

Storm Shadow: Having reflected upon his place in the universe, Storm Shadow now advocates using one's mastery of martial arts to become non-violent. In short, a proper warrior should strive to tame violence and set it aside, resorting to lethal force only as a means of upholding honor.

PLACES TO GO Frusenland: Frusenland's got hundreds of miles of undefended shoreline, but that's largely okay – nothing worse than "rabid sea lions" normally causes trouble. Frusenland leases Arctic bases and conventional weapons testing sites to the United States, providing the Joes with excuses for visiting the country.

STUFF YOU NEED Cobra Commander II's Armor: Equipped with sound mufflers that screen out the fear-generating waves.

HOT WHEELS Cobra Wolves: Arctic attack vehicles equipped with Doppler radar that's calibrated to ignore ground clutter and detect anything more than three feet tall.

THE COMMAND DECISION Oh word, this is the payoff for 14 issues of build-up? Between a lackluster revelation concerning Cobra's Terror-Drome sales and the birth of the fan-loathed Battle Force 2000, the only reason to read issues #67-#68 is a brief but welcome epilogue to the Borovian storyline – and trust us, that's hardly worth the price of admission.

G.I. Joe #69 to #71

Titles: *"Into the Breach" (#69), "Fair Trade" (#70), "Bail-out" (#71)*
Release Dates: *Mar. to May 1988*
Art: *Tony Salmons (#69), Ron Wagner (#70-#71)*

BATTLE ROSTER *Joes:* Wild Bill, Maverick, Hawk, Psyche-Out, Roadblock; *Cobra:* Zarana, Monkeywrench, Thrasher; *Destro:* Destro.

FIRST APPEARANCES *Joes:* Crazylegs (paratrooper, #69); *Destro:* Destro (as Iron Grenadier leader / weapons manufacturer, #69), Iron Grenadiers (Destro's shock troops, #69).

MISSION BRIEF ***Issue #69:*** After the collapse of Cobra's Terror-Drome scheme, several precariously perched dictatorships lose support and fall to insurrectionists. In war-torn Sierra Gordo, the seedy North American Banana Monopoly (NABM) protects its interests by siding with a military leader named General Villavaca – enabling Villavaca to exterminate the country's ruling party. As mobs tear up Sierra Gordo's capital, Hawk takes Roadblock and Psyche-Out to rescue U.S. Ambassador Winthrop from the crumbling American embassy.

Meanwhile, Villavaca continues purging Sierra Gordo of undesirable elements by carving the country's Terror-Dromes to shrapnel. Unable to withstand Villavaca's assault, a Cobra command staff composed of Zarana, Monkeywrench and Thrasher makes a mad dash for freedom in the Dreadnok Thunder Machine.

Nearby, Destro opens arms negotiations with Villavaca and NABM representative Chip Goodfellow. Goodfellow and Villavaca salivate over the prospect of unlimited arms – then discover that Ambassador Winthrop's documents could prove Villavaca's illegal ties to the NABM and effectively destroy the company.

Villavaca's troops surround the American embassy, but Hawk's team grabs Winthrop and drives away. Hawk's group races pell-mell for the local airport, trying to rendezvous with a C-130 transport plane staffed by Wild Bill, Crazylegs and Maverick. Unfortunately, a group of Sierra Gordo refugees arrives at the C-130 first and begs for asylum. Worse, the Dreadnoks drive up and take the refugees hostage – threatening to blow away the assembled men, women and children unless the Joe airmen help them escape.

With little choice, Wild Bill loads the refugees and their pistol-happy Dreadnok captors onto the C-130, firing up its engines. Seconds later, Hawk's gang races onto the airfield, despairing to see the C-130 leaving without them. Wild Bill opens up the C-130's throttle, but Villavaca's men strafe the transport plane and heavily damage its engines.

Villavaca's troops nearly overrun Hawk's party, but Destro – playing all parties in Sierra Gordo against each other – radios pro-American revolutionaries to save Hawk's bacon. While Hawk's band melts into the jungle, Destro calmly retires to his hotel and dons an upgraded uniform – complete with a gold face plate – symbolizing a new era for his family's arms business.

Issue #70: Wild Bill tries to control the careening C-130, but the airship steers like a pregnant cow and crashes into the Sierra Gordo jungle. Crazylegs, Maverick and Wild Bill evacuate the plane's occupants moments before the ship explodes – leaving the Joes stranded with several refugees and a trio of nutty Dreadnoks.

Meanwhile, panic-stricken that Ambassador Winthrop escaped with files that could damn the NABM, Goodfellow pays Destro a hefty fee to dispatch the ambassador. But finding Goodfellow too dishonorable, Destro tracks Hawk's troupe –

MISCELLANEOUS STUFF!

DESTRO'S SELF-EMPLOYMENT

They've come to blows before, both on TV and in the comics, but it's hard to imagine Cobra Commander trying to conquer the world without the shiny Destro at his side. Nonetheless, depicting a shift of allegiance never realized on TV, Destro largely defects the Cobra cause in *G.I. Joe* #55 – evidently feeling there's no room for his (relatively) noble style of leadership in the G.I. Joe/Cobra struggle. Accordingly, Destro returns to his family homestead in Scotland, lazing about until he dons a gold-plated helmet and embarks on a string of lucrative arms deals in *G.I. Joe* #69.

From that point onward, Destro harnesses his family's arms business to make his legions (largely composed of Iron Grenadier and Annihilator shock troops) a match for any Joe and Cobra battalion stupid enough to get in his way. But although Destro easily rivaled his adversaries for military might (notably *G.I. Joe* #74-#76), thoughts of power largely bored him. Unlike Cobra Commander, Destro scoffed at notions of dominating territory and overthrowing governments, almost deeming such endeavors as too *vulgar* and contenting himself mostly with cash flow.

As such, the Joes warmed to Destro much like Batman learned to regard Catwoman – as a valued (if shady) ally given free reign up to a certain point. Indeed, Destro, the Joes and the Baroness (who fully sides with Destro after *G.I. Joe* #76) teamed up on several occasions (*G.I. Joe* #57, #116-#118, #120-#122 and more), grappling with a variety of greater threats. And although Destro briefly resumed command of Cobra from *G.I. Joe* #88-#97, it certainly wasn't to his liking – prompting his quick resignation and return to his Scottish homestead.

Indeed, one gets the impression that Destro would far rather keep out of the Joe/Cobra conflict entirely, selling some arms here and there and banging the Baroness as often as possible. But much like Han Solo in *Star Wars*, events keep conspiring to put Destro in the thick of things – ruining the steel-faced genius' plans for high tea and a relatively quiet life.

cornered in the jungle by Villavaca's forces – and blows up Villavaca's men instead.

Destro introduces himself to El Jefe, the top pro-American revolutionary, and offers to support El Jefe's political standing. In return, El Jefe vows to forcibly seize the NABM's holdings in Sierra Gordo – and award Destro's firm a franchise to run them. Winthrop turns outraged that El Jefe would sell out to an arms dealer like Destro, but Hawk wisely keeps his own council and extradites his team from Sierra Gordo with Destro's assistance.

Issue #71: Stranded in Sierra Gordo with a snowball's chance in hell of escaping, the combined Joe/refugee/Dreadnok brigade commandeers a military bus and desperately tries to avoid capture. General Villavaca disperses his troops to search for the missing C-130 transport plane, but Goodfellow, afraid that Ambassador Winthrop will expose the NABM's illegal ties to the general, advises Villavaca to raid Sierra Gordo's treasury and flee to Switzerland. Villavaca tries to comply, but Destro arrives in force at the treasury with El Jefe's men to arrest the general.

With Zarana behind the wheel, Wild Bill's group spots a roadblock and attempts to plow their way through. Villavaca's men instigate a madcap chase through the streets of Sierra Gordo's capital, causing a series of accidents just as El Jefe tries to leave with the captive Villavaca. Mistakenly believing that Villavaca sold out to El Jefe's cause, Villavaca's own men pump the general full of bullets, gruesomely killing him.

Scrambling for cover, Will Bill's team arrives at the local docks, just as Goodfellow – his briefcase stuffed with money illicitly gained from NABM's bank accounts – tries to depart for Barcelona in his private plane. Wild Bill's group storms the airplane and takes off, but Goodfellow produces an Uzi and tries to take everyone hostage. Unbearably annoyed, Dreadnok Thrasher loses control and tosses Goodfellow off the plane without a parachute, allowing the motley crew of Joes, Dreadnoks and refugees to reach America and go their separate ways.

MEMORABLE MOMENTS In one of the series' most telling moments, Roadblock happens upon a grotty little looter in the desecrated American embassy – who's about to torch an American flag with a cigarette lighter. Roadblock cocks his machine gun and tells the perp: "Sir, you are willfully attempting to destroy United States property. If you persist in doing so... I shall reduce your head to a fine red mist." When the loony wonders why Roadblock's not shooting other thieves who're making off with IBM typewriters, the unflinching Joe responds: "[Because] nobody ever died for a typewriter."

The Dreadnoks provide a near-endless stream of entertainment, especially when Zarana threatens the Sierra Gordo refugees and Wild Bill deadpans: "Lady, I'm putting a black mark next to your name in my book." Thrasher breaks his nose at one point, causing an amusing speech impediment through the rest of the story (Thrasher on his maimed arm: "Arrr! Don't touch id! Id hurts!"). In a surprising twist, Thrasher strikes up a friendship with a Sierra Gordon child and gives a fleeting wave when the refugees depart.

ASS-WHUPPINGS Villavaca's men shoot up Ambassador Winthrop's legs, but Roadblock guts their hideout with machine gun fire. When Villavaca insanely orders an open charge reminiscent of "the Light Brigade," Psyche-Out, Roadblock and Hawk happily gun down their attackers.

Dreadnok Thrasher refuses to strap into his seatbelt – and breaks his nose and right arm when the Joe C-130 crashes to Earth. Thrasher spends the rest of the story in pain but vents his frustrations by clubbing a bus full of Villavaca's troops with an entrenching tool (Crazylegs surveys the damage and asks: "What did they do, let loose a rabid grizzly bear?") For the grand finale, Zarana pistol-whips Thrasher unconscious, ending his rampage.

COMIC TIE-INS The Joes first visited Sierra Gordo in *G.I. Joe* #12, although Snake-Eyes and some Joe buddies laid waste to the country's main Terror-Drome in #54-#56. After this, El Jefe welches on his deal with Destro, leading to conflict in G.I. Joe *Special Missions* #23 and #26.

CHARACTER PROFILE: COBRA Zarana: She's got at least a drop of honor, allowing the Sierra Gordo refugees to leave when the need arises rather than stealing their bus.

CHARACTER PROFILE: DESTRO *Destro:* Destro dons a more elaborate and regal uniform, complete with a gold (rather than silver) faceplate. He commands a legion of shock troops called the Iron Grenadiers. An Iron Grenadier sergeant-major serves as his aide de campe.

PLACES TO GO Sierra Gordo: A country that's been screwed from within and without – by both American monopolies and a string of right-wing dictatorships – for generations.

THE COMMAND DECISION Hysterically funny in parts, issues #69-#71 blend together an inspired roster of characters with the Dreadnoks' constant dementia (especially the wind-'em-up and let-'em-go Thrasher). Additionally, the crisp plot – with Hawk's team fighting for survival even as Destro pushes everyone's buttons – sweetens the deal, making this one of the superior "Joes lost in a gun-riddled locale" stories.

G.I. Joe Special Missions #11 to #13

Titles: *"Sheep's Clothing" (#11), "Airshow" (#12), "Wash-out" (#13)*
Release Dates: *Bi-monthly from June to Sept. 1988*
Art: *Herb Trimpe*

BATTLE ROSTER *Joes:* Slip-Stream, Lift-Ticket, Scarlett, Lady Jaye, Jinx, Low-Light, Dial-Tone, Ace, Slip-Stream, Maverick, Outback, Dusty; *Cobra:* Firefly.

FIRST APPEARANCES *Joes:* Lightfoot (explosives expert, #13), Mangler (unspecified, #13).

DEATHS *Joes:* Mangler (#13).

MISSION BRIEF ***Issue #11:*** In Frankfurt, West Germany, a quartet of revolutionaries robs a lucrative American PX supply store. After a shootout with local police, the robbers hole up in the PX store with three hostages. Simultaneously, the revolutionaries' associates hijack a plane at the Reinmain Flughafen Airport as an escape route.

Led by Chuckles, a Joe team discusses how to best defuse the situation. With two of the hostages respectively suffering from diabetes and a heart condition, Chuckles arranges to swap the prisoners for Joe operatives. Disguised as "harmless nurses," Scarlett, Lady Jaye and Jinx trade places with the hostages. But as the revolutionaries set out for the airport, the Joe women thrash their opponents seven ways to Sunday. Finally, the Joe males don the revolutionaries' clothes, waltzing aboard the aircraft with the captive "nurses" and wiping out the hijackers.

Issue #12: In order to improve the Joes' public relations, Ace, Slip-Stream and Maverick perform a series of high-flying stunts at an Orange County Airport show. But once the Joes land, Firefly and a covert Cobra team filch vital classified components from Ace's Skystriker and Slip-Stream's Conquest X-30. Firefly's group then takes off in Maverick's Vector jet, intending to fly the Joe ship to Cobra headquarters for dissection.

Improvising, Maverick finds a local pilot named Bert Phriem and gives chase in Bert's PT-17 crop duster. Firefly conceals his ship on a barge, but Maverick deduces Firefly's strategy and alerts the Coast Guard. Minutes later, a fleet of Coast Guard ships surrounds Firefly's group, allowing the Joes to safely retrieve their jet components.

Issue #13: Having previously cut deals with the African nation of Trucial Abysmia, the American government frets when a communist regime takes power. The Americans withdraw their personnel and supplies, but in the confusion, a cache of ultra-secret fighter plane electronics gets left behind. Assigned to blow up the electronics depot, Outback and Dusty take freshmen Joes Lightfoot and Mangler on a search-and-destroy mission.

Unfortunately, members of the newly entrenched communist army capture the Joes halfway to their objective. A fiendish, self-serving officer named Aman tortures Lightfoot, forcing him to reveal the electronics cache's whereabouts. Aman sets off to secure the electronics store, leaving his subordinate, Captain Yusif, to kill the Joes. Thankfully, the compassionate Yusif lets the Joes live, suggesting they go 20 miles east to friendly territory.

But once Yusif leaves, the resolute Joes, determined to complete their mission, make their way 40 miles west to the electronics bunker. At the bunker, Aman uncovers a gold mine of guidance systems, keeping back stockpiles of American food stocks – flour, cocoa, scotch and more – to sell on the black market.

That night, the Joes steal a thermate grenade and jury-rig an explosion, blowing the weapons cache to smithereens. Victorious, the Joes make tracks in a stolen armored car, but Aman's armored division gives chase. Sacrificing himself, Mangler jumps off the Joe transport and sprays Aman's drivers with bullets. Blinded, Aman's drivers swerve into a massive pile-up – flattening Mangler in the process. As Aman's superiors punish him for his failure, Outback's trio safely reaches home base and mourns their fallen comrade.

MEMORABLE MOMENTS Maverick brandishes his side-arm, leading nervous civilian pilot Bert Phriem to ask: "Is that gun loaded?" In response, Maverick unabashedly replies: "What good is an unloaded one?"

Mangler carries the wounded Lightfoot piggyback across 40 miles of desert. During his last stand, Mangler stands off against Aman and shouts: "It's your worst nightmare come to life – a 19-year-old American with a machine gun!"

LOVE AND WAR Kidnapper Carlos has unsavory intentions toward "nurse" Scarlett.

ASS-WHUPPINGS A blindfolded Scarlett kicks one of her captors, bonking his head with a rearview mirror. A similarly blinded Jinx pummels the snot out of her opponents, while Lady Jaye gnaws on a thug's wrists. Chuckles gets the coup de grace, blasting holes in one of the kidnappers but taking a bullet wound to his cheek in return. When dealing with the airplane hijackers, Jinx resorts to the time-honored tradition of using one goon as a bullet shield while dicing another with a .45 pistol.

Local military officers beat the stuffing out of Lightfoot for three hours. Some tank treads mangle Mangler, who finishes this story very flat.

GOOFS Firefly gets captured in *Special Missions* #12, but spontaneously shows up at the landlocked freighter on Cobra Island in *G.I. Joe* #98.

COMIC TIE-INS Continuity's rather soupy with regards to the African nation of Trucial Abysmia (SM #13). Previous to this issue, the American government forged a deal with Trucial Abysmia's "emperor," but a communist regime supposedly came to power, ruining the American alliance. That's fine, except that in *G.I. Joe* #108-#115, "Trucial Abysmia" spontaneously becomes a lucrative Middle East oil emirate with a greedy Emir running the show. The country, as most hardcore fans know, plays host to a major battle (*G.I. Joe* #109-#115) that kills off a number of Joes.

Lightfoot goes through Joe boot camp again in *G.I. Joe* #82. Stalker and Rock 'n Roll visit Mangler's gravesite in *G.I. Joe* #145.

CHARACTER PROFILE: JOES

- *Lightfoot:* Lightfoot volunteers information on the Joe mission only after repeated hours of torture, including an agonizing bout with a car battery and some alligator clips. Lightfoot's unbelievably loyal to his fellow Joes, offering to let Captain Yusif shoot him down – thereby removing all proof that the torture session took place – if he'll let Outback, Dusty and Mangler go. (Blessedly, Yusif releases them instead.)
- *Maverick:* His mom flew a PT-13 crop duster with a Lycoming engine all across the Midwest. Maverick claims he just about grew up in the front seat of her airplane.
- *Mangler, Outback, Dusty and Lightfoot:* Of this Joe quartet, Mangler's the strongest, Outback's the leader, Dusty's the desert survival specialist (keeping everyone fat eating little reptiles, etc.) and Lightfoot blows things up. Mangler's appalled when a half-dead, tortured Lightfoot confesses the Joes' intended target, but Dusty and Outback better empathize with Lightfoot's plight.
- *Outback:* Mangler didn't impress Outback as a team player, but he recommends the dead Joe for a posthumous decoration anyway.

ORGANIZATIONS *G.I. Joe:* The Polizei (the German police) and Strassenbahn Commission sometimes give the Joes authorization to operate in West Germany.

PLACES TO GO *Trucial Abysmia:* The former emperor of Trucial Abysmia wasn't graced with good teeth, granting permission for the American government to establish military bases in Trucial Abysmia in exchange for a private dental clinic.

HOT WHEELS *Joe Vector jet:* It's sluggish at low speeds but capable of vertical take-off and landing.

THE COMMAND DECISION Almost by luck of the draw, the hostage-laden *Special Missions* #11 lets its cast inhabit their roles, providing an acceptable – if somewhat slow – read. By contrast, issue #12 never gets off the ground, mired in a lot of pointless flying gimmicks. Finally, *Special Missions* #13 stands as a hardcore story of heroism, with Lightfoot's determination in the face of torture and Mangler's sacrifice keeping you riveted until the tank-crushing finale.

G.I. Joe #72 to #76

Titles: *"Stiletto" (#72), "Divided We Fall" (#73), "Alliance of Convenience" (#74), "Holding Actions!" (#75), "All's Fair" (#76)*
Release Dates: *June to Sept. 1988*
Art: *Ron Wagner (#72-#74, #76), Marshall Rogers (#75)*

BATTLE ROSTER *Joes:* Hawk, Roadblock, General Hollingsworth, Lt. Falcon, Flint, Lady Jaye, Tunnel Rat, Gung Ho, Spirit, Dial-Tone, Mainframe, Psyche-Out; *Cobra:* Serpentor, Cobra Commander II, the Baroness, Zartan, Dr. Mindbender, Tomax and Xamot, the Dreadnoks, Zarana; *Destro:* Destro, the Iron Grenadiers; *Other:* Billy.

FIRST APPEARANCES *Joes:* Wildcard (Mean Dog driver, #72), Skidmark (Desert Fox 6WD driver, #72), Windmill (Skystorm X–Wing chopper pilot, #72), Sneak Peek (advanced recon, #73), Admiral Keel-Haul (*USS Flagg* commander, #73), Ghostrider (Phantom X–19 stealth fighter pilot, #76); *Cobra:* Croc-Master (reptile trainer, #72), the Star Viper (Stiletto pilot, #72).

DEATHS *Cobra:* Serpentor (#76).

MISSION BRIEF ***Issue #72:*** On Cobra Island, Dr. Mindbender completes modifications to the first-ever "Star Viper," a new classification of Cobra pilot with computer-enhanced reflexes. Hoping to attain glory and rip out his enemies' still-beating hearts, Serpentor authorizes the Star Viper to penetrate the Utah-based Pit III and gather intelligence on the Joes' activities.

In Utah, the reflex-enhanced Star Viper conceals himself underneath a Joe Mean Dog attack vehicle, thereby gaining a ride into the Pit III. As the Joes retire for the night, the Star

Viper scours the Pit and steals an ultra-secret "black box" – a data receiver/decoder capable of reading information from every American spy satellite – from the Joe space shuttle *Defiant*. But while making his exit, the Star Viper stumbles across Flint and Lady Jaye groping each other in the Pit's upper level.

The Star Viper thrashes the two lovebirds and steals an AWE-Striker jeep, but the Joes, finally alerted to the intruder's presence, give chase. Out in the Utah desert, the Star Viper leaps onto a BAT-driven semi and clambers into the trailer section – reaching the safety of a Cobra Stiletto jet within. The Joes blow the semi to bits, but the Star Viper rockets to safety – completely outfoxing his pursuers and returning to Cobra Island.

Issue #73-#74: Fearing that Cobra will bypass the stolen black box's anti-tamper devices and eventually decode America's intelligence network, Pentagon officials order Hawk to obtain intelligence on Cobra Island's defenses – potentially paving the way for a major invasion. Accordingly, the *USS Flagg* maneuvers closer to Cobra Island and inserts a six-man recon team, led by Lt. Falcon, using a captured Cobra MAMBA helicopter.

On Cobra Island, the Cobra leadership celebrates the Star Viper's return with a victory parade, enabling Serpentor to gloat about his successes. But all-too-quickly, Cobra Commander II lets his smoldering hatred for Serpentor erupt, leading to a brawl between the Cobra bigwigs. The assembled Cobra officers pull Serpentor and Cobra Commander II off each other, but the two men throw down the gauntlet and declare outright warfare.

The Cobra officers quickly choose sides, with the Baroness, Zartan and the Dreadnoks favoring Cobra Commander II while Dr. Mindbender, the Crimson Twins and their Crimson Guard side with Serpentor. However, Cobra Commander's troops outnumber Serpentor's brigades, forcing Serpentor to withdraw to the relative safety of a landlocked freighter – an formerly sunken ship brought to the surface during the formation of Cobra Island (#41).

With Serpentor under siege, Dr. Mindbender suggests travelling to Washington and bartering the Pentagon's "black box" for American support against Cobra Commander II. Serpentor agrees, helping Mindbender slip past the encroaching Cobra troops and head for the Pentagon.

Superbly blackmailed, the Jugglers order General Hollingsworth and Hawk to marshal every available G.I. Joe – and side with Serpentor's "parliamentary monarchy" against Cobra Commander's "fascist dictatorship." Hawk becomes nauseated at the thought of helping Serpentor but follows orders, preparing to land a massive Joe contingent on the Cobra Island airfield.

Meanwhile, Destro becomes curious about the heated Cobra Civil War and moves several legions of his Iron Grena-

MISCELLANEOUS STUFF!

THE COBRA RIFT

With Cobra ripped asunder between Cobra Commander II's supporters and Serpentor's loyalists, virtually every Cobra officer chooses sides to help guarantee their own survival. Minutes after declaring open war, Cobra Commander II and Serpentor's respective armies divvy up their organization's troops and vehicles along the following lines:

COBRA COMMANDER II: The Baroness (second-in-command), Zartan and his siblings, the Dreadnoks, Vipers, Cobra engineers (Techno-Vipers), communications experts (Tele-Vipers), ground assault vehicles (MAMBAs) and their WORM pilots, and BUGG underwater assault vehicles.

SERPENTOR: Dr. Mindbender (second-in-command), the Crimson Twins and their Crimson Guardsmen, Croc Master, Scrap-Iron, Battle Android Troopers (BATs), RATTLER jets and HISS tanks.

THE JOE RESPONSE

In this story arc, G.I. Joe stages its biggest mobilization since the invasion of Springfield (#49-#50), dividing its members according to their specialties:

- **Sea-Transport and Support:** Admiral Keel-Haul, Cutter, Shipwreck.
- **S-3 Operations:** Hawk, Flint, Lady Jaye and Mainframe (on *USS Flagg*).
- **Air transport and support:** Wild Bill, Lift-Ticket, Slip-Stream, Ace.
- **Mechanized Assault & Combined Aviation (Battle Force 2000):** Maverick, Knockdown, Avalanche, Blocker, Blaster, Dodger.
- **Weapons Team and Field HQ:** Hawk, Roadblock, Leatherneck, Fast Draw, Sci-Fi, Low-Light, Breaker, Doc.
- **Security Team:** Duke, Crazylegs, Beach-Head, SEALs (presumably Torpedo and Wet-Suit), Airborne, Ripcord, Lifeline.
- **Motorized Recon:** Crankcase, Clutch.
- **S-2 Intelligence Recon Team:** Lt. Falcon, Spirit, Sneak Peek, Dial-Tone, Tunnel Rat, Gung Ho.
- **Engineer Team and Demolitions:** Stalker, Trip-Wire, Short-Fuze, Mutt and Junkyard.

diers into the region – awaiting an opportunity to triumph over both groups. Back on Cobra Island, the Baroness drives home an attack on Serpentor's landlocked freighter, hoping for a quick victory, but turns dismayed when Serpy's heavily entrenched forces stand firm against five-to-one odds. As the Joes and Mindbender land on the Cobra Island airfield, Serpentor counter-attacks the Baroness' beleaguered forces – capturing the Baroness and strapping her to his HISS tank.

United, Serpentor's phalanxes and the Joes pummel Cobra Commander II's troops. But just as the battle swings in Serpentor's favor, both sides turn in terror as Destro's Iron Grenadiers rush onto the Cobra Island beach *en masse*.

Issue #75-#76: While the assembled Joe and Cobra troops sensibly beat a hasty retreat, Destro fortifies the beachfront and orders his catering staff to serve the Iron Grenadiers tea. Undaunted, Serpentor relentlessly attacks Cobra Commander II's helicopter air force. But with insurmountable calm, Destro waits for Serpentor and Cobra Commander II's air cover to decimate each other, then rolls his freshly caffeinated troops into the fray and captures the Cobra Island airfield.

With Serpentor and Cobra Commander's armies separated by Cobra Island's main volcano, Destro orders his men to indulge in a hot meal. Meanwhile, the combined Joe/Serpentor army corners and utterly hammers Cobra Commander II's troops, putting Serpentor on the cusp of victory.

Sensing the battle lost, Zartan notches his bow and races onto the battlefield – feverishly scanning Serpentor's tank column for an opening. Calling on his ninja-honed archery skills, Zartan releases his bowstring heavenward. Zartan's arrow eludes detection until the last instant – then skewers Serpentor's head like a candied apple and kills the Cobra Emperor.

Upon Serpentor's death, the craven Dr. Mindbender immediately capitulates – offering to reunite Cobra and reinstate Cobra Commander II. Cobra Commander II agrees, intending to kick Destro off Cobra Island, but Destro strolls up and offers to leave in exchange for the Baroness. Cobra Commander II turns giddy to pay such a small price, relinquishing the battered Baroness and allowing the satisfied (and well-fed) Destro to depart Cobra Island. But as hostilities cease, the Joes realize that Serpentor's death ended the American government's pact with Cobra Island – opening up a renewed age of bloody conflict with the Cobra leadership.

MEMORABLE MOMENTS In one of the comics' most lustful moments, the Star Viper catches Flint and Lady Jaye... err, showing their patriotism by hoisting the flagpole (see Sex and Spirits).

Serpentor advises Dr. Mindbender, who's leaving to force help from the Pentagon: "Try to get as much military aid as possible!" In response, a sarcasm-dripping Mindbender mutters: "What does he think I'm going to ask for? Agricultural tools?"

Thrasher madly (and hysterically) gives his "professional" analysis of Serpentor capturing the Baroness: "Ol' Serpy's got ol' leather-britches herself trussed up like a poached kangaroo." (Cobra Commander II adds: "Remind me to have you lobotomized after this, Thrasher.")

Destro steals most of this story arc's best lines and scenes, conducting an almost nonchalant attack (as he puts it: "No one will fire unless fired upon! We are going to conduct an orderly invasion here!"). Upon taking the Cobra beach, Destro orders the troops to fall out for high tea (noting, "Thirsty work, this [war-making]..."), then folding into a lounge chair and commenting, "Splendid view of the battle. Have the junior officers take notes. Rather informative, actually."

Thrasher develops an inspired method of righting his overturned Thunder Machine – by tossing grenades under it.

Serpentor pontificates about his memories of when the Norman knights won the Battle of Hastings (in 1066) and the Saxon king, Harold, was "laid low by an arrow." Appropriately enough, Zartan's arrow chooses that moment to split open Serpentor's head – a potent death for a series that (ironically) doesn't off many of its main characters.

LOVE AND WAR Fred Smith VII and the Baroness briefly smooch to seal their alliance, but neither fancies the other much. Issue #72, page 13 features Flint admiring Lady Jaye's jugs while she fixes a rocket jet. More tellingly, the Star Viper catches Flint and Lady Jaye in a clinch (and probably about to do the deed) during his escape.

ASS-WHUPPINGS The Star Viper slugs Flint and Lady Jaye, ruining their impending nookie. Tunnel Rat blows away a Cobra tower crew.

Issues #73-#76 feature what's probably the greatest number of Cobra trooper deaths – mind, it's mostly because they're all killing each other. The Joes get by with few casualties, although Lift-Ticket, Crazylegs and Breaker take slight wounds. (Refusing to rest, Breaker adds: "Why lie down? The bleeding's almost stopped!") Joe missile specialist Fast-Draw takes out several MAGGOT vehicles. Lt. Falcon's reconnaissance group, shuttled around Cobra Island's drainage system like a pinball, survive with only a few rat bites and the shame of getting covered in gruel by Destro's chefs.

COMIC TIE-INS Snake-Eyes, Scarlett, Chuckles and Iceberg don't participate in the Cobra Island civil war because they're entangled in Arctic mayhem (*Special Missions* #14-#15). Serpentor's enduring a heightened level of schizophrenia while his progenitors (*G.I. Joe* #49) – notably Genghis Khan, Julius Caesar and Napoleon – compete for attention.

Lt. Falcon's team penetrates Cobra Island security using a

Cobra MAMBA helicopter, captured in *G.I. Joe Yearbook* #4. The Star-Viper's information on the Pit III spurs Cobra to attack the Joe Headquarters in *G.I. Joe* #83. The Star-Viper himself fries to death in *Special Missions* #16.

CHARACTER PROFILE: JOES

• *Ghostrider:* He's stealthy by nature – virtually none of the Joes remember his code-name or can even recognize him by sight. The comic book, in fact, never mentions Ghostrider's code-name (we combed it from his action figure card).

• *Psyche-Out:* Sometimes serves as a section leader.

• *Wildcard:* He's a speed demon, cursed with an amazing capacity to break anything he touches.

CHARACTER PROFILE: COBRA

• *Cobra Commander II:* Despite his partnership with the Baroness, he'd gladly risk a pot-shot at her – if he stood a chance of nailing Serpentor.

• *Croc Master:* Keeps crocs named "Brunhild" and "Kriemhild."

• *Serpentor:* His insistence on sharing battlefield duty with his troops won Serpentor respect – but it also left him vulnerable to Zartan's arrow.

• *The Star Viper:* A masterpiece of electrical engineering, gifted with electromagnetic shunts on the right side of his brain, allowing him to directly plug into a battle computer to heighten his reflexes. Such enhancements grant the Star-Viper near-superhuman response time when piloting his Stiletto rocket-plane and also augment his physical skills (enabling him to leap onto fast-moving vehicles, etc.). Like most Strato-Vipers, the Star Viper's mechanical grafts let him survive G-stresses that'd juice an ordinary man.

CHARACTER PROFILE: DESTRO *Destro:* His legions include bull battalions of armored ground vehicles (DEMONs), anti-gravity assault pods (AGPs) and elite shock troops. He sometimes uses a "legitimate" cruise liner for troop transport. He keeps catering staff on hand (Editor's Note: What does he call them, we wonder? The "Iron Chefs"?).

ORGANIZATIONS *Cobra:* Evidently sells stock.

• *G.I Joe:* Explicit on the point that despite Serpentor's deal with the Pentagon, the Joes operate independently – Hawk's in charge, not Serpentor.

PLACES TO GO *Cobra Island:* It's doubled its radar and aerial infrared detectors in the last year.

• *The Pit III:* The top level's built to house vehicles (presumably for quick deployment). The next level down contains operations rooms and supplies. Hydraulic pistons lower a section of desert floor to ferry the *Defiant* shuttle up to ground level – all other Joe vehicles use a main ramp.

STUFF YOU NEED *Cobra Battle Android Troopers (BATs):* Respond to voice commands and, unlike human troopers, keep fighting even if you shoot away half their mass.

• *The Pentagon's Black Box:* The stolen Pentagon gadget reads and decodes every signal from every American spy satellite. Its main board alone cost $1.5 million (and that's in 1988 dollars). It contains an anti-tamper explosive capable of liquefying everything in a 50-foot radius, but it's entirely possible that Cobra could disarm the device.

HOT WHEELS Cobra MAGGOT Assault Vehicles: Have a greater firing range than the HISS tanks.

• *Phantom X-19:* Probably the sneakiest plane the Joes own, coated with a "Blackball" radar-resistant paint.

THE COMMAND DECISION The glorious, no-holds-barred culmination of everything that's happened since issue #1, "the Cobra Civil War" explodes as the series' most character-filled, complex and downright best epic storyarc. Hama unloads every bullet in his clip at this point, and hell, even the sub-plots – including a quick bit of near-nookie for Flint and Lady Jaye – hold up. Mark our words: Although other *G.I. Joe* stories such as "Snake-Eyes: The Origin" (#26-#27) and "Silent Interlude" (#21) have gained more notoriety over the years, we'll treasure "the Cobra Civil War" as a masterwork, showing what a seasoned *G.I. Joe* series could accomplish.

G.I. Joe #77 to #78

***Titles:** "Aftershocks" (#77), "Payback!" (#78)*
***Release Dates:** Bi-weekly in Oct. 1988*
***Art:** Marshall Rogers (#77), Rod Whigham (#78)*

BATTLE ROSTER *Joes:* Hawk, Roadblock, General Hollingsworth, Lady Jaye, Storm Shadow, Jinx, Grunt, Lola, Rock 'n Roll, Cover Girl; *Cobra:* Cobra Commander II, the Baroness, Dr. Mindbender, Tomax and Xamot, the Dreadnoks, Croc-Master, Zarana, the Star Viper; *Destro:* Destro, the Iron Grenadiers; *Other:* Billy, Dr. Adele Burkhart.

MISSION BRIEF ***Issue #77:*** As the battle-weary Joes set sail for home in the *USS Flagg*, an infuriated General Hollingsworth, Hawk and Roadblock travel to the Pentagon to confront the Jugglers. Hawk and Hollingsworth argue the incompetency of the Jugglers' orders, lambasting the clique of generals for siding with the late Serpentor. But the Jugglers, covering their asses, put the Joe trio under house arrest and begin a smear campaign – claiming the maverick Joes went to Cobra Island without authorization.

The Jugglers' leader, General Malthus, orders Hawk, Roadblock and General Hollingsworth taken under armed guard to an undisclosed hospital for a psychiatric examination. Worried that the Jugglers will arrange a fatal "accident" for them, Hawk and Hollingsworth encourage Roadblock to escape, prompting the Joe machine gunner to snap his bonds and escape into Georgetown.

As Malthus moves swiftly to detain all Joes aboard the *USS Flagg*, Destro grows disgusted at Malthus' lack of honor in politically decapitating the Joes. But as the search for Roadblock continues, the Joe gunner finds shelter at an unlikely location – the home of anti-war advocate Dr. Adele Burkhart.

Issue #78: Conscripting agents from the Domestic Operations Agency (DOA), General Malthus attempts to round up the few Joes at liberty. Thankfully, Dr. Burkhart lets her pursuit of justice override her anti-military sentiments, allowing Roadblock to assemble a task force – including Storm Shadow, Billy, Jinx, Rock 'n Roll and more – at her abode.

Roadblock's Joes track Hawk and General Hollingsworth to St. Lo's Infirmary in Virginia. Unfortunately, the Joes fail to realize that General Malthus, having replaced the St. Lo's staff with DOA agents, deliberately leaked them Hawk's location. By summoning television crews to St. Lo's, Malthus intends to film the Joes attacking a "normal" hospital – forever disgracing the operation. Worse, Malthus plots to make Hawk and Hollingsworth "accidentally" chew bullets in the firefight, thus warding off a drawn-out trial.

The Joes enter the hospital, but Malthus' plan sours when Dr. Burkhart – a noted human rights expert – stands before the assembled broadcasters and charges the government with violating Hawk and Hollingsworth's rights. Sweating buckets, the DOA agents open up a can of whup-ass and lace the hospital lobby with ammunition – forcing the Joes to dive for cover.

Suddenly, a disgusted Destro arrives in a helicopter, refusing to let an honorable officer like Hawk meet such an ignoble end. Accordingly, Destro produces a purchase order and receipt, signed by Malthus, for the ammunition that Destro's arms company sold to the US government for the Cobra Island operation. Holding tangible proof that Malthus authorized the Joes to enter Cobra Island, Destro discredits the general and clears the Joes of all charges.

MEMORABLE MOMENTS With the Cobra Island hostilities ended, Destro retires to his leisure yacht, lazily watches the Flagg pass by and tells his lover: "Wave to the nice aircraft carrier, Baroness! We don't want them to think we're unfriendly!"

Although it's cheap and senseless – actually, *because* it's cheap and senseless – the catfight between Lady Jaye and Zarana in #77 kept us riveted *(see Ass-Whuppings)*. Dramatically, #77's cliffhanger shows Roadblock knocking on Dr. Burkhart's front door and asking for help, to which the good doctor replies: "I think you'd better step inside – before the Feds surround the joint!"

Issue #78 slams home a number of outstanding character moments, with Destro siding with Hawk because, "Sometimes, the soldiers you respect the most are on the wrong side!" Something of a goody-two-shoes, Dr. Burkhart brazenly stands up amid the Joe/DOA shoot-out and screams, "This is an outrage! I am a non-combatant! Stop this senseless shooting immediately!" Finally, Destro whisks the Jugglers' carpet out from under them – ironically becoming the Joes' greatest ally.

LOVE AND WAR Destro and the Baroness resume bumping uglies, but we only know this because – in the typical Marvel Comics fashion – they spend a lot of time lounging around in bathrobes (notably issue #77, although Destro keeps his face mask on). Destro claims he primarily ventured onto Cobra Island to rescue the Baroness – mind, he also needed to test his new troops and gain more information about Cobra Island (ah, young love, it's so... militant).

Zartan's sister Zarana doesn't know what Destro sees in the Baroness, deeming her "worthless trash." Zarana also flirts with Cobra Commander II, but it's more playfulness than anything else.

Grunt first met fellow Georgia Tech student Lola in #56; they're now a couple.

ASS-WHUPPINGS During the Joes' gradual withdrawal from Cobra Island, Zarana goads Lady Jaye with a variety of insults and jabs. Lady Jaye in turn loses her cool and tries to claw out Zarana's eyeballs, instigating a catfight that everyone turns to watch (Roadblock to Hawk: "I wouldn't break this up just yet, sir. At least, not while Lady Jaye's winning!"). Despite Zarana's amazing capacity, as Dreadnok Torch puts it, to "... keep hitting the soles of Lady Jaye's boots with her face," the match ends in a draw.

Cover Girl and Bazooka take bullets during the hospital fracas with the DOA, but again, the Joes mostly get off unscathed.

COMIC TIE-INS Cobra Commander II set Captain Minh up to sleep with the fishes in *G.I. Joe* #64, but Minh survived, living off the Cobra Island marshland for a year. Minh briefly guided Lt. Falcon's reconnaissance group through Cobra Island's sewer system in #74-#76, but stayed behind when the Joes withdrew. In issue #77, Minh tracks down Cobra Commander II and leaps onto his back – threatening to remove the commander's helmet and detonate the anti-tamper explosives within. Minh flirts with the idea of revealing Cobra Commander II's true identity, forcing the commander into giving Minh a Cobra moray boat. Minh flees Cobra Island but later sides with the Joes, eavesdropping on Cobra transmissions in #83.

The Joes rescued Dr. Adele Burkhart twice (*G.I. Joe* #1 and #38-#39), thereby gaining her gratitude. Roadblock calls Burkhart "Lady Doomsday," referring to her Joe-assigned codename from the first operation.

The Jugglers further cause trouble for Storm Shadow and Snake-Eyes in #103.

Issue #77 shows Dr. Mindbender approaching Cobra Commander II – having learned his true identity as Fred Smith VII (*G.I. Joe Yearbook* #4) – and threatening to expose his secret. Cobra Commander II purchases Mindbender's silence by agreeing to let the scientist have Serpentor's corpse for further experimentation. Cobra Commander II and Mindbender rank Zartan as their greatest internal threat, moving against the cowled swamp rat in *G.I. Joe* #84.

Cobra clean-up crews here make a neat little stack of disused BATs aboard the landlocked freighter, but Firefly later modifies the robots to escape his entombment (#98).

CHARACTER PROFILE: JOES

• *Roadblock:* He hasn't been to Washington D.C. in ages, and carries a machine gun that two average-sized men can barely lift.

• *Rock 'n Roll:* Rolls about town in a nifty army car with water-based paint – to throw off his pursuers, he can just drive through a car wash to change the vehicle's color.

• *Storm Shadow and Jinx:* Know a Yagyu "death touch" that renders people unconscious.

CHARACTER PROFILE: DESTRO

Destro: He's upset to learn that grease monkey Fred Smith VII now leads Cobra, bemoaning him as "...more accustomed to giving lube-jobs than orders!"

CHARACTER PROFILE: OTHER Dr. Adele Burkhart: Exceeds normal limits of coolness for a nuclear physicist by riding a Harley.

STUFF YOU NEED Joe Hospital Uniforms: An inspired means of telling friend from foe (prepared for the hospital battle with the DOA), coated with a special dye that's visible to sunglasses with polarized filters (the sunglass-wearing Joes immediately see the words "G.I. Joe" on their allies' uniforms).

THE COMMAND DECISION The perfect chaser to the Cobra Civil War story arc – and a riotous clash of ideologies that ends with Destro oddly showing up to save everyone's ass. It's so good, it's a pity it couldn't continue longer – but then again, a drawn-out "Joes against the U.S. government" plotline could easily violate the series' ideology.

G.I. Joe Special Missions #14 to #15

Titles: *"In From the Cold" (#14), "... and Into the Fire!" (#15)*
Release Dates: *Oct. to Nov. 1988*
Art: *Herb Trimpe*

BATTLE ROSTER *Joes:* Snake-Eyes, Scarlett, Chuckles, Iceberg.

MISSION BRIEF With China tightening its grip on the tiny country of Chomo Lungma, the American government honors various Nixon-era promises and refuses to impede China's progress. To further appease the Chinese government, the government conscripts CIA agent Anderson to find and eliminate Cullen Esterhazy – a former CIA operative who's honing Chomo Lungma resistance into a lethal fighting force.

Anderson recruits Chuckles, Snake-Eyes, Scarlett and Iceberg to "retrieve" Esterhazy, keeping quiet his intention to dust the ex-CIA man. The Joes and Anderson fly to Esterhazy's last known location – an isolated settlement in the Himalayas' "Valley of the Eternal Mist." Unfortunately, Chinese Colonel Peng learns of the Joe expedition and follows Anderson's group to annihilate Esterhazy and his militia. Upon locating Esterhazy, the Joes turn infuriated to learn that Anderson intends to assassinate his prey.

The Joes recoil at the thought of murder, but Colonel Peng's soldiers roll into the Valley of the Eternal Mist and mow down Esterhazy's rebels. The monastery's head abbot – a friend of Esterhazy – surrenders to avoid further bloodshed, compelling Esterhazy to mount a dangerous rescue mission. Snubbing Anderson, the Joes help Esterhazy cut down the abbot's captors.

Esterhazy and his allies nab the abbot and race for freedom, but Colonel Peng blockades the valley's main escape route. After Esterhazy volunteers to slow down their pursuers, the Joes escape on foot with Anderson, the abbot and Esterhazy's lieutenant Tenzig. Esterhazy perishes, but Anderson finds himself moved by the noble ex-agent's sacrifice. As Tenzig and the abbot vow to rally the Chomo Lungma resistance, Anderson "goes native" and stays behind to aid their cause.

MEMORABLE MOMENTS The abbot promises to feed his visitors "a nice cup of tea, laced with most delicious rancid yak butter." Chuckles spots a smirk on the duplicitous

Anderson's face and slugs the CIA man for good measure, declaring: "[That was] just in case you were thinking of saying something!"

ASS-WHUPPINGS In a supreme bit of savagery, Snake-Eyes nails a sentry in the face with a climbing hook. Snakes' whirling sword also makes mincemeat of two soldiers.

GOOFS Anderson downshifts from "completely despicable" to "fighter of oppressed orphans" pretty damn fast. Esterhazy and the Joes make every effort to rescue the abbot but leave the other monks to their own devices. The abbot, supposedly a man of peace, supports bloody revolutions.

COMIC TIE-INS This story occurs at the same time as the Cobra Civil War (*G.I. Joe* #72-#78), explaining the absence of Snake-Eyes, Scarlett, Chuckles and Iceberg from that story. *Special Missions* #18 chronicles the quartet's chronically messed-up efforts to return home. CIA agent Anderson formerly failed to screw over Flint, Low-Light and other Joes in *Special Missions* #8.

CHARACTER PROFILE: JOES

Iceberg: He's a stellar pilot and a decent mountain climber.

CHARACTER PROFILE: OTHER

Cullen Esterhazy: During the Nixon Administration, CIA agent Esterhazy helped airlift 2,000 Chomo Lungman rebels to Colorado, training them there to fight against the Chinese invaders. But soon after, Washington and Beijing struck various deals, cutting off America's support for the Chomo Lungman struggle. Fearing that the Chinese overlords would eradicate Chomo Lungman's culture and religion, Esterhazy resigned his CIA commission to rally his USA-trained brigade. In the current political climate, the CIA deems Esterhazy an embarrassment, slating him for death.

Esterhazy only owns one possession worth mentioning: a copy of Sun Tzu's *The Art of War*. He bequeathed said book to the abbot, who in turn gifted it to Anderson.

THE COMMAND DECISION More in-depth than your typical *Special Missions* story, issues #14-#15 run you through a nice bundle of twists, turns and perils. Mind, Anderson's change of heart doesn't seem very convincing – plus, the optimistic beat belies the communists' victory and the end of an isolated 500-year-old valley civilization. Still, there's something to be said for overall effect, leaving this two-parter worth your time.

G.I. Joe Special Missions #16 to #18

***Titles:** "Tight Circle" (#16), "All in a Night's Work!" (#17), "Extraction" (#18)*
***Release Dates:** Dec. 1988 to Feb. 1989*
***Art:** Herb Trimpe*

BATTLE ROSTER *Joes:* Hawk, Wild Bill, Lady Jaye, Slip-Stream, Ace, Ghostrider, Mainframe, Muskrat, Hardball, Hit 'n Run, Stalker, Dusty, Chuckles, Snake-Eyes, Iceberg, Scarlett; *Cobra:* Cobra Commander II, Dr. Mindbender, Star Viper, Scrap Iron.

FIRST APPEARANCES *Joes:* Shockwave (SWAT specialist, #17); *Destro:* Voltar (Destro's general, #18).

DEATHS *Cobra:* The Star Viper (#16).

MISSION BRIEF ***Issue #16:*** In the aftermath of the Cobra Civil War, Cobra Commander II and Dr. Mindbender suspiciously funnel dozens of unidentified crates through Cobra Island's southern port. Baffled by the irregular shipments, Duke dispatches his best pilots to zip by Cobra Island and collect reconnaissance photos.

While Slip-Stream, Ace and other Joes dog Cobra Island's aerial defenses, Ghostrider slips past in his radar-proof Phantom X-19 jet and snaps a string of photos. Cobra Commander II and Dr. Mindbender send the enhanced Star Viper to take out Ghostrider, but the Joe pilot outflanks his opponent. Pushed beyond his endurance level, the Star Viper's systems short out – causing the Cobra pilot to drown at sea.

The Joes return home, gloating over their success. But that evening, Cobra Commander II and Dr. Mindbender – having successfully diverted the Joes' attention to Cobra Island's south port – oversee the former Springfield populace's departure from the isle's north harbor. Under cover of a moonless sky, the Cobra civilians set out in a non-descript tanker, preparing to land at their new home in Broca Beach, NJ.

Issue #17: Under threat of an audit, Nexus-Tech president Wendell Freen – having rooked the government on his company's defense contracts – panics and forges a deal with Cobra to keep his ass out of jail. Cobra agents coordinate with Freen to stage a highly volatile "hostage situation" that will result in them blowing up the main Nexus-Tech vault, turning the company's financial records into an inferno and keeping Freen from audit hell.

In return, Cobra asks for access to the vault prior to the explosion, hoping to retrieve microfilm plans for a new missile guidance system.

A short while later, a pack of masked Cobra Battle Android Troopers (BATs) raid Nexus-Tech and capture three "employees" – actually Scrap Iron, a Techno-Viper and a Toxo-Viper in disguise. Responding to the situation, Stalker heads for Siliconville, CA with a Joe sniper team. Once there, the Joes enter through Nexus-Tech's roof, guns blazing, and blitz through their opponents. With seconds to spare, the Techno-Viper rolls the microfilm into a watertight capsule and swallows it. The Cobra trio blows up the vault as planned, allowing the Joes to slaughter the remaining BATs and "liberate" the hostages.

Smelling a set-up, Stalker impulsively orders that the three "hostages" get X-rayed for "internal injuries." Scrap-Iron's trio protests, but as Stalker expected, X-ray techs locate the stolen microfilm floating in the Techno-Viper's innards. A subsequent investigation uncovers Freen's ties to Cobra, leading to his arrest.

Issue #18: Enroute home after their Himalayan expedition (*Special Missions* #15), Chuckles, Snake-Eyes, Scarlett and Iceberg find their extraction sites compromised and trek onward to the next (hopefully safe) pick-up zone. Heading down the Mekong River, the Joe quartet spots several thugs, affiliated with a local bandit chief named Big Tep, torturing an old farmer for sport. Unable to simply observe such suffering, Snake-Eyes leaps to the farmer's defense, wiping out most of the goons. Unfortunately, one of the bandits escapes and alerts Big Tep to the Joes' presence.

The old farmer identifies himself as Dr. Krim, a former philosophy department head at a local university. Krim worries about Big Tep returning, but Chuckles pulls out his map, identifying the river bend near Krim's house as the rendezvous point with a Joe helicopter. Events get increasingly complicated when Big Tep forges a pact with Destro, gaining military support against the ruling General Lom in exchange for trade concessions. Simultaneously, Russia's Oktober Guard arrives on General Lom's behalf, intending to keep their communist brother in power.

Chuckles' quartet takes cover in Krim's attic just as Big Tep and General Lom's legions roll into view. General Lom's troops advance on Big Tep's troops, utterly mauling Krim's rice-growing operation in the process. But under cover of a sudden monsoon, Big Tip takes the advantage and kills General Lom. Choosing discretion over getting shot, Oktober Guard leader Colonel Brekhov quickly retreats.

As Destro's troops pursue the fleeing communists, Big Tep's men stay behind to ransack Krim's livestock. Fed up with the wanton destruction of Krim's property, Chuckles plugs Big Tep and his lieutenants. An instant later, Scarlett, Snake-Eyes and Iceberg leap out from hiding, massacring Big Tep's remaining troops to a man. Shortly after, Lift-Ticket arrives with a Joe Tomahawk to retrieve his teammates. Chuckles offers Krim asylum, wanting to help the doctor renew his fortunes, but Krim opts to remain in his blood-soaked homeland.

MEMORABLE MOMENTS Colonel Brekhov frets about political fallout from his mission until General Lom dies in a hail of gunfire, leaving Brekhov to conclude: "Well, that solves the problem of who gets the blame rather nicely."

The aged Dr. Krim refuses to knuckle to the hulking Big Tep, leveling him with: "Do your worst... you cannot take away my honor."

In issue #17, Stalker gets fed up when self-serving FBI agent Saxon withholds information, threatening to pull his tonsils out through his nostrils. Muskrat succinctly conjectures that if the Joes shoot everyone they're ordered to shoot – and leave everyone else alone – then they've done their jobs well.

ASS-WHUPPINGS In issue #16, Cobra Commander II and Dr. Mindbender sacrifice an entire RATTLER jet compliment – purely to divert the Joes' attention from the Broca Beach operation. In #17, the Joes annihilate several BATs.

PREPOSTEROUS PHYSICS Lady Jaye breaks out an in-flight plane's observation window to rifle the Star Viper's ship, again discarding the fact that punctured aircraft have a tendency to depressurize.

COMIC TIE-INS Cobra Commander II's busy re-asserting his authority after the Cobra Civil War (#72-#78). Displaced from their homes in *G.I. Joe* #50, the ex-Springfield populace here sets forth for Broca Beach, NJ, arriving in #81. Sneaky FBI agent Saxon crops up in *Special Missions* #22.

CHARACTER PROFILE: JOES

• *Dusty:* He's often in command during the Pit's night cycle, leaving Duke in charge during daylight.

• *Ghostrider:* He's innately stealthy, able to inadvertently sneak up on otherwise alert individuals. Indeed, most people forget Ghostrider's face unless they're looking directly at him.

• *Mainframe:* His computer systems can mess up radar all the way from Cobra Island to Baton Rogue.

• *Maverick and Wild Bill:* They play a mean game of ping-pong.

CHARACTER PROFILE: COBRA

• *Cobra Commander II:* He never liked the Star Viper much (probably due to Star Viper's unbelievable arrogance) and doesn't mourn his loss.

• *Strato Vipers:* Their synthetically reinforced bodies supposedly withstand more G-forces than ordinary pilots, but it has a tendency to make them over-confident.

ORGANIZATIONS *G.I. Joe:* They often hold jurisdiction in domestic missions involving Defense Department security (i.e. the Nexus-Tech hostage situation), but can't demand help from another agency.

STUFF YOU NEED *Cobra BATs:* Intense light flashes can momentarily blind BATs, but their vision receptors quickly adjust.

HOT WHEELS *Joe Vehicles:* They've been retrofitted to fuel up from Air Force and Navy tankers.

THE COMMAND DECISION A dramatic sign of *Special Missions* relying too much on a single formula, "Tight Circle" (#16) masquerades as a layered dogfight – when it's little more than a bunch of jets going zoom. Issue #17's gains some compelling momentum, although it peters out before achieving much complexity. The best of the bunch, *Special Missions* #18 didn't impress us back in the day, but fares much better from an adult perspective. Dr. Krim in particular gained our sympathies, and Chuckles' group rose to the occasion as well-intentioned heroes out of their element.

G.I. Joe #79 to #83

Titles: *"Dreadnoks Rule!" (#79), "Rolling Thunder" (#80), "Plots and Tracts" (#81), "Weeding Out" (#82), "Road Pig" (#83)*
Release Dates: *Early Nov. to Feb. 1989*
Art: *Marshall Rogers (#79-#82), Ron Wagner (#80, #83), Don Hudson (#82)*

BATTLE ROSTER *Joes:* Cross-Country, Mutt and Junkyard, Law and Order, Outback, Ripcord, Battle Force 2000, Roadblock, Lift-Ticket, Duke, Lightfoot, Grand Slam, Cover Girl, General Hollingsworth; *Cobra:* Zartan, Zarana, Zandar, the Dreadnoks, Dr. Mindbender, Firefly.

FIRST APPEARANCES *Joes:* Charbroil (flamethrower, #80), Hardball (multi-shot grenader, #80), Muskrat (swamp fighter, #80), Hit 'n Run (light infantryman, #80), Rumbler (R/C Crossfire driver, #80), Repeater (steadi-cam machine gunner, #82), Budo (samurai warrior, #82); *Cobra:* Road Pig (Dreadnok, #83); *Other:* Billy's mom (#83).

MISSION BRIEF ***Issue #79:*** Alerted when tax records cite a Cobra holding company as owning Zartan's New Jersey gas station, a pack of Joes take the HAVOC and stake out the Dreadnok base. Meanwhile, as Zarana and Zandar initiate a Cobra-sponsored swindle involving real estate seminars, they order their Dreadnok escorts to return to the gas station and keep out of trouble.

The Dreadnoks comply – but quickly discover the secluded Joes, charging the HAVOC in their Thunder Machine. Luckily, HAVOC driver Cross-Country pops a 180 degree turn and nails the Thunder Machine, rolling over the Dreadnok vehicle with a satisfying crunch. Buzzer wounds Mutt's dog Junkyard, but Law's hound Order captures Buzzer while the other Dreadnoks flee.

Issue #80: When a geological aftershock vomits another hunk of rock into the Gulf of Mexico near Cobra Island, both G.I. Joe and Cobra eye the newborn location as an opportunity to expand their territory. An Outback-led team of Joes aboard the Rolling Thunder attack vehicle engage a landing party of Cobra MAGGOT vehicles, but neither side gains a foothold. Finally, the infant rock plateau settles back into the ocean, forcing the Joes to fly to headquarters while the Cobras tread water and await pick-up.

Issue #81: While Battle Force 2000 runs war games on a Maryland battlefield, Mutt hears reports of a Dreadnok sighting in New Jersey and itches to deliver payback for Junkyard's wounds. Meanwhile, Zarana and Zandar continue their investment scheme operation – acquiring enough capital to purchase the coastal city of Broca Beach, NJ to serve as Cobra's base in America.

With Buzzer sprung from jail on legal technicalities, the Dreadnoks run amok with all the subtlety of an Ozzy Osbourne concert – tearing through a toll booth on the Jersey Turnpike. Mutt and Battle Force 2000 try to pursue, but state troopers – investigating the toll booth mayhem – bar their way and dispute the Joes' authorization.

Itching to capture the Dreadnoks, Mutt guns his accelerator – encouraging Battle Force 2000 to drive forward, demolish the toll booths and chase after the villains. As the Dreadnoks unwisely flee to Broca Beach, a boat carrying the former Springfield residents arrives from Cobra Island. Miraculously, Zarana stifles her urge to bludgeon the buffoonish Dreadnoks for leading the Joes to Broca Beach, hurriedly leading the newly arrived Cobra populace under cover.

Moments later, Mutt and Battle Force 2000 roll into Broca Beach, failing to realize its new vocation as a Cobra mecca. The Joes catch a glimpse of Zarana and Zanzibar aboard a Dreadnok air skid, but state troopers quickly arrive to arrest the Joes for reckless endangerment. Figuring the Joes will endure a legal brouhaha one way or another, Knockdown brings down the Dreadnok skid with a couple of missiles – incapacitating Zarana and Zanzibar but further inciting the state troopers to throw everyone into the federal pokey.

Issue #82: In a remote section of Fort Dix, NJ, top sergeant Duke guts and fillets potential G.I. Joe recruits, boiling out all but the most worthy candidates. After putting the trainees through hell – including a murderous amount of calisthenics and six-hour videos on driver safety/traffic fatalities – Duke forces the survivors to bash each other in a mud pit before declaring privates Lightfoot, Budo and Repeater fit to advance.

Duke awards the three winners a decent night's sleep – but rouses the Joe trainees when unknown forces assault a U.S. military arsenal in Picatinny, NJ. Lightfoot, Repeater and Budo bottle up a main road, but a truck full of Cobra Vipers, hauling anti-aircraft weapons stolen from the arsenal, makes a charge for freedom. The freshmen Joes trounce their adversaries – who reveal themselves to be Destro's Iron Grenadiers, dressed as Vipers to further slur Cobra's name – but a helicopter swoops in and hooks the weapons-loaded truck into the air. Thankfully, Lightfoot plants a mine on the weapons truck, obliterating the Iron Grenadiers and proving the Joe recruits' battle worth.

Issue #83: In New Jersey, a schizophrenic ex-Dreadnok named Road Pig hears news reports of Zarana and Zanzibar's arrest. Graced with two interlaced personalities – the raucous, moronic Road Pig and the loquacious Donald – the infatuated Dreadnok tears off to rescue his lost love Zarana from the local lockup. With the Joes having secured Mutt and Battle Force 2000's release after the Broca Beach debacle, Road Pig dispatches the local constabulary and rescues his colleagues.

Meanwhile, Cobra satellite photos – combined with sketchy reports of the late Star Viper (#72) – confirm a series of oddly placed barracks in Utah as the possible location of the Pit III. When Cobra Commander II sends a helicopter squadron to investigate, Captain Minh, equipped with a Cobra moray watercraft and a radio, eavesdrops on Cobra's radio frequency and warns the Joes of the oncoming assault. Given ample notice, the Joes simply dig up the huts covering the Pit's entrance and move them a mile away. A short while later, Cobra troops level the huts, turning befuddled to find only rock beneath and returning home in shame.

As an epilogue, a strange middle-aged woman arrives at the Joe hideout in San Francisco – pulling a pistol on Jinx, the duty master, and announcing herself as Billy's mother.

MEMORABLE MOMENTS Feeling domestic, Zartan forces the Dreadnoks to sweep their donut crumbs out of his helicopter's hanger.

Duke encourages his trainees to slug each other by crowing: "I want to see some bashing – with heart!"

LOVE AND WAR Road Pig's hot for Zarana (Heaven only knows how that entanglement came about), telling her: "We have come to your aid in your time of need, though you have spurned us in the past and called us vile names!" (She rewards him with a hug.)

ASS-WHUPPINGS The Dreadnoks maim an entire military convoy and saw up a toll booth. Buzzer nips Junkyard with his chainsaw, but Mutt later kicks Buzzer in the face (#81). Cross-Country flattens the Dreadnok Thunder Machine with his HAVOC.

Cobra speeds up its BAT deployment by letting the robots jump from a helicopter – but a lot of 'em go squish. Geological tremors toss several more into the Gulf of Mexico. Ghostrider and Rumbler account for a string of Cobra MAMBAs, MAGGOTs and BUGGs.

The Joe trainees endure an extensive aerobic hell, running dozens of miles and winding up bludgeoning each other in a mud pit. The Viper-disguised Iron Grenadiers wound Grand Slam, but Budo shish-ka-bobs a few with his Samurai sword. Lightfoot's mines eradicate an entire Iron Grenadier platoon.

COMIC TIE-INS Zarana took command of the Cobra Consulate Building in *G.I. Joe* #64, but passed the post to Zartan to continue Cobra's real estate scheme. The Dreadnoks last convened at Zartan's gas station hideout in #60. Cross-Country and his HAVOC formerly played chicken with Thrasher's Thunder Machine in #51.

Issue #79 concerns (literal) aftershocks of the explosion that vomited Cobra Island into the Gulf of Mexico (#40-#41). The Springfield populace, relocated to Cobra Island in #50, departed the isle in *Special Missions* #16 and arrive at Broca Beach.

Lightfoot was wounded (*SM* #13) before completing his training program, so he started over. Captain Minh obtained a Cobra moray in *G.I. Joe* #77 and here eavesdrops on Cobra transmissions. Minh next agrees to help Billy in #97-#98.

Cobra Tele-Vipers remove the MRT-7 micro-radio transmitter that the Joes planted on the Consulate's communications net in *SM* #7.

Cobra mobilizes against the Pit III in issue #83, partly identifying it from the Star-Viper's infiltration of the base in #72. However, the Star-Viper's death in *Special Missions* #16 leaves Cobra without a source of corroboration when they fail here to uncover the Joe Headquarters.

Billy's mother confronts her boy in *G.I. Joe* #84.

CHARACTER PROFILE: JOES

• *Charbroil:* His flame-thrower's equipped with an electrical ignition system.

• *Ghostrider:* He's so innately stealth-prone, even his *mom* can't remember his name.

• *Hardball:* As you might expect, he spouts an obscene number of sports references.

• *Repeater:* Holds seniority over Budo and Lightfoot.

CHARACTER PROFILE: COBRA

• *Firefly:* Firefly wants to ingratiate himself to Cobra Commander II, although it's not clear if he's redeeming some offense or just indulging in brown-nosing.

• *Road Pig:* Like all Dreadnoks, "Road Pig" digs grape soda and chocolate donuts. Conversely, Road Pig's "Donald" persona hates working, finding it too bourgeois.

• *Thrasher:* He eats chocolate donuts – and their packaging. Much like a dog, Thrasher's got a highly acute sense of smell.

• *Zartan:* He's worried that his sister Zarana's getting too arrogant. More radically, he's considering trimming back the Dreadnoks' sugar intake.

CHARACTER PROFILE: OTHER *"Sarge":* Newsstand vendor across from the Cobra Consulate who allows the Joes to run surveillance operations from a secret nook underneath his booth. The military put "Sarge" on medical discharge 20 years ago.

ORGANIZATIONS *Cobra:* Often uses quartz-synchronized automatic frequency hoppers, making Cobra transmissions unintelligible to anyone without a Cobra radio (Captain Minh's boat can tap such frequencies).

• *G.I. Joe:* Sometimes perform field maneuvers on Aberdeen Proving Grounds.

PLACES TO GO *Joe Training Camp:* It sports a 75 percent attrition rate – even higher than ranger school – but that's okay, since the Joes typically only let in 20 members a year. Duke's currently in charge of the camp, assisted by Zap.

HOT WHEELS *HAVOC and Thunder Machine:* The Thunder Machine's faster and steers better, but the HAVOC's got twice the firepower.

• *MAGGOTS:* Have trouble elevating their cannons – you're best off shooting at them from above.

• *Joe Phantom X-19:* Sometimes acquires targets by homing in on enemy radar.

THE COMMAND DECISION How the mighty have fallen. Squandering every drop of momentum from the stellar Cobra Civil War story arc, the lifeless #79-#83 practically drive the series into a brick wall. Issue #79 ineffectually carbon-copies previous Joe/Dreadnok plots, and issue #80's exceptionally worthless, forcing the characters to fight for a landmass that rises up from the ocean, then sinks back down again. Issue #81 at least provides some entertaining chases, but the plot (including Mutt's wooden vendetta against the Dreadnoks) just isn't very satisfying.

The most oddball of the bundle, issue #82 deserves some kudos for drawing on Hama's military experience to portray the Joe training camp, amusingly showing the freshmen Joes watching traffic fatality films and generally beating the crap out of each other. Regrettably, the issue's laudable first half leads into a below-average "deer-in-the-headlights Joes fighting Cobra" skirmish.

Finally, issue #83 introduces the well-spoken, brutish Road Pig, adding yet another level to the cracked Dreadnoks, but the main story, featuring Cobra blowing yet another assault on the Pit, serves only to demonstrate Cobra's increasing ineptitude.

G.I. Joe Special Missions #19 to #21

Titles: *"Getting There" (#19), "Snow Blind (#20), "The Lower Depths" (#21)*
Release Dates: *Mar. to May 1989*
Art: *Herb Trimpe*

BATTLE ROSTER *Joes:* Wild Bill, Lift-Ticket, Muskrat, Repeater, Lifeline, Sneak Peek, Frostbite, Avalanche, Snow Job, Tunnel Rat, Airtight; Cobras: Zandar, Zarana, Buzzer, Road Pig; *Other:* The Oktober Guard.

FIRST APPEARANCES *Joes:* Spearhead (point man) and Max (bobcat, both #21).

MISSION BRIEF ***Issue #19:*** Assigned to retrieve Snake-Eyes' quartet from a landing zone near the Mekong River (*Special Missions* #18), a team of Joes led by Wild Bill set off in a Tomahawk helicopter. But as the Tomahawk passes over a backwater country, a trigger-happy "people's militia" outfit opens fire on the American helicopter. The Joes survive but lose a spare fuel drum in the process – endangering their chances of reaching the Mekong and returning to the *USS Flagg*.

Moments later, HIND attack helicopters attached to the Oktober Guard (also *SM* #19) engage the wounded Joe craft. Evading most of their opponents, Wild Bill and Lift-Ticket perform some gut-wrenching turns and ground a HIND with an air-to-air missile. Always the opportunists, the Joes suck the HIND's spare fuel tanks dry. Once refueled, the battered Joes hook up with Snake-Eyes' unit, exchanging pleasantries before returning to base.

Issue #20: In the frozen Bering Strait, Colonel Brekhov takes his Oktober Guard commandos to conduct a routine ice coring test – hoping to survey which patches of ice could support a Russian armored column. Unfortunately, Cobra troopers in a concealed Terror-Drome panic to find the Oktober Guard snooping about the place. Ideally positioned to douse America and Russia with fear-inducing rays, the Cobra soldiers take to the offensive, hoping to either eliminate the Russians or ruin their survey.

Several Cobra Wolf attack vehicles converge on the Oktober Guard's position, but a group of Joes patrolling the Alaskan border side with the Russians against their mutual enemy. The Russian-Joe team scores several hits, but the Russians poorly drive their transport into icy waters.

While the Joes haul the Oktober Guard to safety, the Cobra Wolves, erroneously thinking their enemies all drowned, return to their secret base. Spitting mad, the Joes unhook their last ski missile and wait until the hidden Terror-Drome opens a ramp for the Cobra Wolves. With precise timing, the Joes pump their missile straight into the Terror-Drome's guts – blowing it to smithereens and preserving relations between America and Russia.

Issue #21: Investigating suspicious Cobra activity in New York's sewer system, Airtight and a team of Joes turn a corner and horrifically discover a tamper-proof Cobra canister conspicuously labeled "nerve toxin." With a square mile of Manhattan and thousands of lives at stake, the Joes dog various Cobra agents, but fail to find a means of defusing the weapon. As the nerve toxin canister's timer reaches zero, the Joes brace themselves for a vicious bio-chemical attack. But surprisingly, the "nerve toxin canister" emits a mere stink bomb.

Scratching their heads, the Joes return to base, wondering what Cobra could have possibly gained. But under cover of the stink gas, Cobra Techno-Vipers tap New York's main telephone station. Given illegal, untraceable access to America's phone network, Cobra telemarketer centers hidden in Arbco Moving Company trucks start dialing up thousands of civilians – raking in a fortune selling crooked pyramid sales schemes, cheap-ass aluminum siding and more.

MEMORABLE MOMENTS When Lift-Ticket optimistically notes that the Russians are firing Gatling guns rather than heat-seeking missiles, Wild Bill snips: "Am I supposed to be relieved by that remark? Is it qualitatively better to be riddled than vaporized?"

Oktober Guardsman Horrorshow cuts short a debate over American/Russian politics with: "No argument! They are wrong and we are right!" (In response, Colonel Brekhov raises an eyebrow and offers: "You missed your calling, Horrorshow. You should have been a political commissar.")

When a homeless vet named Sgt. Gamble grouses about how the military "threw him away," Joe point man Spearhead hotly responds: "You got your medal and your parade! What did you expect, undying gratitude? Grow up!" Later, when Gamble perishes while trying to help the Joes, Tunnel Rat eulogizes: "For a brief moment, [Gamble] remembered what it was like to be part of a team."

The climax of issue #21 left us in stitches, with Cobra telemarketers plying their slimy business to hapless victims across America.

LOVE AND WAR Dreadnok Road Pig thinks Zarana likes him – when she gets annoyed and breaks a bottle over his head. (As Hallmark would say, there's nothing like a broken bottle of Bud to show that you care.)

ASS-WHUPPINGS Lifeline takes some hits on a helicopter mission (#19), but bravely patches up Muskrat and Lift-Ticket before himself. A ski-clad Snow Job blows up a Cobra Wolf vehicle with a satchel charge. Charbroil takes out an albino alligator with his flamethrower. Sgt. Gamble, a grousing old vet, dies from either a coronary or a stroke.

NOW YOU KNOW... If someone pitches a grenade at you, listen for a distinctive "ping" – if you hear it just before the grenade's thrown, your opponent didn't properly "cook" the grenade (i.e. wait for its timing device to tick down), meaning you've got time to throw it back.

GOOFS Homeless people live in John Jacob Boardwalk's disused, high-class private subway station (see Places to Go), but its high-class decorations astonishingly haven't been looted.

COMIC TIE-INS Cobra's still flirting with the idea of using paranoia-inducing rays (first mentioned in #2) to cause political unrest, although the Joes mostly thwarted such schemes in *G.I. Joe* #68. Snake-Eyes' quartet spent three months on the road after their Himalayan mission (*Special Missions* #14-#15). The Oktober Guard previously jousted with the Snake-Eyes' Joes in *Special Missions* #18 and turn up – for a grand finale – in *Special Missions* #26.

CHARACTER PROFILE: JOES

Repeater: He's hauling extremely unique ammunition (designated "Lot #Xm321") – ultra-velocity, armor-piercing slugs made up of depleted uranium cores jacketed with Teflon-coated, tempered titanium steel.

CHARACTER PROFILE: COBRA

Toxo-Vipers: Also known, in Cobra circles, as the "Leaky Suit Brigade."

CHARACTER PROFILE: OTHER

Colonel Brekhov: Brekhov sides with the Joes against Cobra, but nonetheless dubs Americans "the running dog lackeys of the capitalist military-industrial plutocrats and the instruments of their interventionist-adventurist polices to exploit the freedom of loving peoples of the world." (Joe Snowcat driver Frostbite, unsurprisingly, is underwhelmed.)

ORGANIZATIONS *G.I. Joe:* After departing from the *USS Flagg*, Joe pilots can open sealed orders once they've lost sight of the aircraft carrier. The military evidently supplies the Joes with official G.I. Joe digital watches.

PLACES TO GO *Boardwalk's Private Subway Station:* Ritzy little subway stop privately funded by John Jacob Boardwalk, a saltwater taffy millionaire who lost his fortune in the crash of 1931. The subway station closed down, but remains a posh hidey-hole for homeless people.

HOT WHEELS *Cobra Wolves:* Built for ice combat, they're radar-equipped and capable of traveling across Arctic ground twice as fast as Russian vehicles.

• *G.I. Joe Snowcat:* Fires heat-seeking "ski missiles" – missiles literally positioned atop skis that zip over snowy terrain. The Snowcat diverts incoming missiles with infrared flares.

• *Joe Tomahawk:* Holds up under Gatling gun fire decently well – but you'd better worry about them heat-seeking SAM missiles.

THE COMMAND DECISION Oy vey. Launching a pair of take 'em or leave 'em issues, "Getting There" (SM #19) showcases a great cast of Joes – for a lot of mundane aerial gunfights.

A so-so romp through the Arctic, "Snow Blind" (*SM* #20) isn't bad *per se* – it's just not something you'd read a second time. One senses Hama drafting this snow-filled story for the sake of variety, but the choice of locale just isn't enough.

The best of the bunch, "The Lower Depths" (*SM* #21) maps out some crisp underground action, and the story's end is beautiful – with Cobra unveiling its masterstroke of ruling the world through bogus telephone sales. The cast is nicely diversified and Sgt. Gamble, although admittedly a throwaway character, represents the depth to which veterans never forget their military service. Skip the first two comics and go straight for this one.

G.I. Joe #84 to #85

Titles: *"Converging Destinies" (#84), "SFX" (#85)*
Release Dates: *Mar. to Apr. 1989*
Art: *Marshall Rogers (#84), Paul Ryan (#85)*

BATTLE ROSTER *Joes:* Storm Shadow, Jinx; *Cobra:* Cobra Commander II, Zartan, Dr. Mindbender; *Other:* Billy, Mama Billy.

FIRST APPEARANCES *Other:* The red ninja leader (#85).

MISSION BRIEF ***Issue #84:*** Innately sensing that Billy's alleged mom doesn't intend any harm, Jinx escorts the pistol-wielding woman to see Billy and Storm Shadow. Billy indeed identifies the woman as his long-lost mother, defusing the situation and enabling the foursome to share dinner at Storm Shadow's San Francisco apartment.

Meanwhile, Cobra Commander II and Dr. Mindbender deem Zartan too great an internal threat to their ambitions, taking an assassination squad to ransack Zartan's base on Cobra Island. But with a cadre of red ninjas in tow, Zartan easily captures Cobra Commander II. Stating that he learned Cobra Commander II's true identity long ago, Zartan details how he came into the original Cobra Commander's service *(see Sidebar)*.

Billy's mother explains that years ago, her husband – the future Cobra Commander – made off with Billy and began founding his terrorist empire. But when Cobra Commander's reckless older brother Dan died in the same car accident that slew Snake-Eyes' family (#26), Cobra Commander sought vengeance against Snake-Eyes.

Zartan further explains how Cobra Commander contracted him to assassinate Snake-Eyes, already a member of Storm Shadow's Arashikage clan in Japan. Unfortunately, Zartan botched the hit and murdered Storm Shadow's uncle, the Hard Master, by mistake. (*For further details, see issue #26 sidebar, "Snake-Eyes: The Vietnam Years."*)

With storytime over, Zartan releases the hapless Cobra Commander II and heads for San Francisco, determined to eliminate Storm Shadow before the ninja enacts revenge upon him. On a happier note, Billy puts his ninja training on hiatus to spend quality time with his mother in Berkeley.

Issue #85: While browsing a samurai exhibit at the DeJong Museum in San Francisco, Jinx is startled to find a sword belonging to her family, the Arashikage clan. Jinx phones Storm Shadow to report the discovery, but Zartan, staking out the museum, traces Jinx's call and discovers Storm Shadow's whereabouts.

A squad of red ninjas assaults Jinx, who grabs the Arashikage weapon and makes mincemeat of her attackers. Nearby, Zartan and another red ninja pack assault Storm Shadow's martial arts academy, but Storm Shadow skewers most of the ninjas with his bow and arrow. Storm Shadow and Jinx combine their efforts to put Zartan and the red ninja leader on the run, leading to a perilous car chase on the Golden Gate Bridge. Eventually, Storm Shadow shish-ka-bobs the red ninja leader's neck with an arrow, causing him to drive Zartan's van off the bridge. As Zartan, the red ninja leader and their vehicle sink beneath the water, Storm Shadow and Jinx depart for home.

MEMORABLE MOMENTS Zartan equips his red ninjas with high-frequency sound emitters – enabling Zartan's listening equipment to distinguish friend from foe as he fires arrows through obstacles. However, Storm Shadow simply tears one such emitter from a red ninja's chest – fooling Zartan into shafting one of his own men.

ASS-WHUPPINGS Jinx slices open a bunch of red ninjas (indeed, the panels run red with red ninjas). Storm Shadow demonstrates his "Ear that Sees" gift, flinging a sword through a fire door and nailing a ninja. Stormy guts a legion of his opponents, disguising himself as a dead red ninja at one point to lure his adversaries closer. A bow-firing Zartan pincushions one of his ninjas by mistake. The story climaxes with Storm Shadow arrow-pelting the red ninja leader in the back of the neck.

GOOFS We're completely baffled as to how Billy's mother, who to our knowledge isn't an intelligence agent or a super-sleuth, located her son at a classified Joe base. Stretching the realm of memory recall – even for a ninja – Billy last saw his mother at age five but "finds her walk familiar."

It's unclear just *why* Zartan feels a wild compulsion to spill his life story to Fred Smith VII and then release him without even a mention of the assassination attempt.

COMIC TIE-INS Issue #84 reveals Cobra Commander's personal vendetta against Snake-Eyes, elaborating on the deaths of Snake-Eyes' family (first mentioned in *G.I. Joe* #10, detailed in #26) and the Hard Master's murder (also #26). But regrettably, the vendetta's never, ever mentioned again. Moreover, it explains why Cobra hired Zartan to assassinate Snake-Eyes before he became a Joe member.

When Storm Shadow founds a martial arts academy (#84), a sign marking the spot reveals his last name (deemed "unpronounceable" in #26) as "Arashikage." Zartan continues using sound amplification equipment (also #26) to "hear" his opponents and fire arrows at them through obstacles (*a la* Storm Shadow's "Ear that Sees" technique). Zartan's red ninja associates – including the red ninja leader (here wounded by Storm Shadow's arrow) – return to kill Stormy in #90-#91. Zartan himself lays low for a few months, but resurfaces to tussle with the Blind Master in #90.

Zartan lets Cobra Commander II go free here, later attempting to topple him from power in #97.

Storm Shadow continues educating Billy in the ways of "the Void," a nebulous ninja concept first mentioned in *G.I. Joe* #66 (*see Stuff You Need*).

CHARACTER PROFILE: COBRA Zartan: It's suggested that his real name's Dristan.

CHARACTER PROFILE: OTHER Billy, Billy's Mom and Cobra Commander: Billy's mother only found out about her husband's misguided grudge against Snake-Eyes after Billy was born. Soon after, the would-be Cobra Commander sold off his assets, leaving his wife utterly destitute, then made off with his young son. While living out of hotel rooms, Cobra Commander un-creatively told Billy that his mother died in a car crash. Billy claims that his father, totally engrossed in madcap pyramid cleaning schemes and dreams of overthrowing big business, never had time for him. It's still unclear how Billy later left his father's care and joined the Springfield resistance (#10). Mama Billy's name is never specified.

MISCELLANEOUS STUFF!

ZARTAN'S ORIGIN

Before evolving into the algae-coated swamp rat that we all know and love, a red-headed, pool-playing, mercenary Zartan hung out after Vietnam at a Daytona Beach dive named the "Don't Fall Inn." One day, the future Cobra Commander approached Zartan to perform an atypical assassination – the murder of Snake-Eyes, whom Cobra Commander erroneously blamed for his brother's death (*see Story Summary*). Zartan accepted the assignment, intrigued at the challenge of infiltrating the Hard Master's ninja compound to reach his target.

Zartan took a long-term approach, travelling to Japan to obtain a cover identity and camping out on the doorstep of a famed sword-maker named Onihashi. After six months, Onihashi deemed Zartan worthy to apprentice at his forge. Onihashi suspected that Zartan's soul contained a vibrant fire, but hoped to temper it through the art of sword-making.

In time, Onihashi procured a special commission from Storm Shadow's Arashikage clan. Zartan accordingly gained access to the Hard and Soft Masters' household, but the desire to snuff Snake-Eyes strangely left him, replaced by a desire to remain Onihashi's assistant and craft elegant swords.

Unfortunately, Cobra Commander forced Zartan's hand by threatening to expose his duplicity. Zartan moved forward with the hit, but as *G.I. Joe* #26 proved, he killed the Hard Master by mistake. Shamed by his apprentice's misdeeds, Onihashi committed suicide – leaving a double stain of guilt on Zartan's soul. Although Zartan in time became an accomplished criminal and leader of the Dreadnoks, a part of him has always regretted his failure to remain a humble sword-maker.

PLACES TO GO Arashikage Martial Arts Academy: Located at 4498 Zoe Ave., San Francisco.

• *Zartan's Cobra Island hideout:* Zartan's equipped his private lair with hologram projectors, allowing the exterior to shift between a standard Cobra barracks, a swamp-shack or a gas station. The projectors turn trespassers' senses of balance topsy-turvy, giving them waves of vertigo.

STUFF YOU NEED The "Void": Storm Shadow's continuing to refine Billy's sense of "the void" – a mental state that allows ninjas to supposedly sense the infinite layers of "now" (i.e. the multiple states that simultaneously exist between "before" and "after"), thereby clearing their minds for battle. Ironically enough, Storm Shadow notes that the true martial artist must question everything to master his craft – but Billy points out that it seems impossible to clear one's mind with "the void" while questioning everything. Caught in a Gordian knot of his own ninja logic, Stormy concedes that cosmic Zen questions often give him headaches.

THE COMMAND DECISION Proof that endlessly recycling past success is just begging for trouble (well, unless you're The Simpsons), *G.I. Joe* #84 deplorably over-complicates Snake-Eyes' origin story and pinned us to the wall like an Olympic javelin thrower. Granted, Zartan's history throws a couple of interesting curve-balls (we loved him as a pool hall junkie), but Cobra Commander's supposed vendetta against Snake-Eyes doesn't jive with any issue of *G.I. Joe* and smacks of "surprising" us just for the sake of surprise.

A spin-off of the famed "silent issue" (*G.I. Joe* #21), "SFX" (#85) offers a cute and fanciful read, although it's not as interesting or dramatic as it pretends. The fact that fans frequently forget about the silly thing only highlights its lack of innovation.

G.I. Joe #86

Titles: *"... Not Fade Away!"*
Release Dates: *May 1989*
Art: *Marshall Rogers*

BATTLE ROSTER *Joes:* Hawk, Shockwave, Repeater, Muskrat, Stalker; *Cobra:* Firefly, Cobra Commander II, Dr. Mindbender; *Destro:* the Iron Grenadiers.

FIRST APPEARANCES *Joes:* The original G.I. Joe (Joseph Colton), G.I. Jane.

MISSION BRIEF When Destro's Iron Grenadiers besiege a U.S. military lab hidden atop New York's Chrysler Building, Duke takes a six-pack of Joes and rushes to defend the structure. Once inside, the Joes meet a security chief named "Joseph," who explains that the secret military lab houses a "Star Wars" missile defense system, capable of bouncing a particle beam off America's satellite network and obliterating enemy warheads.

Together with Joseph and his assistant Jane, the Joes fortify the particle beam control chamber, retreating inside when the Iron Grenadiers unleash tear gas. But to their horror, the cornered Joes realize that the Iron Grenadiers intend to steal the particle beam system's schematics from a secondary control chamber.

Having gained a moment's peace, the "Iron Grenadiers" reveal themselves as Cobra Vipers, disguised as Iron Grenadiers to defame Destro's organization. Moving about freely, Firefly attaches the particle beam program discs to a passing Cobra drone, then helps the Vipers assemble one-man helicopters to escape. But with America's defense grid at stake, Joseph authorizes a one-time use of the particle beam – obliterating the in-flight Cobra drone and its stolen disks.

Relieved, Duke suggests making Joseph an honorary Joe member. However, Jane starts cackling – revealing that 25 years ago, she and Joseph served on the original Joe team – as G.I. Joe and G.I. Jane.

MEMORABLE MOMENTS Muskrat symbolically makes reference to the original Joe dolls' height advantage over the "Real American Hero" action figures, looking at Joseph and commenting: "Golly! I always thought you were... bigger!"

ASS-WHUPPINGS Muskrat and Repeater suffer flesh wounds.

GOOFS Err... wouldn't foreign governments detect the particle beam that Joseph uses to destroy the computer discs – thereby raising some hackles about the U.S. missile defense net and turning foreign politics higgledy-piggledy?

COMIC TIE-INS This issue celebrates the 25th anniversary of G.I. Joe (1963-1988). Joseph reappears in #127 and returns to active service in #152.

Cobra Commander II orders his Vipers to dress up like Destro's Iron Grenadiers as payback for the Grenadiers impersonating Cobra soldiers in *G.I. Joe* #82.

The Joes coordinate with Domestic Operations Agency (DOA) members to protect Joseph's secret laser project – a decent reconciliation, considering that DOA agents previously hunted down fugitive Joes (#78).

CHARACTER PROFILE: JOES

• *Jane:* She originally served as the Joe team's nurse, but later achieved a doctorate in physics.

• *Joseph Colton:* He still carries an outdated army-issue Colt

.45 M1911 A1.

PLACES TO GO The Chrysler Building: Located in New York, the Chrysler Building secretly houses the "Star Wars" defense grid in its top level. A 2.5-ton steel hatch protects the particle beam's main vault from intrusion. The computer control room lies beneath the particle beam chamber, sealed off by a "sandwich" door of super-hard steel, Kevlar and ceramics.

Beneath that lies a phony DOA-staffed ad agency that's the defense grid's sole means of access to the Chrysler Building. A "dead" floor between the "agency" and the "Star Wars" system contains protective ballistic fiberglass foam.

STUFF YOU NEED Rapid-Pulse Electro: Extremely funky name for Joseph's ultra-secret "Star Wars" defense, equipped with a non-radioactive particle beam that "burns" a hole in its path, preventing energy dissipation in transit through the atmosphere. The particle beam hits its target after bouncing off six geo-synchronous satellites. Properly programmed, the particle beam nails targets travelling at Mach 2 (probably faster).

THE COMMAND DECISION Remembered by Joe veterans and "Real American Hero" fanatics as "that story where the original Joe came back," issue #86 sadly fails to progress beyond the surface-level. Barring the announcement that he served as the original Joe, Joseph isn't much more impressive than any other security officer, leaving this an example of nostalgia winning over substance.

G.I. Joe Special Missions #22 to #25

Titles: *"Decisions" (#22), "Scoop" (#23), "Ladies' Day" (#24), "Forced Play" (#25)*
Release Dates: *June to Sept. 1989*
Art: *Dave Cockrum (#22, #24), Herb Trimpe (#23, #25)*

BATTLE ROSTER *Joes:* Chuckles, Lady Jaye, Shockwave, Hit 'n Run, Stalker, Muskrat, Leatherneck, Scarlett, Cover Girl, Jinx, Hawk, Duke, Ripcord, Lifeline, Dusty; *Cobra:* Cobra Commander II, Raptor, Zarana, Firefly, Voltar.

FIRST APPEARANCES *Joes:* Scoop (combat information specialist, #23); *Cobra:* Crystal Ball (hypnotist, #24).

MISSION BRIEF ***Issue #22:*** At Chicago's O'Hare airport, three masked terrorists lay waste to 17 civilians and flee to a rural town in Iowa. The terrorists quietly capture three members of the Bronsky family (father Laszlo, his wife and son Mikey), holing up in the Bronsky's farmhouse. Soon after, Chuckles and a team of Joe specialists coordinate with the FBI, tracking the terrorists to the Bronsky abode. Unfortunately, FBI agent Saxon confesses the Bureau has no information on what the terrorists or the Bronskys look like.

Working from a snippet of video taken at O'Hare massacre, the Joes match a sadistic grin on one of the killers' faces with a demonic smirk on a man in the Bronsky kitchen. Tagging the American apple-pie-looking duo in the kitchen as Mikey's parents, the Joes ready a pincer movement to plug the grinning man and his accomplices.

With Shockwave, Hit 'n Run and Chuckles serving as snipers, Lady Jaye approaches the main door disguised as a cosmetics saleswoman. But as the operation commences, Saxon learns, from the Bronskys' neighbor, that shrapnel pierced one of Laszlo Bronsky's facial nerves in Vietnam – leaving him with a permanent, sadistic grin called a "rictus."

While Saxon craps bricks, Lady Jaye passes the apple-pie woman (named Mary) a note scribbled with: "We are here to rescue you." In response, Mary – actually one of the murderers – empties an Ingram pistol into Lady Jaye's chest. As Lady Jaye flails backward, her Kevlar vest stopping Mary's slugs, Shockwave pounces and blows away one of Mary's fellow hitmen. Hit 'n Run nearly shoots the insidiously grinning Laszlo, but the remaining male terrorist impetuously pulls a sidearm. Hit 'n Run unloads his rifle into the murderer, forcing Mary to grab young Mikey and haul ass.

The assembled Joes and FBI agents hold their fire for Mikey's sake, but Laszlo – a former instructor at a marine sniper school – boldly grabs Hit 'n Run's rifle. Laszlo gives Mary the option of surrendering, then expertly puts a bullet in her brain. As hostilities cease, the Bronsky family reunites and the FBI begins clean-up operations.

Issue #23: In Sierra Gordo, revolutionary leader El Jefe makes the cardinal mistake of welching on a deal with Destro, leading to Destro's Iron Grenadiers taking El Jefe into protective custody. Determined to ingratiate El Jefe to the United States, Duke assigns Stalker and a ruthless team of Joes to extract the revolutionary from the Iron Grenadiers' clutches. However, Stalker's group collectively groans when the Defense Department assigns a combat information specialist named Scoop to videotape their mission for a Senate committee.

Tunnel Rat accepts Scoop as his assistant gunner, letting the Joe newbie handle the spare barrels and extra ammunition. Upon landing in Sierra Gordo, the Joes seep into the foliage, preparing to ambush an Iron Grenadier convoy. Unfortunately, the Joes' intelligence information completely misses the mark, pitting Stalker's beleaguered group against a massive contingent of Destro's legions.

The Joes fall into retreat, resorting to hand-to-hand combat.

Scoop tries to keep up, but a close-quarters clash forces him to break his camera over an Iron Grenadier's head. The freshman Joe passes out from his battle wounds, later awakening aboard an outbound Joe helicopter. With the mission completely botched, Scoop wonders why the hell his teammates seem so happy – leaving Stalker to explain that however the mission turned out, the Joes escaped with their lives.

Issue #24: When America's president decides to throw the opening ball at a baseball game between the New York "Mites" and the New York "Dandees," Hawk details several Joes to provide extra security. Consequently, four Joe females dress up as Mites' cheerleaders. The Joes stay sharp, but Cobra Commander II – plotting to prove Cobra's power by snatching the president in broad daylight – sends a Cobra hypnotist named Crystal Ball to infiltrate the event.

Crystal Ball's mesmeric, glowing arm shield brings Hawk and Lt. Falcon under his command, leaving the Joes in total disarray. Leaving only the disguised Joe females functional, Cobra Commander II takes the President aboard a Cobra dirigible. Scarlett, Lady Jaye and Jinx jump aboard the blimp just before take-off, leaving Cover Girl to break the Joe males' stupor with her hypno-therapy expertise.

A roaring fight erupts in the blimp's control room, but on Lady Jaye's signal, Cover Girl and Hardball lob a smoke grenade aboard the airship. While the Joe women grab the President in the confusion, rappelling back to Earth aboard a tow cable, the Cobra officers flee in an escape module. In the aftermath, Hawk awards the Joe women a month's leave with double pay.

Issue #25: In Darklonia, a revolutionary group named the Lower Darklonian Separatist Front (LDSF) goads Darklon a bit too much, earning his wrath. Working behind the scenes, Darklon orders his cultural attaché to America, Nobel Peetman, to falsely foster a LDSF plot on American soil – hoping to trigger an incident that incites unholy American retribution and destroys the LDSF.

After returning to Manhattan, Peetman strikes a deal with a crooked Domestic Operations Agency (DOA) director named Skip Bentsen-Barr, offering to help the DOA man round up the LDSF terrorists as a publicity coup. Bentsen-Barr agrees, turning a blind eye as Peetman helps LDSF operatives steal explosives from a Manhattan warehouse. Everything goes according to plan, putting Bentsen-Barr's men in a position to "heroically" round up the terrorists.

Unfortunately, Duke and a team of Joes, summoned to deal with the explosives theft, round up the LDSF soldiers instead. Uneasy about the affair, Duke investigates further and deduces Peetman's true motives. Worse, Duke's Joes realize that Peetman intends to blow up a Catholic school – thereby pinning the incident on the LDSF and to seal the organization's doom.

Alpine, Lightfoot and Jinx catch Peetman in the act of priming a briefcase bomb to blow up the school. Not wanting Peetman's diplomatic immunity to get him off the hook, Alpine's trio haul Peetman – and his bomb – into Bentsen-Barr's office. The Joes inform Bentsen-Barr about Peetman's secret intent to kill Catholic school children, off-handedly mentioning that the bomb will detonate in 60 seconds. Caught with his pants down, Bentsen-Barr tosses Peetman and his briefcase bomb out a multi-story window – killing Peetman and absolving the Joes of blame.

MEMORABLE MOMENTS Leatherneck dismisses Scoop's concerns about being branded an outsider – rather, the gruff Leatherneck worries that Scoop's "lack of experience, stupidity, clumsiness, cowardice or even body odor will get them killed." (Recoiling, Scoop comments: "Well, that certainly cleared the air!")

An LDSF suicide bomber revels in his martyrdom, thinking that school children in lower Darklonia will surely sing his praises. Alas, after the henchmen blows himself to bits, his teammates fail to remember his name.

LOVE AND WAR In her previous career as a model, Cover Girl earned $500 an hour for unveiling her legs. Lady Jaye salivates over beefcake Dandees player Seth Kernandez.

ASS-WHUPPINGS A Kevlar vest saves Lady Jaye's life during the Iowa standoff, but a high-velocity 9 mm round cracks her ribs. An Iron Grenadier sharpshooter nails Hit 'n Run in the knee. Lady Jaye breaks a javelin over Cobra falconer Raptor's noodle and does in one of his birds with a knife.

GOOFS In issue #25, Some Joes and LDSF thugs defy spatial issues by driving their vehicles throughout New York's Natural History Museum.

NOW YOU KNOW... Words of wisdom from Scoop's on-the-field "education" in issue #23: When assigned to a new unit, don't worry about making friends – worry about not screwing up in combat.

Keep your compass in your left side pocket and your maps in your right – that way, your buddies won't waste precious time searching your bullet-riddled corpse for essential equipment. On the other hand, positioning your dog tags isn't important: Just concentrate on getting out alive.

Always test your weapon *before* you reach a hostile landing zone. For that matter, test-slide *every single bullet* into your rifle's chamber. Remember: The government often purchases ammunition from the lowest bidder – and a slightly bulged bullet casing can jam your M16A2 rifle instantly.

When readying an ambush, stealth is imperative for pretty obvious reasons. Tape down your rifle sling so it won't swivel and make noise. Don't let tree branches snap backward – pass them back to the person behind you. If you're going to drink from a canteen, drink it all – the enemy might hear your backwash sloshing. Oh, and munch down *all* of your freeze-dried rations, because the smell might carry.

Learn the silent signals that denote "rest break," "hide" and "radio check." Always make your tripwires from foreign products (Swedish clothespins, Belgian plastic spoons, etc.) so that the enemy won't suspect American involvement.

Ready your bandages in pairs – bullets always leave both an entry and exit wound. Avoid looking into muzzle flashes, because it'll muck up your night vision. Watch your rifle barrel – if it wears away, you'll be spitting bullets with zero velocity. Conversely, shotguns are useful little firearms, because they're geared for a wide dispersal pattern – you don't have to aim with dead-on accuracy.

And for pity's sake, if your buddy doesn't follow any of these rules, force 'em to comply. There's no point in having someone cover your back if they're a bumblefish.

COMIC TIE-INS FBI agent Saxon previously tried to scapegoat the Joes in *Special Missions* #17 – while trying to preserve the FBI's reputation – although he act more benevolently in issue #22.

Sierra Gordo revolutionary El Jefe previously struck a deal with Destro in *G.I. Joe* #69-#71, although the deal evidently soured afterward. Stalker's group fails to rescue El Jefe from the Iron Grenadiers' clutches – but a second attempt causes a *lot* of fatalities in *Special Missions* #26.

Zap comments in issue #24 that "it's great to be back in action," probably alluding to his period as a Joe training instructor (*G.I. Joe* #82).

CHARACTER PROFILE: JOES

- *Duke:* Thinks of DOA director Bentsen-Barr as a "porky little slime-wallower" (among other things).
- *Muskrat:* Muskrat doesn't need to worry about calibrating his shotgun, but he takes part in accuracy exercises – purely to hear the rifles go "bang!"
- *The U.S. President:* He's vaguely rendered to look like George H.W. Bush (in keeping with #24's publication in 1989), but his wife's too young and spry (not to mention good-looking) to be Barbara.
- *Zap:* He's a dyed-in-the-wool Dandees fan.

CHARACTER PROFILE: COBRA

Cobra Commander II: He's still worried about gaining respect from Dr. Mindbender, the Baroness and Destro.

PLACES TO GO *Darklonia:* Allegedly, social classes in "upper Darklonia" oppress the people of "lower Darklonia." (Author's Note: Annoyingly, such terminology mirrors the ongoing political struggle in Borovia, mapped out in *G.I. Joe* #104-#107. In the *G.I. Joe* universe, it's apparently the providence of the "upper" people to smack around "the lower.")

Among other things, the Lower Darklonian Separatist Front (LDSF) wants to restore its people's "ancient right" to drive on the right side rather than the left.

Darklonia keeps official ties with the United States, but holds a national policy of fostering unrest and terror away from home – all the better to encourage the country's armaments business.

ORGANIZATIONS *Joes: G.I. Joe Special Missions* #25 debuts the first use of "Tiger Force" colors – garish blue-yellow hues worn by Dusty, Lifeline and more.

THE COMMAND DECISION A fine jewel in the *Special Missions* crown, "Decisions" (SM #22) holds true to the series' premise of pitting a small team of specialists against wily thugs and cutthroats. Hama's wordplay, meticulously chosen to hide the villains' identities, pulls off a "don't judge a book by its cover" tale that's almost ideal (if quite short) for stage or film.

Another contender for the top *Special Missions* slot, "Scoop" (#23) brings Hama's honed battlefield knowledge to the forefront. The story's masterfully told through newcomer Scoop, who learns that soldiers "win" simply by not dying. Frankly, with this level of detail, even the painful, misbegotten Joe DIC cartoons might look good.

Reverting to type for a non-Hama story (i.e. wretchedness incarnate), the baseball-themed "Ladies' Day" (*SM* #24) gagged us with a mess of kiddie elements (Firefly's exploding hot dogs, etc.). Moreover, the dialogue's awful ("When Crystal Ball zaps 'em, they stay zapped."), and the characters feel the incessant need to blandly… mention… their… every… single… move. Egads.

Finally, "Forced Play" holds quite a bit of merit, but also demands your attention, meaning you can't zip through the issue in 60 seconds. Indeed, Hama saturates the story with several twists, making it a pity that such a readable comic comes wrapped in a dopey "Attack of the Killer Pterodactyl!"-style cover.

G.I. Joe #87 to #88

Titles: *"Assault on Castle Destro" (#87), "Python Patrol" (#88)*
Release Dates: *June to July 1989*
Art: *Tony Salmons*

Now You Know

BATTLE ROSTER *Joes:* Flint, Lady Jaye, Snake-Eyes, Scarlett, Sneak-Peak, Shockwave, Outback; *Cobra:* Cobra Commander II, Dr. Mindbender, Tomax and Xamot; *Destro:* Destro, the Baroness.

FIRST APPEARANCES *Destro:* Darklon (Evader driver/ Darklonia ruler, #88).

MISSION BRIEF ***Issue #87:*** When Destro ratchets up a massive amount of sales on the international arms market – stymieing sales of Cobra-made goods – Cobra Commander II grits his teeth in frustration and resorts to the time-honored tradition of plotting Destro's disembowelment. Accordingly, Cobra Commander II disguises several Cobra battalions as gypsy carnival and trailer park members, positioning his troops on the property that borders Castle Destro.

Sensing the attack, Destro orders his general (named Voltar) to disperse several Iron Grenadier vehicles disguised as giant bales of hay. Consequently, Destro's tank squadrons make mincemeat out of the advancing Cobra forces. As the battle rages, Destro rouses his Nullifier shock-troops and breaks into Cobra Commander II's mobile headquarters.

Cobra Commander II sputters like a teenager caught trying to purchase booze, but Destro, having learned Cobra Commander II's true identity from the Baroness, threatens to expose Fred Smith VII as an imposter. Left with little choice, a cowed Cobra Commander II signs off on extensive ties between Cobra and Destro's corporation – causing troops on both sides to celebrate an increase in their benefits.

Issue #88: Newly united, Destro and Cobra Commander II travel to the country of Darklonia and meet up with its ruler – an elaborately helmeted arms dealer appropriately named Darklon. A major purchaser of Cobra vehicles and equipment, Darklon despairs over his inability to penetrate defenses protecting the bordering country of Wolkekuckuckland. Accordingly, Dr. Mindbender offers to put Darklon's vehicles through a "Python-ization" process, coating them with a radar-resistant substance and rendering them invisible to Wolkekuckuckland's early warning sensors.

In Wolkekuckuckland, a large-scale buyer of American vehicles, General Liederkranz confers with Hawk and other G.I. Joe military advisers about shoring up his country's security measures. But suddenly, Darklon sneaks into Wolkekuckuckland with his Python-ized vehicles, intent on humiliating Liederkranz into purchasing great bundles of overly expensive and shoddy Cobra equipment.

Unfazed by the surprise attack, Hawk's armor teams swat aside Darklon's divisions. Nonetheless, Liederkranz finds himself impressed by Darklon's ability to thwart his detection systems, offering to purchase a wide array of Python-ized vehicles. As the Joes heave a collective sigh of dismay, Destro and Darklon toast the completion of a successful operation.

MEMORABLE MOMENTS Xamot shouts at his disguised (and evidently transvestite) troops, "Take off those silly gypsy costumes and behave like Crimson guardsmen!" As Destro's men surrounds Cobra Commander II, the commander blathers, "Destro! Good heavens! There's been a terrible mistake! You see, we really meant to attack that other castle."

The newfound Cobra-Destro alliance leaves Dr. Mindbender confused about *whom* he's meant to be following. Cobra troops applaud the formalized Cobra-Destro merger with, "Yay!! More benefits!!"

When tight-lipped smugglers refuse to yield crucial information, Snake-Eyes loosens their tongues – by removing his latex mask and showing them his true face.

Finally, Darklon gets a bit over-excited when Liederkranz agrees to purchase Cobra vehicles: "My order book is all atingle with anticipation!"

GOOFS General Liederkranz trusts monitor duty of Wolkekuckuckland's entire perimeter to a snip of a boy named Wolfgang.

NOW YOU KNOW... Hawk advocates never committing all of your forces to a single task – always hold something in reserve for when the battle inevitably screws you over.

COMIC TIE-INS The Baroness informed Destro of Cobra Commander II's true identity in *G.I. Joe* #77. Destro turns increasingly bold from this point on, radically restructuring Cobra's leadership structure in #90.

The original Cobra Commander finds a means of breaching Castle Destro's defenses, spelling its demise in issue #116. Further conflicts in Wolkekuckuckland erupt in #146-#151.

Darklon variously positions himself as Destro's rival and supporter, although Destro entrusts him with the Destro family weapons business (MARS) in *G.I. Joe* #97.

CHARACTER PROFILE: DESTRO

• *The Baroness:* Aside from being a highly renowned international terrorist, she's also a stellar photographer (playing Linda McCartney to Destro's Paul, as it were).

• *Destro:* Destro describes his Nullifiers as "... a grim and trigger-happy lot." The frozen haggis trade hasn't weathered the current economic slump, evidently forcing Destro's neighbor, Lord Malaprop, to raise cash by siding with Cobra.

• *Darklon:* Purchased dozens of Joe X-30 Conquests from a formerly US-friendly country that underwent a coup.

PLACES TO GO Castle *Destro:* Protected, among other things, by 81 mm mortars.

• *Wolkekuckuckland:* A treaty with America allows

Wolkekuckuckland to purchase surplus Joe Maulers, AWE-Strikers, APCs and SLAMs – plus get free technical support from the Joes. In years past, the Americans defended Wolkekuckuckland when the Germans kicked the country's ass.

THE COMMAND DECISION A step in the right direction, blessed with a strong tempo and a heightened role for Destro (he should've outwitted Cobra Commander II long ago). That said, Darklon's impossible to take seriously as a villain – probably because his costume resembles the mutant love child of a car transmission and a banana – and details keep disappearing from Salmons' art, as if we're watching the story through a haze of ether. The final effect leaves this two-parter as average – but even that's an improvement over recent issues.

G.I. Joe #89 to #91

Titles: "Mean Dog!" (#89), "Recurring Themes" (#90), "No Simple Solutions" (#91)
Release Dates: Aug. to Oct. 1989
Art: M.D. Bright (#89-#90), Tony Salmons (#91)

BATTLE ROSTER *Joes:* Clutch, Rock 'n Roll, Hawk, Snake-Eyes, Scarlett, Storm Shadow, Wildcard; *Cobra:* The Dreadnoks, Zarana, Zartan, Dr. Mindbender; *Destro:* Destro, the Baroness, Darklon, Voltar; *Other:* the Blind Master.

DEATHS *Other:* The Blind Master (#91).

MISSION BRIEF ***Issue #89:*** Zarana and Zandar relentlessly expand Cobra's real estate and pyramid schemes, financing Broca Beach's refurbishment into Cobra's new U.S. headquarters. But when a furloughed Clutch and Rock 'n Roll happen to visit Broca Beach, Rock 'n Roll spots a cop wearing a Cobra insignia ring and immediately pressures Clutch to make a quick exit.

The two Joes hop into Clutch's '74 Barracuda and hit the highway, but the Dreadnoks spot them and pursue. Cobra communications experts partly jam Clutch and Rock 'n Roll's radio, but the Joes send a staticky message requesting assistance on the Atlantic City Expressway. In response, Hawk and Scarlett deploy the G.I. Joe Mean Dog attack vehicle to savage Clutch and Rock 'n Roll's pursuers. Unfortunately, Clutch and Rock 'n Roll run afoul of schizoid Dreadnok Road pig, who smashes their car engine and drags the Joe duo back to Broca Beach by the scruff of their necks.

Issue #90-#91: At a former Broca Beach lodge hall, Destro berates the wayward Cobra leadership for pursuing selfish

MISCELLANEOUS STUFF!

RED NINJAS

One of the challenges in crafting a *G.I. Joe* reference guide – although it's admittedly not something Joe readers worried about on a month-to-month basis – is making sense of the seemingly ubiquitous red-clad ninja hordes throughout the series. Much like the ill-fated "red shirt" security guards from *Star Trek*, the red ninjas routinely crop up to get threshed like wheat, retreat to lick their wounds, recruit new members for some months, then resurface to get wantonly slaughtered again in a manner that puts even lemmings to shame.

That'd be fine, except that throughout the years, the red ninjas' motivations and various employers seem as fluid as a butter stick tossed onto a summer highway. So for your perusal, here's a short list of the red ninjas' key appearances and shifting goals:

- **G.I. JOE #21** – The wordless *G.I. Joe* #21 initially debuted a few red ninjas as Storm Shadow's lackey toads, kindly providing Snake-Eyes with cannon fodder to variously gut, grenade and pummel in his quest to save Scarlett. Luckily, the red ninjas' presence nicely pairs with later claims (notably #91) of the red ninjas being renegade second-rate members of Storm Shadow's Arashikage family clan (first seen in *G.I. Joe* #26).

- **G.I. JOE #84-#85, #90-#91** – After "Silent Interlude" (#21), the red ninjas vanish from the series only to later reappear in *G.I. Joe* #84 in Zartan's employ. Regrettably, it's not clear – if you stop to think about it – why the hell they'd obey Zartan, especially considering he slew the Arashikage family head (the Hard Master). A possible explanation lies in #91, where the red ninjas (rather crazily) blame Storm Shadow for the Hard Master's demise – suggesting that they sided with Zartan out of misguided anger at Storm Shadow. Certainly, the red ninja leader holds Storm Shadow accountable, arguing that Stormy set events leading to the Hard Master's death in motion by admitting Snake-Eyes into the family household (#26). However, this seems a fairly pathetic excuse, and it's *certainly* a ridiculous reason for teaming up with Zartan, who skewered the Hard Master like a moth to a piece of corkboard.

CONTINUED ON PAGE 221

agendas rather than rallying for Cobra's benefit. Leveraging his newfound authority with Cobra, Destro radically re-organizes Cobra's command structure, forcing long-running rivals such as the Baroness and Zarana to work together.

Restraining herself from ripping the Baroness' giblets out, Zarana updates her long-running nemesis on various Cobra intelligence projects. In particular, the two of them observe the Dreadnoks strap the captive Clutch and Rock 'n Roll into the late Dr. Venom's brainwave scanner. Moments later, the brainwave scanner – modified by Zarana to implant information rather than extract it – brainwashes the Joes to return to base and destroy the Pit III from within.

In San Francisco, Zartan emerges from hiding after five months, warily searching for traces of the vengeful Storm Shadow. Zartan tries to remain discreet, but the San Francisco-based Blind Master – furious at Zartan for killing his mentor, the Hard Master – tracks the shape-changer and challenges him to a back-alley slugfest.

Zartan lands a few hits, but the Blind Master whips the shit out of Zartan and readies a killing stroke. Suddenly, the Blind Master's newest pupil – a young boy named Tyrone – appears and begs the Blind Master to relent, arguing that Zartan's murder would only corrupt the Blind Master's soul. As Tyrone skulks off, the Blind Master finds wisdom in his words and relents. Unfortunately, the adrenaline-tanked Zartan, caught up in a berserker rage, seizes a knife and stabs the Blind Master in the back.

Dying, the Blind Master repents his savagery, revealing that Zartan's former mentor – Professor Onihashi – forgave Zartan for murdering the Hard Master. The Blind Master expires, but his compassion moves Zartan to recant his past misdeeds. Trying to begin anew, Zartan holographically assumes the Blind Master's identity and meets up with Tyrone.

Oblivious to the Blind Master's death, Snake-Eyes, Scarlett, Jinx and Storm Shadow get word of Zartan's return and regroup at the remains of Snake-Eyes' High Sierras cabin. Unfortunately, Zartan's red ninja associates stalk the Joes. The red ninja leader steps forward and reveals his Arashikage wrist brand, identifying himself as a member of Storm Shadow's crimelord family. But after verbally blasting Storm Shadow for admitting Snake-Eyes into the clan – the act that led to the Hard Master's death – the red ninja leader challenges Storm Shadow to a duel.

Storm Shadow's allies butcher most of the red ninjas, but Stormy and the red ninja leader fall into a roaring stream near a waterfall. Snake-Eyes hauls Storm Shadow to safety, but the red ninja leader disappears – leaving Storm Shadow convinced that his past will always haunt him.

MEMORABLE MOMENTS Darklon zaps the raging Road Pig with tranquilizer darts, eliciting a tranquil monologue from Road Pig's "Donald" personality – "Ahhhh! To sleep, perchance to dream... 'Tis a consummation... " – before passing out. The Blind Master pauses while battering Zartan to comment: "I doubt the soles of my feet will ever recover from the vicious pummeling they have received from your face."

LOVE AND WAR The Baroness feels scorned because Destro crafted the Cobra re-organization plan – and relocated her to Broca Beach – without consulting her. Clutch went steady with fellow student Margaret Boberek during his senior year.

ASS-WHUPPINGS Road Pig thumps Buzzer with a shovel for mouthing off to Zarana. A red ninja nicks Snake-Eyes' wolf Timber with an arrow. The red ninjas slice up Scarlett and make Jinx eat a volley of bullets, but the Joe women survive with only minor wounds. Conversely, the Joes massacre the red ninjas almost to a man. The Blind Master mops the floor with Zartan, but dies after granting the shape-changer mercy.

Cobra's brainwave scanner works Clutch and Rock 'n Roll's brains over from top to toe, allowing the Dreadnoks to gleefully ransack a number of their memories. As part of this process, the Dreadnoks sprinkle the Joes' memories with pro-Cobra conversations, including a cheerleader who teaches about vitamins, household cleaning products and the violent overthrow of democracies. [*Side Note:* Future issues show the brainwashing isn't permanent.]

PREPOSTEROUS PHYSICS The red ninja leader survived an arrow in the back of his neck (#85) – and even for ninjas, that's pushing it.

GOOFS If it's so ultra-important that Cobra conceal its presence in Broca Beach, why do the police strut about town wearing Cobra logo rings? The Blind Master magically knows that Zartan's mentor, Onihashi, forgave Zartan's offense with his dying breath – when the evidence (*G.I. Joe* #84) suggests that Onihashi committed hara-kiri and split his guts in private.

Destro blackmails Dr. Mindbender by threatening to tell Cobra Commander II that the evil doctor's secretly stashing Serpentor's remains, which seems damnably odd, considering Cobra Commander II already knows that Mindbender's keeping Serpy on ice (#77).

NOW YOU KNOW... Cobra POGOs move too fast to properly draw a bead on them – just fill the sky with lead and hope for the best.

COMIC TIE-INS Zartan fell off the Golden Gate Bridge and went missing in *G.I. Joe* #85, but authorities fished him out shortly after. Hurriedly disguising himself as a Russian sailor, Zartan spent five months in custody while diplomatic officials tried to discern his identity. He later escaped, leading to his fateful meeting with the Blind Master. Zartan here assumes the Blind Master's identity, but reverts to his loveable slimeball self – while confronting Cobra Commander II – in #97.

Zartan's sometimes suicidal because he lost his valued apprenticeship to sword-master Onihashi (detailed in *G.I. Joe* #84) after killing the Hard Master. Annoyingly, Zartan killed the Hard Master *by mistake* (#26, #84) – a blunder that's left him haunted for years (Zartan states that the Hard Master's murder happened "20 years ago," although that seems a bit long).

The Blind Master previously accepted a street punk named Tyrone as his new apprentice (#67). Tyrone's clearly a ninja novice – he doesn't sense Zartan's deception until #97-#98.

Snake-Eyes' group returns here to the rubble of his cabin, destroyed in *G.I. Joe* #31 and last seen in *G.I. Joe Yearbook* #3. Shot by Storm Shadow in *G.I. Joe* #85, the red ninja leader claims he contacted Firefly to learn the location of Snake-Eyes' lair (Firefly visited the site in #31-#32). Actually, as #126 reveals, it's a bit more complex than that.

While fighting the red ninja leader, Storm Shadow happens across the skeleton of Fred Smith I (killed in *G.I. Joe* #32), dumped by Spirit behind a waterfall. Still, Spirit carved Fred an epitaph: "Here lies Fred. No matter what he did in life, he died well." Zarana, Zandar and the Dreadnoks established Broca Beach as Cobra's main U.S. base of operations in *G.I. Joe* #81. The Baroness and Zarana started feuding in *Special Missions* #7, although they work together better (under duress) here.

Clutch and Rock 'n Roll previously tangled with the Dreadnoks in *G.I. Joe* #35. Zarana brainwashes the two Joes with Dr. Venom's brainwave scanner (first seen in #10), programming them to obliterate the Pit III. Following orders, Clutch and Rock 'n Roll go postal in #100.

Corpse, corpse, who has the corpse? Serpentor took an arrow to the head in *G.I. Joe* #76, then got iced aboard the landlocked Cobra freighter in #77. Destro here relocates Serpentor's cadaver to Broca Beach to blackmail Dr. Mindbender (*see Goofs*). But at some unspecified point, Serpentor gets re-frozen aboard the freighter, only to get mangled and mistaken for Firefly's remains in #114.

MISCELLANEOUS STUFF!

CONTINUED FROM PAGE 219

Zartan and the ninjas go their separate ways after Storm Shadow and Jinx whup their collective asses in *G.I. Joe* #85, although the red ninjas and their nefarious leader – who spontaneously recovers from his arrow-to-the-neck – try to slit Stormy's jugular in #91. Predictably, that little adventure ends with most of the red ninjas dismembered.

• **G.I. JOE #120-#123** – Naturally, a pack of red ninjas survive the various massacres and set up shop in the Silent Castle, which lay disused after Snake-Eyes raided the place in *G.I. Joe* #21. Oddly enough, by this point, the red ninjas jointly answer to the red ninja leader and Slice and Dice, two advanced ninjas. To our distress, it's entirely unclear who the hell Slice and Dice work for – they clearly don't serve the red ninja leader (Slice insists he doesn't even *recognize* the red ninja leader in #124), but they're not Cobra agents either. Regardless, Slice and Dice and red ninjas assault the castle's various intruders, leading to even more red ninjas getting carved up, blown apart by missiles and pulped between large blocks of stone.

• **G.I. JOE #124, #126, #133, #134** – Further adding to the confusion, Firefly reveals himself as the red ninja leader in *G.I. Joe* #126. Slice, Dice and the red ninjas – disgusted that they've been serving under a collaborator in the Hard Master's death – try to rebel, but Firefly gasses his once-allies unconscious and subjects them to a Cobra brainwave scanner. The zombified red ninjas obey his commands, but Snake-Eyes finally breaks them out of their mental handcuffs in #134. Grateful, the red ninjas run Firefly out of Dodge.

• **G.I. JOE #136-up** – Slice and Dice become Cobra agents, but the red ninjas largely fade from the series entirely – licking their wounds and perhaps obtaining gainful employment as lawn-mowers or Kinko's employees across America.

CHARACTER PROFILE: JOES

• *Clutch:* His car's a slovenly mess. As a high schooler, Clutch cruised "the strip" in Broca Beach. He recalls the town's disused tattoo parlor, poster store, grease-burger stand and, most amusingly, an amphitheater where "Daisy the Diving Horse" amused tourists by leaping off a diving board. Clutch owned a beloved Corvair during high school. His Uncle Arnie ran a local Texaco station and gave Clutch his first job, presumably fueling his love for mechanics.

• *Rock 'n Roll:* Is an ex-surfer.

CHARACTER PROFILE: COBRA
• *The Baroness and Zarana:* Among other things, they're now directing Cobra's phone scams and bogus real-estate deals (as Zarana puts it, "It's easy to make money if you have no conscience and understand basic human nature."). Per Destro's orders, the girls treat each other better, but they sometimes slip into old habits (the Baroness: "Badger barf!" Zarana: "Liberal!").
• *Zartan:* Zartan's holographic projections can, when necessary, disguise him as an ogre.

CHARACTER PROFILE: OTHER *The Blind Master:* Using his sense of smell, the Blind Master "sees" through Zartan's holograms. The Blind Master claims he was a sightless, stranded ex-G.I. rescued from post-war Tokyo by the Hard Master, although this conflicts with *G.I. Joe* #62, which claims that the Blind Master lost his sight at a later point. Still, the Blind Master considers the Hard Master "one of the few good things that happened to him."

ORGANIZATIONS *Cobra:* Under Destro's reorganization scheme, Cobra Commander II and Voltar work toward converting parts of Cobra Island into a giant showroom and luxury resort for wealthy armaments buyers. The Baroness and Zarana jointly run Cobra's funding and intelligence operations from Broca Beach. Most Cobra intelligence specialists report to the Baroness while Zarana keeps the Dreadnoks corralled.

Destro heads up Cobra's sales and marketing division, assisted by Darklon and Dr. Mindbender. Naturally, some friction remains between the various Cobra officers (Dr. Mindbender levels at the elaborately helmeted Darklon: "He could get arrested for impersonating a household appliance!")

PLACES TO GO *Broca Beach:* Cobra command personnel sometimes convene at the Cryptic Order of Benevolent Reptilian Apostates, a former lodge hall. The Dreadnoks spray-paint various Cobra attack vehicles to look like amusement rides at the Broca Beach carnival. The carnival's shooting gallery includes pop-up dummies of various Joe operatives. Broca Lanes, a local bowling alley, houses a detention and interrogation center behind the automatic pin-setters because the bowling balls' thumping makes the place damnably hard to bug. The detention center's prisoners include rival pyramid scam salesmen and IRS investigators who got too close to Cobra's assets.

STUFF YOU NEED *Cobra BATs:* They can pilot Cobra POGO pods. Dr. Mindbender designed and built the BATs (#44), although a little-known subsidiary of Destro's MARS company supplied the androids' logic systems and much of their sealed transmitting gear. Unknown to everyone, Destro took the opportunity to lace the BATs' programming with a special sub-routine – meaning he can override their primary commands at a moment's notice.
• *Dr. Venom's Brainwave Scanner:* Supposedly, the scanner renders its victims' thoughts and memories as "symbolic representations" (i.e. 3D images) for better interaction (meaning Cobra interrogators can smash memories of their choice) although the nature of this process isn't clear.

HOT WHEELS *G.I. Joe Mean Dog:* Can take a direct hit from a 120 mike-mike Sabot high explosive anti-tank round.

THE COMMAND DECISION A valiant effort, with Hama easily flipping his plotlines like a stack of pancakes, simultaneously delivering over-the-top comedy (the Dreadnoks messing with the captive Joes' minds), an examination of vendettas (the Blind Master relenting from slaying Zartan) and refreshing slasher drama (Storm Shadow's band vs. a lot of ninjas). Definitely worth your time.

G.I. Joe Special Missions #26, G.I. Joe #92

Titles: *"Passing of the Guard" (Special Missions #26), "Thunderclap" (#92)*
Release Dates: *Oct. to Nov. 1989*
Art: *Herb Trimpe (Special Missions #26), M.D. Bright (#92)*

BATTLE ROSTER *Joes:* Cross-Country, Rumbler, Stalker, Muskrat, Scoop, Lt. Falcon, Recondo, Shockwave; *Destro:* Voltar; *Other:* The Oktober Guard.

FIRST APPEARANCES *Joes:* Long Range (Thunderclap driver, #92), Backblast (anti-aircraft soldier, #92).

DEATHS *Other:* Oktober Guard members Colonel Brekhov, Horrorshow, Stormavik and Schrage (SM #26).

MISSION BRIEF ***Special Missions #26:*** In Sierra Gordo, Voltar and a brigade of Iron Grenadiers incarcerate revolutionary leader El Jefe – forcibly compelling El Jefe to honor terms of his franchise deals with Destro (#71). Simultaneously, Lt. Falcon, Recondo and Shockwave prepare to snatch El Jefe from Voltar's grasp, hoping to ingratiate America to the revolutionary. But Russia's Oktober Guard, hoping to sway El Jefe to Communism, beats Falcon's group to the punch and spirits El Jefe away.

Lt. Falcon grumbles that El Jefe switches sides faster than Madonna wiggles her hips, but the Joes nonetheless monitor the Oktober Guard's activities. The guardsmen load El Jefe onto a revolutionary-manned train and set out for Sierra Gordo's capital, but Voltar's Iron Grenadiers outflank the Russians and block the train tracks.

Oktober Guard leader Colonel Brekhov leaves flunkies Daina and Dragonsky behind to guard El Jefe, then loads the rest of the Oktober Guard into a pickup truck and charges the Iron Grenadier blockade. In response, the Grenadiers let loose a storm of artillery fire, severely puncturing the Russians. Oktober Guardsmen Horrorshow, Stormavik and Schrage die in the crossfire, but Brekhov survives long enough to reach the Grenadier column and detonate his truck's ordnance – shredding himself along with most of Voltar's troops.

Daina and Dragonsky pale at their comrades' deaths, but the revolutionary train unexpectedly grinds to a halt just outside its destination. To everyone's dismay, Delbert Swinson, a representative of the North American Banana Monopoly (NABM), emerges from the last train car with several soldiers. Swinson offers to help El Jefe secure further political power – in exchange for becoming an NABM stooge. As Daina and Dragonsky turn horrified to hear El Jefe agreeing to Swinson's terms, Swinson's troopers round up the surviving Russians and Falcon's trio.

Issue #92: While Stalker and a pack of Joes covertly enter Sierra Gordo to help Falcon's men, a Joe artillery division takes up position in the neighboring, pro-American country of Punta del Mucosa. Meanwhile, Voltar undauntedly summons reinforcements and prepares to either re-capture El Jefe or thwart his ascension to power.

Swinson and El Jefe withdraw to NABM Headquarters with their Joe and Russian prisoners, but Stalker's cadre disguises their Warthog attack vehicle as a fruit-themed float and approaches the NABM base using the Miss Sierra Gordo parade as cover. El Jefe and Swinson tremble to see a giant pineapple bearing down on them, then flee as the Warthog demolishes the NABM hideout.

As Voltar's regiments, El Jefe's forces and assorted NABM mercenaries play round robin shooting each other, Stalker's team liberates the Joe and Oktober Guard prisoners and runs for the Punta del Mucosa border. A single Iron Grenadier column breaks off and pursues Stalker's group, but the Punta del Mucosa-based Joes fire a shell that wards off Stalker's pursuers – saving their teammates but leaving the fate of Sierra Gordo's leadership uncertain.

MEMORABLE MOMENTS Colonel Brekhov airs his philosophical views: "I don't argue politics, I just shoot people!" During the Oktober Guard's last stand, Horrorshow helpfully props up the bullet-riddled Colonel Brekhov "so he can drive properly." In one of the funniest *G.I. Joe* moments, Stalker's group dresses their Warthog attack vehicle as a gargantuan pineapple float and attacks a warehouse – causing some befuddled guards to cry out: "We're being attacked by giant fruit!"

ASS-WHUPPINGS A moment of silence, please, for the downed Oktober Guardsmen and their loveable Colonel. Russian flame-thrower Dragonsky roasts a FANG II's pilot through an open cockpit. Joe member Backblast downs a Cobra Condor.

GOOFS El Jefe blatantly tells the Oktober Guard that he couldn't care less about Communism, but four of the Oktober Guardsmen nonetheless give their lives in the utterly moronic belief that the self-serving El Jefe will "bring the revolution to Sierra Gordo." (Please. It's blatantly obvious that El Jefe's about as communist as your common lawn gopher.)

COMIC TIE-INS The Oktober Guard debuted in issue #6; a fair chunk of its members perish here. Daina and Dragonsky survive, appearing with replacement Oktober Guard members in #101.

Destro propped up the revolutionary El Jefe as Sierra Gordo's de facto president in *G.I. Joe* #69-#71. After this story, El Jefe returns to power again in #97.

CHARACTER PROFILE: JOES *Long Range:* Spends way too much time calculating statistics.

CHARACTER PROFILE: DESTRO *Voltar:* Although his eyepiece suggests he's missing his right eye, he appears to have both peepers intact – implying that the lens functions instead as a targeting device.

CHARACTER PROFILE: OTHER

• *Daina:* She's studied numerous Joe dossiers, reading up on their histories and specialties.

• *Horrorshow:* He loves the smell of burning tanks.

ORGANIZATIONS *North American Banana Monopoly (NABM):* Currently led by Delbert Swinson, the NABM purportedly owns three US senators and a general – although the general's actually a stool pigeon for the Joes.

HOT WHEELS *Cobra FANG II:* An updated FANG helicopter, equipped with dual helicopter blades and menacing weapons platforms.

• *Joe Thunderclap:* The newest Joe ground assault vehicle, the Thunderclap is essentially a large artillery piece mounted between two mobile tractor treads which specializes in long-distance assaults. It fires an 11-inch shell with a maximum effective range of 20 miles (obviously, you need precise coordinates to aim properly). The Thunderclap's a mean piece of work, equipped with radar and laser range findings. Unfortunately, its weapons propellant generates such high temperatures that the main barrel needs replacing after 100 firings.

THE COMMAND DECISION The two-parter that does in a lot of Oktober Guardsmen – although it's a pretty stupid way to go. Morally speaking, the Russians spend most of *Special Missions* #26 throwing their lives away for no good reason (see Goofs), and #92 – which reads like a drawn-out epilogue – ain't much of an improvement. All in all, it's a tale that relies on shock action, then seems inferior the moment you set it down.

G.I. Joe #93 to #96

NOTE: Issues #94-#96 compose "The Snake-Eyes Trilogy" storyarc.
Titles: *"Taking the Plunge" (#93), "Exterminating Circumstances (or Bern This)" (#94), "No Turning Back!" (#95), "The Hexagram Completed" (#96)*
Release Dates: *Bi-Weekly from Mid Nov. 1989 to Jan. 1990*
Art: *M.D. Bright*

BATTLE ROSTER *Joes:* Snake-Eyes, Scarlett, Storm Shadow, Stalker, Hawk, Lift-Ticket, Doc, Lifeline; *Cobra:* the Baroness, Destro, Zarana and the Dreadnoks; *Other:* Wade Collins.

MISSION BRIEF ***Issue #93-#94:*** In Bern, Switzerland, plastic surgeons develop a radical new reconstructive surgery technique, giving Snake-Eyes the hope of restoring his shrapnel-shredded face to normal. Scarlett accompanies her lover to the Bern Institute of Reconstructive Surgery, watching as skilled surgeon Dr. Hundtkinder – the same doctor who patched up the Baroness' face in *G.I. Joe* #22 – schedules Snake-Eyes for surgery. But hoping to curry favor with his former patient, Dr. Hundtkinder alerts the Baroness to the Joes' presence in his clinic.

Meanwhile, at the Cobra Consulate, the Baroness and Zarana renew their long-term rivalry, indulging in a full-fledged, eyeball-scratching catfight. Relenting for the sake of their careers, the two women collaborate on how to best "return" the brainwashed Clutch and Rock 'n Roll. As scheduled, Zarana and the Dreadnoks attempt to transport the Joe prisoners to a Cobra submarine off Long Island, but the spiteful Baroness tips off the Joes to Zarana's movements. The Joes chase their prey, but the Baroness blows up the Dreadnoks' engine by remote, having mined their van in advance. The Dreadnoks crash in a ball of flames, allowing the Joes to incarcerate most of the felons and "recover" Clutch and Rock 'n Roll.

Simultaneously, Dr. Hundtkinder phones the Baroness, faxing over an old photograph of Snake-Eyes' real face for identification purposes. Glancing at Snake-Eyes' original features, the Baroness recoils, recognizing Snake-Eyes as the man who killed her brother Eugen in Saigon, 1968 (*see Sidebar*). In the weeks that follow, the Baroness bides her time until Dr. Hundtkinder completes six restorative operations to Snake-Eyes' face – vengefully planning to eviscerate Snake-Eyes' newly restored features. As Hundtkinder finishes his work, the Baroness amasses a Cobra helicopter squadron to blitz the Bern clinic.

Cocking her Uzi just as Cobra Alley and Night Vipers storm the clinic, Scarlett bundles a doped-up Snake-Eyes into a wheelchair and runs like hell. But with Scarlett completely surrounded, the Baroness steps forward and plugs the Joe female in the head at point-blank range – taking the unconscious Snake-Eyes prisoner.

Issue #95-#96: The Baroness transports Snake-Eyes to the Cobra Consulate, requisitioning three Cobra interrogators – the Paine Brothers – to torture the captive Joe. Simultaneously, a team of Joe medics airlift a comatose Scarlett back to New York for medical care.

The Paine Brothers diligently heat their branding irons, but Snake-Eyes gets free and engages his would-be torturers. Snake-Eyes dispatches the brothers – but gets nailed in the face with burning coals in the process. Undaunted, the slightly scarred Snake-Eyes dons a mask, raiding a Cobra explosives cache in the Consulate's basement. Snake-Eyes then wrathfully detonates his plundered bombs halfway up the Consulate building, trapping the Baroness and her command staff in the upper levels.

Amid the turmoil, Snake-Eyes' ex-Vietnam teammates – Stalker, Storm Shadow and Wade Collins – arrive to rescue their comrade. With the Cobra embassy in flames, Storm Shadow scurries up the building's exterior while Stalker and Wade summon reinforcements. United, Snake-Eyes and Storm Shadow confront the Baroness, just as the wounded Consulate threatens to collapse.

Fortunately, Destro arrives in a Cobra helicopter to personally investigate the horrendously mangled Consulate. After learning about the Baroness' vendetta, Destro provides an eyewitness account of her brother's murder (*see Sidebar*). Destro explains that Viet Cong troopers shot down the Baroness' sibling, with a pre-scarred Snake-Eyes blundering onto the scene seconds later. Unable to accept the truth, the Baroness insanely tries to fling herself off the Consulate. Partly out of compassion – and also to make the Baroness pay for her crimes – Storm Shadow snags the falling terrorist, tossing her into Destro's helicopter. The Consulate's upper level gives way, but fortunately, a Stalker-summoned Joe helicopter darts forward and catches the ninjas, taking the weary heroes back to base.

MEMORABLE MOMENTS The Baroness bitchily comments that the pink-haired Zarana must "rinse with liquid bubble gum." In a Marvel Universe crossover, Storm Shadow leaps past Spider-Man's nemesis, Daily Bugle publisher J. Jonah Jameson, and screams: "Outta my way, Flattop!"

LOVE AND WAR Scarlett insists that she fervently loves Snake-Eyes despite his mangled looks, but Snakes wants to fix his features… in large measure so that he can gaze upon Scarlett with his proper face. Oh, and it's not exceptionally relevant, but Cobra's top interrogators – the Paine Brothers – dress in black leather and look rather kinky.

ASS-WHUPPINGS Dreadnok Buzzer talks smack about Zarana, so the lovestruck Road Pig pops him one. The explosion at issue #93's climax incapacitates Road Pig and puts Zarana in a coma for weeks. The Baroness plugs Scarlett at point-blank range, but the bullet supposedly (and unconvincingly) deflects off the dome of Scarlett's skull at an "oblique angle," merely putting her into a coma.

During a brawl between Snake-Eyes and the Paine Brothers, Crispo Paine mildly scorches Snake-Eyes' new looks with burning coals. Conversely, Snakes fatally nails Torquemada Paine in the face with a branding iron, then runs Crispo and his brother DeSade through with a sword. For an encore, Snake-Eyes maniacally wrecks havoc throughout the Cobra Consulate, setting off explosions and gutting Night Vipers with his usual efficiency. The Consulate's upper levels collapse, sending the Baroness' command staff falling to their doom. (Author's Note: *Doom!*)

During a flashback in Saigon, 1968, Viet Cong gunfire nails Stalker and Storm Shadow, wasting a US military driver named Corky. Snake-Eyes takes out the gunmen but fails to save the Baroness' brother Eugen (*see Sidebar*).

PREPOSTEROUS PHYSICS The Baroness, a well-armed veteran assassin and terrorist, fails to kill Scarlett by shooting her in the head at point-blank range. Issue #96 ends with a helicopter barrel roll that even the characters involved cite as "impossible."

GOOFS Destro's been lovingly banging the Baroness for years, but never thought to mention: "By the way, I helped mop your brother's bleeding corpse into a bucket." (see Sidebar.) *G.I. Joe* #95-#96 is a textbook example of characters knowing information they shouldn't. When Zarana awakens in the hospital, she tells the Joes about the Baroness' collaboration with Dr. Hundtkinder – even though she never actually overheard their plans. When Destro arrives at the Consulate, he instantly comprehends the Baroness' beef with Snake-Eyes. Conversely, Destro, currently in charge of Cobra, fails to notice Zarana's absence for the entire month between issues #93 and #94.

In issue #94, why does the Baroness spills her intensely personal history to a random Toxo-Viper? The Joes, who conclusively learned that Dr. Hundtkinder stitched up the Baroness' face in *G.I. Joe* #22, don't object to Snake-Eyes jetting off to Hundtkinder's clinic for surgery. Finally, what the hell does Hundtkinder hope to gain by ratting out the Joes to the Baroness anyway?

MISCELLANEOUS STUFF!

DEATH IN SAIGON

On January 31, 1968, Snake-Eyes, Stalker and Storm Shadow arrived in Saigon to receive fresh orders from their higher-ups. However, a random shoot-out with two Viet Cong members left Stalker wounded and Storm Shadow in dire need of a surgeon. Snake-Eyes gave chase, but the sniper duo shot out his jeep, leaving the future Joe pinned.

Meanwhile, the 15-year-old Baroness traveled with her brother, philanthropist Eugen DeCobray, on a relief expedition to aid the victimized Saigon populace. Eugen negotiated with supposedly pro-Western militia members to dole out medical supplies, but Eugen's "partners" – actually the Viet Cong – traded his goods on the black market for firearms. In an ironic twist, the Viet Cong members purchased their ill-gotten wares from Destro's arms-dealing father, who mistakenly believed the thugs represented the South Vietnamese government.

Enraged to uncover the Viet Cong's duplicity, Eugen hotly confronted his two contacts – the same killers who previously ambushed Snake-Eyes' group. Eugen sent his sister from the room to vent his spleen, but in the Baroness' absence, the agitated Viet Cong gunmen riddled Eugen's chest with bullets. Seconds later, Snake-Eyes burst through a window and pasted the two killers. Hearing gunfire, the Baroness rushed into the room and spied Snake-Eyes holding a smoldering pistol above her brother's corpse – erroneously pegging the commando for the crime.

Snake-Eyes quickly departed, but soon after, a teenage Destro and his father arrived to coordinate clean-up operations with the local authorities. Papa Destro lamented Eugen DeCobray's passing, having studied at Eton with the young man's father. Meanwhile, the younger Destro learned the truth about Eugen's murder – revealing the truth years later when the Baroness went gunning for Snake-Eyes.

COMIC TIE-INS Billy previously reunited with his mother in *G.I. Joe* #84, departing to live with her in Oakland, CA and enrolling at Berkeley. But as part of a sub-plot in issue #94, Raptor shows up (presumably spiteful toward Cobra Commander II) and informs Billy of the death of his father, the original Cobra Commander (#61). Motivated to prove Raptor's claims, Billy summons help from Tyrone and Zartan – who's currently masquerading as the Blind Master (#91) – to investigate Cobra Commander's burial site in Denver. Strangely enough, nothing comes of the expedition, but the group nonetheless departs for Cobra Island (#97) to investigate Cobra Commander II's activities.

Dr. Hundtkinder previously glued the Baroness' mutilated face together in *G.I. Joe* #22. Snake-Eyes originally mangled his mug in a helicopter accident (as revealed in #26-#27), but gets patched up here. After this story, Snake-Eyes conceals his semi-wounded face (scorched by Crispo Paine) with bandages, uncovering his mostly restored mug again in #102. Scarlett remains in a coma until #103.

Zarana and the Baroness' deep-rooted loathing for one another hails back to *Special Missions* #7, although Destro recently told them to knock it off and work together (*G.I. Joe* #90). The Baroness tries to keep her vendetta against Snake-Eyes secret from Destro, having violated her lover's orders by getting Zarana incarcerated.

Clutch and Rock 'n Roll got captured in *G.I. Joe* #89, then brainwashed in #90-#91. Enthralled by Cobra, the two hypnotized Joes move to destroy Joe Headquarters in #99-#100.

Despite the Pit II's destruction (#53), senior Joe officials still receive calls at the chaplain's assistants school at Fort Wadsworth.

Wade Collins departed to start a new life in *G.I. Joe* #43, but here returns to help Snake-Eyes. Collins briefly appears in #108 to adopt an orphan that befriends Snake-Eyes.

CHARACTER PROFILE: JOES

Snake-Eyes: Snake-Eyes' shrapnel-ripped face isn't as mangled as you might think, although his left eyeball's protruding like an overripe grape and he's got five or six scars dicing the left side of his head and mouth. Gluing Snake-Eyes' puss back together required six separate operations, skin grafts and cartilage implants.

Snake-Eyes here acquires the fallen Crispo Paine's mask for his own.

CHARACTER PROFILE: COBRA

• *The Baroness:* The Baroness hails from a fantastically wealthy and politically charged family. She attended a high-level Swiss boarding school, journeying to Saigon for her brother Eugen's fateful ass-whupping (*see Sidebar*) over Christmas break. The DeCobrays often wore bullet-proof vests as protection against attackers, although – as Eugen fatefully discovered – such vests couldn't stop a high-velocity AK-47 bullet.

Oddly enough, the Baroness regards her late brother as a philanthropist and man of peace – but claims his wrongful death spurred her career in international terrorism. That's quite a leap in logic (if anything, you'd think she'd become a female version of the Punisher, pasting criminals in revenge), suggesting the Baroness – and this is a technical term – lives in La-La Land. It's not stated, but she possibly operates under the, "Good people relentlessly die! Therefore, I must side with the forces of darkness!" philosophy.

• *Destro:* Destro's named after his father, James McCullen Destro, the 23rd laird of Castle Destro – making the current Destro the 24th head of his family. Destro's daddy also wore a silver mask, although he sometimes conducted business dealings in a foppish, frilly purple business suit (shades of Austin Powers).

A teenage Destro sported blonde hair, although it darkened to brown (*G.I. Joe* #97) later in life. While Daddy Destro rushed about cutting arms deals, a post-pubescent Destro contented himself with playing doubles at Caravelle and lounging about with his American friends.

• *Cobra Tele-Vipers:* Often put Cobra agents on hold, subjecting them to the "mellow melodies" of the Cobra chorus (which includes renditions of John Denver songs).

• *Zarana:* Her hair's naturally auburn-colored.

ORGANIZATIONS *Dreadnoks:* They frequently eat "gummy rats."

HOT WHEELS *Joe Tomahawks:* Can serve as mobile Joe communications centers.

THE COMMAND DECISION Utterly improbable, the sloppy "Snake-Eyes Trilogy" makes so many errors, it's hard to focus on any single problem. The dialogue's agonizing and pompous (the Baroness to Snake-Eyes: "Now you get the payback you so richly deserve, for the senseless murder of my brother!"), there's too much cross-pollination with past continuity and the act of restoring Snake-Eyes' face drains a lot of his mystique. Completely ridiculous.

G.I. Joe Special Missions #27 to #28

Titles: *"Mexican Holiday" (#27), "Condor" (#28)*
Release Dates: *Bi-weekly in Nov. 1989*
Writers: Michael Fleisher (#27), Larry Hama (#28)
Art: *Javier Saltares (#27), Herb Trimpe (#28)*

G.I. Joe Special Missions #27 to #28

BATTLE ROSTER *Joes:* Hawk, Stalker, Outback, Quick Kick, Payload, Hardtop, Admiral Keel-Haul, Slip-Stream, Ace.

MISSION BRIEF ***Issue #27:*** Receiving a cushy assignment – for once – Outback, Stalker and Quick Kick travel to Mexico, delivering top-secret documents to an American drug enforcement agent. Upon the mission's completion, the three Joes start a week's vacation that primarily consists of ogling bikini-clad women.

While Stalker lounges by a pool, Outback and Quick Kick embark on a bus tour of some Mayan ruins. Unfortunately, a revolutionary named Ignazio – leader of the People's Revolutionary Brigade of Mexico – assaults the tour bus as an affront to the American government. Weaponless, Outback and Quick Kick drain some of the bus' gas into pop bottles and pelt Ignazio's men with Molotov cocktails. But the Joes soon lose ground, allowing Ignazio's men to empty the bus and prepare to execute the passengers.

Luckily, Stalker grows concerned over his teammates' absence, commandeering a local helicopter and setting out after them. After spotting the hostage situation, Stalker brashly aims his helicopter straight at the captured bus, bailing out just before impact. Once the subsequent explosion wipes out Ignazio's forces, Stalker's trio helps the rattled tour group return home.

Issue #28: Hoping to boost operations in Sierra Gordo, the Joes equip a base in the neighboring Punta del Mucosa with the latest stealth technology. Unfortunately, Cobra Commander II learns of the secret camp's existence. While the Punta del Mucosa president inspects the Joe base, Cobra Commander II launches a two-pronged attack – blistering the *USS Flagg* and the secluded Joe camp with heavy air strikes. Thankfully, some hotshot aerial piloting on the part of Ghostrider and Dogfight allows the Joes to mop up the Cobra airforce, then return home for brewskies.

LOVE AND WAR Issue #27 spotlights Stalker, Outback and Quick Kick gulping margaritas and undressing bikini-clad women with their eyes. In particular, a foxy black woman named Lydia deliberately botches a high-dive so Stalker can "rescue" her and "apply CPR." The two of them share dinner, although Lydia gets concerned when Stalker – leaving to check on his overdue teammates – hastily leaves the table with a steak knife.

ASS-WHUPPINGS Ignazio's killing crew offs a few bus hostages (notably a UCLA champion javelin thrower), but Quick Kick and Outback's gasoline bombs even the odds. Quick Kick (supposedly a martial arts expert on par with Storm Shadow) takes a rifle butt to the back of the head. A bullet also grazes Outback's face. Stalker ends shoves a helicopter down Ignazio's gullet.

The dogfight in *SM* #28 entails the Joes downing Cobra Stiletto fighters, although the *Flagg* takes a missile hit and literally vents some steam.

GOOFS Hawk briefs Outback, Stalker and Quick Kick on their Mexican expedition in front of everybody – violating the Army's "need to know" policy.

NOW YOU KNOW... Assaulting an aircraft carrier gets a lot easier if you continually fly below the radar horizon, pop upward just long enough to launch your missiles, then hug the water again.

COMIC TIE-INS The Joes previously launched a long-range assault against Cobra from Punta del Mucosa in *G.I. Joe* #92. Stalker, Outback and Quick Kick coincidentally worked together on a Borovian mission in *G.I. Joe* #61-#66. *Special Missions* #28 stands unique among *G.I. Joe* issues for breaking the fourth wall, with Hawk speaking with the reader during the final curtain call for *G.I. Joe Special Missions*.

CHARACTER PROFILE: JOES

- *Stalker, Outback and Quick Kick:* They decline to mention the Mexico debacle to their teammates for humility's sake. Indeed, Stalker claims that Outback – who's sporting a facial bandage as a result of a bullet graze – stupidly fell asleep and rolled off his deck chair.
- *Scarlett:* She's been prepping stealth fighters on the *Flagg* for a week – but still can't remember pilot Ghostrider's name.

HOT WHEELS *Defiant:* The Joe shuttle's fitted with a "Teal Ruby infrared detection system" that spies enemy aircraft through cloud cover. The ship's computer kindly filters out all scheduled commercial flights, preventing the Joes from blowing up, for example, a civilian airliner packed with squealing schoolgirls returning from a trip to Australia. The Defiant's sensors automatically register Joe aircraft, but can't detect Python-ized Cobra vehicles.

- *USS Flagg:* It's heavily fortified, armed with Phalanx radar-directed Gatling guns, diversionary infrared flares and chaff cloud to ward off incoming missiles. The *Flagg*'s guns fire several hundred rounds of depleted uranium-tipped 30 mike-mike, forming a wall of artillery fire between the *Flagg* and its opponents. Most of the *Flagg*'s aircraft – save for the propeller-driven Mudslinger – require a catapult system to lift off.

THE COMMAND DECISION Agony! *Special Missions* #27 doesn't even hold true to the series' title, playing more as a "Mexican revolutionaries whimsically hijack a Joe trio" scenario than an ultra-sneaky "special mission." One senses that this late in *Special Missions*' tenure, the editors hurriedly dumped this issue like a psychotic girlfriend – hoping to quickly and quietly make a fast buck before the series folded.

Ending *Special Missions* with a whimper, issue #28 concerns yet-another aerial slugfest that's best left to the small screen. Creators Larry Hama and Herb Trimpe give it their best, but the final product's little more than shooting, shooting and more shooting. Overall, a lost opportunity to bravely cap off an often-noteworthy series.

G.I. Joe #97 to #100

Titles: *"What Goes Around, Comes Around" (#97), "He's Back!" (#98), "Calm Before the Storm!" (#99), "Seeds of Empire!" (#100)*
Release Dates: *Feb. to May 1990*
Art: *Isherwood (#97), M.D. Bright (#98, #100), Herb Trimpe (#99)*

BATTLE ROSTER *Joes:* Mutt, Spirit, Chuckles, Clutch, Rock 'n Roll, Snake-Eyes, Flint, Lady Jaye, Storm Shadow, Dusty, Wildcard; *Cobra:* Cobra Commander, Cobra Commander II, Zartan, Raptor, Dr. Mindbander, lots of Fred Smiths, Croc-Master; *Destro:* Destro, the Baroness, Voltar; *Other:* Billy, Tyrone, Captain Minh.

FIRST APPEARANCES *Joes:* Steam-Roller (Mobile Command Center operator, #99).

MISSION BRIEF ***Issue #97:*** Exhausted from her recent vendetta against Snake-Eyes, the Baronness decided to travel abroad and ponder her occupation as an international harbinger of terror. Unable to live without his bespectacled, black-leathered mate, Destro shockingly abdicates his position as joint Cobra leader and names Darklon to temporarily head his family arms business.

Meanwhile, Cobra Commander II and Dr. Mindbender feverishly work to boost Cobra's armament sales, hosting an impressive weapons exhibition for visiting dictators and state leaders on Cobra Island. But Billy, Tyrone, Raptor and Zartan (who's still disguised as the Blind Master) decide to ascertain the magnitude of Fred Smith VII's crimes as "Cobra Commander," hiring Captain Minh – and his Cobra moray – to speed them past Cobra Island's defenses.

The Blind Master/Zartan volunteers to reconnoiter a reception for the visiting dignitaries held aboard Cobra Island's landlocked freighter. But once inside, Zartan pulls Cobra Commander II aside, threatening at gunpoint to bounce him back to the ranks of the Crimson Guardsmen. Simultaneously, Raptor approaches Dr. Mindbender, suggesting that the cracked Cobra scientist clone the original Cobra Commander and restore him to power. Dr. Mindbender agrees, but stresses that he needs a sample of Cobra Commander's DNA – compelling Raptor to yield the location of Cobra Commander's burial site in Colorado.

Finally, near a Cobra Island beach, a routine Cobra patrols blows up Captain Minh's ship – forcing Billy, Tyrone and Minh to flee and make their way toward a fateful gathering in the landlocked freighter.

Issue #98: Dr. Mindbender, Raptor and a team of Vipers arrive at Cobra Commander's burial site near Denver, digging like mad for a scrap of the masked fiend's rotting corpse. The Cobra team finishes excavating, but Raptor turns shocked to locate only Cobra Commander's tattered jacket. Seconds later, a cowled, manic and wholeheartedly alive Cobra Commander appears, surrounding Raptor's group with a squad of Fred-series Crimson Guardsmen.

As Dr. Mindbender and Raptor's jaws hit the floor, Cobra Commander explains that he entered a self-induced coma when Fred Smith VII shot him (#61). After Fred VII and Raptor buried Cobra Commander's "corpse," loyalists among the "Fred Smith" class of Crimson Guardsmen retrieved their fallen leader and nursed him back to health. (*For a full explanation, see Sidebar*). Deeming Mindbender and Raptor's return an omen, Cobra Commander loads his Crimson Guardsmen – and their prisoners – into a helicopter, speeding off to topple Cobra Commander II.

On Cobra Island, Billy's group reaches the landlocked freighter and denounces Cobra Commander II as an imposter. While various Cobra officers, including Voltar, hotly dispute Billy's claims, the original Cobra Commander's group secretly lands on Cobra Island and plants a series of explosive charges.

Suddenly, one of the freighter's upper hatches opens, revealing a restored Cobra Commander raving at the assemblage from on high. Giddy to find so many of his rivals in a single place, Cobra Commander disavows any affection for his son, and – after tossing Dr. Mindbender and Raptor below decks – seals the freighter's hatches, trapping everyone aboard.

Frothing at the mouth, Cobra Commander detonates the first set of explosives, funneling sea water into the freighter's dry channel. For the first time in years, the freighter takes float, heading toward the island's extinct volcano. Cobra Commander activates a second charge, blowing an entry point into the volcano, then watches as the freighter slips into the volcano's dormant cauldron. Finally, Cobra Commander detonates one last explosive pack – bringing down tons of rubble atop the volcano opening and sealing his enemies inside.

Issue #99-#100: Zartan swiftly takes charge aboard the buried freighter, organizing his fellow prisoners into work shifts in the hope of digging an escape tunnel before their water and C-ration stocks run out.

Meanwhile, Cobra Commander consolidates his steel-gloved grip, purging a number of Cobra officers and incarcerating Zarana and the Dreadnoks. Striving to keep her head out of the noose, Zarana tells Cobra Commander about her efforts to brainwash Clutch and Rock 'n Roll (#90-#91) as "sleeper" agents among the Joe ranks. Zarana further suggests bathing Clutch and Rock 'n Roll with an ultra-sonic tone – a trigger designed to turn the Joes berserk and make them level their headquarters. Cobra Commander agrees, authorizing Zarana to find the two Joes via Cobra micro-crystals implanted in their skulls.

Simultaneously, Lady Jaye happens across two UFO spotters – 14-year-old girls named Tiffany and Roxanne – camped out near the Pit III. Lady Jaye nabs the two teens, assigning them to Clutch and Rock 'n Roll's custody while she contacts the girls' parents. Unfortunately, Zarana and a pack of Tele-Vipers shortly arrive in a Cobra STUN and blanket the area with ultra-sonic frequencies – shattering the implanted beepers in Clutch and Rock 'n Roll's skulls and releasing a psychosis-inducing chemical.

Zombified, the two Joes level their weapons at the girls. Thankfully, the Cobra programming comes into massive internal conflict with the Joes' personal ethics, rendering them unconscious. As Flint and Lady Jaye rally to apprehend Zarana's troops – although Zarana herself escapes – Joe medics tend to Clutch and Rock 'n Roll.

Meanwhile, a furloughed Mutt and Spirit arrive in Millville, NY, to visit Mutt's ailing Uncle Jeff. The two Joes try to relax, but Cobra Commander – for reasons known only to his demented noodle – moves to quietly capture Millville.

To Mutt and Spirit's horror, Cobra Commander's troops blitz the Millville police station and cripple the town's communications. While Cobra jamming transmissions prevent the Joes from summoning help, Cobra troops proceed to enthrall the townsfolk with a modified version of Dr. Venom's brainwave scanner. Left with little recourse, Mutt and Spirit steal a HISS tank and prepare to flee. But while pausing to collect Uncle Jeff, the two Joes agonizingly find themselves surrounded by Cobra Vipers – led by a brainwashed Uncle Jeff.

MEMORABLE MOMENTS The garishly dressed Dr. Mindbender hypocritically asks the feather-covered Raptor: "Where did you get that silly outfit?" As Cobra Commander pickles his adversaries in the landlocked freighter, raving like a rabid hyena, Billy grimly concludes: "That's my dad, all right!" Foreshadowing the movie Fargo, Cobra Commander II laments shooting his predecessor rather than resorting to a handy wood chipper.

Always dithering about little details, Cobra Commander recommends that the Broca Beach prisons aren't dank enough, demanding more mold on the prisoners' stale bread.

MISCELLANEOUS STUFF!

COBRA COMMANDER'S RETURN

Shrewdly suspicious of his subordinates, Cobra Commander long ago ordered his Crimson Guardsmen to secretly spy on one another. As such, Fred VIII kept vigil as Fred VII plugged Cobra Commander in the back (*G.I. Joe* #61). But displaying a hitherto-unseen talent, Cobra Commander threw his body into a self-induced coma (a trick previously deployed by Snake-Eyes and Storm Shadow), slowing his heartbeat and respiration beyond human detection.

Thinking Cobra Commander dead, Fred VII and Raptor buried his body near Denver. But luckily, Fred VIII followed and dug up his erstwhile leader. Thanks to a string of calls through the Fred Smith hotline, Fred VIII located a Fred series doctor in the Denver area, arranging for Cobra Commander to receive immediate medical treatment.

Once recovered, Cobra Commander tapped money stashed in the Cayman Islands and put himself back in business, using his loyalist Fred Smiths as foot soldiers. Within two years, Cobra Commander opened a series of offices – under the auspices of Arbco Regional – in 10 major cities. Cobra Commander even trafficked in second-hand Terror-Drome components, covering his tracks until his dramatic (and certainly over-the-top) return to power in *G.I. Joe* #98.

LOVE AND WAR Lady Jaye assigns Clutch and Rock 'n Roll to babysit 13-year-old Tiff and Roxy (What the hell was she thinking?), prompting the goofy Clutch – either out of stupidity or kinkiness (it's hard to tell) – to suggest that they visit the motor pool to "lube some steering knuckles." Granted, Roxy seems a bit taken with Clutch, and even Tiff admits he's "kinda cute in an accident sort of way." The boys further demonstrate their formidable wooing skills by showing the girls the main Joe weapons locker.

ASS-WHUPPINGS With his characteristic mania, Cobra Commander returns, entombing several of his enemies to die slowly and horribly. Within the landlocked freighter, a pack of the prisoners roughhouse Fred Smith VII for trying to boss them around.

GOOFS Zartan's piqued at Fred VII's botched assassination attempt on his life in *G.I. Joe* #84 – but Zartan's the boob who declined to plug Fred between the eyes on that occasion. Hama "returns" Cobra Commander to life as a veritable lunatic, discarding truckloads of continuity when it comes to his rehabilitation (notably #55-#61) without a word of explanation (although it's possible that Cobra Commander's short-term burial momentarily deprived his brain of oxygen, leaving him more psychotic than ever).

A word balloon concerning Tyrone watching Zartan fighting the Blind Master back in San Francisco is wrongly attributed to Billy. The landlocked freighter's amazingly seaworthy, considering it sank to the bottom of the Gulf of Mexico before resurfacing during Cobra Island's creation. Raptor appears in the buried freighter with one of his trained birds – but he didn't go in with any. Mutt carries his fierce dog Junkyard about in a container that looks nearly big enough to house a poodle.

In issue #99, Lady Jaye understandably nabs UFO spotters Tiff and Roxy – then throws security protocols to the wind and starts blathering about the ultra-secret Pit's function and features, off-handedly telling the gaping girls such classified tidbits such as, "[The Pit's] underground just so it won't show up on Cobra satellite photos!" Furthermore, Lady Jaye's foolish enough to think that "having a word" with Tiff and Roxy's parents will guarantee the Pit's security.

Err, exactly why does Raptor want Dr. Mindbender to clone the original Cobra Commander? (Revenge on Cobra Commander II, perhaps?) Cobra Commander's Fred-series Crimson Guardsmen disguise themselves in fake Millville police uniforms – which seems pretty pointless, since the Freds all look the same. Zarana's plan to make the brainwashed Clutch and Rock 'n Roll destroy the Pit III seems hopeful at best. Also, Zarana idiotically goes on a stealth mission without Pythonizing (i.e. radar-proofing) her uniform (and naturally, the Joes locate her hot bod via radar).

COMIC TIE-INS Fred Smith VII blew away Cobra Commander in *G.I. Joe* #61 and usurped his identity, although the Cobra leader survived (see Sidebar).

Cobra Commander entombs a laundry list of characters (Zartan, Billy, Cobra Commander II, Tyrone, Dr. Mindbender, Captain Minh, Raptor, Firefly, Croc Master and Voltar) aboard the landlocked freighter on Cobra Island. Zartan and Billy later escape in *G.I. Joe* #116, while Firefly returns in #124 and #126. Everyone else aboard the freighter, as we learn in #114, feasts on a rancid batch of ham and lima bean C-Rations (num, num) and croaks from botulism.

Destro and the Baroness indulge in semi-retirement, briefly surfacing for air in *G.I. Joe* #102. Having learned that Snake-Eyes *didn't* murder her brother (#96), the Baroness re-assesses her role as an international terrorist. Snake-Eyes keeps wearing facial bandages, presumably drawing comfort from them like Linus and his security blanket, even though his restored facial features (#93) only suffered slight damage in #95. The nasty Jugglers scathe the Joes for their botched assault on the Cobra Consulate (#95-#96), *again* threatening to disband the organization.

Ex-Juggler leader General Malthus, implicated in various crimes by Destro (*G.I. Joe* #78), currently resides in Leavenworth Prison. Conversely, Malthus' partner Senator Hegel escaped prosecution and got re-elected.

Zarana and the Dreadnoks brainwashed Clutch and Rock 'n Roll in *G.I. Joe* #90-#91. Cobra lawyers free Zarana and some of the Dreadnoks, captured in #93, on technicalities.

Foreign dignitaries viewing the weapons sales conference on Cobra Island include Prince Ngoto (*Special Missions* #10), General Liederkranz (*G.I. Joe* #89), Colonel Sharif (*G.I. Joe* #1, #58-#59; *Special Missions* #3) and El Jefe (last seen in *Special Missions* #26 and *G.I. Joe* #92).

Captain Minh obtained a Cobra moray from Cobra Commander II in *G.I. Joe* #77, later aiding the Joes in #83.

CHARACTER PROFILE: JOES

• *Lady Jaye:* She claims she's watching her sugar intake.

• *Mutt:* He visited Uncle Jeff's house as a kid, gobbling up Aunt Ida's famous rhubarb pie. After her death, Mutt's cousins moved to California.

• *Rock 'n Roll:* He's traded his standard Joe machine gun for hand-held units that spray bullets like a fire hose. His three older sisters used him for a tackling dummy when he was growing up.

CHARACTER PROFILE: COBRA

• *Croc Master:* His newest reptilian pets are named Chelsea, Melissa and Tara.

• *Zartan:* He carries a portable hologram generator that's separate from his illusion-casting costume gear and powerful enough to disguise an entire hydrofoil.

ORGANIZATIONS *Cobra:* "CarbO Plumbing" serves as another Cobra front.

• *G.I. Joe:* Needs special authority to operate in Canada.

• *The Fred Smiths:* Despite Fred Smith VII's defection, the Fred Smiths are touted as Cobra Commander's most loyal supporters. A variety of Freds numbered VIII through LIX helped resuscitate the commander after his burial, whereas Fred Smith XXIII helped Cobra Commander coordinate the conquest of Millville.

PLACES TO GO Broca Beach: The local high school has "the Rattler" as their mascot.

• *Millville:* So named because it once housed a profitable mill, now disused.

THE COMMAND DECISION Much as we're glad to have Cobra Commander back in the fold, *G.I. Joe* #98-#100 makes for a horrendously contrived and idiotic "resurrection" story, featuring a Cobra Commander who's too over-the-top for now and crowing horrendous dialogue such as "Laugh while you can, you insignificant worms!" Oh, and the brainwashed Clutch/Rock 'n Roll plot's also a total waste of time. Conversely, Hama scores on the superb fate that befalls Zartan's crew, and if nothing else, we'll credit this story arc for picking a direction and sticking with it – which is more than some *G.I. Joe* comics can say.

MISCELLANEOUS STUFF!

COBRA COMMANDER'S KISSER

One of the odder continuity hiccups that occurs in *G.I. Joe* deals with Cobra Commander's face. In issue #98, flashback panels show a wounded Cobra Commander looking exactly like one of his "Fred Smith"-class Crimson Guardsmen, which implies that back in the day, the commander somewhat arrogantly ordered his Crimson Guardsmen to take his face as their own.

Unfortunately, this doesn't jive with *G.I. Joe* #64, where the Baroness, asked to identify the genuine Cobra Commander in private, looks upon Fred Smith VII's mug and immediately knows he's an imposter. Granted, we're only treated to glimpses of Cobra Commander's face throughout the whole of *G.I. Joe* (he notably walks about in make-up in *G.I. Joe* #55-#61) and no one can be certain of Cobra Commander's true looks. Still, even setting aside the Baroness' reaction, it just doesn't seem plausible that Cobra Commander would tailor the Fred Smiths to look like himself – an act that'd surely make it too tempting for one of the Freds to replace him (Fred Smith VII at least had the benefit of wearing a helmet).

Indeed, as further evidence, Cobra Commander's real face serves as the mnemonic that mentally enthralls Destro and Zartan (#145) – and they certainly didn't get hypnotized to see any other Fred Smith faces (Zartan in #97, etc.) As such, we're tempted to ignore the visuals of Cobra Commander's face in *G.I. Joe* #98's flashback scenes, judging them as a continuity glitch spawned from ten-plus years of *G.I. Joe* comics.

G.I. Joe #101 to #102

Titles: *"The New Guard" (#101), "What Did He Say?" (#102)*
Release Dates: *June to July 1990*
Art: *M.D. Bright*

BATTLE ROSTER *Joes:* Mutt and Junkyard, Spirit, Flint, Lady Jaye, Roadblock, Muskrat, Hawk, General Hollingsworth; *Cobra:* Darklon; *Other:* The Oktober Guard (Daina, Dragonsky).

FIRST APPEARANCES *Other:* Lt. Gorky, Sgt. Misha (Oktober Guardsmen, #101), Sioban O'Hara (Scarlett's sister, #101).

MISSION BRIEF Back in New York, Snake-Eyes and Storm Shadow keep vigil with the comatose Scarlett, praying for the merest hint of recovery. But to their complete horror, Scarlett's sister Sioban O'Hara arrives with a court order to enact Scarlett's living will and terminate her life support. Storm Shadow proceeds to bitch out Sioban, but Snake-Eyes, unable to fight the weight of the law, collapses by Scarlett's side. Mustering the tattered remnants of his vocal chords, Snake-Eyes utters Scarlett's name before erupting into tears.

In Millville, Cobra Vipers escort Mutt and Spirit out of Uncle Jeff's house at gunpoint, but a local military vet named Russ slips into the Joes' commandeered HISS tank and rescues them. Russ takes Mutt and Spirit to a nearby hideout, introducing them to Millville's best hope for freedom: a pack of delinquent kids who escaped the Cobra brainwashing sweeps. Mutt and Spirit reluctantly organize the teens into a fighting unit, coordinating surgical strikes against Cobra deployments in Millville.

Meanwhile, lingering anti-Joe elements within the Pentagon threaten again to disband the Joes, but a presidential order wards off the Joes' critics. Longing for a decisive victory to prove the Joes' merit, Hawk and General Hollingsworth assign Flint, Lady Jaye, Roadblock and Muskrat the momentous task of helping a rebel coalition end Cobra and Destro's stranglehold on Sierra Gordo.

To everyone's surprise, Hollingsworth and Hawk order Flint's team to coordinate their efforts with Russia's Oktober Guard, part of a joint East-West effort to liberate Sierra Gordo. A Soviet AN-24 Condor quickly arrives, carrying the survivors of the previous Oktober Guard – Daina and Dragonsky – plus two new members named Lt. Gorky and Sgt. Misha. The Joes and Russians reach Sierra Gordo in the Russian Condor, intending to rendezvous with the rebel coalition. Unfortunately, the Condor finds the rebels disturbingly absent from the Sierra Gordon landing zone. Worse, a Darklon-commanded tank column downs the Russian plane, killing the pilots and forcing the Joes and Russians to run for cover in armored vehicles.

Totally bereft of a plan – and wondering if the rebel coalition sold them out – the Joes and Russians wander into the Sierra Gordon rain forests. A short while later, Flint's brigade meets up with Tucaro headhunters, savages who aided Joe jungle trooper Recondo during a previous mission (*G.I. Joe* #39-#40). Flint's team befriends Danny LeCleir (a.k.a. Anibal), an MIT-educated Tucaro who returned to lead his people to independence.

Unfortunately, Darklon grows weary of the Tucaro resistance movement, selling timber rights to multi-national corporations with the intent of razing the rain forests – and leaving the Tucaros completely without shelter.

MEMORABLE MOMENTS Military veteran Russell, mostly a throwaway character, gives an impassioned speech to Millville's youth center kids about developing pride and respect. His words spur the kids into action, threatening to break Cobra's control of Millville wide open. But later, in a top dramatic moment, Spirit comments how some of the kids enjoyed the combat too much, turning them into adrenaline freaks, while others experienced shell-shock and froze up. Most telling of all, Spirit sagely comments on the mature nature of war, commenting that however the Millville conflict resolves itself, "… these kids can't ever go back to being kids again."

LOVE AND WAR Lady Jaye spends these issues getting a little too cozy with the Russian Lt. Gorky, seizing Flint with the wild desire to take Gorky into a dark alley and club him over the head with a Coors bottle.

Indeed, Lady Jaye accuses Flint of leaving the Russians behind at a crucial juncture merely because Gorky threatens his manhood. Credit where credit is due, Flint turns back for the Russians, justifiably pointing out that the Russkies *certainly* wouldn't have rescued the Joes. That said, the thought of leaving Gorky – and his raging hormones – behind probably made Flint floor the accelerator a little harder. The love triangle mercifully ends harmlessly.

Snake-Eyes spends hours sitting by Scarlett's hospital bed, hoping to somehow facilitate her rehabilitation.

ASS-WHUPPINGS In Sierra Gordo, Flint tries to pop a 180 degree turn to let a Razorback tank skid past him into a yawning chasm. Regrettably, Flint doesn't turn in time and takes the valley head on – luckily leaping across as the Razorback plummets to its doom. Also, the rebels in Millville drop a scrap-iron-filled safe atop two Cobra BUGG pilots.

GOOFS Hawk and General Hollingsworth claim that the Joes' survival rests on the success of Flint's Sierra Gordo mission – which seems wildly overblown, given the almost routine nature of the assignment.

TV/COMIC TIE-INS Scarlett's action figure file card records her as having a father and three brothers, as shown on TV in "Captives of Cobra." The file makes no mention of Sioban, although writer Larry Hama confirms her as Scarlett's legitimate sister. Scarlett's brothers finally show up in *G.I. Joe* (vol. 2) #6.

COMIC TIE-INS Snake-Eyes lost his vocal chords in a helicopter accident (#27) and certainly can't form anything approaching complete sentences. Still, Hama states Snake-Eyes could gasp snippets of words, allowing him to cry out Scarlett's name at the end of #102. On other occasions, such as G.I. Joe #120, we see Snakes stealthily croaking instructions.

Destro's Iron Grenadiers blew away a number of Oktober Guardsmen in *Special Missions* #26, but Daina and Dragonsky survived to recruit replacements. Joe jungle trooper Recondo lived with the Tucaros for a year (circa *G.I. Joe* #39), paving the way for future Joe-Tucaro relations.

Scarlett remains in a coma from the Baroness' bullet (*G.I. Joe* #94) but awakens in #103. At Scarlett's bedside, Snake-Eyes removes his bandages, showing his face only modestly scarred after his brawl in the Cobra Consulate (#95). The Jugglers threatened to disband the Joes (#98), using grievous damage to the Cobra Consulate (#95-#96) as an excuse, but a presidential order keeps the Joes in operation.

Destro first spread his tentacles into Sierra Gordo in *G.I. Joe* #69-#71. Semi-retired as of #97, Destro and the Baroness briefly touch base here with Darklon, fully returning in #116.

CHARACTER PROFILE: JOES Order: Law's dog remains fast friends with Mutt's hound Junkyard.

CHARACTER PROFILE: OTHER

• *Daina:* She doesn't blame Flint for momentarily leaving her group behind (*see Sex and Spirits*), knowing damn well that she'd have abandoned the Joes if the situation were reversed.

• *Lt. Gorky:* He's affiliated with the black sea regiment of the Russia's Naval Infantry and has a limited amount of pilot's training.

• *Sgt. Misha:* Seconded to the Oktober Guard from Spetsnaz, Russia's special purpose troops.

• *Sioban O'Hara:* An attorney-at-law, working from Atlanta, Dallas and Miami Beach, specializing in torts.

ORGANIZATIONS *G.I. Joe and the Oktober Guard:* Were originally slated to rendezvous with the Patriotic Coalition of Sierra Gordo Freedom Fighters, who either perished or simply collapsed amid a string of political movements.

• *The Oktober Guard:* Take their orders from the Stravka, a.k.a. the Soviet High Command.

HOT WHEELS Joe Mobile Command Center: Houses a Desert Fox six-wheel drive vehicle.

THE COMMAND DECISION A tempered and satisfying yarn, even if Spirit seems to have shucked off his American Indian mystique (escaping a tank explosion, Spirit notes: "When [Cobra] doesn't find any crispy critters, they'll be combing the woodwork for us!"). It's slightly mundane, but we enjoyed the Millville escapade's choice moments (Spirit and Mutt pondering how their teenage troops – for better or worse – just became men), and the interaction between the various Joes and Russians (Flint gleefully abandoning the guardsmen, etc.) keeps the story hopping.

G.I. Joe #103 to #108

Titles: *"The Amazing Welkin" (#103), "Hero of the People!" (#104), "Hidden Aces" (#105), "I Lift My Lamp" (#106), "Enter the Night Creepers" (#107), "Apparent Conclusions" (#108)*
Release Dates: *Aug. 1990 to Jan. 1991*
Art: *M. D. Bright (#103-#106, #108), Lee Weeks (#107)*

BATTLE ROSTER *Joes:* Snake-Eyes, Storm Shadow, Flint, Roadblock, Lady Jaye, Muskrat, Hawk, Spirit, Mutt and Junkyard, Stalker, Scarlett, Lt. Falcon; *Cobra:* Major Bludd, Tomax and Xamot; *Destro:* Darklon; *Other:* the Oktober Guard (Daina, Dragonsky, Lt. Gorky, Sgt. Misha), the White Clown, Orlovsky the dwarf.

FIRST APPEARANCES *Joes:* Hotseat (Raider driver, #105), Stretcher (medical specialist, #105); *Other:* General Thurston Crowther (Juggler, #103), Magda (horse rider, Borovian president, #106), the Night Creepers (ninja techno-assassins, #107).

FIRST APPEARANCE AND DEATH *Other:* George Strawhacker (U.S. federal agent, #106).

MISSION BRIEF ***Issue #103:*** In Millville, Cobra Commander becomes increasingly aware of a G.I. Joe presence among the town's revolutionaries and hurriedly issues a pre-programmed code-phrase that suppresses the Millville residents' brainwashing, leaving them entirely ignorant of their actions as Cobra lackeys. Unaware of this, Mutt and Spirit's rebel band waits until dawn, then stages their biggest strike yet, rushing into a Cobra-controlled steel mill en masse with assault rifles held high.

Moments later, Hawk arrives and surrounds the renegade Joes with legitimate police officials – demanding to know why Mutt and Spirit are running amok through Millville with guns and Molotov cocktails. Mutt and Spirit vehemently detail Cobra's brainwashing of the Millville residents, but Hawk – forced over a legal barrel – places the two Joes under arrest. As Hawk's troupe leaves, Cobra Commander spreads a second code-phrase among the Millville populace – re-activating the brainwashing and solidifying the town as a Cobra manufacturing center.

With Scarlett's prognosis looking grim, Storm Shadow feverishly searches for a way to prevent Snake-Eyes from sinking into catatonic despair. Working out of desperation, Storm Shadow locates a government file concerning George Strawhacker, an American operative left to rot in a Borovian gulag. Armed with these findings, Storm Shadow bursts into the Pentagon and confronts the machinistic Jugglers. Stormy "encourages" the Jugglers to assign Snake-Eyes the task of liberating Strawhacker from Borovia, threatening to go public with the Strawhacker file if they don't comply. Faced with the possibility of political fall-out over abandoning Strawhacker to his fate, the generals agree to Storm Shadow's terms.

Stalker objects strongly when Storm Shadow proposes the plan to Snake-Eyes. But Storm Shadow insists that Snake-Eyes holds a personal stake in rescuing Strawhacker – the former fiancé of Snake-Eyes' late sister. Snake-Eyes agrees to undertake the mission, departing with his friends aboard a Joe stealth plane. Storm Shadow cautions Snake-Eyes must use exceptional ruthlessness to survive Borovia's newest outbreak of anarchy. Accordingly, Storm Shadow conditions Snake-Eyes with a ninja trance (called the "Arashikage Mind-Set") – clearing Snake-Eyes of personal concerns and turning him into an unstoppable killing machine.

Although Stalker continues smoldering, Snake-Eyes bails out over Borovia. The Joe plane returns to Washington D.C., but against all odds – and all prognoses – Scarlett suddenly awakens in the hospital and asks for Snake-Eyes.

Issue #104-#105: In Sierra Gordo, the combined Joe/Oktober Guard/Tucaro army hampers Darklon's squadrons, but Darklon makes good on his threat to level the region's rain forests. Logging companies work at a breakneck pace, bulldozing vast amounts of timber and robbing the Tucaro brigade of a fallback position. Thankfully, Joe reinforcements finally arrive with a mobile battle center. As a result, the allies capture Darklon, salvaging the Joes' mangled mission and giving the Tucaros a bargaining chip with which to reclaim their lost territory.

Meanwhile, Storm Shadow and Stalker return to Washington, but the Jugglers – desperate to cover their tracks in the Strawhacker affair – incapacitate the heroes and stash them in a Department of Defense bolt-hole in the Statue of Liberty. Furthermore, the leader of the Jugglers, General Crowther, hires the mercenary Major Bludd to pick off Snake-Eyes or Strawhacker (preferably both) in Borovia.

Now You Know

Landing in Borovian capital of Krogdnsz, a remorseless Snake-Eyes wades into civil struggles between the "upper Borovians" and outgunned "lower Borovians." Snake-Eyes charges into the former headquarters of Borovia's security police, carving up its defenders. Luckily, Snake-Eyes' former allies in Borovia – the White Clown and the dwarf Orlovsky (*G.I. Joe* #64-#66) – spot their ex-colleague and cover his back.

Capitalizing on Snake-Eyes' charge, a racist upper Borovian leader named Metz throws his troops into the fray, helping the berserk Snake-Eyes re-take the building. The White Clown initially despairs as the vicious Metz's reputation swells, but rejoices when police records cite Strawhacker and Magda, a fellow insurrectionist and the White Clown's lover, as prisoners at Gulag 23 near Pvnsk.

Even through his ninja conditioning, Snake-Eyes recognizes the White Clown and Orlovsky as allies and journeys to Pvnsk with them. At Gulag 23, Snake-Eyes waltzes into the camp like an angel of death, wasting everyone who crosses his path. Unfortunately, the dastardly Major Bludd arrives in Borovia, convincing Metz that the Joe ninja poses a threat to his political aspirations. Metz agrees, airlifting Major Bludd to Gulag 23 and positioning him to assassinate Snake-Eyes.

Issue #106: While Snake-Eyes eviscerates every gulag guard present, Strawhacker recognizes his intended brother-in-law and the White Clown happily reunites with Magda. Amid the celebration, Major Bludd tries to bump Snake-Eyes off, but the tiny Orlovsky sneaks up on Bludd and captures him at gunpoint.

Moments later, Metz's upper Borovians rush into the decimated gulag, intending to execute any lower Borovians present. But when the racist Metz acts abusively towards a young lower Borovian girl, Strawhacker objects and slugs the rebel leader. Pumped with adrenaline and hatred, Metz opens up his pistol at point-blank range – riddling Strawhacker's chest with bullets.

With his friend's demise, Snake-Eyes' ninja mantra fades, restoring his compassion. Favoring his chances of survival with Snake-Eyes, the captive Major Bludd deliberately lets slip that Metz hired him to kill the Joe commando. Recognizing Snake-Eyes as a hero, the upper Borovians turn on Metz and prepare to hang the fiend. Magda objects, arguing for democracy and due process, but the bloodthirsty mob refuses to listen. Suddenly, Snake-Eyes steps forward and shoots away Metz's restraints, agreeing with Magda's sentiments that the people must seek justice, not revenge. Having made his point – and with Strawhacker dead – Snake-Eyes sets off for home.

Issue 107 *(NOTE: Storm Shadow and Stalker's escape actually occurs at the tail end of #106, but we've lumped it in with #107 for simplicity's sake):*

When General Crowther sends a team of freelance assassins to rub out Storm Shadow and Stalker at the Statue of Liberty, the heroes easily rough up their opponents and escape. The two fugitives take refuge in Storm Shadow's water tower hideout in Manhattan, attempting to regain their wits and plot their next move.

Meanwhile, Cobra Commander finds himself approached by an affiliation of high-tech ninjas named "the Night Creepers" – a technologically savvy group of martial arts experts hoping to obtain employment from Cobra. Operating from the Cobra Consulate's ruins, Cobra Commander asks the Night Creepers to prove their worth by decapitating the most notorious Cobra traitor – the ninja Storm Shadow.

In an attempt to pit the Joes against one another, General Crowther spills the beans to Hawk and Scarlett that he sent Snake-Eyes to Borovia under threat of blackmail from Storm Shadow. As Crowther predicted, a fuming Scarlett finds the strength to escape from the hospital and head straight for Storm Shadow's lair, plotting to rip out the ninja's gizzard.

Back at Storm Shadow's hidey-hole, Stalker and Stormy hold their own against the first wave of Night Creepers, but the wide-ranging battle takes the combatants into New York's subway system. As the Night Creepers loose a fury of arrows, Storm Shadow comes across an enraged, knife-wielding Scarlett. With little choice, Storm Shadow body-tackles Scarlett and miraculously hauls her aboard a fast-moving train – just as Scarlett drives her blade into the ninja's back. Storm Shadow hastily explains the truth about Snake-Eyes' mission, then passes out from blood loss, leaving Scarlett aghast at her rash actions.

Issue #108: Snake-Eyes returns to Scarlett's hospital, but a breathless Stalker rushes in and details his brawl with the Night Creepers. Wasting no time, Snake-Eyes and Stalker head out to find Scarlett and whisk the fallen Storm Shadow away for medical treatment. At the same time, Stalker identifies a charred layer of concrete dust on a torn piece of Night Creeper clothing as originating from the gutted Cobra Consulate.

Snake-Eyes and Stalker barrel into the Consulate, putting a knife blade at Cobra Commander's throat. With Cobra Commander's life in their hands, Snake-Eyes and Stalker order the commander to end the threat to Storm Shadow's life. Cobra Commander complies, withdrawing his Night Creeper assassins.

While Storm Shadow recovers, Hawk informs General Crowther that the Borovian insurrection ended with Magda being elected the country's president. As a newly entrenched head of state, Magda provides an official affidavit implicating Crowther as the man who hired Major Bludd to kill Snake-Eyes

– effectively ending Crowther's career in disgrace.

LOVE AND WAR Showing her true priorities, Scarlett asks to see Snake-Eyes the moment she wakes up.

ASS-WHUPPINGS In Borovia, Snake-Eyes wipes out a room-full of security troopers with his Uzi and knives, tossing a few of the sliced-up thugs out the window for good measure. He's a veritable avenging angel at Strawhacker's gulag, damn near killing every living thing present save a few prisoners.

Stalker pops a flare into a mercenary's helicopter, crashing it into a goon-filled boat. Storm Shadow and Stalker kill a batch of Night Creepers named Gimel, Resh, Daleth and Taw. Ironically, the only serious injury Storm Shadow suffers comes from Scarlett, who stabs him in the back. In Sierra Gordo, a near-miss blinds Roadblock for a couple issues and showers the Russian Misha's legs with shrapnel.

GOOFS Darklon's affiliate companies bring down vast chunks of Sierra Gordo's rain forests in about 5.3 minutes – fast enough to catch Flint's team of Tucaros by surprise (i.e. "Whoops! Where'd the damn rain forest go?").

Scarlett follows in the footsteps of Harrison Ford and other action stars, becoming fit enough to brawl with a ninja despite her recent emergence from a coma.

Finally, this story arc's main plot sports a number of gaping holes. To wit, does Storm Shadow, however well-intentioned, really think Snake-Eyes is better off as a soulless, trance-induced automaton? If Snake-Eyes cares so much for Strawhacker, why hasn't he noticed his absence all these months? And why, for the love of Pete, don't Snake-Eyes and Stalker kill Cobra Commander when they've got the chance?

COMIC TIE-INS In flashback, *G.I. Joe* #144 details Snake-Eyes' first mission to rescue Strawhacker.

A string of revolutions toppled Borovia's Communist government and two interim administrations since the Joes' last visit (#61-#66). The White Clown and his associate, Orlovsky the dwarf, aided Snake-Eyes in rescuing Stalker's group and escaping on that occasion.

Storm Shadow previously used the Arashikage Mind-Set – which variously calms its subjects or turns them into unstoppable, killing lunatics, depending on your intent (*see Sidebar*) – to ease a wounded Snake-Eyes' suffering during their infamous escape from Vietnam (#26). The Mind-Set also comes in damnably handy for shattering mental conditioning, as witnessed in #131 and #134.

Snake-Eyes keeps a hidden room behind the sensory deprivation tank he frequents at Columbia University (*G.I Joe* #2). The hideout contains various mementos, including the late Kwinn's .30 caliber machine gun and Snake-Eyes' famous collection of spike-knuckled trench knives. Snake-Eyes here leaves a Borovian orphan (*see Character Development: Joes*) with Wade Collins, who last appeared in #97 and returns for the series' curtain call in #155.

Storm Shadow's water tower hideout (first seen in *G.I. Joe* #39) is located above the Montana Towers in New York.

Major Bludd dug his way out of Destro's prison in Scotland (#57), gaining employment from the Jugglers in this story. Darklon here gets captured, but spontaneously resumes business as normal in *G.I. Joe* #146.

Months ago, authorities condemned and closed down the Cobra Consulate, which saw heavy damage in #95-#96. Magda here becomes president of Borovia, aiding Hawk and a group of wayward Joes in #129-#130.

A Joe team rolls into the Middle Eastern country of Trucial Abysmia in #108, readying for a fateful encounter in *G.I. Joe* #109.

CHARACTER PROFILE: JOES

• *Roadblock:* He's not big on the concept of "glory" – deeming it something his mother sings about in church – and would rather collect his pension than heaps of accolades and an early demise.

• *Snake-Eyes and Marina:* During Snake-Eyes' sojourn into Borovia, a little girl named Marina begs him to save her father – who's slated for execution solely because he's an upper Borovian. Entranced by his ninja mantra, the emotionless Snake-Eyes walks past while Metz's soldiers blow the girl's father to shreds. After Strawhacker's death, Snake-Eyes regains his compassion and saves Marina from a similar fate, somewhat making amends by arranging for his ex-war buddy Wade Collins to adopt her.

Under normal conditions, Snake-Eyes won't shoot an unarmed man. Snake-Eyes holds a Combat Infantryman's Badge, a Silver Star and tons of Purple Hearts. His late twin sister, (first mentioned in *G.I. Joe* #26) was named Terri.

• *Storm Shadow:* His middle initial's "S." He's stealthy enough to sneak into the Pentagon, and tosses throwing stars fast enough to plug gun barrels before their owners can fire. Storm Shadow's a talented escape artist and knows how to reset dislocated shoulders. He obtained the George Strawhacker file from the vault at Ft. Leonard Wood, shortly before the records center there burned down.

CHARACTER PROFILE: OTHER

• *Sioban O'Hara:* Sioban seems genuinely concerned for Scarlett's welfare, although a continuing feud about ownership of the family house in Atlanta seems to cloud her motives. Despising Snake-Eyes' shady past, Sioban blaming him for the fact that Scarlett "never took up with a proper gentleman." Scarlett claims she'd have gladly signed over the family house if Sioban wanted it that much – although Scarlett might say that merely out of familial kindness.

• *George Strawhacker:* Former American operative set up to leak false information to Soviet intelligence, then abandoned to a Borovian gulag as part of the deception. Until this point, the Jugglers blocked any possible mention of a rescue mission, fearing that Strawhacker's release would somehow put his disinformation under suspicion (and, more to the point, call their actions into question).

ORGANIZATIONS *The Jugglers:* They don't exist officially, which suggests that they're a merely group of like-minded seedy generals who gang up for their own insidious purposes.

• *The Night Creeper Syndicate:* Mixing ages-old martial arts techniques with modern-day technology, the Night Creeper syndicate offers mercenary services in a variety of combat and financial-related fields. The Night Creepers typically seek freelance work, although they're certainly not above screwing over their employers and don't trust Cobra Commander (the feeling's mutual).

STUFF YOU NEED Arashikage Mind-Set: A ninja mind technique practiced by Storm Shadow's Arashikage clan which alters its users' mental states with a variety of effects. Essentially, the Mind-Set re-orients its practitioners' focus, either A) making them remorseless, unstoppable killing machines, capable of almost superhuman feats of violence, or B) calming them into passive states that suspend the severity of wounds until medical help arrives (although they sound similar, state B isn't related to the omnipresent self-induced ninja coma that Storm Shadow, Snake-Eyes and Cobra Commander have variously employed to simulate death). In state A, the raging ninja assassin in question continues his/her butchery until the completion of a primary mission, whereupon they snap back to normal. Those who perfect the Mind-Set can activate its effect in others by finger-knitting certain hand patterns. Storm Shadow and Snake-Eyes most likely learned the technique from the Hard and Soft Masters.

HOT WHEELS Joe Raider assault vehicle: All the weapons face forward, so indecision spells instant death.

• *Destro Razorback tanks:* Fire jacketed, depleted uranium bursts.

THE COMMAND DECISION Hardly the worst *G.I. Joe* storyarc, although the highly flawed premise (Storm Shadow turning Snake-Eyes into "the Terminator" to abate his suffering) sours the entire cocktail. Also, Hama's interwoven plot threads only water down the story (the well-intended Sierra Gordo warfare dies on the vine), as if he's not sure on a month-to-month basis where plotlines start and stop. That said, we'll credit this story arc's heart for being in the right place – but its brain isn't – making this at best an average performance.

G.I. Joe #109 to #110

Titles: *"Death in the Desert" (#109), "Escalator to Armageddon" (#110)*
Release Dates: *Feb. to Mar. 1991*
Art: *Joe Statema (#109), Ron Garney (#110)*

BATTLE ROSTER *Joes:* Duke, Cross-Country, Breaker, Doc, Quick Kick, Crazylegs, Thunder, Heavy Metal, Crankcase, Wildcard, Rock 'n Roll, Clutch; *Cobra:* Tomax and Xamot, Cobra Commander.

FIRST APPEARANCES *Cobra:* Saw-Viper (heavy machine gunner, #109).

DEATHS *Joes:* Breaker, Doc, Quick Kick, Thunder, Crazylegs, Crankcase, Heavy Metal (#109).

MISSION BRIEF ***Issue #109:*** NOTE: Although the opening paragraph of this summary occurred *G.I. Joe* #108, we've grouped the action together for simplicity's sake.

Operating from the somewhat-friendly Middle Eastern emirate of Benzheen, a team of Joes commanded by Duke and Lt. Falcon grow worried when Cobra fortifies the neighboring country of Trucial Abysmia. Unwilling to let Cobra infinitely stockpile its forces, Duke's platoon enters Trucial Abysmia to obliterate the country's Terror-Dromes. Unfortunately, Crimson Twins' forces surround the Joes with a frightful amount of vehicles. Duke's Joes give it their best, but ultimately surrender to stay alive, throwing themselves on the twins' mercies.

The twins dump the Joe prisoners in a pit for safekeeping, then radio Cobra Commander at the Cobra Consulate for further instructions. Fearing Snake-Eyes' wrath (#108), Cobra Commander recoils at the thought of harming Snake-Eyes' teammates and decides to release the captive Joes. But when Cobra Commander tells Tomax and Xamot to "get rid of their prisoners," the twins mistakenly think Cobra Commander wants the Joes eradicated... for good.

Desperate to avoid complicity in the crime, the twins search their troopers' ranks and happen across a bloodthirsty Saw-Viper. Agreeing to off the Joes for two months extra pay, the Saw-Viper hoists his machine gun toward the pit 'o Joes while the twins' column moves on.

Just as the Saw-Viper reaches the edge of the pit, the Joes boost Doc up to take a look around. Undaunted, the Saw-Viper shoots Doc at point-blank range – instantly killing the Joe medic – then opens up his machine gun full-throttle. In rapid succession, Thunder, Heavy Metal and Crankcase also perish, selflessly throwing themselves in front of their comrades to shield them from the bullet spray.

In the mayhem, Lt. Flacon flings a concealed knife, pegging the Saw-Viper in the chest. The surviving six Joes leave the Saw-Viper for dead and surge to freedom, blowing away the remaining Viper guards with his weapon. Breaker hurriedly radios the Pit III for a rescue detail, forcing Hawk to panic and prep the Joe shuttle *Defiant* for immediate lift-off. Unfortunately, the twins intercept Breaker's transmission, re-rerouting their forces to cut off the Joes from reaching Benzheen.

The *Defiant* soars over the planet and drops Clutch, Rock 'n Roll and Wildcard toward Trucial Abysmia in a Mobile Battle Bunker with a prototype heat shield. Duke's team steals a Cobra RAGE vehicle and makes a run for it, but the Saw-Viper – only momentarily stunned – recovers and gives chase with a herd of Vipers. The Joes blast away at their pursuers, but a direct hit on the RAGE obliterates Breaker, Quick Kick and Crazylegs. As the only survivors, Duke, Lt. Falcon and Cross-Country bring their lone pistols to bear as the Saw-Viper's column rolls closer to mow them down.

Issue #110: On the Benzheen/Trucial Abysmia border, the Crimson Twins ready their forces for an intensive assault to capture Benzheen's lucrative oil refineries. The twins radio Cobra Commander to coordinate the strike, then pale upon realizing that the commander wanted them to release the Joe prisoners.

Nearby, Duke's trio braces for a fatal impact, but the twins hurriedly contact the Saw-Viper and force him to withdraw. The twins roll their forces into Benzheen, even as the Joe Mobile Battle Bunker lands and retrieves Duke's party. But a ballistic Cobra Commander, worried that the Joes' murders will incite unholy retribution, leaves for Benzheen to oversee the operation personally.

The Mobile Battle Bunker crew charges the Saw-Viper's battalion, unleashing a blistering missile barrage that pulps the Saw-Viper's companions. The explosion tosses the Saw-Viper clear, but Duke jumps off the Joe Battle Bunker and flexes his trigger-finger. In a stroke of brilliance, the Saw-Viper flings his hands in the air – realizing that Duke's honor won't let him gun down an unarmed man. Duke sees red for a moment, then turns aside, leading his crew to recover their dead and return to base.

Shortly after, the Emir of Benzheen formally asks for U.S. intervention in reclaiming his country from Cobra. Given official sanction, Hawk amasses a fleet of C-130 Herks and C5A Galaxy transports to fly the bulk of the Joes to Benzheen – readying for all-out warfare against Cobra.

MEMORABLE MOMENTS With four Joes already dead, Quick Kick scoops up a machine gun and wastes most of the

TOP 10

COMIC STORIES

1) "Snake-Eyes: The Origin" (#26-#27) – The definitive *G.I. Joe* story, visceral tragic and making the reader sympathetic to Snake-Eyes' lifetime of pain. Barring a distracting sub-plot with Zartan and a trio of Joes, Snake-Eyes' history left us breathless.

2) The Cobra Civil War (#72-#78) – Graced with a wide-ranging cast, this arc throws dozens of Joes, Cobras and Destro-allied troopers into a whirlpool and watches who sinks and who swims. Although #26-27 undoubtedly deserves the top slot, this story's complexity makes it our personal favorite.

3) "Silent Interlude" (#21) – Certainly the most talked-about *G.I. Joe* comic – this issue's 22 wordless pages, although not as meaty as the top two stories, remain greatly inspiring. And truth to tell, ex-Joe fans often remember this story above all else in the series.

4) The Trucial Abysmia saga (#109-#115) – Much more than just "that story where the Joes got killed," even if it's often remembered as such. An intoxicating seriousness and balls-to-the-wall action permeates this tale, developing it as a true war story.

5) "Crossroads" (#43) – A parallel story of life and death that redeems a scalawag (Wade Collins) and brutally rips apart a compassionate soul (the Soft Master) in a single issue.

6) Snake-Eyes and Storm Shadow assault Cobra Island/"The Invasion of Spring field" (#45-#50) – A glorious bloodbath from start to finish, sparked by intensely riveting character dramas (Ripcord searching for his lost girlfriend, Snake-Eyes and Storm Shadow looking to avenge the Hard Master, etc.).

7) Stalker, Snow Job and Quick Kick tossed in a Borovian gulag (primarily #61-#62, #66, SM #6) – Completely gripping and personal, presuming you ignore the distracting side stories and focus on the Borovian gulag plotline.

8) "Pit-Fall" (#53) – An issue that blindsides you, since there's not a lot of build-up, but it keeps your head in the ballgame until the finale.

9) The Sierra Gordo debacle (#69-#71) – Continual fun as the Joes get lost in a violent, foreign locale – with some saucy Dreadnoks along for the ride.

10) "Cobra Commander Escapes!" (#23-#24) – Partly interesting because the Joes *catch* Cobra Commander, but also due to his madcap escape in issue #24.

Saw-Viper's crew. But afterwards – knowing no amount of payback can return his friends to life – Quick Kick bawls: "I got 'em, didn't I? Didn't I, Crazylegs?" Crazylegs gently replies, "Yeah, you sure did, old buddy. Lemme take that [gun]..."

The over-the-top Cobra Commander's in rare form here, chastising a lieutenant who dismisses Snake-Eyes' threat with: "[Snake-Eyes] got past all of my Vipers and Night Creepers and put his blade to my throat! I am inclined to take his threat seriously!" Cobra Commander later reels to learn of the Saw-Viper's massacre, crying out and cradling his head like the kid from *Home Alone.*

Finally, Duke finds himself unable to shoot the unarmed Saw-Viper – taking the moral high ground in a way that's damnably harder than simply pulling a trigger.

ASS-WHUPPINGS This story features a veritable cattle call of Joe deaths: Breaker, Doc, Quick Kick, Crazylegs, Heavy Metal, Crankcase and Thunder. Duke encourages the Crimson Twins to pound on his ribs, spoofing them into thinking he's helpless. Lt. Falcon sticks the Saw-Viper with a knife and breaks his nose. A pack of Vipers deal Falcon a couple of bullets just before an enraged Quick Kick mows down their entire column. All in all, it's a death fest pretty much unparalleled in the entire series.

PREPOSTEROUS PHYSICS The Mobile Battle Bunker survives a plummet to Earth, but it's only got heat shielding on its underside. (That hardly seems adequate, and what the hell's to stop it from flipping over during free-fall?)

COMIC TIE-INS Snake-Eyes' and Stalker's humiliating invasion of the consulate (*G.I. Joe* #108) motivates Cobra Commander to order the Joes' release. For the Trucial Abysmia operation, Hawk assembles the biggest Joe squadron assembled since the invasion of Cobra Island (#73-#76). The war over Benzheen (an obvious parallel to the Gulf War of the same year) unfolds in #111-#115.

CHARACTER PROFILE: JOES

• *Quick Kick:* He's let his hair grow out (and it's not much of an improvement).

• *Wildcard:* Wildcard's such an immense klutz, Rock 'n Roll and Clutch tie down his hands to stop him from breaking anything or doing something stupid like erroneously hitting the ejection switch.

CHARACTER PROFILE: COBRA

• *The Crimson Twins:* They smoke (although you'd think only one brother would need to puff up at a time).

• *The Saw-Viper:* His armor's composed of seven layers of protective composite fibers, withstanding a talented knife throw with minimal damage.

ORGANIZATIONS *Cobra:* Despite being agents of evil, most of the Cobra troops are not so heartless as to willingly gun down unarmed prisoners.

PLACES TO GO *Benzheen:* Sits atop 10 percent of the world's oil.

• *Trucial Abysmia:* Green with envy over the neighboring Benzheen's built-up petroleum refineries. Cobra obtained permission to build Terror-Dromes along the Trucial Abysmia/Benzheen border. As such, the Joes are in Trucial Abysmia illegally.

HOT WHEELS *Defiant:* The Joe space shuttle runs sophisticated scans from orbit.

• *Cobra HISS II Tanks:* Reinforced Cobra tanks, so tough that only missiles can penetrate their shielding.

THE COMMAND DECISION Highly moving and packed with true grit, *G.I. Joe* #109-#110 (and the subsequent #111-#115) is just about the only *G.I. Joe* story this side of the "Cobra Civil War" that you must on pain of death read. Hama unloads a full round of power cards, juxtaposing such lofty notions as murder and honor with tremendous effect. It's a story so honed, mature and well-crafted, it sets a standard the series can't maintain – but we're thrilled these issues carry such weighty ambition.

G.I. Joe #111 to #115

Titles: *"Probe and Feint!" (#111), "Who's the Hero?" (#112), "Previous Agreement" (#113), "Metal-Head!" (#114), "Counting Coup!" (#115)*
Release Dates: *Apr. to Aug. 1991*
Art: *John Statema*

BATTLE ROSTER *Joes:* Snake-Eyes, Storm Shadow, Scarlett, Flint, Lady Jaye, Roadblock, Hawk, Duke, Dusty, Tunnel Rat, Sneak Peek, Battle Force 2000, Rock 'n Roll, Steeler; *Cobra:* Cobra Commander, Tomax and Xamot, the Saw Viper, Wild Weasel; *Other:* The Emir of Benzheen.

FIRST APPEARANCES *Joes:* Cool Breeze (unspecified, #111), Recoil (long range recon patrol, #111), Ambush (concealment specialist, #111), Salvo (anti-armor trooper, #114), Backblast (anti-aircraft soldier, #115), Rampart (shoreline defender, #115), Dogfight (mudfighter pilot, #115), Dee-Jay (Battle Force 2000 comm-tech trooper, #113); *Destro:* Metal-Head (anti-tank specialist, #114).

G.I. Joe #111 to #115

DEATHS *Joes:* Cool Breeze (#112), Sneak Peak (#113), all of Battle Force 2000 (except Dodger, #113); *Cobra:* Saw Viper (alleged, #112), Cobra Commander II, Dr. Mindbender, Croc Master, Raptor; *Destro:* Voltar; *Other:* Captain Minh, Tyrone (bodies discovered in #114).

MISSION BRIEF ***Issue #111-#112:*** Needing comprehensive data to launch a full-scale Joe assault in Benzheen, Hawk itches for intelligence information on Cobra's troop placements. Accordingly, he orders a ninja team of Snake-Eyes, Scarlett, Storm Shadow and Jinx to sneak into Benzheen and reconnoiter Cobra's defenses. Hawk stresses that the ninjas must remain undetected, thereby preventing Cobra from simply moving its troops and leaving the Joes hanging.

While the ninja team enters the Benzheen capital (helpfully also named Benzheen) Stalker and a team of Joes, including Recoil and Cool Breeze, seclude themselves outside the city as back-up. Meanwhile, in the desert, Flint and Lady Jaye take a Joe armor team and cudgel Cobra divisions with hit-and-run tactics. Unfortunately, a megalomanical revolutionary leader named Faoud and members of his fanatical "People's Resistance of Benzheen" front captures Flint's squad. Faoud boasts how he intends to missile various Cobra nerve centers in Benzheen with the Joe vehicles, but Flint and Lady Jaye realize – with palpable horror – that Faoud's missile strike will kill their ninja allies.

As if things couldn't get any worse, Stalker's team spots a random Night Creeper patrol advancing on the Joe ninjas' position. Panicked, Stalker's team broadcasts a jamming signal on all frequencies – preventing the Night Creepers from radioing for help while Snake-Eyes' hit squad silently dispatches the Night Creepers.

Unfortunately, Cobra Tele-Vipers detect the unauthorized jamming, compelling the murderous Saw-Viper to investigate with a helicopter team. Fearing that a long-range salvo could detonate a nearby ammo dump, the helicopter crew swoops in to stomp the ninjas with a short-range burst. But thankfully, Storm Shadow and Snake-Eyes leap onto the helicopter and dispatch everyone aboard. Leaving the fiendish Saw-Viper for dead, the two ninjas depart.

Meanwhile, Stalker's team happens across the hijacked Joe armor column and rubs out Faoud's associates, taking Faoud prisoner. Seconds later, the Joe ninjas arrive in their captured helicopter. Storm Shadow blows up the Cobra vehicle, making it look like a legitimate crash to cover up the recon team's presence. The Joes set off for home, but as a final act of defiance, Faoud swipes Stalker's gun and tries to plug the Joe ranger. With cat-like reflexes, Cool Breeze shoves Stalker aside – sacrificing himself in a hail of Faoud's bullets and dying almost instantly. Snake-Eyes instantly unloads several rounds and kills Faoud, leaving Stalker's group to return to camp and mourn their fallen comrade.

Issue #113: As fighting in Benzheen intensifies, a Joe recon team composed of Stalker, Dusty, Sneak Peek, Recoil and Ambush find themselves trapped at a Porsche dealership near Abu Talib Square. Hopelessly outnumbered, Stalker radios the Joe base camp for reinforcements. Accordingly, Hawk diverts Battle Force 2000 through Benzheen's reserve oil storage area, gambling that Cobra won't shoot at Battle Force 2000 and risk detonating the valuable oil reserves.

Back at the square, Cobra Alley Vipers capture a Benzheen mother and son, baiting the Joes by tossing the boy's stuffed pony into the crossfire. As the boy walks out to retrieve his toy, Sneak Peek bursts from cover to haul the lad to safety. Predictably, the Alley Vipers dice Sneak Peek with a hail of bullets and release their two hostages.

Unable to venture into the killing zone, a chilled Dusty recalls spending Thanksgiving dinner with Sneak Peek's family, remembering how Sneak Peek's mother implored Dusty to bring her son's body home if he perished in military service. As Stalker desperately reviews his team's dwindling options, a maimed Sneak Peek groans for help.

Meanwhile, the Emir of Benzheen berates Hawk for putting his oil refineries at risk. Conversely, Hawk refuses to prioritize the Emir's wealth over his men's lives. Unfortunately, the Emir secretly contacts Cobra Commander and gives away Battle Force 2000's location, offering $500 million if Cobra will refrain from firing on Battle Force 2000 until they emerge from the reserve oil storage area.

Shrugging off the Emir's offer, Cobra Commander orders a full bombardment – turning the oil tankers into an inferno and annihilating every Battle Force 2000 member save Dodger. Seeing the explosion, Stalker grimly acknowledges the fall of Battle Force 2000 and readies his group for a suicidal charge to freedom. The Alley Vipers sharp-shoot Recoil and Ambush, but Dusty scoops up Sneak Peek and hastily follows Stalker's lead. Luckily, Dodger arrives and tears through several Alley Vipers, wiping out the opposition and saving his comrades.

When Stalker's group returns to base camp, Joe medics scramble to bind Sneak Peek's wounds. But shockingly, the medics discover that Sneak Peek died some time ago – meaning Dusty lugged his friend's corpse through the desert for hours to fulfill his promise.

Issue #114: Miffed that Cobra Commander spat on his previous offer, the Emir of Benzheen re-opens negotiations to purchase his country back from Cobra. The Emir agrees to meet Cobra Commander in the neutral republic of Quagmarh, intending to slay the commander with his desert assassins. But unsympathetic Quagmarh residents – along with Cobra Commander's Night Creeper bodyguards – butcher the Emir's men, leading Cobra Commander to demand a higher buy-out price.

Meanwhile, a Cobra mobile missile launcher named Metal-

Head spars with a Joe infantry team consisting of Dusty, Salvo and Rock 'n Roll. Metal-Head's portable rocket launcher obliterates the Joes' vehicle, but Salvo retaliates with a short-range missile strike that stuns the Cobra missile man. Dusty rushes in to administer a *coup de grace*, but the Joe and Cobra leaders simultaneously enact a cease-fire – announcing that Cobra's accepted the Emir's settlement and will leave Benzheen. In exchange, the Emir voids the Joes' authorization to operate in his country, mandating that the Joes withdraw. Although welcoming a cease in hostilities, soldiers on both sides smolder over enduring Benzheen's bloody conflict with precious little to show for it.

Issue #115: Hawk regroups his forces aboard the *USS Flagg*, convinced that Cobra's still operating out of Benzheen via a private pact with the Emir. Accordingly, Hawk gives Joe pilots Ghostrider and Slip-Stream a set of secret orders, then authorizes them to pilot a stealth jet over Benzheen.

Meanwhile, as Cobra Commander dashes madly about in Benzheen, trying to preserve Cobra's secret presence in the country, Cobra's monitoring system detects Ghostrider's airship launching from the *Flagg*. Ghostrider and Slip-Stream run rings around Cobra stealth fighters, goading Cobra Commander to overheat and order an attack on the Joe jet.

Ghostrider and Slip-Stream nervously make for the heart of Benzheen just as a Cobra Firebat launches from a concealed Terror-Drome. Quick on the trigger, the Joes snap Polaroids of the brightly illuminated Firebat as concrete evidence of Cobra's secret bases in Benzheen. The Joes return to the *Flagg* with their prize, enabling Hawk to bring international pressure to bear against Benzheen and Cobra for treaty violation.

MEMORABLE MOMENTS Trying to avoid Cobra Commander's wrath for the Joe bloodbath (#109), the Crimson Twins try to scapegoat the Saw-Viper for exceeding his authority. However, the Saw-Viper – putting his balls on the table – rebukes his superiors' accusations, arguing that, "I just wasted five times as many Joes in one day as your entire legions have accounted for in nine years!" Unable to fault the Saw-Viper's logic, Cobra Commander recommends the Saw-Viper with a big medal and a party, amusingly asking: "Tell me all about the shooting, Lad! Was it fun?"

Scarlett dithers about Storm Shadow's knife wound – an injury *she* inflicted on him (#107), making Stormy wryly comment that he'd probably have healed by now if the stabber "hadn't been so professional." Cool Breeze echoes our own sentiments about Storm Shadow's effectiveness, claiming he "just has to look at some fool sideways and they drop dead."

Normally as unshakable as the Rock of Gibraltar, Duke falls to pieces over leading his team to their deaths (#109). A mortally wounded Cool Breeze tries to stay brave, crying out, "I ain't cryin', am I, Stalker?" (Stalker's mournful reply: "No, kid. You aren't crying.") Most poignant of all, Storm Shadow says that killing the Saw-Viper has avenged the fallen *Joes:* "... for what it's worth."

LOVE AND WAR Faoud's troopers come across Lady Jaye sweating from close proximity to overheated vehicles, opening her jacket to air out her dripping bosom. Although we appreciated the gesture, the Middle Eastern Faoud tells her: "Cover yourself, woman! Have you no modesty?"

ASS-WHUPPINGS The Joe ninja team garrotes hordes of Night Creepers without firing a shot. Joes Cool Breeze and Battle Force 2000 earn final resting places in Arlington National Cemetery. Ambush and Recoil fall in a hail of bullets and presumably die also (although it's unclear). Dodger, Stalker and Dusty earn some payback by wiping out Cobra resistance in Abu Talib Square.

GOOFS Stalker rails on Cool Breeze, after the fact, for his flawed suggestion of jamming the Cobra radio frequencies. But three pages previous, Stalker himself validated the idea and ordered his team to comply.

COMIC TIE-INS Storm Shadow and Snake-Eyes supposedly do in the cocky Saw-Viper, although *G.I. Joe Battle Files* #2 suggests the fiend survived. The Saw-Viper reiterates that the Joes have hated Cobra Commander ever since General Flagg's death (#16).

Tying up loose ends in #114, Cobra Commander sends a Viper team to see if the prisoners trapped aboard the landlocked freighter on Cobra Island (#98) have kicked the oxygen habit. The Vipers enter the freighter and find a series of bodies, discovering that Cobra Commander II, Dr. Mindbender, Croc Master, Raptor, Voltar, Tyrone and Captain Minh ate a bad batch of C-Rations during their entombment and died in agony from botulism. However, the Vipers find a freshly dug escape tunnel, indicating that Zartan and Billy escaped (they resurface in *G.I. Joe* #116). Dr. Mindbender gets a second lease on life in #139. Firefly also supposedly appears among the deceased, although he crops up in #126.

The Joe ninja team's looking a bit ragged, considering Scarlett just emerged from a coma (#103), Storm Shadow's nursing a knife wound (#107) and Snake-Eyes spent a bit of time as a homicidal lunatic (#103-#107).

Metal-Head here serves Cobra, but his true allegiance lies with Destro (#116).

CHARACTER PROFILE: JOES

• *Admiral Keel-Haul:* Aboard the *USS Flagg*, his orders override Hawk's authority.

• *Cool Breeze:* He's overly arrogant, prone to questioning authority and making snap judgments. Still, he's brave, drawing heat from his teammates at one point by leading a Cobra helicopter into the desert (as it turned out, the helicopter was full of Joe ninjas – making Cool Breeze laugh to find his "self-sacrifice" wasn't necessary). He could've been a superb Joe, given more time and experience.

• *Dusty and Sneak Peek:* They were fast friends right up to Sneak Peek's death. Sneak Peek's grandmother was devastated when his uncle went MIA in Vietnam, leaving her grief-stricken over not knowing his final fate. Remembering this, Sneak Peek's mother asked that Dusty, if needed, bring her dead son home – so she wouldn't have to live with the uncertainty.

• *Ghostrider:* As usual, nobody can remember his name. Slip-Stream just calls him "Stealthy."

• *Snake-Eyes:* Leaping over various rooftops of the Emir's main palace, Snake-Eyes spies the Saw-Viper partying and boasting over his seven kills. Snake-Eyes longs to bury his sword to the hilt in the Saw-Viper's belly, but Scarlett and Storm Shadow insist on prioritizing their mission over revenge. Luckily for them, Snake-Eyes holds back – later gaining the opportunity to gut the Saw-Viper.

• *Scarlett:* Although technically not a ninja, her martial arts expertise (#2) allows her to work with the Joe ninja team.

ORGANIZATIONS *Cobra:* In a definite echo of Saddam Hussein's Gulf War strategies, Cobra rounds up the Benzheen Royal Family and foreign nationals as a human shield against a Joe attack.

PLACES TO GO *Benzheen:* Thanks to its oil revenues, Benzheen boasts the highest per capita income in the world. Accordingly, Benzheen army privates earn a solid $60,000 a year – in Benzheen, even the toilet scrubbers make good coin.

THE COMMAND DECISION Awesomely inspired by the Gulf War of the same year and – when combined with the proceeding two issues – standing firm as the meatiest, most engrossing Joe story from the series' waning years. Already delivering the fanfare of slaughtering Joes wholesale, Hama goes a step further and marbles these comics with maturity, humanism and camaraderie (notably Cool Breeze's demise and Dusty's promise to bring Sneak Peek's body home). Only issue #115 reads as an unnecessary epilogue – but the storyarc's momentum makes even that seem exciting.

G.I. Joe #116 to #118

Titles: *"Destro Must Die!" (#116), "Escape from Castle Destro!" (#117), "Deceptions and Diversions" (#118)*
Release Dates: *Sept. to Nov. 1991*
Art: *Rod Whigham*

BATTLE ROSTER *Joes:* Flint, Low-Light, Hawk, Snake-Eyes, Lady Jaye, Chuckles; *Cobra:* Cobra Commander, Tomax and Xamot; *Destro:* Destro, the Baroness, Metal-Head; *Other:* Billy, Zartan.

FIRST APPEARANCES *Joes:* Big Ben (SAS trooper, #116), Nunchuk (nunchaku ninja, #117), T'Jbang (ninja swordsman, #117), Dojo (silent weapons ninja, #117).

MISSION BRIEF ***Issue #116:*** On Cobra Island, Cobra Commander's Vipers report the results of a second sweep of the entombed freighter (#98), confirming that nearly all of Cobra Commander's rivals gruesomely died from botulism after consuming a spoiled batch of C-Rations. But to Cobra Commander's chagrin, a quick body count fails to locate Zartan or Cobra Commander's son Billy.

Lacking options, Zartan and Billy steal a Cobra aircraft and decide to appeal to Destro, as the most honorable of the ex-Cobra officers, for protection. But by sheer coincidence, Cobra Commander moves forward operations to fulfill a long-running grudge and eradicate Destro for good.

Responding to rumors of an imminent attack on Castle Destro, the Joes dispatch a covert team composed of Chuckles, Flint, Low-Light and Big Ben to monitor the situation and unofficially aid Destro. With the smell of battle palpable, Cobra Commander unleashes the full fury of Cobra helicopters and ground support against Destro's homestead. Destro's Iron Grenadiers hold their ground, but a crashing Cobra jet plows into a neighboring housing development – bursting a house open and spilling out tons of dirt.

Destro reels at the realization that Cobra Commander started moving against him months ago, using the housing development as cover to tunnel under Castle Destro and mine its foundation with explosives. Thankfully, Chuckles extradites Destro and the Baroness just as incendiaries turn Castle Destro into a rubble-filled crater.

Cobra troops surround Chuckles' trio, but Zartan and Billy helpfully steal a Cobra helicopter and take Destro and Chuckles aboard. The Baroness tries to follow, but gunfire singes the bespectacled terrorist and brings her down. Knowing that Destro will turn back and only get himself and the Baroness killed, Billy incapacitates Destro with a ninja nerve pinch. As Zartan and his oddball allies quickly escape, Cobra Commander captures the wounded Baroness as a bargaining chip.

Issue #117: Destro awakens four hours later, enraged over the Baroness' loss but slowly acknowledging the logistics of the situation. In short order, Cobra Commander issues a $20 million international contract on Destro's head. Across the globe, terrorist organizations and bounty hunters, including the Beirut Terrorist Front, the Night Creepers and the Corsican Brotherhood, greedily line up to slit Destro's jugular.

With the American government poised to cut a deal with Destro, Flint asks Snake-Eyes to galvanize the newly formed Joe Ninja Force and protect Destro from the inevitable onslaught of assassins. Accordingly, Snake-Eyes contacts Storm Shadow in New York and calls three secondary ninjas – Nunchuk, T'Jbang and Dojo – into active service.

Meanwhile, Destro's group flees to Marseilles, France, using Chuckles' underground contacts to keep one step ahead of a tidal wave of killers. Finally, Destro's group books passage on a ratty tramp steamer, gaining a respite en route to Destro's safehouse in Beirut.

Issue #118: In Beirut, Snake-Eyes, Storm Shadow and their Ninja Force track down Destro's cadre, who're still dodging Night Creeper snipers at every turn. Storm Shadow proposes evacuating in a C-130 transport piloted by Wild Bill, but Destro insists on visiting his safehouse. There, Destro reunites with Rashid, his top-level computer programmer, and concocts a scheme to end the price on his head.

Wild Bill flies Destro's motley crew to the Night Creeper Headquarters in Zurich, Switzerland. There, Destro's squadron catches the Creepers flat-footed, bursting into their command center. With a few keystrokes, Rashid uses the Night Creepers' advanced computer systems to access Cobra's Swiss bank accounts, activating dormant computer viruses that Destro seeded into the Zurich computers years ago – a safeguard against Cobra Commander's treachery.

Mission accomplished, Destro phones Cobra Commander, demanding he end the bounty on Destro's life, return the Baroness and make a sizeable restitution payment for Destro's trouble. Cobra Commander understandably scoffs at the proposition, but Destro off-handedly mentions that his binary viruses have just erased $10 million of Cobra's wealth at the Credit National Suisse. Cobra Commander double-checks Destro's claims, then trembles as Destro threatens to erase the entirety of Cobra's assets and Cobra Commander's personal accounts. Effectively stripped of his trousers, Cobra Commander agrees to Destro's terms.

MEMORABLE MOMENTS Cobra Commander turns anguished to learn that Billy and Zartan survived, because he's got to put aside his "prime, uninterrupted gloating time!" to deal with them. The Baroness bitches about the lowly stature of her Cobra guards, demanding that she at least warrants a Crimson Guardsman. In Beirut, Destro's group eludes the Night Creepers' infra-red sensors – by hiding in a frozen meat locker.

ASS-WHUPPINGS Cobra Commander annihilates Castle Destro. (In the sage words of Bugs Bunny: "Of course, you realize, this means war!") Failing to nab Destro, Cobra Commander contents himself by kicking the Baroness around instead. Chuckles, Zartan, Billy and Destro knock off overconfident Night Creepers. In a rousing finale to one such slaying, Destro eradicates a Night Creeper helicopter with two wrist-rockets.

GOOFS In *G.I. Joe* #114, a Cobra team discovered the skeletons of the men entombed aboard the landlocked freighter. But in #116, the dead men spontaneously regrow their flesh, appearing as bloated bodies. For that matter, why didn't Zartan and Billy croak from botulism as well?

In Beirut, Storm Shadow and Zartan – who've been mortal enemies for years now (last seen in #85 and #91) – hardly bat an eye upon seeing each other. Snake-Eyes arrives in Beirut about two weeks before anyone has the merest suspicion that Destro's heading there.

COMIC TIE-INS Cobra gained a fortune in stock certificates and oil futures by returning the captured Benzheen to its Emir (*G.I. Joe* #114). After the Joes expose its pact with the Emir in #115, Cobra withdraws from the oil emirate for good.

Destro and the Baroness retired from active service in *G.I. Joe* #97, although they briefly checked in with Darklon in #102. Their neighbor, Lord Malaprop (#88) sold off some of his acreage as his frozen haggis business took another turn for the worse. Metal-Head briefly worked for Cobra (#115) as a spy for Destro. Inspired by Mainframe to learn about computers (#58), a much older Rashid here works for Destro.

Zartan and Billy vanish from the narrative after this point, with Zartan entering Destro's employ in *G.I. Joe* #139. Billy travels around Europe for a time, arriving for dinner (and cookies) with Destro, the Baroness and Zartan in #145.

Slapped on the wrist for destroying Destro's homestead, Cobra Commander surrenders the Silent Castle (formerly seen in *G.I. Joe* #21) to Destro in #120.

With the deaths of the Hard Master (*G.I. Joe* #26), the Soft Master (#43) and the Blind Master (#91), Storm Shadow is now formally acknowledged as the last grand master of the Arashikage ninja clan.

It goes unseen, but Cobra Commander takes the late Dr. Venom's brainwave scanner and puts the captive Baroness' brain on spin cycle, programming her to betray Destro in *G.I. Joe* #120-#122.

CHARACTER PROFILE: JOES

• *Chuckles:* He sometimes uses latex masks as part of his undercover operations, disguising himself as Destro's groundskeeper MacHeath. He's got numerous contacts in the underground, including a French trader named Michel who routinely rats him out to the Beirut Terrorist Front (although Chuckles often uses this to his advantage).

• *Dogo:* Extremely talkative former New York-based pupil

of the Soft Master, gifted with a famous silent backslash.

• *Nunchuk:* Ex-student of the Blind Master, trained with a nunchaku fighting style called "The Screaming Whirlwind."

• *Snake-Eyes:* He sometimes contacts Storm Shadow under the code-name "Mr. Hebime" (roughly the Japanese word for "Snake-Eyes").

• *T'Jbang:* A former disciple of the mystic swordsmith Oni-hashi (#84), sworn to an oath of silence for unknown reasons.

CHARACTER PROFILE: OTHER

• *Zartan and Billy:* They're trained to see in the dark without night vision equipment.

• *Zartan:* He's a qualified pilot. His holographic equipment can, among other things, make him vanish in plain sight or turn into a werewolf.

ORGANIZATIONS *Destro:* The American government's willing to forge a deal with Destro, evidently deeming him a worthy ally, but the agreement's terms go unfulfilled (Destro's too busy running for his life). Most Joes regarded Destro as the only stable element in the Cobra command structure, respecting him as an honorable foe.

• *Joe Ninja Force:* They don't have a battle cry – mostly because their opponents are unconscious or dead before they could hear it.

• *Night Creepers:* They've been trying, among other things, to horn in on Destro's infra-red scanner business with their own products. Like most expert hackers, the Night Creepers thrive on coffee. They've been breaking into Cobra Commander's Swiss bank accounts mostly to check his revenues – and charge him appropriately. Destro figures this out, giving him some leverage over the Night Creepers.

PLACES TO GO Destro's Beirut Hideout: Protected by a laser grid, although shouting the password "frozen haggis" deactivates the system.

STUFF YOU NEED Arashikage Death Touch: Presumably some sort of lethal pinch, although we never see it in action – Billy uses a modified "death touch" technique to render Destro unconscious. A specific counter-touch lets you instantly re-awaken foes rendered senseless in such a fashion, presuming they're strong and healthy.

• *Dr. Venom's brainwave scanner:* A useful little gadget, but beware that a prolonged session might mush your subject's cranium.

HOT WHEELS Joe C-130 transports: The Joes' main class of transport aircraft houses state-of-the-art avionics, radar-defeating "blackball" paint, low-sound signature propellers and infra-red baffles – all in a fairly antiquated frame.

THE COMMAND DECISION Saturated with the thrill of the hunt, issues #116-#118 sees Cobra Commander rise to the occasion and gloriously smack Destro about the place with a tire iron. That said, the Joe Ninja Force members display about as much characterization as a mollusk, serving no purpose other than to overrun the place with ninjas! Ninjas! Hordes of ninjas! Fortunately, the Destro plotline makes up for the Ninja Force's failings, leaving this an above-average three-parter that – if not overly remarkable – deserves a read-through.

G.I. Joe #119

Title: *"Double"*
Release Date: *Dec. 1991*
Writer/Art: *Herb Trimpe*

BATTLE ROSTER *Joes:* Scarlett, Snake-Eyes, Storm Shadow, Hawk.

MISSION BRIEF Cobra Commander spontaneously embarks on yet another cracked master scheme to obtain world domination, directing Cobra's manufacturing plants to pump out high-tech robots that resemble world leaders, intending to put the doppelgangers into power as Cobra thralls. Everything goes smoothly until a Cobra transport team – clearly not even qualified to work at McDonald's – stupidly leaves a crate containing a robotic replica of President Bush Sr. behind at a Long Island airport. Finding the Bush robot more than a little suspicious, Hawk back-tracks Cobra's robotics facility to the Cobra Consulate.

Fearing civilian casualties from an all-out assault, Hawk sends Storm Shadow, Snake-Eyes and Storm Shadow to pin-point the exact location of the robotics factories. Storm Shadow's trio penetrates the Consulate's security, battling through various defenses and unexpectedly grappling with a robotic duplicate of Snake-Eyes. Storm Shadow momentarily loses track of the brawling Snake-Eyes – but uses the genuine article's love for Scarlett to identify the original and blow away the doppelganger. After tagging the robotics plant with a homing device, Storm Shadow's trio hurriedly evacuates, allowing Wild Bill to peg the facility with a smart missile and end Cobra's madcap designs.

LOVE AND WAR Mission accomplished, Snake-Eyes and Scarlett indulge in some celebratory nookie in the back of a C-130 transport.

ASS-WHUPPINGS Storm Shadow unloads a full clip into Snake-Eyes' robotic duplicate. Afterward, Storm Shadow's trio "murders" the Consulate command crew – only to discover they're also robots. The Joes level a Cobra storage facility on an island off Brazil named Atol Das Rocas.

GOOFS/COMIC TIE-INS It's possibly an error, but Snake-Eyes, along with everyone else, cries out "When?" during a briefing with Hawk. It's either an outright mistake or further proof that Snake-Eyes can croak out individual words (*G.I. Joe* #102), even if entire sentences still elude him.

STUFF YOU NEED ECHO (Enhanced Copy Human Original) robots: More sophisticated than Cobra's BATs, crafted to impersonate famous personalities such as then-Russian Premier Mikhail Gorbachev, Iraqi dictator Saddam Hussein, then-American Chief of Staff Colin Powell and famed wrestling manager Don King. However, the fact that we never see the ECHOs in action – save for a Snake-Eyes duplicate who naturally doesn't talk – means we've no proof if the damn things actually work.

THE COMMAND DECISION Utter drivel – an issue clearly crafted as a fill-in for the sole purpose of guarding against blown deadlines. We could almost forgive this comic's run-of-the-mill plot – except for its excruciating dialogue (such as Scarlett's "Yipes! This is weird!", and Cobra Commander's "They fight like demons!" and Storm Shadow's "Somebody's peeking!"), which feels like nails scraping a chalkboard.

G.I. Joe #120 to #122

Titles: *"Return to the Silent Castle" (#120), "Slice and Dice and Everything Nice" (#121), "Transformer!" (#122)*
Release Dates: *Jan. to Mar. 1992*
Art: *Andrew Wildman*

BATTLE ROSTER *Joes:* Snake-Eyes, Storm Shadow, Hawk, Flint, Lady Jaye, Nunchuk, T'Jbang, Dojo, Roadblock, Rock 'n Roll, Big Ben, Dusty, Stalker; Cobras: Cobra Commander; *Destro:* Destro, the Baroness; *Other:* the red ninjas.

FIRST APPEARANCES *Other:* Slice (ninja swordsman, #120), Dice (bo staff ninja, #120).

MISSION BRIEF ***Issue #120-#121:*** Destro meets with Cobra Commander on a Cobra-owned oil tanker, formalizing the commander's reparations for trying to assassinate Destro (#116-#118). Under threat of Destro's computer virus, Cobra Commander apologizes for Castle Destro's destruction by signing over ownership of "the Silent Castle" – a disused Cobra citadel in Trans-Carpathia. Cobra Commander also surrenders the Baroness, but not before re-programming her, via the Cobra brainwave scanner, to betray Destro upon hearing a specific ultra-sonic signal.

Anticipating the Baroness' mental conditioning, Destro quietly collaborates with his G.I. Joe allies. In short order, Destro and the Baroness airdrop into the Silent Castle – the Cobra stronghold where Snake-Eyes rescued Scarlett in issue #21 – to examine its potential as a new headquarters. Meanwhile, Hawk, the Joe Ninja Force and various other Joes take up position near the castle, preparing to haul Destro's ass from the fire as needed.

Unknown to everyone, a pack of red ninjas – renegade members of Storm Shadow's Arashikage clan – long ago usurped the abandoned castle as a hideout. Led by a pair of ninja masters named Slice and Dice, the red ninjas brace for conflict against the newcomers. But at that moment, a Cobra Condor jet, racing past the castle per Cobra Commander's instructions, transmits the ultra-sonic transmission that activates the Baroness' brainwashing.

The Baroness tries to club Destro with a wrench, intending to lug his unconscious carcass into a brainwave scanner concealed in the Silent Castle's basement. Fortunately, Destro blocks the Baroness' blow – only to turn as a tidal wave of red ninjas attack.

Issue #121-#122: When Destro fails to give a pre-arranged signal, Hawk grows concerned about his ally and brings forward his Joe Brawler and Battle-Wagon assault vehicles. But to further complicating matters, Cobra Commander arrives with an assault team, planning to seize the Silent Castle after the Baroness incapacitates Destro. Hawk's brigade falls on the Cobras, battling Toxo-Vipers, Heat-Vipers – indeed, every flavor of Viper imaginable – and slowing their advance.

Inside the Silent Castle, Destro and the Baroness elude the red ninjas and reach the Silent Castle's control chamber. Rather than harm his duplicitous brainwashed lover, Destro unexpectedly crawls into the Silent Castle's brainwave scanner. The Baroness engages the device, but as Destro predicted, the Baroness' love for him overcomes Cobra Commander's programming. Snapping her mental shackles, the Baroness frees Destro from the machine.

As the Joe Ninja Force madly dashes about, variously laying waste to the red ninjas and the Cobra troopers, Destro and the Baroness reach a series of giant gears in the Silent Castle. Having originally served as the castle's architect, Destro throws a secret lever and puts the castle's inner clockworks into motion. With a giant rumble, the Silent Castle transforms itself into a replica of Castle Destro – the seat of Destro's power – flattening a number of the red ninjas in the process.

Cobra Commander abandons his goals of maiming Destro and – mostly for the hell of it – tosses the remainder of his forces at the Joes. Agonized at abandoning the Joe Ninja Force, Hawk orders his team to flee into a nearby forest. As Destro and the Baroness enjoy an eerie sense of quiet in the combatants' absence, Slice and Dice scour the countryside for red ninja survivors.

LOVE AND WAR Flint suggests that Destro might let his "wild passion" for the Baroness run rampant and forget to signal his Joe allies. But Lady Jaye counter-suggests: "Destro's not like you, Flint. He thinks of other things from time to time."

Destro recalls telling the Baroness how the permanence of Castle Destro symbolized his love for her. Castle Destro's destruction (#116) might seem to shatter this analogy, so Destro here "rebuilds" his homestead.

ASS-WHUPPINGS The Baroness sums up her feelings as Cobra Commander's prisoner – by kicking him in the happy sacks. Destro and the Baroness shoot, stab and blow up red ninjas. The Silent Castle's sudden re-configuration into Castle Destro makes several red ninjas very flat.

GOOFS Destro previously claimed (*G.I. Joe* #31) that he owned the Silent Castle, but this storyarc conclusively establishes that it belonged to Cobra Commander.

Baroness comes upon Destro's chess set – depicting her as his queen – and seems startled to realize Destro's feelings for her stretched back that far (except that, err... Destro and the Baroness were making out several issues before the chess set made an appearance).

TV TIE-INS Trans-Carpathia serves as the setting for the spook-filled "The Phantom Brigade."

COMIC TIE-INS "The Silent Castle" first appeared in *G.I. Joe* #21, although its name, clearly symbolic of the "silent" nature of that issue, isn't used until this story. Cobra Commander abandoned the castle after Snake-Eyes rescued Scarlett from its dungeons (also #21), disgusted because it served as a constant reminder of his vulnerability.

Cobra Commander relinquishes control of the Silent Castle as reparation for turning Castle Destro into itty-bitty pebbles (*G.I. Joe* #116). The red ninjas took up residence there sometime after their last battle with Snake-Eyes (#91). The Joe Ninja Force flees from the Silent Castle here, running afoul of the red ninjas and their leader in #124 and #126. Meanwhile, Hawk's Joes make their way into Borovia (last seen in #103-#107) in #128-#129.

Destro once hired a Brooklyn sculptor – the same man who carves the miniatures used by credit card companies for their holograms – to forge Destro's prized chess set (first seen in *G.I. Joe* #21). Cobra Commander, formerly oblivious to the Night Creepers' penetration of his computer files (#118), now knows about their offense.

Slice and Dice mostly operate as freelance ninjas, entering Cobra's employ in *G.I. Joe* #136. The Silent Castle's "transformation" ability later draws attention from the evil Decepticon leader Megatron of *Transformers* fame (*G.I. Joe* #138).

Slice knows a formidable ninja move called the "Scorpion Cut" (possibly a one-man derivation of the larger "Scorpion" strategy, seen in #133-#134).

PLACES TO GO The Silent Castle: Easily defensible because it's damnably hard to reach, set in a mountain range with an abominable lack of ground access. A single, winding gravel road leads to the castle – and even that's mined and fitted with retractable tank traps. The castle sports state-of-the-art radar and infrared detector systems, although it's almost unnecessary, since strong winds around the castle foil most airborne assaults. Moreover, the castle doesn't contain landing pads for helicopters or VTOL aircraft, so your best bet's to reach it using one-man helicopter harnesses. Destro, primarily a military engineer, designed the Silent Castle with a "Spartan elegance."

• *Trans-Carpathia:* A traditional stomping ground for vampires and werewolves.

STUFF YOU NEED Destro's Facemask: Contains an integral combat computer and sensors that sweep for explosives.

THE COMMAND DECISION An unmistakable sign of *G.I. Joe* having overstayed its welcome, "Return to the Silent Castle" and its ilk solely exists to put its characters on the table, then make them pointlessly dance about like screeching gibbons with high-velocity rifles. The red ninjas only serve to get threshed like wheat – oh, and let's not even talk about the transforming castle at story's end. A massive disappointment.

G.I. Joe #123 to #126

Titles: *"Shots in the Dark!" (#123), "Triptych!" (#124), "Diptych!" (#125), "Firefly!" (#126)*
Release Dates: *April to July 1992*
Art: *Andrew Wildman*

BATTLE ROSTER Cobras: Cobra Commander; Firefly: Firefly.

FIRST APPEARANCES [NOTE: In keeping with the ongoing Hasbro toy line, several Joes gain new specialties throughout *G.I. Joe* #123-#125. These aren't "first appearances" as such, but we're listing their new positions anyway.] *Joes:* Shockwave (as SWAT specialist), Cutter (as sea operations specialist), Mutt and Junkyard (as K9 officer and attack dog), Bullet-Proof (DEF leader, #124), Flint (as Eco-Warrior commander), Ozone (ozone replentisher trooper, #123), Clean-Sweep (anti-tox trooper, #123); *Cobra:* Cesspool (chief environmental operative, #123); *Other:* Headman (drug kingpin, #124) and the Headhunters (Headman's narcotics guard, #124).

MISSION BRIEF ***Issue #123:*** Hawk's Joes flee from the Silent Castle, sharpshooting a group of Cobra pursuers and driving onward. Soon after, Duke arrives in a C-130 transport, re-assigning Flint to command a Joe toxic enforcement team named "the Eco-Warriors." While Flint takes off with his new crew – a pair of environmental experts named Clean-Sweep and Ozone – Hawk's party stays to search for the Joe Ninja Force.

Meanwhile, Cobra Commander radios a Cobra helicopter for pick-up, growing miffed to receive unsavory reports from various Cobra strongholds. On Cobra Island, Zarana warns that a chemical weapons expert named Cesspool, hired as an independent contractor, has overzealously covered the isle with his toxic sludge refinement facilities.

Cobra Commander also learns that the Headman, a drug kingpin, has started trafficking massive amounts of narcotics through Broca Beach, banking on the fact that Cobra won't risk exposure by summoning federal drug agents. At Broca Beach, Fred Smith LXV angrily finds his son Sean wasted on drugs, grabbing his Crimson Guard assault rifle and rushing to confront the Headman. Unfortunately, the Headman's guards, creatively named "the Headhunters," waste Fred LXV in the bat of an eye – signaling that the Headman won't surrender Broca Beach peacefully.

Issue #124-#125: Foreswearing allegiance to Cobra, Fred Smith LXV's widow tips off the newly founded G.I. Joe Drug Elimination Force (DEF) to the Headman's operations. Still oblivious to Cobra's presence in Broca Beach, the DEF team storms the Headman's hideout. Although Mrs. Fred dies in the crossfire, the Joes rally to drive the Headman's band away.

Meanwhile, Flint takes the Eco-Warriors to reconnoiter an off-shore Cobra toxo-lab that's built to manufacture weapons-grade Plasmatox sludge. The Eco-Warriors box in Cesspool and his Sludge-Vipers, but a Plasmatox tank ruptures in the process. Cesspool's troops capture Flint and Clean-Sweep in the resultant confusion, but Ozone escapes, threatening to return with the Joes' "secret weapon."

Cesspool froths at the mouth, intending to dunk his captives in a Plasmatox vat, but Ozone returns with Mr. Jones from the Attorney General's Office. Mr. Jones blisters Cesspool with a bureaucracy attack, hitting the sludge-loving fiend with a tsunami of injunctions and environmental violations. Reeling from the financial blow, Cesspool releases his prisoners.

Finally, back in Trans-Carpathia, Slice and Dice regroup the surviving red ninjas and make for a secondary base in a nearby forest. The Joe Ninja Force follows, but an inevitable ninja smackdown oddly ends with the red ninja master stepping forward and unmasking himself…

Issue #126: The assembled ninja combatants freeze in their tracks, staggered to identify the red ninja leader as the

MISCELLANEOUS STUFF!

FIREFLY'S HISTORY

During the 1940s, Firefly's father – a plantation owner and anti-Japanese guerrilla in French Indochina – opted to spare a young Japanese officer. The Viet Minh murdered Papa Firefly for showing too much mercy, but the officer's father – a Koga ninja clan Grand Master – benevolently adopted young Firefly into his family. Training with the Koga clan, Firefly became the first non-Japanese person to master a ninja skill.

In time, Firefly apprenticed to the mystic swordsmith Onihashi (first mentioned in *G.I. Joe #84*). Achieving even greater ninja prowess, Firefly gained access to the Arashikage household as "the Faceless Master," a Koga sensei whose face, on the rare occasions that he unmasked, appeared as a blur (*see "Unmasking the Faceless Master" sidebar*). "The Faceless Master" formally held a rank equal to Storm Shadow and Snake-Eyes, learning knowledge of the secret Arashikage forms and earning a family wrist tattoo.

Some time later, Cobra Commander contracted the money-grubbing Firefly to rub out Snake-Eyes (*see G.I. Joe #84*), likely pegging Firefly (a high-ranked outsider in a ninja household) as someone open to greed. Firefly brashly spent Cobra Commander's loot, then came to the uneasy realization – during an Arashikage training session – that he couldn't defeat Snake-Eyes if Snakes lost both his arms in a chainsaw accident.

Indulging in sweaty panic, Firefly convinced Cobra Commander to hire an outside contractor – the pool hall rat known as Zartan – and equipped Zartan with sound-amplification equipment to mimic Storm Shadow's famed "Ear That Sees" talent. Zartan murdered the Hard Master by mistake (*see G.I. Joe #26*), fleeing aboard a Cobra helicopter piloted by Firefly. Soon after, Firefly took up gainful employment as a saboteur, abdicating his position as the Faceless Master and leaving the Arashikages to mistakenly pin Storm Shadow for the Hard Master's death.

Cobra saboteur Firefly. Enraged at the thought of Firefly – who lacks any ninja credentials – leading the red ninjas, Slice and Dice rush their would-be warlord. However, Firefly displays a number of fighting techniques unique to Storm Shadow's Arashikage family clan, batting his opponents aside.

Storm Shadow cagily holds his ninjas at bay, curious to know how Firefly escaped the landlocked Cobra freighter (#98). Firefly explains that while Zartan's group started digging their way out by hand, Firefly re-programmed a stack of slightly damaged BATs (#77) to dig an escape route. Firefly then put his uniform on Serpentor's frosty corpse, mauling Serpy's face to suggest that "Firefly" met an untimely demise. As a final act, Firefly raided the freighter's computer banks, learning of the defunct Silent Castle and making it his base of operations.

Firefly explains his history (*see Sidebar*) up to the present day, bragging how he's upgraded his arsenal to accentuate traditional ninja skills with cutting edge laser and toxin technology. Green at the gills thanks to Firefly's ramblings, the assembled ninjas brace themselves to rush their common foe. Unfortunately, Firefly's re-programmed BATs appear, unleashing a tremendous gas attack. The ninjas fall unconscious, leaving Firefly to enthrall his captives via a stolen Cobra brainwave scanner.

MISCELLANEOUS STUFF!

UNMASKING THE FACELESS MASTER

G.I. Joe #62 established that sword-maker Onihashi's first assistant (later called "the Faceless Master," #126) kept his true appearance secret by making his face look like a blur. Storm Shadow theorized that the Faceless Master used a hypnotic effect on anyone looking at his mug, thereby canceling the impulses between his victim's optic nerves and cerebral cortex.

The talent obviously wouldn't fool photographs, although Firefly suggests that he avoided the problem, during any given photo session, by simply "moving his head."

Unfortunately, this entire theory, as Peter Sellers once put it in *Murder By Death*, suffers from a simple problem: "Is stupid... is most stupid theory we ever heard." Never mind that many of Firefly's acquaintances were ninja masters and immune to such instantaneous brainwashing. But frankly, we're hard pressed for a better explanation, so do the best you can.

MEMORABLE MOMENTS Hawk memorably explains why the Joes aren't celebrating their victory over a Cobra tank division: "When a soldier wins, somebody gets killed or something gets destroyed. It's not something you can take a lot of satisfaction in – and stay sane – for too long."

Likely reflecting writer Larry Hama's opinion (and ours) regarding the Eco-Warriors, Flint nearly pukes to see the "garish hue" of the Eco-Warriors' uniforms. A drenched but still glib Cobra Commander, priming himself for bad news, lets his lackeys wring out his mask before they "assail him with the depressing tidbits."

Finally, Fred Smith Jr. – a hopeless junkie who's just witnessed the Headhunters gun down his mother and father – frets more about continuing his drug habit than crying for his parents. Indeed, young Freddie pawns his mother's assault rifle to continue his habit – a sad commentary in the war against drugs.

ASS-WHUPPINGS The Headhunters pump Fred Smith LXV and his rifle-toting wife full of lead. Flint drops a Toxo-Viper into a Plasmatox vat, stripping his flesh more effectively than a dose of E Coli. Firefly knocks out a couple of Dice's teeth. A bundle of Cobra Paralyzer tanks shatter while following the Joes down a steep slope.

GOOFS Cesspool's construction workers apparently possess inhuman speed, erecting sludge plants on Cobra Island so fast that Cobra Commander doesn't notice the construction until it's too late. A couple of DEF Joes notice a proliferation of Cobra-made rifles in Broca Beach, but moronically never take the hint that it's a Cobra base of operations.

Balancing the stupidity scales, Cesspool's crew lets the captive Flint and Clean-Sweep keep their radio head-sets, allowing the Joes to communicate with the at-liberty Ozone. In issue #124, Slice and Snake-Eyes fight each other as "champions" for their respective parties – without setting any terms for victory/loss.

Finally and most important, why the bloody hell would Firefly spontaneously unmask and spill his guts, knowing it'll piss everyone off?

COMIC TIE-INS Issue #126 reveals that Firefly, as the red ninja leader, previously partnered with Zartan (*G.I. Joe* #85) and fought Storm Shadow to a draw (#91). Firefly was entombed aboard the landlocked freighter on Cobra Island (#98), although #126 explains that Firefly tunneled to freedom using partly-damaged BATs (stacked like cordwood in the disused freighters after the Cobra Civil War in *G.I. Joe* #77). Firefly paused to take Serpentor's defrosted body (stowed aboard the freighter in *G.I. Joe* #77, briefly moved to Broca Beach in #90, then taken back to the freighter at an unspecified point) and maul its face, covering it with

Firefly's gray jammies to fake his death.

As an associate of the Arashikage household, Firefly called himself "the Faceless Master" (first mentioned in #62, *see Sidebar*), learning secret ninja techniques including the Hard Master's "Cloak of the Chameleon" (#26).

The Arashikage hexagram tattoo (#21) contains a secret – and undisclosed – meaning.

Cobra Commander torpedoes the Headman's drug trade in *G.I. Joe* #127.

CHARACTER PROFILE: JOES

• *Bullet-Proof:* So named because he wears a bullet-proof vest. (*Author's Note:* Lucky he didn't wear a diamond-studded jock strap.)

• *Flint:* His serial number's Wo-2, 307-6290-DF07.

• *Ozone:* He carries an ozone emitter. (*That's* certainly useful in battle – "Don't move, or I'll pump you full of ozone!")

CHARACTER PROFILE: COBRA

• *Cesspool:* Formerly CEO of a major corporation, Cesspool embarked on a lucrative career as a ruthless, morally bankrupt industrialist. But eventually, a veritable army of federal marshals, attorney general's office inspectors, IRS agents and EPS inspectors descended on him. Cesspool tried to dump some incriminating evidence – namely few tons of toxic waste – but a weakened pipeline ruptured, dousing him with sludge. Much like Batman's nemesis, "the Joker," the accident left Cesspool extremely intelligent – and mad.

Cesspool habitually refines concentrated toxic waste, selling the resultant weapons-grade Plasmatox to weapons traffickers. He's outsmarted seven federal investigating committees so far, but bureaucracy still makes Cesspool piddle in fear. His gun shoots weapons-grade sludge, capable of dissolving a Cobra Hammerhead attack vehicle.

• *Sludge Viper:* Cesspool's troopers, who carry Plasmatox slime-firing weapons.

CHARACTER PROFILE: FIREFLY

Firefly: In issue #126, Firefly "integrates" ninja methodology with new technologies. Frankly, we've little idea what the hell that means, but in layman's terms, Firefly operates as a ninja master with extreme knowledge of electronic and biotoxic weaponry. Or to put it another way, he's a technologically savvy martial arts expert *a la* the Night Creepers.

ORGANIZATIONS *The Arashikage Clan:* Among other things, the Arashikage clan knew answers to various Zen koan (supposedly impossible riddles).

• *G.I. Joe:* A Navstar/GPS satellite system helps the Joes fix their ground position. A hand-held laser enables them to target the enemy in misty or murky conditions.

• *Joe Drug Enforcement Force:* Presumably all wear bullet-proof vests.

• *Joe Eco-Warriors:* The Eco-Warriors typically fight "polluters, rain forest defilers and wasters of natural resources." They're equipped with toxic waste-neutralizing compounds. Their suits provide shielding against such corrosives, although they sometimes forget to insulate their battle copters.

• *Joe Ninja Force:* Has never heard of Firefly.

THE COMMAND DECISION A storyarc so ungodly, we wanted to wear sackcloth and ashes, *G.I. Joe* #123-#125 teleports you into a world of pain. One senses that even writer Larry Hama found the Hasbro-created Drug Enforcement Force and Eco-Warriors concepts tough to swallow, although his efforts split the action – for the purpose of casting the characters aside – as fast as possible – only triggers a maelstrom of confusion.

The truly poisonous seed of the bunch, the Firefly retcon in #126 turns Snake-Eyes' laudable origin story into a veritable train wreck. It's a mystery where the reader barely understands the questions at times, let alone the answers, and most of it fails to make a lick of sense. Overall, a bad idea that does the series few favors.

G.I. Joe #127 to #129

Titles: *"Playing with the Big Boys!" (#127), "Winds of Change!" (#128), "Standoff" (#129)*
Release Dates: *Aug. to Oct. 1992*
Art: *Andrew Wildman*

BATTLE ROSTER *Joes:* Joseph Colton, Duke, Stalker, Snake-Eyes, Storm Shadow, Lady Jaye, Hawk, Bullet-Proof, Cutter, Mutt and Junkyard, Shockwave, Roadblock; *Cobra:* Zarana, Cobra Commander, Road Pig, Cesspool; Firefly: Firefly; *Other:* the Headman, the White Clown, Magda.

MISSION BRIEF ***Issue #127:*** Outraged at the amount of drugs flowing through Broca Beach – but unable to compromise Cobra's operations there – Cobra Commander flounders for a way to squelch the Headman's narcotics business. But in short order, the commander learns about the "Star Wars" defense system (SDI) secretly housed in New York City's Chrysler Building, deeming it his chance to wipe out the Headman.

As a ruse, Cobra Commander fortifies a base in the New Jersey marshlands and "clumsily" taps into the "Star Wars" system's communications net. Soon after, SDI security chief Joseph Colton – the original G.I. Joe – summons Duke and Stalker to plug the leak. The three men rip through the Cobra base in a Tomahawk helicopter, but amid the chaos, Cobra Commander and two Techno-Vipers hang-glide onto a vulnerable point in the Chrysler Building's defenses.

As the Headman approaches Broca Beach via cargo liner with a record haul of narcotics, Cobra Commander's Techno-Viper team briefly usurps the SDI system's circuitry – pinpointing the drug lord's ship and obliterating it with a satellite-bounced particle burst. After the Joes haul the Headman and his lieutenants out of the Hudson River, they rush like mad back to the SDI system. But in a sweet turnabout, Cobra Commander's group strips to their civilian clothes and discreetly exits the building – leaving the Joes unaware of Cobra's involvement in Broca Beach.

Issue #128-#129: In Trans-Carpathia, Hawk's group abandons hope of locating the missing Joe Ninja Force and makes their way to the Borovian capital of Krogdnsz. Unfortunately, Hawk's team arrives in Borovia just as renewed civil conflict unseats President Magda's pro-US government.

While most of Hawk's team hides out in an abandoned rock quarry, Hawk and Lady Jaye attempt to procure train tickets to Austria. Unfortunately, lower Borovian snipers mistake the Joes for state security goons, grievously wounding Hawk with a sniper shot. Lady Jaye rescues Magda and Snake-Eyes' sometime-ally the White Clown from certain execution, but continued violence forces Lady Jaye's crew to scoop up Hawk and dodge trigger-happy lunatics at every turn.

Hawk partially recovers, informing Magda that U.S. intelligence satellites spotted a cache of gold bouillon hidden in the Krogdnsz soccer stadium – a treasure trove stolen from the state treasury by Borovia's former Communist regime. Lady Jaye's team reaches the stadium and recovers the bouillon, giving Magda the financial clout to stabilize Borovia and grant Hawk's team safe passage out of the country.

Meanwhile, in Trans-Carpathia, Firefly makes good on his threat to create a zombified ninja task force, treating his Joe and red ninja captives (#126) to repeated doses of the Cobra brainwave scanner. Most of the ninjas capitulate to the scanner's effects, but Snake-Eyes and Storm Shadow show exceptional resistance. Regrettably, multiple zaps from the brainwave scanner chip away at the two ninja's defenses – ultimately turning them into Firefly's slaves.

Firefly launders Storm Shadow's noggin for more information, twitching with glee when the brainwave scanner dredges a detailed map of the Pit III. Crafting yet another master scheme, Firefly contacts Cobra Commander and travels alone to Cobra Island in a stolen Trans-Carpathian airliner, asking $2.5 million for the Pit III's location. When Cobra Commander agrees, Firefly surrenders his data – but true to form, the evil one promptly tosses Firefly back into Cobra Island's extinct volcano, the site of his former entombment (#98).

Cobra Commander immediately mobilizes his armies and departs for Utah, leaving a skeleton crew to run Cobra Island. But soon after, Storm Shadow, Snake-Eyes and Firefly's other enthralled ninjas awaken from self-induced comas aboard the Trans-Carpathian jet, pre-programmed to rescue Firefly from Cobra Commander's treachery.

MEMORABLE MOMENTS Spoofing Hasbro's Joe action figure line, Bullet-Proof mentions that the Joes' battle-copters are easy to assemble if you, "... don't read the instructions and skip the decals." In a delicious little twist, Stalker, Duke and Colton walk right past a civilian-garbed Cobra Commander, who denies their inquiries about seeing armed men in masks (Cobra Commander: "Most assuredly not!"). Firefly suggests that the schizophrenic Road Pig "could be his own team on Family Feud."

LOVE AND WAR Err... the title to issue #127.

ASS-WHUPPINGS Cobra Commander detonates the Headman's drug-filled ocean liner, but the druggie guru and his troopers survive. Hawk takes a bullet to the chest in #128 but lives with minimal damage. Lady Jaye guns down some Borovian security enforcers.

GOOFS In the Krogdnsz soccer stadium, Magda, Lady Jaye and the White Clown dig an absurdly large hole – with their bare hands – to uncover the hidden gold bullion reserves.

COMIC TIE-INS Joseph Colton, the original G.I. Joe, originally appeared in the 25th anniversary issue (*G.I. Joe* #86). The White House summons him for an ultra-important conference in #152. Magda became president of Borovia in *G.I. Joe* #107. She and the White Clown return for a final outing in #145. The drug-trafficking Headman usurped Broca Beach as his distribution hub in #124-#125.

Firefly enthralls Snake-Eyes, Storm Shadow, Slice, Dice, the Joe Ninja Force and the red ninjas here, having nabbed 'em all in #126. Storm Shadow previously used "The Sleeping Phoenix" – a ninja technique designed to slow heartbeat and respiration – in #47.

The awakened ninjas, as promised, rescue Firefly and run amok on Cobra Island like a bunch of ninja frat boys in *G.I. Joe* #130-#131, when Firefly's data prompts Cobra Commander to assault the Pit III. Cobra Commander's remained willfully blind about the Pit III's location, crazily believing a tidal wave of evidence citing Utah as the Pit III's home state (*G.I. Joe* #72, #83 and #100) was a gigantic red herring designed to throw him off the trail.

Cobra retains unprofitable interests in Sierra Gordo (last seen in *G.I. Joe* #92), Frusenland (#68), Borovia (here) and Trucial Abysmia (#108-#115).

CHARACTER PROFILE: JOES *Spirit:* Often volunteers for guard duty in the Quonset hut above the Pit III for meditation purposes.

CHARACTER PROFILE: COBRA

Cobra Commander: He lusts after increased weapons sales in Asia, Siberia and Russia. Cobra Commander still fears Destro despite the arms baron's semi-retirement.

ORGANIZATIONS *Lower Borovian Separatist Front:* They're supposedly pro-democracy. But considering grudges and guns make for a dangerous mix in Borovia, you're better off not trusting anyone.

• *Ninjas:* They're damnably hard to hypnotize, capable of segmenting off parts of their brains to shield them from mental corruption. It's rumored that ninja masters (such as Snake-Eyes and Storm Shadow) can segment their minds even further, effectively copying large parts of their minds like computer back-ups.

PLACES TO GO Borovia: Contains oil fields.

• *Trans-Carpathia:* Contains bauxite mines.

THE COMMAND DECISION Presuming you've even half-heartedly followed the series up to this point, issues #127-#129 read like a tired rehash of what's come before – replicating #86 (Colton's return) and previous Borovian excursions with preciously little charm.

G.I. Joe #130 to #131

Titles: *"Point and Counterpoint!" (#130), "Last Stand" (#131)*
Release Dates: *Nov. to Dec. 1992*
Art: *Andrew Wildman*

BATTLE ROSTER *Joes:* Spirit, Duke, Scarlett, Airtight, Barbecue, Snake-Eyes, Storm Shadow, Dogo, T'Jbang, Nunchuk, Trip-Wire; *Cobra:* Cobra Commander, Zarana, Cesspool; Firefly: Firefly, Slice, Dice.

FIRST APPEARANCES *Joes:* Heavy Duty (heavy ordnance specialist, #131).

MISSION BRIEF Using a prototype anti-radar system, Cobra Commander's battalions elude detection by the U.S. defense grid and pound on the Pit III's doorstep. The Joes fend off attacks from a myriad of Viper squadrons and BATs, enduring a hellish amount of close-quarters combat. Improvising at a critical juncture, Duke catches Cobra Commander napping and wipes out his ground support. But as the Joes gain momentum, Cobra Commander gathers his troops aboard a Cobra helicopter squadron and withdraws.

On Cobra Island, Storm Shadow's ninja brigade frees Firefly from the dormant volcano – affording Firefly a pre-planned opportunity to capture the isle in Cobra Commander's absence. Zarana and Cesspool rally a squadron of Paralyzer and HISS tanks to attack the intruders, but the brainwashed ninjas kill the tank crews and make for the island's main citadel.

With the air reeking of slaughter, Snake-Eyes marshals his inner defenses and snaps Firefly's conditioning against all odds. Snakey then leaps in front of his allies and molds his fingers into the Arashikage Mind-Set (#103-#108), freeing the Joe Ninja Force from Firefly's mental shackles. Abandoning Firefly's mad schemes, the Joe Ninjas steal the parked Trans-Carpathian airliner and employ their wayward piloting skills to haphazardly return to America.

Firefly's remaining forces, including Slice and Dice, overrun the Cobra citadel, capturing Zarana and Cesspool. Firefly gloats as Cobra Commander returns home, offering to return Cobra Island for a sizeable ransom. But unexpectedly, Cobra Commander reveals that the raid on the Pit III was solely intended to document the efficiency of Cobra's new anti-radar system. Anticipating that sales of the anti-radar system to America's enemies will make Cobra ludicrously wealthy, Cobra Commander shockingly lets Firefly keep Cobra Island and his captives. As Cobra Commander's troops depart, Firefly – who never intended to *keep* Cobra Island – flounders for a response.

MEMORABLE MOMENTS Firefly performs an elegant little soliloquy from Hamlet, using Dr. Mindbender's skull as a prop. The mad Cobra Commander returns home from raiding the Pit III and, upon seeing the smoldering damage and mayhem on Cobra Island, remarks: "That's still no excuse to cancel [my victory] band."

ASS-WHUPPINGS Spirit shoots a bunch of Vipers, takes cover and dismembers them with a blanket-covered grenade. Airtight and Barbecue flame a bunch of Laser-Vipers. A group of BATs fling one of their cut-in-half comrades over the Joe battle lines – allowing the BAT's upper half to graze Outback and Torpedo with bullets. Trip-Wire smears a bunch of BATs with explosives. The ever-testy Cobra Commander slays an overly negative Techno-Viper.

PREPOSTEROUS PHYSICS Spirit's eagle Freedom supposedly has talons sharp enough to tear a Viper's metal helmet to pieces.

GOOFS In *G.I. Joe* #126, Firefly said his damaged BATs (stockpiled in #77) weren't serviceable for battle, but here they reinforce the ninjas' ranks and overrun Cobra Island.

COMIC TIE-INS Firefly plundered Storm Shadow's memories, offering the Pit III's location to Cobra Commander in *G.I. Joe* #129. But true to type, Cobra Commander "rewarded" Firefly by dumping him in Cobra Island's landlocked freighter. Firefly had previously been trapped in the freighter (starting in #98), but escaped by re-wiring a group of BATs deactivated after the Cobra Civil War (stacked aboard the freighter in #77).

Snake-Eyes counters Firefly's mental conditioning with the Arashikage Mind-Set, first used in *G.I. Joe* #103. Zarana and Cesspool end this story as Firefly's prisoners, but he tosses 'em in a dungeon – meaning they sit out the carnage in #132-#134 – and play their get-out-of jail cards in #135.

CHARACTER PROFILE: JOES

• *Storm Shadow and Snake-Eyes:* Can barely – and let's stress *barely* – pilot a 747.

CHARACTER PROFILE: COBRA

Cobra Commander: It should surprise nobody to learn that the Melodramatic One is fond of Wagner's "Ride of the Valkyries."

PLACES TO GO The Pit III: Is protected by internal steel, Kevlar and ceramic sandwich layers.

STUFF YOU NEED Cobra BAT II: I*t costs less to forge a BAT than to train and maintain a Viper. BAT IIs come equipped with guns on their right hands. They're resilient to 7.62 mike-mike firepower, but a 40 mike-mike rifle slug does the trick. You're better off not holding back when combating a BAT – if you blow their lower halves away, they'll crawl forward to gut you.

• *Arashikage Mind-Set:* Ninjas adept at the Arashikage Mind-Set can use it to influence other practitioners almost instantly.

THE COMMAND DECISION A real mixed bag, considering the act of Cobra invading Joe Headquarters almost seems passé by this point. Granted, Cobra Commander's goons nicely grill the Pit-based Joes, but the milquetoast Cobra Island sub-plot proves far less enthralling (indeed, Firefly seems more buffoonish with every page flip). Still, we'll credit this two-parter for at least keeping our attention – and the fact that it's surrounded by a steaming heap of lackluster Joe issues makes it all the more desirable.

G.I. Joe #132 to #134

Titles: *"Bump in the Night" (#132), "Recon by Fire!" (#133), "Throw Down in the Citadel!" (#134)*
Release Dates: *Jan. to Mar. 1993*
Art: *Rurik Tyler (#132), Andrew Wildman (#133-#134)*

BATTLE ROSTER *Joes:* Duke, Snake-Eyes, Lady Jaye, Roadblock; Firefly: Firefly, Slice, Dice, the red ninjas.

MISSION BRIEF ***Issue #132-#134:*** Miffed about Cobra's assault on the Pit III, Duke takes Snake-Eyes, Lady Jaye and Roadblock and sets off to retaliate against Cobra Island. Unaware that Firefly now controls the Cobra nation, Duke's quartet parachutes into the island's marshy region, heading straight for the main Cobra citadel.

Snake-Eyes enters the Cobra stronghold first, intending to sniff out any booby traps, but Firefly's ninjas blitz him *en masse.* Unable to contain the Joe commando, Firefly orders his red ninjas to deploy a secret Arashikage clan battle tactic called "the Scorpion." Standing on each other's shoulders and moving in unison, the red ninjas link their bodies into a scorpion-like mass with Firefly placed as the scorpion's stinger.

Despite the Scorpion's renowned invulnerability, Snake-Eyes nimbly leaps up and carves a vulnerable point in the Scorpion's tail – killing a red ninja or two and collapsing the entire Scorpion network. The Joes and ninjas resume slaughtering each other in a whirlpool of blood, but Snake-Eyes finds Firefly in the citadel's control center.

Firefly brashly activates the base's video system, intending to humble Snake-Eyes before everyone present, but Snake-Eyes takes the opportunity to finger-weave the Arashikage Mind-Set over the TV system – snapping Firefly's conditioning over Slice, Dice and the red ninjas. Firefly craps himself as his one-time allies boil with anger and body-tackle him, enabling the Joes to quietly depart Cobra Island.

MEMORABLE MOMENTS Searching for concealed ninjas, Snake-Eyes impulsively stabs his sword through the floor – and toothpicks his weapon through Slice's hand. But with way cool ninja reserve, Slice doesn't scream out.

Duke tells Roadblock that Snake-Eyes will signal "one long burst on the Uzi" if he's in trouble.

LOVE AND WAR Err… we'd be remiss to not mention the title of issue #132.

ASS-WHUPPINGS Snake-Eyes scraps an obscene number of BATs, cheerfully slicing a door in half and carving up a BAT on the other side. Lady Jaye pops a thermite grenade inside a damaged BAT's chest cavity.

Red ninjas concealed behind a curtain (in the finest Shakespearean tradition) try to impale Snake-Eyes in the gut, but Snakes leaps up, aims high with his sword and halves the ninjas' heads. Snake-Eyes also tricks two red ninjas with the old "make 'em follow the detonator cable" routine, blowing them up at point-blank range.

GOOFS Pardon our asking, but what the hell does Firefly want at this point? There's no real point in his occupying Cobra Island, and he's not out for revenge per se... so essentially, he's just lounging about and getting attacked a lot.

Then again, the Joes think Cobra Commander still rules Cobra Island at this point... so why the hell would Duke send in a *four-man* strike team against Cobra Commander's legions?

Firefly raves about the red ninjas' "unbeatable" Scorpion maneuver – a boast that might seem credible, except that Snake-Eyes solves the problem with a single cut to the Scorpion's "tail." (Apparently, the Scorpion's "unstoppable" – unless you counter-attack.)

Duke spontaneously grows a mess of stubble between issues #132 and #133. Slice and Dice are never established as Arashikage ninjas, but somehow know the Arashikage Mind-Set.

NOW YOU KNOW... If you're going to toss a grenade, get rid of it relatively quickly – the military often contracts such goods from the lowest bidder, meaning your grenade might lack a proper fuse.

COMIC TIE-INS Duke's team seeks to retaliate for Cobra Commander's attack on the Pit III (*G.I. Joe* #130-#131), only to find that Firefly and his mesmerized ninja band captured the isle in #131. *G.I. Joe* #135 reports that although his ninjas turn on him, Firefly eludes capture. Snake-Eyes frees Slice and Dice from Firefly's brainwashing, but they reappear as Cobra Commander's agents in #135-#138.

CHARACTER PROFILE: JOES

• *Roadblock:* He's not fond of night HALO (High Altitude Low Opening) jumps from airplanes – but likes it better than creamed chipped beef on toast.

• *Stalker:* He sometimes serves as jump master on parachute missions.

CHARACTER PROFILE: FIREFLY *Firefly:* He accorded his brainwashed ninjas a mote of autonomy to preserve their fighting edge, but it leaves them chattier as a result. Firefly knows a number of Arashikage secrets and can ignore the Arashikage Mind-Set at will.

STUFF YOU NEED BATs: You can crank up your BAT's aggression levels, but it drains their batteries quicker.

HOT WHEELS Cobra Paralyzer Tanks: They easily repel 5.5 mm military ball ammo, but their armor's not effective against Roadblock's .50 caliber machine gun.

THE COMMAND DECISION The story we wanted to headline, "Dear G.I. Joe. It's over. Please die," *G.I. Joe* #132-#134 barely sports enough plot for one issue, let alone three. Firefly's utterly worthless at this point, and his supposedly invulnerable "Arashikage Scorpion" contains about as much oomph as a beheaded chicken. We finished this story wishing – indeed, praying – we could at least hold it up alongside Marvel series *Rom* as "one of our favorite bad comic stories," but it's not even worthy of that.

G.I. Joe #135 to #138

Titles: *"Ninjas Own the Night" (#135), "Reversals and Betrayals!" (#136), "The Traitor Strikes!" (#137), "Unfoldings!" (#138)*
Release Dates: *Apr. to July 1993*
Art: *Andrew Wildman*

BATTLE ROSTER *Joes:* Scarlett, Snake-Eyes, Storm Shadow, T'Jbang, Dojo, Jinx, Nunchuk, Hawk, Psyche-Out; *Cobra:* Cobra Commander, Zarana, Road Pig, Slice, Dice; *Destro:* Destro, the Baroness.

FIRST APPEARANCES *Cobra/Other:* Dr. Sidney Biggles-Jones (scientist, #135).

MISSION BRIEF ***Issues #135-#136:*** When Pentagon officials order Hawk to plant a high-level mole in Cobra's ranks, the Joe commander assigns Scarlett the duty of "spontaneously" defecting. Accordingly, Scarlett tosses a hissy-fit during a Joe Ninja Force training session, "angrily" denouncing the ninjas for treating her like an outsider and storming off. Snake-Eyes follows, genuinely confused about Scarlett's actions, but Scarlett adamantly goes AWOL and departs for a skiing holiday in Switzerland.

Meanwhile, in an attempt to pump up Cobra's international arms sales, Cobra Commander dispatches Slice and Dice – hired as Cobra agents after the Firefly debacle – to uproot Destro and the Baroness from the newfound Castle Destro in Trans-Carpathia. Surprisingly, the two ninjas take Destro and the Baroness with ease, allowing Cobra Commander to claim Castle Destro as his headquarters.

Emboldened, Cobra Commander contracts the freelance Night Creepers to acquire massive amounts of weapons technology for Cobra's technical division. Most importantly, the Night Creepers kidnap a ballistic scientist named Dr. Sidney Biggles-Jones and steal her prototype rail gun – a projectile weapon with seemingly limitless capabilities – to boost Cobra's arsenal of destruction.

Soon after, Night Creeper computer hackers turn up financial records noting that Scarlett recently ditched Snake-Eyes as her insurance beneficiary in favor of her sister Sioban. After confirming that Scarlett deserted the Joes, Cobra Commander offers the "traitorous" Joe – and Dr. Biggles-Jones – employment as Cobra agents. While Biggles-Jones accepts out of contempt for her sneering male peers, Scarlett signs up "for revenge" against her ex-teammates.

Issues #137-#138: The ever-suspicious Cobra Commander demands Scarlett and Biggles-Jones prove their new-found allegiance to Cobra – ordering Biggles-Jones to sabotage a Joe-guarded kinetic weapons project at the White Sands testing range. Simultaneously, Cobra Commander hands Scarlett the juicy duty of assassinating Hawk. But as Scarlett and Biggles-Jones depart with their Cobra escorts for White Sands, the Baroness and Destro escape detention, taking refuge in the castle's hidden passages.

Destro radios his Joe allies for assistance and – having overheard Cobra Commander's ravings – warns of Scarlett's impending mission to slay Hawk. Upon arrival at White Sands, Biggles-Jones maims a prototype kinetic energy cannon with her rail gun while Scarlett – forced to give a good show to her Cobra observers – "misses" Hawk by a whisker's length. Luckily, the forewarned Hawk and Stalker fake their deaths, making it look like Scarlett detonated their jeep engine.

Hawk finally reveals Scarlett's true loyalties to the Joe Ninja Force, sending Snake-Eyes and Storm Shadow to extract Destro and the Baroness from Castle Destro. Simultaneously, Cobra Commander blows a gasket and sends every available agent – including Scarlett and Biggles-Jones – to flush Destro and the Baroness from Castle Destro's secret passageways.

Desperate to shake off pursuit, Destro reaches Castle Destro's gearbox and half-transforms the edifice, leaving it in a jumbled arrangement halfway between its "Silent Castle" mode and "Castle Destro" configuration. With the sudden rearrangement of the castle's passageways and corridors hampering Cobra Commander's troopers, Destro's battle helmet maps a safe route up to the roof for himself and the Baroness. Scarlett and Biggles-Jones reach the castle controls and return the building to its "Silent Castle" state, then chase after the Destro and the Baroness like mad.

In the confusion, Snake-Eyes and Storm Shadow parachute onto the Silent Castle's roof from a Joe C-130 transport, setting up an extraction rig with hot air balloons. Destro and the Baroness arrive seconds later, strapping themselves into the extraction rig's harness, but Scarlett and Biggles-Jones race onto the scene and draw their weapons. Unable to simply ignore Scarlett for fear of blowing her cover, Snake-Eyes slices his sword through his lover's torso – specifically aiming his blow to miss her heart and other vital organs.

As Scarlett falls, slick with blood, the Joe C-130 swoops back and pulls Snake-Eyes' group to safety. Cobra ninja Slice remains unconvinced about Scarlett's loyalty – knowing full well that Snake-Eyes would *never* miss a target at point-blank range – but Cobra Commander validates Scarlett's actions and summons Cobra medics to bind her wound.

LOVE AND WAR The Baroness wiggles a panel on Destro's face plate open – with her tongue. Dr. Biggles-Jones is surely the hottest physics scientist to ever detonate someone's ordnance.

ASS-WHUPPINGS Snake-Eyes tricks a group of increasingly impotent Night Creepers into wasting each other (see Goofs). The Baroness and Destro kill two Eels underwater and take their uniforms, leaving the Cobra divers' stripped bodies to bob to the surface. As Castle Destro reconfigures itself, some Vipers take a plunge worthy of the Hindenberg. Snake-Eyes runs Scarlett through, but kindly misses her heart.

GOOFS Okay, wait a minute… Scarlett, one of the original Joe members, having staunchly fought Cobra without fail for more than 10 years, decides to defect to Cobra… and Cobra Commander – not to mention Storm Shadow and Snake-Eyes – think it's for real? Are they completely out of their minds?

By the way, Scarlett whines that Storm Shadow and Snake-Eyes never invited her into the "family business," when… err… their "family business" died years ago in Japan.

Two guards, who were surely hired as dumb-ass cannon fodder, stand about and debate Dr. Biggles-Jones' experiments with the proficiency of Sir Isaac Newton ("You see, the aluminum coating turns to plasma and pushes…" etc.).

In issue #136, the Night Creepers – famed martial arts experts – surround Snake-Eyes in a circle… then shoot each other when he jumps. For that matter, why do the Night Creepers attack Storm Shadow's lair at all? (It's dubbed a "pre-emptive strike," but that doesn't jive with the rest of the story.)

Slice and Dice capture Destro and the Baroness appallingly easily compared to previous outings at Destro's homestead (#87, #116-#118, etc.).

Later, during an escape attempt, Cobra Commander says he predicted that the locked-up Baroness and Destro would try to swim their way to freedom – so why the hell did he let them try?

Scarlett and Dr. Biggles-Jones – who isn't a soldier by any stretch of the imagination – magically know to dodge a concealed weight-triggered floor trap. In issue #138, Megatron (*see Comic Tie-Ins*) converses with unknown identified Decepticon allies – but he crashed alone in Canada in *Transformers* #79.

COMIC TIE-INS Firefly captured Zarana and Cesspool (and Road Pig, off-screen) in *G.I. Joe* #131 but tossed them into a dungeon – meaning they missed the bloody battle between Firefly's troupe and Duke's task force in #132-#134. After Firefly's defeat, Slice and Dice released the chained-up trio. Faced with insurmountable opposition (i.e. a horde of ninjas hell-bent on tying a knot in his neck) in #134, Firefly's escaped for parts unknown.

Destro and the Baroness secured the new Castle Destro as their new home in *G.I. Joe* #122 and tried (somewhat foolishly) to continue their early retirement. Upon seizing the castle, Cobra Commander tosses the duo into the same prison cell that once housed Scarlett (#21).

In issue #138, the Silent Castle's "transformation" draws attention from a giant robot and Decepticon leader named Megatron in #139-#142.

CHARACTER PROFILE: JOES

• *Snake-Eyes:* As a ninja master, Snake-Eyes' senses outstrip those of regular ninjas. He knows such ninja positions as the Iron Horse and the Low Praying Mantis.

• *Storm Shadow:* Back in the day, Storm Shadow could only carve a Makiwara practice board (essentially a stationary post) apart about 10 percent of the time. But after he taught the skill to someone else, he nailed it every time.

• *Snake-Eyes and Storm Shadow:* Think less of Hawk for sending Scarlett on her covert mission to infiltrate Cobra.

• *T'Jbang:* He's mute, but sometimes "speaks" through sign language.

CHARACTER PROFILE: DESTRO

• *Destro:* He can remove his wrist-rockets, planting them with an eight-second delay detonator.

• *The Baroness:* Wears "Eternity" perfume.

ORGANIZATIONS *The Night Creepers:* Their membership's divided between the combative Field-Creepers and the nerdy Night-Hackers.

STUFF YOU NEED *Destro's Face Mask:* Contains a short-burst eye laser that responds to voice commands. The mask's polarized eye lenses project light and enable Destro to detect ultraviolet paint, helping him identify booby-trapped floor stones in the Silent Castle. Even more usefully, the mask features a holographic display that assists in strategy-planning.

• *Dr. Biggles-Jones' Rail Gun:* The rail gun coordinates superconductor magnets to fire slugs that're clear, lensatic and coated with aluminum. In short, the magnets propel the slugs to unbelievable velocities – turning their aluminum coating into plasma. As such, the slugs prove frighteningly accurate, able to tear through steel plating like tissue paper. Dr. Biggles Jones carries a hand-held version of her rail gun that, like the larger version, fires magnetically accelerated projectiles.

THE COMMAND DECISION Vying for the questionable title of the worst *G.I. Joe* story ever, issues #135-#138 feature an atrocious premise (Scarlett becomes a "traitor" for the flimsiest of reasons), ungodly dialogue (Slice: "We'll hack them into luncheon meat, Cobra Commander!"), and a groin-kicking disregard for 11 years of Joe comics (the fox-like Destro and the Baroness are overpowered in about 45 seconds). Indeed, Hama seems so atypically off his game, one suspects that series editor David Wohl heavily doctored the script – especially since the tone and tenor here highly evokes Wohl's future work on *Witchblade*. Whatever the case, trust us: If there is a hell for *G.I. Joe* comics, this is it.

G.I. Joe #139 to #142, Transformers: Generation 2 #2

Titles: *"Realignments" (#139), "Goin' South," (#140), "Sucker Punch" (#141), "Final Transformations" (#142), "All or Nothing!" (#2)*
Release Dates: *Aug. to Dec. 1993*
Writers: *Larry Hama (G.I. Joe issues), Simon Furman (Transformers: Generation 2 #2)*
Art: *Chris Batista (#139-#140), Steven Leiber (#141), Jesse Orozco and William Rosado (#142), Manny Galan (Transformers Generation 2 #2)*

BATTLE ROSTER *Joes:* Scarlett, Snake-Eyes, Storm Shadow, Hawk, Tunnel Rat, Spirit, Mutt, Roadblock, Airtight, Rock 'n Roll, the Joe Ninja Force; *Cobra:* Cobra Commander, Dr. Mindbender, Zarana; *Destro:* Destro, the Baroness, Zartan; Decepticons: Megatron; Autobots: Hot Spot, Brawn, Chase, Override, Steeljaw, Skydive; *Other:* Dr. Biggles-Jones, Spike Witwicky.

FIRST APPEARANCES *Other:* Night Creeper leader (ninja supreme master, #141).

DEATHS Autobots: Brawn, Chase, Override, Steeljaw, Hot Spot (all #142), Fortress Maximus; *Other:* Spike Witwicky (both TF: Gen 2 #2).

G.I. Joe #139 to #142, Transformers: Generation 2 #2

MISSION BRIEF ***Issue #139-#142:*** (Author's Note: Megatron actually arrives at the Silent Castle in issue #138's climax, but we've lumped the Transformers-relevant material here.)

Stranded in Canada (*American Transformers* #79) with the remains of the Autobot flagship named the Ark, the severely wounded robot conqueror named Megatron scans for his lost Decepticon shock troops. Registering a transform signal emanating from Trans-Carpathia, Megatron investigates in the hopes of finding a fellow Transformer robot. But upon arrival, an annoyed Megatron discovers that the signal originates from the multi-mode, non-sentient Castle Destro.

But when evil finds lemons, it makes evil lemonade. Before long, Megatron strikes up a deal with Cobra Commander, offering to trade the fallen Ark and its futuristic technology for a complete overhaul and systems upgrade. Working from Megatron's schematics, Cobra technicians strip Megatron down and rebuild him as a tank-mode Transformer equipped with Dr. Biggles-Jones' high-velocity rail gun.

Megatron helps a Cobra retrieval squad transport the Ark from its resting place to the Cobra-subdued town of Millville, but the Joes get wind of the operation. Using a trans-dimensional communicator entrusted to them by the Autobots, the Joes alert their allies on the robotic planet of Cybertron to Megatron's return. While Megatron repairs the Ark and secretly prepares to welch on his deal with Cobra, Protectobot leader Hot Spot takes an Autobot commando squad to Earth.

With Cobra Commander absent, Destro takes the Baroness and Zartan – who's now in Destro's employ – and re-captures Castle Destro. Back in Millville, Dr. Biggles-Jones approaches the bed-ridden Scarlett and – suspecting that the redhead still harbors loyalties for the Joes – confesses her own role as a double-agent for an American security agency.

Just as Cobra Commander agrees to release Biggles-Jones to Megatron for continued technical assistance with his newly forged body, Hot Spot's group drives home their assault. Megatron turns the Autobot assault squad – save Hot Spot and Skydive – into scrap, then kidnaps Biggles-Jones. Scarlett tries to rescue her new friend, ruining her cover as a Cobra operative, but Megatron takes his prize and launches to freedom in the Ark. Both Skydive and Spike Witwicky (the Autobots' primary human ally) smuggle themselves aboard before takeoff, leaving Hot Spot behind as the sole Autobot on Earth.

In the aftermath of Megatron's escape, the Joes flood into Millville, rescuing Scarlett and breaking Cobra's hold on the town. As Cobra Commander and his lieutenants retreat, a space-borne Megatron gloats over his victory.

Transformers Generation 2 #2: Stowed away on the Ark and feeling the weight of the world on his shoulders, Spike roots through the ship and hooks up with his former Autobot symbiote, the gigantic battle station known as Fortress Maximus. (*Author's Note:* Don't ask us how it got there. It's complicated.) While Fortress Maximus/Spike fights a losing battle with Megatron, Skydive frees Biggles-Jones.

Meanwhile, on Earth, Protectobot leader Hot Spot struggles for a course of action when Cobra tries to make off with the alien technology they procured from Megatron. Concerned that such advanced weaponry could plunge Earth into chaos, Hot Spot transforms to vehicle mode and scorches Cobra's tanks with his fireball cannons. Hot Spot succeeds in wrecking Cobra's technology store, but the effort leaves him drained, weaponless and surrounded by Cobra HISS tanks. Cobra Commander threatens to dissect Hot Spot – which would more than make up for the lost technology – but Hot Spot denies Cobra the chance to study him by self-destructing.

Aboard the Ark, Megatron carves through Fortress Maximus, spilling the Autobot's silicon guts onto the floor. As Skydive swoops in and draws Megatron's fire, Fortress Maximus/Spike tosses himself into the Ark's antimatter conversion chamber. Registering the antimatter breach, Megatron hurls himself to safety in an escape pod while Skydive jets to freedom with Biggles-Jones. Seconds later, Fortress Maximus and Spike succumb to the antimatter explosion that vaporizes the Ark. Skydive safely returns Biggles-Jones to G.I. Joe, grieving for his lost comrades.

MEMORABLE MOMENTS A cloned Dr. Mindbender (see Comic Tie-Ins) turns awe-struck to realize how the world's changed during his "demise": "A Democrat in the White House? Cheers got cancelled? What happened to Michael Jackson's face?... The world is more unhinged than ever! All the better for my plans!"

LOVE AND WAR It's never blatantly stated exactly why Megatron wants the hottie Dr. Biggles-Jones to accompany him back to Cybertron, although Megs mentions: "Perhaps I can find a way to bend her talents to my ends!"

ASS-WHUPPINGS Megatron blows up all members of the Autobot command squad save Skydive and Hot Spot – who fireballs a number of Cobra HISS tanks, then self-destructs.

Scarlett whaps ninja Dice with his own fighting stick, then swings about and shatters Slice's helmet. She also damn near beheads a couple of Alley-Vipers and guts an Frag Viper. Oh, and she kicks Cobra Commander and Zarana around for the sheer hell of it.

Snake-Eyes slices up several Alley-Vipers and bests the Night Creeper leader in one-on-one combat. Fortress Maximus and Spike sacrifice their lives to detonate the Ark (but miss nailing Megatron in the explosion).

GOOFS Joe member Tunnel Rat spies Megatron and remarks, "A large Decepticon – one I've never seen before!", but we're hard pressed to think when Tunnel Rat has ever seen a Transformer. Dr. Biggles-Jones, apparently a mole within Cobra's ranks, builds the terrorist group a hell of a lot of artillery. It transpires that she's a double agent – but we never learn which security agency employs her. At the climax of issue #141, Scarlett – presumably recovering from Snake-Eyes' near-mortal sword wound – whups a whole lot of ass for a recovering invalid.

The Ark's automatic defensive systems only react to active Transformers, not deeming deactivated ones like Fortress Maximus a threat (which seems like a gigantic oversight).

At the end of #142, Megatron laces Cobra's ill-gotten Transformer technology with a computer virus, rendering it useless and making Hot Spot's sacrifice in *Transformers: Generation 2* #2 entirely unnecessary. (One presumes Hama and Furman separately crafted solutions to divest Cobra of futuristic technology, but it generates a continuity glitch).

COMIC TIE-INS In *G.I. Joe* #139, Cobra Commander arranges for the same equipment that spawned Serpentor (#49) to generate a clone of the cracked, extremely bald and very dead Dr. Mindbender – although it's not clear why (it's hinted that Mindbender programmed the machine with his DNA, meaning it could only be used by bringing him back to life first).

Dr. Mindbender is briefly pissed at Cobra Commander for entombing him aboard Cobra Island's landlocked freighter (#99), leading to Mindbender's death from botulism (reported in #114), but he eventually tosses aside the animosity when money's waved at him.

Hawk here briefly meets with Destro, the Baroness and Zartan on Cobra Island (deserted since #134), confirming that Cobra Commander snitched the aforementioned cloning equipment and torched the bodies aboard the landlocked freighter.

Cobra initially subjugated Millville in *G.I. Joe* #99; the Joes liberate it here.

Last seen in *G.I. Joe* #118, Zartan resurfaces – having gained Destro's gratitude for assistance rendered in #116-#118 – as Destro's agent. Scarlett infiltrated Cobra as a double agent in #135-#138. Snake-Eyes holds a tiny grudge toward Destro because rescuing him and the Baroness (#137) forced Snakes to skewer Scarlett as part of her cover.

The Ark crashed in Canada, with Megatron aboard, in American *Transformers* #79. (For a full explanation, read that breathtaking Transformers guide called *Prime Targets* – available from Mad Norwegian Press).

Spike previously merged with Fortress Maximus to rough up Galvatron in American *Transformers* #79 but retired (so he hoped) from the role.

The Autobots at some point supposedly entrusted the *G.I. Joe* team with a trans-dimensional warp communicator, possibly in the apocryphal *G.I. Joe and the Transformers* mini-series, but more likely after a fracas with Megatron in the somewhat-more legitimate *Action Force* #24-#27.

CHARACTER PROFILE: JOES Snake-Eyes: He knows an arcane technique called obake no odori – the "dance of the demons."

CHARACTER PROFILE: COBRA

• *Dr. Biggles-Jones:* Deems Cybertronian technology as not very efficient.

• *Dr. Mindbender:* It's speculated that the original Mindbender covered his bets by encrypting the cloning apparatus that created Serpentor (*G.I. Joe* #49) with a complex algorithm that would've forced anyone using the machine to clone Mindbender back to life. The cloned Mindbender's metabolism slowly returns to normal, meaning he sits about for a while in a bathtub full of ice.

CHARACTER PROFILE: OTHER Aleph: He's studied two thousand forms of martial arts methods created by ancient masters, as well as reciprocating defense techniques.

HOT WHEELS Joe C-130 transports: They're the only aircraft capable of being refueled by both Air Force and Navy tankers.

STUFF YOU NEED Dr. Biggles-Jones' Rail Gun: A rail-gun fired-projectile – shot at Megatron to defend Castle Destro – is slowed by passage through Megatron's body and still attains orbit.

• *Dr. Mindbender's Cloning Device:* Contains inert organic tissue percolating in an electrolyte-rich protein bath with a pure oxygen aerating system.

THE COMMAND DECISION Good enough for the purpose of putting Megatron back together, although *G.I. Joe* #139-#142 is really a G.I. Joe story with some Transformers thrown into the mix. We'll credit the Joe creators for offering a four-parter that's lightyears beyond the woeful *G.I. Joe and the Transformers*, although it was a pretty lousy means of getting comic readers excited about *Transformers: Generation 2* (an extremely short-lived Transformers revival back in 1994). Worse, the Transformers plots seem enthralling compared to the Joe-orientated stuff, wasting our time with tripe such as Dr. Mindbender's return and Scarlett's profitless infiltration of Cobra.

G.I. Joe #143 to #144

Titles: *"Dark Island" (#143), "Snake-Eyes: The Tale Untold!" (#144)*
Release Dates: *Dec. 1993 to Jan. 1994*
Writers: *Eric Fein (framing sequence, #143), Vic Sutherland (flashback, #143), Larry Hama (#144)*
Art: *Jesse D'Orozco (framing sequence, #143), Tom Mandrake (flashback, #143), William Rosado (#144)*

BATTLE ROSTER *Joes:* Snake-Eyes, Scarlett and Hawk (present); *Joes:* Snake-Eyes, Scarlett, Grunt, Rock 'n Roll and Breaker (flashback).

MISSION BRIEF ***Issue #143:*** In a flashback sequence from the Joes' early days, Hawk assigns Breaker and Rock 'n Roll to aid Scarlett on her first mission as a Joe field operative. Hawk briefs the trio on the "Safe House," a Caribbean island run by the vicious Madame Umbra, that coordinates prisoner exchanges for powerful nations. Suspecting Umbra of rerouting her fees to terrorist organizations, Hawk orders Scarlett's group to blow the lid off Umbra's game and destroy her base of operations.

Accordingly, as part of a scheduled prisoner swap, Scarlett disguises herself as an incarcerated Soviet spy – with Breaker and Rock 'n Roll as her "escorts." Unfortunately, Umbra uncovers Scarlett's deception, forcing the redhead and Rock 'n Roll to shoot their way out while Breaker slips into the base's control center. Pocketing evidence of Umbra's terrorist ties, Breaker hotwires the Safe House's command systems, thereby blowing the base to smithereens.

While the Joes and Umbra's staff evacuate to the beach, an American submarine moves in and cuts down Umbra's guards. With Scarlett's gun drawn on her, the weaponless Umbra – choosing death over a dishonorable surrender – draws close enough to the novice Joe to pull the trigger. Shocked, Scarlett laments her inability to anticipate Umbra's suicide, but Hawk ultimately applauds his team's efforts.

Issue #144: Given a lull in clean-up efforts at the recently liberated Millville (#142), Snake-Eyes and Scarlett quietly recall the helicopter accident that shredded his vocal chords …

When Cobra kidnaps an American agent in the Middle East, Snake-Eyes, Scarlett, Grunt and Rock 'n Roll meet up with an American helicopter team to stage a rescue attempt. The Joes set out, but a back-up chopper experiences engine trouble and crashes into the Joes' ship. Grunt and Rock 'n Roll bail out to safety, but one of the craft's doors slams shut – unexpectedly snagging Scarlett's harness and immobilizing her. Snake-Eyes pauses long enough to cut Scarlett free, but the other helicopter detonates, shredding his face with shrapnel.

While Grunt and Rock 'n Roll extinguish the smoldering ninja and haul the unconscious Scarlett clear, Hawk arrives with a medical team. Hawk ponders aborting the mission, knowing full well that the kidnappers will spirit away their hostage soon, but Snake-Eyes insists on moving forward.

Rock 'n Roll and Grunt take Snake-Eyes to rendezvous with an undercover Stalker, who helps Snake-Eyes barge into the Cobra captors' hideout. Snake-Eyes wastes the opposition, liberating a federal agent named George Strawhacker – the man engaged to Snake-Eye's sister Terri. The two of them and Stalker escape, pleased over Strawhacker's rescue – but burdened with the grim knowledge that nothing can ever restore Snake-Eyes' face.

ASS-WHUPPINGS At the Safe House, Rock 'n Roll finds a guitar – and breaks it over a guard's face. Breaker rigs booby-trap bombs with the proficiency of a grown-up Dennis the Menace.

The helicopter accident that mauls Snake-Eyes' vocal chords also slags him with third degree burns and major head trauma. It's suggested that had Snake-Eyes undergone emergency surgery after the accident – rather than stubbornly continuing his rescue mission – doctors might have been able to patch his face. As such, Snake-Eyes partly holds blame for his ongoing disfigurement, although one can't help but suspect that doctors simply couldn't have stitched him up *too* well in any event. (It's not like he only needs a Band-Aid and some iodine.)

Although Snake-Eyes fillets his Cobra opponents with the usual efficiency, Stalker takes a bullet wound in the crossfire. Still, in a show of brotherhood, Grunt and Rock 'n Roll sharpshoot rooftop opponents to cover their buddies.

GOOFS Upon seeing Snake-Eyes' shredded face for the first time, Stalker – Snake-Eyes' longtime friend and teammate – displays about as much emotion as a fire hydrant, casually asking, "What happened to Snake-Eyes' face?", then completely ignoring his friend's trauma.

Evidently a huge fan of James Bond villains, Umbra favors fighting the cornered Scarlett in hand-to-hand combat rather than just plugging her. Umbra also shows off her concentration by punching a hole in the floor (good grief, she's not the Hulk). Umbra's supposedly aware of Scarlett's reputation, even though Scarlett's a newbie and hasn't hurt a fly by this point.

Given the injuries that Snake-Eyes sustained in the chopper accident (*see Ass-Whuppings*), it's moronic to think that a commanding officer Hawk to send him into battle afterwards. We're talking third-degree burns and *head trauma* here, folks.

In #144, two Vipers shed their uniforms and sit around the tied-up Strawhacker – with the intent of plugging Snake-Eyes while he's figuring out which one's the hostage. It's a stupid plan for several reasons, not the least of which being that two pages earlier, one of the Vipers displays a distinct Cobra tattoo on his bicep. But setting aside Snake-Eyes' personal relationship with Strawhacker, wouldn't the rescue squad members *know* what Strawhacker looks like?

G.I. Joe #143 includes a framing sequence that supposedly takes place immediately before Scarlett's "defection" in #135. In the framing shot, Scarlett bitches to Hawk that she doesn't feel welcome among the Joe Ninja Force. That'd be fine, except that it's pointless lying to Hawk – since he assigned her the mission.

COMIC TIE-INS Issue #144 fleshes out the helicopter accident that cost Snake-Eyes his voice and face – an adventure mentioned in *G.I. Joe* #10 and previously detailed in #27. We've already seen George Strawhacker perish at a Borovian Gulag in #106. Strawhacker doesn't recognize Snake-Eyes during the flashback story but does identify him during the Borovian escapade (#106), suggesting the two shared an association even after the death of Snake-Eyes' family (#26).

CHARACTER PROFILE: JOES

• *Scarlett:* Scarlett's currently continuing her ninja training, acting like the wet-eared Luke Skywalker in *Star Wars* and deflecting a drone's laser bursts with her sword. Scarlett sometimes serves as a Joe silent weapons specialist and occasionally carries resin guns to thwart metal detectors.

• *Snake-Eyes:* Snake-Eyes served two tours of duty as a long-range recon patrol member, famed for walking right up to an enemy without detection.

THE COMMAND DECISION A horribly unnecessary experiment, with preciously little to say and no conviction for its flashback episodes (Stalker barely bats an eye at seeing his longtime friend Snake-Eyes so disfigured).

G.I. Joe #145 to #148

Titles: *"Threads and Resolutions" (#145), "Immovable Objects" (#146), "Oblivion Express!" (#147), "Irresistible Forces" (#148)*
Release Dates: *Feb. to May 1994*
Art: *Phil Gosier*

BATTLE ROSTER *Joes:* Snake-Eyes, Scarlett, Flint, Lady Jaye, Stalker; *Cobra:* Cobra Commander, Destro, the Baroness, Billy, Zartan, Dr. Mindbender, Zarana, the Dreadnoks, Slice, Dice; *Other:* the Oktober Guard (Daina, Dragonsky).

FIRST APPEARANCES *Joes:* Duke (as Star Brigade commander, #145), Space Shot (combat fighter pilot, #145), Roadblock (as space gunner, #145), Sci-Fi (as star brigade laser sniper, #145), Payload (astro pilot, #145); *Other:* Colonel Krimov (a.k.a. Red Star, the Oktober Guard).

DEATHS *Destro:* Darklon (#146); *Other:* Magda, the White Clown (#145).

NOTES *G.I. Joe* #145-#148 contain widely differing plot threads – the Star Brigade's efforts to stop a runamuck asteroid and Cobra Commander's invasion of Borovia, respectively – that don't have a thing to do with one another. As such, we've separated out the two plotlines for your reading convenience.

MISSION BRIEF *"Star Brigade Plot":* When scientists discover an asteroid hurtling pell-mell toward Earth – threatening to wipe out all life on our little blue-green orb – Duke hastily assembles the "Star Brigade," a space-trained Joe team consisting of Roadblock, Sci-Fi, Payload and Space Shot. In short order, the Star Brigade takes space shuttle Defiant and links up in Earth orbit with a Russian shuttle bearing the Oktober Guard.

The Joes are re-introduced to Daina and Dragonsky as well as newcomers such as space commander Colonel Krimov and a lookalike of the late Colonel Brekhov. In due course, Krimov explains that the Russian military embarked on experiments to seed asteroids with teams of robots equipped to divert the giant rocks from their conventional orbits. If successful, the experiments would gain Russia a tactical weapon capable of obliterating military targets anywhere on Earth.

Unfortunately, the chief specialist in charge of the operation unexpectedly went bonkers, pre-programming a robot team to send a 15 mile-wide asteroid heading toward Earth. Trying to intercede before impact, the Joe and Russian shuttles stage separate landings on the runaway lump of rock. But within minutes, the haywire robot drones – pre-programmed to eliminate all opposition – fall out to laser the invaders to pieces.

The robots annihilate the *Defiant*, but the Joes and Russians hold their own as the asteroid speeds toward Earth. Luckily, Payload and Dragonsky determine that the robots' programming only allows them to attack armed humans. By laying down their weapons, the Joes and Russians walk past the robots into their makeshift command center – activating the base's self-destruct. As the Joe/Russian task force loads into the Russian shuttle and sets course for home, the asteroid harmlessly fragments into billions of tiny bits.

Borovian Plot: In Borovia, Cobra Commander's forces dethrone Magda's democratic administration and set up rebel leader Metz as a puppet ruler. Recalling how the duo previously saved his life (#106), Metz advocates sparing Magda and her consort, the White Clown. But Cobra Commander impulsively guns down Magda and the White Clown, completely silencing opposition to Cobra's newfound rule.

Meanwhile, after returning from travels abroad, Billy happily dines with Destro, the Baroness and Zartan at Castle Destro. Unfortunately, the Borovia-entrenched Cobra Commander starts longing to besiege Castle Destro, conveniently located in the neighboring nation of Trans-Carpathia. To that end, the cloned Dr. Mindbender off-handedly mentions that during his previous life, he secretly implanted Destro and Zartan with mind-control chips as a safeguard to guarantee their loyalty. After learning that the sight of his unmasked face will trigger the implants, Cobra Commander drives up to Castle Destro's door and whips off his hood – immediately enthralling Destro and Zartan to obey his lunatic whims. Intending to rescue their entranced allies, the Baroness and Billy gird for battle, but Destro and Zartan capture the duo after a brief chase.

Mentally re-programmed to work for Cobra's betterment, Destro and Zartan advocate a Cobra invasion of Eastern Europe. As a first strike, Destro triggers one of his hidden intercontinental ballistic missiles – eradicating his once-ally Darklon in nearby Darklonia. Afterward, Destro and Zartan effortlessly roll several Cobra columns into Darklonia, intending to invade Wolkekuckuckland and convert it into Cobra's main manufacturing center.

In Wolkekuckuckland, General Liederkranz (#89) summons G.I. Joe members to serve as military advisers and strategists. Hopelessly outgunned, Hawk, Stalker, Flint, Lady Jaye and other Joes pull every trick that springs to mind, but all their efforts do little to slow Cobra's inexorable advance.

MEMORABLE MOMENTS Cobra Commander shows up on Destro's doorstep with all the verve of a comedy club performer, explaining his visit with: "I was just over in the next country, undermining the moral fiber of the new government and I thought I'd drop by…."

Flint pretty much sums up our feelings about this ridiculous four-parter: "We parachuted into this cluster foul-up [Wolkekuckuckland] just to be on the receiving end of a massacre while the world gets K.O.-ed by an asteroid."

ASS-WHUPPINGS Cobra Commander wastes Magda and the White Clown with a savagery that upsets even the slimy Metz. The Joes in Wolkekuckuckland resort to the time-honored method of sneaking under Destro and Zartan's tanks, attaching shape charges and running away like adrenaline-tanked weasels. Destro mashes Darklon with a missile.

PREPOSTEROUS PHYSICS At one point, Dr. Mindbender looks into the sky and comments on the approaching asteroid – but if it were truly that close, Earth would be irrevocably doomed.

GOOFS Dr. Mindbender claims that he implanted Destro's mind control device after knocking him out to remove a bad tooth. (Author's Note: You mean Destro, who's obviously loaded, would let the crazed Dr. Mindbender serve… as his dentist?)

Even allowing that he's spent some time pushing up daisies, why didn't Dr. Mindbender reveal Zartan and Destro's implants before now? (They might have come in awfully handy in *G.I. Joe* #84, for example, when he and Cobra Commander II set out to *kill* Zartan). Dr. Mindbender keys Destro and Zartan's implants to activate upon seeing Cobra Commander's unmasked face – except that Dr. Mindbender has never learned, to our knowledge, what Cobra Commander looks like (it's not exactly the sort of information you'd find lying about in a Cobra computer bank, along with the Baroness' favorite recipes for chocolate mousse).

The Joes continue using the Pit III, even though Cobra knows its location (#130-#131).

We never learn anything about *how* exactly the robot workers divert asteroids through space. The runamuck asteroid's variously cited as being 15 and 23.6 miles in diameter.

NOW YOU KNOW… Stalker reflects how the Chinese warlord Sun Tzu commented that "any commander who doesn't try every possible avenue before committing troops to battle isn't fit to lead." Furthermore, Stalker believes that a soldier's job is to "do the unspeakable and be forgotten" – except by his comrades-in-arms.

COMIC TIE-INS Snake-Eyes and Scarlett, tired of maiming and slaying Cobra troops like lambs, journey here to the High Sierras for a lengthy vacation. Regrettably, Storm Shadow shatters their slaughterless interlude in *G.I. Joe* #149.

It's not particularly relevant, but the Joe Ninja Force members – sans Snake-Eyes and Storm Shadow – renovate the Soft Master's former restaurant ("Comidas Chinas," first seen in #26) and start offering free martial arts classes, teaching their students the value of non-violent defense techniques.

Ex-Borovian President Magda spared Metz's life in *G.I. Joe* #106, advocating a newer, gentler Borovia with fewer public hangings – although the White Clown predicted (accurately, as it turns out) that letting Metz live would bite them in the ass. It's not much consolation, but Metz gets smeared into a bloody paste in #151.

The discovery of Millville as a Cobra hideout (#142) motivates authorities to vindicate Mutt and Spirit for their previous killing spree (#99-#103). Grunt, who enrolled at Georgia Tech in *G.I. Joe* #54, holds a master's degree in engineering but claims he's been "looking for work for four years."

In issue #145, Stalker and Rock 'n Roll visit Arlington Cemetery and pay respects to the graves of Breaker, Doc, Crankcase, Crazylegs, Heavy Metal, Quick Kick, Thunder (all killed in #109), Cool Breeze (#112), Avalanche, Blaster, Blocker, Knockdown, Maverick (#113), and Mangler (*Special Missions* #13). Dodger, the only Battle Force 2000 member who survived *G.I. Joe* #113's bloodbath, also appears on the casualty rolls and evidently perished on another occasion.

Billy formerly saved Destro's metal-plated mug in *G.I. Joe* #116-#118, departing shortly afterward on a foot tour of Europe afterward. Zartan ingratiated himself to Destro on the same occasion, formally entering Destro's employ in #139. Destro's troupe regained control of the Silent Castle/Castle Destro in #140.

It happens off-stage, but Dr. Mindbender evidently implanted Zartan with a mind-controlling device while Cobra medics stitched up his wounds (sustained when Zartan infiltrated the Pit II in #48-#51). Dr. Mindbender pegged Destro with a similar device while removing a tooth (*see Goofs*).

Destro's chess board (last seen in #120) now contains updated pieces that look like various Cobra officers and rival military leaders. The October Guard last appeared in *G.I. Joe* #101-#102.

Cobra Commander graciously releases Zarana, last seen in #131, from his service, allowing her to reunite with the Dreadnoks at their new hideout in New Jersey (the Joes ransacked the original in #79) and tear about the place like Hell's Angels.

Darklon formerly got captured in *G.I. Joe* #105, but escaped in the interim. Wolkekuckuckland, General Liederkranz and his treacherous lackey-boy Wolfgang first appeared in *G.I. Joe* #88.

CHARACTER PROFILE: JOES

• *Hawk:* He badly speaks Darklonian (specifically, Hawk awkwardly asks some restaurant diners how to get to the "secret stuffed cabbage").

• *Roadblock:* He loathes space duty, claiming he'd rather jump into a bullet-filled landing zone than "go orbital in a frisbee covered with bathroom tile!"

• *Rock 'n Roll:* The late Breaker's fondness for gum-popping previously bugged Rock 'n Roll, but now he misses it.

• *Sci-Fi:* He's never worked with the Russians before. (*Side Note:* The Sci-Fi "Star Brigade" toy actually lists him as a pilot, not a laser trooper.)

CHARACTER PROFILE: COBRA

• *Cobra Commander:* He wears a pony-tail under his mask.

• *Destro:* Plagued by a noble streak, he's been disposing of assorted chemical weapons for the good of humanity.

CHARACTER PROFILE: OTHER

• *Colonel Krimov:* His code-name's Red Star – a moniker accorded him before the term became politically embarrassing.

• *Daina:* She's actually a Czech who secretly lusts for a free and democratic Czechoslovakia. On space missions, Daina serves as a laser-rifle sniper. (She cheekily tells her counterpart Sci-Fi: "You don't worry, Mr. American Laser Sniper, there's plenty of work for both of us.")

ORGANIZATIONS *Joes:* Evidently Lord of the Rings fans, as they sometimes signal to each other in Orcish. One such recognition signal is: "asch nazh gimbaul," with the countersign: "Asch nazh durbatulik" (which amusingly enough translates to Tolkien's infamous "One ring to rule them all..." motto).

STUFF YOU NEED *Dr. Mindbender's Implants:* Given a certain stimulus, the implants convert their subjects into zombies. When a pre-determined trigger word is also applied (such as "Niagara Falls"), the implants override the victims' ethical/moral codes, making them crafty, evil geniuses bent on world domination in Cobra's name.

PLACES TO GO *Borovia:* After Cobra's invasion, Borovia renames itself Borigia/Franzy-Marengo – and no, we couldn't explain why at gunpoint.

• *Darklonia:* It's technically a principality (a small state ruled by royalty, often part of a larger empire), not a nation.

• *Castle Destro:* Destro's fortified it with a super-rocket, so try to avoid pissing him off.

• *The Pit III:* The current password for entry: "Bobby Heinlein."

• *Wolkekuckuckland (a.k.a. W-Land):* It's hailed for producing clocks and chocolate – the name Wolkekuckuckland, in fact, means "cloud-cuckoo land." The country also sports an international underground banking center, *a la* the Cayman Islands, and an industrial base that's ideal for Cobra's needs.

HOT WHEELS *The Defiant:* Reasonably compatible with its Russian counterpart – considering the Russians evidently nabbed a lot of their space technology from us.

THE COMMAND DECISION Dear word, is the series over yet? Beating Armageddon to the punch, *G.I. Joe* #145-#148 offers up the lamest of "Asteroid! Dead ahead!" plots, refusing to even lower itself to explain how the robot workers diverted the asteroid in the first place. There's an endless wave of shortcomings, including Magda and the White Clown's ignoble deaths issue #145, plus some of the most heart-stabbing cover slogans ("It's mayhem on the moon as the Joes ride the Oblivion Express!", etc.) you're ever likely to see. All in all, you could burn every copy in existence and we just wouldn't care.

G.I. Joe #149 to #151

Titles: *"Heroes and Medals and Things" (#149), "Slam Dance in the Cyber-Castle!" (#150), "Cobra Renewed!" (#151)*
Release Dates: *June to Aug. 1994*
Art: *Phil Gosier*

BATTLE ROSTER *Joes:* Snake-Eyes, Storm Shadow, Flint, Lady Jaye, Stalker; *Cobra:* Cobra Commander, Dr. Mindbender, Slice, Dice, Destro, Zartan, the Baroness, Billy.

DEATHS *Other:* Metz (#151).

MISSION BRIEF ***Issue #149-#150:*** In Trans-Carpathia, Cobra Commander's Cyber-Vipers take an electronic pick-axe to the Baroness and Billy's mental defenses with repeated brainwave scanner treatments. Billy briefly "capitulates" to the scanner's effects, "proving his loyalty" by showing Cobra Commander one of Destro's hidden control centers. But once inside, Billy touches a control, firing off one of Destro's maverick ICBM missiles. As Billy expected, Cobra Commander's troops bring down the missile a short distance from the Silent Castle, but American satellites detect the explosion.

Cobra Commander flings Billy back into the brainwave scanner and puts his brain on spin-cycle, but in the Pit III, a concerned Storm Shadow examines the telemetry reports of the ICBM explosion. Activating hidden scanners left behind in the Silent Castle, Storm Shadow spots Billy writhing in the brainwave scanner and vows to rescue his one-time protégé. Stormy briefly stops in the High Sierras to confer with Snake-Eyes and Scarlett, who are desperately trying to enjoy a well-earned vacation. Respecting his friends' desire to avoid active combat for a time, Storm Shadow sets off to rescue Billy alone.

Meanwhile, Dr. Mindbender equips Cobra Commander with a sleek body armor, making the commander super-strong and nigh-invulnerable. Storm Shadow easily enters the Silent Castle, but Mindbender disorientates the ninja's enhanced senses with vertigo-inducing holograms, allowing Cobra Commander to whupp Storm Shadow's ass and capture him.

Back in the Sierras, Snake-Eyes inwardly pops for leaving Storm Shadow to his fate, departing for the Silent Castle but stopping off in Wolkekuckuckland to borrow heavy assault weapons from Hawk's team. A short while later, Snake-Eyes forcibly bursts into the Silent Castle's control center, guns blazing. Snake-Eyes disrupts Dr. Mindbender's holograms with a smoke grenade, then neutralizes Cobra Commander at point-blank range with a high-velocity flechette round and phosphorus burst combination. Although the double whammy puts the commander out of commission, Snake-Eyes turns to face his new opponents: the brainwashed trio of Billy, Storm Shadow and the Baroness.

Issue #151: Feverishly improvising, Snake-Eyes hauls up the fallen Cobra Commander, using the Cobra leaders' bullet-proof battle suit to ward off a continual volley of firepower. Thankfully, Hawk, Flint and Lady Jaye divert from their ongoing mission in Wolkekuckuckland to rescue Snake-Eyes and flee, leaving Storm Shadow and their other allies in Cobra's clutches.

Back in Borovia, Zartan disguises himself as General Liederkranz's craven assistant Wolfgang, then blows up Borovian President Metz. As expected, the real Wolfgang takes the heat for the murder, apprehended while trying to sell black market items. But to Wolfgang's surprise, the Borovians praise him for "assassinating" the imbecilic Metz, hoisting Wolfgang up and proclaiming him president of Borovia.

MEMORABLE MOMENTS Stalker sweetly claims that the only heroic thing the turncoat Wolfgang ever did was "remember to flush."

Cobra Commander comes unglued after Billy fires off Destro's ICBM to alert the Joes, shouting: "This kind of behavior is totally unacceptable, Billy!", to which Billy replies: "That line didn't work on me when I was *five*, Dad!"

Far more dramatically, Scarlett muses over Snake-Eyes' need to rescue Storm Shadow: "The bond between those who've been through combat is a brotherhood sealed in blood, watched over by the ghosts of those who fell."

LOVE AND WAR Scarlett, it seems, hopes to abandon ninja intrigue and spend her days bumping uglies with Snake-Eyes.

ASS-WHUPPINGS Cobra Commander kicks the captive Baroness around a bit. Snake-Eyes butchers a pack of Vipers and nails Cobra Commander with a flechette round (essentially a giant shotgun shell loaded with steel darts – a piece of extremely useful ammunition forbidden by the Geneva Convention), then follows up with a white phosphorous burst (normally primed to explode at a distance, but rigged by Snake-Eyes to ignite on impact). The improvising Snake-Eyes – who gets our vote for a guest spot on Whose Line Is It Anyway? – then ingeniously uses the commander as a bullet-proof shield.

GOOFS Issue #151 opens with Snake-Eyes' hands in flames, supposedly due to his punching a phosphorous-torched Cobra Commander in #150 – except that in the previous issue, Snake-Eyes' hands were flame-free. Even if

Storm Shadow left Snake-Eyes and Scarlett to their own affairs, wouldn't summoning assistance from the other Joes make sense? (They surely share a vested interest in rubbing out Cobra Commander's lair.)

It's entirely irrelevant to the plot, but in #151, Hawk discourages a pack of Cobra pursuit vehicles by phoning veteran Joe member Joseph Colton (#86, #127) and asking him to discharge America's ultra-secret "Star Wars" defense grid – bouncing a particle beam off various satellites to swipe at the Cobra troops. The ploy works, but there's several difficulties involved: A) Even Hawk shouldn't have the authority to fire such a top-level weapon, B) The defense grid's supposedly for use only in the most dire of emergencies (say, a volley of nuclear missiles), and not for something menial like a Cobra vehicle riding up your butt, and C) Once again, we'll mention the small diplomatic fallout from firing such a particle beam and screaming to the nations of the world, "Neener! Neener! Look at our newest toy!"

Snake-Eyes and Storm Shadow supposedly left eavesdropping devices behind during their previous visit to Castle Destro (#138), even though they never actually entered the edifice (damn ninjas – they get into everything).

Why would Cobra assassinate Borovian President Metz, their sniveling toady and ally, and blame Wolfgang? Is it because Cobra wants to provoke warfare between Borovia and Wolkekuckuckland? But why bother with that pretense, since they already control Borovia? Most importantly, what's to stop this story from ending in a complete and utter quagmire?

COMIC TIE-INS Issue #151 climaxes with the White House summoning the original G.I. Joe, Joseph Colton (last seen in #127), back to Washington – he travels there in #152.

Borovian President Metz, here pasted by Zartan, rose to power with Cobra's backing in *G.I. Joe* #145. Cobra Commander hypnotized Destro and Zartan into his service in #145, then netted the Baroness and Billy in #146. For the fate of the villains in the Silent Castle, *see G.I. Joe #55: Closing the Pit III Sidebar*.

CHARACTER PROFILE: JOES

• *Snake-Eyes:* The Pentagon's awarded him yet another medal that he won't receive until the Joes get declassified.

• *Storm Shadow and Snake-Eyes:* They catch fish with their bare hands. Storm Shadow deems Snake-Eyes as retired from active service, although nothing's official.

CHARACTER PROFILE: OTHER

• *The Baroness:* She's a world-class pistol shot.

• *Billy:* His ninja training makes him somewhat resistant to the brainwave scanner.

PLACES TO GO The Pit III: Officially, it's designated a "chaplain's assistants' supply depot" in Utah, although you'd think that'd enable Cobra to rifle through government files and spot the obvious similarity to the Pits I and II.

STUFF YOU NEED The Brainwave Scanner: Dr. Mindbender augmented the brainwave scanner to rewrite its subjects' loyalties, leaving their personalities and fighting skills intact.

• *Rapid Pulse Electron Beam:* Hawk gives Joseph Colton the password "little green apples" when requesting use of America's "Star Wars" defense system.

THE COMMAND DECISION A trio of issues that's about as tired as we feel. We should go on record stating that we adore *G.I. Joe* and would love to deliver nothing but great reviews. But *G.I. Joe* #149-#151, with its appalling art, pointless battle scenes, complete lack of passion and tendency to run on automatic, only makes us wish Marvel had pulled the plug on the series sooner.

G.I. Joe #152

Titles: *"... Just Fade Away"*
Release Dates: *Sept. 1994*
Art: *Phil Gosier*

BATTLE ROSTER *Joes:* Joseph B. Colton.

MISSION BRIEF En route to Washington to answer a White House summons, the original G.I. Joe, Joseph Colton, recalls a previous situation from his early days as a first lieutenant. During a special forces mission in Vietnam's central highlands, enemy firepower whittled down Lt. Colton's team until only Colton, Sgt. Wenzel and specialist Angel Vasquez remained. A bullet grievously wounded Vasquez, but Colton and Wenzel carried their dying friend to an extraction zone and escaped aboard a CIA helicopter.

In flight, Lt. Colton suggested airlifting Vasquez to the nearest base camp for medical treatment, but the helicopter pilot overruled him, citing Pentagon-level orders to shuttle Colton on a two-hour trip to Tonsonhut base. Colton protested to no avail, but Vasquez, recalling a grotesque army practice of leaving dead soldiers on a tarmac for processing, begged his friend for a proper burial.

Vasquez died halfway through the journey, but at Tonsonhut, Colton blatantly disregarded an executive order to travel to Washington and immediately carried Vasquez's corpse to the army's graves registration department. After personally overseeing Vasquez's processing and internment, Colton continued his journey and arrived in the Oval Office.

Snake-Eyes' Vietnam Buddies

In airing his views about warfare, Snake-Eyes elaborates on the histories of his Vietnam comrades – including the late Ramon Escobedo and Dickie Saperstein – first heard of in *G.I. Joe* #26. Naturally, the group also included Wade Collins himself, but *G.I. Joe* #43 pretty much encapsulates his story. What follows is new information regarding the original soldiers who served with Snake-Eyes during his Vietnam tenure.

• **Stalker** – After Stalker's two brothers died – presumably due to gang warfare – in Detroit, Stalker grew more and more desperate to escape and begin a new life. Stalker enrolled in the military, but feared his mother, having already lost two sons, would worry too much. Thankfully, Stalker's cousin, an engineer in Darmstadt, Germany, helped Stalker concoct a cover story and routed his mother's letters. The ruse fooled Stalker's mama into thinking he was snug in a German personnel office. Although proud of his military service, Stalker doesn't regard it as a great adventure – preferring to think that tooling around in Germany might have been a far better quest.

• **Storm Shadow** – Storm Shadow's mentors selfishly looked upon the Vietnam War as a chance to hone their star pupil's prowess, and if truth be told, Storm Shadow's ninja senses and abilities greatly benefited from the field experience. Mind, he only got through the ordeal by resorting to sheer badness, and Snake-Eyes points out that by large measure, Storm Shadow became a "tightly wound psycho killer, desperately needing martial arts discipline to keep him in check."

• **Ramon Escobedo** – Ramon stood a fair chance of getting out of Vietnam unscathed, but as his tour of duty drew to a close, his kid brother finished basic training and got an infantry posting. Ramon magnanimously extended his tenure, sparing his kid brother under military rules forbidding that two family members serve in the same war zone. Two weeks later, Ramon's benevolence came to naught when enemy bullets killed him. As Snake-Eyes put it, "Ramon didn't look all that heroic when he died. He just looked surprised."

• **Dickie Saperstein** – In a decently frightening parallel, Dickie had two months of duty left before returning home. Regrettably, Dick's father lacked the money for a badly needed heart valve dilation. Dickie re-enlisted and paid for the operation with his re-enlistment bonus – a sadly fruitless act, given that his dad died on the operating table. Dickie could've potentially rotated home on a "compassionate" clause for his dad's death, but he took the "honorable" route and stayed put. But honor, as Snake-Eyes points out, didn't do Dickie much good when a landmine later tore him to shreds.

• **Snake-Eyes** – He's still searching for reasons to remain a soldier. Certainly, Snake-Eyes never got parades or medals upon returning home from the Vietnam War, although he memorably recalls spitting pro-peace advocates accusing him of being a child killer. He concedes that he wavered in trying to find a new identity, including his "disastrous" time spent with Storm Shadow's family in Japan. Stalker and Hawk later talked Snake-Eyes back into the military fold, but things hardly improved. After the helicopter accident that savaged his face (*G.I. Joe* #27), Snake-Eyes spent some time in a burn unit – listening to the screams of his fellow burn victims. The experience left Snake-Eyes with some perspective, however: As opposed to the other patients, he still possessed *most* of his face.

Despite all this, Snake-Eyes holds no regrets about becoming a soldier, taking solace in the fact that the occupation engenders camaraderie like no other. However, he's quick to point out that a soldier's fare, as young Sean Collins wants to claim, holds little honor.

There, Colton met with President John F. Kennedy, intrigued to hear the commander-in-chief's proposal for the creation of a new army unit directly accountable to the presidency. Kennedy asked Colton to head the unit, deeming it "a cadre of knights errant fit for a modern Camelot." Although Kennedy died before fulfilling his newest project, Colton accepted the president's offer – and thereby helped give rise to G.I. Joe.

MEMORABLE MOMENTS In a surprisingly visceral moment, a dying Vasquez recalls an occasion at Ban Me Thuot, when American officials temporarily lined up bodies of dead soldiers on the tarmac and covered them with ponchos. But every time a helicopter tried to land, the ponchos blew off the bodies, making the cadavers grotesquely flop about. It's a tremendously macabre fate, and one Vasquez hopes to avoid by asking Colton: "You ain't gonna let them leave me out on the tarmac like that, are you, lieutenant?"

Naturally, Colton agrees to Vasquez's request, later reflecting that if he'd known he was violating White House orders at the time, he "would have thought twice, but I still would have done it."

LOVE AND WAR Sgt. Wenzel threatens to "console" Jane (#86, #127) if something happens to Colton – suggesting romance between Colton and the so-named G.I. Jane.

ASS-WHUPPINGS Specialist Angel Vasquez goes to the Great Beyond, but Colton at least arranges for a proper burial.

NOW YOU KNOW... Jet pilots routinely shave their beards to guarantee a good seal if they've got to don an oxygen mask in a hurry. Ejecting simultaneously poses collision hazards, so make sure you bail out before or after your co-pilot. Colton sagely notes that payback never makes up for the deaths of your buddies, no matter how many enemies you mow down.

COMIC TIE-INS The White House summoned Joe Colton, the original G.I. Joe, in *G.I. Joe* #151, likely with the intent of reinstating him back to active service. Unfortunately, Marvel's *G.I. Joe* series ended shortly thereafter, leaving Colton in character limbo.

CHARACTER PROFILE: JOES

- *General Joseph R. Colton:* Officially he's a general, although he regards it mostly as a pay grade. He last sat in a combat jet (specifically, an F-4 Phantom) on the final leg of his White House trip in 1963. Colton's evidently got a decent amount of flight training – modern-day officials waive his re-certification in an altitude chamber.
- *President John F. Kennedy:* He formerly commanded a PT 109 wave-skimmer, but a Japanese destroyer sliced it in half during a conflict in the Pacific.

THE COMMAND DECISION A glowing highlight from the Joes' swan song year, *G.I. Joe* #152 deftly renders Colton's relationship with President Kennedy. More importantly, it displays the cut of Colton's jib, with his personal mandate to honor Vasquez's last request winning the day. Overall, a gem of a story that's worth celebrating.

G.I. Joe #153 to #154

Titles: *"Shadow of the B.A.T." (#153), "Flying the Unfriendly Skies" (#154)*
Release Dates: *Oct. to Nov. 1994*
Writers: *Eric Fein (#153), Peter Quinones (#154)*
Art: *Peter Quinones (#153), Ernie Stiner (#154)*

BATTLE ROSTER *Joes:* Scarlett, Roadblock.

MISSION BRIEF ***Issue #153:*** While Scarlett wanders about Salt Lake City pining for Snake-Eyes, a female Cobra engineer named Knox builds a lethal Cobra Battle Android Trooper (BAT) variant and sets her new creation after the red-haired Joe. Scarlett combats the new BAT all around town, desperately trying to avoid civilian casualties while staying one step ahead of the Terminator reject. Finally, Scarlett mangles the BAT in a city garbage compactor, ruining Knox's schemes and allowing Scarlett to enjoy a well-earned cup of coffee.

Issue #154: Granted shore leave, a gleeful Roadblock dresses himself in Western wear and departs for the airport, intending to grill his opponents in a chili cook-off contest. Unfortunately, Cobra espionage agents identify Roadblock as a Joe member and re-route him onto a plane stocked with a dizzying array of Cobra assassins and scalawags. Unable to simply blow Roadblock away – which would rupture the plane's cabin pressure – the motley crew tries to kill the Joe with a variety of knives, poisoned needles and taser weapons.

Roadblock plays cat-and-mouse with the Cobra agents, discovering that the plane's cargo hold contains illicit anti-tank missiles bound for various Cobra bases. Roadblock parachutes off the plane, obliterating the jet with a portable anti-tank launcher, then consumes his pouch of canned beans while waiting for the Joes to arrive at the plane's smoldering wreckage.

LOVE AND WAR Scarlett's itching to return to the High Sierras and resume making headboard-knocking sounds with Snake-Eyes. A couple of Vipers admire Knox's shapely posterior.

ASS-WHUPPINGS Scarlett crushes her BAT stalker like a frat brother flattening a beer can with his forehead. Roadblock douses one terrorist with chili powder, then smacks Cobra goon Igor in the face with a microwave. For an encore, Roadblock blows up the plane with a missile launcher, also tossing Igor overboard (and making the thug very flat).

PREPOSTEROUS PHYSICS At a construction site, Scarlett punctures an in-flight Cobra helicopter – with a rivet gun. The souped-up BAT throws a pickaxe at Scarlett, but it merely bounces off her leg and goes "BONK!" Knox's BAT survives when Scarlett drops several iron girders on his noggin, but doesn't withstand a city-ordnance garbage compactor. Roadblock clearly kicks a Cobra goon named Igor off the plane, but four pages later, Igor shows up again and Roadblock comments, "Igor, you old blowhard. You survived the wind tunnel!" (Author's Note: Screw the supposed "wind tunnel." He fell off the bloody plane.) Just for the record, Roadblock later makes Igor plummet to his doom a second time.

GOOFS Knox, supposedly an expert Cobra engineer, looks about as intellectual as Britney Spears. Scarlett walks around Salt Lake City with a trenchcoat covering her skimpy battle outfit and high-powered assault rifle (no, that's not conspicuous). When the BAT grabs a bystander, Scarlett plows a garbage truck into the robot – and miraculously fails to harm his hostage. The cover to #154, evidently drawn in advance by the lovely Amanda Conner (Soulsearchers and Company), shows Roadblock and Scarlett plummeting to their doom – even though Scarlett doesn't appear in the issue.

The supposedly cultured Roadblock's headed to compete in a chili cook-off, even though he previously slagged on chili (#22) as being woefully commonplace. For that matter, Roadblock claims in *this* issue that he hates canned chili – but carries it with him anyway.

COMIC TIE-INS Cobra recorded Scarlett's brainwaves off-panel while she recuperated in a Cobra-controlled hospital (#140-#141), enabling Knox's BAT to track her down. Knox's revamped BATs are simply an upgrade of the skeletal variant of BAT (a.k.a. BAT IIIs), first seen in *G.I. Joe* #132.

CHARACTER PROFILE: JOES

Roadblock: His serial number is RA 538-20-3485. Roadblock learned his cooking skills at Escoffier school in France. His Grandma Hinton allegedly possesses more secret spices than Colonel Sanders.

PLACES TO GO *The Pit III:* It's evidently located near Salt Lake City (one presumes Scarlett didn't drive hundreds of miles across Utah just to mope about a Salt Lake City sidewalk).

THE COMMAND DECISION A work so amateurish it nearly burned our fingers, the amateurish issues #153-#154 contain a spine-snapping amount of action flick dialogue (a Cobra goon radios Knox: "BATer up"; the normally tough-as-nails Scarlett hacks at the BAT while commenting, "You axed for this!") – not to mention some surface-level motivations. The final result's 10 to 15 minutes of your life that you'll never get back.

MISCELLANEOUS STUFF!

CLOSING THE PIT III

For anyone who stuck around for the end of the Marvel series, the Pit III's abrupt closing understandably left a few readers scratching their heads and asking, "What the hell happened?" Indeed, it wasn't immediately clear if the Joes or Cobra had won the war, although one largely suspects the former, given that the American government would hardly shut down the Joes and let Cobra run amok throughout the country. Certainly, *G.I. Joe* #155 offers no explanation for G.I. Joe's de-activation, although the upcoming *G.I. Joe: Frontline* will likely fill in some of the gaps. Furthermore, *G.I. Joe* (Image) #4 offers that the government initially closed the Pit III as a ploy to give the remaining Cobra forces a false sense of security. The plan supposedly worked, with the Jugglers supposedly shutting down the Joes for real a year later in 1995.

Also a cause of confusion, Marvel's *G.I. Joe* ends with Destro, the Baroness, Zartan, Billy and Storm Shadow still under Cobra Commander's mental thrall. In the seven-year gap between the Marvel run and *G.I. Joe* (vol. 2) #1, Destro, the Baroness and Zartan throw off their mental shackles and pretty much resume business as normal (*see Sidebar: Bridging the Seven-Year Gap in the Image write-up*). Billy also gets free, but falls into an emotional tailspin for years of abuse at Cobra Commander's hands. Finally, Cobra Commander treats Storm Shadow to even more rounds with his brainwave scanner, compelling Stormy to return to service as Cobra Commander's bodyguard in *G.I. Joe (*vol. 2) #4.

As for the heroes, a footnote in writer Larry Hama's farewell speech in *G.I. Joe* #155 mentions – although it's never seen onstage – that Snake-Eyes and Scarlett retire to the High Sierras after the Pit III's closing. However, the upcoming *G.I. Joe: Frontline* series will likely drop details about their activities afterward (for pity's sake, one presumes they didn't take up knitting or croquet).

G.I. Joe #155

Titles: *"A Letter From Snake-Eyes"*
Release Dates: *Dec. 1994*
Art: *Phil Gosier*

BATTLE ROSTER *Joes:* Snake-Eyes (present), Stalker, Storm Shadow (flashback); *Other:* Wade and Sean Collins.

MISSION BRIEF Happily living in an unspecified American town, Snake-Eyes' former teammate Wade Collins feels his gut tighten when his adopted son Sean, aged 17, announces his desire to enlist in the army. Sean asks Wade to sign his enlistment papers, but Wade, recalling the trials of his military service, implores his son to reconsider. Unable to persuade the rebellious teen to think otherwise, Wade proposes that Sean write his "uncle" Snake-Eyes for a second opinion.

Sean agrees, sending Snake-Eyes a letter just as the mournful Joes mothball the Pit III, preparing to retire from active service. Snake-Eyes reads Sean's inquiry, contemplating the passionate boy's belief that soldiers must adhere to heroic ideals. But in response, Snake-Eyes writes that concepts such as "honor" and "glory" count for preciously little on the battlefield.

Driving home his point, Snake-Eyes profiles the laudable men who served in his original Vietnam recon patrol – and how their heroism didn't mean spit when they died (*see Sidebar*). Snake-Eyes deftly stresses that even for the survivors, there's little gratitude and glory to be found upon returning home. At best, a soldier lives to earn a pension, but he shouldn't expect anything else.

Ultimately, Snake-Eyes implores Sean to look upon soldiering as a *national trust* rather than a call to duty, insisting that there's far more to lose than to gain. While Snake-Eyes doesn't regret his time as a soldier and fondly remembers the camaraderie he's experienced, he'd hardly label his occupation as "honorable."

Shortly afterward, Wade graciously offers to sign his son's enlistment papers, but Sean, reflecting on Snake-Eyes' words, asks for more time to decide about military service. Simultaneously, in Utah, the Joes hold a private ceremony to commemorate the Pit III's closing, folding an American flag to symbolize the end of G.I. Joe.

MEMORABLE MOMENTS Mostly tailored as a letter, *G.I. Joe* #155 doesn't offer many "moments" as Snake-Eyes' narration smoothly flows from one topic to the next. It sounds trite, but the entire issue almost is a Memorable Moment in itself – an intimate view into Snake-Eyes' very soul. If we're forced to choose a top moment, it's a tie between the Joes saluting the American flag for a final time and young Sean Collins deciding to put off his enlistment – a telling commentary on how sometimes, guns and violence don't make a finer world.

GOOFS The late Quick Kick, Crankcase and Breaker (who ate lead in *G.I. Joe* #109) appear with the other Joes on the cover of #155 – although it's possibly symbolic of their souls looking over the gathering. Less plausibly, Storm Shadow – brainwashed by Cobra Commander in *G.I. Joe* #150 – also puts in an appearance.

Scarlett claims Snake-Eyes hasn't received any correspondence since his family bit the dust (*G.I. Joe* #26), although that sounds like a nutty claim. (Do we seriously think Snake-Eyes hasn't received a letter in 20 years? From anyone? Not even Publisher's Clearing House?)

Snake-Eyes' narration states that Hawk and Stalker initially recruited him to join G.I. Joe, although the artwork shows Stalker and Storm Shadow in that role. Also, the original depiction of this scene (*G.I. Joe* #27) showed Snakes carrying a dead rabbit, not an axe.

COMIC TIE-INS On the transition between the Marvel and Image *G.I. Joe* series, see Sidebar. Wade Collins' family last appeared in *G.I. Joe* #108, when Snake-Eyes dropped a Borovian orphan on their doorstep (a bottle of milk – or indeed, a fruit basket – might have been preferable).

CHARACTER PROFILE: JOES Snake-Eyes: He couldn't sing, even before his accident.

PLACES TO GO The Pit III: The Joes retire their headquarters, but rig it for re-activation at a moment's notice.

THE COMMAND DECISION An unbelievably poignant finale, simultaneously bidding a sweet farewell to old friends while divesting anyone present from reveling in bloodshed. "A Letter to Snake-Eyes" makes for Larry Hama's swan song as well as the comic's finale, coming off as one of the most genuine examinations of war ever put to paper. Falling when it does at the series' finale, this ironically makes you see the previous 12 years of G.I. Joe comics in a more mature light.

Action Force #1 to #9

***Titles:** "Gun Boat!" (#1), "Cut and Run" (#2), "Run to Ground" (#3), "Coils of the Serpent" (#4), "Snow Chase" (#5), "Terror Tower!" (#6), "Fast Feud!" (#7), "A Bomb in Wardour Street!" (#8), "Holding the Baby!" (#9)*
***Release Date:** Mar. 3 to May 2, 1987 (weekly)*
***Writers:** Simon Furman (#1-#3, #7-#9), Mike Collins (#4-#6)*
***Art:** Kev Hopgood (#1-#6, #8-#9), Geoff Senior (#7)*
***Included reprints:** "Best Defense," G.I. Joe #50 (AF #1-#2); G.I. Joe #34 (AF #3-#4); G.I. Joe Special Missions #1 (AF #5-#6); G.I. Joe Special Missions #4 (AF #7-#8); G.I. Joe #25 (AF #9)*

BATTLE ROSTER *Joes:* Lady Jaye, Flint, Footloose, Barbecue, Shipwreck, Snake-Eyes, Scarlett, Alpine, Dusty, Airtight, Bazooka, Gung Ho; *Cobra:* Storm Shadow, Cobra Commander, Destro, the Dreadnoks.

Bridging the Marvel/Image Gap

[NOTE: The original version of this guidebook, released in 2002, wasn't able to incorporate much of the Devil's Due/Image series (2001-2005) that followed on from the Marvel Comics run. Rather than commit to a massive update, we've decided to leave things alone and tie things off with the Marvel series. The following sidebar, however, does flesh out what happened to many of the characters in the Marvel-Image gap, so seems worth reprinting here.]

After G.I. Joe disbanded (*G.I. Joe* #155), the Joes and Cobras largely went their separate ways, indulging in a variety of military and personal pursuits. The Image series pretty much establishes how the characters spent their time between the two *G.I. Joe* series, although the reference-minded *G.I. Joe Battle Files* #1 and #2 fill-in a lot of the gaps from the seven-year interim. The text that follows combines information from the two sources, spelling out where our heroes and villains went before their call to battle in *G.I. Joe* (vol. 2) #1.

THE JOES

• **Ace** – Performed stunt flying for movies (often summer blockbusters).

• **Airtight, Barbecue and Beach-Head** – They largely remained with the Army, quietly gaining promotions.

• **Bazooka** – Bazooka got old, bald and fat, bumping around from one security guard position to the next. He failed to pass the reformed G.I. Joe's physical requirements, but remains a Joe associate on detached status.

• **Clutch** – The mechanic-minded Clutch worked in a pit crew on the Indy Racing League circuit, earning numerous wins.

• **Duke** – He disappeared entirely after G.I. Joe folded, supposedly working as a black ops member for a government agency (possibly the CIA). Hawk's among the few who're aware of Duke's activities during this period. After turning up evidence of Cobra's revival (issue #5), Duke found himself hand-picked to serve as General Hawk's right-hand man. As such, he's technically the Joes' No. 2 leader, but he usually yields field command to Stalker, Gung Ho and Scarlett.

• **Dusty** – Dusty sharpened his skills on a tour of duty in Israel, but eventually tired of the locale. Recalled to America, Dusty teaches Joe recruits survival tactics.

• **Flint and Lady Jaye** – The two married several years after G.I. Joe folded, settling down in Ft. Meade, Maryland. While Lady Jaye entered semi-retirement, Flint continued working at the Pentagon. Hawk offered Flint a top slot as Joe field commander, but Flint declined, preferring to remain the team's primary tactical planner.

• **Frostbite** – Re-posted to Alaska, he was stationed at Ft. Greely Cold Regions Test Center.

• **Gung Ho** – Gung Ho remained with the Marines, later accepting a Joe field command position when Flint declined.

• **Hawk** – The Pentagon promoted Hawk to Lieutenant General, although the former Joe leader attained membership in the Jugglers – in order to keep tabs on the organization – through blackmail. Now sporting gray hair, Hawk does his damnedest to keep Joe operations hidden from the Jugglers' purview.

• **Heavy Duty** – Heavy Duty relocated to Chicago and started up a home recording studio, performing classical guitar music. He enjoyed the life, only reluctantly returning to the Joes.

• **Jinx** – Jinx took up gainful employment as a Tokyo-based bounty hunter, largely severing ties with the Joes and the remnants of the Arashikage clan. Relishing her new position and power, she flipped out when the Joes penetrated her aliases and tracked her down. Although she keeps quiet about her dealings in Japan, Jinx helps train new Joe recruits.

• **Lifeline** – After Doc's death (#109), the military offered to upgrade Lifeline's medical training. Lifeline enrolled at Johns Hopkins University before the Joes disbanded, later graduating and working at Walter Reed Medical Center.

• **Low-Light** – Night sniper Low-Light worked for the Criminal Investigation Division (CID).

• **Mainframe** – Mainframe developed software in Seattle.

• **Recondo** – He served several tours of duty in the African bush, busting up black market ivory trading rings.

• **Roadblock** – Roadblock became a veritable Emeril Lagasse, furthering a career as a nationally recognized gourmet chef. He's a *New York Times* bestseller, having

CONTINUED ON PAGE 269

Now You Know

NOTE As far as dating these stories goes, "Cut and Run" (#2) cites itself as happening on March 5, 1987.

MISSION BRIEF ***Issue #1:*** When the British Ministry of Defense learns that Cobra Commander's arranged to receive a sizeable weapons shipment from Destro, the English branch of G.I. Joe – code-named "Action Force" – readies itself to prevent the arms from reaching the open sea. Unfortunately, Cobra Commander and Destro arrange for the swap to take place aboard a legitimate yacht party, hosted by the wealthy David Bryant. Not wanting to injure the innocent partygoers, the Joes conspire to blow up the ship without civilian casualties.

Meanwhile, Cobra Commander and Destro secretly board the yacht while it's moored in the Thames' West India dock section. As Joe firefighter Barbecue slips below decks to plant incendiaries, naval officer Shipwreck sets off a series of smoke bombs. Dressed as civilians, Action Force members Flint and Lady Jaye evacuate the partygoers amid the mayhem. Cobra Commander and Destro's forces rally against the heroes, but Storm Shadow – his alliance to Cobra wavering – secretly helps Barbecue prime his explosives. The ninja warns Cobra Commander and Destro about the impending explosion, thereby covering his ass and allowing everyone involved to flee just as the bomb rips the ship to shreds.

Issues #2-#3: When Snake-Eyes and Scarlett arrive for duty at Action Force's hidden base in London, they run a simulated practice session in the facility's SIMCOM room. Flint guides Snake-Eyes and Scarlett through a falsified Cobra frogman ambush in order to hone their battle skills. Unfortunately, a *real* frogman (captured by Footloose in *Action Force* #1) escapes the base's detention block. Snake-Eyes and Scarlett dispatch their facsimile opponents, but the genuine Eel harpoons Scarlett's arm and momentarily stuns Snake-Eyes, fleeing into the Thames.

Flint and Snake-Eyes bind Scarlett's wound, then trail the runaway Eel into London. But the crafty frogman thrashes some street punks, stealing their clothing and making for a Cobra hideout in a Tastee Burgers restaurant. While Flint stops to radio for reinforcements, Snake-Eyes, scouring the Tastee Burgers roof for the frogman's escape route, spies a helicopter piloted by Cobra Commander and Destro. Leaving Flint behind, Snake-Eyes hitches a ride with the Cobra leaders, hoping to infiltrate their base of operations.

Issues #4-#5: Cobra Commander and Destro come home to roost at Castle Destro in the Balkans, completely oblivious to their ninja stowaway. Meanwhile, Snake-Eyes eavesdrops on the Cobra leaders' conversation, learning that they intend to destroy the Eiffel Tower – the first strike in a new tidal wave of terror.

Snake-Eyes attempts to flee, but a routine Cobra patrol raises the alarm. Gunning his way to freedom, Snake-Eyes makes for the snowy mountain passes near Castle Destro. Unfortunately, Dreadnoks Buzzer and Ripper give chase, grazing Snake-Eyes with a bullet from afar. Bleeding profusely, Snake-Eyes reaches a local hotel and faxes Cobra's assault plans to Joes in Geneva. The two Dreadnoks gut the hotel, but Snake-Eyes upends their motorcycles with a trip-wire. After stealing Buzzer's bike in the confusion, the Joe ninja slowly makes his way back towards base.

Issues #6-#7: Warned by Snake-Eyes' fax, a quartet of Joes arrive in Paris to guard the Eiffel Tower. Lady Jaye and her colleagues bushwhack a pack of Crimson Guardsmen, preventing the elite Cobra troopers from scrapping the tower with a thermite grenade. Regrettably, a successful Cobra bombing in Rome dampens the Joes' victory, hailing the opening volley of a Cobra onslaught.

Taking back the offensive, Flint leads a Joe platoon against the Tastee Burgers restaurant in St. James' Park. The Joes kick the stuffing out of a Crimson Guardsmen troupe, capturing Storm Shadow in the process. Unfortunately, the Joes also locate a well-detailed map of London's busiest shopping district – undoubtedly marking the next target in Cobra's terror campaign.

Issue #8-9: Flint fails to convince local authorities of the threat posed by Cobra, leaving Action Force the frenzied duty of scouring Wardour Street for explosives. In short order, Lady Jaye happens across a female Crimson Guardsman pushing a stroller containing a "baby" made from sticks of dynamite. Footloose quickly apprehends the Cobra agent, but Lady Jaye unwisely lifts the "baby" out of its stroller – starting its countdown and activating a motion-sensitive trigger. Frozen to the spot, Lady realizes she daren't move for fear of blowing up the "baby" – and herself.

Action Force engineers frantically examine the bomb, but fail to disarm it. As the timer approaches zero, an inspired Flint handcuffs the captive Cobra agent to Lady Jaye's wrist. Panicked, the Crimson Guardswoman tells Flint to snip the bomb's blue wire, ending the threat. Afterward, Lady Jaye asks Flint what he would've done if the Cobra goon hadn't cracked, forcing Flint to admit he'd already flipped a coin to make his decision – and would've cut the red wire instead.

MEMORABLE MOMENTS An amusing warning on the opening to *Action Force* #2 cautions: "Scarlett and Snake-Eyes are highly trained Action Force personnel – on NO account should you play on London Underground tracks."

A sweating, dynamite-holding Lady Jaye ponders if her world will end in pain – or simply a blinding flash of light. Finally, Flint wryly confesses how he'd chosen the wrong deto-

Bridging the Marvel/Image Gap

CONTINUED FROM PAGE 267

written several cookbooks, and endorses an entire line of cooking products bearing his name. But for returning to the Joes, Roadblock would've probably hosted a nationwide cooking show.

• **Rock 'n Roll** – The scruffy Joe machine gunner became a training instructor at Ft. Meade, Maryland, doing his best to ignore the facility's stringent dress code. Rock 'n Roll currently runs the Joes' weight training program.

• **Scarlett and Snake-Eyes** – The two of them got engaged, but Snake-Eyes wigged out on Scarlett a few weeks before the wedding (*see Love and War*). Plagued by cold feet, Snake-Eyes fled to his Sierra cabin. At an unspecified point, he assumed the mantle of "the Silent Master," accepting ninja novice Kamakura as his pupil. Scarlett currently holds a high-ranking Joe field command position along with Gung Ho and Stalker.

• **Shipwreck** – He retired from the military, mostly running a lucrative tour guide service across the globe. Shipwreck also developed a feared reputation among international criminals, helping the military bust up modern day pirate rings and small-time drug traffickers. Today, Shipwreck drills the Joes' naval recruits into shape.

• **Spirit** – Spirit returned to a reservation in Taos, New Mexico, attempting to elevate the residents out of poverty. He now trains freshmen Joes.

• **Stalker** – He maintained some military service but moreso devoted himself to his wife and two boys in Detroit, MI. Stalker currently shares field command with Scarlett and Gung Ho.

• **Tunnel Rat** – Tunnel Rat returned to his native Brooklyn, helping to motivate neighborhood kids from disadvantaged backgrounds. He's returned to G.I. Joe on reserve status.

• **Wild Bill** – If you can believe it, Wild Bill pursued a country singing career in his hometown of Brady, Texas.

COBRA

And just so you know, here's how the Cobra elite spent their seven-year sabbatical:

• **Cobra Commander** – After Cobra's collapse, Cobra Commander roamed the globe as an international fugitive. Allying himself with anti-American terrorist factions and dictatorships, Cobra Commander largely rebuilt Cobra's army from the likes of Middle East youth, displaced Cuban refugees and jaded American soldiers.

• **Big Boa and Copperhead** – The boxing Big Boa and hovercraft pilot Copperhead never cropped up in Marvel's *G.I. Joe* series. Nonetheless, they're both apparently Cobra veterans, with Big Boa – who supposedly owes Cobra Commander some type of debt – responsible for whipping Cobra cadets into shape. Having racked up a staggering debt, Copperhead now heads Cobra's naval forces as a means of dodging creditors.

• **Dr. Mindbender** – He consulted as a freelance engineer to some of the world's top weapons manufacturers, including Destro's MARS corporation.

• **Firefly** – After the red ninja fiasco (#132-#134), Firefly returned to his saboteur roots. He's been spotted several times around the world, but his whereabouts are unknown.

• **Major Bludd** – After Cobra's dissolution, Major Bludd was captured in 1995. Officials sentenced him (presumably for life) to Ft. Leavenworth prison, but Bludd escaped in 1997 after inciting a riot. He's worked for several dictators and terrorists, holding some involvement with former KGB official Colonel Nakita.

• **Saw-Viper** – Snake-Eyes and Storm Shadow left the Saw-Viper, who killed a frightening number of Joes in *G.I. Joe* #109, to die in #112. However, *G.I. Joe Battle Files* #2 suggests the bastard survived the experience. If he's alive and kicking, the Saw-Viper's likely working as a mercenary in Europe.

• **Scrap Iron** – His whereabouts are unknown.

• **Storm Shadow** – Cobra Commander treated the already brainwashed Storm Shadow (#150) to extensive doses of the brainwave scanner, wringing out the ninja's brain like a tea towel. Inflicted with complete amnesia, Storm Shadow's resumed his role as Cobra Commander's bodyguard.

• **Tomax and Xamot** – They resumed running their Extensive Enterprises corporation full time, escaping Cobra's dissolution unscathed.

• **Wild Weasel** – He became a smuggler, illegally exporting a myriad of substances into the Americas. Wild Weasel currently commands Cobra's air division.

CONTINUED ON PAGE 271

nator cable, capping this storyarc with an edge of seriousness.

LOVE AND WAR Destro welcomes the Baroness to his castle, naughtily mentioning that his family prides itself on "meeting the needs of its guests."

ASS-WHUPPINGS Shipwreck plugs a Cobra guard at point-blank range. Snake-Eyes and Scarlett tear a bunch of simulated Eels to pieces, while a real Cobra frogman harpoons Scarlett in the arm. On the streets of London, said frogman dispatches a mohawked street gang. Snake-Eyes sprays a bunch of Cobra guards with his Uzi, but Dreadnok Ripper pegs the fleeing Joe commando in the arm.

GOOFS In *Action Force* #8, the Crimson Guard saboteur walks down the street with only a trenchcoat covering her Cobra uniform – a somewhat obvious giveaway for an espionage mission.

COMIC TIE-INS The Cobra elite here operate out of "Castle Destro" – evidently the same edifice seen in "Silent Interlude" (*G.I. Joe* #21). Keep in mind that the American run first tagged this location as "Castle Destro," with later issues (*G.I. Joe* #57 and #121) retroactively citing it as a separate location named "the Silent Castle." As such, it's best to detach your brain and realize that the American comics put "Castle Destro" in Scotland, but the British *Action Force* plants it in the Balkan Mountains. (Of course, Destro claims to own "many houses.")

As *Action Force* #1 demonstrates, Storm Shadow's already lamenting his work for Cobra, foreshadowing his future change of heart in *G.I. Joe* #38 or *AF* #41 (depending on which you favor). In *AF* #7, Scarlett sees Storm Shadow's wrist brand for the first time, but fails to recognize his relationship with Snake-Eyes.

Cobra keeps an official consulate in London, similar to the New York Consulate (first mentioned in *G.I. Joe* #55).

CHARACTER PROFILE: JOES

• *Barbecue:* Given enough time, he can arrange blast-resistant screens to contain explosions.

• *Crankcase:* Serves as Action Force's artillery expert.

• *Footloose:* This version's much more lucid than his US incarnation – a highly effective field agent with a Scottish brogue.

• *Flint:* Designated as Action Force's leader.

• *Lady Jaye:* In addition to soldiering, Lady Jaye's worked as a scholar and an actress. She's been with the Joes for a few years and is proficient in 18 languages. Lady Jaye's frightfully competent with an M-16 assault rifle or crossbow, and she knows a wealth of disguise skills.

• *Scarlett:* Possesses oodles of ninja skills, but she's not a proper ninja.

• *Shipwreck:* Supplies Action Force with naval intelligence.

• *Snake-Eyes and Scarlett:* Mostly affiliated with the American-based Joes, they're only on temporary attachment to Action Force.

• *R. Trent:* Action Force's liaison with the British Ministry of Defense, he's Flint's superior when Action Force operates in the British Isles.

CHARACTER PROFILE: COBRA

• *The Baroness:* She's loyal to Cobra Commander – at least, more than she is to Destro.

• *Cobra Commander and Destro:* Destro's first and foremost a businessman out for profit. As such, Destro views Cobra as a blunt instrument that tries to gobble up power without worrying about the outcome. He worries when Cobra Commander blathers about overthrowing the current order, since near-anarchy and governmental upheaval isn't always conducive to good business. Destro's hoping to refine Cobra's agendas and goals, or, failing that, simply eliminate Cobra Commander and take over.

Destro briefly considers, then dismisses working for Action Force – both because they're "ridiculous idealists" and because they don't pay well. A pulled-back shot of the unmasked Cobra Commander and Destro suggests they're both bald.

ORGANIZATIONS *Action Force:* Usually acts independently, although it can quickly summon help from the United States or Geneva when needed.

• *The Destro family:* The Destro clan's conducted business with all levels of tyrants and despots ever since the Crusades. A 17th century Destro sold weapons to Swedish aggressors. Another Destro helped Frederick the Great arm Prussia to become the strongest military state before Napoleon's France.

PLACES TO GO *Action Force's British Headquarters:* It's concealed near the Westminster Tube stop on the London Underground. A palm-scanning device allows Action Force members and affiliates to enter through a hidden door.

• *Castle Destro:* Castle Destro has stood since the 13th century. In the 1930s and 1940s, it decorated itself with Nazi swastikas and the German imperial eagle.

THE COMMAND DECISION Adequate enough for the purpose of introducing the Action Force cast, although its episodic format – understandably forged to keep readers engaged on a week-by-week basis – feels crude when read together. As such, you'll fare better if you look at issues #1-#9 as elaborate set pieces. Thankfully, the unpolished storyarc climaxes with a sweet cliffhanger in #8 (Lady Jaye holding a baby bomb), and Flint's delicious confession about how he nearly blew them all away.

Bridging the Marvel/Image Gap

CONTINUED FROM PAGE 269

THE DREADNOKS

• **Zartan, Zarana, the Dreadnoks and Zanya** – Shaking off his brainwashing (suffered in *G.I. Joe* #145), Zartan furthered the Dreadnok cause for his own gain. The Dreadnoks soon embarked on a nationwide crime spree, rising to become America's most feared biker gang. Dreadnok chapters sprung up in more than 30 states, but Zartan couldn't fully enjoy his organization's success. Years of genetic tinkering, used to refine his disguise talent – finally caught up with Zartan, leaving him with a debilitating skin disease. The Dreadnoks presumed Zartan would hand the torch of leadership to his sister Zarana, but Zartan surprisingly favored his daughter Zanya. Pissed at her brother, Zarana cut off all ties and now runs the Chicago Dreadnok chapter.

In exchange for Zartan's services, McCullen (Destro's son) programmed some nano-mites to heal Zartan's skin condition. Although Zartan's health could still take a turn for the worse, he's largely stabilized.

• **Torch** – Dreadnok Torch inherited his Uncle Winkin's hard grape soda company, surprisingly nurturing it into a thriving business. (Mind, it helps that the Crimson Twins manage Torch's portfolio.)

... and NEARLY EVERYONE ELSE

• **Billy (a.k.a. William Kessler)** – Billy also freed himself from Cobra Commander's brainwashing (#145-#151), although the effort – combined with years of a less-than-desirable upbringing – left him an emotional wreck. Billy disappeared for much of the 1990s, hiding out in Scotland until Spirit and Kamakura recruited Billy's help in freeing the briefly captured Scarlett and Snake-Eyes (*G.I. Joe* vol. 2 #3). Kicked into action, Billy formally enlists with the Joes in *G.I. Joe* vol. 2 #6.

• **The Night Creepers** – They're dutifully employed tossing CEOs out open windows on behalf of unscrupulous corporations.

• **The Oktober Guard** – They largely disbanded when the Soviet Union fell, although the survivors united under the command of a Russian colonel codenamed "Red Star." (*G.I. Joe* #145-#148)

Action Force #10 to #13

Titles: *"Moroccan Roll!" (#10), "Rigged!" (#11-#12), "The Man in the Silver Mask!" (#13)*
Release Dates: *May 9 to 30, 1987*
Writer: *Mike Collins*
Art: *Kev Hopgood (#10, #13), Geoff Senior (#11-#12)*
Included reprints: *G.I. Joe #25 (AF #9-#10); G.I. Joe #26 (AF #11-#12); G.I. Joe #27 (#13)*

BATTLE ROSTER *Joes:* Flint, Lady Jaye, Alpine, Dusty, Footloose, Shipwreck, Wild Bill, Cutter, Bazooka, Quick Kick; *Cobra:* Destro.

MISSION BRIEF In Casablanca, Action Force members Dusty, Lady Jaye and Alpine meet with Farouk, a Cobra defector offering then vital information. The trio manages to speak with Farouk for all of three seconds before Cobra assassins peg the traitor with a venom-tipped dart. Farouk warns the Joes that Cobra Commander intends to assault an Argent Corporation oil rig – as an opening gambit toward snagging control of the global oil market – then expires.

Flint immediately capitalizes on Farouk's information, leading an Action Force platoon to savage a Cobra phalanx already aboard the oil rig. Action Force easily prevails, but to Flint's horror, Destro steps forth as the legitimate owner of Argent Corporation. Having falsely leaked information through Farouk to discredit Action Force's reputation, Destro asserts his rights as a fully accredited businessman. In short order, a secondary Cobra team rounds up Flint's crew for piracy on the high seas, securing them aboard the oil rig.

News footage of the illegal assault spreads like wildfire through Britain, forcing anti-Action Force elements in Parliament to curtail the group's authority in the British Isles. Unwilling to leave his teammates at Destro's mercies, silent weapons expert Quick Kick infiltrates the oil rig and liberates Flint's team. Destro willingly allows the rescue, figuring that Action Force's escape will further dampen their credibility. Furthermore, Destro travels to Morocco and meets with the "late" Farouk – a Cobra loyalist who faked his death to mislead the Joes. With Action Force already under heavy scrutiny from

British officials, Destro capitalizes on the heroes' lack of attention to North Africa and other regions, allowing him to spread his arms-dealing empire to those regions.

ASS-WHUPPINGS Over-zealous Cobra assassins defy capture by gulping down venom capsules. The Joes carve through Cobra troops on the Argent oil rig. Destro kills an Action Force informant with a wrist-fired crossbow bolt.

GOOFS Dusty knows that a landing helicopter contains the owner of Argent Corporation – which seems strange, since it's not as if there's a sign proclaiming, "Hello, I run Argent."

COMIC TIE-INS Destro says he formerly served as his father's apprentice, running guns for the Arabs, although *Action Force* #45 fleshes out his true relationship with Daddy Destro. *AF* #44-#46 also takes place in Casablanca – with grave consequences for Destro and Farouk.

The British government curtails Action Force's activities here, although the Joes resume full operations in *AF* #22.

CHARACTER PROFILE: JOES

• *Alpine and Dusty:* Alpine speaks French, but Dusty doesn't.

CHARACTER PROFILE: COBRA

• *Destro:* He's publicly known as a legitimate arms dealer (if there is such a thing). Highly adept at hand-to-hand combat, he believes that his career as a master weaponsmith requires keeping his own body in tip-top condition.

• *Farouk:* He works for Destro's MARS corporation, but he hasn't seen Destro in 10 to 15 years.

ORGANIZATIONS *Action Force:* British officials worry about Action Force, an international organization, working in the U.K. without directly answering to the British government. It also doesn't help matters that Action Force agents mask their true identities with code-names. In Parliament, Elwyn Jones (MP for Llatwon, South Wales) is Action Force's biggest critic.

• *Cobra:* These issues portray Cobra in a cult-like fashion, with Cobra agents willing to commit kamikaze runs or take suicide pills in order to aid the organization's cause.

• *MARS:* Destro chiefly runs his family business, MARS, but also funds a global subsidiary business named Silversmile. Thanks to its union with Cobra, MARS has greatly expanded Destro's Middle East enterprises. Cobra/MARS keeps an underground headquarters in Casablanca.

THE COMMAND DECISION Standard military action lathered with a veneer of irrelevance (despite legal sanctions imposed on Action Force, life continues as normal).

Action Force #14 to #17

Title: *"Cold Comfort"*
Release Dates: *June 6 to 27, 1987*
Writer: *Simon Furman*
Art: *Steve Yeowell (#14-#15), Simon Furman (#16-#17)*
Included reprints: *G.I. Joe #27 (AF #13-#14); G.I. Joe #28 (AF #15-#16); G.I. Joe #29 (AF #17)*

BATTLE ROSTER *Joes:* Quick Kick, Flint, Wild Bill.

MISSION BRIEF With British officials scrutinizing Action Force's movements at every turn, Quick Kick despairs when Valerie Anke, wife of longtime friend and fellow stuntman Michael Anke, contacts him to say that Michael's disappeared. Valerie details how a fanatical, anti-American cult named "the Two-Headed Serpent" seduced her husband, prompting his sudden relocation to China. Quick Kick immediately goes AWOL, tracking his friend to an abandoned monastery in the Himalayas.

Quick Kick identifies "the Two-Headed Serpent" as a breakaway Cobra group, outlawed by the Cobra elite. After stealing a guard's uniform, Quick Kick infiltrates the cult's hideout – only to find Michael serving as the renegades' all-too-willing leader.

Shortly afterward, Cobra pinpoints the cult's hideout and unleashes a massive air attack, hoping to bring the insurrectionist sect to heel. While Cobra forces slaughter the cult members almost to a man, Michael makes a run for his private helicopter. Quick Kick intercepts his former friend, leading to a duel atop the cult's stronghold. In the course of the skirmish, Quick Kick pitches Michael aside – accidentally throwing the cult leader to his death.

An Action Force detachment led by Flint soon arrives, having tracked the absent Quick Kick to the monastery. Flint tries to console Quick Kick, insisting that he acted in self-defense, but Quick Kick shrugs off Flint's words, despairing over having killed the man he tried to save.

MEMORABLE MOMENTS *Action Force* #16 unloads a spellbinding cliffhanger, with Cobra phalanxes showing up to pound the Two-Headed Serpent into submission. Sadly, there's little time in #17 to see the fracas unfold.

ASS-WHUPPINGS Quick Kick missiles one FANG helicopter, grenades another and knocks a bunch of Serpent members unconscious. Michael stretches Quick Kick on some stakes on a freezing mountaintop, but QK escapes. Michael finishes the story very flat.

GOOFS Similar to TV's "The Pyramid of Darkness," Quick Kick demonstrates an astounding ability to wander around frozen mountaintops while shirtless and shoeless.

COMIC TIE-INS Action Force's activities were curtailed in *AF* #12, meaning Quick Kick and Flint are operating here without legal authority.

CHARACTER PROFILE: JOES

• *Flint:* He threatened to quit Action Force if it meant getting Quick Kick back safely, netting Trent's unofficial assent for a rescue mission.

• *Quick Kick:* Quick Kick's father taught him that friendship pretty much transcends all considerations, fueling his personal mission to redeem Michael. Papa Quick Kick also instilled in his boy that one learns martial arts to prevent violence, not sire it. Quick Kick previously found employment as a Hollywood stunt man, but tired of the life and accepted Flint's offer to join Action Force. He's fast enough to grab thrown knives and hurl them away.

CHARACTER PROFILE: OTHER

Michael Anke: A complete and utter dirtball despite his past friendship with Quick Kick.

ORGANIZATIONS *The Two-Headed Serpent:* Establishing themselves as a breakaway Cobra faction, the Serpent members wear a two-headed adaptation of Cobra sigil. They're primarily in China to recruit and train communist fanatics for suicide missions against American interests.

THE COMMAND DECISION The best Action Force arc since the series' launch, this story drives home Quick Kick's wrenching failure to save Michael. It's a pity that *Action Force* didn't explore the notion of Cobra splinter groups further, since it's such an interesting track to follow.

Action Force #18 to #22

Titles: *"Dummy Run!" (#18), "Doppelganger!" (#19-#22)*
Release Dates: *July 4 to Aug. 1, 1987*
Writers: *Steve White (#18), Ian Rimmer (#19-#22).*
Art: *Geoff Senior (#18), Kev Hopgood (#19-#22).*
Included reprints: *G.I. Joe #29 (AF #18-#19); G.I. Joe #30 (AF #20-#21); G.I. Joe #32 (AF #22-#23).* ***NOTE:*** *Action Force Summer Special #1 reprinted G.I. Joe #31.*

BATTLE ROSTER *Joes:* Shipwreck, Flint, Lady Jaye, Crankcase, Heavy Metal, Footloose; *Cobra:* Destro, Copperhead.

MISCELLANEOUS STUFF!

BRITISH CONTINUITY CONNIPTIONS

Presuming you're already fluent with the American *G.I. Joe* comics, combing through the *Action Force* material proves problematic, even nightmarish. Put simply, it's crucial to remember that British creators crafted *Action Force* solely for a UK audience. As a result, the continuity's hopelessly futzed to hell – but you'd only know this if you're an American.

The root of the problem stems from the haphazard manner in which *Action Force* reprinted the American *G.I. Joe* series. For whatever reason, the American stories got sufficiently randomized, forcing the British-only stories to apply a hopeless amount of continuity glue to keep UK readers from getting confused.

To wit, *Action Force* reprints *G.I. Joe* #25 (showing Storm Shadow's imprisonment on Alcatraz Island), but never bothers to publish *G.I. Joe* #24 (where he wounded Gung Ho and got apprehended in the first place). To explain the discrepancy, "Fast Feud!" (*Action Force* #7) lets Storm Shadow carve up Gung Ho a second time and – you guessed it – get nabbed in the process.

Continuity only nosedives from there. *Action Force* reprinted "Silent Interlude" (*G.I. Joe* #21) way, way late in the game, forcing "Prologue" (*Action Force* #37) to explain how Storm Shadow kidnapped Scarlett in the first place (thereby contradicting with the American explanation in *G.I. Joe* #22). Also, Storm Shadow's shifting loyalties throughout the scrambled American reprints force UK stories in *Action Force* #38, #40-#41 to massage Storm Shadow's beliefs, finally arriving at the point where he and Snake-Eyes storm Cobra Island (*Action Force* #44-#50 or *G.I. Joe* #45-#47, depending on which you prefer).

P.S. The UK editorializing wasn't limited to *Action Force*'s original stories – the American reprints underwent some surgery too. British letterers replaced all dialogue references to "G.I. Joe" with the words "Action Force," and some continuity splicing also occurred – for instance, a reprint of *G.I. Joe* #25 makes Cobra Commander talking about Wild Weasel instead of Major Bludd, since Bludd virtually never appeared in the UK run. It's a wacky solution for a wacky world.

MISSION BRIEF ***Issue #18:*** At a weapons range on Salisbury Plain in southwest England, Flint, Lady Jaye and Heavy Metal prepare to test their refitted Mauler tank's capabilities. Unfortunately, Destro disguises himself as a hippie and directs a Cobra helicopter assault against the Joe tank. Flint's crew pulps their attackers with the Mauler's prototype anti-helicopter missiles, but Destro, having arranged the assault purely to check the Joe missiles' efficiency, makes a note to steal one of the missiles and replicate it in his arms factories for enormous profit.

Issues #19-#22: With the oil-rich nation of Ishmali firming up relations with Britain, Cobra marks Ahmen Hassan – slated to become the first Ishmali ambassador to England – for assassination, hoping to discredit the West. Flint learns of the plot, but with Action Force's jurisdiction in England still being questioned (*AF* #12), Ministry of Defense liaison Trent orders the Joes to refrain from action.

Going against Trent's wishes, Flint and a covert team monitor Hassan's arrival at Jefferson Military Base in England. To bolster their security, the Joes swap a disguised Shipwreck for the real Hassan. Unfortunately, Cobra jeeps attack Hassan's escort, making off with Hassan/Shipwreck and a random policeman as hostages.

The Cobra heads with their captives toward an underwater base, but a Cobra guard spots Shipwreck's wrist tattoo – blowing his cover. The sailor slugs his opponents, then steals a Cobra hovercraft and charges to freedom. A merry chase on the Thames ensues, but Flint finally swoops in with a helicopter, saving both Shipwreck and the kidnapped policeman. Cobra abandons their bid to kill Hassan, but even more fortuitously, the Joes identify the rescued policeman as Reece Jones – the son of Elwyn Jones, their chief opponent in Parliament. Forced to soften his anti-Action Force stance, MP Elywn Jones arranges to lift the legal sanction blocking the Joes from operations in the United Kingdom.

MEMORABLE MOMENTS Issue #18 features Destro dressed as a 1960s hippie, waving at the Joes and drawling, "Peace, man."

ASS-WHUPPINGS A fleeing Shipwreck causes a huge hovercraft pile-up.

COMIC TIE-INS Parliament here lifts legal sanctions against Action Force (imposed in *Action Force* #12).

CHARACTER PROFILE: JOES

Shipwreck: He genuinely looks like Ambassador Hassan, merely requiring some hair dye and a change of clothes to complete the part. Shipwreck's got a sailor's tattoo (an anchor of some sort) on his wrist. He's unfamiliar with the controls on a Cobra hovercraft, but he figures it out during a crisis.

HOT WHEELS Joe Mauler Tank: Able to take direct hit from a FANG helicopter and keep moving.

THE COMMAND DECISION Issue #18's a cute little one-off story, worth the price of admission just to see Destro dressed up as a Woodstock reject. Regrettably, issues #19-#22 waste creative serum with every installment. The fact that purely by happenstance, Action Force rescues the one policeman in all of England who can help their legal cause, makes you smack your forehead and cry, "D'oh!"

Action Force #23

Title: *"Gas Masque"*
Release Date: *Aug. 8, 1987*
Writer: *James Hill*
Art: *Brett Ewins*
Included reprint: *G.I. Joe #32.*

BATTLE ROSTER *Joes:* Heavy Metal, Flint, Quick Kick, Alpine; *Cobra:* Destro.

MISSION BRIEF When a Cobra operative named Tony Lander steals a lethal nerve gas canister from a military installation in Dartmoor, Action Force madly gives chase. When the Joes corner Lander on the rooftop of an abandoned warehouse, Joe driver Heavy Metal recognizes Lander as an old school chum.

Heavy Metal tries to reason with his friend, but the suicidal Lander – completely unhinged from his experiences as a Cobra trooper – makes ready to kill himself and half of southwest England with the nerve gas. But in a blur of motion, Quick Kick bats Lander's nerve gas canister aside. Lander moves for the deadly toxin, but Heavy Metal threatens to shoot his former classmate if needed. Faced with a stalemate, Lander hesitates and ponders his choice.

Suddenly, Destro appears in a helicopter and mercilessly shoots Lander through the heart. While the Joes gape in response, Destro cites Lander as an insane maverick who should've been culled from Cobra's ranks a long time ago. The metal-faced one departs, leaving Heavy Metal to thirst for vengeance against Destro – yet acknowledge that their steel-plated adversary may have saved thousands of lives.

MEMORABLE MOMENTS The final showdown, with Heavy Metal glaring at Destro but unable to act, grips your chest in an iron gauntlet.

ASS-WHUPPINGS Destro fills Lander with lead.

CHARACTER PROFILE: JOES

Heavy Metal: Heavy Metal feels he owes Lander for protecting him from school bullies.

CHARACTER PROFILE: COBRA

Destro: He's not automatically opposed to the thought of murdering thousands – it's just that he'd only commit such an act for a *purpose*, be it power, glory or conquest. Senseless death and violence offends Destro's sensibilities.

THE COMMAND DECISION A winner, proving what one can accomplish in a scant five pages, "Gas Masque!" marshals a sizeable amount of characterization and emotions (when Heavy Metal looks upward in the last panel, you can feel every shade of anger racing through his head).

Transformers (UK) #125, Action Force #24 to #27

Title: *"Ancient Relics"*
Release Dates: *Aug. 8, 15, 22, 29; Sept. 5, 1987*
Writer: *Simon Furman*
Art: *Geoff Senior*
Included reprints: *G.I. Joe #32 (AF #24); G.I. Joe #33 (AF #25-#27)*

NOTE Although we're counting *Action Force* as *G.I. Joe* apocrypha, this G.I. Joe/Transformers crossover forms an important part of Transformers continuity.

Once again, there's no time here to explain the conflict between the heroic Autobots and evil Deceptions (transforming robots from the planet Cybertron, for those of you that slept through the 80s). Suffice it to say that this story helps bring Decepticon leader Megatron back from the dead. Also, Autobot leader Grimlock's currently fuming over the defection of Blaster and Goldbug, who object to Grimlock's increasingly tyrannical leadership style. With that in mind, read on:

BATTLE ROSTER *Joes:* Flint, Scarlet, Airtight, Barbecue, Bazooka, Wild Bill; Autobots: Grimlock, Centurion, Blades; Decepticons: Megatron.

MISSION BRIEF Autobot leader Grimlock dispatches his henchmen around the globe to locate the missing Blaster and Goldbug (who defected in American TF #28) – fully intending to punish the two deserters. Hovering above London as part of his sweep, Protectobot helicopter Blades detects an unidentified Transformer life-form in Roman-built tunnels beneath the city. Meanwhile, reports of a "robotic monster" in the tunnels also prompt a swift response from Action Force.

Blades and Action Force separately explore the tunnels, stumbling across the eviscerated, highly confused Megatron (still recovering from injuries inflicted in American *TF* #25). Megatron shoots Blades in the back, then pursues the Action Force team. Outclassed, Flint's group withdraws to the surface and hits Megatron with a futile tank, helicopter and plane assault.

Arriving in response to Blades' request for back-up, Grimlock and fellow Autobot Centurion engage Megatron near a natural gas refinery. Acknowledging Grimlock's benevolence, Flint nonetheless readies a Skystriker jet assault to blow up the refinery and end Megatron's threat to the civilian population – even if it means ending Grimlock's life. Judging himself more expendable than Grimlock, Centurion wrestles Megatron into position while Blades pulls Grimlock clear. Action Force's Skystriker missiles devastate the refinery, chucking both Megatron and Centurion into the Thames. Failing to find either their friend or Megatron, Grimlock and Blades return to the Ark while Action Force heads back to base.

MEMORABLE MOMENTS In a nicely terrifying moment, Heritage Society members search London's tunnels and spot Megatron's half-torn face. Action Force members flee the tunnel system with Megatron in hot pursuit, only to emerge and find the human-hating Grimlock chewing them out – for being human.

ASS-WHUPPINGS Megatron brings down a tunnel roof, killing three people exploring to find relics for the London Heritage Society. Centurion apparently gets blown to bits. Megatron once again "dies," but that's hardly a surprise.

GOOFS During a momentary misunderstanding, the Joes – including the veteran Scarlett – think they can shoot Blades down with assault rifles.

COMIC TIE-INS Megatron supposedly kicked the bucket in American Transformers #25, but he reappears here as the first step of his return to evil leadership. Decepticon Shockwave dredges up the submerged Megatron yet again in British Transformers #160.

CHARACTER PROFILE: JOES

Wild Bill: Wild Bill recalls a last-ditch rescue mission that entailed him piloting a chopper into a Southeast Asian jungle. The rescue party saved six troopers, but a seventh went missing. The commanding officer refused to turn back, unwilling to risk the entire team for a single person. Bill can't judge his superior as wrong – but the fate of the seventh man often keeps him awake at night.

THE COMMAND DECISION The most successful and convincing G.I. Joe / Transformers crossover, ditching the notion of pointless character interaction (designed only to make so-and-so Transformer meet so-and-so Joe member) and featuring good, old-fashioned slugfests instead. That alone puts it ahead of the competition, although this storyarc's limited page count admittedly doesn't allow much room for the plot to maneuver.

Action Force #28 to #31

Titles: "Gunpoint!"(#28), "Sky Strike!" (#29-# 31)
Release Dates: *Sept. 12 to Oct. 3, 1987*
Writers: *Steve Cook (plot, #28), Ford Alan (script, #28), Steve White (#29-#31).*
Art: *Anthony Williams (#28), Martin Griffiths (#29-#31).*
Included reprints: *G.I. Joe #36 (AF #28-#30); G.I. Joe Yearbook #2 (AF #30-#31); G.I. Joe #37 (AF #31).* ***NOTE:*** *Action Force Winter Special #2 was a reprint of G.I. Joe #35.*

BATTLE ROSTER *Joes:* Ace, Lady Jaye, Flint, Footloose, Wild Bill.

MISSION BRIEF ***Issue #28:*** At Churchfields Comprehensive School in England, snoopy young student Gary Turner shockingly discovers a Crimson Guardsman uniform stashed away in a storeroom. Exposed as a Cobra agent, a teacher named Perkins takes a roomful of children and the school's headmaster hostage. Action Force quickly surrounds the joint, but Perkins, feeling trigger-happy, offs the headmaster.

Perkins turns his attention to the children, but Gary stands his ground, staring straight down Perkins' barrel. Gary rebukes Perkins, stressing that murdering schoolchildren won't make the world any better for Cobra. Having children of his own, Perkins yields to the abhorrent nature of his actions and surrenders. Flint consoles Gary afterward, knowing full well that the incident will probably give the youngster nightmares for some time.

Issue #29-#31: In South America, Ace and Lady Jaye load themselves into a Skystriker, intent on bombing a hidden Cobra supply base. Flint and Wild Bill provide back-up in a Dragonfly helicopter, leading to an entanglement with Cobra battalions. Finally, the Action Force members level the munitions dump and return to the *USS Flagg. Fin.*

MEMORABLE MOMENTS Gary Turner displays testicles of titanium, listening to the gun-totting Perkins blathering about sacrifices and retorting, "Well sacrifice me, then. Just don't think of your own kids when you do it." What unbelievable grit.

NOW YOU KNOW... If your Skystriker stalls out, drop the nose a thousand feet and open up the throttles to full power.

COMIC TIE-INS *Action Force* #29-#31 evokes the Ace/ Lady Jaye team-up seen in *G.I. Joe* #34 (reprinted in *AF* #3-#4).

THE COMMAND DECISION Intensely gripping, "Gunpoint!" (#28) hinges on a compelling dynamic (the Joe/Cobra war as seen through a child's eyes), saying a great deal in a short amount of time. Conversely, "Sky Strike!" (#29-#31) fails to capitalize on the previous Ace/Lady Jaye pairing in *G.I. Joe* #34, pathetically stretching what should be a two-page story over three issues.

Action Force #32 to #34

Titles: *"Runaway Train" (#32), "Sunday Drivers" (#33-#34)*
Release Dates: *Oct. 10 to 24, 1987*
Writers: *Ford Alan (plot, #32), Ian Rimmer (script, #32; #33-#34)*
Art: *Antony Williams (#32), Phil Gascoine (#33-#34)*
Included reprints: *G.I. Joe #37 (AF #32); G.I. Joe Yearbook #2 (AF #33-#35); Sierra Gordo and Professor Appel material, G.I. Joe #38 (AF #33-#34)*

BATTLE ROSTER *Joes:* Barbecue, Airtight, Flint; *Cobra:* Buzzer, Ripper.

MISSION BRIEF ***Issue #32:*** Aided by Cobra agents, a man named Timpson hijacks a train filled with nuclear waste containers and takes the wheel. Already dying of cancer, Timpson prepares to drive the train pell-mell into Paddington Station in London. Action Force operatives conclude that the reinforced containers probably wouldn't rupture on impact, but they send Barbecue and hostile environment expert Airtight to leap aboard the train and storm the conductor's booth anyway. Undone, the terminal Timpson leaps to his death to avoid capture, allowing the train to grind to a grisly stop.

Issue #33-#34: At Stonebury Weapons Testing Range, Bazooka prepares to test a new support gun's capabilities. Unfortunately, Dreadnoks Buzzer and Ripper get the drop on the missile specialist, stealing the gun and making for the hills. Bazooka pursues them in an jeep, leading to a frenzied chase through a nearby shopping district. Thankfully, a decorated, retired military officer named Alfred Taylor makes the Dreadnoks' motorcycles skid out with a well-aimed oil can. Although Bazooka easily retrieves the weapon, the Dreadnoks escape. Pleased at his success, Bazooka later learns that the prototype gun never worked in the first place.

MEMORABLE MOMENTS The inside cover of *Action Force* #34 carries a stellar teaser for #35, bearing the slogan: "Who's for the bullet? Flint? Destro? Jaye? Find out next week – in *Action Force* #35!"

LOVE AND WAR Bazooka crashes his jeep through a lingerie store, scattering a series of naughty mannequins.

ASS-WHUPPINGS Timpson throws himself from a train.

GOOFS Timpson's motives don't make a lot of sense. He picked up cancer from a nuclear power plant accident, so why does he now want mass droves of people to die horrendously in a radiation burst? Also, considering everyone pretty much agrees that the hijacked canisters won't rupture on impact anyway, stealing the train seems a pretty profitless thing to do.

CHARACTER PROFILE: JOES

- *Airtight:* He carries Geiger counters that register radioactivity.
- *Barbecue:* He likes pizza and carries a foam-squirting pistol.

THE COMMAND DECISION Wrapped in a cool – albeit misleading – cover (Barbecue asks the rifle-armed Airtight to "atomize" their enemy), "Runaway Train" illogically plods along. The playful "Sunday Drivers" (*AF* #33-#34) fares better, although it's too crowded with action shots to focus on anything like, say, characterization. Also, the fact that the whole story revolves around testing a weapon the military knows doesn't work made us go cross-eyed.

Action Force #35 to #38

***Titles:** "Violent Lives!" (#35-#36), "Consequences" (#37), "Truth" (#38)*
***Release Date:** Oct. 31 to Nov. 21, 1987*
***Writers:** Richard Alan (#35-#36), Steve Alan (#37-#38)*
***Art:** Bryan Hitch*
***Included reprints:** G.I. Joe #39 (AF #35-#36); G.I. Joe Yearbook #2 (AF #35); G.I. Joe Special Missions #8 (AF #36-#38); G.I. Joe #21 (#37-#38)*

BATTLE ROSTER *Joes:* Flint, Lady Jaye, Snake-Eyes, Scarlett; *Cobra:* Destro, Storm Shadow, Cobra Commander.

MISSION BRIEF ***Issues #35-#36:*** Intent on seizing new weapons technology, Destro marshals his troopers to raid a military testing range in Stonebury. Destro easily pilfers a folder of classified weapons schematics, but Lady Jaye moves to catch him in the act. With cat-like reflexes, Destro whirls around and skims Lady Jaye's skull with a bullet – knocking her into a coma.

Flint rushes Lady Jaye to an intensive care ward, then comes completely unglued. Crying vengeance, Flint barrels into MARS' London branch and smacks Destro's bodyguards aside. Pummeling Destro within an inch of his life, Flint unholsters his gun and prepares to plug the fiend between the eyes. But at the last minute, Flint relents, unwilling to cross a certain moral line and become a murderer. As Flint quickly departs, Destro mentions off-handedly that if positions were reversed, he'd have pulled the trigger.

Issues #37-#38: Unwilling to let Flint's act of aggression go unpunished, Destro dispatches Storm Shadow to kill the warrant officer at a pre-arranged Action Force rendezvous. But Flint fails to make the meeting, skipping out to visit Lady Jaye in the hospital. As a consolation prize, Storm Shadow nabs Scarlett instead, fleeing with her to Castle Destro.

Snake-Eyes rapidly follows, freeing Scarlett as recorded in "Silent Interlude" (*G.I. Joe* #21). Afterward, Storm Shadow and Destro come to verbal blows over the ninja's lackluster performance, prompting Storm Shadow to bash Destro around. Finally, Storm Shadow demands to know the identity of the Hard Master's killer, and Destro – having goaded the ninja into "forcing" a confession out of him – claims Action Force murdered the Hard Master as a ploy to discredit Cobra. Suitably fooled, Storm Shadow heads off for his next assignment, mentally preparing to gut and fillet Action Force.

MEMORABLE MOMENTS Flint's narration (#35) poignantly conveys the pros and cons of his violent life with Lady Jaye. Destro razors the Joe at the climax of #36 with the point that he certainly wouldn't have spared Flint's life.

LOVE AND WAR Although the Action Force series mostly downplays the American comics' romance between Flint and Lady Jaye, Flint here claims that Lady Jaye's fantastic on the battlefield, able to "...kill with a smile and wound with her eyes."

ASS-WHUPPINGS In issue #35, Lady Jaye wastes Cobra troopers with terrifying efficiency. Destro's bullet puts Lady Jaye in the hospital, prompting Flint and Destro to trade blows in #36.

GOOFS Destro somehow blames Cobra Commander for "a serious mistake" related to Flint's rampage, but we have no idea as to what he's talking about. Considering the Dreadnoks walked off with a supposedly advanced weapon there (*AF* #33-#34), Action Force idiotically fails to beef up security at the Stonebury testing range. Action Force's late-night rendezvous – the one that Flint fails to attend – never gets explained.

COMICS TIE-INS In a Gordian Knot of continuity, Scarlett claims that her scuffle with Fred Smith II (*G.I. Joe* #36, reprinted in *AF* #28-#30) took place a few days ago. That's fine, except that seconds after she makes that comment, Storm Shadow kidnaps her and makes off for Castle Destro – instigating events from *G.I. Joe* #21 (*AF* #37-#38).

AF #38 suggests Destro knows the identity of the Hard Master's killer, although there's no evidence in the American run that he possesses such information. Snake-Eyes here upgrades his costume and dons a modified visor, matching his battle togs seen in *G.I. Joe* #45 (*AF* #44).

THE COMMAND DECISION Kicking *Action Force* into high gear, issues #35-#36 throw Flint, Lady Jaye and Destro into a thundering clash of personalities and philosophies, deploying the old argument of "if a hero kills the villain, does he become like the villain?" to great effect. For comic book fans, it's a bonus to witness how Bryan Hitch (*The Authority, The Ultimates*) draws like mainstay artist John Byrne (*Superman, Fantastic Four*) at this point in his career.

Issues #38-#39 add new levels to the fan-prized "Silent Interlude" (*G.I. Joe* #21), although *Action Force*'s patchy continuity might leave you feeling like you've just stared at a Picasso for several hours. They're hardly bad stories, but purely for continuity's sake, it's probably best to delete them from your memory.

Action Force #39 to #43

Titles: *"Coma!" (#39), "Law of the Jungle!" (#40-#41), "Rage!" (#42), "Silent Night" (#43)*
Release Dates: *Nov. 28 to Dec. 26, 1987*
Writers: *Richard Alan (#39, #42), Mike Collins (#40-#41), Steve White (#43)*
Art: *Geoff Senior (#39, #42), Mark Farmer (#40-#41), Dougie Braithwaite (#43)*
Included reprints: *G.I. Joe Special Missions #8 (AF #39-#40); G.I. Joe #42 (AF #39-#40); Storm Shadow and Billy material, G.I. Joe #38-#42 (AF #41); G.I. Joe #43 (AF #42-#43); G.I. Joe Special Missions #5 (AF #43). NOTE: Action Force Annual reprinted the creation of Cobra Island from G.I. Joe #40-#41.*

BATTLE ROSTER *Joes:* Snake-Eyes, Lady Jaye, Flint, Footloose, Frostbite; *Cobra:* Storm Shadow, Destro, Cobra Commander.

MISSION BRIEF ***Issue #39:*** Still comatose, Lady Jaye nightmarishly envisions herself fighting a giant talking cobra. After finding the inner resolve to kill the serpent, Lady Jaye snaps out of the coma – to the great relief of Flint and her attending doctors.

Issue #40-#41: Handed new orders, a Cobra team led by Storm Shadow heads for the Asian sub-continent, hoping to retrieve a fallen European satellite named Bilal and sell its intelligence data to the highest bidder. Fortunately, Snake-Eyes arrives and wastes Storm Shadow's group to a man – then turns to engage the Cobra ninja.

The two adversaries slug it out, stalemating each other until a tiger arrives and starts chomping on Snake-Eyes. Storm Shadow grabs the satellite's information-laden data core, then finds himself unable to abandon his former brother-in-arms. Brandishing a knife, Storm Shadow skewers the tiger to death, saving Snake-Eyes' life and regaining his humanity. Sick to death of sparring, Snake-Eyes and Storm Shadow agree to blow up Bilal's data records, then tell their respective superiors that the satellite was damaged beyond retrieval on impact.

Issue #42: At Action Force's London base, an enraged Lady Jaye slugs Flint after learning that he backed down from killing Destro (*AF* #36). Although Lady Jaye insists that Action Force exists to eliminate the bad guys, Flint counters that he's a soldier, not a murderer, and that unrestrained violence never solves problems. Unable to accept his excuses, Lady Jaye storms out and insists that the next time Destro kills someone, it'll be on Flint's head. Flint quietly acknowledges his responsibility in letting Destro off the hook, nursing guilt for future casualties stemming from the arms dealer's actions.

Issue #43: On Christmas Eve, a patrolling Footloose and Frostbite stumble upon a Cobra patrol inside the Norwegian Arctic Circle. The Action Force members eliminate their oncoming attackers, but a final volley flings a single surviving Cobra trooper into freezing waters. Seizing the moral high ground, Footloose adheres to some seasonal goodwill and hauls the Cobra trooper to safety – citing mercy as a quality that separates Action Force from Cobra.

ASS-WHUPPINGS A tiger rips up Snake-Eyes like a bolt of fabric, although he somehow only gets by with flesh wounds. Lady Jaye and Flint smack each other around to prove their respective points about violence. A missile hit knocks Frostbite unconscious.

PREPOSTEROUS PHYSICS A splash page in issue #42 shows a nostril-flaring Lady Jaye apparently knocking Flint to the floor – with a rolled-up piece of paper.

GOOFS Hospital workers don't bother removing all of Lady Jaye's blood-stained battle togs – they just dump her comatose carcass into a bed.

COMICS TIE-INS In *AF* #38, Destro schnookered Storm Shadow into thinking that Action Force authorized the Hard Master's death. Stormy's encounter with Snake-Eyes in *AF* #40-#41 motivates his final defection from Cobra, leading to his rescue of Billy (*G.I. Joe* #38, reprinted in *AF* #41).

Spy satellite Bilal stopped transmitting on August 15, meaning *Action Force* #40-#41 must occur near the same date (although the year isn't specified). Footloose delivers a similar "We don't recklessly murder the enemy" speech in *G.I. Joe European Missions* #6.

CHARACTER PROFILE: JOES

Lady Jaye and Flint: With the Zen calmness of Yoda, Flint claims that no-holds-barred anger only leads to murder. Lady Jaye insists that while it's one thing to adhere to a moral code, it's berserk to hold back from killing Destro – who's just about as close to pure evil as you can get. In short, Lady Jaye believes Flint neglected his duty to take out Destro, meaning Flint's indirectly responsible for anyone Destro kills from this point.

THE COMMAND DECISION "Coma!" (*AF* #39) isn't anything special, forming your typical "I must kill this giant snake to emerge from my coma" sort of tale. Issues #40-#41 emerge as a forlorn tale of two ex-brothers-in-arms, with writer Mike Collins playing Storm Shadow's change of heart like a well-tuned lyre. The heated Flint/Lady Jaye confrontation from #42 solidly compresses a huge argument into its five pages, laudably fleshing out its central dilemma ("When is a soldier's violence justified?") but smartly letting the reader come to their own conclusions. Finally, "Silent Night" (#43) makes for a somewhat leisurely interlude, driving home a moral point that's poignant, but somewhat redundant when stacked against the Flint/Lady Jaye row of #42.

Action Force #44 to #46

Title: *"Destro: Down and Out!"*
Release Dates: *Jan. 2 to 16, 1988*
Writers: *Mike Collins*
Art: *Bryan Hitch*
Included reprints: *G.I. Joe Special Missions #5 (AF #44, #46); G.I. Joe #45 (AF #44-#45); G.I. Joe #46 (AF #46)*

BATTLE ROSTER *Cobra:* Destro.

MISSION BRIEF ***Issues #44-#46:*** In Casablanca, Morocco, a battered and bloodied Destro awakens in an alley with no knowledge of his past or identity. Staggering into the streets, Destro runs into a 19-year-old girl named Jenna Miseva, who takes him to the abode of Hajid, her grandfather.

Naming the amnesiac Destro "Silver," Jenna and Hajid nurse him back to health and treat him like an honorable man. As "Silver," Destro develops a fondness for Jenna, slowly accepting her image of him as a heroic figure. Unfortunately, treacherous Cobra troopers inexplicably following Destro trail their quarry and murder Hajid. Bashing his attackers aside, Destro flees with Jenna and tries to avoid detection.

Fearing for Jenna's safety, Destro urges her to leave his company, but the girl, who's become increasingly smitten with "Silver," insists on remaining with him. Shortly afterward, yet another Cobra trooper shows up. Destro brawls with his attacker, but in the confusion, the soldier's gun accidentally discharges and mortally wounds Jenna. Destro smacks the trooper down, then rushes to Jenna's side. With her dying words, Jenna validates Destro's heroism, then expires.

His true identity flooding back, Destro picks up the would-be assassin's weapon and ruthlessly plugs him in the head. Donning the hit man's uniform, Destro returns to Cobra's secluded base in Casablanca to confront his ex-associate Farouk. Destro recalls in full detail how Farouk summoned him to the Cobra base two weeks ago – part of a set-up on Farouk's part to rub out Destro and win Cobra Commander's gratitude. As such, Farouk's men bludgeoned Destro, leaving him for dead in an alley.

Farouk fanatically validates Cobra Commander and his dream of world conquest, accusing Destro of deliberately hampering Cobra's operations. Destro argues that if Cobra Commander is left unchecked, his greed for power will incite military retribution far greater than Action Force's. A slow and sure rise to power – balanced with the intuition to handle it – will win Cobra the world, Destro insists, not brash military action.

Fast as lightning, Destro impales Farouk, then hauls his corpse before the base's troops as an offering to Cobra Commander. Rhetorically whipped into action, the Cobra soldiers cheer their leader – leaving Cobra Commander to think that Destro's just rooted out Farouk as a traitor from the ranks. Privately, Destro places a wreath on Jenna's grave, mournful because the heroic "Silver" – the man Jenna loved – died with her. Saddened, Destro comments to himself, "But now Silver is dead too. Now there is only Destro. And he is no hero."

MEMORABLE MOMENTS Pretty much this entire arc constitutes a Memorable Moment – particularly Jenna's jaw-dropping demise, Destro's recollection of his father's murder (see Character Profile) and the tearful epilogue with Destro standing over Jenna's grave (*AF* #46).

LOVE AND WAR Keeping in mind that *Action Force* never explored Destro's relationship with the Baroness – or even reprinted American stories dealing with their romance – Jenna's bravery, affection and warmth are all new experiences for Destro. The final scene at Jenna's grave brings an unprecedented outpouring of emotion from the metal-visaged one.

ASS-WHUPPINGS Upon regaining his identity, Destro kills his opponents with a Herculean proficiency. The deathfest ends with him snapping Farouk's walking stick in half and goring him to death.

COMIC TIE-INS *AF* #10-#13 debuted Cobra's underground base in Casablanca and introduced Farouk as Destro's longtime associate. Destro's murder of his father (see Character Profile) fiercely clashes with a more benevolent view of Daddy Destro in *G.I. Joe* #96.

CHARACTER PROFILE: COBRA

Destro: Back in the day, Destro's father – a towering figure who also wore a silver mask – harangued his son for some shady business dealings that "disgraced the family name." Consumed by ambition, Destro shot his father to death, donning Daddy Destro's mask and expanding his business operations.

Destro recuperates from battle wounds quickly. His face mask serves as an integral part of his identity – indeed, he considers himself nothing without it.

THE COMMAND DECISION The crowning achievement of the entire *Action Force* run, "Destro: Down and Out!" (*AF* #44-#46) fiercely peels away Destro's identity layer by layer, unveiling him as a formidable force that – much like Dr. Doom – must persevere at all costs. It's a web so intricate, we finished it with bated breath, greedily lusting for more.

Action Force #47 to #50

Title: *"Venetian Blinds"*
Release Dates: *Jan. 23 to Feb. 6, 1988*
Writer: *Simon Furman*
Art: *Kev Hopgood*
Included reprints: *G.I. Joe Special Missions #5 (AF #47-#48); G.I. Joe #46 (AF #47-#48); G.I. Joe #47 (AF #49-#50); "Bystander," Yearbook #4 (AF #50).* ***NOTE:*** *After AF #50, the British Transformers title (starting with #153) took up the American G.I. Joe reprints.*

BATTLE ROSTER *Joes:* Flint, Lady Jaye, Quick Kick, Footloose, Shipwreck; *Cobra:* Destro, Cobra Commander.

MISSION BRIEF In Venice, Cobra moves to horn in on the Italian mob's business, spontaneously assassinating a number of Mafia bosses. Not fully understanding the conflict, Action Force flounders for a response, but Lady Jaye comes unhinged when Destro – the man who shot her – offers to provide the Joes with intelligence information on Cobra's movements.

Destro selfishly explains that a Cobra victory could diminish his arms sales to the Mafia bosses, but adds that it's also in Action Force's interests to stop Cobra making such headway in Venice. Begrudgingly accepting that their goals coincide with Destro's, the Joes capitalize on his tip-off to a planned assassination of high-ranking Mafia representative Tito Meira.

Led by Flint, Action Force members systematically wipe out Cobra agents threatening the mob goons, then race like mad for Meira's residence. Although the Joes prevent a Cobra detachment from wasting Meira, Cobra Commander escapes in the confusion. A vengeful Lady Jaye briefly considers dropping Destro with a "stray bullet," but instead turns aside to help Flint at a crucial juncture. Destro runs off, leaving Action Force to pat itself on the back and return to England.

Shortly afterward, Cobra Commander, Meira and Destro gather at Meira's house, having staged the entire Cobra-Mafia conflict as a means of diverting Action Force's attention from Italy. With the Joes now oblivious to Cobra's operations in Venice, Cobra Commander, Destro and Meira continue their long-running (and profitable) business deals in complete secrecy.

LOVE AND WAR While monitoring Cobra Commander's activities, Flint and Lady Jaye indulge in a romantic gondola ride (mind, Footloose serves as the gondolier, so the trip's pretty platonic).

ASS-WHUPPINGS Quick Kick nails a Crimson Guardsman in the back with three throwing stars. Lady Jaye savagely clubs another Guardsman – an effective way of venting her spleen about having to work with Destro.

Flint impales a Cobra frogman on his own harpoon and Lady Jaye knifes another. Flint also guns down several of Cobra Commander's bodyguards, but fails to snag the commander himself.

COMIC TIE-INS There's lingering resentment on Lady Jaye's part toward Destro (for shooting her, *AF* #35) and Flint (for sparing Destro's life, *AF* #36).

CHARACTER PROFILE: COBRA

Destro: He claims that the Mafia families purchase more guns from him than Cobra, although he's probably lying to further the deception against Action Force.

THE COMMAND DECISION Topping off the *Action Force* run in a tepid fashion, issues #47-#50 offer a promising set-up but fail to cross the finish line in a meaningful fashion. Lady Jaye's left dangling for want of revenge, Destro manipulates Action Force (but then, that's hardly a surprise) and Cobra Commander continues raking in his ill-gotten loot. All told, it delivers little closure.

MISCELLANEOUS STUFF!

THE MONTHLY REBOOT

After the demise of the weekly *Action Force* series, the monthly *G.I. Joe European Missions* continued the Joes' British adventures with pretty much the same characters and set-up, adding in a few newcomers such as Sci-Fi, Lifeline and the Crimson Twins for variety's sake.

That said, the monthly series pretty much ditched any loose ends from the previous 50 *Action Force* issues, probably to make the story accessible for newcomers. Accordingly, *European Missions* almost entirely forgets details such as Lady Jaye's wrath against Destro (*AF* #35), and the arguments between Lady Jaye and Flint (*AF* #42). As a result, *European Missions* detaches itself pretty definitively from *Action Force* (save for Trent's demise in the second issue), meaning you're better off rebooting your brain before reading these issues.

P.S. Although *Action Force* never saw publication in its weekly reincarnation in America, its monthly successor appeared in Britain as *Action Force Monthly* and in the States as *G.I. Joe European Missions* (the two were virtually identical, save for the cover logo). As such, we've stuck with the *European Missions* tag, since it clings to American fans' minds better than the *Action Force Monthly* moniker.

G.I. Joe European Missions #1 to #2

Titles: *"Double Bluff" (#1), "Double Cross" (#1), "Death or Glory" (#2)*
Release Dates: *June to July 1988(monthly)*
Writers: *Ford Alan (plot, "Double Bluff"), Dan Abnett (script, "Double Bluff"), Ian Rimmer ("Double Cross"), Simon Furman (#2)*
Art: *Dougie Braithwaite (#1), Bryan Hitch (#1)*
Included reprints: *"Ancient Relics," British Transformers #125.*

BATTLE ROSTER *Joes:* Flint, Lady Jaye, Roadblock, Footloose, Sci-Fi, Leatherneck, Shipwreck; *Cobra:* Tomax and Xamot, the Dreadnoks.

MISSION BRIEF ***"Double Bluff" (#1):*** In London, the Crimson Twins attempt to kidnap Ambassador Trent, Action Force's liaison officer to the British Ministry of Defense. But in response, a Flint-led Action Force safeguards Trent, deliberately letting the Crimson Twins trail them to Action Force's headquarters as a test for their base's defenses.

As expected, the Crimson Twins take a BAT squadron and assault Action Force's headquarters. The Joes satisfactorily dice the twins' robots to pieces with their laser defense grid, forcing them to withdraw. Unfortunately, the Cobra brothers rummage through Trent's office at the base and discover that the liaison officer has a daughter. Returning home, the twins ponder kidnapping Trent's daughter to force top-level secrets from the liaison officer and curry favor with Cobra Commander.

"Double Cross" (#1): In the Mediterranean, a seaman named Thornton helps the military triangulate the probable location of a German WWII airplane shot down by his father. Action Force sailor Shipwreck comes along to lend his expertise to the experimental salvage procedure, using heavy-duty balloons hoping to float the wreck to the surface. Just when the salvage looks to be successful, Thornton suddenly reveals himself as a Cobra operative and kills his fellow crewmen.

Taking a bullet in the arm, Shipwreck dives underwater and surfaces aboard the Nazi vessel. Once inside, Shipwreck finds a cache of Nazi gold – the object of Thornton's desire. Thornton travels from his sailing vessel to the floating Nazi plane in a small dinghy, hoping to plug Shipwreck and secure the treasure. But Shipwreck dives underwater yet again, deflating the balloons that hold the plane aloft. The gold-laden Nazi plane quickly sinks – with Thornton aboard – allowing Shipwreck to return to the mainland aboard the dinghy.

"Death or Glory" (#2): Having learned that the Crimson twins intend to kidnap Trent's daughter Amy, Zartan ponders a subtle way to one-up the brothers and retain his standing as Cobra Commander's favorite. But the Dreadnoks, hoping to "do Zartan a favor," impetuously nab Amy for him. The Dreadnoks demand that Trent turn over various classified military documents, but Trent – a former military man – dons his old fighting togs to get his daughter back.

Trent guns for the Dreadnoks at their scheduled rendezvous, but Monkeywrench, wounded by one of Trent's bullets, plugs the Joe liaison officer in the chest. The Dreadnoks to grab Amy and race for the hills, leaving Trent to die from his wounds. The next day, Action Force tracks Trent's killers. The Dreadnoks try to hand off Amy to a Cobra RATTLER – still intending to use her as a hostage – but the Joes fall on the Dreadnok pack.

Flint recovers Amy, then draws a bead on Monkeywrench. But in that instant, the RATTLER jet makes an attack run on Hawk and Snake-Eyes. Torn about between letting Trent's killer run free, Flint nonetheless turns aside, shooting down the RATTLER and saving his friends. Decently battered, the Joes take Amy home and vow to save lives in lieu of pursuing vengeance whenever possible.

MEMORABLE MOMENTS Flint concludes that Trent's military motto of "Death or glory" isn't really adequate – it's more important to live, grow and evolve.

ASS-WHUPPINGS Roadblock sprays some Crimson Guardsmen with bullets. Sci-Fi lasers a hole in a Crimson Guardsman's chest from two miles away. A laser defense grid at Action Force Headquarters eviscerates a lot of BATs. A RATTLER bullet gets Snake-Eyes in the leg. Shipwreck drowns turncoat Thornton and a Cobra hovercraft pilot. Most importantly, Trent shoots Monkeywrench in the arm, but the Dreadnok offs Trent in return.

GOOFS Action Force isn't familiar with the Crimson Twins, conflicting with their debut in *G.I. Joe* #37 (reprinted in *AF* #31-#32).

COMIC/TV TIE-INS The Crimson Twins remain telepathically linked (*G.I. Joe* #37), although unlike in the TV series, they don't feel each others' injuries. (Footloose hits Xamot, but Tomax doesn't feel the blow.)

CHARACTER PROFILE: JOES

• *Flint:* Flint maintains his position as Action Force's commander, although Hawk sometimes flies in to lend assistance. Flint claims to have "complete faith" in Her Majesty's Government. Hawk offered Flint the late Trent's position as Ministry of Defense liaison, but Flint declined, wanting to remain a field leader.

• *Roadblock:* He's strong enough to bash a BAT's head off.

CHARACTER PROFILE: OTHER

The Crimson Twins: They're increasingly worried that Zartan's gaining too much authority as Cobra Commander's favorite.

THE COMMAND DECISION Incredibly primitive, "Double Bluff" (*EM* #1) looks like a warped mirror of the Joes you've come to know and love – hampered by art that's better suited to caricatures than actual human beings. The story's horribly clunky, sacrificing innovation to "ease" new readers into the British Joes' stories. Blessedly, the admittedly short "Double Cross" (also *EM* #1) gets across Shipwreck's inner timbre, making good use of the level-headed sailor's use of cutthroat tactics to counter Cobra's plans.

A vast improvement over "Double Bluff," "Death or Glory" (*EM* #2) at least runs through the motions and bow-wraps a neat little moral (Flint's prioritizing his teammates' lives over vengeance) at story's end.

G.I. Joe European Missions #3 to #4

Titles: *"Old Scores" (#3), "The Cold Zone" (#3), "The Devil and the Deep Blue Sea" (#4), "Betrayal" (#4)*
Release Dates: *Aug. to Sept. 1988*
Writers: *Grant Morrison ("Old Scores"), Ian Rimmer ("The Cold Zone," "Betrayal"), Richard Alan and Steve White ("The Devil and the Deep Blue Sea")*
Art: *Mark Farmer ("Old Scores"), Jerry Paris ("The Cold Zone"), Robin Smith ("The Devil and the Deep Blue Sea"), Kev Hopgood ("Betrayal!")*
Included reprints: *Action Force #24-#25.*

BATTLE ROSTER *Joes:* Snake-Eyes, Hawk, Cutter, Sci-Fi, Wet-Suit, Dusty, Flint; *Cobra:* Storm Shadow, Wild Weasel.

MISSION BRIEF ***"Old Scores" (#3):*** Embarking on a vengeance quest, Storm Shadow trails an ex-Vietnamese general named Loi to a southeast Asian island. Once there, Storm Shadow recalls how his friend Donald Jefferson died, after being tortured over a series of four months, at General Loi's hands during the Vietnam War. With ruthless efficiency, Storm Shadow butchers the general's bodyguards, drawing closer to Loi's sanctum. Loi freaks as Storm Shadow avoids his myriad of "invincible" defenses, allowing the ninja to confront the Vietnamese military man face-to-face. Having proved General Loi's weakness – and wracking Loi with fear – Storm Shadow swiftly turns and exits. But Loi, unable to live with his newly proven vulnerability, commits suicide in Storm Shadow's wake.

"The Cold Zone" (#3): In a desolate, frozen forest in North America, Snake-Eyes learns of a Cobra plot to steal a rare computer decoder from a military research base. Snake-Eyes quickly hides the decoder, then lies in wait for his attackers. Soon after, a group of Cobra snow troopers arrive, aided by a treacherous researcher named Chattle. Snake-Eyes easily makes mincemeat of the Cobra goons, but Chattle reaches the base's experimental arsenal and dons a terrifyingly powerful pair of hand-held, rapid-fire artillery projectors. Chattle's guns wound Snake-Eyes, forcing the Joe commando to flee into the forest and stake a bundle of sharpened branches in the ground. Chattle pursues him, but the ever-crafty ninja pushes Chattle from behind – skewering the traitor on the branches and leaving Snake-Eyes master of the terrain.

"Deep Blue Sea" (#4): In the Straits of Hormuz, an Action Force WHALE helps escort a Kuwaiti tanker named the *Pegasus Star* into hostile waters. Cobra RATTLERs deploy several mines, trying to blow up the *Pegasus Star* as a show of terror. Thankfully, the Joes prematurely detonate the mines with pinpoint accuracy, downing the Cobra RATTLER squadron. Although their hovercraft takes on water and sinks, the victorious Joes lazily swim back to the *Pegasus Star* for brewskies.

"Betrayal!" (#4): On a routine patrol in the Middle East, desert trooper Dusty miraculously gets thrown clear when a Joe HAVOC drives over a landmine. A Cobra platoon swoops in for the kill, slicing through Dusty's teammates before driving off. Slowly recovering, Dusty searches the carnage and proves unable to locate HAVOC driver Julia Kreig. Vowing to save his teammate, Dusty tracks the Cobra vehicles' tire tracks.

Pitilessly, Dusty shoots down the Cobra troops to a man. But while looking for Julia, Dusty spies her body among his kills – dressed in a Crimson Guardsman uniform. Realizing that the traitorous Julia arranged the whole ambush to return to Cobra, Dusty loses faith and contemplates quitting Action Force. Thankfully, Flint talks Dusty through his aggression, helping the desert trooper find the inner steel to remain a Joe warrior.

MEMORABLE MOMENTS Pissing himself at the thought of Storm Shadow sneaking up on him undetected, General Loi holes up in a room ringed with strands of bells. You can imagine the general's horror when he hears a single bell ringing, then turns around to see Storm Shadow inside the bell barrier, grimly tapping one of the bells to get Loi's attention.

ASS-WHUPPINGS Snake-Eyes and Timber savagely rip through a bunch of Cobra guards. Snakey also sharpens branches, surprises Chattle and pushes him onto the spikes.

Wild Weasel's RATTLER attack nails Hawk in the shoulder.

CHARACTER PROFILE: JOES

Cross Country: He's currently on leave, leaving the turncoat Julia serving as a HAVOC driver.

CHARACTER PROFILE: OTHER

Storm Shadow: Seventeen years ago, a Viet Cong ambush led by General Loi took Storm Shadow and an 18-year-old soldier named Donald Jefferson prisoner. Loi tortured Storm Shadow and the Philadelphia-borne Donald over a four-month period, but although Storm Shadow's ninja training gave him the resolve to endure, Donald died from either a fractured skull or gangrene. Stormy escaped shortly afterward.

Storm Shadow defeats General Loi's bodyguard Han, a master of Korean *tae kwon do* and an adept of fourth *dan jeet kune do*, nunchaku and bo fighting. The Hard Master taught Storm Shadow an "invisibility" technique that allows him to match his opponent's moves exactly, thereby staying at the edge of his rival's blind spot and becoming unseen and untouchable.

THE COMMAND DECISION The unquestionable highlight of the entire European Missions run, "Old Scores" examines Storm Shadow's character from every facet – but then, you'd expect little else from writer Grant Morrison (*Invisibles, JLA*). It barely qualifies as a G.I. Joe story, but "Old Scores" undeniably molds Storm Shadow into more than just a nutty ninja with a sword.

"The Cold Zone" dramatically leaves its mark thanks to Snake-Eyes' inspired impaling of Chattle at story's end – which paints the visceral difference between the American and British G.I. Joe stories. If there's a fault, it's that Chattle's body armor seems a bit silly, but the core of the story – Snake-Eyes' ability to master a remote terrain – won us over.

Regrettably, "The Devil and the Deep Blue Sea" (*EM* #4) washes out as a waste of time – the sort of filler that pops your brain cells with a bundle of shoddy action sequences. Redeeming the mix, "Betrayal" deftly conveys Dusty's need for trust on the battlefield, startlingly cracking his resolve for the murder – on his part – of a close friend.

G.I. Joe European Missions #5 to #6

Titles: *"Gunships!" (#5), "As Thick as Thieves!" (#6), "Killer Instinct" (#6)*
Release Dates: *Oct. to Nov. 1988*
Writers: *Steve White (#5), Mike Collins ("As Thick as Thieves"), Dan Abnett ("Killer Instinct")*
Art: *Robin Smith (#5, "As Thick as Thieves"), Bryan Hitch ("Killer Instinct")*
Included reprints: *Action Force #26-#27*

BATTLE ROSTER *Joes:* Snake-Eyes, Flint, Beach-Head, Dial Tone, Roadblock, Leatherneck, Lift Ticket, Hawk,

Scarlett, Lady Jaye, Dusty, Footloose; *Cobra:* Destro, Serpentor, Tomax and Xamot, Cobra Commander; *Other:* Pythona.

MISSION BRIEF ***"Gunships!" (#5):*** When The United States military runs a test-flight of its Northrop B2 jet, Cobra blows up the ship, forcing the pilots to eject over Indonesia. Hawk and Flint quickly scramble a rescue party, hoping to keep Cobra from interrogating the pilots and learning the plane's specifications. Heavy Cobra firepower brings down a number of Joe Tomahawk helicopters, but Flint's team perseveres and rescues the missing three-man crew. Mission accomplished, Action Force returns home.

"As Thick as Thieves!" (#6): At the London branch of MARS, Destro dismays when his researchers brief him about the Broadcast Energy Transmitter (BET), a device capable of transmitting energy across the globe. Fretting that such a device could make oil prices plummet, Destro makes efforts to blow the BET to bits.

Meanwhile, Action Force escorts the BET to an island in the Pacific Ocean, warming up the device for a test run. However, Destro brings his personal Cobra retinue to bear against the Joes, hoping to slag the BET in the crossfire. The Joes repel Destro's soldiers, but Destro secretly plants a homing device on the BET.

Soon after, the Cobra elite brings Destro up on charges, curious as to why he acted alone to "capture the BET for Cobra." Destro unconvincingly lies through his steel-plated teeth, claiming he rashly sought the BET as a token of esteem for Serpentor. But while preparing to pass sentence, Serpentor unexpectedly experiences a vision of a alien-looking woman.

Answering the woman's siren-like plea, Serpentor agrees that Cobra desperately needs the BET. Snapping back to reality, Serpentor absolves Destro of wrongdoing and retires to his chambers. Relieved – but slightly puzzled – over his acquittal, Destro informs the Cobra officers about his homing device. Finding that the Joes have relocated the BET to the Himalayas, Cobra prepares a heavy assault to retrieve the device.

"Killer Instinct" (#6): Discovering a Cobra plan to severely cripple Britain's national power grid, Joe infantry trooper Footloose unmasks a local "power station worker" as a Crimson Guardsman. Footloose guns down the Cobra agent, preventing him from flicking a detonator and blowing the whole place to bits. Station manager Edmunds blanches to witness Footloose killing one of his "employees," then learns how close Cobra came to eradicating the entire complex.

Suddenly, a second Crimson Guardsman tries to seize his fallen comrade's detonator switch. Footloose thumps the newcomer unconscious, but Edmunds cries out for Footloose to kill the villain. Explaining the difference between self-defense and cold-blooded murder, Footloose warns Edmunds to ditch any thoughts of harming their unconscious adversary. Relenting, Edmunds apologizes for his lapse of judgement, allowing other Action Force members to secure the area.

LOVE AND WAR Hallucinating about Pythona, Serpentor tells her: "You are the woman of my dreams – whatever you desire I'll gladly give." Of course, Serpentor fails to realize that he's really looking at Destro. The Baroness frets that if something happened to Destro, she would "lose a valuable chess opponent."

ASS-WHUPPINGS Cobra firepower brings down two Joe Tomahawks. Lift-Ticket's co-pilot bites it. Snake-Eyes sticks a grenade down one Viper's boot and nails another in the chest with throwing stars. Beach-Head smears a Viper with a pair of grenades. Destro knocks Hawk unconscious with a drug-laced dart, then brawls with Flint.

TV TIE-INS The story lines set up in "As Thick As Thieves" (*EM* #6) are picked up in *G.I. Joe: The Movie* (which makes it comic apocrypha, given how the American comics refuse to acknowledge the movie's events). Serpentor's already experiencing dreams about a "serpent city and a beautiful serpent woman," an obvious reference to Cobra-La and Pythona (also *G.I. Joe: The Movie*).

COMIC TIE-INS Footloose previously delivered a "Don't murder the bad guys" sermon in *AF* #43.

CHARACTER DEVELOPMENT: COBRA

- *Cobra Commander:* He testifies as to how Destro never follows orders (a curious juxtaposition, considering Cobra Commander's similar horsewhipping in *G.I. Joe: The Movie*).
- *The Crimson Twins:* Serve as prosecutors for Destro's trial.

ORGANIZATIONS *Action Force:* Houses some of their Skystrikers at Kadena, Japan. They also work out of Darwin Airbase, North Australia. One Action Force Skystriker squadron answers to the code-name "Razorback."

- *The United Nations:* Authorizes Action Force missions in Indonesia.

STUFF YOU NEED *The BET:* It works by bouncing an energy stream off several satellites in orbit over receiving stations. The satellites duplicate the energy beam like a reflective mirror, generating an output of 6 to 1. In the near-vacuum of space, energy loss from dissipation amounts to almost zero.

THE COMMAND DECISION Dreadfully pointless, "Gunships!" (*EM* #5) represents a startling lack of creativity

– essentially depicting the Joes going into the jungle, grabbing some lost airmen and coming out again. Woo-hoo. Cigars, everyone.

Conversely, "As Thick As Thieves!" (*EM* #6) excels as a prelude to *G.I. Joe: The Movie*. Certainly, Pythona seems at home in a comic book environment, and Destro's double narrative (his lies to Serpentor vs. the truth) steal the show. Finally, "Killer Instinct" succeeds as yet-another five-page story happily forced to focus on character rather than overheated gun barrels. Footloose drives home an incredibly succulent point – the difference between self-defense and murder – putting this compassionate tale among the A-level *European Missions* tales.

G.I. Joe European Missions #7 to #8

Titles: *"Smooth Operators" (#7), "Mark of the Assassin!" (#7), "Nuclear Winter!" (#8)*
Release Dates: *Dec. 1988 to Jan. 1989*
Writers: *Dan Abnett ("Smooth Operators"), Ian Rimmer ("Mark of the Assassin!"), Steve Alan (#8)*
Art: *Kev Hopgood ("Smooth Operators"), John McCrea ("Mark of the Assassin!"), Robin Smith (#8)*
Included reprints: *Action Force #1*

BATTLE ROSTER *Joes:* Lady Jaye, Flint, Frostbite, Iceberg, Dial Tone, Low Light, Lifeline, Hawk; *Cobra:* Destro, Storm Shadow, Cobra Commander.

MISSION BRIEF ***"Smooth Operators" (#7):*** In northern Italy, Lady Jaye pockets intelligence information from two dead Joe operatives and races on a motorcycle toward her teammates in Lugacelli. As Cobra Ferret ATV drivers take off in hot pursuit, Joe communications chief Dial Tone and sniper Low Light prepare for Lady Jaye's arrival. Lady Jaye bursts into town minutes later, reaches a phone and transmits her data – the location of Cobra's bases in Italy – to London via Dial Tone's secure channel. Low Light picks off the remaining opposition, allowing the three Joes to hook up outside of town and return home.

"Mark of the Assassin!" (#7): Confident in his power, Cobra Commander asks Storm Shadow to assassinate T.P. Dexter, a millionaire who's been slow to ally his business with Cobra. But finding the assignment lacking any honor or merit, Storm Shadow forewarns the Joes with an anonymous tip. Braced for anything, Action Force disguises a Kevlar-wearing Dial Tone as Dexter. Soon after, Storm Shadow arrives and bow-shoots the disguised Joe "to death," then escapes. Cobra Commander turns gleeful as the evening news reports Dexter's murder, allowing the genuine article to live underground without fear of reprisal.

"Nuclear Winter!" (#8): Destro's mouth waters when Professor Alec Peter Gilmore, a weapons research expert, develops a new stealth missile code-named "Project Omega." Unable to buy Gilmore's loyalty, Destro sends his agents to kidnap Gilmore aboard a private flight. But the hijack mysteriously goes awry, causing Gilmore's jet to crash in Greenland.

Suspecting Cobra involvement, Flint takes a team to rendezvous with Joes already stationed at Apogee Base in Greenland. A Cobra helicopter squadron arrives, keeping the main Action Force party busy while Destro makes for Gilmore's plane. Flint gives chase in a Snowcat, running Destro aground but overturning both their vehicles in the process. Finally, the two men concede their need to work together, hauling Destro's transport upright to prevent both of them freezing to death.

The ill-matched duo finds the wreckage of Gilmore's plane, but the treacherous Destro bashes Flint unconscious. Entering the ship, Destro learns that Gilmore shot the Cobra pilot, then erased the Omega blueprints to prevent Cobra obtaining the weapon. Gilmore killed himself shortly after, fearing he might crack under Cobra interrogation. His tremendous effort come to naught, Destro laughs while Flint recovers and kerwallops the Cobra weapons guru unconscious.

ASS-WHUPPINGS When nosy Tele-Vipers tap into a hotel's phone lines, Dial-Tone sends out an ultrasonic, high-decibel feedback that kills one of them. Dial-Tone also strangles a Tele-Viper intent on stabbing him in the back. Lady Jaye crashes one Cobra Ferret vehicle and missiles another.

COMIC TIE-INS The captured Destro is forcibly interrogated in *EM* #13. Both *EM* #8 and #13 imply that Destro's face is horribly disfigured (Flint here recoils in horror upon seeing Destro's mug) – but that clearly contradicts Destro's handsome features, shown in *G.I. Joe* #97 and *AF* #18.

"Mark of the Assassin" (*EM* #7) obviously takes place during Storm Shadow's tenure with Cobra (he defects to the Joes in *G.I. Joe* #38/*AF* #41)

PLACES TO GO Apogee Base: An Action Force camp located at latitude 72.10 north by longitude 40.10 east.

STUFF YOU NEED "Project Omega": The most advanced stealth cruise missile ever created. It's invisible to radar and infra-red sensors and armed with multiple nuclear warheads.

THE COMMAND DECISION Going down your gullet like a blackberry smoothie, "Smooth Operators" (*EM* #7) adheres to a great sense of tempo. Likewise, "Mark of the Assassin!" (EM #7) crisply features a still-turncoat Storm Shadow's quiet efforts to help Action Force, graced with supple pencils by John McCrea (Hitman).

Full of steel, "Nuclear Winter!" (*EM* #8) resorts to the successful Flint/Destro dynamic previously shown in Action Force, savagely pitting the two of them against each other in an edgy fashion. It's a layer of character shading we're happy to see, which leads to the similarly successful "The Prisoner!" in *EM* #13.

G.I. Joe European Missions #9 to #10

Titles: *"Diamond Lies!" (#9), "Blood Brothers" (#10), "War Correspondence!" (#10)*
Release Dates: *Feb. to Mar. 1989*
Writers: *Simon Furman (#9), Ian Rimmer ("Blood Brothers," "War Correspondence!").*
Art: *Robin Smith (#9), Stewart Johnson ("Blood Brothers"), Andy Wildman ("War Correspondence!").*
Included reprints: *Action Force #2-#3*

BATTLE ROSTER *Joes:* Cover Girl, Flint, Low Light, Leatherneck, Beach-Head, Roadblock, Lifeline, Hawk, Sci-Fi, Wild Bill, Scarlett, Flint, Snake-Eyes; *Cobra:* Serpentor, Copperhead, Tomax and Xamot, the Dreadnoks.

MISSION BRIEF ***"Diamond Lies!" (#9):*** Raising a collective eyebrow when Cobra starts stealing diamonds across the globe, Action Force concocts an espionage operation to learn more. In Amsterdam, Cover Girl poses as model Courtney Krieger, openly flaunting the completely fictionalized (but heavily publicized) "Watchstar Diamond." Suddenly, a Cobra hovercraft crew shows up and nabs Cover Girl.

Action Force members quietly give chase, but Weaponsmith, Cobra's chief munitions expert, takes Cover Girl to an abandoned windmill. Weaponsmith unpacks his "Stone Killer" rifle – an energy weapon that refracts a laser beam through a number of diamonds, amplifying a laser to 100 times its normal potency. Needing to field-test his newest invention, Weaponsmith starts smearing the Joes upon their arrival. Thankfully, Flint frees Cover Girl and body-tackles Weaponsmith, knocking his laser rifle aside. As Flint leaps aboard a passing Dragonfly helicopter and escapes, Cover Girl picks up "the Stone Killer" and – out of revenge for the indignity of being tied up – uses it to obliterate Weaponsmith.

"Blood Brothers" (#10): In the quiet English town of Little Meldon, Tomax and Xamot order one of their undercover Crimson Guardsman – a bank executive named Simon Weller – to rob his place of employment. Simon immediately dons his Crimson Guard uniform and proceeds to plunder the bank's vault, but Action Force swiftly surrounds the joint. Hoping to avoid casualties, Hawk asks Robert Weller – Simon's brother – to make his sibling see reason. Robert convinces Simon to surrender, but the Crimson Twins, disgusted with Simon's poor performance, conk Beach-Head unconscious and steal his sniper rifle. The twins plug Simon at long-range, leaving Robert to believe Action Force gunned his brother down. The Joes begin clean-up operations, but Robert, traumatized by his brother's passing, accepts Cobra's offer of employment as a Crimson Guardsman.

"BATs out of Hell" (#10): When Cobra rolls a van with explosives onto London's Tower Bridge and demands that Action Force release its various prisoners, Hawk despairs to find a team of android BATs guarding the bomb-laden vehicle. Afraid of setting off the explosives, Hawk recalls laser trooper Sci-Fi from Germany. With expert precision, Sci-Fi lasers through the bomb's detonator cables, ending the threat.

"War Correspondence!" (#10): A photographer named Steve feels his nuts clench in excitement when *Trooper!* magazine offers him $15,000 for a picture of Snake-Eyes' unmasked face. Steve legitimately gains access to Action Force's weapons testing range, awaiting his opportunity.

Suddenly, the Dreadnoks – having stolen a stack of classified documents – roar past in their Thunder Machine. Snake-Eyes and Flint give chase, destroying the stolen papers, but a spontaneous brawl rips off Snake-Eyes' face mask. Aghast at Snake-Eyes' mangled features, the Dreadnoks floor it and escape. Simultaneously, Steve feels doubly nauseous at seeing Snake-Eyes' true features, compassionately destroying his negatives.

LOVE AND WAR A random journalist ponders the genuineness of the Watchstar Diamond, to which Cover Girl replies, "Honey, believe me, everything you see here is real!"

ASS-WHUPPINGS A Crimson Guardsman garrotes one of Cover Girl's bodyguards. Cover Girl wipes out Weaponsmith and his entire damn windmill with "the Stone Killer."

CHARACTER PROFILE: JOES

Cover Girl: She hopes to never resume her modeling career. Still, the Amsterdam assignment nets her a cover shot on *Life* magazine.

CHARACTER PROFILE: COBRA

Zarana: She raided Action Force's personnel files at some point, giving Cobra access to the Joes' likenesses.

THE COMMAND DECISION Harshly screwball, "Diamond Lies!" (*AFM* #9) relies on sandpaper-grating, improbable plot points (a Cobra engineer fine-tuning his laser rifle with celebrity diamonds), that we thought we'd escaped when the TV series folded. Conversely, "Blood Brothers" (*AFM* #10) pumps itself up with a personalized take on the nature of brotherhood, although it could have used additional pages to flesh out its characters. "BATs out of Hell" (*AFM* #10) isn't anything to write home about, relying on the sort of sniper tension (i.e. "Will Sci-Fi hit the target?") that's better left to film. Oddly enough, that leaves "War Correspondence!" (*AFM* #10) to shine through as a silent tale that makes good use of the comic book format, with a beaut of an ending as photographer Steve decides he shouldn't make Snake-Eyes' true face public.

G.I. Joe European Missions #11 to #12

Titles: *"Wild, Wildlife!" (#11), "Super Trooper!" (#12).*
Release Dates: *Apr. to May 1989*
Writers: *Dan Abnett (#11), Steve Alan (#12).*
Art: *Robin Smith (#11), Stewart Johnson (#12)*
Included reprints: *Action Force #4-#5*

BATTLE ROSTER *Joes:* Outback, Psyche-Out, Flint, Lt. Falcon, Hawk, Super Soldier; *Cobra:* The Dreadnoks.

MISSION BRIEF ***"Wild, Wildlife!" (#11):*** With Action Force survivalist Outback hot on the Dreadnoks' trail in the Australian desert, Hawk assigns Psyche-Out to complete Outback's annual psychological exam in the field. Observing Outback's obsession with hunting down the Dreadnoks, Psyche-Out grows concerned about the Joe survivalist's increasingly reckless strategies.

Finally, the two Joes run their quarry aground at a stop-over bar named Blue Pete's. While Psyche-Out distracts the Dreadnoks by calling them stupid, Outback herds the captive bar patrons to safety and steals a Dreadnok Thunder Machine. Psyche-Out hops aboard, leading to a wild chase through the Australian outback with the Dreadnoks in hot pursuit. Finally, the supposedly "obsessive" Outback keeps a level head – luring the Dreadnoks closer, then unleashing pre-made gas canisters to knock the Cobra ruffians unconscious. Psyche-Out amends his former opinion of Outback, filing a good report at headquarters while Outback takes the Dreadnoks into custody.

"Super Trooper!" (#12): Hoping to launch soldiering to a new level, the military opens a new "Super Soldier" program to produce an "all-purpose, new age warrior." Starting out with 15 recruits, the "Super Soldier" project soon pares itself down to two long-time friends: captains Joe De Niro and Glenn Goddard. Hawk asks Flint to serve as drill instructor for the last phase of De Niro and Goddard's training, which requires that the "Super Soldier" candidates endure lengthy endurance trials and stress tests.

As a final test, Flint orders the captains to fly a Skystriker against pilotless RATTLER drones. The captains perform well, but a final hit wounds their Skystriker. With the falling ship heading for a village, the "Super Soldier" candidates realize one of them must stay aboard to keep the plane's nose up, preventing civilian casualties. Goddard remains adamant about remaining, forcing De Niro to eject. De Niro is enraged over Goddard's subsequent crash and death, but Flint reminds the captain that a "Super Soldier" must be self-sufficient above all else. Honoring Goddard's memory, De Niro graduates from the "Super Soldier" program as the military's top combatant.

ASS-WHUPPINGS Outback whacks Road Pig over the head with an iron bar, but the lumbering Dreadnok just shrugs it off. Ever resolute, Outback gives it another try, this time bashing Road Pig unconscious. Psyche-Out also tosses Monkeywrench through a window.

Super Soldier Goddard dies during a training exercise.

GOOFS Flint off-handedly mentions that "there could only be one Super Trooper," confusingly suggesting that the military rigged the Skystriker dilemma to ferret out the true Super Soldier recruit. But even if the military didn't predetermine Goddard's crash, holding training exercises near a village is a pretty stupid idea.

CHARACTER PROFILE: JOES

Outback: Outback claims he experienced a quiet childhood. He mostly liked being alone, but sometimes, the continued solitude made him suddenly yell at the top of his lungs. Psyche-Out dubs this "primal scream therapy," although Outback prefers the more technical term of "hollering."

Outback's been trailing the Dreadnoks for eight months, making him prone to nightmares of fire, smoke and Dreadnoks, always *Dreadnoks!* Psyche-Out spends most of this story wondering whether Outback's isolation and obsessive search have unhinged his mind, although he ultimately concludes that Outback's craziness is an act. Psyche-Out's final report cites Outback as possessing unusual courage.

P.S. Outback hears gunfire from two miles off.

ORGANIZATIONS *The Dreadnoks:* Psyche-Out's reports describe Buzzer as smart, but easily offended; Monkeywrench as a psychotic vandal fixated on his mother; and Thrasher as dense (although calling him stupid usually stirs up a hornet's nest of violence). Zanzibar simply reeks.

• *The Super Trooper Program:* Designed to breed a new generation of ultra-lethal, ultra-adept, all-purpose warriors. The initial Super Trooper recruits numbered 15, although the intense training requirements quickly whittled them down to two: Captain Joe De Niro, age 31; and Captain Glenn Goddard, 35.

Captain De Niro trained in the Apennines and specialized in covert operations. Endowed with a fanatical zeal for the military, De Niro could quote the manual blindfolded. As part of De Niro's training, the military buried him alive in a pothole for two months. He somehow survived, liking it enough to stay down there for four weeks afterward.

Infantry specialist Captain Goddard saved De Niro's life a few times during their SAS days. Goddard's supreme accuracy allows him to fire at a moving target from his hip.

THE COMMAND DECISION A story with its head on straight, "Wild, Wild Life" (*EM* #11) soars as more than just another Dreadnok tale, featuring a strong dynamic between the intellectual Psyche-Out and the somewhat berserk Outback. Conversely, the drawn-out "Super Trooper!" (*EM* #12) comes packaged with a twist that's momentarily interesting, then immediately forgettable.

G.I. Joe European Missions #13 to #15

Titles: *"The Prisoner!" (#13), "War Beneath the Waves" (#14), "Nights in Armor" (#15), "The Mission" (#15)*
Release Dates: *June to Aug. 1989*
Writers: *Steve Alan (#13), Simon Furman (#14), Dan Abnett ("Nights in Armor"), Ian Rimmer ("The Mission!")*
Art: *Robin Smith (#13), Robin Smith (#14), Stewart Johnson ("Nights in Armor"), John McCrea ("The Mission!")*
Included reprints: *Action Force #6-#7*

BATTLE ROSTER *Joes:* Flint, Lady Jaye, Lifeline, Mainframe, Dial-Tone, Lt. Falcon, Wet-Suit, Lifeline, Cutter, Heavy Metal, Cross Country, Backstop, Crazy Legs, Hit 'n Run, Roadblock, Tunnel Rat, Fast Draw, Snake-Eyes; *Cobra:* Destro, Cobra Commander, Wild Weasel.

MISSION BRIEF ***"The Prisoner!" (#13):*** While Action Force members interrogate Destro (captured in *EM* #8), Cobra Commander and a MAMBA squadron arrive in London to demand the steel-faced goon's release. Tracking a homing device in Destro's mask, Cobra Commander's troops batter down Action Force's front door and run rampant through their headquarters. The Joes retaliate, but Destro hurriedly sheds and detonates his plastique-laden mask, then escapes into the London Underground. Cobra Commander withdraws his forces and reunites with Destro, horrified at the sight of Destro's facial deformity but welcoming him back into the Cobra fold.

"War Beneath the Waves" (#14): In the Atlantic Ocean, an advanced Cobra sea warrior named a "Hydro-Viper" captures an Action Force quartet and their WHALE hovercraft. Stripping the WHALE clean, the Hydro-Viper's subordinates steal a Tactical Analysis Computer System (TACS) – a device capable, with the proper access codes, of deciphering the Ministry of Defense's classified files. The Hydro-Viper's team returns to an underwater Cobra base with the captive Joes, plotting to use the TACS to plunder and sell Europe's military hardware specs. Meanwhile, Lt. Falcon's Action Force team pursues their missing teammates, leading to a major slugfest.

The captive Joe foursome breaks loose and evacuates, but computer expert Mainframe stays behind to deal with the TACS. Terrifyingly encountering an armored Cobra Commander, Mainframe dashes about the base's control room like a mad ferret and nabs the TACS unit. Mainframe holds still just as Cobra Commander mis-times a punch, bashing the TACS device to itty-bitty pieces. Opting not to press his luck, Mainframe rejoins his teammates, leaving a despairing Cobra Commander to once again escape.

"Nights in Armor" (#15): Stationed in a Middle East oil emirate, Lt. Falcon mounts up an Action Force armor team to wrest a captured oil field from a Cobra squadron. Falcon's team encounters a blistering amount of resistance, drawing Cobra's firepower long enough for the *real* attack – a sneaky pack of Joes led by Tunnel Rat – to sweat blood racing through the oil field's main pipeline. Narrowly avoiding an oil flow, Tunnel Rat's team emerges and surrounds a group of Techno-Vipers planting explosive charges. Mainframe deduces the bomb's deactivation code, allowing the Joes to end Cobra's gambit.

"The Mission" (#15): Drastically short-handed, Hawk sends Snake-Eyes alone to reconnoiter – and preferably wipe out – a covert Cobra laser research station off the Swedish coast. Landing on an otherwise uninhabited isle, Snake-Eyes opts to knife a Cobra Viper team and swipe a RATTLER jet. Snake-Eyes daringly floors the RATTLER, driving the Cobra vehicle into the base's main laser cannon and escaping with only seconds to spare. The Cobra research center erupts in a tremendous explosion, allowing Snake-Eyes to casually swim to his rendezvous with an American submarine.

MEMORABLE MOMENTS In the finest tradition of Monty Python's Flying Circus, a sea-faring Mainframe spies Cobra frogmen (a.k.a. Eels) and cries out, "My hovercraft is full of Eels!"

G.I. Joe European Missions #13 to #15

LOVE AND WAR European Missions #13 provides the British comics' only hint of a Flint/Lady Jaye romance, although Lifeline dubs the relationship as "young and dewy." For all her rancor toward Flint (see Character Profile), Lady Jaye's overcome with joy when he survives an explosion.

ASS-WHUPPINGS The Baroness' troops seize Albert Hall in London, causing some entertainers named the "Bubblebath Brothers" to get the receiving end of (as the Baroness claims) a "small accident with an MK46 acoustic homing projectile." Destro's final gambit with his plastique-laden face mask singes Flint a bit. A Cobra Eel takes a harpoon in the hand rather than let Mainframe scrap the WHALE's TACS.

A shoot-out entails a Joe HAVOC erupting in an explosion of metal guts. Joe armament expert Fast Draw missiles a couple of Cobra MAGGOTs.

Snake-Eyes guts a pack of Cobra troopers almost to a man, then blows up their base with an exploding RATTLER.

COMIC TIE-INS Further widening the continuity chasm between the American and British G.I. Joe comics, Cobra Commander's battle armor (later worn by Cobra Commander II) makes a "first appearance" here. Mind, that completely contradicts events in *G.I. Joe* #58-#61, where Cobra Commander "died" before wearing the armor more than a few minutes.

As with *EM* #8, issue #13 hints that Destro bears some hideous facial deformity, but the American series (*G.I. Joe* #97) later shows off his good looks. *European Missions* #13 sloppily retreads old arguments between Flint and Lady Jaye from *AF* #42.

CHARACTER PROFILE: JOES

• *Airtight:* His costume's resistant to flame bursts.

• *Flint:* He's inwardly drained by the continued struggle against Cobra. Claiming that he never really wanted to join the Army, Flint fears that positions of power invariably bring out the worst in people.

• *Flint and Lady Jaye:* They disagree on the best way to beat information out of Destro – Lady Jaye favors electrical and chemical brainwashing, but Flint argues that Destro deserves more respect. Lady Jaye outwardly considers Flint as arrogant, pig-headed, self-righteous and incompetent, but she clearly harbors hidden feelings for him.

• *Lifeline:* Unlike his wholesome TV and American *G.I. Joe* incarnations, the British version of Lifeline comes off as an unshaven, foul-mouthed boozer.

CHARACTER PROFILE: COBRA

• *Destro:* Destro's helmet works like a Chinese puzzle – you've got to hit the right pressure points in sequence to open it up, or it'll electro-shock you. Flint's fisticuffs with Destro in *EM* #8 opened the helmet purely as a lucky fluke.

Lifeline abandoned efforts to draft up a personality profile on Destro, mostly because Destro's raving egotism left the medic unsure how to proceed.

• *Hydro-Vipers:* An advanced form of Cobra frogmen, surgically altered with body insulation, webbed hands and feet for deep-sea diving.

ORGANIZATIONS *Cobra:* It's allied with terrorist factions in Libya and South Africa.

STUFF YOU NEED *"Directive Eight":* An order originating, if needed, from the British Prime Minister, mandating the total destruction of Action Force Headquarters to ward off a battle or ransom scenario in London.

THE COMMAND DECISION Brutal, but highly effective, "The Prisoner!" (*EM* #13) ignores Flint, Lady Jaye and Destro's previous entanglement (*AF* #35 and onward) but nonetheless triumphs as a round robin slugfest throughout Action Force Headquarters. Writer Steve Alan uses his expanded page count to maximum effect, making us long for more Action Force tales of this proficiency.

Meanwhile, "War Beneath the Waves" (*EM* #14) features a beginning, middle and end, but basically nothing else unique to recommend. We'd wish for a better conclusion to the Joes' British endeavors, as "Nights in Armour" (*EM* #15) comes off as woefully lackluster – a run-of-the-mill exercise that sees Action Force beating someone up, then heading home. Whoopie.

The Crucial Bits (the Sunbow TV Show)

... being a quick and dirty rundown of the salient bits of the *G.I. Joe* TV show and comics, so one can more easily find the trees for all the forests.

• **THE M.A.S.S. DEVICE** – Cobra hooks up a matter teleporter to a super-fast global satellite, creating a death ray. Attempting to thwart Cobra with their own teleporter, the Joes race about the world searching for three rare elements.

• **THE REVENGE OF COBRA** – Cobra creates and loses a device that controls the world's weather. The Joes run about the planet battling Cobra for the device's component parts. Zartan, Shipwreck and some giant creeper vines make their debut.

• **THE PYRAMID OF DARKNESS** – Cobra captures a Joe space station and positions giant cubes around the world, forming an energy-draining "Pyramid of Darkness."

• **COUNTDOWN FOR ZARTAN** – Disguised as a big-nosed French scientist, Zartan tries to blow up an anti-terrorist conference.

• **RED ROCKET'S GLARE** – Cobra plants warheads atop a nationwide chain of fast food restaurants.

• **SATELLITE DOWN** – The Joes team up with a bunch of Neanderthals, fighting Cobra to retrieve a fallen surveillance satellite.

• **COBRA STOPS THE WORLD** – After hamstringing the world's energy supplies, Cobra makes off with an oil tanker convoy.

• **JUNGLE TRAP** – Cobra kidnaps a scientist in an attempt to control the world's molten lava flows.

• **COBRA'S CREATURES** – Cobra uses brainwashed animals as weapons of war.

• **THE FUNHOUSE** – Cobra Commander tortures a handful of Joes in a psychedelic funhouse.

• **TWENTY QUESTIONS** – A Geraldo Rivera-inspired TV crew annoys the Joes by claiming that Cobra's a hoax.

• **THE GREENHOUSE EFFECT** – Cobra overruns Chicago with giant vegetables.

• **HAUL DOWN THE HEAVENS** – Cobra pulls down the Aurora Borealis, hoping to melt the polar ice caps and flood the Earth.

• **THE SYNTHOID CONSPIRACY** – Cobra replaces a bunch of Pentagon officials – and Duke – with artificial "synthoids," planning to ruin the Joes' funding and support.

• **THE PHANTOM BRIGADE** – Cobra Commander terrorizes the Joes with a trio of ghosts.

• **LIGHTS! CAMERA! COBRA!** – While a movie director films *The G.I. Joe Story,* Cobra agents try to recapture a top-secret stealth jet.

• **COBRA'S CANDIDATE** – Cobra sponsors a candidate for mayor, hoping to spread (more) evil into municipal politics.

• **MONEY TO BURN** – Cobra incinerates the world's money, attempting to refinance the planet with "Cobra currency."

• **OPERATION MIND MENACE** – Cobra trains a legion of psionic shock troops on Easter Island.

• **BATTLE FOR THE TRAIN OF GOLD** – Cobra loots Fort Knox.

• **COBRA SOUNDWAVES** – Cobra constructs a giant sonic cannon in the Middle East.

• **WHERE THE REPTILES ROAM** – Western-dressed Joes investigate a Cobra-controlled Texas dude ranch. (Yee-haw!)

• **THE GAMESMASTER** – A psycho engineer kidnaps a handful of Joes and Cobras, forcing them to fight to the death.

• **LASERS IN THE NIGHT** – A brainless but nubile martial arts expert named Amber falls for Quick Kick, causing the Joes a lot of trouble. Cobra Commander attempts to carve his face on the moon.

• **THE GERM** – A mutant germ-turned-giant-blob wreaks havoc.

• **THE VIPER IS COMING** – A speech impediment hoodwinks the Joes.

• **SPELL OF THE SIREN** – The Baroness gets her hands on a legendary seashell that mesmerizes males.

• **COBRA QUAKE** – Cobra wracks Japan with earthquakes.

• **CAPTIVES OF COBRA** – While going after some highly explosive crystals, Cobra brainwashes the Joes' relatives into its service.

• **BAZOOKA SAW A SEA SERPENT** – Cobra Commander terrorizes the sea lanes with a giant, ravenous mechanical sea serpent.

• **EXCALIBUR** – Storm Shadow plays King Arthur.

• **WORLDS WITHOUT END** – A Joe team arrives on a parallel Earth, where Cobra has exterminated G.I. Joe and conquered the planet. Steeler, Clutch and Grunt remain behind to fight evil in the alternate timeline.

• **EAU DE COBRA** – A love potion causes trouble at a rich bachelor's yacht party.

• **COBRA CLAWS ARE COMING TO TOWN** – Destro uses shrunken, toy-sized Cobra troops to capture Joe Headquarters. Thankfully, a giant parrot saves the day.

• **AN EYE FOR AN EYE** – A victimized father goes on a vengeance quest against Cobra.

• **THE GODS BELOW** – While looting an ancient Egyptian tomb, Cobra encounters some seriously old deities.

• **PRIMORDIAL PLOT** – Cobra clones and brainwashes dinosaurs on a remote island.

• **FLINT'S VACATION** – Planning to wipe out the world's plant life, Cobra brainwashes an entire town into serving its evil will.

The Critical Bits

• **HEARTS AND CANNONS** – A couple of Joes rescue a captive scientist from Cobra's clutches in the Middle East.

• **MEMORIES OF MARA** – Shipwreck falls for a genetically created ex-Cobra mermaid.

• **THE TRAITOR** – A desperately destitute Dusty defects to the dark side.

• **PIT OF VIPERS** – A computer takes command of G.I. Joe. Meanwhile, Cobra prepares to gut Joe Headquarters with a giant drill.

• **THE WRONG STUFF** – Cobra dominates the world through subversive television programs.

• **THE INVADERS** – Milk-drinking aliens invade Earth.

• **COLD SLITHER** – Making like "Twisted Sister," Zartan and the Dreadnoks become rock stars.

• **THE GREAT ALASKAN LAND RUSH** – With Cobra's help, a used-car salesman seizes control of Alaska.

• **SKELETONS IN THE CLOSET** – When Destro cheats on the Baroness, she brings his ancestral manor to ruin. Lady Jaye and Destro are revealed as distant cousins.

• **THERE'S NO PLACE LIKE SPRINGFIELD** – In an elaborate interrogation scheme, Cobra royally screws with Shipwreck's head.

• **ARISE, SERPENTOR, ARISE!** – Cobra makes an emperor named "Serpentor" from the DNA scraps of famous dead people.

• **LAST HOUR TO DOOMSDAY** – While Lady Jaye impersonates the Baroness, Cobra blackmails the world with giant tidal waves.

• **COMPUTER COMPLICATIONS** – Cobra goes after a fallen antimatter pod, Zarana and Mainframe fall in love and the *USS Flagg* goes under.

• **SINK THE MONTANA** – Desperate to save his ship from retirement, a US Navy admiral signs up with Cobra.

• **LET'S PLAY SOLDIER** – Cobra attempts to control the world through mesmeric chewing gum.

• **ONCE UPON A JOE** – A wacky Shipwreck-spun fairy tale comes to life.

• **THE MILLION DOLLAR MEDIC** – A rich bubble-head falls for Lifeline.

• **COBRATHON** – Cobra broadcasts a telethon to sponsor its criminal endeavors.

• **THE ROTTEN EGG** – One of Leatherneck's old trainees goes renegade.

• **GLAMOUR GIRLS** – Cobra funds a fashion magazine as a front for a youth-sucking enterprise.

• **ICEBERG GOES SOUTH** – Iceberg is turned into a giant killer whale.

• **THE SPY WHO ROOKED ME** – A James Bond clone aids the Joes in safeguarding a deadly nerve toxin.

• **GREY HAIRS AND GROWING PAINS** – Cobra turns several Joes into little kids and old geezers.

• **MY BROTHER'S KEEPER** – A Cobra-sponsored quantum physicist learns the value of brotherly love.

• **MY FAVORITE THINGS** – Serpentor races around the globe stealing his ancestors' possessions.

• **RAISE THE FLAGG!** – While trying to retrieve the sunken *Flagg,* the Joes run into a tyrannical Cobra chef.

• **NINJA HOLIDAY** – Sgt. Slaughter kicks ass at a martial arts tournament in the South Pacific.

• **G.I. JOE AND THE GOLDEN FLEECE** – An alien hyperdrive coil transports the Joes back to ancient Greece.

• **THE MOST DANGEROUS THING IN THE WORLD** – Cobra hackers promote three Joes without a drop of leadership ability to the rank of colonel.

• **NIGHTMARE ASSAULT** – Cobra plagues the Joes with fiendish nightmares.

• **SECOND HAND EMOTIONS** – An emotion-manipulating device wreaks havoc at Lifeline's sister's wedding.

• **JOE'S NIGHT OUT** – Cobra launches a dance club into outer space (and somehow thinks the world will care).

• **NOT A GHOST OF A CHANCE** – While Cobra denies shooting down a stealth jet, the Joes race to find two missing pilots.

• **SINS OF OUR FATHERS** – Cobra Commander hires Destro's family monster to eat Serpentor.

• **IN THE PRESENCE OF MINE ENEMIES** – Slip-Stream and a Cobra babe get marooned on a desert island with an icky blob.

• **INTO YOUR TENT I WILL SILENTLY CREEP** – Thieving robots lead Cross-Country to uncover a secret Cobra brotherhood.

• **G.I. JOE: THE MOVIE** – An ancient civilization named Cobra-La – the culture that spawned Cobra from behind-the-scenes – attempts to retake the planet. Duke and Lt. Falcon revealed as half-brothers. Origin of Cobra Commander, who turns into a serpent.

• **OPERATION DRAGONFIRE** – A jilted Baroness restores Cobra Commander, who reassumes control of Cobra, Back to human form. Serpentor transformed into a primitive lizard-thing.

The Crucial Bits (the Marvel Comics)

• **G.I. JOE #1** – First appearance of G.I. Joe (1980s incarnation) and the terrorist organization Cobra.

First appearance of the original clutch of Joes, including Snake-Eyes, Scarlett, Hawk, Stalker, Breaker and Clutch. First appearance of Brigadier General Flagg and Major General Austin.

First appearance of Cobra Commander and the Baroness. First appearance of Dr. Adele Burkhart and Joe Headquarters ("the Pit"). First hint of romance between Snake-Eyes and Scarlett.

• **G.I. JOE #2** – First appearance of special ops freelancer Kwinn.

• **G.I. JOE #5** – First mention of Springfield, a Cobra-controlled U.S. city.

• **G.I. JOE #6** – First appearance of Russia's top commando squad, the Oktober Guard.

• **G.I. JOE #10** – First appearance of Cobra scientist Dr. Venom and his ubiquitous brainwave scanner. First appearance of Cobra resistance cell member Billy. First full appearance of the Cobra-controlled city of Springfield. First hints about the helicopter crash that mauled Snake-Eyes' face and the auto accident that killed his family.

• **G.I. JOE #11** – First appearance of Joes Gung Ho, Doc and Wild Bill. Cameo appearance by Cobra weapons supplier Destro.

• **G.I. JOE #12** – First appearance of Cobra courier Scar-Face and the wartorn nation of Sierra Gordo.

• **G.I. JOE #14** – First full appearance of Destro. First appearance of hotshot Joe Skystriker pilot Ace and Arbco, a long-running front for Cobra's business operations.

• **G.I. JOE #15** – First appearance of Cobra mercenary Major Bludd.

• **G.I. JOE #16** – Cobra Commander and Major Bludd attempt to kill Destro. The Baroness gets severely maimed foiling their scheme.

• **G.I. JOE #19** – Deaths of General Flagg, Dr. Venom, Kwinn and Scar-Face. The Pit damaged in an explosion that destroys the Fort Wadsworth motor pool.

• **G.I. JOE #21** – First appearance of Cobra ninja Storm Shadow and the (as-yet unnamed) Silent Castle. Identical wrist tattoos denote a bond between Storm Shadow and Snake-Eyes.

• **G.I. JOE #22** – First appearance of Joes Roadblock and Duke, who's promoted to G.I. Joe's top field commander. General Flagg and Kwinn laid to rest. The Joes start renovating the Pit into the Pit II.

• **G.I. JOE #23** – Plastic surgery restores the Baroness' face to normal.

• **G.I. JOE #24** – First appearance of Cobra saboteur Firefly. Cameo appearance of Cobra disguise artist Zartan.

• **G.I. JOE #25** – First full appearance of Zartan and his Dreadnoks (Buzzer, Ripper and Torch). First appearance of the *G.I. Jane* freighter.

• **G.I. JOE #26** – Detailed history of Snake-Eyes' Vietnam tour of duty with Stalker and Storm Shadow. Deaths of Snake-Eyes' family, his ninja training and the murder of the Hard Master (his mentor) outlined. First appearance of Snake-Eyes' other sensei, the Soft Master.

• **G.I. JOE #27** – Chronicle of Snake-Eyes' romance with Scarlett, plus the helicopter accident that rendered him mute and ruined his face. Storm Shadow reveals his quest to find the Hard Master's murderer.

• **G.I. JOE #29** – First appearance of the Cobra Crimson Guard and undercover Cobra agent "Fred Smith."

• **G.I. JOE #30** – The Baroness and Major Bludd ally with Billy, plotting to assassinate Cobra Commander.

• **G.I. JOE #31** – First appearance of Joe tracker Spirit.

• **G.I. JOE #32** – First appearance of Joe covert operations agent Lady Jaye. Death of Fred Smith I. First appearance of Fred Smith II.

• **G.I. JOE #33** – Billy revealed as Cobra Commander's son. First appearance of Candy (a.k.a. Bongo the Balloon Bear).

Scarlet, Breaker, Zap, Grunt, Short-Fuse, Rock 'n Roll, Stalker and Flash promoted to the Pit's administrative arm. Hawk promoted to full commanding officer of the Joes and the Pit. Duke takes much more active role as top Joe sergeant.

• **G.I. JOE #35** – The Joes capture Dreadnok Buzzer.

• **G.I. JOE #36** – Destruction of the *G.I. Jane* freighter. First appearance of the *USS Flagg* aircraft carrier.

• **G.I. JOE #37** – First appearance of Joe warrant officer Flint and Crimson Guard commanders Tomax and Xamot.

• **G.I. JOE #38** – Storm Shadow turns against Cobra, freeing Billy. Cobra Commander's rise to power partially detailed. First appearance of Candy's father (Professor Appel), who's revealed as a Crimson Guardsman.

• **G.I. JOE #39** – Storm Shadow starts training Billy as a ninja warrior. First appearance of Storm Shadow's watertower hideout in Manhattan.

• **G.I. JOE #40** – First appearance of Joe sailor Shipwreck. Dreadnok Buzzer escapes with the Pit's location.

• **G.I. JOE #41** – Cobra tricks the Joes into detonating a major fault line, creating an island in international waters. Cobra dominates the landmass, legitimizing "Cobra Island" as a nation-state.

• **G.I. JOE #42** – Fred Smith II revealed as Wade Collins, Snake-Eyes and Stalker's ex-military associate. Major General Austin suffers a heart attack.

• **G.I. JOE #43** – The Soft Master learns the identity of the

Hard Master's killer, transmitting the information to Snake-Eyes. Deaths of the Soft Master and Candy. Billy severely wounded.

First appearance of Cobra armament expert Scrap Iron. Wade Collins' history revealed. The late Fred Smith's family embraces Wade as one of their own, departing for points unknown.

• **G.I. JOE #44** – First appearance of Cobra scientist Dr. Mindbender.

• **G.I. JOE #45** – Zartan revealed as the Hard Master's killer. Major General Austin retires as Pentagon-level commander of G.I. Joe. Hawk promoted to Brigadier General, retaking Joe field command.

• **G.I. JOE #46** – Death of Professor Appel. First appearance of Cobra's Terror-Drome defense installations.

• **G.I. JOE #47** – The Baroness apparently kills Storm Shadow.

• **G.I. JOE #48** – One of the few *G.I. Joe* issues where nobody fires a single shot.

• **G.I. JOE #49** – First appearance of Cobra Emperor Serpentor. Hawk recalls the original Joes to active duty, bringing the Joes' military might against Springfield.

• **G.I. JOE #50** – Cobra yields Springfield to the Joes, who suffer political fallout from overrunning an "innocent" American town. Storm Shadow gets over his apparent death, claims he's "feeling much better now." First appearance of Zartan's sister Zarana.

• **G.I. JOE #51** – First appearance of Dreadnok Thrasher.

• **G.I. JOE #52** – Cobra Commander botches an assassination attempt on Serpentor's life, solidifying Serpentor's authority.

• **G.I. JOE #53** – Destruction of the Pit II. First appearance of Gen. Hollingsworth, who reinstates the Joes as a nomadic unit. First appearance and deaths of General Ryan and Admiral Dyson.

• **G.I. JOE #55** – Cobra Commander reunited with a comatose Billy. Grunt retires from active Joe service and enrolls at Georgia Tech. First mention of the Cobra Consulate Building in Manhattan.

• **G.I. JOE #56** – First appearance of Lola, his fellow student and future love muffin.

• **G.I. JOE #58** – First appearance of Fred VII, who forges new body armor for Cobra Commander.

• **G.I. JOE #59** – First appearance of ninjas Jinx and the Blind Master.

• **G.I. JOE #60** – First appearance of Joe members Lt. Falcon and Chuckles.

• **G.I. JOE #61** – Apparent death of Cobra Commander. Fred Smith VII dons Cobra Commander's armor. First appearance of Borovia.

• **G.I. JOE #62** – First mention of Professor Onihashi, an acclaimed sword-smith who worked for the Hard Master. First mention of Professor Onihashi's assistant (later revealed as Firefly).

• **G.I. JOE #63** – Storm Shadow reunited with Billy.

• **G.I. JOE #64** – Fred Smith VII becomes Cobra Commander II, striking up a silent partnership with the Baroness.

• **G.I. JOE #65** – First appearance of the White Clown.

• **G.I. JOE #69** – First appearance of Destro's gold-plated head, updated costume and Iron Grenadiers. Destro becomes more aggressive in asserting his own agenda, furthering his family's armaments business.

• **G.I. JOE SPECIAL MISSIONS #13** – First appearance of the African nation of Trucial Abysmia.

• **G.I. JOE #73** – Serpentor and Cobra Commander II throw down the gauntlet against one another, instigating a Cobra Civil War.

• **G.I. JOE #76** – Death of Serpentor, which ends the Cobra Civil War. Destro reunited with the Baroness.

• **G.I. JOE #81** – First appearance of Broca Beach, NJ, a Cobra stronghold.

• **G.I. JOE #83** – First appearance of Dreadnok Road Pig and Billy's unnamed mother.

• **G.I. JOE #84** – Origin of Zartan. Partial origin of Cobra Commander and his grudge against Snake-Eyes. Billy reunited with his mother. Storm Shadow's clan name identified as "Arashikage."

• **G.I. JOE #85** – First appearance of the red ninja leader.

• **G.I. JOE #87** – Destro renews his allegiance with Cobra.

• **G.I. JOE #90** – Destro heavily reorganizes Cobra's command structure.

• **G.I. JOE #91** – Death of the Blind Master.

• **G.I. JOE SPECIAL MISSIONS #26** – Deaths of Oktober Guard members Colonel Brekhov, Horrorshow, Stormavik and Schrage.

• **G.I. JOE #94** – Snake-Eyes' face restored to normal. Details of the Baroness' history revealed.

• **G.I. JOE #95** – Snake-Eyes' face somewhat lacerated by hot coals.

• **G.I. JOE SPECIAL MISSIONS #28** – Final *G.I. Joe Special Missions* issue.

• **G.I. JOE #97** – Destro abdicates leadership of Cobra and his family business, MARS, entering semi-retirement with the Baroness.

• **G.I. JOE #98** – The original Cobra Commander returns to power and buries numerous rogues, including Zartan, Billy, Dr. Mindbender and Cobra Commander II, aboard a landlocked freighter.

• **G.I. JOE #99** – First appearance of Millville, subverted by Cobra as a manufacturing mecca.

• **G.I. JOE #101** – First appearance of Oktober Guard members Lt. Gorky and Sgt. Misha. First appearance of Scarlett's sister, Sioban O'Hara.

• **G.I. JOE #103** – Scarlett revives from her coma.

Now You Know

• **G.I. JOE #106** – First appearance and death of George Strawhacker, formerly engaged to Snake-Eyes' late sister.

• **G.I. JOE #107** – First appearance of the Night Creepers, freelance techno-assassins.

• **G.I. JOE #109** – Deaths of Joes Breaker, Doc, Quick Kick, Thunder, Crazylegs, Crankcase and Heavy Metal. First appearance of the murderous Saw-Viper.

• **G.I. JOE #112** – Deaths of Joe member Cool Breeze. Alleged demise of the Saw Viper.

• **G.I. JOE #113** – Deaths of Sneak Peek and Battle Force 2000 (save Dodger). Probable deaths of Joes Recoil and Ambush.

• **G.I. JOE #114** – Bodies of Cobra Commander II, Dr. Mindbender, Croc Master, Raptor, Voltar, Tyrone and Captain Minh located.

• **G.I. JOE #116** – Destruction of Castle Destro.

• **G.I. JOE #117** – First appearance of the G.I. Joe Ninja Force.

• **G.I. JOE #120** – First appearance of ninjas Slice and Dice. Cobra Commander signs possession of the Silent Castle over to Destro.

• **G.I. JOE #122** – Destro "transforms" the Silent Castle into a new Castle Destro.

• **G.I. Joe #123** – First appearance of Cobra chief environmental operative Cesspool. Flint reassigned to lead the Joe Eco-Warriors.

• **G.I. Joe #124** – First appearance of the Joe Drug Enforcement Force, a drug kingpin named Headman and his Headhunters.

• **G.I. Joe #126** – Revelation of Firefly's position as red ninja leader and early days in the Arashikage household. Further details about the Hard Master's murder revealed.

• **G.I. JOE #131** – Cobra Commander willingly surrenders Cobra Island to Firefly.

• **G.I. JOE #134** – The Joes drive Firefly from Cobra Island, leaving it largely deserted.

• **G.I. JOE #139** – Cobra rebuilds Decepticon leader Megatron, granting him a tank mode.

• **G.I. JOE #140** – Cobra Commander restores Dr. Mindbender to life.

• **G.I. JOE #142** – Cobra abandons Millville. Megatron breaks off his alliance with Cobra.

• **G.I. JOE #144** – Detail of the mission that ruined Snake-Eyes' voice and face.

• **G.I. JOE #145** – Cobra Commander brainwashes Destro and Zartan back into the Cobra fold. First appearance of the GI Joe Star Brigade. Deaths of the White Clown and Magda.

• **G.I. JOE #146** – Death of Darklon.

• **G.I. JOE #147** – Destruction of the *Defiant.* Cobra Commander additionally mesmerizes the Baroness and Billy into his service.

• **G.I. JOE #150** – Storm Shadow also succumbs to Cobra Commander's brainwashing charms.

• **G.I. JOE #152** – The White House summons Joseph Colton (the original G.I. Joe), likely to discuss his reinstatement.

• **G.I. JOE #155** – Marvel's ongoing *G.I. Joe* title folds after 12 years. The U.S. government closes the Pit III, decommissioning the G.I. Joe team.

PUBLISHER / EDITOR-IN-CHIEF
Lars Pearson

DESIGN MANAGER / INTERIOR DESIGN
Christa Dickson

ASSOCIATE EDITORS
Marc Eby
Chris Lawrence
Joshua Wilson

COVER ART
Richard Martinez/Art Thug

TECH SUPPORT
Robert Moriarty
Mike O'Nele

4606 Kingman Blvd.
Des Moines, Iowa 50311
madnorwegian@gmail.com

Printed in Great Britain
by Amazon

26837845R00165